CARNIVAL

He hurled hi... ...to the shadows, out of the headlights, tearing at his useless priest's disguise to find his Mauser. Before he could get it loose, several men came running at him. One of them dealt him a blow to the chest with his rifle butt that sent him toppling backward into the street.

Laid out on his back, he summoned enough strength to send one of his assailants flying with a hard left kick. He got the gun out and fired widly. He heard the tinkle of glass as one of the car headlights blew out. Then they were all over him. They wrestled the Mauser away from him and one of them rammed it up against his closed teeth so he could taste the steel of the muzzle.

The one in charge sauntered down the hill and stood over him. Behind his captor, beyond the vast bay of Guanabara, a narrow slash of pink had appeared in the eastern sky.

Captain Honorio Schmidt, the chief of the Special Police, studied his prize with satisfaction and decided to allow himself one of his slim Bahian cigars. One of his assistants sprang forward to strike a match. Captain Honorio huffed life into the cheroot and remarked, 'It's Ash Wednesday, Father.'

Also by the same author,
and available from Coronet:

MOSCOW RULES

About the author

Robert Moss is the author of MOSCOW
RULES and DEATH BEAM, and the co-author
of THE SPIKE and MONIMBO. He is a
prize-winning journalist and a former lecturer
in history at the Australian National
University. He is currently a visiting lecturer at
a number of universities and NATO military
academies including the Royal College of
Defence Studies. He lives in New York State.

Carnival of Spies

Robert Moss

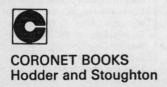

CORONET BOOKS
Hodder and Stoughton

Grateful acknowledgement is made to Random House, Inc., to reprint excerpts from the Poem 'The Panther', by Rainer Maria Rilke, from *The Selected Poetry of Rainer Maria Rilke*, translated by Stephen Mitchell. Introduction copyright © 1982 by Robert Hass. Copyright © 1980, 1981, 1982 by Stephen Mitchell. Used by permission.

First published in Great Britain in 1987 by Hodder and Stoughton Limited

Coronet open market edition 1988

Printed and bound in Great Britain for Hodder and Stoughton Paperbacks, a division of Hodder and Stoughton Limited, Mill Road, Dunton Green, Sevenoaks, Kent (Editorial Office: 47 Bedford Square, London WC1B 3DP) by Richard Clay Limited, Bungay, Suffolk. Photoset by Rowland Phototypesetting Limited, Bury St Edmunds, Suffolk.

British Library C.I.P.

Moss, Robert, *1946–*
    Carnival of spies.
    I. Title
823'.914[F]   PR6063.O83

    ISBN 0-340-42249-1

The most important thing in life
is love, duty, The most important thing in work
is beauty, discipline.

MARLENE DIETRICH*

---

*One of Dietrich's directors, Rouben Mamoulien, kept a book
in which he invited his guests to write their 'innermost
thoughts'. This was Dietrich's contribution

CONTENTS

CARNIVAL OF SPIES

Prologue:

Ash Wednesday

(1936)

What is done out of love is beyond good and evil.

— Nietzsche

She rode in a chariot drawn by sea horses. A sickle moon and a shower of stars glittered above her crown. Ropes of make-believe jewels cupped her breasts and snaked around her belly. But her body was burning gold, brighter than these. She moved tirelessly, hypnotically, to the voluptuous rhythm of the samba. Around her, across the width of the avenue, the dancers darted and flashed like fireflies and birds of paradise. Tomorrow she might be back in a tumbledown shack on a muddy hilltop in the Northern Zone or trudging off to work with a broom and a mop in the houses of the rich. But tonight she was Queen of the Nile, goddess of the waters, empress of desire. She arched her back, and the dream-ruby at her navel turned little circles. She danced so Ash Wednesday would never dawn, so that Carnival would never end.

In front of the Copacabana Palace Hotel, a crowd of young swells got up as harlequins and Arabian princes paraded in an open car and squirted the girls with cheap cologne. 'Cocococococoró, Coco-coco-cocoró!' They crowed the chorus of one of the new songs that had caught the pulse of Rio. It carried all the laughter and all the sadness of the last night of Carnival:

> The cock of the night is singing
> Everyone wants to see
> What he has to tell.
> When the little rooster replies
> Cocococococoró
> Cocococococoró
> The little hen dies.

On the streetcar bound for Botafogo they were chanting the March of the Little Rooster too, and the tram swayed from side to side under their pounding feet. Along the mosaic sidewalk, a man in a black cassock and flat black hat picked his way through the throng. The words of the song seemed to trouble him, or perhaps it was merely the moist tropical heat that rose from the ground and opened every pore, and the sight of so much naked flesh. He looked unnaturally pale, and his eyes were searching for something beyond the streamers and the travelling hips of the mulatto girls. He trod on a mass of gold paper without noticing that it was the crown of a King of Angola. People didn't want to look at him. It was not the night for priests and Portuguese saints. Their season would come soon enough.

But a dark, pretty girl who was resting at the corner of one of the narrow streets that wound into Lapa, a quarter that lived for the night in all the seasons of the year, stretched out her hand and offered something to him. He paused to look down. It was half a lemon, from the stock she had brought with her in a little string bag so she wouldn't have to pay for *guaraná* from the street vendors. Caught off guard, he took the fruit and sank his teeth into it, watching the girl warily with his intent grey eyes as if she might pose some danger to him. She had been crying. Perhaps she had lost something precious in the riot of Carnival.

She whispered, 'Bless me, Father.'

He frowned, mumbled a few words and waved his hand over her upturned face.

She couldn't make out what he said. Perhaps he was one of those Dutch fathers who came to Brazil. She watched him with a puzzled expression, and he stumbled on up the street, into a neighbourhood where the services of priests were rarely required. He was such a big man, with powerful shoulders and fists like a prizefighter's. The cassock looked silly on him. And there was something wrong with the way he walked. His right leg swung stiff from the hip. She saw him limp past half-shuttered windows from behind which women's voices lapped out, softly propositioning, at the passersby. Then he stood out in bold profile, listing noticeably to starboard, against the illuminated sign of the Babylônia Club.

Zé Pimenta, the keeper of the door to the Babylônia, didn't like being on duty on the last Tuesday of Carnival, even if the tips were good. By the time the patrons inside were done, it would be too late to show off his finery – he was decked out as a Turkish pasha, complete with turban and baggy pants and pasteboard scimitar – to his girlfriends in the Mangue. They would all be sleeping it off. Zé had been consoling himself with a few fingers of *cachaça*. He could sneak imported hooch from the bar, but he preferred the raw, potent cane alcohol of his own country. Its effect, after a while, was as hallucinating and enervating as the steamy heat and the relentless beat of the samba drums. He was half asleep when he saw the man in black rise up in front of him like a monstrous crow.

'*Dá licença*, Zé,' the priest addressed him, pleasantly enough.

'Excuse me, Father.' Zé hastily adjusted his sash. 'You wouldn't want to go in there. It's dreadful what goes on. Human nature, I'm afraid.'

But something in the priest's face – was it the strange, set smile or the strong, almost brutal, features? – made Zé step aside. 'We don't see a lot of cassocks in the Babylônia,' he mumbled as the priest walked into the club.

They didn't play sambas inside the Babylônia. Half the clientele was foreign, and the band alternated between tangos and German and American favourites. As the priest entered, a singer with a powder-white face and vocal chords that had been gutted by chain-smoking was attempting a rendition of Lola-Lola's song from *The Blue Angel*. A few of the German syllables got transposed, but nobody in this crowd seemed to mind. Girls in bright satin with plunging necklines were trying to prise drinks from the regulars who hung along the bar like vampire bats. Few of the couples who revolved on the dance floor had arrived together. The fancy dress on display was mostly compliments of the house – party hats and clowns' red bubble noses. But there were a few men in formal evening dress with stiff collars, looking for company that was certified hygienic. The management of the Babylônia discreetly advertised the claim that its girls were inspected by a qualified doctor once a day.

The whirring propeller fans overhead did not dispel the haze of cigar and cigarette smoke; they distributed it evenly to every corner of the room. The walls were adorned with baroque mirrors and a mural depicting an ancient orgy among hanging gardens. One of the women, dancing with a drink in her hand, shuddered when the reflection of the man in black loomed up suddenly behind her shoulder. Another tittered and called out mockingly, 'Coco-coco-coco-cocoró!'

In the mirror he saw the girl he had come for. The candlelight caught the silvery whorls of her butterfly mask and the long white curve of her throat. She was at a corner table with her back to the wall. The two men with her were both wearing dinner jackets. The one he could see in profile was lean and equine and looked mildly bored. The other, squeezed up against the girl, was heavy and flushed and bellowed snatches of Lola-Lola's song in between gulps from his tankard.

Ich bin von Kopf bis Fuss
Auf Liebe eingestellt . . .

A waiter swooped around them, pouring champagne. Before he replaced the bottle in its silver bucket, he flipped it upside down, and a few inches of champagne disappeared into the ice. It was one of the management's little tricks to speed up consumption. Nobody noticed except the man who was glued to the mirror.

The girl looked up, and their eyes met in the glass. She pulled away from her admirer, as if to leave the table. The priest made a motion with his hand for her to stay.

He completed a half circle of the dance floor, trying not to let his right foot drag, and came up behind the men at her table.

'Alms for the poor,' he suggested in a wheedling voice.

'Ach, it's unbelievable,' the ruddy-faced German complained, shifting his bulk to stare at the source of the petition.

The one who looked like a racehorse turned his mouth down and busied himself by screwing a cigarette into a tortoiseshell holder.

'Have you no charity, mein Herr?'

The heavy one turned a deeper shade of red and said, 'Piss off.'

'Oh, give him something,' the other German said wearily. 'It's a country of beggars.'

The first German made a disgusted face and threw some money on the table. 'Now piss off,' he repeated. His speech was thick and slurred, and he had pulled out his top stud so his collar flapped loose. He swore more violently when he saw that the priest was still perched at the table like a bird of ill omen.

'Do you have something for me, Fraulein?' the man in black said to the girl.

'Of course.' But instead of reaching for her purse she extended her hand to the priest, who took it and raised it to his lips.

'It's unbelievable!' the first German spluttered. He pawed at the girl's shoulder and said, 'Do you know this holy-water man?'

'He's my favourite confessor,' she replied with a little smile that dimpled her cheek. She had clear, translucent skin and an oval face framed by waves of fine-spun coppery hair.

'Wait a minute!' the first German slurred. 'I know you!' He dragged back his chair and got up to get a better look at the priest. 'It's Johnny, isn't it? Johnny Gruber! I thought you'd left Rio.'

'It's a hard city to leave. Engineer Hossbach and I used to live in the same guesthouse in Copacabana,' the priest explained to the girl, as if he were rounding out introductions at a garden party.

'So I've found out your little secret!' Hossbach roared at Johnny. 'You like to fuck in a priest's skirts!'

'I'm afraid our friend Hossbach has had too much to drink,' Johnny said to the table.

'Yes,' the other German intervened curtly. 'Sit down, Hossbach, and apologise to the lady for your language.' He had a metallic, rather high-pitched voice that reminded Johnny of a blade being sharpened.

Hossbach did as he was told.

'Wolfgang Trott,' the second German introduced himself. 'From the embassy. I take it you are living in Rio, Herr Gruber?'

Johnny nodded.

'I'm surprised we haven't met.' Trott paused, inspecting Johnny's costume more closely. The cassock was several sizes too small. 'I must say, Hossbach has a point,' the attaché went on. 'Do you often go about dressed like that?'

'It's Carnival.' Johnny shrugged as if this explained everything.

'Sit down and have a drink, Johnny,' Hossbach interjected, brandishing a bottle.

'I'm afraid I've kept Sigrid waiting too long already. She has to be home before her husband.' Johnny winked.

Hossbach snorted and returned to mauling the girl. He got one of his meaty fists on her thigh, but she wriggled free.

'It's become quite a ritual in Rio,' Sigrid said coolly, on her feet and smoothing her dress. 'Husbands and wives go to different parties during Carnival. But there are still certain courtesies that must be observed.'

'Of course,' Trott agreed, rising to kiss her hand. 'I've been told that it is no crime in Rio for a man to blow out the brains of his wife's lover. Is that so, Herr Gruber?'

'I've heard something about it,' Johnny mumbled. There was menace in Trott's icy poise.

'I'm sure we'll have the pleasure of meeting again,' Trott said as they shook hands. He wore the Nazi party emblem under his lapel, Johnny noted. The stem showed through.

Johnny took the girl's arm and squired her around the dancers, towards the exit behind the piano.

'It's not right to keep so much woman to yourself!' Hossbach bawled after them.

When they had reached the stairs, she clutched his arm tighter. 'In God's name, Johnny,' she said in an urgent whisper, 'What held you up? And who are those men?'

'Later,' he responded sharply. Her voice was still steady enough, but he could feel the trembling in her arm. She was frightened and angry and probably half dead with fatigue, and it was taking all her reserves to keep up a mask of composure.

There were half a dozen rooms above the Babylônia Club that could be rented by the hour or the night. The toll collector was a blowsy woman with dyed red hair who sat in a booth at the top of the stairs eating chocolates. She dealt matter-of-factly with the priest and the girl in the butterfly mask. After all, she had seen strange goings-on at the Babylônia. Just the same, she crossed herself after taking their money and giving them the key to a room at the end of the hall – a room where a federal deputy, no less, had gasped his last while pleasuring two lively brown girls from Bahia.

Johnny locked the door behind them, flung his hat on the bed and took her in his arms. Her mouth tasted of wine and wild strawberries. The edges of her mask chafed his skin, so he pulled it off. In the murky orange light of the bedside sconces he could see the dark rings of worry and fatigue around her eyes. The irises were a pale sea green, the green of pebbles at the bottom of the water. There was a small red scratch mark in one of her eyes, close to the cornea, as if a tiny blood vessel had burst. All the same, she was painfully beautiful.

He pulled her closer, till the contours of their bodies were locked tight together. He was breathing heavily. He did not conceal his quickening desire.

'Johnny –'

He was half waltzing, half shoving her backwards onto the bed. Her body moved in rhythm with his, straining to meet him, as if there was no world, no terror, but this. By an effort of will, she wrenched herself free. The sudden motion caught Johnny off balance. His right leg collided with the brass bed frame, and he winced in pain.

'What's the matter? Are you hurt?'

He shook his head. 'Just an old wound,' he grunted. He sat down heavily on the bed, nursing his leg.

She folded her arms under her breasts and studied him. 'You're lying,' she said. 'Let me see.'

Without waiting for his approval, she hitched up his cassock until she found a rough strip of bandage, crudely knotted above the knee. It was caked with blood.

He did not resist when she stripped away the bandage and probed the blackened trench the bullet had dug across his thigh. But the faint flush that had returned to his cheeks drained away when she started dabbing at the wound with a handkerchief soaked in perfume from her bag. She pulled the covers off the bed and made a new bandage with a strip of linen torn from the sheet. She knotted it tight and said, 'It may have chipped a bone. I'll take you to Eusebio. He'll be home by now.'

Eusebio was a socialist and a doctor, one of the few who had eluded the police over the last few months.

Johnny tested the bandage and shook his head. 'It's not worth the risk. I've found us a boat. It sails in the morning. We can go direct from here to the docks.'

'But Johnny, we can't. We have orders –'

'Forget the orders,' he snapped. 'All orders are cancelled. Don't you understand? We're finished in Brazil. The revolution is defeated. *Kaput*. Our only duty now is to save our skins.'

She stared at him, and the unspoken question was clear from her expression, a compound of fear and suspicion.

'The police were waiting for me,' he said quietly. 'They waited for me to walk right inside the sack. There were men all round the block. I got away over the rooftops. There was a church – a priest who was ready to help.'

'A priest?' Her surprise was understandable. In that year of revolution, few men of the cloth were on the side of the rebels.

'A man of God,' he said impatiently. 'It doesn't matter for now.'

22

'What about the others?'

'Max is safe enough,' he said bitterly. 'We can be sure of that. His kind know how to look out for themselves. By now he'll be drinking at the bar of the Crillón in Buenos Aires. What I want to know is who told the police about the safe house.'

She thought about this for a moment. With her dress disarranged, hanging partway off her shoulder, and the fabric stretched tight to reveal the upward tilt of her breasts, she looked wickedly – discordantly – sensual.

She said, 'It could have been Emil,' and instantly bit her lip, as if to choke back the words. Emil was the chief of the conspiracy, and he had been in jail since Christmas, two full months. What they had done to him in the barracks of the Special Police was almost beyond imagining.

'No,' Johnny said flatly. 'It wasn't Emil. He never knew the address.'

She mentioned the names of other prisoners, the handful of men and women who had been privy to the secrets of the envoys of the Comintern in Rio – the 'Grey Cardinals', as one of the Brazilians jeeringly described them – and Johnny dismissed them one after another.

'Only three people knew that house,' he said curtly.

He watched the cloud pass across her face. What it left behind was a deeper layer of fear.

'Johnny, you don't think – ' she faltered. 'You don't think it was *me*?'

'If I believed that,' he said carefully, 'I think I'd go out in the street and shoot myself. Or possibly both of us.'

He covered her hands with his own. 'We'll leave it for now,' he said softly. '*Das wird auch abgerechnet*. The account will be settled later.'

It had been this way since the failure of the rising, since the mutineers in the army barracks on the pretty beach of Praia Vermelha, at the foot of the Sugarloaf, had been bombed and strafed into submission. The surviving con-spirators – 'Communist bandits', according to the government-controlled press – had been stalking each other, hunting for police spies. Now he was bone tired and wounded and fighting back the blackest doubts about his own mission. For an hour or two at least, he wanted a truce, a sanctuary.

'Sigrid,' he said, coaxingly. 'I'll never doubt you. I hope you believe me. You must never doubt me either. Promise me that.'

'Johnny, you'll never have to ask for that.' Her eyes were full of pain and bewilderment.

'Promise me,' he insisted.

'All right, I promise. But I don't know what you're saying.'

'Whatever I have done – whatever I may have to do – is for love of you.' He seemed on the point of making some larger statement. Instead, he nestled his head on her breast. When he plucked at the fastenings of her clothes and tossed them across the room like whirling leaves, she did not resist. There was a great wind in the room whose deliberate violence gathered them together and shut out all the commotion from the dance floor below and the Carnival that was spending its last energies outside.

Afterwards, she fell into a deep sleep and he smoked and listened to the thud of insects beating against the screen in the window and the twang of a single-stringed instrument someone was playing in the street below. Sexual arousal is the last reflex of a hanged man. The thought flicked maliciously, repetitively at the edge of his consciousness, so that sleep, when it came, was shallow and haunted by fearful images.

He dozed until a hammering at the door shook the dresser he had pushed against it to reinforce the simple lock. Still half asleep, with the girl clutching the sheet to her throat while he grabbed for the ten-shot Mauser he had hidden under a pillow, he imagined he was in another city and called out in German, 'Who's there?'

In the babble of words from beyond the door he recognised the voice of the woman who collected the rent.

'Forgive me, Father,' she was saying. 'But the police are downstairs. A raid during Carnival! Whoever heard of such a thing?'

He rushed to the window. There was a truck blocking off one end of the street and men in red kepis, carbines at the ready. Special Police. So it wasn't a matter of checking that the tarts' medical papers were in order.

He tucked the gun back into the waistband of his shorts and slipped the cassock over his head.

'Listen,' he said to Sigrid. 'They're after me, I'm sure of it. I may have been followed. I want you to stay here till the search is over.'

She started to protest, but he put a finger over her lips and went on, 'You'll be all right. They'll think you're one of the working girls. I'll fix it with the woman outside.'

'But what about you?'

'I'll find a way. Whatever happens, you must be at this place at six o'clock.' He made her memorise the address on a street near the Praça Maua. 'There'll be a man waiting. You must do whatever he says.'

'How will I know him?'

'He'll know you. Whatever happens,' he repeated, 'you must be on that boat.'

'Johnny –'

'You promised you would trust me.'

'It's not that. I just want you to kiss me.'

He had words with the woman in the booth, and money changed hands. She made sympathetic clucking noises over the plight of a married lady discovered by chance under such circumstances and pointed the way to the fire escape. Leaning from the window over the iron steps, Johnny saw more red caps along the alleyway behind the Babylônia Club. The police seemed to be checking everyone who came and went – but only the men, he noted, were asked for their papers.

The music was still blaring from the dance floor, which suggested that the police were not being over-assertive on the premises of the club itself, and a plan began to shape itself in Johnny's mind. It was insane, just insane enough to work.

He went back down the stairs into the Babylônia Club. He could spot the policemen at once, from their hats and the way their double-breasted jackets were buttoned tight across their midriffs. One had taken off his hat, and his hair was stiff and shiny with cream. They were moving from table to table.

He marched over to the table where the Germans were sitting. The wine waiter, or the intrusion of the police, must have dissatisfied them, because they had sent for their bill. A heavily rouged woman hung on Trott's arm but was clearly getting nowhere.

'I didn't expect to see you again tonight, Herr Gruber,' Trott greeted him, shaking off his female companion.

Johnny sat down without waiting to be invited.

Hossbach, who had been sunk in torpor, rallied himself to make a coarse remark about sexual staying power. 'I'll go and finish the job,' he announced. 'Show her what a real German is made of.' He launched into a graphic description of what he had in mind.

'By the way,' Trott interjected, 'what have you done with the lady?' The man from the German Embassy had screwed an eyeglass into his face, and it stayed there as effortlessly as if it were grafted to the skin.

'She went out the back way,' Johnny lied. 'She was terrified that her husband would find out.'

Trott did not comment. He tossed a thick pile of Brazilian banknotes onto the saucer on top of the bill.

'I see you're bored with the Babylônia,' Johnny remarked. 'I know a superior establishment that is quite diverting, on the Rua Alici.'

'Hah!' Hossbach chimed in. 'I bet I know the one. You can get anything you want.' He dug Trott in the ribs. The attaché looked pained but also mildly inquisitive.

'It's not far,' Johnny prodded. 'I'll show you the way if you like.'

Trott gave a little nod and stood up, indicating the decision was made.

The police stopped them only at the door, and their profuse apologies were amplified when Trott showed his embassy credentials. The inspector peered at the man in the priest's cassock curiously.

'This is our embassy chaplain,' Trott announced without the shadow of a smile. Johnny was not asked for his papers.

'These people lack formation,' Trott said, when they were outside, waiting for Zé Pimenta to summon the embassy driver. 'I'm sure that if I had declined to show my papers they would never have insisted. They can't conceive that a subversive could be dressed in a dinner jacket. We Germans know better, don't we, Herr Gruber? We have a great deal to teach them. But they're a weak race,' he added reflectively, 'a mongrel race, leached by the climate of the tropics. Hossbach was telling me just now that the reason that half the Brazilian men hold the cup with their left hand when they're drinking their eternal *cafezinhos* is that they are terrified of syphilis. They think that by holding the cup in the wrong hand, they'll avoid sipping from the same spot where a syphilitic might have pressed his lips. Have you seen that?'

'Yes, I've seen it,' Johnny acknowledged. He watched the red caps patrolling the street from the corner of his eye.

'But since so many of them do it, they defeat the whole object of the exercise!' Trott observed triumphantly. 'And they don't even see their own absurdity! They're worse than Italians. It will take an iron man to change them.'

Hossbach puffed himself up as if he thought he were a candidate for this role.

Trott's powerful black Mercedes was waved through the roadblock and purred to a stop in front of them, with Zé Pimenta on the running board. Zé excelled himself, holding his pasteboard scimitar in front of his nose with one hand while the other fished for tips.

To Trott's surprise, Johnny did not accompany them into the house on the Rua Alici, pleading sudden fatigue.

'I'm sorry,' he said. 'I think I've overdone it.'

'My man will drive you home,' Trott suggested solicitously. 'What's your address?'

'No, but thank you. I'll walk for a while to clear my head.'

Trott squinted at him through the eyeglass, which gave him the aspect of a man inspecting an unidentified organism through a microscope.

Johnny set off in search of a taxi. There were always a few on the prowl in this neighbourhood, which was home to the most exclusive bordellos in the city. His head was light, but the sky had clouded over. He could no longer see moon or stars, only the great statue of the Redeemer, arms outstretched, lit up on top of the hunched peak of Corcovado. The cobbled street he was following sloped down the hill into a well of darkness where the street lamps were sparse. He must have mistaken his direction. He wheeled around to retrace his steps.

At the same instant a car on the slope above him turned on its headlights. For a moment he stood blinded by the high beams. It occurred to him that Trott might have sent his chauffeur after him.

But it was a Brazilian voice that called out, 'Good morning, Senhor Gruber.'

He hurled himself into the shadows, out of the headlights, tearing at his useless priest's disguise to find his Mauser. Before he could get it loose, several men came running at him. One of them dealt him a blow to the chest with his rifle butt that sent him toppling backward into the street.

Laid out on his back, he summoned enough strength to send one of his assailants flying with a hard left kick. He got the gun out and fired wildly. He heard the tinkle of glass as one of the car headlights blew out. Then they were all over him. They wrestled the Mauser away from him and one of them rammed it up against his closed teeth so he could taste the steel of the muzzle.

The one in charge sauntered down the hill and stood over him. Behind his captor, beyond the vast bay of Guanabara, a narrow slash of pink had appeared in the eastern sky.

Captain Honorio Schmidt, the chief of the Special Police, studied his prize with satisfaction and decided to allow himself one of his slim Bahian cigars. One of his assistants sprang forward to strike a match.

Captain Honorio huffed life into the cheroot and remarked, 'It's Ash Wednesday, Father.'

I

Bolsheviks

(1913–1934)

We are fighting for the gates of heaven.
> *— Karl Liebknecht,*
> *murdered leader of the*
> *Spartacist rising (1919)*

1

The Call

Man is the only animal who refuses to be what he is.
— *Albert Camus*

1

When he stood by the window, he could hear the sirens
from the harbour, calling him. At times they were women's
voices, keening on the wind. The siren voices came from
places with magical names, across shining oceans, from
Ceylon and Madagascar and Manaus. It was all he could
do not to drop everything and run out the door, out of that
overheated room with its fat-bellied stove and the dark,
heavy furniture that seemed to close in on him, squeezing
out the air and the life, like someone forcing a pillow down
over his face.

'Johann!' his mother barked at him. 'Be careful with
those!'

It was a few days before Christmas, and he had been
conscripted for women's work, helping his mother and his
sister Bertha to trim and decorate the *Tannenbaum* that
occupied the middle of the front parlour. It was a grey,
cheerless day outside, and the light was nearly spent, but
that wouldn't have stopped him rushing down to the docks.
He liked to hang around the ferry landing and watch the
seamen going back and forth to the giant wharves across
the river where the ships of the Hamburg-Amerika Line
came in. He played games of pirates around the godowns,

which smelled of tea and spice. He loved the bustle of the fish market at St Pauli. More daring, he and his friends would range the streets above it, past tattoo shops with pictures of big-hipped tropical girls in the window, down alleys where the naked girls in the windows were real and where pimps and policemen came running to shoo the boys away.

But here he was, fussing over Christmas decorations. It was part of his punishment. He had been sent home from school early with a note from the headmaster after giving Willi Rausch, the school bully, a black eye. Willi Rausch was a swaggering lout who was suffered by the masters because his father was a boss of the Shipowners' Association. That morning, he had pushed Johnny too far. He started by crowing that Johnny's pants were too short. Then he put two fingers above his head, like horns, and cackled that Herr Lentz was a capon who didn't know who was doing it with his wife. When Johnny went for him, he got out his penknife, but it didn't help him a bit. Johnny knew how to use his fists, and he knew when to ignore the rules. He had learned all about that in the back alleys behind the harbour.

His mother had ordered him to stay inside until his father got home. There would be a reckoning, she promised. And tomorrow Johnny would have to make a formal apology to Willi Rausch and his parents. The Rausch family were important people, and Hermann Rausch was his father's employer.

Herr Lentz was unusually late coming home from the office that night. Johnny did not fear his anger. In that household the mother was the angry one. She seemed to tower over her husband, a big-boned woman who twisted her thick blonde hair into a coronet. She never tired of telling him that she had married beneath her, that he was dragging her down in the world. Johnny often thought of his father as a wounded bird. He wasn't made to walk on the ground, but his wings wouldn't work. He was a shy, unassuming man who went about in a dove-grey tie and striped trousers like a government functionary. His stoop and his pince-nez made him look smaller than he was. He could sometimes be heard tinkling on the harpsichord in the music room. This expensive instrument – as Johnny's mother frequently recalled during family squabbles – had been purchased with *her* money.

The Lentz family, like the street in Hamburg where they lived, had come down sharply in the world. Only Frau Lentz's inheritance kept the bailiffs away. When she had married Gottfried, Johnny's father, he had been thought to be a fine young musician with a brilliant career. But he had wasted years writing experimental pieces that no orchestra wanted to perform, and his brilliant career had receded further and further into the future. By day, he was reduced to toiling as a clerk in the great gloomy hall of the Ship-owners' Association down by the docks. By night, he gave himself over to his secret world. Johnny would sometimes wake in the early hours to hear him working on some strange, discordant composition with plunging gaps in the scales, as sombre and unsettling as the black well under the trapdoor leading to the coal cellar. Then he would hear his mother's angry tread, her voice raised shrill in anger and, as often as not, the thud of blows rained on his father's unresisting back. She would fly at the failed composer with anything that fell to hand, even a poker. He never fought back. Herr Lentz was a pacifist.

'We're going for a walk,' he had announced to his wife one Sunday afternoon, clutching Johnny's hand. They had walked as far as a coffee-house, where six or seven men were assembled in a back room. Johnny recognised the family doctor and the director of a funeral parlour. They greeted Gottfried Lentz warmly, and Johnny was proud that, here at least, his father commanded respect.

A plump fellow with a Polish accent gave a talk on how technical progress had made war obsolete. In the age of the telegraph and steam shipping, he asserted, the countries of the world were all interdependent; for one to make war on another would be like setting out to burgle your own home. Furthermore, the instruments of slaughter had become so lethally effective – witness the invention of the magazine rifle – that soldiers would never consent to fight each other.

There was a good deal of applause, and Johnny's father got up and made a short speech on the brotherhood of man, garnished with quotations from Fourier in the original French.

'Well, what do you have to say?' Gottfried Lentz asked his son on the way home.

'You can't remake men overnight. Men are made to fight.'

'That's not so! We only fight because of the kind of society we live in. When we change the social order, when we abolish class tyranny, everything will be different.'

'And do you think that can happen without a fight?' A small troop of hussars came clattering past, splendid in their blue dolmans. 'They think your Fourier is just another Frenchman to be put to the sword.'

'They're dinosaurs,' Gottfried Lentz murmured with quiet contempt. 'We have to kill the Prussian in all of us.' This was a backhand swipe at his wife, whose family came from East Prussia. 'I'll give you some books to read, so you can begin to understand. But Johnny –' Their corner had come into view. 'Not a word about this to your mother, do you hear?'

Dutifully and secretly, Johnny had struggled with the tracts of the utopian socialists, but they were too bloodless for his taste. He preferred the mythic romances of his own country – Wolfram's *Parzifal* in particular, with its tale of heroism in a magical quest to rescue a dying kingdom. He liked the Wild West adventures of Karl May, but above all he loved stories of the sea. His imagination was filled with the exploits of Raleigh and Klaus Störtebecker, the buccaneer from Hamburg. He thrilled with pride when he went with a school party to watch the launching of one of Germany's splendid new battle cruisers. His father detested the Kaiser, with his bristling moustaches, as a noisy war-monger, but Johnny could picture himself in the smart uniform of a German naval officer. In his imagination the sea meant release from the drab taboos of family life, from his father's albino abstractions, his mother's petty tyranny and his sister Bertha's tireless pursuit of a comfortable bourgeois marriage.

He was thinking of the sea now, as he worked his way through his mother's box of Christmas ornaments. At fourteen, he was tall enough to reach the topmost branches of the tree without use of the stepladder. His rope-coloured hair, wide, chiselled mouth and candid blue-grey eyes came from his mother's side of the family. So did the fussy set of lead crystal angels, trumpets and wings outstretched, that he was disentangling from the shrouds of crepe paper.

He yawned and wondered whether there would be time left before dinner to visit one of their neighbours on the Valentinskamp, a young man called Heinz Kordt, who wore a seaman's cap and had sailed on the ships of the North German Lloyd. Frau Lentz disapproved of Heinz Kordt. She called him a 'ruffian' and (on one occasion) a 'desperado' and had forbidden Johnny to visit his lodgings – a prohibition Johnny cheerfully ignored. With his bold gaze, his ruddy cheeks and his flourishing jet-black beard, Heinz Kordt was, in Johnny's eyes, a very fair imitation of a pirate. Johnny could picture him storming the walls of Cartagena and getting royally drunk on Spanish wine with a pair of black-eyed girls as the flames leaped from the rooftops. Kordt wove wondrous tales of lost islands in the Pacific, mutiny on the high seas and knife fights in the Boca – the red-light district – of Buenos Aires. He fed the boy's fascination by opening up the huge metal trunk that occupied most of his room and showing him souvenirs from his voyages. One night he pulled out a tiny shrunken head, not much bigger than a walnut, with matted dark hair festooned with shells and parrot's feathers. Kordt said he had bought it from headhunters along the banks of the River of Death, somewhere in the jungles of Brazil.

Johnny was thinking about the shrunken head and the way it felt like baked clay to the touch, when he heard the jangle of the front door.

'Gottfried?' his mother called. 'Is that you?'

The man who staggered into the living room was barely recognisable as the prim little clerk of the Shipowners'

Association or even the Sunday *philosophe*. His starched collar flapped wide. He was hatless, and his lank, thinning hair hung down to his eyebrows. His pince-nez was precariously suspended above the bulging tip of his nose, which was suspiciously empurpled. His overcoat trailed daringly from his shoulders.

'Gottfried?' Frau Lentz sniffed the air. 'Have you been *drinking*?'

Between a belch and a cough Johnny's father mumbled something that might have been, 'It's that time of year.'

'*Gottfried*! Have you no decency?'

'That's not all,' Herr Lentz piped up. 'I am no longer in the employ of the Swindlers' – that is, the Shipowners' – Association.'

'Have you taken leave of your senses?'

Pink, bouncy Bertha came in from the kitchen and goggled at her father.

'How will you fend for poor Bertha, who is all but engaged?' Frau Lentz pursued. 'How will we pay for Johann's school, where he spends all his time brawling? Do you want to disgrace us? Do you want to live in the gutter? You must wash out your mouth and go to Herr Rausch at once –'

Johnny pictured Willi Rausch's father, a bloated version of the son, a walrus with thick moustaches who fancied himself a ladies' man and had flirted with Frau Lentz at office parties.

'Herr Rausch is a fair man,' Frau Lentz insisted.

'I did not resign.' Gottfried Lentz drew himself up to his full height, till he seemed in danger of toppling backwards.

'What are you saying?' Frau Lentz's eyes widened. Then her arm shot out, pointing straight at Johnny. 'It's because of him, isn't it? Because he was picking on the Rausch boy, the godless savage. We must go to them at once and apologise. Bertha, get my shawl –'

'It won't do any good.' Johnny's father's lips were curled in a blissfully vacant grin. 'I was sacked for expressing dangerous political ideas.'

'That can't be true. It's because of the boy. Bertha –'

'Not only true, my dear, but to emphasise my point I told Rausch he could stick my miserable pittance up his backside. Then I stuck *this* in his fat mug.' He winked at Johnny and displayed a row of shiny knuckles.

'You're drunk! You're insane!' Heidi Lentz looked ready to faint. An extraordinary mewling sound came from Bertha, whose heart was set on snaring the eldest of the Rausch boys.

Johnny became so excited that he let slip the lead crystal angel he had been trying to fasten to the Christmas tree. It flew to the stone apron of the fireplace and shattered into a dozen shards.

This diversion revived Frau Lentz and provided a momentary reprieve for her husband.

'Johann!' Frau Lentz shrieked.

'I'm sorry – I didn't mean it –' Johnny stammered, but the awesome force of his mother's wrath was now trained on him.

She lashed out with the first object that came to hand – the pair of shears they had used earlier to trim the tree. Johnny dodged the blow, seized hold of his mother's wrist and wrenched until the metal tool fell from her hand.

For a moment she seemed bolted to the ground, stunned by this new rebellion. Then the blood rushed into her cheeks, and she yelled at her husband, 'Deal with your son, you miserable excuse for a man!'

Johnny didn't wait to see what response this would bring. Without saying a word he ran to the kitchen, grabbed his ulster from its hook and banged out the side door.

Oblivious to his mother's screams and his sister's wails, he raced down the steps and then west along the Valentinskamp in the direction of St Pauli, through a fine mist of rain. It was already dark, and the street lamps cast sulfurous pools of light on the wet pavement. He paused half a block away from the house, until he saw his father come out onto the porch.

'I wish I'd been there to see it,' Johnny said when his father had caught up.

Gottfried Lentz smiled. For the first time Johnny could remember, his father looked like a free man.

'But it *was* because of my fight with Willi, wasn't it?' Johnny went on.

His father's face clouded. 'It would have come to the same thing. So long as the bosses can treat people like replaceable parts. Someday we'll change all of that. But for now –' he sighed. 'Life goes on. We'd better go inside.'

'I can't go back.'

'Don't be silly. It's not the end of the world. It's not your fault. I'll find another job.'

'I've been thinking about this for a while, father. I'm old enough to take care of myself –'

'You're fourteen! What can you do without a school certificate? Work as a navvy down at the docks? There are worse bosses than Rausch, I can tell you.'

'I've got friends. I'll be all right. Please go inside, father. You'll catch cold.'

They heard Frau Lentz's harsh voice raised from the porch. Involuntarily Johnny's father shuddered.

'Don't be too hard on her,' he said to his son. 'She's not a bad woman, you know. She just can't help herself.'

'I know. I have to go, that's all.'

Johnny waited for his father's response. He couldn't go back into that house, where he felt his lungs were bursting. He couldn't go back to that expensive school, where the teachers sided with Willi Rausch because his father had money and rode around in a fancy carriage, puffing his cigar. Besides, he knew the school fees had been crippling for his father. Now it would be worse. By leaving he would be doing all of them a favour.

He refused to live as his father had lived, a man with a dream that was broken daily on the wheel. His father had had his moment of glorious revolt, and in that moment Johnny had felt closer to him than ever before. But his father's words suggested that the moment had already passed. 'Life goes on . . .'

I'm not going to wait until I'm past forty to punch the Rausches of this world in the nose, Johnny told himself.

'But where will you go?' his father repeated.

'I've got friends. I'll manage. Don't worry yourself.'

'You'll write? At least you'll write?'

'Of course I will.'

Gottfried made no effort to invoke parental authority. Perhaps he felt his own actions earlier that day had made a mockery of all that. Perhaps he felt it would be more than mildly ridiculous for him to tell this strapping youth, a head taller than himself, that he would not be able to fend for himself. Perhaps he even felt a tinge of envy.

Johnny tried not to recognise the pain in his father's face. I'm doing them a favour, he reminded himself.

Gottfried blinked myopically through his spectacles, which were beaded with rain. Then he rummaged in his vest pocket and pressed something into Johnny's hand. A bank note. He moved as if to hug his son, then stiffened in embarrassment and stuck out his hand instead. This friend of abstract humanity had always shied away from physical contact.

'If only I were younger –' he began, then cleared his throat.

The boy swallowed and walked quickly away.

'Proudhon!' his father's reedy voice wafted after him. 'Don't forget to read Proudhon!'

Two blocks farther on, Johnny crossed the street and ran up the steps into the building where Heinz Kordt had his lodgings. Once the mansion of some Hanseatic burgomaster, it was now a disreputable apartment house, only a cut above a tenement.

In the lobby he nearly bowled over a sallow, furtive man in a fedora and an oversized overcoat that billowed around his ankles. The stranger thrust his hand into his pocket, and Johnny imagined that he saw the bulge of a revolver. For an instant their eyes met. The stranger's quick stare was feral, the gaze of a hunted animal ready to round on its pursuers and tear. A low rumble came from the man's throat. Then he was gone.

Johnny's imagination was fired up by this brief encounter. He saw the roof of the Shipowners' Association blown off by an anarchist bomb. He had spotted other wary, vaguely foreign men coming and going at all hours from an office at the back that was rented by a socialist group. These socialists did not look much like his father's circle of henpecked philosophers. Maybe they were Russians. In one of his father's tracts he had come across a reference to 'the propaganda of the deed' – the method of the Russian revolutionaries who had blown up a Tsar and a grand duke. The world called these Russians terrorists, yet Johnny thought they were the reverse of cowards. They gladly put their own lives at risk, believing that by offering to sacrifice themselves they would demonstrate the purity of their cause.

The boy who had pictured himself in the uniform of a naval officer (not much chance of that now) could also daydream of joining a party of bomb throwers. He was of an age, and a temperament, in which the call of adventure, not flags or philosophies, was supreme. He wanted to live each day as if it were his last.

He climbed the stairs, and found that the lightbulb on Kordt's landing had burned out. He stood in darkness and tapped gently on the door. There was no response. But he could see, from the chink along the bottom, that the light was on inside the sailor's room, and he could hear gusts of music from a gramophone. He rapped louder on Kordt's door. There was a scuffling sound and a groan that might have been bedsprings.

A sleepy voice called out, 'Go away!'

The boy knocked again. 'Heinz! It's me. Johnny.'

There was an odd smell on the landing, like burning rope. He leaned his ear up against Kordt's door. He heard low whispers, a ripple of laughter and another creak from the bedsprings.

The door was flung open without warning, so abruptly that Johnny went spinning headlong into the room and landed on a heap of pillows that had been dumped providentially on the floor. Kordt's lodgings were suffused with pink light, the effect of the makeshift shade the sailor had constructed by tossing the top of an old pair of red pyjamas over his bedside lamp.

The first thing Johnny saw, as he tried to reorient himself, was a narrow, sloping calf in a black fishnet stocking. He raised his eyes higher. All the girl was wearing apart from the stockings was a garter belt and a tart's brassiere with holes snipped out to show off her nipples. Her straight blonde hair was cut tight around her head, like a helmet. Despite her outfit, he guessed she was not much older than he – fifteen or sixteen at most. Her breasts were barely formed, and her slender body, straight as a boy's, was almost hairless. He stared at her, open-mouthed.

She burst out laughing and puffed smoke in his face as he tried to scramble to his feet. She was smoking a knobbly pipe, one of Kordt's. Again there was that odd aroma of burning rope.

Heinz Kordt was laughing too. He clapped Johnny on the shoulder and said, 'What's the matter, boy? Haven't you seen a girl's backside before?'

Johnny blushed to the roots of his hair, and the seaman laughed louder. He was wearing only his red pyjama bottoms. He had various tattoos on his arms, among them a sea monster inscribed in marvellous detail and a cruder design of a South Seas girl in a grass skirt.

Kordt flung his arm around Johnny's neck. 'You like the look of her? Her name's Helene. You can play with her, if she lets you.'

The girl made a face like a cat preparing to spit.

'She's a little spitfire, all right,' Kordt said indulgently. 'But she's clean, I'll warrant you that. She's from Berlin. I found her at the station. A runaway, just asking for trouble. I'd thought I'd better bring her up here before she ran into somebody worse.'

Helene marched up to Johnny and tweaked his nose. 'How old are you?' she demanded. Her voice was surprisingly deep; it might have been a ventriloquist's trick. There was a disturbing vacancy about her ice-blue eyes.

Johnny swallowed and said, 'Seventeen.'

'Liar,' she hissed.

'It's true,' he protested.

'Then let me see you smoke this.' She offered him the pipe, and he wasn't scared to take it. He had tasted tobacco before in Kordt's room and in secret corners of the school-yard and down at the fish market. But he had never tasted tobacco like this. After a few puffs, inhaling the way she did to show he was every bit as grown up, the room started to blur and he thought he saw Kordt's red pyjama tops burst into flame above the lamp.

'Indian hemp,' Kordt remarked mysteriously and confidentially. 'Never touch it myself.' He confiscated the pipe and added, 'You'd better be running back to your own folks. I've met your mother and that's one lady I wouldn't care to cross.'

'I'm not going home,' Johnny said flatly.

'One drink,' Kordt responded with mock severity. 'Then it's off with you. Helene and I have unfinished business.'

'I mean I've left. For good.'

While Kordt stared at Johnny, the girl waggled her finger and chortled, 'He's a runaway!'

'Let's see if I've got this straight,' Kordt said to Johnny. 'You've left home for good?'

Johnny nodded.

'Why? You've got a decent home, you go to a decent school. The whole world is ahead of you. But not if you drop out.'

'You told me when you left home, you were younger than me,' Johnny countered accusingly.

'I didn't have any choice. I didn't even know my father's name, and my mother was generally too drunk to remember mine. What's your excuse?'

Johnny tried, haltingly at first, then with passion, to explain. Heinz growled when Rausch's name was mentioned.

'I know that bastard,' the sailor grunted. 'He had me on a blacklist once. For tossing a couple of scabs overboard. If the workers ever get their way, he'll be one of the first to go.' He rubbed his chin. 'All right. So what's your next step?'

'I'm going to sea.'

'Just like that, huh?'

'I thought you might help me find a boat.' He stared at the floor, partly to avoid the spectacle of Helene, who had stretched out on the bed and was kicking her legs in the air.

'Listen.' Kordt – who had given the boy a couple of boxing lessons – feinted a right jab at his face. 'You'll find shits like Rausch on board ship as well as onshore. It's no romance, working a merchant steamer. The officers treat you like dogs, and the men aren't much better. You mustn't go by my stories. You'll learn that whatever you're running away from has a habit of catching up with you.'

'I have to go, Heinz.'

'What do you expect to find?'

'Myself.'

He looked Kordt in the eyes then, and the seaman must have read something he approved of, because after a while he nodded. Then he was on his feet, grabbing for his clothes. He gave the girl on the bed, who had rolled over on her belly, a smack on the rump.

'Put something on, will you? I've a mind to show the boy the town.'

They went to a dive where Heinz seemed to be well known, on the border of St Pauli and the workers' district of Altona. An exotic name was picked out in multicoloured lights at the top of a rickety flight of steps. From the street Johnny thought the sign read 'Ali's Bar'. Closer up, he saw that the bulbs in the frame of the first letter had been smashed. The place was the Kali-Bar, named for a Hindu deity.

'There's the old girl herself,' Kordt remarked as they entered a dark, cavernous loft, pointing at a weird statue of beaten tin and silver paper daubed with gaudy enamels. It was a female figure with pointed dugs that hung to its waist, a lolling, pointed tongue and a necklace of death's heads. 'Time the devourer. Chews her men up, that one. Pretty, isn't she? Some of the black-asses who come here think she's their patron saint.'

He shot a sidelong glance at Johnny, to see if the boy was shocked.

Johnny was drinking up the whole scene. Under the smudged light of blue lanterns filtered by hessian sacking, scores of men and women groped and gyrated to a scratchy recording. There were seamen from every port, with a high proportion of lascars and Chinamen. Some of them danced together, others with heavily rouged tarts or pale, overgrown girls who were bussed in at the end of their shifts from the big cement works at Altona. A sinuous creature of indeterminate sex wafted towards them. A pale arm flashed out and, before Johnny realised what was happening, the apparition was trying to shake hands with his private parts.

He pushed the thing away, revolted.

'Pretty, pretty,' it hissed at him.

'Go away,' Helene said, draping her arm around Johnny's shoulder. 'He's taken.'

Johnny felt the warmth as his cheeks flushed red. Helene was laughing at him again, and he was furious that his embarrassment showed. He wanted to prove to Heinz that he was the equal of any experience life might throw in his path, not some callow boy who belonged back in school.

Heinz found them an empty corner at a huge trestle table, and an Indian waiter brought foaming steins of Bremen beer.

'You dance with Helene for a bit.' Heinz nudged Johnny. 'There are some men I have to talk to.'

The girl looked older in her red dress. It was real silk, one of Heinz's trophies from the Orient. As they danced, she ground herself against his body. The insistent, repetitive pressure against his thigh became unbearable. He looked into her face, into those eyes like drowning pools. There was no hint there that she was remotely conscious of the physical effect she was having on him.

Dammit, he thought. Is she trying to make me look a complete fool?

He was rescued by Kordt, who got up from the table

where he had been playing dice with a rough-looking crowd and signalled to him.

'Johnny, this is Ernst.' Kordt introduced a man who was built like a beer keg. His head bulged out of his trunk with only the faintest suggestion of a neck. His stubby legs seemed to have been tacked on as an afterthought. His eyes were dark, narrow slits; the whites didn't show at all.

'There's a Norwegian ship at the Kaiser Quai leaving for Frisco Bay tomorrow,' Kordt reported. 'Ernst is chief stoker. He can get you signed on if he likes the look of you.'

Ernst sized Johnny up and spat a wad of tobacco on to the floor. 'Too soft,' he muttered, turning away.

Johnny was outraged. He clutched at the stoker's shoulder. 'What do you mean, too soft?'

Ernst grabbed his wrist, twisted it round, and pointed at the soft skin of the palm.

'Smooth as a baby's bottom,' he complained, addressing himself to Kordt. 'He's never done a day's work in his life. You should know better than to bring me spoiled puppies like this.'

'He'll learn,' Kordt said. 'Let's have another beer.'

The stoker rubbed the coarse stubble on his chin. 'Pretty boys don't last out the first watch on my tub,' he said, staring rudely at Johnny. Without warning, he struck out with his fist, aiming straight at Johnny's face. He flattened the palm at the last moment so that he merely patted the boy's cheek. 'You know what I'm talking about?' he said mockingly.

Johnny put his fists up straight away and delivered a quick jab to the stoker's belly before he had got his guard up. Ernst swore and took a swing that would have laid the boy out had he not leaped nimbly aside. Johnny feinted with his right and landed two hard left punches. The stoker was winded and angry and came after Johnny with his arms outstretched. For a moment he had the boy caught in a bear hug, and Johnny felt his breath being squeezed out of him. But he wriggled free and a moment later landed a blow to the stoker's jaw that sent him reeling backwards.

He crashed into a table, sent the beer mugs flying and landed on his back, bellowing and flailing his stocky legs. His friends came running over, one of them armed with a bottle.

Kordt pushed between them and Johnny.

'I said the boy would learn,' he reminded Ernst as the stoker struggled to his feet, puffing, and began to dust himself off.

'All right, he'll do,' the stoker agreed grudgingly and shook Johnny's hand.

'And what do you say?' Kordt asked Helene, who had watched the scrap as if it were part of the routine entertainment at the Kali-Bar. She was tapping her foot in time to the music and munching at a big salted horseradish that had been served with the beer.

She moved over to Johnny, light and surefooted as a cat, put her hands on his shoulders and purred, '*Du bist eine Kanone.*' Her voice sounded remote, and her hands were unnaturally cool. Her teeth were slightly irregular, and this gave her a primeval, almost animal, look. She opened her mouth so wide he could see its pink roof. Then she pounced on him, biting the side of his neck. It was a real bite, not a love graze, for when he put his hand to the spot he found a bead of blood on the tip of his finger.

2

Heinz saw him off at the docks after making him swallow a raw egg and a nip of brandy. 'It's the best antidote for a night like that,' the sailor assured him. Helene came too, and when Johnny, bundled up in the old pea jacket Heinz had given him as a going-away present, hugged both of them, he felt, more keenly than the night before, that he was leaving his family.

The squat figure of the chief stoker appeared at the top of the gangway, yelling at Johnny to get on board. He waved to his friends and patted the pocket where he had concealed another gift, a little tattered book with a red cover.

'It's about sharing,' Heinz had said.

It had been a night of initiations, a night when everything was more important than sleep. The scent of the girl still travelled with him, so he imagined, in the folds of his skin. Heinz had left them alone for a few hours, to return before dawn with a couple of bottles and an immense thirst for strong liquor and stronger conversation.

'Hey, give a man some room!' Heinz had boomed at them, lunging for the bed so unexpectedly that Johnny had had to hurl himself to one side to avoid his bulk. The sailor squeezed both of them and pulled the cork out of one of the bottles with his teeth. As he passed it back and forth, he studied each of them with an amused, assessing stare.

'She likes you,' he pronounced at last. 'Are you still set on going to sea?'

'Yes.'

But when the girl shrugged and said, 'It's all the same to me' between gusts of acrid smoke from a Turkish cigarette, Johnny felt bitterly disappointed. She was Heinz's girl, but even so . . .

'Let's talk!' Heinz roared. 'Let's talk of what is and what ought to be!'

For the rest of that magical night, he left no corner of silence where the sadness of parting could take root. He talked of things Johnny had never heard before, of organising a seamen's strike, of rum running across the Baltic, of staging a jailbreak in Batavia to get a comrade out of the hands of the Dutch colonial authorities. Johnny realised now that if his friend was a pirate, he was a pirate in the mould of the new century – a revolutionary ready to make war on the flags and totems of every nation in the old, decaying world. Heinz spoke with real passion, even eloquence, about a coming world upheaval that would sweep away all the doddering crowned heads of Europe, the monocles and the chimney barons, the paunchy capitalists of the Hamburg Shipowners' Association. Seamen would be in the vanguard, according to Heinz, because their travels freed them from the narrow life of the tribe.

But before revolution came, Heinz predicted, there would have to be war.

'That's where your father's wrong,' the sailor pursued. 'The system won't collapse under its own weight. But the kings and the capitalists are lighting a bomb under their own backsides. Wait and see. Europe is a heap of loaded rifles. Move one, and all the rest will go off. *Then* it will be our turn.'

Johnny was drunk on the words, even more than on the brandy Heinz kept pouring down his throat. Bright yet indistinct, like a flash of sheet lightning over the brow of a hill, he could see a mission shaping itself for him.

'And you?' he questioned Heinz. 'What will you do?'

'Oh, I'll make myself useful somewhere or other. Now drink up! Any sailor knows it's terrible luck to put the cork back in a bottle.'

Before they left for the harbour Heinz pressed the dog-eared pamphlet into Johnny's hand.

'Here. Stick this in your pocket. But don't let the officers see you, or they'll turn you off the boat.'

Johnny saw the title. *The Communist Manifesto*.

'It's about sharing,' Heinz went on. 'But handle it gently. It's not a book. It's a bomb. A case of dynamite wrapped in forty pages. If you want to talk to someone about it, talk to Ernst. He's a son of a bitch, but he's on our side.'

On board the Norwegian freighter *Ula* Johnny studied Marx and Engels in the breaks from heaving coal into a glowering furnace until his muscles ached and the sweat poured into his eyes. He found a sheltered spot in the lee of a lifeboat and read and reread the *Communist Manifesto*. He was excited by its coiled power. In a handful of pages the authors had compressed an arching theory of world history, a devastating indictment of a society made for the Rausches – a society founded on selfish calculation – and a programme for revolutionary action. 'Let the ruling classes tremble . . .'

Johnny began to think of himself as a communist. When the *Ula* docked at San Francisco, Ernst took him to a meeting in a smoky hall where twenty men disputed in half a dozen languages. Johnny could follow some of the Yiddish; it was close enough to German. The rest was lost on him. A Javanese seaman got up and jabbered in a tongue that nobody else could understand. But when it was explained that he was pledging the support of the peoples of the Dutch East Indies for the anti-imperialist struggle, he was hailed with rapturous applause.

They gave him leaflets to hand out to the men on the docks. Usually he was rebuffed, sometimes with blows and oaths. The harbour police came to chase him away, but each time he went back. He enjoyed the game of hide and seek. He told himself he was striking a blow for the cause.

But when war came, the call of the tribe – as Heinz had called it disparagingly – was stronger than the canons of Karl Marx.

He was in a honkytonk in Panama drinking with Ernst, who had picked up a pair of olive-skinned girls. They had had to get off their last boat in a hurry after Ernst had led a mutiny against the first officer, a strutting martinet who would flog a man because he didn't like the shine on the deck. The captain had broken out the rifles and threatened to shoot the troublemakers.

Now they were looking for another boat and talking about the carnage in Europe that was reported in the American papers. Johnny felt edgy sitting in foreign bars, sailing under foreign flags, while his own people were fighting and dying in tens of thousands – whether or not the war was just. The Royal Navy was the most powerful on earth, and its arrogant admirals were trying to impose a blockade to starve the Germans into submission. His own family might go hungry. Germany needed sailors, needed them desperately, and a small voice inside him argued that he belonged there, not in a cheap bordello in Panama.

There were French seamen at the next table, six or seven of them, all several sheets to the wind. Johnny heard muttering about *les sales Boches*, obviously directed at them. One of the Frenchmen got up and started bellowing the *Marseillaise*, beating out the rhythm on the table with his fist. The others joined in a ragged chorus.

'Hey, you!' the first Frenchman called over. 'Sausage-face! Stand up when we're singing our anthem.'

'Go fuck yourself,' Ernst spat.

Another French sailor jumped up and made a grab for Rosita, the girl sitting next to Johnny.

'Get away from her!' Johnny snapped.

The Frenchman pushed a paper into the girl's hands.

'Are you going to sit with these *saligauds*? See what they do?'

Johnny snatched the paper away. It was a crude piece of war propaganda. The cartoon showed hoggish German soldiers in pickelhaube helmets skewering French babies on their bayonets.

'They lie to you,' he appealed to the Frenchman in broken English. 'Don't believe this shit.'

The Frenchman either did not understand or did not care. He looked like a real Marseilles harbour rat, spoiling for a fight. He clamped his paws round Rosita's waist and started dragging her away. Johnny jumped to his feet, fists clenched. The sailor dropped the girl like a used rag and peeled a knife out of his sock.

Johnny ducked the first lunge and got his hand around the sailor's wrist, struggling for the knife. Other men's shadows fell over him, closing in.

Ernst did not waste any time. He seized the rum bottle in front of him by its neck, knocked off the bottom against the table edge, and advanced on the Frenchman behind a ring of jagged glass. The shadows started to recede.

'Come on,' Ernst hissed. 'Let's beat it.'

That might have been the end of it, but the barroom patriot wasn't ready to call it a night.

He hurled himself at Ernst as the stoker turned his back to go out the door.

'Ernst!'

Before Johnny's warning had left his lips, the stoker,

warned by some sixth sense, had wheeled round with an agility surprising in a man of his girth to meet the Frenchman with the broken bottle. Johnny saw the man's face explode like a ripe watermelon hurled off a cart.

'*Klugscheisser*,' Ernst swore. 'Smart-shitter.' Then, to Johnny: 'What are you gaping at? Run, before the cops arrive.'

Johnny found himself running the way he had always run, towards the sea, sickened by the criminal waste of what had happened inside the bawdy house. Those men had been ready to cut out his liver for no better reason than that he spoke German. Now one of them had lost his face. This was the madness that was convulsing Europe. The war had followed him here.

He now knew what he had to do.

There was a German ship in port, bound for Hamburg.

'Go your own way, then,' Ernst growled when Johnny announced his intentions.

The stoker shook his head, but he lingered on the wharf, watching the boy clambering along the hawser, hand over hand. In the bright moonlight, Johnny should have been spotted at once; the lookout must have been snoring drunk.

They were three days out into the Atlantic before he was discovered, living off bananas in a forward cargo hold crawling with spiders and cockroaches the size of his thumb.

The captain was all for putting Johnny in the brig. But when the boy announced that he had stowed away because he wanted to get home to enlist in the Kaiser's navy, the captain's long brown face softened.

'How old are you?'

'Eighteen,' Johnny lied, promoting himself three years.

'All right. You can work your passage. Germany needs lads with your spirit.'

3

The war changed Johnny and everything else.

He sailed on the battleship *Thüringen* into a night of black horror off the coast of Jutland. Blinded by the North Sea fogs and the smoke blown back from their own stacks by the howling headwinds, the German navy battled the full might of the British Grand Fleet.

'We're on the devil's anvil,' one of his shipmates muttered under the thunder of bursting shells.

They were on deck trying to rescue the drowning men from a battle cruiser the British had sent to the bottom.

The next instant, the sailor was silenced by a piece of flying shrapnel. Johnny caught the falling body and clasped his hands around his friend's chest, trying to prop him up. The sailor was curiously light. He stumbled with him towards shelter, oblivious to the warm stickiness that was seeping through his trousers.

'Idiot!' one of the officers snapped at him. It was Lieutenant von Arnim, a wasp-waisted dandy who thought he was a ringer for Prince Rupprecht and who made the men's life a hell. 'Throw him over the side!'

Dazed, Johnny staggered on with his burden.

Klaus Behring, another Hamburg man, came hopping over the rolling deck and said gently to Johnny, 'I'll take him.'

Only then did Johnny realise that he was carrying a detached trunk. The shrapnel had sawed his friend in two, just below the waist.

The German battle fleet made its escape to its boltholes at Kiel and Wilhelmshaven, and the admirals came with boxloads of medals. The men were paraded in their bonnets, the ribbons flapping in the breeze, and told they had won a famous victory for the Fatherland.

Johnny got an Iron Cross for bravery under fire.

What kind of victory? he thought sourly – with thousands of good men dead, a dozen ships sunk and the British in command of the seas, while at home German families gnawed on scraps of leather, waiting for shipments of food that will never come?

Idleness was more subversive than action. Johnny had come home to fight, but after Jutland there was precious little fighting to be done in the German navy. Only the

U-boats slunk out through the British patrols to prey on Allied shipping. The battle fleet stayed cooped up like a set of toy boats in a bathtub. The days passed in mindless, mechanical routine, drilling and scrubbing, with von Arnim lying in wait to reward the tiniest slip with a vicious flogging. In their free hours, denied home leave, the men were left to stew in fetid metal boxes. They were fed on slops while the officers dined on foie gras and fine wines. There was a contest to see who could count the largest number of maggots in his meat. Klaus Behring claimed the prize with a count of thirty-seven, but his record was soon broken.

Johnny came to live with hunger, a dull ache that never went away.

But he did not yet know real hunger. He saw it in the street the day the peace marchers came to the docks. He was lounging near the gates with Klaus when he heard a low buzzing in the distance, more purposeful than angry, like a swarm of borer bees at a crack in the timbers of a house.

The first civilians to appear in the street were women, haggard and shapeless, the loose skin of their faces hanging off the bones, some clutching their suckling infants. Men too old to be called up shuffled along behind them. Some of these granddaddies' faces, grey and set as if they had been rough-etched into stone, terrified Johnny. A red flag trailed from a pole, lifeless as the men's faces. There were a few younger fellows, Johnny noticed, keeping well to the back, one in a sailor's uniform, but hatless – perhaps a deserter. They started singing the *Internationale*.

'Give us bread!' the women croaked.

Johnny went closer to get a better look at the crowd, and one of the women shoved her baby in front of his nose. He saw the unnatural, distended belly, the puny limbs, limp and pale as cold macaroni.

'Give us bread,' the mother implored.

'Down with the Kaiser!' men's voices chimed in. 'Stop the war!'

The sentries formed a line bristling with bayonets.

'I've got an idea,' Johnny said to Klaus. 'Quick! Before the officers come!'

Klaus grumbled but trotted along at his heels. As he ran, Johnny scribbled on a card.

Klaus clutched at his arm when he realised they were headed for the storeroom where the officers' provisions were kept.

'We can't go in there,' he objected. Indeed, there were armed guards posted outside. At Kiel, in the third year of the war, food was more valuable than artillery shells.

But when Johnny announced 'Orders' to the guards, they let him through. One even winked at him. They had been on the *Thüringen* together and had met once or twice in the shipyard latrines, where some of the sailors held secret meetings with socialist activists who slipped into the base from the outside.

A civilian clerk was inside, checking his inventory. He looked like a thoughtful hamster.

Johnny came smartly to attention and presented the card. On the front, embossed in gothic lettering, were the words

ERICH VON ARNIM
Oberleutnant zur See

The clerk frowned over the scrawl on the back.

'Two smoked hams?' he sniffed. 'Six tins of paté?' He inspected Johnny over the rims of his spectacles. 'This is highly irregular. Why didn't your lieutenant fill out the necessary forms?'

'His apologies, sir. Oberleutnant von Arnim has a pressing social engagement.'

The clerk squinted more closely at Johnny. 'I remember you. You fetched him a case of champagne only a few days ago. Also without the proper requisition order. Perhaps your Oberleutnant should be reminded that this is a war station, not a catering establishment.'

'I believe –' Johnny lowered his voice '– that a royal personage is involved.'

This phrase had an immediate effect. The clerk rapped

out orders to his assistant, who rushed up and down the aisles with a trolley.

'I can let you have only two bottles of champagne.' The clerk jabbed his finger against the last items on the list. 'And the schnapps you must order from the mess.'

'Very good, sir.'

'Naturally, Oberleutnant von Arnim will be personally liable for the expense.'

'Naturally, sir. Thank you very much, sir.'

As they pushed the trolley back towards the gates, Klaus whispered, 'Have you gone out of your mind? Von Arnim will have your guts for garters. And how did you get his card?'

'He had a spare one on his desk. I thought it might come in handy.'

'You'll get both of us court-martialed,' Klaus muttered unhappily.

At the main gate things had come to a standstill. The crowd was singing revolutionary songs but had no forward momentum. A young lieutenant had taken charge of the guard. He had a frank, open face and ginger hair. Johnny recognised him. His name was Knorr, and he was assigned to their flagship, the *Baden*. His men said he was not a bad sort. Knorr's sailors looked unhappy, hoisting their bayonets against women and children.

'What the devil do you want?' Lieutenant Knorr snapped at the two men with the trolley of provisions.

'Oberleutnant von Arnim's compliments, sir. These are for the people.'

'For them?' Knorr looked at the crowd with misgivings. It had swelled in Johnny's absence. Some of the women were drumming on empty cooking pots.

'Yes, sir. Sort of a goodwill gesture, sir.'

'A bayonet charge would be more like Erich von Arnim's idea of a goodwill gesture,' Knorr remarked.

Johnny's eyes remained level with the ribbon of the Pour le Mérite, Germany's highest military decoration, on the lieutenant's tunic.

'Very well.' Knorr opened his cigarette case. There was

55

a faint smile of understanding at the corners of his mouth as he added, 'Get on with it, then.'

Johnny advanced into a warm tide of human flesh. The smell of the crowd as it washed over him was sweet and stale. It reminded him of the odour of a dead mouse behind the wainscot of his bedroom on the Valentinskamp, multiplied twentyfold. The sentries goggled and grumbled when they saw the hams, the cheese, the tins of sardines and foie gras – things that never graced their common tables. A girl threw her arms around Johnny's neck. Hands plucked at his bonnet, his scarf. But when the supplies ran out, an angry, hollow roar rose from the body of the crowd.

It's the voice of Germany, he thought.

Erich von Arnim assembled the crew of the *Thüringen* on deck to witness a public flogging. He stood off to one side, tapping the palm of his left hand with his riding crop in rhythm with the blows of the cat-o'-nine-tails. Of course, it was a notable breach of decorum for a naval officer to go about with a riding crop, but the captain of the *Thüringen*, impressed by von Arnim's aristocratic connections, interfered with him as little as possible.

When Johnny blacked out, they sloshed salt water over him until he revived. Von Arnim did not call off the flogging until his back had been skinned as neatly as a rabbit's.

'Some of us are fixing to get even,' a sailor whispered through the barred porthole of the ship's brig that night.

Johnny, lying belly down, could only grunt.

'It won't be long now. They say Lenin's taken power in Russia.'

Despite the pain, Johnny pushed himself up from the bench with the palms of his hands and propped himself against the door.

'Lenin?' he croaked. 'Is it true?'

'It's soldiers and sailors who put him in. He's going to stop the war. Liebknecht says we can do the same here.'

There was a heavy footfall on deck, and the sailor scuttled away.

In the gloom of his confinement Johnny felt as if a candle had just been lit. There had been wild rumours from Russia early that year, when Kerensky had taken over. But Kerensky, like Ebert and his gang in Germany, was a war socialist, ready to fight the battles of the ruling class for them. Lenin! Now that was different. Johnny had read some of his articles in underground papers put out by Liebknecht's followers that passed from hand to hand inside the shipyards. The Russian looked like a schoolmaster, with his pasty face and his little pointed beard. But he had a mind like a razor. He dissected the crisis of civilisation that was killing and starving millions for the sake of profiteers like Rausch and predators like von Arnim. He offered cures for the plagues that were ravaging Johnny's generation: war, hunger and spiritual exhaustion. Above all, he offered hope. In Russia, fighting against impossible odds, he had just proved his own dictum: 'There are absolutely no impossible situations.'

Johnny thought, We have found our compass.

The German revolution came almost a year after Lenin's, and Johnny was in its front ranks.

He made no more quixotic gestures. To all appearances he had learned his lesson and become a dutiful German sailor, suitably deferential to his superiors. But in secret he joined the Spartakus Bund, named for the hero of the celebrated slave revolt against the Roman republic, and plotted mutiny with handpicked socialists from other ships. Soon the conspirators had organised cells on every warship in the harbour.

A champagne party gave them their signal.

Germany was defeated, everyone knew that. There was talk that Kaiser Wilhelm had abdicated and run away to Holland. But that night, Admiral Hipper and his officers sat up in their wardrooms, clinking champagne flutes and toasting the Death Ride of the Fleet.

'*What* did they call it?' Johnny asked the orderly who brought word to the men crowded below on the *Thüringen*.

'The Death Ride of the Fleet,' he repeated. 'They say the British will seize all our ships when the surrender is signed. They want to take on the British and go down with all guns blazing, if that's what it comes to. For the honour of the navy.'

'Honour!' Johnny echoed the word with contempt. '*Their* honour. Not ours. Not one ship leaves harbour. Right?' He stared around the circle of worried, intent faces. 'Klaus, you go to the *Baden*. Make sure the men are with us.' He gave similar instructions to the others. They accepted his orders without question, without resentment. He was the youngest among them, yet he had already acquired a natural authority that had nothing to do with age or epaulettes.

In the morning the sailors doused the furnaces and downed anchors. On the flagship *Baden*, mutineers barricaded themselves in the forward hatches and sang the *Internationale*. On the *Thüringen*, Johnny and a dozen others broke into the armoury and passed out rifles.

'Back to your posts,' a voice rang out. The voice was confident and superior, the eternal voice of command.

Johnny turned and saw Lieutenant von Arnim in full dress uniform with his monocle and his riding crop. He had to admire the man's coolness. The sailors hesitated.

'You! Lentz! Stand to attention!'

Even Johnny, drilled for months to obey that voice without hesitation, started instinctively to respond. But instead, he leveled his carbine.

'Oberleutnant, you are under arrest. The ship is in the hands of the revolutionary committee.'

Von Arnim laughed. In the face of a mutiny, he seemed to be utterly without fear.

'You goddamned little Red,' he said softly. 'I knew I should have had you shot.'

He flicked the riding crop and drove a diagonal welt across Johnny's cheek. The men murmured but started to back off. Erich von Arnim, with his total self-confidence and his riding crop, personified the power that had regimented their lives better than a company of marines with fixed bayonets.

Johnny knew the illusion had to be shattered, or the revolt on the *Thüringen* would end at that moment. If only his hands would stop shaking . . . He tried to recall the pain of his flogging, the haunted faces of the grey women with their empty cooking pots.

He held the carbine in front of him, steadying the barrel with his left hand. When he pulled the trigger, the butt slammed back into his stomach.

Von Arnim pressed his hand to his chest between the collar bones, where a scarlet patch, vivid against his dress white, flowered like a new decoration. His eyeglass dropped from his face and rolled on its edge across the deck. He flailed at the air with his riding crop, but his body crumpled under him.

'Come on!' Klaus Behring rallied the men. 'We're in this together! We're going to Hamburg!'

'And then to Berlin!' someone else bellowed.

All along the harbourfront women were waiting to garland them with red sashes and red cockades. One of them tied a paper flower into the ribbon of Johnny's hat. The sailors reversed their hatbands and slung their rifles butt upwards. What better symbol that the world was turning upside down?

They commandeered every car and truck they saw, piling on to the running boards, the hoods, even the roofs.

'To Hamburg!' Klaus yelled in Johnny's ear.

Johnny nodded his agreement.

There's no turning back now, he told himself. We win or we die.

4

The rebel sailors called themselves the *Volksmarine*, the People's Navy, and the world belonged to them in those autumn days of 1918. Johnny went home to Hamburg with them. An elderly general at the head of a column of reservists and policemen marched out, revolver in hand, to order them back to their ships. Klaus Behring, warming to his new role, kicked the revolver out of the general's hand, and the Volksmarine paraded through the port city in triumph. Girls fought for the privilege of bedding a sailor with a red cockade in his hat, and Johnny was not ashamed to take advantage of their liberated spirits. The sailors decked their girls out in silks and furs plundered from the fashionable stores. Johnny was nervous about this orgy of looting. Surely this was not the way to win the people; and the time would come when the middle class, however lethargic and cowardly, would fight for its property. Still, they had announced the formation of a Workers' and Soldiers' Council; perhaps that would impose revolutionary discipline.

For all his scruples, he was not above taking a hamper of 'liberated' delicacies with him when he went back to the Valentinskamp to visit his family. From the intermittent letters from his father that had reached him at Kiel, he gathered that the family was living close to the edge, scraping by on the pickings of a lowly clerical job Herr Lentz had found at the cement factory at Altona.

Johnny was shocked to see how they were living. They had all lost weight, even Bertha. The music room and his old bedroom had both been given over to lodgers. The living room was dominated by an ancient Singer sewing machine, which his mother and Bertha took turns operating, stitching party dresses for neighbours who could still afford to pay.

Heidi Lentz scowled at her son's muddied uniform and the sailor's hat with the band reversed, and averted her face when he tried to kiss her cheek. Bertha gave him the briefest squeeze.

'They don't approve,' his father whispered when they were alone together in the kitchen. It smelled of lard and boiled cabbage. Herr Lentz's face was the colour of old ivory, with two bright, unnatural points of colour in the cheeks. He was sweating, despite the chill in the room. Each breath seemed to cause him an intolerable effort.

'Father, you're not well. You must go to a doctor. I have some money –'

'No time for all that,' Herr Lentz barked. 'I need your advice. You've seen something of what's going on. Will it last?'

'I can't say.'

'It's too soon, Johnny. You and your sailors – what have you been up against so far? A few tired reservists. Wait till the frontline troops get home and the General Staff takes over. The Social Democrats won't shed any tears for you. They'll lead the slaughter. They're good Germans, after all. Good Germans believe in order.'

'We've got Russia behind us.'

'Russia!' Gottfried Lentz snorted. 'Lenin is on top because the German General Staff put him there. He won't last much longer than your friend Liebknecht, not with the British and the White generals against him. Tell me I'm wrong.'

'You're wrong, father.' Johnny talked about the war that had chased three dynasties from their thrones and turned Europe into a gigantic graveyard. The old order was smashed beyond repair. Old conventions – even the old religions – were dying. History belonged to those with the courage to seize the reins, as the Bolsheviks had done in Russia.

'Well, it's no good arguing with a believer. I see that's what you've become.'

'Is it wrong to have a cause?'

'Only if it becomes an ersatz religion. That's what Proudhon thought was wrong with Marx, that he wanted to found a new religion, a religion of the state.'

'You said you wanted my advice.'

'Oh, yes. Our local Lenins – the Workers' and Soldiers' Council, they call themselves – summoned me to see them. I suppose somebody must have it in for me. I found a lot of drunks carousing in a grand salon. They even had a fire going in the middle of the floor. They scared me more than General Ludendorff.'

'What did they want?'

'They wanted me to take charge of popular education. I gather I might be paid if they stay in for more than a week. Should I do it?'

Johnny suddenly felt cold. He could gamble with his own life, but not with his father's.

'Father, it's not for me to say –' he began lamely.

'I mean, do you think I might do any good?'

'You might be a restraining influence,' Johnny admitted, thinking of the looters running amok in the stores. 'They need educated men.'

'Then I'll do it!' Herr Lentz announced with a grin. 'That will give old Rausch something to worry about. Let's have a beer to celebrate!'

'What about Mother?'

For an instant, his father's head seemed to withdraw between his shoulders. Then he bounced back.

'I am the master of this house,' he announced defiantly.

To prove his point, he called to his wife, 'Heidi! Bring us two beers!'

Johnny watched in some trepidation as his mother walked heavily into the kitchen. Her expression was thunderous, but, to Johnny's amazement, she brought the beer.

The revolution had entered the house on the Valentinskamp.

5

In Berlin, Johnny saw the red blanket draped over the Kaiser's balcony at the imperial *Schloss*, which the rebel sailors had turned into their barracks. He saw the crowds rip the epaulettes off any regular officer who dared to present himself in uniform in the streets. The girls were as welcoming as they had been in Hamburg.

But the carnival did not last long. Soon the streets rang under the boots of endless columns of stern-faced men in steel helmets and field grey, troops coming home from the front. When the crowds sang 'Death to hangmen, kings and tyrants!' these soldiers did not join in.

Former cavalry officers caught Karl Liebknecht and Rosa Luxemburg, the two shining names of the German revolution, shot them in the back of the neck, dumped their bodies in the canal and made a marching song out of their exploit.

The Social Democrats in power, Ebert and Noske, turned to the monocles of the General Staff, just as Johnny's father had foreseen. They even appealed to the ultranationalists and out-and-out monarchists of the *Freikorps* – the volunteer detachments – who hated their new rulers as much as they did the Bolsheviks, and possibly more. Together they shelled the rebel sailors out of the Schloss and marched from city to city, liquidating Workers' Councils. Bremen, a Red fortress, was assaulted with heavy artillery.

Johnny returned to Hamburg as a hunted man, disguised in the cloth cap and drab overcoat of a worker.

He approached the family house cautiously. Instead of police agents, he saw a movers' truck outside. Bertha puffed down the steps, carrying the lamp from his old room.

He whistled to her.

'You –' she gaped at him. 'You must go away at once!'

'Have you been evicted? Where's father?'

'Go away! Mama mustn't see you!'

'Answer me, Bertha!'

'We're going to Mama's family in East Prussia,' she said nervously, looking over her shoulder.

'What about Father?'

'He's gone.' She looked ready to burst into tears.

'Tell me!'

'They came for him. They had a list.'

'Who?'

'Freikorps. General Maercker's detachment, I think. Willi Rausch was with them. They shot him at the front door.' Her chest heaved, and she could hardly get out the last words. 'They put him down like a dog. Now go. Please. Before she comes.'

It was too late. Johnny's mother was already hurrying down the steps.

'Bertha!'

'It's Johnny, Mama.'

She turned her face away. 'I have no son.'

'Mother –' Johnny appealed to her.

She faced him then, for an instant, and he saw that she had grown terribly old.

'*You* pulled the trigger,' she said.

He drank into the night at a whores' bar off the Reeperbahn, where the lights of the honky-tonks burned brighter than ever, despite the misery outside. In that dead port you could buy any kind of sex for money or chocolates or cigarettes, or merely a bed and a chance of breakfast.

I have lost everything, he told himself. My family. God. (Nietzsche, before Marx, had persuaded him that God was dead, and even if he had never read either, the war might have had the same effect.) Country. Profession. Everything except my comrades and that will-o'-the-wisp – the revolution. All the more reason to cling tight to them.

It was past midnight when he went to the Rausch residence, on an elegant boulevard near the Binnen-Alster. He still had his pistol, confiscated from an unlucky member of the Berlin police. At least he could settle one score.

He banged on the door knocker until Herr Rausch leaned out of an upstairs window in his nightcap.

'What do you want?' he shouted down. 'Go away or I'll call the police.' The sight of the big man in a cloth cap made him nervous.

'Willi told me to come!' Johnny called back.

'Willi?' Herr Rausch's flabby features creased in puzzlement. Then he added with pride, 'Willi's on the eastern border, fighting the Reds!'

One more stupidity, Johnny thought. He had heard that some of the Freikorps had gone east, dreaming of the Teutonic knights. That account would have to be settled later.

Trudging back to his bolthole, Klaus Behring's dingy room in the Gängeviertel, he was accosted by a trembling woman with a daughter about his own age. The woman had a decent, homely face.

'We have nowhere to go,' she said. 'You have a kind face. Will you help us?'

'I wish I could.' He thought of the rising damp on the walls of Klaus's room.

'My husband was killed in the war. My daughter could warm your bed,' the woman implored. 'Or I could, if you prefer.' The girl kept her face hidden.

'Here – take this –' he blurted out, handing them his last pack of cigarettes. He rushed on into the dark.

My God, he thought, has it come to this? His head was pounding. There must be tens of thousands of such women all over Germany. He had seen the packs of orphans by the docks, fighting over scraps of rotting fish. He had to help change all of that. But he would need to be part of an organisation of professionals. The mutiny in the fleet, the risings in Hamburg and Berlin, had been a glorious amateur stunt and had captured the imagination of the country – for about as long as a travelling circus. Next time, it would be different.

When the Communist party of Germany was formed as the German section of a world movement, the Communist International, Johnny was one of the first to join. They gave him a membership card in his own name, and a pocket calendar with a questionnaire on the first page headed, 'Important: To Be Filled in Immediately.' He gnawed on his pencil as he studied the page. 'This book belongs to . . . (space for name). Address . . . Membership number . . . Union . . .'

He tore the calendar into strips, lit a match and watched it burn. Then he chopped the membership card into tiny pieces with his pocketknife and tossed them into the toilet. They were still amateurs – or worse, good Germans, sticklers for form. How could he, a man on the run with blood on his hands, go about with these lethal documents on his person?

Since the party was unable, or unwilling, to support him, he survived by doing odd jobs, first around the waterfront in Hamburg and later in the steel mills of the Ruhr. He made himself useful to the cause in little ways. He organised self-help groups, flying squads of men on bicycles who could be called in to save tenants from being evicted. Even the police were scared of them. He went on a gun-running assignment in the Baltic in a leaky old forty-footer, the *Lisl*. They met a disguised Soviet freighter in the middle of the night and collected a pile of antique tsarist rifles bundled up in tarpaulins and cartridges buried in barrels of flour.

The party gave him the sense of security that comes from belonging to a large family, and the women were easy. Many of them thought him handsome, now that the lines of his face had sharpened. More compelling than mere looks was the sense of danger that travelled with him. 'When I kiss you,' one of his girls said, 'I smell gunpowder.'

Committee meetings bored him with the endless quibbling over petty points of doctrine, and as the months passed his impatience grew. He felt that for some reason he had been marooned in the outer circle. He wanted to be *inside*. And he needed action.

6

He found lodgings nearer the harbour, above a curio shop. When he came home that night, the gas lamps were sputtering. The wail of a ship's siren floated in from the sea, lonely and plaintive like a cat begging to be let in from the cold. He clenched his fists inside his pockets. He was restless and angry; as winter came on, he felt the days slipping through his hands. He had been out on recruiting work, trying to persuade the men coming off a freighter of the North German Lloyd to come to a party meeting. The sailors were nervous; they wanted to get home to their wives or girlfriends. Johnny recognised one of them, an old shipmate from the *Thüringen*. In the winter of 1918 the man had been ready for anything. Now all he could do was to mumble that he had mouths to feed and couldn't risk getting his name on the blacklists. He fled from Johnny as he might have fled from a mugger.

They'll become mules without action, Johnny told himself. We must have *movement*.

Greta, the landlord's daughter, came out into the hall as soon as she heard the latch and fluttered her eyelashes at him.

She was round as a pumpkin and had no waist at all, but she was soft and giving and good to hold on a raw night when the harbour mists rose above the windows.

'How are you, Lovie?' He gave her a quick kiss on the lips, turning his hips as she slipped her arms around him so she would not feel the angular bulge of the pistol that lay flat against the small of his back, hidden in the waistband of his trousers.

'Father's out,' Greta announced, looking suggestively at the open door behind her. 'And I've got some cherry brandy.'

'Later. I have work to do.'

'Those stuffy old books can wait.' She hung on his neck.

How could he explain to her that he was ravenous for the stack of dog-eared, broken-backed books that formed a barricade beside his bed? Books were weapons, no less than the gun he had carried since the mutiny. He had to master so many, with so little time. He had to make up for the schooling he had lost and prepare himself for the next stage of the fight. He had already worked his way through the two volumes of a selected edition of Marx. He revelled in the Promethean defiance of the early writings, the sense of stealing fire from heaven. From Marx he had learned to see history as a process of constant struggle. From Engels, from the *Anti-Dühring*, he obtained the answer to the moral question. Nothing was final, absolute or sacred; everything was relative. History, only history, would decide whether a man's actions were good or evil. The murder of a thousand Erich von Arnims was justified if it accelerated the march of history.

From Lenin, Johnny learned what revolution required: an elite corps of legionnaires, secret and disciplined, utterly divorced from the sticky web of comforts and constraints that made lesser men slaves of the social order. He believed his own destiny belonged with that secret order.

But here was little Greta, grazing on his neck.

'Later,' he repeated.

'I know what's on your mind,' she pouted. 'You've got a new one, haven't you? Your taste's gone off a bit. Black as a witch and flat as an ironing board. Four eyes to boot. My poor mother used to say men will make love to the back of a bus.'

Johnny was mystified. 'What the hell are you talking about?'

'She came round here looking for you, didn't she?'

Johnny's alarm showed in his face. Nobody knew his address except Klaus and Harold Beer, the district party chief.

'What did she want?'

'Don't look at me like that, Johnny.' His expression scared the girl. She dipped into her bodice and pulled out a folded square of paper. 'Here. She left you this.'

Johnny snatched it from her.

Nothing more than a place and a time. He knew the place, a hall in a workers' district just outside Altona.

'What did she say?'

'Nothing – just her name.'

'What name?'

'Ula. She said you'd remember. Silly kind of a monicker, if you ask me.'

Johnny remembered. The *Ula* had been his first boat. He consulted the paper again. Eight o'clock. That gave him less than an hour.

There were guards outside the hall, and one of them wanted to frisk Johnny before letting him in. He was rescued by a girl in wire-rimmed glasses and a short leather coat, with kinky black hair that flew off in all directions from under her beret.

'You're late,' she greeted him.

'And you must be Ula.'

68

She didn't return his smile. 'I'm Magda,' she said curtly, and wrung his hand like a man trying to prove something.

She might be pretty, he thought as he followed her past the guards, if she were ever prepared to let on she's a woman.

He sat next to her, on the aisle. The faces around him were those of workers and seamen like himself, people living on the waterline. It would take little to sink them, but then again they had nothing much to lose. The man on the platform, however, looked different. He wore a decent suit and a watch chain across his vest and talked through his nose about the theory of surplus value.

There was some whispering behind the rostrum. Then the chairman got up, tugged at the speaker's coat tails to signal that his time was up and announced, 'The comrade from Russia is here!'

This revived the audience. While the pianist banged out a few bars of the *Internationale*, people craned to get a good look at the new arrival. A burly figure in a brown leather coat like Magda's, his cap rakishly askew, he marched across the stage and vaulted right onto the table at which the party leaders were seated, sending pencils and ashtrays flying.

'We sit talking while Germany starves!' he roared at his audience. 'But every one of us knows what's required! The rich must die so the poor can live!'

The previous speaker fidgeted and rubbed his nose, but several men jumped up and chorused their approval. Johnny got on his feet too, trying to get a better look at the speaker. The beard was gone, except for a bluish shadow. The face was leaner and harder, with deep lines scored between nose and chin. But there was no mistaking the man. The comrade from Russia was Heinz Kordt.

'You know my voice!' Kordt went on. 'It's the voice inside every one of you. A man can take so much before he breaks – or breaks out. I've been in Petrograd, and in Moscow. I've seen the future. I've seen a country without monocles or profiteers, where men are equal and earn the fruits of their labour. I've seen a place where children don't go hungry while their mothers hawk their bodies for bread.

'Comrades, the revolution in Russia is still imperilled. The capitalist world, terrified of the future, has conspired to strangle it. The Russian people need our help. Their final victory, which is inevitable, will bring ours closer — until a Soviet Russia and a Soviet Germany stand together as the mightiest power on earth! Then no cabal will be able to stand against us. Together we shall ignite the world! It's not a dream of the next century, it's a dream of tomorrow!

'But the monocles and the profiteers and their lapdogs in Weimar won't give up without a fight. We must arm! We must build a Red Army in every German city! Each man among you, every woman, has to make your choice. *Es geht im die Wurst.* The sausage depends on it.'

The old man sitting in front of Johnny nodded his head at this. But at the end of Kordt's speech, which returned to the theme of a new man in a new society, he tugged at his beard and muttered, 'And ye shall be as gods.'

Curious, Johnny tapped his shoulder. 'What did you say?'

The old man turned in his seat. His eyes were watery. He sucked on his pipe and said, 'It's what the serpent said to Eve. It's what they always promise. You'll see what comes of it.'

'Fool!' Magda snapped at him. 'You don't belong here.' She jogged Johnny's elbow, coaxing him into the aisle.

She took his arm and steered him around the crowd, through a side door.

The old man's words left a sour taste.

It was my father's warning too, Johnny thought. Beware of building a false church. But they're wrong. Of course they're wrong. If only my father had lived to see Russia . . .

'You must call him Viktor,' Magda was saying.

She escorted him across a courtyard, up a treacherous flight of steps. The biblical gloom evaporated the moment Heinz Kordt erupted from a circle of admirers and seized Johnny in a bear hug.

'Let me get a good look at you.' He thrust Johnny back,

still hanging on to his arms. 'By God, you're a man. Isn't he, Magda?'

'There's no contrary evidence,' she shrugged, and sidled off to the table where tea and whiskey were laid out.

'She's from Cracow.' Kordt watched her trim backside as she moved away. 'A cold-assed bitch, but very reliable.'

'Heinz – I mean Viktor –'

'Listen. We drink. Then we get rid of the others and we talk, you and me. I've got plans for you.'

The night was as long as the last one they had spent together almost six years before, in the world before the war. Sometime before dawn, Kordt dragged out a Victrola and put on a recording of the mercenary marching songs of the Thirty Years' War. He hooked one arm around Magda's, the other around Johnny's, and turned a little jig, as he boomed out the chorus of the famous song of *Der verlone Haufen*, the Lost Band:

Let the flags blow wide,
We are going into battle . . .

This was the Heinz Johnny remembered.

'I got your address from Harold Beer,' Kordt announced at one point.

'I guessed as much.'

'Harold says you're a good man, but impatient.'

'Beer's an old woman. He spends all his time bitching about his rivals. He's scared to move. He won't understand that this business is like riding a bicycle. If you stop pedaling, you'll fall off.'

'I see you've learned a thing or two.' Kordt stared at the younger man for a moment, appraising. He seemed to like what he saw. He turned up the volume on the Victrola and leaned close to Johnny. 'I've been sent here on a special job,' he confided. 'We're going to build a Red Army here in Germany. A hundred thousand armed men, enough to sweep the monocles into the Baltic. The Russians are sending their best instructors. Trotsky promised me personally that he will arrange shipment of all the rifles we need. I'm in charge in Hamburg. Within a year – two years at the outside – we'll be ready to seize power, with twenty times the resources the Bolsheviks had when they took St Petersburg. We can't fail. What do you say?'

Johnny was on his feet, his eyes shining. 'Tell me what I can do.'

For the next two years he worked for Kordt in the underground party – the *Apparat* – building a revolutionary army. In the woods outside Hamburg he helped train recruits for the Red Hundreds, the workers' militia, under the scrutiny of a tall, imposing Russian Jew who called himself Waldemar. It was rumoured that Waldemar had seized the telegraph office in St Petersburg in 1917 and routed the cossacks in the civil war. Under his direction each clump of trees became a barracks, a police station, a government office.

Again and again Waldemar hammered on the theme that political struggle was different from conventional war.

'Psychology is the key,' he told Johnny. 'A military setback can be a psychological victory, if it mobilises support for our side. When you take on the police, make sure there are lots of people around. Get them in the middle if you can. If innocents are killed, the workers will be outraged and join us in their thousands.'

When the French sent their troops into the Ruhr – Germany's industrial heartland – on the pretext that the Weimar government had not kept up with the schedule of tribute imposed at Versailles, Johnny went too, at the head of a combat squad, to organise armed resistance. The sight of giant smelters shut down, of swollen, sullen breadlines, told him the revolution could not be long delayed. What he saw on his return to Hamburg made him sure of it.

By late October 1923 the daily wage of a worker on the Hamburg docks was seventeen billion marks. Hungry mobs broke into bakeries and food stores. Near midnight, on his way to an emergency meeting called by Kordt, Johnny passed a crazy old woman who was burning currency in a rust-eaten gasoline drum to warm herself. Everyone knew the French were to blame. When they had marched into the Ruhr, they had starved the German government of money, and the government had turned to the printing presses. Day and night the presses spewed out paper money, with more zeroes on every bill every time you looked. It was the death of the currency and the death of the middle class. A man who had spent his life salting away his savings in bonds and bank deposits was now worth less than his drunken brother who had saved the bottles his booze came out of. It was a good season for speculators – and for the Communist party.

The meeting room, a pistol shot away from the Kali-Bar, was crowded and overheated. They had three or four trestle tables pulled together. Heinz and Waldemar presided together at one end. The men who squeezed in along the sides were not ordinary party members. They were chiefs of Red Hundreds and cadres from the M-group, the party's professional combat organisation. They whispered to each other as they waited for the meeting to come to order. It had been a week of wild rumours and false alarms. The political bosses of the German Communist Party were meeting in Chemnitz, on the other side of the country. As far as Johnny was concerned, the only item on their agenda that mattered a damn was whether to order an armed insurrection. The German leaders were said to be divided; so were the observers from the Comintern. So, it was rumoured, were the Russians. While telegrams were fired back and forth to Moscow, the men in this room worried at their leash.

Heinz looked drawn and tired. As Johnny watched, Magda crossed the room and whispered something in Kordt's ear. Immediately his face seemed to regain colour and life.

He got to his feet and banged his fist on the table.

'Comrades! A courier has just arrived from Chemnitz by train. They've made their decision! By God, I believe it's the right one! We move at first light!'

He made the clenched-fist salute. The next instant, every man in the room was on his feet.

'Red Front!' a dozen voices chorused.

Heinz and Waldemar rehearsed the targets assigned to each group.

There was at least one doubter in the room, a shoemaker from Barmbek who sat across the table from Johnny.

'We can't fight with broomsticks,' he pointed out. 'My group has only got three revolvers and a few hand grenades.'

There were sympathetic murmurs from some of the others. Despite Trotsky's promise, weapons were in short supply.

'If you need a gun, Georg —' Kordt wagged a finger at him '— you catch a policeman. We'll take what we need from the enemy. All right?'

'What if the government sends troops?'

'The honourable Minister for War will be busy saving his own rear end,' Kordt said contemptuously. 'There will be simultaneous risings in Berlin, Leipzig, Frankfurt, Bremen – where are reinforcements going to come from?'

The shoemaker sucked on his pipe, apparently pacified.

But a young seaman spoke up with a different complaint.

'We can't count on anyone around the docks except our own men,' he said. 'Not since the strike.'

This touched a raw nerve. The communists had called for a total shut-down of the port early in the summer. The strike had been a success to begin with. Then hunger had started to wear down the strikers' resistance. Finally the communists themselves had decided to break the strike. Secret orders had gone out: party members should go down to the docks at first light and get themselves signed up for any job that was going. By this cynical device, the communists had hoped to turn half the ships in the harbour into floating fortresses. But in the eyes of a lot of angry, unemployed men around the waterfront, they were blacklegs. Johnny had heard the ugly word hurled at him. He didn't like the way it sounded. In their ignorance, in their misery, those angry men could not be expected to understand that what looked to them like a sordid manoeuvre would help them in the long run – by building workers' power.

Heinz might have made a speech along these lines, but it was not a night for speeches. He simply growled at the young sailor, 'The Hamburg docks belong to *me*! Let any man try to prove otherwise.'

Then Waldemar got up, and a deep hush grew around him. They were all in awe of him, this man who had fought with Lenin and Trotsky.

'I know a bit about revolution.' His voice was warm and protective. 'On the eve of revolution, there are always voices that say, "The masses aren't ready." On the night before, they are probably right. It doesn't matter a damn. Once we strike, the masses will follow.'

With that, all hesitation seemed to leave the room.

The first target for Johnny's group, in the early dawn, was a police station within sound and smell of the harbour. He had twenty men, including Klaus Behring. Only a few were armed with rifles. The rest had to make do with revolvers, bottle bombs, kitchen knives and spiked clubs. Inspecting his ragtag army, Johnny wondered again what had happened to Trotsky's shipments.

By the time they converged on the station, they had two more guns. With knives at their throats, the policemen they ambushed weren't reluctant to part with their Sam Browne belts. But one of them was less cooperative when Johnny ordered him to strip. Johnny knocked him out cold with a blow to the back of the neck. The uniform was a reasonable fit.

He stopped at an all-night café a few blocks from the station, to use the telephone.

'Police? I want to report a rape. Yes. It's still going on. The screams are terrible. Please hurry.' He gave a made-up address and hung up.

In the cold morning light he watched two more police-men pedalling off in the direction of the reported crime. The odds were narrowing by the minute. But the men at the station weren't asleep. They had turned their post into a blockhouse, with rolls of barbed wire and a machine gunner up on the roof.

Johnny deployed sentries at the street corners and massed the rest of his men in an alley in the lee of a boarded-up dress shop.

'Can you throw straight?' he asked a muscular young stevedore with a brace of hand grenades in his belt.

'Straight as an arrow.'

'Very well. As soon as you hear shooting inside, aim for the machine gun. And don't forget to take out the pin.'

Johnny strolled into the police station as if he lived on the premises. He and his companion were wearing the green tunics and shakos of the Hamburg police.

Inside the building, several men were dozing on camp beds. The others were hunched around a table, playing poker.

'Who the hell are you?' the duty sergeant addressed Johnny, turning his attention from a busted straight.

'You've been expropriated, friend.' Johnny flourished a pistol in one hand and a grenade in the other. 'This station belongs to the people.'

'*Leck' mich am Arsch,*' said the sergeant, unimpressed. He grabbed for a rifle from the rack.

He had his hand on it when Johnny shot him behind the ear. The somnolent forms at the back of the room began to stir. Johnny yanked the pin from the grenade with his teeth and lobbed it towards them. Everyone rolled for cover. The building rocked with a double explosion, from inside and overhead. Streaked white with plaster dust, the surviving policemen gave up meekly enough. One of them, cooler than the rest, plucked the scattered playing cards off the floor and said, 'Do you mind if we play another hand, Your Excellency?'

Johnny let them go on with their game in the cells. He left the station with enough rifles for all his men and a few to spare for the volunteers who started bobbing up out of nowhere. He did not spare a thought for the sergeant he had killed; history would justify him. All the same, he avoided looking at the man's clumsy body. It was easier to kill when the enemy was impersonal.

By midday it was obvious that things were going badly wrong. In some areas – especially in the working class citadel of Barmbek – the people joined the rising in great numbers. But they fled from the armoured cars that shoved their ugly snouts over the barricades, spitting machine gun bullets.

Johnny saw Kordt, riding on the running board of a truck, shouting orders.

'Heinz! Any news from Berlin?'

'Nothing.'

Heinz let himself drop from the running board.

'What about the fleet?'

He shook his head. 'Listen. To fight the armoured cars, we must have explosives. You know the dynamite factory?'

Johnny remembered. It was west of the city and heavily guarded.

'Can you take it?'

'I'll try.'

'Good luck.' Heinz clapped him on the shoulder and ran after the truck.

The navy got to the factory first. Johnny and his men were pinned down by a hail of fire from blue-uniformed German sailors. These were not the sailors of 1918. The rumour spread that a battle flotilla was steaming up the Elbe, ready to shell the rebels into submission if they captured the port or the business quarter.

Klaus Behring made a mad dash for the blockhouse commanding the gates and was caught in a murderous crossfire. Johnny saw his old shipmate fumble forward and lie still in a pool of his own blood.

Someone will pay, he promised himself, emptying his magazine at the line of sailors that was inching steadily, relentlessly forward.

Finally Magda came on a bicycle with a message from Heinz.

He saw her beside the road, her mouth opening and

closing. He couldn't make out the words. He ran towards her, ducking and weaving.

'Give it up!' she yelled. 'We've been stabbed in the back!' Before he could reach her she was speeding away, her head bent low over the handlebars.

He was reduced to running to save his skin. The old instinct drove him back towards the harbour. He found the waterfront swarming with police. They were checking anyone who tried to cross to the Free Port by bridge or tunnel. He slipped behind a warehouse and found a dinghy that had been hauled up for repair. It had sprung a leak, but it might hold out long enough to serve his purpose.

Paddling and bailing by turns, he crossed the inner harbour and spotted a passenger boat that was just getting up steam. It was flying the Dutch flag. In the chaos of departure, he was able to haul himself up on deck without being spotted. But almost at once he saw one of the ship's officers strolling his way. Where could he hide? If he were discovered here, they would turn him over to the police. He saw only one chance – the manhole cover a few yards away, in the bow of the boat. He sprang at it and hauled it open. Even as he jumped inside, he realised his mistake.

He was inside the chain locker. Once he had pulled the cover back over his head, he was left squatting uncomfortably on a great iron anaconda – the coiled anchor chain, hundreds of feet long. Still, he would be safe enough until they got out to sea, when he might be able to find a softer berth.

He had not slept for two days and he soon dozed off, lulled by the familiar reek of bilge water and the vibration of the hull against his side. It was an uneasy sleep. In his dream he was being prodded up a cattle run behind Heinz Kordt and a dozen other men he knew from the *Thüringen* and the Hamburg underground. They were all bent over, running on all fours like brutes. At the head of the cattle run stood a masked man with an iron mallet, waiting to brain them one by one. *Stabbed in the back*, Magda's words came into the dream. *Stabbed in the back . . .* Now the feet were thudding harder, faster, threatening to trample him unless he hurried. A tremendous howl burst against his eardrums – and he snapped awake.

Above, the foghorns wailed. He heard the creak of a windlass. Disoriented, still half in the grip of the dream, he stared at the vertical length of chain beside him, trailing from the hole in the hull. Suddenly he was on his feet, wrestling with the manhole cover.

For some reason – the fog on the river? – the ship was going to drop anchor. When the crushing metal weight was loosed, the coils of chain that had made his bed would lash up at him and batter him to pieces. The cover wouldn't shift. He pounded and clawed, but he couldn't move it an inch. Someone must have secured it from above.

Desperate, he hammered on the metal with both fists.

'For the love of God –'

'For the love of God, is it?' The cover was pulled back and Johnny found himself looking up into a ruddy face embellished with thick white eyebrows.

At the same instant, he heard the splash of the anchor. The chain kicked and sawed, and he clutched at the edges of the manhole, swinging his legs up under him.

His rescuer seized his forearm and dragged him up on deck.

A white-jacketed purser came running. 'Need any help, sir?'

'No, I reckon he'll be docile for a bit.'

Johnny realised he was dealing with the skipper himself.

'You'll be one of them Reds, I venture? Well, come along with me. I want to hear all about it.'

For once luck was on Johnny's side. Captain Jan Gallagher, Irish on his father's side, took a liberal view of human foibles and didn't mind other men's politics – even the Bolshevist sort – as long as they didn't try to spread them on his boat. He also had a liberal hand with his *genever*. He poured both of them a few glasses in his cabin, eager to hear a firsthand account of the Hamburg rising.

'What happened in Berlin?' Johnny asked him. 'Did you hear any news?'

'None of your comrades lifted a finger, in Berlin or

anywhere else. They left you lot in Hamburg to swing by yourselves.'

Johnny was stunned by this information. This must have been what Magda had meant. They had been stabbed in the back. Even if they had won in Hamburg, the government would have been free to throttle them with fresh troops from all over the country. They had been led on a dance of death. But why? Had the party leaders changed their minds? Were they cowards? Had the groups in other cities been betrayed?

He thought of Klaus Behring, face down in his own blood. Someone would have to atone for that and all the other wasted lives.

Captain Gallagher looked at him with a sort of pity.

'Here. Have another drop of gin. I'll take you to Rotterdam if you're willing to work your passage. But I won't have any politics on my ship. Agreed?'

It was not a hard promise to keep. On that voyage Johnny was in no mood to play the apostle.

7

'It was a fuck-up.' Heinz delivered his postmortem six months later. 'The orders were changed at the last minute. The rising was called off. The couriers had already left the party congress in Chemnitz. They sent men to stop them. But when they got to the station the messenger for Hamburg had left. They could still see the lights of his train.'

'Wait a minute.' Johnny leaned across the table. 'What are you telling me? That we spilled our guts because nobody bothered to tell us the operation was cancelled? Couldn't they have sent another messenger by car? Don't they even know how to drive?'

He sat back, furious and mildy nauseous. They were in a booth at a restaurant on the Hedermanstrasse in Berlin, shielded by panels of frosted glass. The place served excellent bratwurst and latkes, but it hadn't been chosen for its cuisine. The owner was a member of the N-group, one of the most secret components of the underground party *Apparat*. The 'N' stood for *Nachrichten*, or intelligence. He was said to have an unerring nose for police spies.

'It was a fuck-up,' Heinz repeated, fanning his hands. 'It's not the end of the world. There'll be plenty more battles to fight.'

'Not for Klaus Behring,' Johnny said savagely. 'Or a lot of other good men.' By the end of the rising one in three Communists in Hamburg had been killed or captured. 'It was Thälmann who lost his nerve, wasn't it?' he pressed on. Thälmann was emerging as the biggest of the *Bonzen*, as the party leaders were unflatteringly described by the rank and file.

'It was the Bonzen,' Heinz half confirmed.

Johnny had spent half a year on the run from Rotterdam to Marseilles, where he had washed up at the Comintern liaison office, which operated under the cover of a seamen's club down at the docks. They had given him odd jobs to do, running around as a messenger boy with an envelope glued to the skin of his back. Then the telegram ordering him to meet Heinz in Berlin had come. He hadn't hesitated. Whatever he might think of the Thälmanns, he would cross oceans for Heinz.

'Have you got something for me?' Johnny asked.

'That depends on the man you're going to meet.'

'Do I know him?'

'You may have imagined him,' Heinz replied oddly.

'Is he German?'

'No. Though he speaks better German than Thälmann.'

'Russian, then.'

'He speaks that, too. Someone told me once that he was born in Riga. Also that he went to school with the Jesuits. I don't know if it's true. I know he was with Dzerzhinsky, when he defeated the plot against Lenin.'

'So he's a chekist.' The word was widely used in party circles, as in Russia, to describe a member of Soviet intelligence. It derived from the original name Lenin had given to his secret police.

'He is a man who lives in shadow country,' Heinz responded. 'He has his own network in the West. He told me once that it extends from Iceland to the Cape. In Germany, he controls the N-group. Also the T-groups.' The 'T' stood for 'Terror'. 'Max is the most extraordinary man I have ever met. A man like that breeds myths wherever he goes. But let me tell you one story about him I can vouch for. He had a Polish girl once, called Zinka. She was a poetess, quite beautiful. She fought with him in Russia. When the Bolsheviks won the civil war, she insisted on going home to Lvov, to make the revolution for her own people. But there was a spy in her circle, and he warned the police. They were waiting for her at the railway station. She was a Jew, and you know the Poles are not always subtle with Jews. They invaded her body with a hot iron. I imagine she talked. Inevitably she died. When word reached Max, he went to Lvov dressed as a Polish priest, travelling alone. He stalked the police torturer to his home and shot him on his own doorstep. He traced the spy and gave him the same rites that Zinka had received. In other words, he rammed a red-hot poker up his backside. This is the man you are going to deal with.'

'Why does he want to meet me?'

'I recommended you.'

A girl squeezed into their booth. She was a svelte brunette, elegantly dressed.

She said to Heinz, 'He's coming now.' She was attractive and conscious of it. She flirted with Johnny by affecting to ignore his existence.

'What's the matter, Johnny?' Heinz teased him, noting his interest in the girl. 'Why don't you say hello to Magda?'

'Magda? It's not possible –' But it was. Take away the clothes and the makeup, add wire-rimmed glasses, and he was looking at the mannish guerrilla he had briefly encountered in Hamburg. 'I like you better this way,' he said, laughing at his own confusion. 'Can I buy you a drink?'

'A glass of red wine.' Even the voice was softer.

'Heinz?'

But Heinz was sliding out of the booth. 'I'll see you later.' An ironic salute, and he was gone.

'Well,' Johnny turned back to the girl. 'I see Berlin has had an agreeable effect.'

'For you, too, I trust.' This new voice startled Johnny. It was identifiably foreign, but only because of the perfect weight that it gave to every vowel. It had a metallic timbre. The effect was not harsh, but it suggested – at least to Johnny – a distance between what was said and what was intended.

The newcomer slid into Heinz's place before Johnny realised he was there. It was the eyes Johnny saw first. They reached out and touched him with such force that he felt, for an instant, that he had been physically struck. He had to will himself not to look away. Under that violent stare, he felt completely exposed.

He thought, I've got to control myself. He tried to make a rational inventory of the stranger's appearance. The man was of medium height, compact and strongly built. His clothes were dark and conservative, discreetly well cut. The index and second fingers of his right hand were tawny from nicotine. He was already lighting another cigarette. Black tobacco, the kind that smells like camel dung. A commanding forehead. Straight black hair, worn rather long, slicked back from a widow's peak. The slant of the cheekbones, above cavernous hollows, gave the whole face a vaguely oriental cast. The eyes were black – or brown. No. They were violet.

I'm losing my balance. No man has violet eyes.

'I've been looking forward to this meeting,' said Max.

The mutual inspection had taken something less than twenty seconds.

Max wanted the story of his whole life. He acted as if he had no other concern in the world, on that bright spring afternoon, than to listen to the hopes and disappointments of a man twenty years his junior. He interrupted Johnny only to order brandy and cigarettes. When Johnny paused, it was 'Go on' or 'What happened then?' – so that after a time the younger man forgot all about his initial, inexplicable panic and talked more freely than he had talked to anyone, even Heinz. When he got to Klaus Behring's death and his own flight from Hamburg, he stopped.

Max nodded and said, through a blue haze, 'The problem is, some of your countrymen mistook the second month of pregnancy for the ninth. But a good deal was gained, all the same. Don't overlook that just because you lost a friend. Any revolt, any uprising, is *ein Fanal*. A beacon. It helps to show the people that the order of society can be changed. It's a training for the revolution we shall win. And it helps us to know our own.

'You read, don't you?' he suddenly changed tack. 'What do you read?'

'Marx. Lenin –'

'Marx. Very well, then. Do you remember what Marx wrote to the French workers in 1850, when all his prophecies for a proletarian revolution next week had gone up the spout? No? He told them they would have to go through fifteen or twenty or fifty years of civil war in order to change themselves, to render themselves fit for political domination. Do you understand?'

'I hope we don't have to wait fifty years.'

'Ah, we've learned how to hurry things up. I'm saying, be thankful for Hamburg, Johnny. Yes, I'm serious. Be thankful for anything that tests you. That's how we know our own,' he repeated. 'The fire that melts the butter tempers the steel. Now I've got a special question for you.'

'Anything.'

'Who is the greatest enemy of the German revolution?'

Johnny considered for a moment. Not square, ponderous Stresemann, with his face like a side of beef. The chancellor was just a front for the financiers and the industrial barons and the Prussians on the General Staff.

'Seeckt,' he decided, picturing the confident, monocled face of the chief of the General Staff, the face of an Erich von Arnim with ten times the brains and a thousand times more low cunning. 'General von Seeckt.'

'Let's suppose you are right,' Max went on. 'What effect

do you think General Seeckt's assassination would have on the correlation of forces in Germany?'

'It would increase the contradictions within the ruling class.' Johnny thought rapidly. 'It would disrupt the secret rearmament programme. It would lead to reprisals – probably indiscriminate reprisals. More people would be forced to choose between us or the reactionaries.'

'Agreed. So. If I sat General von Seeckt down in front of you, at this table – would you be man enough to blow his brains out?'

Johnny was conscious of Magda watching him closely. Her lips were slightly curled. Was she mocking or encouraging?

He met Max's eyes and said, 'Yes.'

'Why?'

'Because I have nothing to lose.'

Magda took Johnny back to a lavish apartment with a view of the Tiergarten. Her lovemaking, that night, was like the furniture: elaborate and impersonal. Afterwards she scrubbed herself all over, repeatedly, with a deodorant soap, as if she wanted no trace of another individual on her body.

It occurred to Johnny that this was the second of Heinz's hand-me-downs he had enjoyed. He felt a wave of nostalgia for the first. He wondered what had happened to Helene, with her lust for life. He must find out from Heinz, when he came.

But this time, Heinz did not come.

In the morning Magda shook him awake.

'Get dressed.'

'What's happening?'

'You must go to the Anhalter station before eleven. Seeckt is returning from Weimar by train.'

She gave him an Ortgies pistol. He had used one before, and it had jammed. He wanted to take his own gun, the Mauser, but she refused.

'There must be nothing that can be traced.'

She checked his pockets, removing anything that could

be identified. Then she gave him some odd bits and pieces – a death's-head badge to wear under his lapel, a membership card with a false name and the crest of a Fascist secret society.

'What's all this?'

'In case you're shot,' she replied blandly. 'You're ready for that, aren't you?'

'Of course.'

He loitered at the Anhalter station near the entrance to platform four. Seeckt's train was late. No, it was merely his nerves.

There he was now. For a moment he saw the general's head beyond a press of military aides and station guards. In a minute he would be coming this way. But wait. Seeckt had stopped. He stared around, then spun on his heel and marched back to his Pullman. What had happened? The stationmaster, flustered, ran puffing towards his office.

Ten minutes later, a troop of regular soldiers tramped through the station and joined their general. When Seeckt descended from his carriage, he vanished behind a ring of steel. There was no chance of getting a clear shot at him.

Johnny hesitated, his hand toying with the flap of the satchel in which his pistol lay concealed. If only they'd given him a bomb . . .

He heard a low whistle from nearby. He turned, and saw a man with his hands in his pockets. The stranger cocked his head and said, 'Leave off. The bastard's got a sixth sense.'

Johnny realised then that for every second since he had left the Hedermanstrasse Max had had him watched.

Under the full moon, Felseneck was beautiful. It was just a huddle of modest cottages with communal plots in the midst of the wasteland between Berlin and the neighbouring town of Reinickedorf. But tonight even the scruffy rows of onions and radishes had a kind of dignity, and the sweltering garbage dumps to the north glowed with unearthly fire.

By day or by night, appearances here were deceiving.

Felseneck was a virtual military colony of the Communist party, complete with armed lookouts and concealed machine gun posts. Max, it seemed, liked to be very sure of his ground. Or perhaps he had other business.

Magda waited with the car at the house of the district organiser while the two men walked side by side past cabbage patches and compost heaps.

'Do you think Seeckt was warned?' Johnny asked.

'It's possible.'

'Your watchdog said he's got a sixth sense.'

Max ignored the spin Johnny put on his words. 'Seeckt has got luck,' he commented. 'Napoleon said that's the most important quality in a general. We tried before, you know. It was an excellent plan. Seeckt goes riding in the morning, in the Tiergarten, flanked by his spruce young ruffians with duelling scars. We got a girl to make a pass at one of these cavaliers. It looked very promising. She agreed to help us smuggle an assassin into the stables. Do you know what we forgot? No? A handsome young man like you should get to know women better. We forgot about a biological compulsion called love. Women, one gathers, are unusually vulnerable. The girl fell in love with her Prussian hussar and betrayed her contacts to the police. Naturally, we had to get rid of her.'

Max struck a match.

Remembering the story of Max's Polish woman and the risks he had taken to avenge her, Johnny wondered how much of his cynicism was feigned.

'By the way,' Max turned back to him, 'do you have a woman of your own?'

'No attachments.'

'You should keep it that way. Revolutionaries can't afford the luxury of emotional entanglements. Piatnitsky will tell you the same thing.'

'Piatnitsky?'

'Yes. You'll see him in Moscow. You'll take him some little presents from me.'

Johnny stared at him. Russia! It was what he had dreamed about since he had first heard the news that the Bolsheviks had seized power. But war of one kind or another had always kept him away.

'I made up my mind about you the day we met,' Max announced. 'The rest was merely a test. I've learned caution, these last years.' His eyes were intense, but the violence was no longer directed at Johnny. 'You've experienced more than many men go through in their whole lives, and learned more from it, too. But in some ways you're still unformed. In Moscow we have special schools. You'll be joining a very unusual elite recruited from all over the world. You belong on a bigger stage than this – this German cabbage patch.' He swung his foot at the vegetables. 'You'll learn we have worse enemies than Seeckt.'

Max was silent for a time, apparently lost in his own thoughts.

'Can you be more specific?' Johnny pursued.

'What? Oh, yes. The British are the worst. The British are reactionaries without complexes, but not without subtlety. The *Intelligence Service* –' he pronounced this phrase in English – 'is our most fanatical opponent, and the most deadly. You'll learn.'

8

Johnny's road to Moscow began in a cigar store in the Wedding district of Berlin.

'You know what they say in Russia,' said the little man behind the counter. 'We don't go by the passport, we go by the face.'

Alfred's business seemed to be languishing. His shelves were half empty. He was coatless but bustled around with his hat on the back of his head. He produced a cigar box and pushed it across the counter.

Johnny inspected the contents. The passport looked real enough. It made him out to be a Dutch commercial traveller born in Eindhoven. There was bric-a-brac to support his cover: letters addressed to him under his assumed name,

Dutch guilders, a snapshot of a girl with plump cheeks he had never seen.

The railway tickets were first class. 'Always travel first class if you can,' Alfred counseled. 'The police give you an easier time, and you get a better dinner. There's one thing more.' He went into the back room and returned with two handsome cowhide suitcases, secured by straps.

'Your samples,' he explained. 'Whoever heard of a commercial traveller without samples?'

'What am I selling?'

'Douches.' Alfred's round face was positively cherubic.

'To the Russians?'

'You're crossing Poland,' Alfred said wickedly. 'The Poles are in dire need. Have a cigar, my dear fellow.'

The suitcases had false bottoms. Johnny was sure of it. But they were expertly constructed, like his passport. The only way you could tell for certain was to cut open the lining. Neither German nor Polish customs officials would dream of doing that to a first-class passenger's luggage, not without a tip from a very good source.

He boarded the train at the Friedrichstrasse station and had a sleeper to himself. The amenities were even better than Alfred had promised, starting with morning tea on a silver salver and ending with a casual flirtation over champagne with a Baltic countess of violently anti-Bolshevik opinions. There was a two-hour stopover at Warsaw Central. Johnny got off the train and breakfasted in the station buffet. Elegant painted ladies were bidding farewell to paramours in uniforms with lots of gold braid.

He had fallen into a half sleep when he was roused by a faint rattle at the door. Someone was trying the handle. Then there was the scrape of a passkey being inserted in the lock, and the door opened. Two men in broad-brimmed hats and mufflers that concealed part of their faces rushed in. One of them flung himself on top of Johnny, who glimpsed the flash of a steel blade. The other reached for the luggage rack, making a grab for the suitcases.

Johnny wrestled with the first assailant, trying to turn

the knife back against its user. Flat on his back, with his attacker's knee on his chest, he was at a serious disadvantage. The knife point ratcheted down until it was inches from his face. He suddenly jerked his attacker's hand closer, twisting so the knife missed his cheek, and sank his teeth into the man's wrist. The man yelped and let the blade fall. In the next instant Johnny had his thumbs on his assailant's throat under the square-cut beard, pressing until the oxygen was cut off and the man fell back inert.

The second intruder was halfway out the door with Johnny's bags. Johnny seized his revolver – he had always gone armed since he had started working for Kordt – and gave pursuit. The thief dropped the suitcases and ran. Johnny let him go. He hauled his bags back into his compartment and secured the door. His first assailant was still laid out, shoulders on the bunk, legs on the floor. Johnny opened the window, got a grip under the man's armpits, and hoisted the body up until the head was lolling over the sill. It was going to be a tight squeeze. The man began to revive as Johnny forced his torso through the window. Johnny's last sight of him was of a pair of thick, flailing legs. An obscure oath was swallowed up in the rush of wind outside the carriage, and Johnny was left holding a patent leather boot. He tossed it after the body. Breathing hard, he flung himself back into his seat. Who were his assailants? Common criminals, or agents – possibly British agents – who knew that he was carrying secret material for the Comintern? He would report the episode as soon as he got to Moscow. He promised himself one thing: nothing would come between him and his mission.

Several hours later, they reached the border. Johnny stayed in his compartment until the train was nearing the Soviet customs post at Niegorelodzhe. They passed under an arch with a Cyrillic inscription: 'The Revolution breaks down all barriers.' Ahead was a giant's cabin, a large building of rough-hewn logs rearing up against the grey sky. He saw a sentry with a greatcoat down to his ankles and a star on his tall, peaked cap. There were bright murals depicting stalwart workers and peasants wielding their tools. They had odd, tubular physiques. Tin men, Johnny thought.

'We're in Russia,' the attendant announced. He pocketed his tip and added, '*L'Europe est finie.*'

9

'What language did they speak?'

The man asking the questions was short, stubby and grizzled, like a small, energetic bear. He scribbled constantly as he talked. He wore a military tunic, unbuttoned, without badges of rank, and worked at a rough wooden table littered with files that was utterly out of place in that enormous, echoing room. With its marble floors and tapestries, its gold leaf and ormolu, it might have served as a ballroom for the Tsars, and no doubt had.

'I only heard a couple of words. Curses,' Johnny specified, trying to summon up the dying gasp of the man he had pushed out the window. 'It could have been Polish.'

'Or Russian,' Osip Piatnitsky suggested. 'Poland is full of Whites who are still fighting the civil war. They hire themselves out to Western special services and gun down our agents for fun. Many have sold themselves to the British secret service. There's only one answer for these retrogrades. Shooting.'

The little light bulb on the desk beside the telephone flashed red. Piatnitsky picked up the receiver, listened for a moment, and hung up without speaking. He scrawled a note. 'I expect you had a brush with the *Intelligence Service*.' Like Max, he pronounced the last phrase in English. 'The first of many, perhaps. Great Britain remains the most fanatically anti-Bolshevik power in Europe.'

He refilled their glasses with scalding tea from the samovar bubbling beside his table.

'You delivered your packages,' he said. 'That's what counts. And you did whatever was required to protect them. I don't forget these things. Max Fabrikant wasn't wrong about you.'

It was the first time anyone had mentioned Max's surname. Johnny had no means of knowing whether it was merely another cover. Max had hinted that Osip Piatnitsky was his ultimate boss and the man he most respected in the headquarters of the Communist International. Johnny had gleaned a few crumbs of information about the elusive Comintern chief from the other foreign guests at the Hotel Bristol.

Piatnitsky was the chief of the Orgbureau and the man most feared by party officials in other countries. He was the man who paid their salaries, and who decided when to dump them. Piatnitsky's domain included the OMS, which was talked about in hushed tones. 'OMS' stood for *Otdel Meshdunarodnoi Svyasi*, the 'International Communications Department'. The title was a masterpiece of understatement. The OMS was the heart and lungs of the Comintern. It provided the means for agents to operate all over the world. Its assets included diamond dealers in Antwerp and London, a forgery factory on the Lindenstrasse in Berlin, a smuggling ring based in Copenhagen, a battalion of radio operators and a liaison man in every major port. Beyond all this, Piatnitsky's men kept watch over the others.

'We've learned the lesson of Hamburg,' Piatnitsky said. 'One of our mistakes was that we failed completely to infiltrate the armed forces and the police. The revolution cannot succeed unless the so-called forces of order are demoralised and divided. We have to undermine the foundations before we can bring the fortress down. Insurrection is a science; there are rules that must be followed. We are opening a new school to teach those rules. You're one of the lucky ones. You'll attend the first course.'

Listening to Piatnitsky then and later, in seminars for all the students from the M-school, Johnny began to realise the vastness of the enterprise on which he and his comrades were embarked. Piatnitsky talked of Shanghai and Bucharest, Java and Capetown, as if they were suburbs of Moscow – or vegetable plots in the garden of his dacha. Events separated by thousands of miles, societies made even more remote from each other by differences of language, colour and religion, all proved to be intimately connected.

A Chinese student told him about preparations for an armed revolt in the Dutch East Indies. This, he learned, was the opening gambit in a complicated game plan. The Comintern hoped that risings in Java and Sumatra would tempt the voracious Japanese to intervene. This, in turn, would stir the British to assert themselves to defend their own stake in the Far East. If the exercise succeeded, two imperialist powers opposed to Russia would be locked in conflict with each other. With Britain and Japan diverted, Russia would have a free hand to pursue its main objective in the Orient: revolution in China.

'We are at war with the whole of the capitalist world,' Piatnitsky declared in the course of a three-hour speech at the M-school. 'The war can end only with the triumph of the world revolution.'

Viewed from such commanding heights, setbacks like the collapse of the Hamburg rising were parochial and unimportant. Today Russia was the besieged citadel of the world revolution. But it would not be alone for long.

The M-school occupied a Red Army barracks on Pokrovskaya Street. The 'M' stood for 'military,' and the courses included bomb making, marksmanship and street-fighting tactics, as well as all the techniques of clandestine operations: codes and ciphers, secret inks, dead-letter boxes and so on.

One of the instructors was a Russian general, Petrenko-Lunev. He had fantastically detailed knowledge of bridges, telephone exchanges and armaments plants in Germany and Great Britain. He talked as if he had personally reconnoitered each one to see where best to lay the charges. When the general talked, he had a curious habit of rubbing his right thumb and forefinger close to his ear.

'It comes from checking fuses in the dark,' Petrenko-Lunev explained sheepishly one day, when he caught Johnny watching him closely.

He referred to Germany with affectionate insolence as

Wurstland, and his German pupils didn't seem to mind. Some of them even picked up the habit.

The Russian general wasn't much older than his students, and his heart was set on going to Shanghai, where the next revolution was expected to start.

The dream exploded the day he took a bottle bomb from a Czech student in Johnny's class, the German-speaking group. Petrenko-Lunev wanted to demonstrate how the bomb should be thrown to make certain of blowing up a tank. The flustered Czech had got confused about what type of fuse he had attached to the bomb, the slow-burning or fast-burning type. It cost the Russian instructor his right arm to set him straight. The bomb went off as he reached down to pick it up. He gave a terrible scream and fainted dead away, while Johnny and one of the girls in the group tried to stanch the torrent of blood from the socket of his arm. The Czech doubled over and retched for a very long time, making a sound like a cistern that wouldn't shut off. To Johnny's amazement, Petrenko-Lunev reappeared before he finished his course, brandishing his pointer with his left arm instead of the right, paler but still enthusing about a mission to Shanghai. The Russian general, with his right sleeve pinned across the breast, seemed living proof of what all of them felt: they were indestructible. Destiny had joined the party.

Another intriguing instructor was the German who called himself Emil. He was a big, hearty man with vivid blue eyes set deeply under his bulging forehead. One of Emil's driving themes was that there was no room in the movement for narrow nationalistic feelings – for *Lokal-patriotismus*. Theirs was an international cause. They were members of a World Party, of which all the individual Communist parties were merely 'sections'. They had no homeland, no loyalties, except the world revolution.

But when Emil got together with the German students over a few beers, his line was somewhat different. 'It will all be decided in Germany,' he would say. He was scornful of most of the German party leaders, especially Thälmann, the dubious figurehead of the Hamburg rising who had emerged from the rubble stronger than before. 'A top sergeant,' Emil dismissed him. 'A wooden-headed, strutting little zealot.' Emil was impatient with those in Moscow and Berlin who insisted that the Social Democrats, not the Fascists, were the party's main enemy. 'One day,' he prophesied, 'we're going to have to join ranks to stop the Fascists. You have to forget about family feuds when the whole damn house is on fire.'

Emil left for the United States before Johnny's course was over. He had lived in New York before and after the war, and it was rumoured that he had been the virtual dictator of the Communist Party, USA. Tired of the endless wrangling inside the American party, the Comintern was sending Emil to crack heads together.

'We go where we're sent,' Emil said to Johnny in the midst of a farewell party. '*Moskauer Fremdenlegion*. That's what they call us, isn't it? Moscow's Foreign Legion. But don't forget Wurstland, Johnny. One of two things is going to start there: the next revolution or the next world war. Maybe both.'

By day they memorised the basic commandments of conspiratorial work. You confided in no one who did not have a clear need to know. You tried to be invisible, to fade into the background. You lived like a bird of passage, constantly changing lodgings and meeting places and always checking on the neighbours. You shared nothing with outsiders, including ordinary Communist party members, because you belonged to an elite, exacting underground: the *Apparat*. You trusted no one entirely.

By night the rules were abandoned, and they flocked together for wild parties at the Bristol and the other Comintern dosshouses, with girls and vodka and impromptu entertainments. One of the favourite games had been dubbed 'The Jumble Sale'. As many men and girls as could fit crowded into a room and started swapping clothes – sometimes in the course of a few hands of strip poker, often at random, as the mood took them. The men would wriggle into skirts and stockings, the girls into baggy pants and soldiers' tunics or peasant-style blouses. Then, at a piercing whistle, the lights were turned off. You had until the lights came on again to retrieve your own clothes — wherever they happened to be. This resulted in much groping and whooping and some unexpected anatomical combinations.

At one of these parties, Johnny was still scrambling about on the floor, squeezing various legs in search of his trousers, when the lights snapped on. At eye level he found a young Red Army instructor called Jacob happily grazing at the ample bosom of a large pink Danish girl.

'We have a better name for this sport in Russian,' Jacob hissed.

'What's that?'

'*Kogo zgreb, togo yevyob.* You fuck the one you grab.'

Johnny was still looking for his trousers. He was sure he had lost them to the dark girl with frizzy hair who tried to hide her looks behind wire-rimmed glasses. She made a face at him and showed her empty palms.

'The people's tribunal will now convene,' announced another young German, one of the few men in the room who had recovered his clothes.

'Citizen Fritz!' he barked. This was addressed to Johnny. Like all the other Comintern recruits, he had been required to adopt a cover name. He had picked the name of a sailor he had known on the *Thüringen*, Fritz Mattern. This was the name on his new party card and the name under which he was registered at the M-school. Members of the *Apparat* changed their names more often than some people changed their shirts, but this one would stay with him; it was reserved for contacts inside the party.

Johnny got off his hands and knees and stood bare-legged with his shirt tails hanging out. Some of the girls started giggling.

'The charge is bourgeois indecency!' the self-appointed prosecutor continued. 'The case is proven! Citizen Fritz is indecent, but not obscene! That, by definition, is bourgeois. The people's court will now deliberate the sentence.'

'Hit him!' a woman's voice rang out. It was deep and strident, like the first bar of a gypsy song. It was also oddly familiar. It brought back something of the past, as the sound of foghorns in the Moskva river brought back boyhood memories of the great ocean steamers on the Elbe.

'So decided!' Johnny's judge pronounced, and they set a tumbler of vodka to his lips and made him drink it down. He spluttered and coughed, and a rivulet of alcohol coursed down from the side of his mouth to his chin.

'Hit him again!' the same woman called out. He was craning around to find her among the press of bodies, but already they were making him tip his head back to swallow another four fingers of vodka.

'*Budem zdorovy!* Jacob said encouragingly. 'Cheers!'

The second tumbler of vodka went down more smoothly than the first.

'Again!' the woman urged. Now he spotted her, bouncing up and down on one of the iron-frame beds so the springs twanged beneath her. Her white-gold hair fell to her shoulders. She was wearing a high-necked, tight-fitting sweater and rumpled grey trousers that were unmistakably his. She seemed much taller, and her body was fuller, her features sharper and more defined. But he knew her at once from her ice-blue eyes and her mocking, infuriating self-confidence.

'Give it to *her*,' he said to the boy who was pressing the third tumbler on him. 'She's wearing bourgeois pants!'

She laughed, slipped out of his trousers and tossed them across the room. 'No, I'm not!' she sang out, with no more embarrassment than she had displayed the night they had met in Heinz Kordt's room in Hamburg.

'I'm going to spend the night with this one,' Helene announced to the room, draping herself around Johnny's neck.

10

Romantic attachments were frowned upon in their circle in Moscow. Sex, on the other hand, was accepted as a necessity, and there were only two regulations that had to be observed: proletarian frankness and the higher interest of the party. If you wanted to go to bed with someone you said so, just as Helene had done. If the two of you found you were compatible and wanted to stay together, you didn't talk about marriage; that was a relic of a defunct bourgeois morality, like religion. The correct procedure was to say, 'I want you to be with me as long as the party permits,' or words to that effect.

This wasn't exactly what Johnny said to Helene, but by the time he had finished his course, it was clear to everyone that they were a couple. Not an orthodox couple, since their lives were pledged to a cause that transcended personal loyalties; and also because spending time with Helene was like standing under a shower with a broken faucet: you never knew whether the water was going to run hot or cold.

In matters of sex she continued to take literally the party's prescription that there were no taboos. She would vanish for days, and each time he suspected a different man. One was Jacob, who, she told him, was being promoted to the British section of the Fourth Department – Soviet military intelligence. Once he went to her room, opened the door without knocking, and found her cuddling with the dark, frizzy-haired girl from the Lenin School. He found the spectacle both disgusting and disturbingly erotic.

'What's the matter with you?' Helene asked coolly. 'Girls are human, too.'

In these ways, Helene was still inhabited by the same demon he had encountered in Hamburg. In bed she was insatiable. After a wild night of lovemaking she would hurl herself on top of his spent body at dawn, clawing him awake, demanding to ride him. When they fought, which was often, her words flicked at him like a whip. And she used more than words. When she bit or scratched, she drew blood.

Yet there was a stronger force that was driving Helene, and it was this that held him to her. He was astonished to discover a depth of intelligence and commitment that he would never have suspected in the runaway Kordt had picked up at the railroad station, a more natural candidate – it seemed then – for the whorehouses of the Reeperbahn than the Communist underground.

She talked eagerly about what she learned at the Lenin School and had mastered more of Marx than he had even attempted. Once, when she left off grappling on the bed, she launched into a dissertation on the theory of imperialism.

Another time he arrived at her room unannounced and saw a painting leaning against the wall on top of the dresser. It showed street musicians performing with a fiddle and an accordion in a dark, almost medieval courtyard. People were hanging out of their windows to listen, while an old woman crouched by a fire in an open drum. It was a scene of poverty, yet it was suffused with tremendous warmth and life. The dominant colours were rich, earthy shades of russet and green.

'That's very good!' he exclaimed. 'Who is the artist?'

But already she was hiding the picture away in a drawer.

'It's nothing,' she said curtly.

'But I think it's wonderful. Why don't you hang it on the wall, where it belongs?'

'Because there are things I don't want to be reminded of.'

So she had personal secrets after all. It was only after several months that she confided that the artist was her sister.

'You never mentioned your family before,' he pointed out.

'There's nothing to be said about them.' Her face contorted, and she was a child again, on the brink of a temper tantrum. 'My mother's a bitch.'

They were both strays, Johnny thought. But he no longer felt this force of animus against his own mother, even though she had rejected him so totally. The hatred that remained was directed at Willi Rausch, the man who had broken up the family and murdered his father. When he thought of his father, it was to remember his moment of heroism, the fleeting, precious moment when Gottfried Lentz had found wings.

'And your father?' he asked Helene.

'I don't have a father!' Her eyes glistened. 'I don't want to talk about it.'

He let it go. Let her tell him in her own time. Oddly, she chose to return to the subject on an outing to Leningrad, as they were strolling through the splendid halls of the Hermitage museum.

'You know, my father was a Prussian officer,' she remarked. 'He didn't wait to see the baby. My mother says she got married so I wouldn't be born a bastard. But I was, all the same, wasn't I?'

She said the bit about the Prussian officer with a kind of pride. Johnny pictured the type he had suffered under in the Kaiser's navy, the type that recognised only three kinds of people – officers, women and civilians, the last an inferior breed whose wives and daughters were fair game. Perhaps there was something of the father in the daughter.

What was most dangerous in her was something he recognised in himself, though in him it was less voracious, less indiscriminate. She needed to plumb the depths of experience, both physical and mental. The same drive, the *Drang nach Absoluten*, propelled her in sex, in rehearsals for violence – she was proud of her prowess in unarmed combat – and in ideological debate.

'Man is a process of overcoming,' she said to him one afternoon, when they were sitting in the Alexander Gardens. 'And the end of that process is communism.'

She gave form to his own deepest instinct.

Despite all they had lived through – or perhaps because of it – they really believed they were invincible.

2

Homecoming

Of course, the Fascists are not asleep, but it is to our advantage to let them attack first; they will rally the entire working class around the movement . . .

Besides, all our information indicates that in Germany, fascism is weak.

— *Joseph Stalin(1923)*

1

For the next seven years Johnny's homeland was the world revolution.

He was sent to Romania as military adviser to the communist underground. Helene was invaluable to his cover. They posed as a pair of fashionable idlers dripping with money. They hired a yacht and sailed up and down the Black Sea coast south of Costanza. Helene mixed cocktails and sunbathed half nude – which scandalised the Romanians – while Johnny coached underground leaders in the organisational techniques he had mastered in Moscow. His best student was Saul, a Bessarabian Jew and a wool spinner by trade. Within a few weeks Saul had set up a network of cells inside the army and Johnny was schooling civilian recruits in bomb making and marksmanship at a firing range within sight of King Carol's summer palace. For a time the revolt prospered, and in Moscow the Fourth Department was delighted with the intelligence windfalls.

One of Saul's men, an employee of the government printing office, supplied them with copies of secret orders and manuals of the Romanian General Staff before they came off the press.

But suspicion fell on one of Johnny's couriers, an itinerant vendor of soybeans and sunflower seeds. The Romanian secret police operated on the old-fashioned principle that a man is put in jail in order to confess. After the unhurried removal of several of his fingernails, the greengrocer confessed everything. Saul was shot. Johnny owed his escape to Helene, who flirted with a lieutenant at the border while he crouched in the trunk of the car, holding his nose in order not to sneeze.

'You make perfect working partners,' Max Fabrikant congratulated them afterwards.

In theory Max had no direct authority over Johnny. Max belonged to the OGPU, or Unified State Political Administration – in short, the Russian secret police. Johnny was an agent of the Comintern, the general staff of a world movement that was supposed to be independent of the Soviet government.

But if the frontiers were clear on the map, they were invisible on the ground. Most of the Comintern's military experts were seconded from the Red Army, and General Berzin, the head of the Fourth Department, took a close interest in their activities. Since Stalin had driven out Trotsky and his supporters, the number of chekists in the corridors of the Comintern had increased; often they seemed to be the ones giving the orders. In practice Johnny found himself carrying out assignments for all three agencies – the Comintern, the OGPU and the Fourth Department.

To complicate matters further, the power struggle that was raging in the heart of the Kremlin spilled over into the vast, ramshackle headquarters of the Comintern in Ozhod-Niriat, in the suburbs of Moscow. At one level it was a fight over tactics: whether to pursue the dangerous, solitary road of armed insurrection or, instead, to form fronts and alliances with rival political groups. At another level it was a conflict between old guard Bolsheviks and a new generation of apparatchiks who owed everything to Joseph Stalin.

The most decisive of these shadow battles was played out in 1927, soon after Johnny's return from Romania. There was tragic news from China, where Borodin – one of the most daring of the Old Bolshevik adventurers – had been sent to make a revolution in alliance with the nationalist forces of Chiang Kai-shek and the Kuomintang. The omens were against him from the beginning. Borodin arrived (so Johnny heard in Moscow) in a cattle boat full of stinking carcasses. The ship had been caught up in a terrible storm, and most of the animals, hurled back and forth against the slats of their wooden pens, had perished during the night. Now it was the turn of the Chinese Communists. Chiang took them by surprise. Paid off by the Shanghai financiers and their Western friends, he betrayed his Communist allies. Striking without warning, soldiers and squads of killers toured the streets of Shanghai in the dead of night, machine-gunning Reds.

Someone had to take the blame for the costly mistake of trusting Chiang Kai-shek. From Moscow directives went out denouncing 'conciliators' wherever they might be found. At the end of November Bukharin, the President of the Executive Committee of the Comintern and a senior member of the Soviet Politburo, was abruptly removed, and his fall crushed hundreds of lesser men who had hitched their wagons to his star. The party line was struggle without compromise, no deals with class enemies or 'class traitors' like the Social Democrats in Germany. Within the Comintern, power came to rest in the hands of a curious Balkan duo: Georgi Dimitrov, a Bulgarian, and Dmitri Manuilsky, the son of a Greek Orthodox priest from Tarnopol.

In these treacherous times, Max counseled Johnny, the secret of survival was 'Bolshevist elasticity' – and, it seemed, a willingness to inform on your friends. When their paths crossed in Moscow or a foreign capital, Max frequently asked Johnny to report his impressions of fellow agents, including their sexual proclivities, their drinking habits and other pecadilloes. Johnny usually complied. He knew that foreign secret services, especially the British, would try to exploit a man's weakness to induce him to betray his comrades. Still secure in his own revolutionary faith, he was genuinely outraged when he discovered that some of those he was ordered to work with were cynical parasites, not above pilfering from operational funds or fabricating reports. When he told Max about them, he did not feel like a sneak; *they* were the ones who were betraying the cause.

But Johnny's sense of rectitude did not survive an encounter with a moon-faced man in a fur hat who collared him at the Hotel Lux in Moscow and introduced himself as 'Drozhdov, a friend of Max.' The year was 1930, and the first snows were falling outside. Although it was only mid-morning, Drozhdov insisted on squiring him to the best table in the restaurant and plying him with vodka and caviar and salty river crabs.

'I heard from another friend,' Drozhdov said confidentially, 'that you spent an evening with Emil Brandt.'

'Why, yes. I had dinner with him last night. He was my ideological instructor when I was at the M-school.'

'Yes, yes. We know all that. What was the content of your conversation?'

'It was personal.' He had decided immediately that he did not care for Drozhdov. The Russian's tone was prurient, like that of a man asking to see dirty photographs in the back room of a shop. And Johnny was worried about Emil. He remembered his fellow German as a big, rollicking fellow, quick with a joke, brimming with life – a man who was said to have a tremendous future ahead of him. It was even whispered that he might oust Thälmann's crowd and take over the leadership of the German Communist Party. They had met quite by chance when Johnny had been strolling with Helene in the Arbat. Emil had called out to them. But for that, they might have walked on without seeing him. The man had not only aged enormously; he seemed to have shrunk. In the Azerbaijani restaurant where they had gone for dinner, he had insisted on sitting with his back to the wall, and his face was contorted by a tic Johnny had never noticed before. Each day, Emil confided, he had to present himself at the Central Committee. He was the subject of an investigation.

'Did Emil Brandt discuss the state of affairs in Germany?' Drozhdov pursued.

'We may have talked about Germany,' Johnny conceded. 'After all, we were both born there.'

'Naturally, naturally.' Drozhdov sucked on his teeth. 'And of course, you must have discussed party policy in relation to the Social Fascists and the Hitler movement.'

'We may have. I really don't remember the details.'

'I am sure you would not forget any references to Comrade Manuilsky,' the chekist purred.

'We did not discuss Comrade Manuilsky,' Johnny said flatly. 'It was an innocent reunion of old friends. I don't see that it can be of any interest to the Organs –' this was one of the euphemisms for the secret police in circulation in Moscow.

'Our interests are quite catholic, I can assure you, Comrade Lentz.'

Johnny wanted to ask Drozhdov what charges were pending against Emil. But he was worried that by asking he might provide the Russian with a lever he could use to prise out details of the previous night's conversation that might do harm to Emil.

Johnny made a show of consulting his watch. 'I have an appointment at Ozhod–Niriat.'

'Of course.' Drozhdov was positively ingratiating. 'It's been a pleasure. I do look forward to meeting you again.' He sucked his teeth. 'And please give my regards to the lovely Helene.'

'You don't know when to be afraid,' Max Fabrikant reproached him two months later in Berlin.

'I didn't like him.'

'Dear me! And Drozhdov prides himself on being the most cultivated man in Moscow.'

'What are they doing to Emil?'

'Oh, that! It's all been settled.' Max rubbed his hands and went hunting for a fresh pack of cigarettes. 'Emil has recanted. He has written a full letter of apology. I believe it's in the current issue of *Imprecor*.' This was the news bulletin of the Comintern. 'He admits that the Social Democrats – excuse me, the Social Fascists – are the main enemies of the working class in Germany and that it was a grave tactical error to call for a popular front with class traitors. He quotes the Greek three or four times. *Where* are those damn cigarettes? Ah.' He found a reserve carton on the bookshelf, wedged between copies of Gide and Malraux. 'So you see, all is forgiven. You made an enemy out of Drozhdov for no reason.'

'I thought –'

'*What* did you think? Really, Johnny, I'm disappointed. I didn't think you were so naive. Do you actually imagine that Drozhdov needed *you* to tell him what Emil said to you at that idiotic dinner? That story about the Greek, for example –'

For an instant Johnny saw Emil again at the table, regaining his old *élan* as the wine flowed. He saw Emil telling a hilarious story of how the Greek, Manuilsky, had tried to lay down the law at a gathering of German Communists. Several of the Germans, street fighters spoiling to take on the Brownshirts, had yelled out 'Go back to Moscow!' Then a gnarled old man, a Bremen delegate, had got up and bawled, 'He's no good for anything except shish kebab!' Manuilsky had left swearing he was going to break heads in the German party . . .

The implications of what Max had said suddenly dawned on him. They had picked the restaurant at random. It was frequented by Russians, not foreigners. It was hard to believe their table had been bugged – unless there were microphones at every table. That was possible, but there was a more likely explanation. Johnny remembered Drozhdov's parting remark.

It was Helene, he realised. Helene had told Drozhdov everything. Even though she was exposing me at the same time. I mustn't take it personally, he told himself. I mustn't let Max see me look bitter. She's a professional, doing her job. That's the beginning and the end of it. And of our relationship. I'm a fool if I ever forget that.

'Emil was a good man,' Johnny said to Max, turning his emotion into a different channel.

'He's a better man now. He forgot about *Parteibefehl*. Party orders. What kind of army allows every man to question orders? Be sure you never make the same mistake, Johnny.'

'But Emil may have been *right*, dammit. The Popular Front —'

'— is not for discussion by you and me.' Max cut him off. 'Don't overreach yourself, my friend. We're Marxists, aren't we? Then we know that history cannot be understood from surface events. There's a deeper level of meaning, accessible to only a few, with the science and the knowledge required. Don't you imagine that Stalin may know things that are concealed from you?'

'Of course.'

'Well, then.'

2

Marlene Dietrich swirled off the screen in the leather coveralls of an aviatrix, her goggles pushed back on top of her head. She reappeared in sequins and satins, the brazen finery of a *poule de luxe*. She was a spy, a mantrap employed by the Austrian secret service. One of her victims appeared on the screen, a man who had sold his country to be betrayed, in turn, by love. He had a revolver; he was preparing to shoot himself. 'What a charming evening we might have had,' he whispered, 'if you had not been a spy and I a traitor.'

'Then,' she observed calmly, 'we might never have met.'

A woman in the row behind Johnny started sniffing.

A man slipped into the empty seat on his left and murmured without looking at him, 'The Hollywood idea of espionage.'

Johnny didn't respond. He stared up at the screen. It was impossible not to think of Helene. There were the visual echoes: the wide, hooded eyes, the tartar cheekbones, the legs that scissored across a room. The character Marlene Dietrich played in *Dishonored* was a prostitute, recruited by her Austrian spymaster because of her allure and her remarkable sangfroid. 'I'm not afraid of life, though I'm not afraid of death, either.' It wasn't hard to imagine Helene in the role, despite the vagaries of the unlikely plot. This mental association deepened his sense of unease, which encompassed the mission that lay ahead of him, the unknown courier who was sitting at his left hand smelling of onions, the homecoming to Berlin, a place of lengthening shadows, and the woman who resembled Dietrich and was described on three separate passports – Swiss, Belgian and American – as his wife.

The courier belched quietly and whispered a time and an address in the Moabit district. Then he was gone, leaving Johnny with the fleeting impression of a round-shouldered figure in a soft hat.

Johnny stayed in the cinema until the end of the film. In the last scene, the Dietrich character, faced with a firing squad, insisted on dying in her streetwalker's clothes. She was shown going to meet her maker with the same eagerness – or indifference – with which she might encounter a new lover.

The theatre was hushed, apart from the woman in the row behind, who started snuffling again, and Johnny himself, who made a stifled sound between a sneeze and a snort. The next instant, he was laughing uncontrollably. He was as surprised as the sentimentalist behind him, who muttered, 'Shame.' He pressed his hand across his mouth and rushed for the theatre exit.

The white October light gave everything sharper edges: the ominous young men wearing lipstick and rouge who patrolled the Ku'damm, the crowd of Brownshirts daubing swastikas on the windows of a Jewish-owned furniture store, the block-long red banners that festooned the Communist party headquarters on the Bülowplatz. But the scant light that leaked down to the inner courtyard of the peeling workers' tenement in Moabit seemed to have got there by mistake, like water through rotted sacking.

Heinz was true to old habits, Johnny thought as he made his way through a series of low arches. He picked boltholes in places where the neighbours looked after their own kind and had no great love for the police. Nobody challenged him on his way to Kordt's hideout, on the third floor at the back. But a dozen pairs of eyes marked every step, and he was received at the door by a young tough with a pistol in the waistband of his trousers.

Kordt pounced on Johnny, grinning from ear to ear. 'I'm glad I found you,' he exclaimed. 'It's been a long time. I wonder if you can still speak German.'

'Only with a Hamburg accent.'

'Hamburg!' Kordt's eyes lit up for a moment, but then his smile vanished. 'We'll never see times like those again.'

Johnny was shocked by how much his friend had aged. Deep lines were gouged across his forehead and down his cheeks, as if the flesh had been sucked back into the bone. His cropped hair was like steel wool.

'You're older too,' Kordt said, reading his thoughts. 'You look like a man who's found out what the world is about. Let me see. You'll be thirty now. Am I right?'

'Thirty-one,' Johnny corrected him.

'Oh yes, that's right. Born with the century, isn't it? Look at Karl here.' He aimed his jaw at the boy with the gun. 'All of eighteen, and ready to shoot Hitler and take both our jobs. Aren't you, Karl?'

Karl looked at the floor and shuffled his feet.

'Come along, old man.' Kordt threw his arm around Johnny's shoulder and steered him into the kitchen. 'We've got a lot to catch up on.'

They sat across the kitchen table from each other with the blind drawn, and Kordt poured beer. They lolled and drank and nodded at each other for a bit, in a comfortable silence.

'You've filled out,' Kordt said.

'You're thinner. Our average weight must be the same.'

'Tell me about Helene. I heard you two got hitched.'

'We're partners,' Johnny said hastily and tried to change the subject.

Kordt jabbed him with the stem of his pipe. 'Johnny, this is *me*. Remember? I know you're fond of the girl. I could see you were right for each other that first night at my place in Hamburg. I sent her to Russia, and in a roundabout way I did the same for you. Like it or not, I've got a lot invested in both you kids. So talk to me.'

'She's very good at her job. She's a brave girl.'

'But you're not happy with her, are you? What's the matter? Is she sleeping around?'

'It's not that.' Johnny looked at the tangle of dark hair on the back of his friend's hands and remembered that first night in Kordt's room on the Valentinskamp. No, he wasn't jealous. The capacity for jealousy had been drilled out of him, he thought, in his years with Helene. Perhaps that meant the capacity for love had been burned out of him too. In Helene's presence he felt something more subversive than jealousy. He felt vulnerable.

The night after his last conversation with Max, she had come into his bed, scented from her bath. He had taken her roughly, selfishly, trying to punish her without telling her why. Later, he lay awake for a long time, his head propped up against the heaped pillows, smoking and staring at the sullen panorama of barracklike brick walls beyond the window. In the dark they seemed hostile, pressing forward into the room. He looked at Helene's face, composed in sleep, and thought, even now, even behind closed eyelids, you are watching me.

Kordt waited.

Johnny finally said, 'I've had a few problems.'

He described his Moscow encounter with Emil Brandt and his reasons for believing that Helene had been reporting on him to the OGPU.

'I heard about Emil,' Heinz growled. 'They put the poor bastard on the grill. Luckily, there are a few of us left who don't broil so easily.'

He rattled around, fetching more bottles.

'We're having a few problems here, too,' he went on. 'I expect you've got the picture by now.'

'I've been in Berlin barely a week,' Johnny said. 'But I've learned one thing. It's easier to get in to see Stalin than to find Heinz Kordt.'

The first signal from Heinz had been a message on a piece of rice paper inside a box of matches Johnny hadn't wanted to buy from a legless street vendor who pursued him on his trolley and pushed it into his hands anyway. Then came a rendezvous with a courier in Neukölln; a last-minute change of address; and finally the assignation in the UFA cinema.

'I have to watch my back these days,' Heinz grinned. 'So, it would seem, do you.'

'The police?'

Kordt's pipe wheezed asthmatically. He blew into it vigorously, scattering ash and live cinders. 'The police aren't my worry. Not here in Berlin, anyway. We've got friends on the inside. I can usually count on a tip-off if a big raid is being planned.'

'The Nazis?'

'They want my head, all right,' Kordt agreed. 'But that's not the whole story. Some of our comrades would like to give it to them.'

'Thälmann?'

'Him for one. He's the one who denounced Emil. Wollweber's no better. We've got a civil war going on now, inside the party. What it comes down to is that some of us want to fight Hitler and others haven't got the balls or the brains to do it. Thälmann and his cronies think everything is just fine. They think Hitler's a bag of hot air, a help to us because he's helping to drive people one way or the other. They think if Hitler gets too rowdy the monocles and the financiers will sit on him until all the air goes out, *phttt*! They're completely out of touch. You ought to go to a Hitler rally, Johnny. The whole thing grabs you by the throat. You want to tear yourself away, but you can't. It's like witnessing a sex murder. There's the whole crowd, made delirious by the lights and the music and the tramping feet, suddenly sunk in a deathly hush as the great man makes his entry between a forest of standards. He plays with them, ravishes them, lashes them to an orgiastic frenzy, until he stands with the body of the crowd at his feet.'

'Hypnosis was a German invention,' Johnny commented.

'It has found its master. That's why Hitler could take the country. The monocles are starting to realise it, too. You heard what just happened? Hindenburg invited the Bohemian corporal – that's what he calls him – to tea. He turned up like a bandy-legged penguin with his tails flapping over his bum, and people thought it was funny. Well, it doesn't matter whether the Bohemian corporal knows how to knot his bow tie. He's a master of mass psychology and a master of organised terror. That's why he's going to win – if we let him. There are over a hundred Nazi deputies sitting in the Reichstag, and there could be twice as many after the next elections. He's getting all the money he wants from Hugenberg and Thyssen and other chimney barons. And what are we doing about it? We spend most of our time smashing up Social Democrat rallies. You know the theology. The Nazis aren't a threat to us. The Social Democrats are the main enemy of the working class. I believed that when we were fighting in Hamburg and the Social Democrats were attacking us with armoured cars. I don't believe it any more. If we don't stop Hitler, he'll drink our blood.'

On another occasion, the expression would have seemed ludicrous to Johnny. But he sat silent, hanging on Heinz's words.

'If we are going to stop Hitler,' Kordt went on, 'we have to do two things. We have to meet terror with terror. Every time they kill one of our boys, we knock off two of theirs. And we've got to swallow some of the theology and do a deal with the Socialists. I don't even rule out a pact with the centre parties. What matters is beating Hitler.'

He paused to drain his glass.

'I tried to make Thälmann see sense, but he wouldn't listen. He talks as if Hitler is the best recruitment agent the party ever had.'

'I heard that party membership *is* growing fast,' Johnny observed.

'Granted. But we're not growing as fast as the Hitler movement, and we're not putting down proper roots. We're just spreading like a ground creeper. We're losing the veterans, the union men, the sailors who were with you at Kiel. We're getting trigger-happy kids off the streets like Karl Vogel out there. And I'll be frank with you about that. It's just accidental that a tearaway like Karl comes to us instead of the Brownshirts. He's not like you, Johnny. He doesn't read. He doesn't question the reasons for his actions. He was down and out, jobless. He wanted a few kicks. I know other kids like Karl who got bored with us and went off and signed up with the jackboots. But they're not our problem. Our problem is *die Bonzen*. The bosses.'

'Who else have you talked to?' Johnny asked.

'I talked to Emil. He said he was going to talk to Stalin in Moscow. We saw what came of that.' Angry, Kordt knocked his pipe out against the edge of the table, and hot ashes flew about the room.

'Did you talk to Dimitrov?'

'I'm afraid we move in different social circles,' Heinz responded with heavy sarcasm. 'You know he's the boss of bosses here in Berlin. Have you met him? Are you going to see him?'

Johnny hesitated. He had an appointment with Georgi Dimitrov the following day in the headquarters the Comintern chief maintained behind the urbane façade of a conservative publishing house in the embassy district. Indeed, this appointment was the principal reason for his visit to Berlin. They had told him in Moscow that Dimitrov would give him specific instructions for his next foreign assignment. What harm could there be in revealing this to his friend? But he did not tell Heinz. His recent experience with Emil and the habits entrenched by years of operating under legends and cover names on hostile territory had made him cautious.

Heinz must have smelled this out, because he rushed on. 'Don't tell me if you don't want to. No hard feelings, eh? But if you *do* stop in to see the Bulgarian, be sure to hold your nose. He smells worse than a Turkish bathhouse.'

He raised another bottle of beer to his lips and sloshed half the contents down his throat. He belched noisily and rubbed his stomach.

He's putting on a show, Johnny thought. I've offended him.

'I got a letter from old Georgi the other day,' Heinz sailed on. 'A copy went to all the party organisers. I used it for toilet paper. I wish I'd held on to it now. Do you know what Dimitrov said?'

'I have no idea.'

'Dimitrov ordered united action – those are the exact words, Johnny – *united action* between the Communist party and the Hitler movement. The aim of this united action –' he half closed his eyes, summoning up the words neatly typed on the page '– is to accelerate the disintegration of the crumbling democratic bloc that governs Germany.' He blinked and fixed Johnny with his stare. 'What do you make of that?'

'I don't know.' Johnny was bewildered. It was hard to believe that Dimitrov, who knew conditions in Germany and was also privy to Stalin's thinking, could have issued such a directive. But why would Heinz make the story up? 'Perhaps there was some misunderstanding,' he suggested hopefully.

'No misunderstanding,' Kordt was flushed. 'I've got a story I've been saving up for you, Johnny. It concerns an old pal of yours. Do you remember Willi Rausch?'

Johnny sucked in his breath. The name conjured up the bulging, oily face of the schoolyard bully Johnny had trounced in the winter before the war. He had often pictured Willi Rausch since then, not in school uniform but in the helmet and brassard of a Freikorps officer, stinking of booze as he climbed the steps to the front door of the Lentz family house, crowing as he pumped bullets into a defenceless old man – Johnny's father.

'What about Willi Rausch?'

'I saw him last month. Not here. In Bremen. I was sent there on a Z job. The Bonzen may not like me, but they know that's one thing my group does better than anyone.'

Johnny was familiar with the shorthand. The 'Z' stood for *Zersetzung* or 'Disruption'. The Z-groups, which specialised in terrorising and sowing confusion among rival political parties and trade unions, were one of the most lethal elements in the underground organisation of the German Communist Party.

'The transport workers were having their national congress in Bremen,' Heinz went on. 'It was supposed to be a really big production. The Social Democrats were running everything, so naturally we had to bust it up. Now wait for this, Johnny. The night before the official opening, I got orders to go to a secret meeting with – who do you think? The area Nazi high command. Shut your mouth, Johnny, you're making a draught. There's better to come.

'I thought it could be a trap, so I went with Karl and some of my kids. We all had automatics and machine guns. The Brownshirts weren't taking any risks either. They picked the right locale – a brewery outside town. The Nazi in charge was a great ugly brute about your age. An Untersturmführer, I think they said. I don't pay much attention to their comic opera ranks. His name didn't click straight away either. But I worked it out later when we'd had a couple of beers and he told me he was from Hamburg.

'I'll give Willi Rausch credit for one thing. He said he didn't like his orders any better than me. We pretty much agreed that if we ever saw each other again, one of us was going to end up a dead man.'

'I don't understand,' Johnny interjected. 'What were the orders?'

'I'm getting to that. Try to picture this, Johnny. We're all inside the hall the next day, Rausch and his goons on one side of the gangway, our lot on the other. We're sprinkled around in groups of four and five, minding our manners, because the stewards have got their eyes on us. The band strikes up, everybody starts singing, and then the chairman is at the rostrum talking about the rights of labour. Then they bring on one of the bigwigs from the Social Democratic party, and I get up on my hind legs and start blowing my lungs out. Soon all my boys are doing the same. The stewards start moving in, and my lads bring out their coshes and iron bars. Someone runs to fetch the police. Things are really livening up, when all hell breaks loose on the other side of the gangway. Rausch jumps up and calls the people on the platform a bunch of ass-lickers, and the Brownshirts go charging at the rostrum. They collared the speaker and threw him out the window. He broke both arms and dislocated his shoulder. They brought the cops in by the truckload, but by that time the congress was wrecked. I got a thank you note from Wollweber later. A job well done, he said. I didn't feel much like looking at myself in the shaving mirror, though.'

Johnny sat immobile through most of this, suspended between rage and disbelief.

'You're telling me you had Party orders –'

'*Parteibefehl*,' Kordt agreed.

'It's obscene – it's criminal –'

I'll tell Dimitrov, he thought. Obviously he has not been informed of what is happening. Stalin must be told. He's been preoccupied with other things – with famine in the Ukraine, with the Japanese invaders in Manchuria who are threatening Russia itself. Stalin and Dimitrov will put things right. Mistakes have been made in Germany. No, worse than mistakes.

He remembered the Hamburg massacres.

There are traitors in the German party, he told himself. Stalin must be told.

'Tell me, Johnny.' His friend had his feet up on the table. 'If you'd been me, in that congress hall, what would you have done?'

For an instant Johnny's caution abandoned him. 'I would have shot Willi Rausch.'

'You know what? I'd sleep better if I'd done just that.'

3

Johnny walked back to the rooms his Comintern contact had arranged. Shaken by his conversation with Kordt, he lost his way twice, and it was past midnight when he found the building, a few blocks east of police headquarters on the Alexanderplatz. The place had the solid, satisfied look of a strongbox. The manager, Frau Hügel, matched the building in appearance, but she was in the pay of the OMS.

She startled Johnny in the entrance hall.

'I've been waiting up for you, Herr Stoltz.' This was the cover name Johnny had been assigned for his trip to Berlin.

'Is something wrong, Frau Hügel?'

'Come inside.'

He followed her into her kitchen. Copper pots and cast iron skillets marched along the walls in orderly files.

'The police were here,' his landlady whispered.

'Looking for me?'

'No.' She took off her spectacles and rubbed them nervously against her quilted robe. Naked, her eyes were bright and never still, like a magpie's. 'There was a robbery in the house,' she reported. 'The widow Teller, on the second floor. The police are questioning everyone in the house. They wanted to search your room.'

'What did you tell them?'

'I said I couldn't permit them unless you were present. They said they'll be back.'

'Thanks, Hilde.' Johnny abandoned formality. 'We'll leave tonight.'

Frau Hügel hooked her glasses over her nose and said, 'Perhaps you will take a small glass of schnapps with me, Herr Stoltz. Frau Stoltz is not yet home.'

'I see.' He glanced up at the cuckoo clock. He had no idea where Helene was or when to expect her back. It was possible she was doing a job for Max. He knew she had seen Max at least once in his absence. It was equally possible she was warming another man's bed.

'Just a small one,' he said to Frau Hügel. But he borrowed

what was left in the bottle and took it up to his room.

Afterwards he packed all their possessions into three small suitcases – one for him, two for Helene. It was strange to think that at thirty-one all his property in the world, apart from the books he had left in a steamer trunk in Moscow, could fit into one bag.

When he had finished packing, he finished Frau Hügel's schnapps.

Nearly 3:00 AM. Helene might not be coming back at all. How long should he give her? Until dawn?

He was getting angrier with her by the minute. He told himself it was only because her nocturnal habits were exposing them both to unnecessary danger.

But there was something else. His friend's story about Willi Rausch had shaken the certainties Johnny had lived and fought by since the war. How could he reconcile his revolutionary faith with the appalling reality of what the party was doing in Germany?

In that moment of doubt, he felt very alone. He wanted Helene with him. She had never been fully his and never could be. She was her own creature, beautiful but inconstant, shining and remote like a distant star. But their lives had raced close together on parallel tracks. They had shared danger and good times, too. She – and Heinz Kordt – were all the family he had.

When she slipped in at 3:20, he said mildly, 'Nice of you to drop in.'

'Are you still up?' she responded coolly. 'God. It smells like an ashtray in here.' She opened a window and started picking cigarette stubs off the rug.

'Did you do anything interesting today?'

'I saw my sister. It's her birthday this week.'

This might be a half truth, Johnny decided. Better than an outright lie.

Helene walked towards the bedroom. She looked as fresh as she had done the previous morning.

'We're both invited to dinner,' she called back.

'You told your sister about me?'

'I said you were a travelling salesman. That's true, in a

way, isn't it?' She turned on the bedroom light.
What have you done with our clothes –'

'I was going to mention that. Do you think your family
would mind if we made it breakfast instead?'

They could have gone to Alex, Johnny's Comintern contact, or simply to a hotel. But Alex would be less than over
joyed at being rousted out of bed before dawn, and checking
into a hotel at an odd hour increased the risk of attracting
the attentions of the police. Besides, Johnny was curious
to take a look at Helene's family.

Their apartment building was on a pleasant street in
Charlottenburg with lime trees dotted along the pavement.
They arrived shortly after five, after stopping for coffee
and the morning papers at the Friedrichstrasse station,
where no one except a panhandler swilling wine out of a
paper cup appeared to take the slightest interest in them.

Helene rang the bell. A dog in a neighbouring house
started snarling and snapping.

Johnny rapped on one of the frosted glass panes in the
door.

A light came on inside, and the door opened a crack.

'Who is it?'

'Sigi?'

The girl inside peered through the crack, disbelieving.
Then she pulled the door shut. There was a rattle of chains,
the door flew open, and she flung herself into Helene's
arms.

Over Helene's shoulder, Johnny glimpsed a face with the
soft, smudged beauty of a child just roused from sleep. The
sisters moved apart, and the tawny light from the hall lamp
played on the bold contours of the girl's body under the
filmy nightgown. She looked up, and the colour rose in
her cheeks when she saw how freely the stranger's eyes
ranged over her. She pulled the flaps of her flowered robe
together.

'This is Johnny,' Helene announced.

Sigrid let him take her hand. Her touch was raw silk. He
could see her face more clearly now. It was almost heart

y a wild mane of red-gold hair. Her lips
er than Helene's. Her eyes were a magical
ith hazel and gold.
t the suitcases.
in trouble,' Helene said. 'Can we stay?'
d a man's hoarse voice raised from an inner
roo id? What is it? Who's there?'

'It's all right, Father,' she called back. Suddenly brisk
and practical, she snatched up their bags, dragged them
inside, and relocked the door. 'The lodger's got your old
room. You can have mine.'

'No, Sigi. What about the room at the back? The sewing
room?'

'There's just a sofa. And it's such a mess –'

'It doesn't matter.'

Sigrid ran lightly ahead of them down the corridor,
gloomy in the half light with its suffocating, wine-red
wallpaper. They found her gathering up canvases, turning
an easel to the wall.

'This is your studio,' Johnny said. The room was small
and bright and smelled of oils and turpentine. The blend
was not unpleasant. Johnny wanted to look at the pictures,
but Sigrid hoarded them shyly under her arm.

'Helene.' The new voice was husky, even deeper than
Helene's.

Johnny turned and saw an extraordinary apparition. The
woman's body seemed slender and supple as either of her
daughters, but her hair was completely white. The face was
Helene's, seen in a cracked mirror.

A stocky man with a red, jowly face barrelled into the
doorway beside her.

'So she's back, is she, the little slut?'

'Shut up, Hermann.'

'She's not staying here with her fancy man.'

Johnny looked anything but fancy, in his hat and shapeless overcoat.

'He's my husband,' Helene said.

Johnny saw no reason to amend this statement.

'Probably a fucking Red, like you.'

'It's my room,' Sigrid interjected. 'I told them they could stay.'

Hermann Eckhardt appealed to his wife. 'For all we know, they've got the cops on their tails. I'm not having them under this roof.'

'Shut your face,' Helene's mother said. She looked at him like something that ought to be trodden underfoot. 'I'll decide.'

'It's just for a few nights,' Johnny spoke up. 'I'm sorry for the inconvenience. Of course, we'll pay for your trouble.'

'Bloody right you'll pay.'

'Go to bed, Hermann.' The mother's voice was oddly compelling. It wasn't the anger or disgust it might have conveyed; it was the absence of emotion.

Hermann grunted and shuffled off along the corridor, muttering to himself.

Clara Eckhardt looked from Helene to Johnny. 'You've come from Russia,' she said. It was not a question. 'You mustn't bring any of that into this house. There are no Communists here.'

'We won't,' Johnny promised.

'Sigrid,' she instructed her daughter, 'bring sheets and towels.'

As soon as the girl was gone, she said to Helene, with sudden ferocity, 'And you leave her alone, do you hear me? Don't go putting anything in her head. Things are hard enough for her as it is.'

There wasn't room for both on the sofa, so Johnny lay on the floor, his head resting on his bundled overcoat, and watched the moonlight slanting through the window. He started rehearsing what he would say to Dimitrov when he kept his appointment later that morning. But he found that Sigrid kept drifting in and out of his thoughts. She had something of her sister, but it was softer, unstudied. Something a man could hold on to. Helene reached down and snapped her finger against his cheek.

'What my mother said was meant for you, too,' she said quietly.

'What?'

'About Sigi. I saw how you looked at her.'

'Well?'

'She's not like us. She can be hurt. I want you to leave her alone.'

It was the first time Johnny had ever seen Helene play the big sister, the protectress. He liked this human side, this confession of weakness, and instead of sleeping he made love to her eagerly in the early light. But when he let his eyelids fall, the face he saw was Sigrid's.

4

The offices of the Führer-Verlag were on the Wilhelmstrasse. Civil servants and foreign diplomats from nearby chanceries would pause on their way to lunch to peer into the windows of the ground-floor bookshop. Johnny would not be mistaken for one of them in his tweed coat, soft collar and comfortable gabardine trousers. But he might very well pass for a writer on his way to discuss a contract. He walked through the bookshop, nodded at the man in a cubbyhole at the back and went up by the service stairs.

There was an atmosphere of frenzied activity on every floor – couriers and copyboys coming and going, type-writers clacking, telephones jangling. There were armed men posted on every landing, because this building housed the headquarters of the Westbureau, the nerve centre of Comintern operations in Europe.

Georgi Dimitrov's sanctum smelled and looked more like a cigar humidor – a very expensive one, with sides of dark, polished wood – than a Turkish bath. A portrait of Bismarck in a funereal black frame hung over the immense mahogany desk. The Iron Chancellor looked like a petulant bulldog. There was a glass-fronted bookcase filled with rich leather bindings, the kind of volumes that are ordered by the meter.

The figure that blossomed from behind the desk was sleek and olive skinned, dandyish in a silk smoking jacket.

Dimitrov advanced in a haze of tobacco and attar of roses and extended a plump hand garnished with an enormous ruby ring. His eyes were moist. His whole body moved with the rhythms of his speech.

He waved Johnny into a studded leather chair and dipped into a plain manila file.

'You've travelled a good deal, Johann Lentz,' he addressed Johnny. 'Romania. Scandinavia. France. South America. The Far East. You've never been to Great Britain?'

'No.'

'Britain is a special hobby of mine. I asked Moscow to find me a man who has no record with the British authorities. I asked for a military expert, the best available expert in the area of AM measures. They sent me a list of candidates, and I picked you. Did I make the right choice?'

'I'm honoured, of course.'

'AM' stood for 'Anti-Military'. Under the statutes of the Comintern, every Communist party was required to maintain its own AM *Apparat*. These secret networks were responsible for recruiting sympathisers and inciting mutiny inside the armed forces, under guidance from Moscow. In his years as a Comintern military adviser Johnny had directed AM operations against the Romanians, the Belgians and the French.

'Do you know why I picked you?' Dimitrov went on. 'Not because of that Romanian mess. No, don't say a word. I know it wasn't your fault. I picked you because you're a sailor and because your record doesn't start with Costanza, or even with Hamburg. It starts with the mutiny in the Kaiser's fleet. I want you to go to England and do the same thing in the Royal Navy.'

'That's quite an undertaking.'

'It's quite an opportunity,' Dimitrov corrected him. 'Do you read the newspapers? Do you know what's going on in England?'

'I know there was a mutiny in the British fleet. At a base in Scotland.'

'At Invergordon. The government tried to cut the sailors'

pay, and a strike was called. For several hours, the battle fleet was paralyzed. The British lion was changed into a helpless pussycat. Then the government panicked. It restored full pay and tried to hush everything up. The ringleaders were removed without publicity. And do you know when I received the first report from our comrades in the Communist Party of Great Britain? Four days afterwards!'

Dimitrov got up and waved his cigar like a baton.

'Think of it, Lentz!' he went on. 'We had a historic opportunity! What holds the British Empire together? The navy! For a few hours the empire lost its sword and shield. The situation demanded strong, ruthless leadership, the shooting of officers, action to bring things to a boil. And what did our British comrades do? They sat in their semi-detached cottages swilling their tea. I know Comrade Pollitt and the rest of that crowd. The British Communists are sluggish and complacent. They run their party like a grocery store. They think that revolution is good business.

'I want you to go and light a fire under them. Don't be scared to throw your weight around. Your credentials are being prepared now. I want you to examine them closely. You are going to Britain as an inspector of the Comintern. Do you know what that means? It means that *you*, Johann Lentz, have the power to issue any orders you like. If you tell Pollitt to shine your boots, he's obliged to do it. If they give you any trouble, hit them where their hearts are – in their hip pockets! Tell them you'll chop off their subsidies. That will bring them around in short order! Every letter they send to Moscow ends with a chiselling demand for money. Tell Harry Pollitt we want value for money, and if he won't give it we'll find someone who will!'

Dimitrov threw himself down on the sofa and inspected his audience.

'Well? What have you got to say?'

'I'd rather be doing the same job in Germany,' Johnny said quietly.

'You needn't concern yourself with Germany,' Dimitrov responded, with faint annoyance. 'The German party has a quarter of a million members, and this department is not exactly idle.'

'That doesn't seem to be bothering Hitler,' Johnny ventured. The remark bordered on open insolence, but he was determined to test what Kordt had told him about the party line on the Hitler movement. He recounted Kordt's story about the Bremen congress, trying to keep his emotion in check.

The Bulgarian's eyelids narrowed. 'Where did you hear these things?'

'Friends.'

'You should be more cautious who you talk to,' Dimitrov warned him. 'The German party is a snake pit.' He made an effort to revive his earlier bonhomie. 'Look, I know you're German. And you've been away from home for a long time. Naturally you're concerned about certain things. But you're really in no position to pass judgment. A foot soldier doesn't see what a general can see.'

But the general's mistakes are much deadlier, Johnny thought. Didn't the war teach us that?

'I'll tell you something in confidence,' the Bulgarian pressed on. 'Just in case you imagine we're asleep at the wheel. I have it from an irrefutable source, a man high up in the General Staff. If Hitler is ever in a position to attempt to seize power, the Reichswehr will prevent him by force. You see? Hitler is a marionette. He can be broken like that.' He snapped his fingers and looked triumphantly at Johnny.

Johnny knew at that moment that it was useless appealing to this man. Dimitrov was part of the problem.

I mustn't push it any further, Johnny told himself. Not here. That was Emil's mistake.

Perhaps, after all, he would be better off in England.

He walked north up the Wilhelmstrasse in the perfect afternoon light. It played on the decorations of bankers and high officials and the jewels of their expensive women as they streamed from their phaetons to a grand reception at the Adlon. In the shadow of the great hotel, on the side next to the kitchens where there was an inescapable aroma of cooking oil, the British flag flapped on its staff in front of the former mansion of a railroad millionaire.

A man came out of the side entrance of the embassy and walked briskly towards a waiting sedan. Johnny glanced at him through the wrought-iron gate. Tall, straight-backed, he wore his civilian clothes like a military uniform: homburg, dark chesterfield with a velvet tab on the collar, scrolled umbrella. He moved with utter self-assurance, the model of a defender of the Raj. This is the enemy, Johnny thought, as he watched the Englishman swing into his car. He had had it drilled into him in countless briefings and study sessions in Moscow: Great Britain was the main enemy. His Majesty's Intelligence Service, which had tried to overthrow Lenin, was still the most ferocious of the secret opponents of the revolution. The Englishman was speaking to his chauffeur. There was something enviable about the man's total composure.

Johnny quickened his stride as he turned up the wide boulevard Unter den Linden. He barely registered the romantic triumph of the Brandenburg Gate, flung up against the sky. He needed time and space to sort out his emotions. He had instructions to go to a house in Grünewald, where the Westbureau hid its British section, to start his detailed briefings. That could wait till tomorrow. He rambled on into the Tiergarten without fixed purpose.

5

He stopped at the zoo on his way back to the family flat in Charlottenburg. He found something relaxing in the presence of wild animals; possibly it had to do with their simplicity, their lack of a moral sense. He spent some time inspecting a small herd of blackbucks from southern Africa. The dominant male was distinguished by his black face and neck. As he grew older and weaker, one of the younger bucks would start to acquire this distinctive colouring as he rose in status. One young buck in this herd was well advanced; his head and neck were almost completely black. The old leader watched him warily, waiting to lock horns with his own death.

Johnny rambled on towards the cages of the big cats. There was a girl bent over a sketchbook on one of the benches. She wore a loose beret over her fine-spun red-gold hair. Her ankles were neatly crossed under the calf-length skirt. He knew her before he even saw her face. She looked up from her stub of charcoal to the animal that was padding silently around the narrow ambit of its cage, its shoulders rising and falling rhythmically. It was a panther, black as diamond dust.

He walked quietly along the slope of the path till he was standing just behind her. He stared at the white curve of her neck, at the hunted eyes of the panther, and recited

Sein Blick ist vom Vorübergehn der Stäbe
so müd geworden, dass er nichts mehr hält.
Ihm ist, als ob es tausend Stäbe gäbe
und hinter tausend Stäben keine Welt.

His vision, from the constantly passing bars,
has grown so weary that it cannot hold
anything else. It seems to him there are
a thousand bars; and behind the bars, no world.

She turned without haste, without fear, and studied him as if she were considering him for one of her sketches. He felt awkward with his big hands dangling at his sides.

'You don't look like someone who would know Rilke,' Sigrid said.

'And you look like a woman who does.'

One of his yawning afternoons in the schoolroom in Hamburg had been brought alive by a young teacher who had introduced his class to Rilke, reciting from the *Neue Gedichte* with the fire of a convert. The terrifying image of the panther behind bars had lived with Johnny ever since.

He sat down beside her on the bench, so close he could

feel the warmth of her thigh. She did not draw away, but he felt her body tense, her legs press together.

'May I?'

He seized the sketchbook before she could close it.

The drawing of the panther was arresting; you could see the muscles rippling beneath the hide.

'You know what it's like to be caged,' he said. He looked at her with such intensity that she turned away from him. She didn't exactly blush, but he could sense the heat in her face. It excited him.

'Yes,' she murmured.

'You have a gift. Have you been to art school?'

She shook her head. 'Father's been out of work for so long,' she said by way of explanation. 'And now I have to work in the restaurant. When I get a half day off, I come here or go to the exhibitions.'

'Will you show me your paintings?'

'If you like.'

'I don't know much about art. But I met Grosz once.'

'Georg Grosz? His work is wonderful but – so brutal.'

'He's an educator. He trains us to see things as they are. And to see why things have to be changed.'

'I couldn't draw that way. Not to pass judgment.'

'The artist can't be neutral. Neutrality is an illusion. To be neutral means to be on the side of the powers that be.' He instantly regretted this statement. It sounded clumsy and pontifical.

She weighed this for a moment. 'Is it true what Father says – that you're a Red?'

'I'm a member of the Communist party.' He smiled. 'Does that offend you?'

'I'm not political. I don't find it easy to take sides. Father votes for the Social Democrats, though I don't know whether he will next time. He says Stalin's worse than Hitler.'

'He doesn't know what he's talking about.'

'You met Helene in Russia?'

'Yes.' He saw no reason to tell Sigrid about her sister's early life in Hamburg.

'You know, she ran away from home.'

'You must have been very small.'

'I remember her bending over my bed, late at night. She left me with something of hers, something that was close to her. A teddy bear with one eye missing. I still have it. She sent letters, sometimes, from all over the world. She never mentioned you. How long have you been married?'

Johnny hesitated. 'We're not married.'

'But Helene said – oh, I see.' She dropped her eyes, embarrassed.

'It's not quite what you think. We're partners, workmates if you like. You see, the party is our family.'

Sigrid's face brightened. 'You're involved in secret work, is that it?'

'I'd rather not talk about it.'

'Let me see your hands.'

'I beg your pardon?'

'Let me see your hands.'

He held them out obediently. She bent over them, studying the ridges and raised veins. She turned them over and traced the lifeline with her finger. Her hand looked small and soft as a child's inside his broad, calloused palm.

She said, 'I'd like to paint you.'

'Really? Like your models in the zoo? I'm flattered. Tell me, which of your animals do I resemble?'

'Oh, that's easy,' she replied. 'That one.' She pointed at the panther. 'Strong, very dangerous – but caged.'

Startled by her own boldness, she slammed her sketch-book shut. A loose page flew out, and she darted after it. Johnny moved faster.

As he handed it to her, he let his arm graze her waist, as if by accident.

He said, 'Are you sure the bars will hold?' and she started to blush as though she felt he was comparing her, not himself, to the animal in the cage.

6

'Kipling's books are decorated with swastikas,' Max Fabrikant remarked. 'They spin the other way from Hitler's,
anticlockwise. The swastika is a very ancient symbol of
the oriental mystics. I am told it is also a symbol of the
Freemasons – hence, perhaps, Kipling. There are even
those who maintain that the Christian cross is a sawn-off
swastika.'

They were strolling along the Ku'damm into the cabaret
district. Johnny glanced back at the swaggering crowd of
Nazis who had blocked the pavement on the other side.
Max led the way into a street where lone men drifted
among lurid signs advertising sex shows and porno
films.

'Hitler is plumbing something atavistic in the human
psyche,' Max went on. 'That is the secret of his appeal. He
can't be defeated on the level of reason, because he draws
directly from the unconscious, from the reptile brain that
is older than thought.' In the blue light that fell from the
neon sign above, Fabrikant's mouth seemed to be moulded
into a leer. 'But you discussed all of that with Heinz Kordt
didn't you?'

'How did you know?'

Max shrugged. 'I know what Heinz thinks. And I knew
you were bound to seek him out. You're loyal to your
friends. That's not always a failing.'

Johnny had asked for this meeting. He had also suggested
that Helene should not be present. But the choice of locale
belonged to Max.

The spymaster glanced up at the sign above their heads.
The neon lights picked out the exaggerated profile of a
naked woman lowering herself into a tub. *Die Badewanne*,
flashed the words underneath. The Bathtub.

'In here.'

A person in a blonde wig with breasts like hunting horns
led them to a table. Johnny was struck by the legs that
showed through the slits in the dress; they were as sturdy
as his own, with knobbly knees. He was reminded, for a

moment, of a night at the Kali-Bar in Hamburg. The night he had met Helene.

The floor show had already begun. There was a real bathtub on stage, surrounded by people of both sexes in varying stages of nudity. The centrepiece was a young man wearing only a black hood and a studded collar, who was being led around on a chain like a dog.

Max ordered Dom Perignon. He seemed determined to enjoy himself.

'Why here?' Johnny shouted above the din.

'Why not? It's so uplifting, don't you think? The Decline of the West in two acts, with live sex.' As if on cue, a masked man with impossible pectorals came onstage and started cracking a whip. He seemed to be a great hit with this crowd.

'About Heinz —' Johnny leaned closer, so as not to shout.

'Well?'

'He thinks we're not doing enough to stop Hitler. I think he's right. I talked to Dimitrov. He seems to be living in some imaginary country.'

'Drop it, Johnny. You're talking like a German.'

'I *am* a German.'

'Don't give me that crap, that *Lokalpatriotismus*. You know better than that. You belong to a world movement. That's your only loyalty.'

'I'm worried about Heinz.'

'I'm fond of Heinz. You know that. He's a good man to have with you in the trenches. But you should tell him not to make so much noise. The wind carries it further than he imagines.'

The wine waiter came up and fussed over them. Max tested the champagne and indicated his approval.

'To London!' he proposed, clinking glasses. 'To the girls along the Serpentine!'

'How long have you known?' Johnny asked.

'Longer than you, I expect. I have a piece of advice for you. When you get to England, buy yourself a decent suit. Never mind what it costs.'

'Is there something wrong with my clothes?' Johnny

glanced down at his grey flannel suit, bought off the peg in Bucharest years before.

'Not from my point of view. But you must come to terms with the English psyche. In the eyes of an Englishman, a man who goes to the right tailor is above suspicion.'

'I'll try to keep that in mind.' His eyes flitted up to the semi-nude dancer who was gyrating onstage with her pet boa constrictor around her belly.

'You asked for this meeting,' Max reminded him. 'It's always a pleasure to see you, of course. But was there something in particular you wanted to say?'

'It's about Helene.'

'Yes?'

'I'd rather she didn't come to England with me.'

'That's not my province.'

'But she works for you –'

Max silenced Johnny with a subtle but sudden flick of his wrist. The young man followed his gaze and saw a newcomer, smartly attired in a broad pinstripe and a bow tie, with a red rose in his buttonhole. The stranger murmured something to the transvestite waiter and was rewarded with giggles. His manner was languid, but his eyes flicked warily from side to side as he crossed the room to join a poised, very fair young man at a corner table. As Max and Johnny watched, the snake-dancer, minus the boa constrictor, threaded her way through the drinkers and sat down at the same table.

Max allowed himself a small sigh of satisfaction.

'A friend of yours?' Johnny tried to provoke him.

'That, my dear fellow, is the head of British Intelligence in Berlin.'

Johnny took another look at the Englishman, trying to memorise the face.

Max reached for the champagne bottle, found it empty, and pushed it back nosedown into the bucket.

'About Helene,' he remarked, studying the chemistry between the British spy and the colourful crowd at his table, 'I may have a solution for you. A temporary one, at any rate.'

'Yes?'

'It occurs to me that I may need to borrow her for a few weeks.'

7

Sigrid waited on tables in the Palace Café Mondays through Saturdays from eleven until eight, with Wednesday afternoons off. There was a brisk trade at lunchtime (secretaries and clerks from nearby government offices) and in the early evenings (cinemagoers dining out on their way to the UFA theatre up the street). In the slack times, in the middle of the afternoon, she would sketch the faces around her. Some of the customers, discovering her hidden talent, would slip her an extra mark for their portraits. It was in those lazy hours that Johnny took to drinking coffee at the Palace Café. Once he brought her a leaflet about the conditions of German workers. It was illustrated with a drawing of a street sweeper, his face corrugated by a lifetime of toil, trudging off to work.

She refused to speak to Johnny for the rest of the day. The sketch was hers, something he had asked for. He had no right to have it printed without her consent, least of all in such a publication. At the bottom of the leaflet was the long-winded title of some organisation she had never heard of. She presumed it was something to do with the Communists, and when she questioned Johnny later, he didn't bother with denials.

'Did you read it?' he demanded. 'Is there anything you disagree with?'

She had to shake her head.

'Well, then, be proud you're part of something that *matters*. Publications like this are important. People have to be made aware of how the workers are forced to live, of what the Fascists are doing. They have to be made to *see*. Your picture says more than all of the text. They'd like to use more of your work, Sigi. You don't need to worry. Your name won't be used. And they'll pay you, not much, but enough to pay for the best materials you can buy. It's a start, isn't it?'

She had the use of her studio again. The lodger had moved on, and Johnny and Helene had taken over his room. Her father had said he wouldn't stand for it. When drunk, he even threatened to go to the police. But he was scared of his wife, and his grumbling subsided when Johnny handed him twice the usual rent, for a whole month to boot. With the additional allowance Johnny had received from Dimitrov's people, he had no shortage of funds. Now there was meat on the table every night and money for Hermann to loaf all day in his *Lokal*. And morning and evening, Johnny was there, under the same roof. In fact, he was at home far more often than Helene, who would vanish without explanation for days at a time.

His presence disturbed Sigrid. When he entered a room, he seemed to fill it. She could feel his nearness on her skin, like a physical caress. His eyes were changeable as the sea, sometimes calm and gentle, sometimes a violent tide that threatened to envelop her. She wished he would leave. She promised herself to speak to her mother, to make them go. She had the ominous sensation that he was about to tear open the padlocks that secured a sealed room deep inside her, where some nameless, terrible thing thrashed in its chains, striving to break loose. Yet at the Palace Café, when the afternoon wore on and he had still not appeared with his battered hat and his puckish grin, she began to feel empty, almost desolate. And when he suggested little outings, she did not refuse.

These excursions were harmless enough, considered singly: a visit to the UFA cinema after work or to a rehearsal of the new play by Bert Brecht, or a Wednesday afternoon on the Wannsee. That day he hired a boat, and they sculled to the farther shore, where he scrambled onto a rock and squatted, his arms dangling over his knees, his face turned up to the sun.

'You look like a seal, with your nose pointing up like that,' she laughed at him. She turned the sketch she had begun into a caricature, with a feminine hand dangling a fish over Johnny's nose.

'It's not the fish I'm pointing at,' Johnny said, snatching the drawing away from her.

She made out that she hadn't heard. But rowing back across the Wannsee, half blinded by the late sun that burned on the waters, she was frightened, less of him than of herself.

He had flung off his jacket and rolled up his sleeves. The light traced the flex of his arms, which were strong but not brawny. He leaned forward to point something out, and he smelled like the sun. He bent over her, and all of her body rushed to meet him. He found her lips. His touch scalded, but it took all of her strength to wrench herself away. She sat in the prow of the boat, quivering, her head erect, poised for flight.

'Why?' His tone wasn't entreating or accusing. Slowly she turned back to him. He cocked his head and she wanted to laugh, because now he looked like a dog trying to puzzle out the strange speech of humans.

She said, 'Because of Helene,' and tried to smooth her dress. It felt unnaturally constricting, pressing so tightly against her bosom she could hardly breathe.

'I told you already,' he said gently. 'I'm not married to Helene.'

'But you sleep together.'

'Sometimes.' He held her gaze. 'But there are no commitments. Except for the mission we share. And that is something I hope one day to share with you.'

The boat drifted closer to the home shore, and a copse of fir trees on a rise swallowed the sun. She felt a sudden chill.

'I'm not Helene,' she said. 'I couldn't live like that.'

'You're saving yourself for the man you'll marry?'

This was treacherous ground. She wasn't sure she believed in marriage, not after what she had seen between her parents.

She moved onto safer slopes. 'Helene is my sister,' she pointed out.

A maddening smile plucked at his lips. 'You're not accountable for an accident of birth.'

'It's not proper,' she said. 'It's *unanständig.*'

She made this last remark with such a determined imposture of bourgeois rectitude that he burst out laughing, and it horrified her to find that she wanted to join in. The mood was so convulsive that she had to turn her back on him, so he would mistake the spasms for a different sentiment and not take them as an invitation to return to the attack. What was the matter with her?

She knew, of course, that the situation was hopeless. Johnny was a man on the run, a dangerous agitator likely to spend the rest of his life – which might not be long – behind bars. Further, he was married (well, if not exactly married, then at least pledged) to her sister. In any case, he might be leaving Berlin at any moment for God-knows-where. To cap it all, he was a sailor by trade, and everyone knew how far you could trust sailors with women.

Yet when he reached for her again, she didn't move quickly enough to avoid him (did she move at all?) and when he crushed her against him, her body betrayed her. She should have been stiff and unyielding, wooden as a plank, but every part of her hastened to receive him. She could feel his breath on her neck, his circling hands invading her secret places. With an effort of will she grabbed the side of the dinghy – which rolled dangerously, so that water sloshed over their feet – and dragged herself away.

She moved through the rest of that week like a sleepwalker. Forms had lost their usual weight and density. In bed, she fell into a shallow, restless sleep. It was like lying on shifting sands, with a gauzy curtain blowing over her face. Waking, she went about her chores like an automaton. At the restaurant she got orders mixed up and dropped a tray, and the manager threatened to fire her.

'There are thousands of girls in Berlin!' he screamed. 'Don't think you're anything special.'

Johnny turned up at her side one morning at the Ethnological Museum – had he followed her or come with her? – and they wandered among the displays of primitive art. Johnny was fascinated by some of the masks. He stopped in front of a Kwakiutl mask from British Columbia. It showed a frontal view of a face with an enormous, tragic eye, sheared off along the ridge of the nose so that it was suddenly transformed into a dark profile.

They looked at Yoruba initiation masks, at a towering Senufo headdress that was a whole alphabet of hieratic signs, at the abstract Oceanic figures she told him had influenced Giacometti.

'The mask is not just decoration,' she told him. 'The man who puts on the mask is no longer himself. He dies to the old life to become the god, or the ancestral spirit. The mask belongs to a higher order of reality than the man who wears it.'

He considered this without comment, but his face darkened. He strolled away with his hands in his pockets to stare at some shrunken trophy heads from South America. Sigrid shuddered at the sight of one of them, a nut-brown face with black oblong stones for eyes, draped with plaits of dried flowers and blue-and-red feathers. It had a coil of string in its mouth, with a length left dangling underneath like a hangman's noose.

'I saw something like this once before.'

'Come away,' she said, taking his arm.

'All primitive art is for use,' he remarked, when they were standing on the museum steps. 'Superstitious use, it's true, but the service of something greater than the individual artist.'

'Are you preaching at me again?'

He smiled and patted her hand. 'No, but they'd like some more of your drawings for a new magazine. What would a trophy head of Goebbels look like?'

Then a couple of days passed when she didn't see him. Helene flew in and out of the flat to fetch some clothes. She was in a filthy temper and wouldn't exchange more than half a dozen words. Hitler made a violent speech promising revenge for the assassination of a storm troop commander by the Communists. In her free time Sigrid busied herself with the Nazi caricatures Johnny had requested for the magazine. The likenesses weren't bad. Some of them –

especially the sketch of Himmler, the poultry farmer, as a turkey with wattles drooping over the collar of his SS uniform – were quite funny.

Wednesday came around, and Johnny still hadn't re-appeared. His absence made a wasteland of her afternoon off. Keep away, she had told herself, knowing that she could be only a passing diversion in the life of a man like him. She was bound to lose him soon enough, inevitably and irrevocably. But now she was terrified by the fear that he had been snatched away even sooner than she had calculated, before she had had time to make up her mind about everything. Had she been right to refuse him, that afternoon on the lake? Was it right to spurn something your whole being cried out for because you couldn't have it for keeps? She didn't know the answers, not for sure.

That Wednesday night, long after her parents had gone to bed, she went to the lodger's room. The door was locked, but she opened it with the key to her own room; all the locks inside the apartment were the same.

She examined the familiar furnishings of the room – the ponderous armoire against the wall, the china jug in its bowl on the washstand, the painting of a stag with a pack of dogs at its heels, the double bed with its massive headboard. Nothing was out of place. There was no personal touch to suggest the room was even occupied. The bed cover lay flat and smooth, the ashtray on its brass stand had been wiped clean. Overcome by a kind of panic, she rushed to the cupboard and flung the doors open. His clothes were still there: a couple of suits, the tweed coat he had worn that day on the lake.

A measure of calm returned, and with it insuperable weariness. She lay on the bed, *his* bed, and let sleep take her.

His breath was hot against her face. She smelled raw alcohol and wood smoke. The mattress sagged under the double weight.

He murmured, 'Oh, my love.'

Coming out of the dream, she realised he had pulled up her nightgown. The fabric lay bunched beneath her armpits while his lips moved to her breasts.

She clawed at him, and there was a dull thud as his shoulder hit the wall.

Then his full weight was on her, pinning her. She opened her mouth and formed words, but no sound escaped.

She stopped wrestling and listened to the rasp of his breathing. When he forced his way between her legs, she stayed the same, not yielding, not resisting. She bit her lip at the first stab of pain and tasted her own blood.

He was bucking and sawing, but then his movements became slower, coaxing and circling as he tried to lead her like a dance partner. She relaxed a little, and began to enter into the rhythm.

But before she had learned it, he was lunging inside her. She saw his face lifted over her, flushed and triumphant, gleaming with sweat.

He whispered, 'My love.' The rough stubble pricked her skin as he rested his head against her neck.

She slid away from him and went to the washbasin.

In the moonlight he could see the dark patches on the sheet.

'Sigrid,' he said hoarsely. 'I didn't know. You're a woman made for love. I thought –'

He broke off at the sight of her calmly hoisting her nightgown over her head and shoulders. Without shame, she walked back to the bed and stood over him, examining his body as if she wanted to see how each part worked.

'*Noch einmal*,' she said. 'Do it again.'

He stared at her. The light showed the thrust of her breasts, the long, voluptuous slope of her belly.

'You took something from me,' she said. 'Something I dreamed of sharing. You owe me something now. I want to know what it feels like to be a woman.'

8

The Austrian passport was two years old. It was dated October 1929, the year and month of the Great Crash. The name of the holder was entered in a confident copperplate hand: Ludwig Dinkelmeyer. According to the information entered on the second page, his profession was *Kaufmann* – 'Merchant' – and he had been born in Vienna in 1894. Oval face, blue eyes, dark blond hair, no visible distinguishing marks.

Johnny's face looked out of the photograph on page three. He was respectably dressed in a dark suit, his tie perfectly in place, his hair slicked back, the image of a successful tradesman. A matching photograph of Helene, described as his wife, Erna, had been inserted next to his. She wore her hair in tight waves and a dress with a broad collar and fashionably padded shoulders. They shared the imprint of the same rubber stamp.

'The shoes are a nice fit, wouldn't you say?' the man in the tailor shop remarked to Johnny. 'Scotland Yard has a nose for dummy passports. But they're not magicians. They'll never fault this.'

They were in a back room equipped with a pair of ancient Singer sewing machines and piled high with bolts and remnants of cloth.

'Your credentials,' the tailor said, showing Johnny a linen square bearing a dozen lines of black type. 'Give me your jacket.'

Johnny handed over his coat, and the tailor inspected the lining. He took a pair of scissors and made a brisk incision around the left armpit. He plied his needle, and in a couple of minutes the job was done. Unless the British customs men decided to tear Johnny's clothing apart, they would never find his secret credentials from the Comintern.

'What am I selling this time?' Johnny asked.

'You're in luck, my friend. You're a wine merchant. I'm only sorry I won't have the chance to inspect your samples. You'll pick them up in Hamburg.'

'You're a woman for life,' he had told her.

And Sigrid had replied, 'But you – you're the man of Sesenheim.'

He had not understood the allusion, so she had had to remind him. Goethe had had a tempestuous affair with an innocent

140

country parson's daughter, Friedericke Brion. He had made no effort to guard her reputation, flaunting her as his mistress. But when the poet had decided to leave Sesenheim, he had dropped the girl like a plaything he had outgrown. He had met her on horseback and hadn't even dismounted to say good-bye. He had just leaned over from the saddle and shaken hands. The girl had never looked at another man.

'It's not true,' Johnny protested. 'I'll come back for you. I'll find a way for us to be together.'

'Don't make me any promises,' she said, shaking her head. 'You're a soldier under orders. Isn't that what you told me? Let's just live in the time we're allowed.'

It was stolen time. He had known that all along. So far he had contrived to keep the affair secret from Helene. But in time she was bound to find out. He didn't feel guilty in relation to Helene; on the contrary, he was ready to stand his ground with her. But he could only guess at what Helene would say to her sister, at the weapons she might use to turn Sigrid against him.

He had found excuses to prolong his stay in Berlin, but the excuses had run out. When the signal to leave for England finally came, it was peremptory. His instructions were to take the express from the Lehrter station – less than two hours away – to keep a rendezvous in Hamburg that same night.

He rushed to the Palace Café. Sigrid's face lit up when she saw him.

'Can you come outside for a minute?' he asked.

She saw his expression, and her face went blank. She asked one of the other girls to take over her post, took off her apron and followed him outside. The bite of winter was in the air.

'It's now, isn't it?' she said in a whisper.

'I'm not on horseback.' His attempt at a joke fell like a stone. 'I'll write. And I'll be back. But I don't know when. I can't possibly ask you to wait for me.'

'I won't wait,' she said. 'I won't even know if you're alive or dead. But I'll be here, just the same.'

3

The Lost Band

Out of the ruins of the Communist revolution we built in Germany for Soviet Russia a brilliant intelligence service, the envy of every other nation.
— *Walter Krivitsky, In Stalin's Secret Service (1939)*

1

It was raining when Johnny's plane from Hamburg bumped down onto the runway at East Croydon. It rained steadily over Greater London for the next sixteen consecutive days, out of a sky that closed over the rooftops like a saucepan lid.

His passport raised no questions. The customs inspector waived duty on his case of wine samples. A police constable whose muttonchop whiskers gave him the benign aspect of an Old English sheepdog showed Johnny the way to the train station and asked if he was South African. Everything but the weather was accommodating.

Following instructions, he took the train to Victoria and checked into a small, sooty hotel frequented by travelling salesmen and illicit lunchtime lovers. He bought himself an umbrella, dined on warm beer and cottage pie in a pub up the road and wrote his first letter to Sigrid before he turned in for the night. Two days away from her, he felt her absence as an aching hollow, demanding to be filled.

In the morning he went to the post office to mail his letter. It did not include a return address. He would look for a safe mailing address when he found more permanent lodgings.

When he returned to the hotel, a young man in a rather loud plaid suit was chatting up the girl receptionist. Johnny checked his watch against the clock above the desk – 9:27 A.M. He was two minutes fast.

The young man followed Johnny into the elevator, whistling an old music-hall song. He pulled the gate shut behind them and unfolded a copy of the *Sporting Guide*. It increased his resemblance to a racetrack tout. Then Johnny noticed the date on the paper. It was a week old.

The stranger's nose popped over the top of his paper.

'You wouldn't have the time, would you, squire?'

'Certainly.' Johnny did not consult his pocket watch. 'It is precisely quarter to five.'

'George Mikes,' the young man grinned and stuck out his hand. 'At your service.'

George Mikes was as good as his word. For the next two weeks he played guide, chauffeur, drinking crony, racing tipster, amateur pimp and general aide-de-camp. He was the London organiser of the party's AM *Apparat* – a word he pronounced to rhyme with 'plate'. He had a bedsit in Hampstead, where he brewed Irish coffee over a single gas ring, but he drove Johnny in his little green Austin to new digs on the other side of the river, in Shepherds Bush.

Johnny's hosts were the Roses – Norma and Ernie. Norma was a big, blowsy, warm-hearted girl, the daughter of a Polish baker in Stoke Newington. Every morning, she cooked huge fry-ups for the two men before boarding her bus to the city, where she had some kind of secretarial job. When it wasn't raining, Ernie spent much of the day pottering round his pocket-handkerchief garden. On Saturdays, religiously, he went bowling. He told Johnny that he had once worked as a piano player at the cinema down the road, interpreting the moments of passion on the big screen.

But his job had vanished with the demise of the silent movies. Now he did part-time work as a glassblower – a job that seemed to Johnny to have an equally precarious future.

Norma and Ernie were both party members, which made Johnny uneasy, since he had been warned in Berlin that the British Communist Party was crawling with police spies. He became even more nervous when Norma had a couple of sherries too many and let slip that she knew Johnny was in England on a secret Soviet mission.

The second Saturday, he came back to Shepherds Bush in midafternoon in a blazing fury. George had taken him to Paddington to inspect the secret printing press that was used to crank out *Soldier's Voice*, a party publication aimed at enlisted men. Johnny approved of the location in the basement below a shoe-repair shop, where the rumble of the press was camouflaged by the hammers and the sewing machines overhead. But he was unhappy about an unexpected discovery. He had found a door, half hidden by piles of newsprint. George hadn't wanted him to look inside. It was just a storage closet, according to George. He looked inside anyway – and found a good-sized room, filled from floor to ceiling with bundles of *Soldier's Voice*. The issues dated back more than twelve months. Moscow paid for every copy that was printed – and the British Communists left them to gather dust. They were lazy and corrupt, just as Dimitrov had said. This wasn't the first evidence he had stumbled across, despite George's assiduous efforts to divert his attention to pubs and pliable female sympathisers. Johnny demanded a meeting with Pollitt and was reminded that it was the weekend.

'What are you? Shopkeepers?' Johnny exploded. 'You get word to Pollitt I want to see him tomorrow, even if it is bloody Sunday. Do you think the revolution has licensing hours?'

He declined George's offer of a lift and walked to a nearby bus stop. There was a long line and only a few seats on the first bus that came. But nobody jostled or tried to jump the queue. A second bus came, and Johnny climbed on top. The people around him chatted about soccer teams and Christmas shopping.

He remembered a line he had read in Engels. 'Even the British proletariat is bourgeois.' He wanted to yell at them, to make a scene.

He changed buses twice and walked the last half mile to the Roses' terrace house, to make sure he wasn't being followed. Rounding the corner of Holly Street, he stopped short.

A sleek, powerful car was double-parked in front of the house. It looked like a Bristol. It didn't belong in that modest street. As Johnny watched, Norma Rose slid out of the passenger seat and blew a kiss to the driver, who pushed his foot down on the gas pedal so hard that the tires complained as he sped off down the street.

Johnny walked round the block, trying to make sense of what he had just seen. A boyfriend Norma had picked up at a cinema or a tea dance? She was a very physical woman, and available – she had suggested that, without much subtlety, to him. Her marriage to Ernie seemed to be fairly sexless. There were no children, and Ernie complained of having to go in for a hernia operation.

The other possibility was the police. But the English police, by Johnny's observation, did not drive around in Bristol motorcars. And they would hardly be so inept as to show themselves at the front door of an agent of the Communist party.

Johnny decided to confront Norma. He was in the mood for a confrontation with someone.

He let himself in with his key and found her in the bedroom, half out of her dress. She had her back to him. As she bent over, he could see the tops of her breasts, swollen and milky white, in the cheval glass on the far side of the room.

She glanced up, gave a stifled squeal, and clapped her hand to her chest.

'You gave me quite a turn.'

'Have you been out?'

'I had to go in to the office. There's a bit of a panic on.'

She was smiling but her eyes looked puffy and sore, as if she had been crying.

'Is something the matter?'

'No. 'Course there isn't.' She went to the dresser and blew her nose.

'I see you got a lift home.'

For the first time, she looked scared. 'You won't tell Ernie, will you?'

'Why should I?' He paused. 'Your friend drives a very fancy car.'

'It's not his. It's an export model. He's trying it out. No harm in that, is there?'

'I couldn't say.'

'Arkady said –'

At the mention of the Russian name, Johnny froze. '*Arkady*?'

'Oh, Jeez. I thought you knew.'

'Who is Arkady?'

'He's my boss. I work for Arcos. Jeez. You're not having me on, are you? I mean, I thought you'd know, you two being Russians and all –'

Johnny swore in German and stormed out of the room.

His anger was not allayed by the knowledge that it was partly his fault. He had never bothered to inquire where Norma worked; he had counted on George Mikes and his organisation to be able to take care of *something*. As a result, he had been living for nearly two weeks at the home of a woman who was not only a party member but an employee of the Soviet trading company, Arcos, which had been the target for a famous police raid a few years before and was publicly identified by Scotland Yard as one of the centres of Russian espionage in Britain. To cap it all, Norma was evidently having an affair with her Russian boss, whose sense of security was clearly as exiguous as her own.

It would be little short of a miracle, he realised, if the police had not had him under observation since he first lugged his suitcase up the Roses' front steps.

He decided to move house immediately. And this time he would find his own lodgings.

He found them in the Sunday classifieds – a pair of good-sized rooms in a boarding house in Richmond that seemed to be largely patronised by theatrical gentlemen who wafted around in dressing gowns at all hours of the day. The bohemian atmosphere appealed to him; a man with a foreign accent and unusual hours was unlikely to draw comment. He paid a month's deposit in cash and moved in with a newly bought suitcase stuffed with newspapers the same day. He told George to collect his bags from Shepherds Bush and meet him on neutral ground. He did not wish to set foot in the Roses' house again.

George Mikes was nervous and full of apologies that night, as they drove – interminably, it seemed – across south London. Walworth was the name on the last sign Johnny noticed. George parked the Austin in front of a neat semi-detached cottage behind a picket fence. There was a doctor's shingle above the door.

'What is this place?' Johnny demanded.

'It's all right. The doctor's a Socialist. He was our candidate in the last general election.'

Johnny swore copiously. 'Haven't you idiots ever heard of a *yafka*?' In his agitation, he slipped into the jargon of his training courses in Moscow.

George blinked at him.

'A safe house!' Johnny translated. 'Don't you know what a safe house is? You'll get all of us arrested!'

'You'll be safe enough here,' George assured him. The man looked totally bewildered. 'Doctor Pratt is a good friend of Harry's.'

Johnny sighed and went inside the house. He found Harry Pollitt in the sitting room, warming his backside in front of a gas fire. The leader of the Communist Party of Great Britain was smooth and freshly barbered, soberly but smartly turned out in a dark suit that minimised his girth. His greeting was unctuous. He pressed Johnny's hand for too long.

Pollitt was a former boilermaker, Johnny had read in the files.

Johnny thought, he looks like a minor evangelist getting ready to pass the collection plate.

Pollitt settled himself in an armchair and wasted twenty minutes reminiscing about his visits to the Soviet Union. He waxed eloquent about a holiday at Stalin's private villa on the Black Sea and dropped the names of a dozen other Moscow officials. The message was crude, but impossible to miss; he wanted Johnny to know he had powerful protectors.

A pretty, dark-haired girl brought tea and biscuits.

As she left, Pollitt winked at Johnny and said, 'Good-looking bint, isn't she? If there's anything you're missing to make your stay comfortable, you needn't be shy with us. Brother George here is just the man to fix you up.'

Johnny said nothing, and Pollitt looked at the teapot with mock dismay. 'I think our guest must be in need of something stronger, Georgie.'

George Mikes dashed out and returned with a bottle of Dimple Haig.

Johnny accepted a glass but let it sit.

You smug bastard, he thought, watching Pollitt. You'd love to get something on me, wouldn't you? Something you could use with your big friends in Moscow. I won't give you that satisfaction.

He resolved to seize the initiative.

'Comrade Pollitt. You know my authority –'

'We don't stand on ceremony here, brother.'

'– and you know the urgency of my mission. It is possible that Russia will be at war with Japan in a matter of weeks. It is equally possible that the Western Powers will exploit the opportunity to intervene on the Japanese side while the Soviet Union is isolated. It is imperative that we should have a network in Britain that is capable of paralysing any war mobilisation.'

'We know our duty. Our AM *Apparat* –'

'– exists only on paper.'

Pollitt appealed mutely to George, who shuffled his feet.

'I've seen what you're doing in the London area,' Johnny pursued. 'You're printing appeals to soldiers and sailors that are never distributed. You haven't begun to capitalise on the Invergordon mutiny. You don't have a single party cell inside the barracks."

'London's tricky,' George spoke up. 'Wait until you see what we're doing in the provinces.'

'I've seen your lists,' Johnny glowered at him. 'I've also noted you've found one excuse after another to delay my visits to Portsmouth and the north.'

'There are always security considerations,' Pollitt observed piously.

'Security!' Johnny snorted. 'None of you seem to know what the word means! Since I've been here, your people have done everything to blow my cover short of delivering me to Scotland Yard.'

Pollitt professed to be shocked.

'I took a day trip to Portsmouth on my own,' Johnny announced.

It was George's turn to look shocked. His reaction, at least, was genuine.

'I went to the address of your AM organiser in Portsmouth,' Johnny continued. 'Billy Shar. Wasn't that the name, George? They'd never heard of him. But it was an interesting establishment. I believe some of your countrymen would refer to it as a knocking shop.'

George Mikes squirmed.

'Surely there's some mistake,' Pollitt interceded. 'George?'

'Er – I'll look into it.'

'It gave me an idea, all the same,' Johnny said, relaxing a bit now he had scored a point. 'When I was in Belgium, we ran a bordello that was popular with army officers. We developed some useful friends. It's one of the ideas I want to work on here.'

'Well, you're the expert, of course.' Pollitt cleared his

throat. 'I'm not qualified to discuss these – ah – technical matters.'

'It's going to require money. Like some other ideas I've got.'

'Now, that could be a problem.' Pollitt was back on home territory. 'We're not a wealthy party, you know. Times are hard, and a lot of our lads are on the dole. We scrape by as best we can.'

'We gave you more than eighty thousand pounds last year.'

'Steady on, now. The figure was nothing like that.'

'I've seen the paperwork,' Johnny pressed on, implacable. 'Thirty thousand in direct grants, the rest fudged in one way or another. Like subscriptions to all those copies of the *Daily Worker* and *Soldier's Voice* that nobody ever reads. And how much of this cash goes on AM work? Sixty bloody quid a month.'

He paused to see if either would contradict him. Neither did.

Pollitt poured another drink and said, 'I'm not used to being talked to like this.'

'I apologise for being direct. I'm impatient to get my job done and get back to where my friends risk getting shot simply because they are Communists. I'm sure that would suit both of us.'

Pollitt seemed to like this better. 'What do you need?'

'I want to pick new men to run the AM network. And I'll need money. Two thousand to start with.'

Pollitt opened his mouth to protest, but Johnny said curtly, 'It's already been authorised. You can check if you like.'

Pollitt's expression finally resolved itself into a smile. 'I'll see what we can do.'

Johnny thought, I'll have to watch my back with this bastard.

Johnny had his own channels of communication, and naturally they had nothing to do with the British party. His
regular post office was a rare bookshop near the British
Museum, a location that suited him because he could steal
an hour or two, upon occasion, in the reading room that –
or so he indulged himself – still harboured the ghosts of
the authors of the *Communist Manifesto*. Sitting there leafing
through old editions of the forerunners – Saint-Just, Buon-
arroti's strange account of the Conspiracy of the Equals – he
sought to renew his revolutionary faith. He had memorised
two telephone numbers. One belonged to 'Smollett', the
resident director of Red Army intelligence; the other was
to be used only if he needed to arrange sudden flight. But
the post office that meant most to him, as his lonely weeks
in England turned into months, was a corner newsagent
five minutes away from his bolthole in Richmond. It was
the sort of place that had grubby filing cards in the window
advertising secondhand bicycles and models who gave
French lessons. He got on friendly terms with the owner,
stopping in to buy his cigarettes and his copies of the
Manchester *Guardian* and the Tory press. He told the man
he had to travel a lot in his job and would be glad of
someone to receive his mail while he was away. Whether
or not the newsagent saw through this excuse, he was
happy to oblige.

From then on, intermittently, Johnny received envelopes
from Germany addressed to 'D. Green'. The tone of Sigrid's
first letters was cheerful, if forced. She thanked him for the
small gifts he had sent – a book of Elizabethan poetry, a
poster from the Tate – and told him she had been able to
increase her earnings as a commercial artist and would soon
be moving to a place of her own. He interpreted this to
mean that she was doing regular work for Willi Münzenberg's agitprop organisation in Berlin.

In the later letters Sigrid's tone turned sombre, even
desperate. She chronicled the daily signals of Hitler's ascent,
small things she witnessed in the streets, beatings of Jews,

the defection of neighbours – even, it seemed, her father – to the Hitler movement. In the shadow falling over Germany, she seemed to read the death of love, of any hope of private fulfillment.

'Now I begin to understand you,' she wrote. 'In the world as it is, there is no room for individuals, that is to say, neutrals. I will give up my art and work only as a draughtsman for the cause.' Then she added, in anguish, 'But isn't this another small triumph for the destroyers? I see Germany at the mercy of terrible legions that will trample everything human in the name of an abstract, impossible humanity. Some of them are singing the *Internationale*. On the day I join the party, I will destroy my canvases. Even the ones of you.'

He wrote back across the aching distance, begging her not to lose hope. 'I'm coming for you,' he promised.

Sigrid's letters never mentioned Helene. He found this vaguely ominous, though he tried not to brood on it. He had enough to worry about, trying to lick the British network into shape. He found an energetic man called Jim Straw, a carpenter by trade who had fought on the Somme and knew what wars were about, to take over from George. Together they located some of the sailors discharged after the Invergordon mutiny and put them to work in pubs near the docks at Southampton and Portsmouth. They recruited a sergeant at Catterick camp who had already formed an active cell. With help from Communists in the railwaymen's and transport workers' unions, Johnny roughed out plans for lightning strikes to prevent troops and war materiel from reaching the docks. But less than three hundred pounds of the money he had demanded from Pollitt had been forthcoming and he was reduced to running to 'Smollett', the lugubrious Fourth Department man in London, for funds to pay his own rent.

He sent report after report to Berlin, describing his progress while excoriating Pollitt and the leadership of the British Communist Party. He half hoped that Pollitt was complaining loudly enough to get him recalled. Though he threw himself into his assignment, he felt on the sidelines

152

in Britain. He belonged in Berlin, in the thick of the battle, with Heinz – and with Sigrid.

Besides, the more he saw of the British, the more his conviction grew that Engels was right. Here even the proletariat was bourgeois. The trade unions remained resolutely reformist, and the police and armed forces – for all his efforts – seemed almost impervious to Communist teachings. Even in the sour, smoky slums of the industrial north, in human slagheaps cast off by factories whose machines were half a century out of date, the workers weren't signing up for any revolution. The British Empire was doomed – wasn't the writing on the wall, for all to see? – yet the working class, more than any other social group, seemed to be lulled by the romance of the Raj. Throughout the nation the birthday of the dead Queen-Empress Victoria, May 24, was still celebrated as Empire Day.

On Empire Day 1932, Johnny watched hundreds of schoolchildren dutifully chanting Kipling's hymn of dedication,

Land of our birth, we pledge to thee
Our love and toil in years to be

and found that in part of himself he envied them for their uncomplicated faith, their primitive sense of belonging.

Unlike Germans or Russians, the Englishman was allergic to abstract causes. Johnny remembered Max Fabrikant's grudging admiration for the British as 'reactionaries without complexes'. It would take more than his efforts or those of a thousand like him to bring down the foundations of the British Empire. Only the British themselves could do that, if they ever lost their nerve.

3

In a larger plan the British Communists had their uses. Their seamen's organisation smuggled Comintern agents to India and all of the garrison colonies – Malta, Gibraltar, Aden, Hong Kong. Johnny saw it at work when Smollett called on him for a professional favour.

They sat side by side on a bench on Hampstead Heath. Beyond the trees men were hammering tent pegs and setting up booths, getting ready for a summer fair. Englishmen who had escaped from their offices to catch a few precious rays lay prone on the grass or lounged in deck chairs, jackets and ties discarded.

'We're having trouble with Ved Gupta.' The Russian wiped his long, pendulous nose. He was getting a summer cold, the most maddening kind. 'Do you know him?'

'Only by reputation. He runs the East Indian Seamen's Association, doesn't he?'

'He's a greasy Hindu from Bengal,' Smollett said charitably. 'Round and dumpy as a piece of *nan*.'

'What's the problem?'

'We ordered him to move his headquarters to Calcutta. The bloody babu won't go –'

Smollett broke off to stifle a sneeze.

'Perhaps he's afraid his ex-wives will catch up with him,' Johnny suggested.

'I think he's been lining his nest. He's got his nose into some nice little rackets he doesn't want to give up. Look, I know this isn't really your parish, but I could do with some help.'

'What do you want me to do?'

'Pay him a visit. Find out what the score is. Then remind him who's paying for his lifestyle and put some fear of God into him.'

'And if he won't be persuaded?'

The Fourth Department man considered this. 'Then we'll have to get rid of him,' he concluded. 'I wouldn't put it past him to go crying to the police. Let me know what happens. Do you need any help?'

'I'll manage with my own boys.'

Johnny's personal network was expanding fast. He had rented rooms in Poplar, near the town hall, where he held training sessions for his best recruits. He had found a wiry

Tasmanian, Barry Flynn, who had been to the Lenin School in Moscow, to take charge of the docks. He had promoted a thrusting young British Communist, John Gollan, to help run the national *Apparat*.

He told Flynn to pick a couple of sturdy young men who weren't scared to use their fists and to meet him near the entrance to the Blackwall Tunnel the following night. The babu lived and worked above the seamen's club on the East India Dock Road.

Under the uncertain glow of the streetlamps, the street had the grainy, sepia look of an old photograph. There was a stir outside the club. A crowd of lascar seamen, some incoherently drunk, were apparently in the midst of a party.

Johnny led the way around the back and up a fire escape. He had already reconnoitered his ground.

He shouldered his way past the male secretary who tried to stop them at the door and found Ved Gupta in the midst of a business transaction. The Indian's comfortable bulk overflowed a splendid mahogany desk as he scrabbled to sweep several wads of banknotes – American dollars – into the top drawer. There were two other men in the room: a turbaned Sikh, impassive and watchful, and a Cockney with a pinched, nervous face, who clutched a leather satchel and looked ready to jump out the window.

'Relax,' Johnny said to him. 'We're not the police.'

'I've seen this one before,' Barry Flynn remarked, pointing his thumb at the Cockney.

'Nice place you've got here,' Johnny said to Gupta, examining the lavish appointments of the room. He pulled back a louvered folding door and found a row of steel cabinets. 'Are these your files?'

'I say, you can't go in there! This is not at all seemly!' The babu's voice trembled.

'I quite agree. I think we ought to talk privately, don't you?'

Flynn was puzzling over the Cockney.

'I've got it!' he suddenly announced. 'It's the Ferret, isn't it? Ferret Friedman! They had you up for dope running!'

Friedman ran for the inside door.

'She'll be apples!' Flynn whooped at Johnny. He sprinted after Friedman and brought him down with a rugby tackle.

In a moment Flynn had the briefcase open. It was packed full of little oilcloth packets. He opened one, took a pinch of the powder inside, sniffed, then dabbed it on his tongue to make sure.

'Opium,' he pronounced.

'Did you get it from him?' Johnny demanded, pointing to Gupta.

The Ferret's response was not very helpful. Flynn kicked him just once, in the kidneys.

'Yes,' Friedman grunted.

'How many of these deals have you done?'

'This is the first, I swear – blimey!'

A second, more vicious kick, brought the confession that the Ferret had done business with Gupta over a period of more than a year.

'All right,' Johnny said to him. '*Out*!'

The Ferret did not need a second invitation. Once he was gone, Johnny identified himself, and the babu's trembling became more violent.

'I'm curious to see how much you've been making,' Johnny went to the desk, pushed Gupta aside and wrenched open the drawer. It was full of currency – at least four thousand dollars in American bills plus smaller amounts in British, German and Japanese notes.

'I can see now why you weren't keen on moving to Calcutta,' Johnny said.

'Upon my word, sir, those are party funds. I can account for every penny.'

'Then you won't object if we examine your financial records.'

'I am entirely at your disposal, sir. But my records are kept in Sanskrit. Perhaps you have studied the language?' The Babu displayed a gleaming row of teeth.

'Barry –' Johnny turned to Flynn. 'Start clearing out those files, will you?'

'What'll we put them in?'

'That will do for a start.' Johnny indicated the most expensive of the oriental rugs.

'You're making a very great mistake,' Gupta protested, in high agitation. 'Such behaviour is not tolerated in London. All my activities have the approval of the very highest authority.'

'Indeed? And who might that be?'

'I have had tea with Mr Pollitt,' Gupta said triumphantly.

'I don't doubt it.' Johnny called Smollett's private number.

'Yes?'

'You were right. He's turned the place into an opium den. I'd say he's been pocketing five thousand a year.'

Smollett didn't waste any time. He issued instructions that wound up the affair the same night. Gupta was bound and gagged and driven to Harwich by Flynn in the back of a van. Smollett's agents were waiting at the harbour. They chloroformed the Indian, nailed him inside a packing crate and stowed him on board a freighter bound for Leningrad, via Antwerp.

'I'd like to see his face when he gets to the other end,' Smollett remarked to Johnny afterwards.

The episode deepened Johnny's skepticism about his assignment. Everywhere he turned, he found the British Communist movement suppurating with corruption and betrayal. Activists like Flynn, willing to take risks without thought of personal gain, were exceptions. There might be few men as venal as Ved Gupta in Pollitt's crowd, but there were even fewer revolutionaries.

4

'I'm glad to be able to repay a favour,' Smollett told him. 'I've got good news for you.'

'You mean I've been recalled?'

'What are you thinking of? No, your woman's coming.'

It was Sigrid's face that leaped into his mind; so vivid

157

that his own features lit up. The light was gone the next instant.

It's Helene who is coming, he realised. Max is passing her back to me – and his OGPU friends in London.

He said, 'When?'

'Thursday. She's coming on the night-boat from Antwerp. You don't look exactly overjoyed. Found a new one, did you?'

Johnny's eyelids narrowed.

'It's none of my business, I know,' the Russian backed off. 'Good luck all the same.'

Cecil Hitchcock, the elderly thespian who presided over the boarding house in Richmond, expressed mild dismay at the news that his foreign lodger was about to acquire a roommate whom Johnny described evasively as 'his fiancée from the Continent'. It was not clear whether Mr Hitchcock disapproved because the couple were unmarried or simply because the new lodger was to be a woman. Whatever its source, his disapprobation evaporated within an hour of Helene's arrival. He waxed rhapsodic over her accent and her clothes – she appeared in a close-fitted suit with puff shoulders and a hat that dipped low across her forehead – and made her promise to take part in the musical soirées he held in his own apartment 'for the pleasure of a few very discriminating friends'.

They walked in the park that afternoon. Across the greensward a herd of royal deer kept pace with them.

Helene stretched out her hand to him, and he took it. Her skin was cool and dry.

'Sigrid told me everything,' she said, not looking at him. 'I expect you know that.'

'As a matter of fact, I didn't.'

'You might have told me first.'

'I was going to –'

'I would have thought you owed me that much. We've shared a few things together, you and I.'

'I never asked you about your lovers.'

'This is different.'

He did not contradict her. He watched her throat move as she swallowed. She was trying to bring herself to some kind of resolution.

After a long silence, she said, 'We'll go on as before. We both have work to do, responsibilities. But you must promise me that it's over with Sigrid.'

'It's not over. I'm in love with her.'

'Then you're making a fool of yourself!' she burst out. She turned her face to the deer and he thought that she might be on the edge of tears. It struck him that he had never seen her cry.

He felt a surge of consuming tenderness towards this woman who had always seemed so utterly in command.

'Sweetheart –' he put his arms around her. 'I've never meant to hurt you.'

'It's not *me* who'll be hurt!' she flew at him.

He steeled himself for the rest – the impassioned, protective speech about the child sister he had seduced and exposed to danger. He was not prepared for what she said next.

'*You're* the one who will suffer!'

She had the sun behind her, and he had to squint to look at her. Her eyes were very deep, but clouded.

'You can't mean what you're saying,' he said gently. 'Sigrid feels for me the way I feel for her.'

'What do you know about her? That she's a pretty girl who came alive in bed with you like a night flower? That she has dreams? You don't know her, Johnny. She doesn't know herself yet. Neither of you can possess what you imagine you see. Bring her into your life, and you'll find you're living with a different woman – one you never wanted, one who doesn't belong to you at all.'

She stopped to pick a late foxglove and crushed it between her fingers.

When Johnny tried to argue with her, she smiled bravely and took his arm.

'You'll choose your own course,' she said. 'I knew that in Berlin. I wanted to warn you, all the same. But I promise not to repeat myself. Now I'd like you to show me the inside of an English pub.'

Another warning from Helene – a warning of a different kind – brought an end to Johnny's stay in England.

Mr Hitchcock had given them tickets to the Richmond Theatre for a performance of Bernard Shaw's *Candida*.

'You absolutely *have* to go,' Mr Hitchcock said. 'My friend is in the third act. No excuses, now!'

They agreed to meet at the theatre. Helene was coming back from Cambridge, where Johnny suspected she was servicing an agent for Kagan, the chief of the OGPU in London. She was as tight-lipped as ever about her own work, but Johnny was intrigued by the idea that Soviet intelligence had found an entrée to the privileged world of Oxbridge.

When they dimmed the lights, Johnny was still waiting. He took his seat and tried to concentrate on the play. Halfway through, one of the characters quoted La Rochefoucauld: 'There are convenient marriages but no delightful ones.'

It was a fair summation of the years they had spent together, Johnny thought. But perhaps not entirely fair. He had known passion with Helene and later the steady warmth of comradeship. But never full trust, and never the dizzying fusion of spirits he had discovered with Sigrid, when all senses were joined in a single shaft of light.

His mind returned to the conversation he had had with Barry Flynn earlier in the day. If Flynn was right, they were about to make a major breakthrough. Flynn had struck up acquaintance with a Royal Navy lieutenant in a Portsmouth pub. The man expressed socialist leanings and lusted after women and racehorses – and was chronically short of cash because of both these fixations. According to Flynn, the lieutenant was willing to talent spot and to provide information, which could be valuable, since he was an expert on torpedoes. In return for a small advance he had supplied a specimen blueprint that excited Smollett.

The lieutenant had already been awarded a code name: 'Fisher.'

There was one catch. Though Flynn claimed he had played it all close to his chest, never letting on who Fisher would be working for, the lieutenant had come right out and said he wanted to 'deal directly with the Russians'.

It's a trap, said one voice in Johnny's head.

Let's run with it, said another.

He had more or less decided to take the gamble. He had authorised Flynn to set up a meeting with Fisher in Portsmouth in the morning. He would take the early train.

When the curtain came down for the interval, Johnny lingered inside the theatre. He stood up to let a couple pass. Then he felt a light tug on his sleeve.

'Have you given up smoking?' Helene teased him.

He rose and followed her out. She skirted the crush at the bar and went out into the night air.

'Are you enjoying the play?'

'So-so. I haven't seen Hitchcock's friend yet.'

'Fine. Then let's go and find something to eat. My tummy's rumbling and we need to talk.'

They found a chophouse, and Helene ordered the biggest steak on the menu.

'You're going to Portsmouth. Am I right?'

'How did you know?' The meeting had only been set up that morning. 'Or should I ask, how did Kagan find out?'

'Doesn't matter.' She tore into her steak and went on talking with her mouth full. 'You mustn't go. You've been set up.'

'You mean the man in Portsmouth is a plant.'

'No, that's not it. One of your friends in the party tipped off the police. You've made powerful enemies.'

'Who are you talking about? Not Flynn? George Mikes? Pollitt?'

She shook her head. 'I don't know any names. Someone high up. Someone who's out to destroy you.'

It could be Pollitt, Johnny thought. The last report I sent stripped the son of a bitch naked. Or someone who's got his nose out of joint because of the Gupta affair. Hell, I wouldn't put it past any of them.

Helene's plate was clean. She speared some potatoes from his and tossed off a glass of claret. Danger always enlarged her appetites.

They collected their bags and moved to the flat in Poplar that Johnny used for his training courses. Fortunately, Mr Hitchcock was engrossed in one of his cultural evenings. By the time he emerged in his caftan, they were already boarding a taxi.

Johnny tried repeatedly to reach Flynn from a public telephone box down the street. There was no answer. He called Smollett, who said he would try to get a message through and told him to phone again in the morning.

The pubs had just opened the following day, when Johnny heard Smollett say, 'Your information was correct.'

'What happened?'

'The police got both of them. You know the procedure.'

They followed Ved Gupta's path to Leningrad, minus the chloroform and the packing crate. Three days later, they stood in the bow of the steamer, as the storied battlements of the Fortress of Peter and Paul hove into view.

Helene raised her glass and said, 'Home!'

5

There were beggars on the slow train from Leningrad and droves of them at the station. Even in Moscow people looked grey and half starved, shuffling to work under giant images of Stalin and triumphal banners proclaiming the successes of the Five-Year Plan. There were disturbing rumours from outlying areas – stories that in the fertile Ukraine, the peasants' seed grain was being stolen from them by security troops so it could be sold abroad, that millions had been condemned to die of starvation in the midst of plenty.

'Is it true?' Johnny asked Jacob, his friend from the Fourth

Department, when they met for lunch at the Hotel Lux.

'It's all been blown out of proportion by Western propaganda,' Jacob responded. 'Besides, you don't see anyone going hungry here, do you?'

Johnny glanced around at the crowded tables. The Lux had become a miniature League of Nations, packed with Comintern guests from Peru to Indochina and delegations of favoured trade unionists and literati from the West. There were no shortages at the Lux – and no mention of famine on the radio or in the newspapers, which were full of breathless accounts of the horrendous plans for economic sabotage concocted by six British contract engineers who had been arrested as spies.

Johnny had other things to preoccupy him. He had completed his final report to the Comintern on his activities in Britain, and he had not pulled any punches. He accused a member of the national executive of the British Communist Party of betraying him to the police. He had even speculated that Pollitt may have personally authorised this treachery in return for Johnny's attacks on his leadership.

Johnny did not have to wait long for the Comintern's response. He received the summons from Piatnitsky two days later.

He found the chief of the Orgbureau in a new office, smaller and untidier than before. Bulging folders tied up with string rose from the floor on all sides of his desk. Piatnitsky's skin was as pink as a child's under the mane of white hair.

He pumped Johnny's hand.

'This is one of the best reports I've ever read,' he announced, waving a copy of Johnny's memorandum. 'I sent a copy to the boss.' He half turned his head to the full-length portrait of Stalin hanging on the wall behind him.

'Of course, we will make a full investigation,' Piatnitsky pursued. 'But I can't guarantee what will come of it. Britain, as you observed, is difficult territory for us. And whatever might be said against Comrade Pollitt, you can't fault him in one respect.'

'Sir?'

'He has an unerring sense for which ass to lick.' His eyes glided to the door, leather-padded like an old chesterfield sofa to foil possible eavesdroppers. 'I think you've earned a vacation,' he went on briskly. 'I've given instructions that you are to be permitted to use one our villas near Livadia. The climate is perfect at this time of year.'

'I'm grateful, of course, but –'

'Don't tell me. You're the kind that doesn't take holidays.'

'I'd like to make a request.'

'I'm listening.'

'I request to be reassigned to Germany.'

'Personal reasons?'

'In the sense that I'm a German.' He tried to express his fears about the rise of the Hitler movement, his conviction that he could serve the party best by working to rebuild a fighting organisation in his own country. He did not mention the women.

Piatnitsky heard him out and said, 'I won't make any promises, except to mention this to Starik.' Starik was a familiar sobriquet for General Jan Berzin, the head of the Fourth Department. 'He may have something for you. But you must make me one promise.'

Johnny waited.

'You'd better not go shooting your mouth off to Thülmann – or Dimitrov – the way you did to Pollitt. The boss takes a special interest in Germany.'

From inside his gilded frame, Stalin smiled down on them enigmatically. The snowcapped mountains in the background seemed to elevate him to a heroic height. The pockmarks that disfigured his face had been tactfully airbrushed out.

Piatnitsky was as good as his word. Within the week Johnny was summoned to Starik's headquarters and briefed on his new mission. The job was the one he knew best: he would serve as an adviser to the underground military arm of the German Communist Party, which had been reorganised as the Red Front Fighters' Federation, or

RFKB. He was informed that he now held the rank of major in the Red Army. He noted that the man who gave him his orders wore four little diamond-studded stars on his collar. The days when Bolshevik commanders wore no badge of rank except the red star of the revolution had long passed.

'You be careful,' Helene said to him through the train window, as the conductors ran along the platform, slamming doors. 'I won't be there to look out for you this time. Here –' she reached up and passed him a coat with a fur collar, something of her own. 'Give this to Sigi. You won't always be there to keep her warm.'

As the great wheels of the locomotive started to turn, he tried not to let Helene see what he felt: a sudden lifting of the heart, the marvellous beating of wings.

6

Sigrid carried out her threat. On the day she joined the Communist party she destroyed her paintings, all the ones that were personal to her. The slashes across the canvas were self-inflicted wounds.

They had been living together for almost a month. They had an apartment to themselves in the Neukölln district – two rooms and a kitchen, which Johnny paid for out of operational funds.

He had had to renew his courtship. The first time she had set eyes on him, she had seemed to glow. But she had held back. Why? And why hadn't she replied to his last letters? Was there another man?

'You'll leave me again,' she told him. 'You'll always be leaving. Helene warned me of that. It would be death by a thousand cuts, each one deeper.'

He made promises, argued, implored. When she consented to make love in the cold hollow of the morning, an hour before dawn, she held her body in check, forcing him to use her like a mannequin.

They reached a watershed on Yom Kippur, the Jewish

Day of Atonement. He had gone round to see her at the Palace Café, where she continued to work, and found Sigrid and most of the customers out in the middle of the street.

'It's Herr Silbermann's shop,' Sigrid said to him, pointing. 'We have to do something, Johnny. The family is upstairs.'

Half a dozen Brownshirts were gathered outside a second-hand furniture store. They had smashed in the windows and were allowing casual looters to climb in and out, taking what they pleased. They had daubed swastikas and anti-Jewish slogans on the door. There was not a policeman to be seen, and the large crowd of spectators was impassive.

'Come out of your rats' nest!' the Brownshirt leader bellowed up at the windows above the street. 'Come down before we burn you out!'

Johnny saw scared faces peeking out from behind the curtains – faces of children and a man with a heavy beard. The Silbermanns had spent the holy day fasting and in prayers and were assembled for the solemn meal that would be served when the sun went down.

Johnny thought quickly. He could use the telephone in the restaurant to summon help, but there was no telling what would transpire before it arrived. If he tried to step in by himself, he risked being beaten and searched. But he had no compromising documents on his person, except for the scrap of rice paper in the ticket pocket of his trousers that contained several clandestine addresses. And he was armed. He also had one useful item of camouflage: the badge of the Stahlhelm, the militia of the rightwing National Party, under his lapel. It had proved useful in one unexpected encounter with the Berlin police. Perhaps it would help him here.

He moved closer to the back of the crowd around the furniture store. One of the Brownshirts had a bottle bomb. He waved it aloft, with matches in the other hand, threatening to light the wick. Johnny could feel Sigrid's eyes burning into his face.

He stepped forward and said to the SA leader, 'Haven't you taught those Yids enough of a lesson?'

'What's it to you?' The tough rounded on him suspiciously.

Johnny flipped back his lapel to show the Stahlhelm badge.

'Just like you shitheads,' the Brownshirt spat. 'Not man enough to show your colours.' He slapped his armband and puffed out his chest.

Johnny moved closer and said in a confidential tone, 'Why don't you take care of that shyster Lifshitz, the pawnbroker? I owe him money.' He added a fictitious address to the made-up name.

The SA leader roared with laughter and thwacked his rubber truncheon against his leg.

'We'll see about Lifsheiss later,' he promised. 'I want to finish with these ones first. They've got plenty to atone for. Go on, Fritz!'

Johnny saw the flash as the match was struck and raised to the fuse, the Brownshirt's arm sloping upwards and back. He reached for his Mauser.

'Look out, he's got a gun!' someone yelled.

As Johnny squeezed the trigger, the troop leader's truncheon crashed down on his forearm. The shot went wide, and the gun tumbled from his limp fingers onto the road. At the same instant, the bottle bomb exploded inside Silbermann's store. A sheet of flame swallowed the looters' debris like dry kindling. A child's high, plaintive scream carried from the floor above.

Johnny drove his foot into the troop leader's groin. The man shrieked and was lost from sight as the others flung themselves at Johnny. He dived for the gun, rolling sideways to avoid the first rabbit punch angled at his neck. A jackbooted foot swung at his kidneys, and the pain lanced through his body.

Through the tumult he heard Sigrid's voice, keen and accusing: 'Are you men? Are any of you Germans? Are you going to let those poor people burn to death?'

They were hammering at his back with fists and feet, but he kept rolling and weaving. He got one of them by the leg and pulled him down. Then his hand closed on the butt of his pistol. One of the Brownshirts took a running jump and came down hard on top of Johnny, flattening him under his weight. Gasping for air, Johnny tried to wriggle free. But someone had got his head in a vice. They had him.

'Johnny!' It was her voice again. It seemed very distant. He couldn't breathe. Everything around him was shaded red and black, pulsing like the coals of a ship's furnace.

She came whirling into the mass of human flesh that bore down on him, raking with her nails and a kitchen knife that must have come from the café. Taken off guard, the Brownshirt who was trying to break Johnny's neck released his grip.

In that moment of grace, Johnny rallied his last reserves. He lashed out with the snout of his gun. He heard a hoarse yelp, and the weight on his back was gone. In the next instant he was on his feet, ready to open fire.

But something almost miraculous was happening. Shamed by the girl's courage, men were coming out of the crowd in twos and threes and attacking the Brownshirts with their fists. The SA men were already outnumbered by better than two to one. Johnny looked at the Brownshirt leader. He had a gun, too. He had also weighed the odds, and found them unsatisfactory.

'I'll remember you,' he promised Johnny. 'You better not show your mug round here any more.'

He and his toughs straggled away. Half a block on, they launched into a marching song.

'Thank you,' Johnny took Sigrid by the shoulders and kissed her cheek. Her blouse was in shreds, and she had a welt along the side of her neck. He handed her the Mauser. 'Here. You stand watch. Remember, the safety is off.'

'With you, the safety is never on,' she said, with a brave attempt at humour.

He covered his nose and mouth with a handkerchief and rushed into Silbermann's store.

The smoke was worse than the fire. He fought it all the way up the stairs, groping at the bannister until the railing collapsed under his touch.

He found the Silbermann family in a prayer circle in the sitting room.

He announced, 'I'm going to take you out of this.'

'The unexpected things decide your fate,' Sigrid said afterwards. 'Or perhaps the unexpected *is* fate. Like shooting over a crossroads at night in a car travelling at high speed, without knowing it was possible to go a different way until the chance is gone.'

She moved into Johnny's apartment in Neukölln the same night. The choice was made for her by events. The Brownshirts knew her face, and the manager of the Palace Café, who was not to be relied on, could give them her name. Out of concern for the Silbermanns, who meant nothing to her except a kindly old man who occasionally bade her good morning and a brace of children who were never allowed to play in the street – and the sense of shared humanity – she had committed herself. Not yet to the party, but to a life in hiding. *His* life.

Johnny refused to let her go back to the restaurant or her previous lodgings. He sent a messenger to collect her things and settle up with the landlady. She found she had to adjust to the routine of a nocturnal animal. Johnny came and went at all hours, and house guests appeared without warning to camp out on the twin mattresses in the spare room. Their faces sometimes frightened her: the faces of men who had burned their bridges. She sketched them in secret, until she had a collection worthy of Hieronymous Bosch.

The central figure was missing. She realised that only when he arrived at their doorstep.

Johnny was away. He had told her not to wait up; he would not be back until morning, perhaps not for another day. This was what she had expected, and she knew it had nothing to do with other women. His overnight absences, and the night callers, were already familiar.

But this caller was different. In the half-light from above, the face was a death mask, with great hollows of darkness under the eyebrows and the flaring cheekbones. Unlike the others, he didn't bother with a *Parole*, a password; Johnny made her memorise a new one every few days.

He merely said, 'You are Sigrid. You do not resemble your sister.' The words, oddly grammatical, were delivered in a voice she judged to be foreign not because of any identifiable accent, but because of the utter absence of one. 'What are you looking at? Are you going to let me in?'

'Wh–who are you?' she stammered.

'I am a friend of your sister. Also of Johnny. My name is Max. Perhaps he mentioned me?'

'No – I don't think so.' Johnny had said little about his secret work for the party, but he had talked a great deal about a boyhood friend, a sailor from Hamburg with a lust for life who had fought with him on the barricades. She remembered Johnny's disappointment when he had found that his friend was not in Berlin and could not be reached immediately. She was sure this vaguely menacing stranger could not be the same man. She said, 'Is Johnny expecting you?'

'I wanted to surprise him.'

He moved forward into the light, and she saw his eyes. They seemed to reach out and touch her.

She wanted to close the door in his face. She couldn't do it. She was frightened, but fascinated too. She sensed she was in the presence of a tremendous power, a concentrated force of will.

'Johnny's not here,' she said, too sharply. 'I'll give him a message if you like.'

'I don't wish to trouble you. I'll wait for him.'

The security chain was still in place. She touched it with her hand, making sure. She felt he was watching her fingers, mocking her caution, though his eyes never travelled from her face.

'It would be pleasant to talk about Helene,' Max suggested. 'I saw her only a few days ago. In fact, she gave me a letter for you.'

He plucked it from the folds of his coat and held it up, so she could see the handwriting on the envelope. It was Helene's.

Sigrid released the chain and drew back the door.

Max lay on the sofa, chain-smoking and drinking Johnny's whisky. Sigrid perched on the edge of the armchair, putting records on the Victrola when he asked for them. She had brought a boxful with her when she moved in. They were mostly classical, which suited Max. His tastes were operatic. Their conversation was now accompanied by the third act of *Aida*.

It was less a conversation, she realised, than an interrogation.

The style of the questioning was casual, even languid. But the flow was unremitting.

Which of Johnny's friends did she know?

Did Johnny talk about his work for the party?

Had he ever mentioned Heinz Kordt?

Did she take an interest in politics? What about her parents?

Helene's letter said that Max should be treated as one of the family and that his instructions were to be obeyed without question. Max must therefore be a general in the shadow army in which her lover and her sister were enrolled.

She tried to carry out Helene's wishes. She answered Max's questions, played him records and, when he said he was hungry, went out to the kitchen and cooked eggs and sausage.

The first time she rebelled was when he asked if she would show him her pictures.

She said, 'I'd rather not.'

She had been working on a portrait of Johnny, a surprise for his birthday. It showed him in a sailor's blue jacket with the sea behind him.

'Why not? I've heard you have an exceptional talent.'

'I'd rather not, that's all.' How could she explain? There was something of the artist in this man, who understood music and quoted Goethe and Heine in between the questions. Yet her whole spirit revolted at the idea of admitting him to the private world of her art, as if she would be letting in something that would blot out the sun.

'I'll relent on one condition,' Max announced.

'Which is?'

'That you draw *me*.'

The eyes were the hardest part. The pencil could not translate the intensity of that stare. But she persevered until she had a certain likeness. She puzzled over it for a time. It reminded her of someone else. Who was it?

Of course.

She scribbled a couplet from Goethe across the bottom and handed him the sketch.

'You've caught something –' He paused over the words, then recited them out loud with his eyes closed:

When I shall introduce you at this revel,
Will you appear as sorcerer – or devil?

Max threw back his head and laughed. 'Faust to Mephisto-pheles!' he exclaimed. 'My dear Sigrid, I'm flattered!'

By 2:00 A.M., she could hardly keep her eyes open.

'Do you mind if I go to bed?'

'Not at all. Would you like some company?' His tongue flicked lightly at the corner of his mouth.

'I'm afraid I'm a reactionary,' she responded, making light of it. 'My natural proclivity is towards monogamy. Anyway, I'm too tired.'

It was another little test, she realised. He was probing her, not pursuing something he particularly wanted.

When he bent to kiss her hand before she retired, his lips never grazed the skin.

She woke to the murmur of voices from the living room.

She threw back the shutters. The sun had not yet risen, though the sky to the east, where it was visible between the squat workers' tenements, was salmon pink.

She slipped out of bed and crouched by the door, trying to make out what the two men were saying.

172

'I would trust her with my life.' That was Johnny. He sounded wounded and angry.

'You are a fool. You are risking everything.'

'For God's sake, Max. She's Helene's sister.'

'But you're not with Helene. And I am not asking you why. That is immaterial. What matters is the girl is not even a party member.'

'She's been doing work for Münzenberg's operation. She did the artwork for that new poster that's all over Berlin.'

'You are evading the issue,' Max went on, implacable. 'You are putting men's lives in danger.'

'What men?'

'You and me. The others who have been here. Who knows the whole list? Who knows how much you let slip in the course of this – infatuation?'

'You don't understand.'

'On the contrary. I understand only too well.'

Sigrid wrapped herself in the fur-trimmed coat Helene had sent from Russia and burst into the front room.

'If you have something to say about me –' she challenged Max Fabrikant '– then say it to my face.'

'You see?' Max turned to Johnny. 'She's spirited. Too spirited to run without guiding reins.'

'Sigrid – darling –' Johnny moved to hold her, but she stepped around him and pushed up against Max. There was barely a wrinkle in his suit, though he had been lying on the sofa all night long. But a blue-black shadow rose from his jawline all the way to the cheekbones.

'What do you want of us?' she demanded.

'I'm sorry we disturbed your rest,' Max responded. 'That was thoughtless.'

'What do you want?' she repeated.

'You must ask Johnny. He knows well enough.' Max ground a cigarette into the ashtray. 'For the moment, you will please get dressed and leave. There are private matters we have to discuss.'

She was stunned by this sudden brutality. What right did this intruder have to order her out of her own home?

'It's not necessary,' Johnny said to Max. 'We can go to

Müller's place. It's safe enough, and they'll make you a decent breakfast. Sweetheart, why don't you go back to bed and get some sleep?'

'I'm up,' she said coldly. 'And I want some fresh air.'

When she came back, Johnny was alone, and he was so gentle and so patient with her that she knew something terrible had happened.

He let her exhaust her complaints about Max's behaviour before he said, 'They want you to join the party. It's not at all a complicated business, if you agree to do it. You'll be interviewed, of course, but that's just a formality.'

He said this matter-of-factly, as if it was a question of catching the right bus. But she could see the anxiety in his face.

She said, 'He gave you an order, didn't he?'

'A very direct order,' Johnny said quietly.

'For God's sake, what right does that man have to come into our home and tell us how to live? How can he order you to tell *me* what to do? Does he think I'm your property? What right –'

'He has every right,' Johnny interrupted her. His tone was soft yet firm. 'Listen to me, Sigrid. Max is an extraordinary man, perhaps the most extraordinary man I know.'

'He's a spy, isn't he?'

'He is a Soviet officer. It is his duty to guard our secrets. From traitors and from – carelessness. The lives of hundreds, perhaps thousands, of men and women depend on him. In the pursuit of his duty, he is totally honest and absolutely ruthless. In all the years I have known him, I have never known him to do anything for trivial or selfish reasons.'

'Am I under suspicion? Does he think I'm a police informer?'

'No, of course not. He knows you belong on our side. But you're not fully committed. Suppose I told you that I am a major in the Red Army? Suppose I told you that the men who were here the night before last have been smuggling Belgian rifles into Germany so we can fight the Fascists?'

174

'Do you think I'd betray you?' she came back fiercely. 'Do you think I'd love you any less?'

'I know you wouldn't. But to be involved in secret work requires training and discipline. If you are going to share my life, you will have to share the discipline that makes it possible. That's why Max is right. I suppose I recognised that from the day I fell in love with you. I just wanted to postpone the day when you would have to make your choice. I've been ordered to bring you into the party –'

'And if I refuse?'

She sat clutching her knees. He lay his hands over hers, covering them. He said, 'Then I am ordered to leave you.' He bent and kissed both her hands. 'It is your choice,' he pursued. 'I can't make it for you. I love you more than my life. But if you refuse, I *will* leave you, because I am fighting for a cause that matters more than you or me or the happiness of any individual.'

She shook herself like someone in a restless dream.

He did not try to comfort her when she got up and went padding barefoot into the kitchen, her hair tousled and wild.

There was a constant pounding above his eyes, and his tongue was swollen. It hurt him to swallow. He had spent hours wrangling with the organisers of the Red Front Fighters' Federation before he came home to face Max. A rapid inspection of the party's combat units in Berlin and the south had persuaded him that the sanguine reports Willi Leov, the front's burly president, had been sending to Moscow were lies – more deadly lies than Pollitt's. Leov told Moscow what he thought would reflect credit on himself, leaving Johnny with the task of trying to turn a paper army into a real one.

The burden that weighed on his shoulders seemed crushing. But he must not – would not – stumble under it. There were a few of them, only a few, who had the courage and the stamina to overcome the morass of cynical accommodation and appeasement that threatened to engulf the party and deliver Germany to Hitler. Max was one of them. Heinz was another – God, how he yearned to see Heinz, to be with a man who had never run from a battle! Heinz would have known what to say to Sigrid.

Because they were so few in number, they had to demand vastly more of themselves than other men. That was the penalty for belonging to their order – and the reward. That was why Max was right.

If only Sigi could understand . . .

He leaned back against the arm of the sofa, resting his eyes.

He woke with a start and had no idea whether he had been asleep for two minutes or twenty. In his dream Putzi, the cat he had played with as a boy, was raking its claws up and down the arm of his mother's prize sofa, lacerating the crewel upholstery.

The sound of scratching was coming from the bedroom.

Then he remembered the letter and rushed to the door.

She was standing in the middle of the room. In her hand was the chopping knife she had used on the Brownshirts outside Silbermann's store. At her feet were her paintings, hacked to shreds. His own left eye stared back at him from a flapping strip of canvas. At one side he recognised a fragment of Sigrid's portrait of her sister, rigged out in a silk hat and a man's tailcoat like the heroine of a Dietrich film.

Sigrid's face was flushed, her hair spilling over her eyes.

Her chest heaved as she turned to confront him.

She said, 'I'm ready now.'

7

She joined more than the party, and did so with her eyes open. Already the keeper of a safe house, she became a courier for the underground, ferrying messages around the city on a bicycle, servicing dead-drops. She took to wearing a knife on these missions – not a kitchen utensil now but a switchblade, something worthy of a backstreet hoodlum – taped to her leg under her long skirt. Three nights a week, she went to a special school for members of the *Apparat*. They taught her ideology, and they taught her how to kill with her bare hands. The rare nights she and Johnny were at home alone together, she immersed herself in the same books he had struggled with years before, when he was still a novice burning to unlock the secret of history.

Johnny was proud of her; yet the cold frenzy that began to possess her troubled him. He recalled the strange words of warning Helene had used in England. The night she spurned his advances in favour of an unfinished chapter of Lenin, he asked himself whether in winning her to his cause he had not already begun to lose her.

That's nonsense, he thought. I can't be jealous of what I have made her.

And an hour later, when she crept into his arms, sleepy but loving, he told himself Helene was wrong. Sigrid was his, more completely than before. They had lost nothing; they had added a new dimension.

Johnny went to Hamburg to report on the reorganisation of the party's combat units and found the man he most needed to see.

The newspapers were full of the results of the latest elections. Hitler had stumbled. The Nazis had lost two million votes, compared with the last elections. The Communists had gained ground. Thälmann and the party's propaganda machine trumpeted the news that six million Germans had voted Communist. They boomed out a new slogan: 'Hitler's ship is sinking!' They did not dwell on the fact that while the party's strength had increased, it had still attracted only half as many votes as the Nazis.

'Some victory!' Kordt snorted.

They walked by the Alster Pavilion in the tawny afternoon light. It was the perfect hour for discreet liaisons. Courting couples twittered along the railings, their conversations masked by the Viennese waltzes that echoed from the bandstand inside the pavilion.

Heinz had suggested this meeting place. They strolled along the smart promenade to the Binnen-Alster and stood side by side watching the swans and the little screw steamers bobbing on the water. Twenty paces behind, Karl Vogel, the young tough Johnny remembered from Berlin, slouched along with his hands in his pockets.

'Do you always go around with a bodyguard?' Johnny asked.

'Always. And I never spend two nights in the same bed. Lucky for me, there are plenty of friendly beds in Hamburg.'

He slapped Johnny on the shoulder. 'You needn't look like a dog just pissed on your foot. I still know how to look after myself. You're the one who should worry. It's not smart to be seen with me.'

'Don't be silly.'

'Haven't they told you?' Heinz looked at him quizzically. 'They called a special leadership meeting to discuss my conduct.'

'Why?'

'I'm a fighter, Johnny. You know that. I judge men by whether I can count on them if I get cornered, not by the smell of their aftershave. I've built the best anti-Nazi fighting group in the country. You know what the others are like. Tell me I'm wrong. What the bosses don't like is, I'll give a lad a gun even if he can't tell Uncle Joe Stalin from a boiled potato – as long as he's ready to use it on a Nazi.'

'What happened?'

'I wasn't supposed to be at the meeting, but I got wind of it and went along anyway. I reckoned nobody else would say much on my behalf. Emil Brandt was leading the pack. He was halfway through his spiel when I got there – and the sight of my mug fairly took the wind out of him, I can tell you. But he pulled himself together again. He called my boys adventurists, terrorists and provocateurs – and half a dozen other things I can't remember. Claimed I was consorting with anarchists and known Trotskyites. I think they were fixing to throw me out of the party, but they didn't dare, not with me staring them in the face. They said there's going to be an inquiry.'

'Emil Brandt. I can't believe it. He used to be my instructor.'

'They gave him a pretty good working-over in Moscow. Weren't you the one who told me about it? Now he sings whatever music they're handing out.'

'Are you saying that Emil was speaking for Moscow?'

'Oh, I used to tell myself the problem was Thälmann and all our pocket Stalins in Berlin. I didn't understand very much in those days, Johnny. You now, you've become a world traveller. You must know all about it. Did you ever meet Neumann?'

Johnny remembered an arrogant, opinionated party leader, the son of a grain millionaire, who treated girl secretaries as if he had the droit du seigneur. He had instantly disliked Neumann as a man but knew that, like Heinz, he believed in fighting the Nazis with any weapon that came to hand.

'Neumann thought everything would be put right if he explained the situation to Stalin. He said it was all a problem of Stalin getting the wrong advice from Berlin. So Neumann went to Moscow. He told Stalin we have to join up with the Social Democrats – the devil if necessary – and break Hitler before he breaks us. Stalin knew better. You know what he told Neumann? He said he doesn't believe Hitler will take power but, if he does, it won't matter because Hitler will spend all his time fighting with Britain and France. The way I look at it, if Stalin *wanted* Hitler in power, he couldn't do much more to help him get in.'

It's not possible, Johnny told himself.

But looking out across the water, he felt momentarily dizzy. The solid row of buildings on the far side seemed to sway like a pasteboard facade. His surroundings seemed utterly insubstantial.

If Heinz is right, he thought, my whole life has been wasted.

The cynicism and corruption he had found among local party leaders from London to Berlin; the waste of lives in failed insurrections from Hamburg to Shanghai; the famine in the Ukraine; the flight of Trotsky from Russia – all of that could be explained and subsumed in a larger perspective. None of it touched the core of his revolutionary faith. But the idea that Stalin, the leader of world communism, might *knowingly* collaborate with Hitler . . .

'It's monstrous,' he said. 'It's a lie.'

What he might have said – but was unwilling to face – was that if it were true, he had been living for a lie. And had just committed the woman he loved to the same lie.

He wrestled with his friend for a while, until Kordt squeezed his arm and said, 'Don't let's waste all our time arguing. You and I have got serious drinking to do. You'll come to see it my way, I'll bet on it. We can't trust the Russians. Whatever chance we've got depends on fellows like you and me, punch-drunk fighters who care about Germany and don't give a shit about the odds. *Die verlorenen Haufen.* The Lost Band. If some smartass had said this to me ten years ago, even five, I would have punched him in the throat. But we'll have to choose whether we're German Communists or Russian Communists. And if we wait too long, the Austrian corporal will choose for us – whether we go to the headsman or the hangman.'

8

'Johnny!' Sigrid shook him again. 'There's someone at the door.'

He snapped awake, sprang from the bed and groped for his trousers and the Mauser under his pillow. He prised open the window and peered down over the fire escape. As far as he could see down into the well of shadow, that way was clear.

'Get dressed,' he told her. 'If there's any trouble, don't hesitate. Take the fire escape.'

He went to the door.

'Who's there?'

'Heinrich Himmler.'

He knew that voice, edged with irony, vaguely foreign but without any identifiable accent.

He opened the door, and Max Fabrikant swept into the room. He looked as if he had just come from a job, with his collar turned up and his hat rammed down over his eyes. He had a bodyguard with him, who was told to wait outside.

Max inspected the flat. He went into the bedroom and stared at Sigrid, who was buttoning her blouse. He said, 'You wait outside, too.'

'For God's sake, Max.' Johnny protested. 'It's past three in the morning.'

But Sigrid said, 'I'm used to it,' and wrapped herself in her camel-hair coat.

'I'm sorry to disturb your love nest again,' Max said, when she was gone. He flung himself full length on the sofa without bothering to take off his hat or coat. He lit up a cigarette while Johnny poured whisky.

'*They* don't care what time it is in Berlin,' Max went on, leaving Johnny to guess that he was referring to his controllers at the centre. 'I've got instructions that have to be acted on immediately. They involve you.'

Johnny's eyes moved to the door, and Max followed them. 'Don't worry,' Fabrikant said. 'You can leave her out of this. It's about our friend Heinz.'

'What about him?'

'The centre has received information that he is a police spy, a provocateur.'

'That's a lie!' Johnny erupted. 'Heinz risks his life every night, fighting the Hitler movement.'

'Also that Kordt is associating with known Trotskyites and other enemies of the party.' Max had adopted the impersonal manner of a court official reading from a charge sheet. 'Also that he was responsible for the arrest of two of our most valuable agents.'

'Who's putting out this crap? You know what it's worth.'

Max exhaled and watched the smoke circles waft towards the ceiling. 'Perhaps you should ask Emil Brandt.'

'Emil? What has he got to say about it?' Johnny resolved not to say anything that would reflect his conversation with Heinz, barely a week before.

'It's my understanding that Brandt made the denunciation.'

The sniveling bastard, Johnny swore inwardly. The irony of the fact that he had once tried to shield Emil from Max's colleagues in Moscow chafed at him. Emil had sacrificed his beliefs and become a sideshow performer, ready with a song-and-dance routine for any occasion.

'Did *you* put Emil up to this?' Johnny suddenly challenged Max.

The spymaster remained unruffled. He said, 'I'm sorry to disappoint you. I had nothing to do with it.'

'Then why is Emil spreading these lies?'

'Perhaps he is still trying to prove his own loyalty. I seem to recall that the most vigorous members of the Spanish Inquisition had Jewish blood in their veins.'

'It's indecent!' Johnny exploded.

'Do you understand the nature of belief? I wonder.' Max closed his eyes, and in the long pause that followed Johnny started to wonder whether he had dropped off to sleep. The ash on his cigarette reached his fingertips, and he let the burning stub fall to the floor.

Johnny got up and stamped it out. There was a sour odour of combustion as Max went on. 'The medieval inquisitors had a manual called the *Malleus Maleficarum*, the Hammer of Witches. Perhaps you have heard of it? No? Well, it is written there that some of the crimes attributed to witches are real and many are illusions. However, the illusions are created by the devil at the behest of the witches. So even if the witch's crimes are illusions, the witch is guilty nonetheless.'

'Is that what chekists are taught?' Johnny asked, shocked and astonished. He remembered the rumour that Max, like Stalin, had once studied in a religious seminary.

'I warned you once before that Heinz makes too much commotion. Emil isn't the only one who has reported against him. Heinz insults Thälmann and Ulbricht to their faces and bitches all the time about the party line. Someone was bound to report sooner or later that he is attacking Stalin. Stalin *is* the party line. Furthermore, Kordt has gone on the rampage. He launches madcap forays and gets good men shot. He's got waterfront scum, petty criminals, anarchists, even Trotsky sympathisers in his organisation. He's set himself up in Hamburg like a gangster in an American movie. Something has to be done. I stand corrected. Something *is* to be done.'

'Yes?'

'He's been summoned to Moscow to account for his actions.'

'You mean, to answer the witch finders?'

Max shrugged. 'Perhaps. If he can only stop playing the fool, he'll be safe enough. He may even return stronger. He's still got friends in Moscow. Piatnitsky's one of them. There are some in my organisation, too. I want you to go to Hamburg and give him his marching orders.'

'Why me?'

'You're friends. He trusts you.'

'He won't agree to leave Germany. Not in the middle of the fight.'

'Remind him about *Parteibefehl*. Party orders. This isn't a matter for discussion.'

'What if he refuses?'

'You'll report to me.'

Johnny was on the morning train.

'If I go to Moscow,' Kordt said to him that night. 'I know I won't be coming back.'

They were in a room above the Bunte Kuh, a whores' dive in St Pauli. Kordt was paring his nails with a long hunting knife.

'You don't have any choice,' Johnny reminded him.

'I used this last night,' Kordt said. He held up the knife so the reflected light from the naked bulb overhead shone in Johnny's face. 'On a snitch we caught visiting the Nazis.'

'They'll expel you from the party,' Johnny warned.

'So let them.'

'Heinz, that's only the beginning. You know people like us can't just walk away.'

'What are you trying to tell me, Johnny?' He drew the

tip of the knife lightly across his throat. 'Is that what you mean?'

Johnny said nothing.

Kordt burst out laughing, rocking back and forth in his chair. 'I know death too well,' he said. 'He's as close to me as you are. I can't be scared off that way. But tell Max he's welcome to try. This is my town. My people will protect me.'

'People like the Baron?' Johnny had seen the man they called the Baron, a notorious pimp and dope peddler, at the bar downstairs.

'Why not? At least he's not siding with Hitler.'

'If you won't follow orders,' Johnny said deliberately, 'then get out. Get out tonight.'

'And go where? My duty is here.'

Johnny gave up trying to argue with him. 'At least say you'll sleep on it,' he suggested.

'I have better things to do at night than sleep.'

'I'll come tomorrow.'

'Come if you like. My answer will be the same.'

He overtook Johnny on his way to the door and embraced him. 'You're still my friend,' he said. 'But they always send someone you trust, don't they?'

They were waiting for him at the safe house, a comfortable apartment on the Johanniswall kept by a not-so-old widow called Magda whose hospitality was legendary in certain circles. They were eating Magda's pastries, washed down with kirsch, while she flustered over them like a mother hen, apparently unconcerned that one of them, a fellow with a nose like white sausage and a neck that bulged over his collar, had his feet up on the polished rosewood dining table.

'Krichbaum,' he introduced himself. He extended a hand without bothering to rearrange his feet. 'This is Hirsch.'

The one called Hirsch was wiry and compact. There was an unpleasant sheen about his face and clothes.

A real river rat, Johnny thought.

Hirsch contributed nothing to the conversation. Either

he had nothing to say, or he didn't understand German. His hands tended to stray towards the middle button of his jacket.

Krichbaum produced his credentials. *Osobiy Otdel*, 'Special Department'. These two were specialists, all right; the kind of chekists who were hired to shoot men in the back of the neck.

'From Berlin?' Johnny inquired.

Krichbaum wiped the crumbs off his cheek with his thumb. 'We've been sent to speed things up,' he reported. 'You saw Kordt?'

'Yes.'

'What did he say?'

Johnny hesitated for only a second. 'He said he'd give me an answer tomorrow.'

'Why not tonight?' Krichbaum swung his feet off the table. 'You know where he is, don't you?'

'I – I'm not sure.'

'What do you mean? You were just with him.'

'He moves around a lot. He never spends two nights in the same place.'

If I can just hold them off for tonight, Johnny was thinking. For long enough to warn Heinz.

'Don't play games with me, smart-shitter,' Krichbaum snarled at him. 'You were at a whorehouse called the Bunte Kuh. You're going to take us there now.'

'He just uses it for meetings. He's probably left by now.'

'We'll just have to make sure, then, won't we? How many guards does he have?'

'I don't know. Three or four, maybe more.'

'Well, you'll make it simple for us. They trust you. They shit at the Bunte Kuh, don't they?'

'I suppose so,' Johnny replied, startled.

'Where's the john?'

He described the layout. The lavatory was on the ground floor, at the back of the stairwell.

'So we'll play it this way,' Krichbaum said. 'Hirsch and me, we'll take a look at the meat downstairs while you speak to Kordt. Find a reason to get him into the bathroom

– tell him you've got a message, anything you like. We'll do the rest.'

As Johnny stared at them, the silent one pulled out a straightedged razor, opened it and tested the edge with his thumb.

'It's a piece of cake,' Krichbaum said. 'Hirsch used to be a barber.'

Johnny prayed that Kordt had left the Bunte Kuh and gone to another of his haunts. But Heinz was still there, holding court upstairs with some of the complaisant ladies of the house.

Johnny went in first. Krichbaum and Hirsch followed after a few minutes' interval, making a reasonable impersonation of drunken patrons.

Karl Vogel was squatting on the landing, his bony legs straddling the steps. He made Johnny wait until he had checked with Kordt.

'You again?' Kordt greeted him, less friendly than before. The colour in his cheeks had come straight out of a bottle. 'I told you not to waste your breath. What is it this time?'

'Not here.' He looked at the half-naked girls, one angular, the other rosy and plump, like a pile of heaped pillows. Heinz had become omnivorous.

'Tell him to fuck off,' the thin one suggested to Kordt.

But Kordt was already on his feet. 'I'll come in a minute,' he told the girls, and gave the fat one a resounding smack on the rump. '*Zuversichtlichst.* Most confidently.'

Johnny's heart was thumping so hard that he felt sure Kordt must hear it. He had put off considering the choice that confronted him – to betray his friend or his superiors – in the hope that something would simply turn up. Now that the choice was unavoidable, he chose his friend – although he knew he might be inviting the same kind of retribution the OGPU had planned for Heinz.

'There are two men downstairs,' he told Kordt. 'Chekists. I've seen their credentials.'

Kordt's eyes narrowed. 'You brought them here?'

'I had no alternative. I'm supposed to get you into the men's room.'

Kordt gave a dry chuckle. 'This isn't that type of establishment.'

'They're armed. One of them likes to use a razor.'

'He does, does he?' Kordt's face brightened. He called to Karl and gave him some whispered instructions.

'How's your bladder?' he said to Johnny. 'I feel a terrible need to water my horse.'

Afterwards, Johnny's mind turned on what Sigrid had said: that you passed the major crossroads in life before you were aware of them.

He went downstairs with Kordt and made a little signal to Krichbaum, who was quaffing beer while a tart groped around inside his fly.

There was a man in the washroom taking a long time to rinse his hands.

'Out!' Kordt ordered.

The man blinked myopically. Johnny had the fleeting impression of a moon-round face, a watch chain stretched across a copious paunch, a pair of gold-framed spectacles glittering on the edge of the sink.

Then the door banged open.

Hirsch came through first. Kordt saw the light on the open blade and flung himself clear, leaving the stranger at the washbasin in the line of attack. The man stood frozen in bewilderment or terror. At the last instant he put up his hands to protect his face.

Hirsch was unable to arrest his forward momentum. His arm came down like a javelin. The razor slipped between the fat man's fingers and sliced deep into the palm. He screamed as blood spurted in all directions, spotting Johnny's shirt.

Hirsch was cursing in Russian, ducking and circling, looking for Kordt, who had slipped behind the stalls.

Krichbaum rushed in, a silencer attached to his pistol. 'He squeals like a stuck pig,' he said with disgust. 'Hurry up –' he addressed this to Johnny as well as Hirsch '– somebody may come.'

He had his mouth open to add something, but no more words issued. His face darkened, and as he clutched at his throat, only hoarse gargling sounds came out. His eyes bulged, and his tongue swelled out between his teeth.

As Karl twisted the piano wire tighter, beads of blood erupted from Krichbaum's coarse neck, and his weapon fell to the floor.

Hirsch saw nothing of this because, as he circled the stalls, Kordt lashed out with a short length of iron bar and broke his arm. Johnny didn't turn away when he saw his friend pick up the cut-throat razor and begin to do the barber's job for him. He felt unnaturally warm but also oddly detached.

When Heinz stabbed a finger towards the weeping man at the washbasin and said, 'Take care of him,' Johnny didn't ask what kind of care he had in mind.

'We'll pin it on the Nazis,' Kordt announced over cognac in his room. 'It won't be the first time. You'll be covered.'

Johnny put off thinking about whether this was true. 'You're burned,' he told Kordt. 'Even if they never prove what happened, they'll blame it on you. And those two won't be the last ones they'll send for you.'

Kordt considered this for a while. 'I must admit your friend the barber has done a lot to convince me,' he conceded at last.

'I'll have to report to Max tomorrow,' Johnny said. 'I can only delay for a few hours. You've got friends in the port. Get on a boat – any boat – and leave with the first tide.'

'All right.' Kordt jumped up. He stretched out a hand and then, thinking better of it, clasped Johnny in a bear hug. 'But I'll be back. We'll make quite a team, you and I.'

'Where will you go?'

Kordt shrugged. 'Any port is home to a sailor, isn't that so? But somewhere warm, I think. Maybe I'll call on

Trotsky. He might be able to explain what insanity spawns people like Barber Hirsch.'

9

All foreign legions have the same motto: March or Die, *Marschier oder Krapier*. The man who asks questions is lost. Johnny had done more than question. He had saved a life that had been claimed by the party. If his role were discovered, he would face the same fate that had been dictated for Kordt. Yet he boarded his train back to Berlin – and Max Fabrikant – without the slightest hesitation. Because of Sigrid, but not only because of her. Whatever he had done, whatever retribution might lie in store for him, he still belonged to the party. For the whole of his adult life it had been his church, his profession, his family. It was his compass. He had no direction, no purpose, without it.

In Berlin things were both better and worse than he expected. He did not have to face an immediate inquisition over Kordt's escape, because Max had left the capital on one of his mysterious errands. When Max reappeared a few days later, he seemed oddly unconcerned about the whole affair. He asked a few perfunctory questions and seemed content to accept Johnny's answers at face value. It was difficult to understand why Max was so indifferent to a case that had been a consuming obsession earlier that week. Perhaps, lacking evidence of Johnny's part in the escape, he was laying a trap. Perhaps he had larger matters on his mind.

Johnny's own mission in Germany had become impossible. He was supposed to build a fighting underground, but his local chief, Willi Leov, refused to supply him with guns or money. Young activists – the kind who had rallied to Kordt – complained that their orders were always the same: to wait. Instead of trying to mobilise the working class against Hitler, the party instructed Communist railroad workers to join with the Nazis in a strike designed to discredit the Social Democrat union bosses. The strike fizzled out after a few days, leaving a yawning chasm between the Communists and the rest of the anti-Hitler movement. Any militant who presumed to criticise these policies was reminded that he could not see 'the big picture' – only Stalin knew what it was – and threatened with expulsion.

By the end of January 1933, Johnny had concluded that if the Communists had set out to install Hitler in power, they could hardly have done a better job.

'Grandmother is dead!'

In the early hours of January 30 the phrase was flashed across the country, and convoys of Brownshirts from Hamburg and Dresden, Munich and Leipzig, joined the march on Berlin. Count Helldorff, the leader of the storm troops in Berlin, rushed in and out of the Kaiserhof issuing orders. Goering waddled about in his gorgeous sky-blue uniform, his wide-cut trousers flapping like wings.

'Grandmother is dead' was the prearranged Nazi code for the seizure of power. But Hitler did not have to take power by force. He was handed it on a silver salver by the archintriguers around the president. At 11:10 A.M., Hindenburg named the man he had once reviled as 'the Bohemian corporal' Chancellor of Germany. Twenty thousand storm troops turned out to ensure that nobody had second thoughts. They set the proper Wagnerian mode with a night of flaming torches.

Johnny listened to the thud of their jackboots as they marched up the Wilhelmstrasse, past the Reich Chancellery, where Hitler, flushed in triumph, took the salute. Anonymous in the crowd, borne along by its tide, he saw the torches licking at the columns of the Brandenburg Gate.

'Everything will be different!' a woman shrilled. She was pleasingly plump with a clear open face, the model German housewife.

Within twenty-four hours the phrase was blazoned in neon lights across the grand façade of the Gloria Palast, the flagship of the UFA cinema chain: EVERYTHING WILL BE DIFFERENT — ADOLF HITLER.

Johnny reeled home that night with the sinking sensation that all of Kordt's fears had taken flesh. He had a bottle with him. Sigrid said nothing when he proceeded to pour glass after glass, but he could read something beyond reproach in her eyes. Her father had used the same crutch until it had become his supporting limb. At the thought, he felt revulsion for himself but drank long after Sigrid had gone to bed, until the bottle was empty.

When he lurched into the bedroom, she lay with her eyes closed, pretending to be asleep. He rolled onto the bed and started fumbling with the straps of her nightgown.

'Stop,' she said calmly, quietly, sadly. 'You'll tear it.' She sat up and eased the garment over her head.

In the light from the street lamp across the road, her body was ivory, lovingly, exquisitely hewn.

But what followed was squalid.

He thrust himself on her, reeking of booze and stale sweat, his breathing harsh and constricted. His desire ebbed away as soon as he entered her. Soon he was panting apologies.

'It won't happen again,' he promised. His tongue felt thick and furry.

'Nothing's the way it used to be,' she murmured, running her hand through his hair. 'Oh, Johnny. What's to become of us?'

'We'll survive.' He swallowed. 'We're going to survive.'

She pursed her lips and said, 'Is that all?'

The survival instinct was not highly developed in Karl Liebknecht House, the headquarters of the German Communist Party. The following day, Johnny received orders to prepare for an armed insurrection in Berlin. It would be timed to coincide with a general strike. The instructions came from Willi Leov, his nominal boss – the same man who had refused him the guns and the money he had demanded to prepare an effective underground army.

'You'll be sending men to their deaths,' Johnny protested.

'We have two thousand trained fighters in Berlin. Only half that number are armed. And the general strike will never take place.'

Willi Leov glowered at him over his spectacles. 'Are you refusing a party order?'

'I'm telling you how things are.' He looked with contempt at Leov's red, puffy face. It was criminal, he thought, that parasites like this sat back and gave orders while Heinz was on the run from OGPU killers.

'You're sailing close to the wind, let me tell you.'

'I'll do what you say,' he said, in order to get out of the room.

He did nothing of the kind. When the general strike was called, the fighting cells under his command stayed at home. He had no intention of delivering them up to an act of blood sacrifice.

The German people did not respond to the party's belated call. The general strike stirred hardly a ripple. Rank-and-file trade unionists were not disposed to risk their necks for the party now. Who could blame them? Johnny asked himself.

Sigrid came home on her bicycle and announced, 'They stormed the Bülowplatz.' She described the scene of hundreds of grey-uniformed police and booted storm troopers attacking party headquarters. 'They caught a man who was trying to destroy party documents,' she reported. 'The idiot was throwing the pieces out the window. They threw him out after them. I saw the Nazis carrying out whole cabinets of files.'

The fools, Johnny thought. They must have known this was coming on the day Hitler took power, even if they were blind before. Couldn't they even salvage the party records?

'The fight isn't over,' he promised Sigrid. But he expressed more confidence than he felt. The party had failed. To build a true resistance to Hitler, he would have to find an alternative – even if it meant fighting Stalin, too. But when he tried to work out the next step, his mind veered away.

It was hard, in any event, to plan for the future when

everything revolved around surviving the next twenty-four hours. Soon terror reigned in Berlin. All over the city suspected Communists were dragged from their beds in predawn raids. Presses were wrecked, offices gutted. Some of those arrested informed on their friends and their families in the hope of saving their skins. Others, out of fear or disgust, volunteered their services to the new regime. The Gestapo's net widened.

Johnny and Sigrid abandoned the Neukölln apartment – it was known to too many night callers whose fate was unknown – and lived like vagrants, dossing down in dank, airless rooms in the 'rental barracks' of Moabit and Wedding. When they left their places of hiding, often in the late mornings, after working through the night, their partings were tender. They never knew whether that day's farewell would be the last.

He wanted to tell her about Heinz and the larger doubts that wracked him. In the precious few hours they spent together, he did not have the heart. Her courage, her confidence – in defiance of everything – was immense. How could he deprive her of that, when all he could offer were questions without answers?

The whiplash of winter was in the air as he trudged back to Moabit, his chin buried in a wool muffler. The jail over to his left was a landmark, a great Victorian pile whose barred windows were dressed up with wrought iron as if they were trying to stop burglars from breaking in rather than prisoners from getting out. He crossed the street to dodge a troop of beery SA men, out looking for girls to squeeze or Jews to beat up. Between the street lamps, the darkness was almost impenetrable.

He turned into a quieter street and sensed, rather than saw, a shadow move with him. He ducked up the first alley and pressed himself flat against the wall, waiting and listening, his hand searching for the butt of his Mauser. To begin with, he could hear only the scream of police sirens and, closer, a warm-blooded scream – hard to say if it was a woman or a cat.

There.

It was a light, scurrying sound.

A rat poked its snout out of a mound of garbage and scuttled across his foot. He stayed motionless, listening.

There.

A shadow flitted across the mouth of the alley. A man was coming after him, a slight figure in workman's clothes, advancing almost noiselessly on crepe-soled shoes. Perhaps he was only a common pickpocket. Johnny willed himself invisible.

The stranger let out a low whistle – a signal to confederates? But he was almost abreast of Johnny before he spotted his quarry. He jumped, but Johnny was faster and heavier. He got hold of his pursuer's arm and screwed it up behind his back until the man yelped in pain.

'What do you want?' Johnny let him see the gun.

'Alfred, it's me –'

Johnny was startled to hear himself addressed by a work name he had used in Hamburg. The fellow could be a police spy after all.

'Don't you recognise me?' the stranger pleaded.

Johnny hauled him back into the light. The face was narrow, almost vulpine.

Johnny remembered the young tough on the stairs at the Bunte Kuh. Heinz Kordt's bodyguard.

'It's Karl, isn't it?'

The boy nodded and Johnny let him go.

'What are you doing here?'

'Party orders, what would you expect? We're screwed, wherever we are.'

'Why did you follow me?'

'I saw you at the station. I've got some stuff for you.'

'What stuff?'

'From Heinz.' The boy pulled up his sweater and brought out two small packages he had tucked under his belt. 'He made me promise to bring these to you if anything happened to him.'

'If anything happened –' An icy hand closed over Johnny's heart. 'What is it? What have you heard?'

Karl stood there mute, holding out the brown paper parcels. One of them had the shape and heft of a book.

Johnny reached out and gripped the boy's wrists instead of the packages.

'Please. You have to tell me. He's my friend, too.'

'You know someone called Max, don't you? You ought to ask him.'

They were moving in a macabre dance, Johnny following as Karl backed away towards the street.

'*Tell me.*'

Johnny squeezed tighter. Karl looked at his hands as if they didn't belong to him.

'I'm cold,' the boy said. 'And I haven't eaten all day.'

'We can go to my place.'

'Not there.' Karl shivered and glanced furtively at the street. The boy was running scared.

They went to Müller's. It hadn't been raided yet, even though it was popular with factory militants in the area. The bar had been shut for several hours, but Müller could always produce a drink and a sandwich for an old comrade. Karl wolfed down everything that was put before him, cramming the food into his mouth with both hands. Müller set an open bottle of wine on the table and said, 'I'm turning in. Lock up after you.'

Johnny watched Karl guzzle some of the wine and said, 'I'm waiting.'

'It's like this.' Karl wiped his mouth with the back of his hand. 'Heinz got away from Hamburg, all right, on a tub bound for Rotterdam. But there was trouble at the other end. The police nearly nabbed him on the docks. I guess that's when Max's people got on to him, though I can't say for sure. Anyway, Heinz stowed away on a French cargo boat, the *Antoinette*. It was bound for Algiers. Heinz figured he'd be able to find a berth on another ship and get to South America. He hid under a lifeboat. But they caught him out. The captain was a real son of a bitch. He locked Heinz up in a cabin and said he'd have him deported to Germany once they got to Algiers.'

'How do you know all this?' Johnny interrupted.

'One of the seamen from the *Antoinette*.'

'Go on.'

'Max beat him to Algiers.'

'Max? There's some mistake.' But even as he spoke, Johnny recalled Max's sudden disappearance after his trip to Hamburg and his curious loss of interest in the topic of Heinz Kordt.

'Listen, the name I heard was Max,' Karl insisted. 'If you don't want to hear the rest of it, that's fine by me.'

Johnny picked at details, hoping the boy's story would fall apart before he reached its conclusion. Not knowing exactly where it would lead, he was already besieged by a creeping horror, colder than the night outside. Colder than any night there had ever been.

'How could Max have beaten the *Antoinette* into port?'

Karl shrugged. 'Maybe he took a faster boat. Maybe the French tub had to stop for repairs. Maybe he found a plane. What the hell does it matter?'

Johnny reached for the wine, but his hand was shaking. His glass tipped over, and a pool of red spread across the bare wooden table.

Karl stared at it balefully and went on, 'When the *Antoinette* came in, Max was waiting on the dock. He'd hired a gang of layabouts and armed them with axes and sledgehammers. They muscled their way straight up the gangplank. Only a few of the sailors put up any fight. Once he found out he wasn't being hijacked, the captain was only too pleased to show them where Heinz was being held. They didn't wait for someone to fetch the key. They broke down the door right away.'

Karl paused. His eyes were damp. His lips barely moved, and Johnny had to strain to make out every word as he said, 'From what I was told, Max finished the job himself. With a sledgehammer. Myself, I've only seen a sledgehammer used on wood or cement. I don't reckon a man's skull would hold up for very long.'

Johnny sat without speaking for a long time. The spilled wine, unattended, had spread to the edge of the table. The drops made a plopping sound as they hit the linoleum.

Karl's brittle mask of cynicism had cracked. His shoulders were heaving, and he turned his face away to hide the tears.

After a while, he asked, 'Why did they do it?'

Johnny felt numb. 'It's a time of madness,' he whispered.

'He was the best man we had.'

'I know.'

Heinz and one other, he amplified this inside his head. The one who had murdered him.

Karl's expression was a mixture of disgust and disappointment. He looked at Johnny the way a child might look at a clockwork toy with a broken spring.

'I'm off,' he announced, scraping back his chair.

'Where will you go?'

'It's all the same,' Karl said, his mask again in place. 'We're screwed wherever we are.'

The boy's parting shot, Johnny understood later, was the demotic version of the line Heinz Kordt had inscribed on the first page of his diary. The diary was inside the larger of the two packages Karl had brought from Hamburg. It had been recorded in an old ship's logbook. The cover was mottled and warped, and some of the pages had been torn out in haste or anger, leaving jagged rows of paper teeth. Kordt wrote in an oversized, awkward script, like a schoolboy. Johnny leafed through the later sections. The diary was the chronicle of a mind being pushed over the edge, a prolonged howl of rage and pain. 'What is the difference between communism under Stalin and national socialism in Germany?' one passage read. 'Answer: only that Stalin has yet to settle "the Jewish problem". Once he does that, he will be indistinguishable from Hitler.'

Johnny turned back to the epigraph. It was a phrase from Leviné: 'We Communists are all dead men on leave.'

4

The Walk-in

It is not Germany that will turn bolshevist, but Bolshevism that will become a sort of national socialism. . .
Besides, there is more that binds us to bolshevism than separates us from it.

There is, above all, genuine revolutionary feeling, which is alive everywhere in Russia except where there are Jewish Marxists. I have made allowance for this circumstance and given orders that former Communists are to be admitted to the party at once. The *petit bourgeois* Social Democrat and the trade union boss will never make a National Socialist, but the Communist always will.

— Adolf Hitler(1934)

1

Adam de Salis strolled up the Wilhemstrasse towards the British Embassy. It was a warmish afternoon, and he had draped his topcoat nonchalantly over his shoulders. This, together with the brown trilby and, above all, the brown suede shoes, gave him a somewhat louche air, despite the perfectly pressed Savile Row suit and the monocle that swung on its cord above the third button of his waistcoat. Louche was the appropriate style for a foreign correspondent, de Salis thought. But while the nameplate on his door, a short canter south on the same avenue, blazoned the title of Fleet Street's noisiest patriotic tabloid, journalism was only his part-time vocation. Adam de Salis, formerly Lieutenant Commander de Salis, RN, was the chief of British Intelligence in Berlin.

The ambassador's Rolls was waiting at the main entrance to the embassy.

Here comes the old fart now, de Salis thought as a peevish-looking man in a homburg hurried towards the car.

'Good afternoon, sir,' said de Salis, touching the brim of his hat.

The ambassador returned his greeting with the most distant of nods. He was the quintessential Foreign Office type, in de Salis' estimation. In his impossibly grammatical missives to London, the ambassador frequently protested the use of his embassy as a postbox for messages sent in codes that he couldn't read by people whose methods, he opined, were unworthy of gentlemen.

The cable de Salis had in his pocket was flagged 'CX', which meant that it was for the personal attention of the chief of the Secret Service. De Salis had served under C – a former admiral – on a dreadnought in the North Sea during the Great War, and he made use of the direct channel when he wanted to make a point.

'How are you, Sandy?' he greeted the cipher clerk. 'Still keeping the Fräuleins happy?'

He handed over his text, which he had encrypted himself, and watched while Sandy transcribed it into another numerical code.

He had taken some pains with this report.

The main part dealt with the terrible fire that had gutted the Reichstag in the early hours of the morning. The Nazis had bagged a deranged Dutchman and were blaming the act of arson on the Communists. On that pretext they were rounding up thousands of their critics. In de Salis's opinion, the whole business was a transparent hoax. He cited a curious piece of evidence. One of his sources, an elegant young ex-cavalryman who had ingratiated himself with Himmler, had been to a big party the night before, hosted by Hanussen, the

Führer's court astrologer. At the witching hour, the stargazer had gone into an apparent trance and announced to the throng, in a melodramatic basso: 'I see a blood-curdling crime committed by the Communists. I see blazing flames! I see a terrible firebrand that lights up the world!'

The Reichstag fire was a fraud, but in terms of British interests – so de Salis maintained – it had already had some useful effects. For years the Comintern had used Berlin as its forward command post. Now the Soviet cause in Germany was a busted flush. The Gestapo had hunted down that Bulgarian trickster, Georgi Dimitrov, and put away scores of his best agents. Some of the Westbureau's secret files had fallen into Nazi hands, and de Salis was hoping to get a look at them through the good offices of the same friend who had told him about Hanussen.

But the best thing about the whole episode, de Salis reported, was that it brought an end to a whole era of secret German–Soviet collaboration. The German General Staff had helped to install the Bolsheviks. The Soviets had returned the favour later on by assisting the Germans to rebuild their army illegally on Russian soil. In de Salis's view, the greatest threat to the status quo was an alliance between Germany and Russia. Herr Hitler had put paid to that.

De Salis knew that some of his colleagues at Broadway Buildings were less sanguine about developments in Germany. Colin Bailey, for one, talked as if Hitler were as much of a menace as the Communists. Hitler was a vulgar upstart surrounded by beerhall louts, no argument on that score. Not the sort of chap you asked to dinner. But de Salis had long contended that Hitler's bad manners and his silly obsession with the Jews were no reason to neglect his usefulness in dealing with the main enemy. He felt completely vindicated.

De Salis appended a shorter message, requesting the transfer of a new man to work in the Passport Control Office. Until recently, the passport office – a mile away from the embassy, at the other end of the Wilhelmstrasse – had provided satisfactory cover for British secret operations. Staff duties were relatively light, and the visa fees collected were a useful supplement to the niggardly budget from headquarters. Herr Hitler and his well-publicised views on the Jewish question had changed all of that. Every day, the passport office was mobbed by would-be emigrants, mostly Jews. A lot of them were Poles who had come to Germany because they thought they would be safe from pogroms. Some were bound to be Comintern agents. Normal business had been hopelessly disrupted. The passport office had been forced to hire local clerks, and who knew where that would lead? Some of the Jews were willing to pay almost any amount to get a visa for Palestine. The Firm operated on trust, not routine bookkeeping, and that trust was being subjected to new strains.

De Salis dallied for a couple of gins with the naval attaché and walked out of the embassy into a powdery dusk. His flat was only a few blocks away. He had plenty of time for a bath before he dined with his latest conquest, an aristocratic lady who made up with experience for what she lacked in youth and enjoyed the most remarkable entrée into Berlin society. De Salis was separated from his wife, which allowed him an agreeable latitude in his extracurricular activities. He found it amusing that both the Russians and the Gestapo had drawn certain conclusions from his bachelor status and had sent young women – and occasionally young men – to try to take advantage of his presumed vulnerability. He had fallen for the oldest trick in the world once, just once. The girl was a stunner. When she did her hair a certain way, you might have mistaken her for Marlene Dietrich. In the act of love, she had shown him things even he had never imagined, and he had discovered reserves of stamina he had never known were there. He was horny for her at breakfast, in the middle of the day, at teatime, like a randy teenager.

She had come to him in the most banal way, looking for a job as a stringer with his newspaper. She was too perfect, in bed and everywhere else. He must have realised what she was, but he did not admit it to himself till he woke in the middle of the night after hours of lovemaking and found her rifling his safe. She got away, and though he put traces out for her he never found her. Her last name was phony, of course. But perhaps not the first name. Helene.

He was thinking of her now, as he turned off the Wilhelmstrasse, heading east, when he sensed that he was being watched. He made a few detours and reversed direction abruptly in front of a department store. He failed to spot anyone. All the same, he decided to turn down the steps of a Bierkeller. Frequented by minor officials from the government offices along the Wilhelmstrasse, it was almost deserted at this time of day.

De Salis settled himself in a booth by the far wall and ordered Berlinerweisse. In his first years in Berlin, he had found the taste of the raspberry syrup in the pale lager offensively sweet. It had grown, like the city, to suit his palate.

A big man in a raincoat came in and surveyed the rows of trestle tables. His eyes fastened on de Salis's table. Then he moved off to the right, slowly circumnavigating the room.

De Salis marked him discreetly. Fair hair. Six-two, maybe six-three. Built like a prize fighter, though the face was alert and intelligent. He was good looking in a primitive sort of way, de Salis thought. The type Lady Chatterley would go for. Not the sort you would want on your tail in a dark alley. Not a Slav. Almost certainly a Hun, or perhaps a Scandinavian. He might be from Himmler's mob – they had put a tail on de Salis once or twice.

The Englishman raised his newspaper like a rampart.

He expected the stranger to seat himself at a strategic remove, somewhere between his table and the door. There were plenty of empty seats.

To his surprise, the man walked up to his booth.

Bloody cheek, de Salis thought. He *must* be Gestapo. Russian agents tend to show a bit more form.

'May I?' The stranger gestured to the bench opposite.

'Be my guest,' de Salis said smoothly. He did not look up from his paper.

'Do you know Richmond-on-Thames?'

De Salis put aside his paper and gave the stranger a closer inspection. The man spoke passable English. There was a touch of the East End in his voice, on top of that Germanic rumble. There was nothing shifty about those eyes.

De Salis thought, he looks at me as if he knows me.

'I've been to Richmond,' de Salis conceded. 'But how did you know I was English?'

'Your clothes.' The stranger's glance encompassed de Salis's bold pinstripe, the watch chain across his vest, the violet silk handkerchief exploding from his breast pocket. 'Only an Englishman dresses like that. Do you know the Richmond Theatre? I have friends there. Actor friends.'

'Really?' The Englishman's tone was neutral.

What is this? he asked himself. Another provocation? Perhaps the bugger was merely rough trade, the kind that thought that anyone who went to a public school was a pederast.

'I saw a first-rate production of *Candida*, by George Bernard Shaw, in Richmond last summer.'

The fellow was getting tedious.

'Look here,' said de Salis, 'this is all frightfully interesting, but I'm afraid I have a date.' He folded his newspaper.

'I do wish you'd stay, Commander. I promise not to detain you for long.'

De Salis raised an eyebrow at the use of his old navy rank.

'You are Commander Adam de Salis, MBE, DSO.'

'You seem to have me at a disadvantage, my dear chap. But since you mention it, it's a CBE.'

'Our records must be out of date. I congratulate you.'

'Perhaps you'd care to introduce yourself.'

'I am a major in the Red Army, currently assigned to the Comintern in Germany,' Johnny said in an undertone.

'I thought your lot had all scarpered after the Reichstag fire.'

'Not quite all. As you see.'

'What can I do for you?'

'I am in a position to supply you with certain information. Extremely valuable information.'

'You intrigue me, Mister – er –' Johnny did not fill in the name.

'But perhaps I should warn you,' de Salis resumed, 'the rag I write for is pretty stingy about paying for stories.'

'Can we stop playing games? I've seen your dossier.'

'Might I ask where?'

'At the British section of the Westbureau, here in Berlin. You were also pointed out to me once at a nightclub, by a friend of mine called Max. I imagine you have a file on him somewhere. You probably know him as André, or André Bloch.'

The mention of this alias excited de Salis. He knew that a man code-named André was one of the most dangerous Russian agents in Europe, responsible for the murder of several British operatives. He had tried repeatedly to run André to ground. Instead, the Russian – or so de Salis suspected – had planted a female spy in his own bed.

De Salis tried to keep up a mask of indifference. This could be another of André's tricks.

'Could you be more specific about this information you are willing to part with?'

'I can give you the names and whereabouts of the principal Russian agents in Britain. I can give you a complete description of Communist sabotage units and the underground organisation that is working to incite a mutiny in the Royal Navy. I created them myself.'

To de Salis, a former navy man, this was pure gold. He knew that C would feel the same way. But he kept his guard up.

'What about André? Can you give me André?'

'That, too.'

The German spoke quietly, but something flashed in his eyes. Pure hatred, de Salis thought.

Dammit, the Englishman told himself, I'm going to push my luck.

'Do you happen to know a woman called Helene?' He described her quite vividly.

'No.' The German touched his collar, as if it were too tight for him.

Is he holding something back? de Salis asked himself. Of course he was. He'd be an idiot not to. But perhaps the girl was too much to hope for.

'I don't suppose you're doing this for love,' de Salis suggested.

'I have made a list of conditions,' Johnny said. 'They are not for negotiation.' He brought a copy of a German paper out of his raincoat. It was the *Völkischer Beobachter*, the most vicious of the Nazi hate rags. He slipped it under the table, onto de Salis's lap.

'You realise I'll have to consult on this.'

'Of course. Your people will need to check my credentials. You will find something in there —' he angled his chin towards the paper he had slipped to de Salis. 'You may also tell them that when I landed in England in 1931 I used a passport in the name of Ludwig Dinkelmeyer.'

'That may help.'

He's a professional, de Salis told himself. No doubt on that score.

The German was rising from the table.

'Wait a bit, won't you?' de Salis appealed to him. 'How can I contact you?'

'You can't. I'll contact you.'

'What do I call you, for God's sake?'

'Call me Johnny.'

'Is that German?'

The big man smiled. 'As German as possible.'

2

'Thank God.'

As Johnny closed the door behind him, Sigrid threw herself into his arms. He caressed her hair and felt her tremble against him. Her face was burning.

'You're running a fever,' he said gently. 'I'll put you to bed.'

'I was scared for you, Johnny. I had a premonition —'

'I'm here.'

'They took Müller,' she told him, shivering. 'I saw them from across the street. There was a police informer, in a hood so I couldn't see his face, jabbing his dirty finger at the people they dragged out of the bar. They took nearly everyone.'

'What were you doing there?'

'I was told to meet a man.'

'What man?'

'Someone from Max.'

Always Max, lying in wait at every turning. My nemesis. You took Helene, he addressed Max mentally. You won't take this one.

'Was the man there?'

'I can't say. I didn't see him. I went to Münzenberg's place, but the police were there too. I didn't know where to turn. So I came back here.'

It was his turn to say, 'Thank God.'

I'm not going to lose you now, he promised himself.

She sat on the window seat, swaying lightly as she talked, as if she were trying to keep her balance in a driving wind. The amber light from outside made a soft aura around her head and shoulders. In the penumbra of the room, her lips were purple, almost black, dark as the plums he'd so often stolen from an orchard on boyhood outings to the country. This mental association tugged at his heart, because it brought with it images of a parallel life they had never shared, a life that had room for children's laughter, and the smell of new-mown hay in the sun, and the heart's leap at the sight of a wisp of smoke from their own chimney as dusk settled over the fields. It was the life he had denied her, the life she might have had with a different man. It was the ordinary life of ordinary people, and at that moment, in that occupied city, he yearned for it with every fibre of his being.

'Listen to me,' he said to her. 'I think I've found a way to get us out. It may take a few days. You must stay here. Don't go out, not even for groceries. I'll take care of everything.'

She tried to argue, talked of duty and responsibility.

'Half the people we know are under arrest,' he reminded her. 'Most of the others have fled or turned into snitches for the Gestapo.' This was reasonably accurate. Gurevitch, the Fourth Department chief, had got out the same morning. He had told Johnny that Max Fabrikant had slipped away to Copenhagen on the eve of the Reichstag fire, alerted by a sixth sense or, more likely, by information from his own spies which he did not choose to share with those who depended on him. 'It's all falling apart,' Johnny went on. 'Trust me. I'll get us out of this.'

He carried her into the bedroom and tucked her under the covers.

'I'll make you a toddy,' he announced.

'There's only one medicine I need.' She opened her arms to him, and he made love to her slowly, tenderly, till a warm tide swallowed both of them.

When she fell asleep, he sat up in a chair beside the bed, watching her.

Helene was wrong, he told himself again. We are still the same.

Later, in another country – in England, perhaps, or France – he would be able to explain everything to Sigrid. It would not be easy, he had no delusions about that. It would take time for the wounds to heal, time for understanding to grow. He imagined the conversation they might have if he simply announced, 'I'm working for the British.' She would spurn him as a traitor, and until two weeks ago – until he learned how Heinz had died – he would have agreed with her.

He would have to begin by explaining, painstakingly, everything along the road that had led to this tremendous watershed in his life. He would have to describe the macabre dance of death he had helped to lead, of revolutionaries betrayed by the corruption and stupidity of their commanders. He would have to show her the proof that men who paraded as paladins of the anti-Fascist cause were secret collaborators with the Nazis. He would tell her why Heinz had died – because he cared more about fighting Hitler than about licking Stalin's backside – and who had killed him.

It would take time, nonetheless. Faith was stronger than facts, and he had watched her faith in the Communist cause grow stronger in these weeks of playing hide-and-seek with the Nazis. It had been reinforced by Max, who had asked her to perform some minor chores – which she had accepted over Johnny's protests. It had disturbed him to see the repulsion she had at first expressed for Max give way to a kind of fascination with the spymaster and his deadly games. Johnny had intimate experience of how that fascination grew, and where it led.

I want Max dead, he had told himself over and over, after Karl had come to him with the story of Heinz's end. Even now, in the silence of the bedroom, beyond Sigrid's shallow breathing, he seemed to hear the sickening crunch of bone under the executioner's iron mallet.

Emil, too, the same voice said inside his head. Emil Brandt was more guilty than Max. He was the one who had denounced Heinz for crimes he had once been charged with himself. And I lied to Max's people to protect that bastard.

Before he had walked in on Adam de Salis, he had deliberated how much he would offer the British. He had been ready to give them Max and Emil – those two had earned anything that might be coming to them – and the British network, which was riddled with cynicism and corruption. But there were large areas of his life that he would not betray, comrades who had fought with him and had given him their trust. And he would let nothing touch the two women who meant most to him. It troubled him that de Salis had asked about Helene.

He had chosen the British because the Intelligence Service – so his briefers in Moscow had never tired of repeating – was the most professional and most dedicated opponent of the Soviet cause. Also because, in his time in England, he had come to admire the unflappability of the English and their visceral distaste for the abstract reasoning that cloaked the crimes of a Stalin or a Max Fabrikant. Most of all because, if he and Sigrid were going to start over, they would need help – a place on which to stand.

Sigrid rolled over in her sleep, uncovering her back, and he pulled the sheet up to her shoulder.

He thought, I'll give de Salis three days.

Colin Bailey liked to walk to the office. From his Mayfair pied-à-terre, three rooms above a French bistro, he would stroll down Curzon Street past Trumper's – his barber's – duck through Shepherd's Market, deserted at that hour, into Piccadilly, and proceed down St James's Street to his club, where he would sometimes stop for bacon and eggs. Diana didn't care for breakfast and, in any case, had taken to spending most of the week in Devon. Bailey's club, the Senior, was largely patronised by retired army officers and colonial officials, to both of which castes he belonged. It stood across Waterloo Place from the Atheneum, much loved by Anglican bishops, and the Travellers, which most of his colleagues preferred.

The best part of the walk was across St James's Park. Following the winding path across the footbridge, he had a choice of views – the palace to the right, Whitehall to the left – and stood about equidistant from both, which was precisely where he placed himself in the invisible order of things. On the far side of the park, he waited for a troop of Life Guards to canter past. They were in full dress, horsehair plumes tossing, early light glinting on steel. It was a sight for the camera-toting Americans who descended on London in larger numbers every year, but Bailey was old-fashioned enough to find it comforting.

When he climbed Cockpit Steps and emerged into Queen Anne's Gate, he found the street empty, apart from the milk cart making its stops. It was really absurdly early, and it was quite unlike C to issue a dawn summons. But Bailey was not given to idle speculation; the cause would reveal itself soon enough. His mind turned on the party that had kept him up much too late. Over the port he had allowed himself to get into an argument with a languid viscount, one of Diana's endless cousins, who was a prop of the Anglo-German Fellowship. The man refused to believe, of all things, that white men could possibly be descended from the ape. Bailey knew something of ethnology and had followed the debate over Raymond Dart's discoveries in

South Africa. He ventured to suggest that Herr Hitler and his admirers were proof positive that man not only had evolved from the killer ape Dart had dug up but was in imminent danger of reverting to his former condition. This remark was not well received.

From his homburg and his starched collar to the mirror-like polish of his shoes, Bailey looked the model of the army officer in mufti; he had swapped one uniform for another. But inside him was something that could never be regimented – a wild Celtic streak from his mother's side of the family, mad Irish through and through. Try as he might, he could never keep it buttoned down for long. It had caused a minor scandal in Calcutta. It popped out at dinner parties after a bottle of claret. It delighted Diana, who called it his leprechaun, and his daughters, for whom he wrote nonsense rhymes.

The ferrule of his scrolled umbrella rang against the paving stones as he marched briskly past the weathered statue of Anne Regina and up the steps of number twenty-one. It was one of a row of elegant five-storey townhouses, with gargoyle heads along the façade and carved foliage over the portico.

Bailey tapped the brass knocker, and a nuggety little man in a black coat opened it at once.

'Morning, Spooner.'

'Morning, Major Bailey. Bit early for you, is it?'

Spooner had been the chief's orderly during the war and had stuck to him ever since. He treated all C's subordinates with the same cheerful insolence.

He helped Bailey off with his chesterfield and said, 'They've just sat down to breakfast.'

'They?'

'Mr de Salis is here from Berlin. Took the boat train, I believe.'

Bailey was mildly annoyed that he had not been fore-warned. De Salis presumed too much on his personal relationship with the chief. But then, the head of station from Berlin never had been one of Bailey's favourites. There was an element of professional jealousy. For too many years de Salis had been allowed to run the most important SIS station as his own fiefdom. Predictably, he had started to go native. His Germanophilia seemed more pronounced since Hitler had taken power. His latest report provided arguments to sustain what, on the part of upper-class twits like the one at Diana's party, was merely uninformed prejudice. Bailey was second to none in his detestation of Bolshevists. He had helped to frame the plot to sink Lenin and had accompanied the British expeditionary force that had landed at Murmansk. But he viewed the Hitler movement with equal suspicion and contempt, not solely because of the Nazis' bad manners. Hitler, he was convinced, was no less of a revolutionary than Stalin and would prove to be no more of a dictator. Britain and the Empire must be ready to take on both. There were few men in England who understood this, fewer still in North America. Churchill was one of the few, and his reward was to find himself blacklisted by the BBC. De Salis's reports did not help.

Bailey followed Spooner into the dining room and found C sprinkling sea salt into his porridge.

'Ah, there you are, Colin. Good of you to come.'

C made a habit of addressing men who were acting under orders as if they were doing him a personal favour. His diplomacy, like his comfortable, bluff exterior, could be misleading, as a Labour prime minister had discovered. C had once called on Ramsay MacDonald and informed him that, unless he had his way, he would draw on the resources of friends in the City and set up an independent intelligence network, answerable only to the King. His bluff – if it was a bluff – had never been called.

De Salis made as if to rise from the table.

'Please don't trouble yourself, Adam,' Bailey said. 'How are you?'

They shook hands.

'Adam's been travelling all night,' C explained. 'He washed up on my doorstep like a shipwreck.'

'I thought it best not to wait,' de Salis said, quite un-ruffled. 'In view of the prime minister's request.'

'Quite so,' C agreed. 'Colin, do have something to eat, will you?'

Obediently, Bailey set about slathering Gentleman's Relish onto a piece of toast.

'Might I ask what request that would be?' he said, without looking up.

'It came up in December. You know what I'm talking about, don't you?' C looked mildly embarrassed, and Bailey immediately knew why.

The prime minister had asked the Secret Service to put together a paper on Comintern activities in Britain. The job had been assigned to Bailey's department, and he had only just completed the draft report. The whole affair was hypersensitive because, in theory, the Firm was not permitted to embroil itself in domestic matters. Communist subversion in England was the preserve of its sister service, MI5. The government was looking for political ammunition, and C – for reasons of his own – had decided to be accommodating. But the whole investigation was supposed to be kept under wraps. De Salis could only have heard about it from the chief.

Bailey felt his blood pressure rising. He set down his knife and played with the crumbs on his plate.

C recovered briskly. 'Adam, why don't you bring Colin up to date?'

'I have a potential defector,' de Salis reported. 'A walk-in, as it happens. He is a military specialist for the Comintern and was previously stationed in Britain. He knows all the Communist bosses here – Pollitt, Gollan, the lot. He has given me a digest of his activities in England. I don't think I'm overegging it if I say it will enable us to destroy the most dangerous fifth column that is operating in this country. This is the best catch we've had in years.' He glanced at C, who did not contradict him.

'I've had a quick look at the material,' C observed casually. 'I think they'll be quite interested at the Admiralty.'

'I take it this chap's a Russian,' Bailey interjected.

'German. But he's done the Red Army intelligence course in Moscow.'

'I assume you've checked his bona fides.'

'That's one of the reasons I'm here.'

De Salis reported the traces that Johnny had given him – the cover name he had used to travel to Britain, the dates of his various postings, the identities of other agents and operatives he had mentioned.

Bailey made a few notes inside the cover of his cheque-book.

'We'll need to check some of this with the Sisters,' he remarked.

'You won't give them any inkling what it's about, I hope,' de Salis said, in some agitation.

Bailey gave him a basilisk stare.

'Well, he *is* our property,' de Salis subsided.

'I'll try to keep that in mind,' Bailey said drily. As the man who handled day-to-day liaison with the Security Service, Bailey was well aware that there was no love lost among siblings. 'I'll go down to Cromwell Road myself.' He directed his words to C. 'Max Knight owes me a favour.'

Bailey decided to indulge in a poached egg.

'Perhaps I could ask one or two questions, Adam,' he said, when he had deployed the egg to his satisfaction on top of a piece of toast.

'Of course.'

'What's your chap like?'

'A rough diamond. Self-educated, but bright.'

'What does he want?'

'He wants out. I expect he's in a bit of a funk, though he doesn't show it. The Reds have been blown out of the water in Germany. There's also some question of a girl. He wants a British passport for her.'

'Oh, he does, does he? I expect he also wants money.'

'He mentioned the figure of ten thousand pounds.'

Bailey snorted. This was more than a tenth of the budget for the whole Secret Service. 'Did your chap also mention a knighthood and an audience with the King?'

'It's not inconceivable something could be arranged,' de Salis suggested. 'This man's information could be worth a damn sight more than that to the government and certain sections of Fleet Street. I could talk to Bunny,' he added, using the family nickname of one of the most powerful and jingoistic of the press barons.

Only now did Bailey begin to appreciate the extravagance of de Salis's ambitions. He wanted to ingratiate himself with the government by creating a tremendous splash – a red scare of the proportions of the Zinoviev Letter that would guarantee a Tory victory in snap elections. Perhaps de Salis even had his eye on C's job.

Bailey was by no means allergic to the use of propaganda, black, grey or even white. But his first instinct was operational. If the Berlin walk-in was genuine and not a fabricator or an agent provocateur, then he would be more valuable in place than fulminating against the Comintern in the pages of the Tory press.

'I'll need a little time,' he said, looking at C. 'I'll want to examine all of Adam's material. And of course Adam will want to put in an appearance at his newspaper.'

De Salis looked distinctly peeved.

'Very well.' C drew back his chair, signalling that breakfast was over. 'Why don't we regroup next door later on. Shall we say eighteen hundred? I'll have the lift waiting.'

Bailey's designation on interoffice memos looked like the name of an old school form: Va. It meant that he was chief of Section V, the counterintelligence department. Some of his juniors called him the Fakir, a jocular sobriquet that could not be explained by his appearance; he was of middling height, wiry and compact, his wide, domed forehead capped by tight waves of dark brown hair that was just starting to grey. He had acquired his nickname because of his time in India in the intelligence branch of the police. His first experience of Russian intrigues, in those years before the war, had involved Tsarist plotters on the northwest frontier. On his first undercover mission, he had blackened his face and donned the flat turban and loose trousers of a Pathan tribesman to ride through the mountain passes to Kandahar, and found it was harder for an Englishman to pass for a native than it had been in the pages of his favourite story, *Kim*. His sojourn in Kipling country had ended when his family had learned of his romantic involvement with an Indian girl and brought pressure on his superiors to send him home. It had taken him the whole summer to recover from that love affair and a serious bout of malaria. By the end of that summer, there was no time for convalescence: Europe was hurtling over the terrible watershed of the Great War.

The colonial police was an odd career choice for a Scholar of Winchester; there were other oddities in Bailey's makeup. His friend John Buchan, with whom he lunched occasionally at an obscure writer's club that convened on alternate Tuesdays, described him as a model for the 'practical mystics' who peopled his tales of adventure. His library, which had outgrown his country house on the borders of Dartmoor as well as the flat in town, ranged from ornithology to the occult.

If Bailey lived in a certain degree of comfort, it was thanks to Diana's inheritance. Secret Service salaries were paid in cash and mercifully free of tax, but nobody could live on one without independent means, a military pension or an aptitude for embezzlement. Bailey had met Diana – Lady Diana Vavassour, as she then was, in the first spring after the war, on the day Mansfield Cumming, the original C, informed him that he had been accepted for the service. He was roaming the corridors of Broadway Buildings, looking for his section. It was lunchtime, and most of the rooms were deserted. He threw open a frosted glass door, hoping it was the right one – and found a tall, generously proportioned girl sprawled full-length on the rug.

'Good God!' Bailey exclaimed.

He had rushed to the girl and knelt over her. Her pulse was still beating. He tried to remember his first aid as he started to undo the top buttons on her high collar.

Suddenly he found himself looking down into two wide, china-blue eyes.

'Do you generally molest women, or just the ones you haven't been introduced to?'

The girl sprang up. She was nearly as tall as Bailey.

'I'm sorry,' Bailey stammered. 'I thought you'd fainted. Or something. Are you sure you're all right?'

'Oh spiffing, thank you.' She straightened her dress and smiled at his red face. 'I like to take a catnap when I've been burning the candle at both ends.'

That was his introduction to Diana. At that time she was the secretary to one of the directors of the Firm, the kind it favoured then and since: a girl with good legs and equally good social connections. It didn't take long for her to cure him of his lingering oriental infatuation. Within a year they were married, and she left the Firm to bear the first of their daughters. It was a pretty good marriage, as marriages went. They made space for each other. Diana spent a good deal of her time in the country, charging over the moors on her favourite hunter, tearing up the roads in the cheeky red Austin roadster he hadn't wanted her to buy. That was no bad thing, Bailey thought. If she were in London more, she would exhaust the social scene and then be demanding to be sent off to overthrow some foreign potentate.

Bailey himself had tried his hand at overthrowing more than one such potentate. But he did not think of himself as 'political'. Adam de Salis was political, and that was a defect in an intelligence officer; it corrupted his judgment. Bailey believed instinctively in a natural order of things that included the rule of law, civility, and the absolute right of Great Britain, as the principal custodian of both, to defend her interests, wherever threatened, by whatever means fell to hand.

What he most detested were political abstractions. Ideologies, people had taken to calling them – no doubt thanks to the Germans, who had invented the worst of them.

At the same dinner party where he had had to suffer the fool from the Anglo-German Fellowship, he had encountered another typical specimen of the times: the Trinity College Bolshevist. The boy had just come down from Cambridge, full of theories, and had proceeded to thrill his hostess with lurid accounts of what would happen to the ruling class when the inevitable revolution dawned.

'Perhaps you could intercede for our dear hostess,' Bailey had suggested.

The Cambridge revolutionist had glowered at the Turner over the mantel. 'In Russia,' he declaimed, 'this house would be expropriated by the people and used to accommodate eight needy families.'

He had spoken with such utter lack of humour that Bailey had burst out laughing.

'It's all very well for you to make fun,' the young man had said huffily. 'The Establishment can afford a sense of humour.'

'My dear boy, it's our last line of defence.'

'It's obvious you're a Tory.'

'I find politics rather a bore. But I'm against the revolution.'

'You mean the Russian Revolution?'

'Absolutely.'

'Then I suppose you're against the French Revolution too.' The Trinity man's tone had been that of a prosecutor marshalling the points of an indictment.

'No question,' Bailey had countered blandly. 'I don't know if people still read Burke at Cambridge, but I think he polished off the French Revolution rather well.' He had been about to cite one of his favourite passages from Burke about the presumption of those 'who think of their country as carte blanche, on which they may scribble as they please' – when Diana had decided to head him off at the pass.

'Actually,' she'd purred, 'Colin doesn't see the point of the agricultural revolution of four thousand B.C.'

On the way home, he protested, 'I was just starting to enjoy myself.'

'Honestly, darling, one can't take you anywhere.'

'I thought I was on my best behaviour.'

Diana started giggling. 'You'll cross swords with anyone, from Freddie the Fascist to the Trinity Terrorist.'

'They sounded pretty much the same to me.'

'Oh, Colin, be serious.'

'But that's the point, my love. As I get older, I find there are only two parties worth a damn – the one that's got a sense of humour, and the one that hasn't.'

Bailey returned to the office shortly before six. The temperature had dropped, and the rain that had started coming down in midafternoon, as he left the club, was turning to sleet. Bailey crossed the road from the underground station and hurried up the steps of a greyish, undistinguished office block called Broadway Buildings. He had to squeeze through a crowd of shoppers and commuters taking shelter from the weather under the eye of a uniformed commissionaire on the other side of the glass doors.

The commissionaire opened the door for Bailey.

'Lift's waiting, Major.'

Bailey took the reserved elevator that went direct to the fourth floor. According to the directory on the wall in the lobby, the tenant on that floor was the Minimax Fire Extinguisher Company. Bailey had always thought this a rather apt cover name for the Intelligence Service.

He found de Salis smoking a cigarette in C's outer office.

They had barely exchanged greetings when the red light above the padded door went off and the green light came on.

C was engaged in mixing his staple draught: gin and bitters, diluted with soda rather than plain water. Bailey couldn't stand the stuff. He asked for scotch, and C produced a bottle from among the dummy bindings on the lowest shelf of his bookcase.

The office would have passed for a well-to-do, but quite unexceptional, Edwardian sitting room, except for the model warships in glass cases and the imposing iron safe in the corner. Bailey liked to fancy that inside that quarter ton of metal were things that could make the empire tremble, blood secrets from the time of Elizabeth and Anne and every monarch since.

'Well, Colin,' said the owner of the safe. 'Do we have a verdict?'

'It's not conclusive.' Bailey laid a hand on the tattered file, secured by ribbons, that he had brought with him. 'We can't match Adam's chap up with anyone in our records. I did find a reference to a Comintern bomb-thrower identified only as "Alfred" in the material we got from the French after that nasty business in Brussels. It may fit this chap. Or again, it may not.'

'What about the wireless traffic?'

'Nothing of interest.'

'What did the Sisters have to say?'

'On this occasion, the Sisters were quite helpful. It seems a Herr Dinkelmeyer did visit this country on the dates Adam's man suggested. The Home Office still had the landing and departure cards. Special Branch reported a meeting between Jim Straw of the CPGB and an unidentified foreigner at King's Cross Station. The foreigner gave them the slip. But he seems to match our man's description. I gave Max Knight a few of the highlights from our man's report on subversion in the armed services – edited of course – and he got quite excited. The names and addresses are right, and it all seems to fit the m.o.'

Bailey paused for a sip of whisky.

'Frankly, sir,' he went on, 'it's the connection with André Bloch that interests me. Or perhaps we'd better call him Max, since he seems to be running with that monicker now. What exactly did your chap say again, Adam?'

'He said he'd give André to us. Or words to that effect.'

'Only that?'

'I didn't have time for a leisurely chat, Colin.'

'What do you suppose your fellow – Johnny – had in mind?'

De Salis thought about this for a bit. 'There's bad blood there,' he suggested. 'I had the sense Johnny might be ready to have Max killed, even to do the job himself. I must say, I wouldn't mind having a potshot at the bugger myself. At the least, I think Johnny can tell us where to find him.'

'I know where Max is,' Bailey said mildly. 'He's in Copenhagen, rebuilding his organisation. And the last thing I think we should do is to have him killed.'

C waggled his tufted eyebrows.

'What did you have in mind, Colin?'

'If we can play Johnny back against Max – and whoever else he reports to – we're home and dry. With luck, we'll know everything their lot is cooking up against us before they do any damage. Needless to say, Adam, I'm speaking on the assumption that your chap is genuine. The best way to find out for sure is to run with him and see how he performs.'

'In other words, you want to play him long,' C suggested.

'I want to run him as an agent in place.'

'You don't look happy, Adam,' C remarked.

'I'm not at all sure Johnny will go for it. He's suggested a one-time business arrangement. He gives us specified information, we give him enough money to retire somewhere in the sun. He says his terms are non-negotiable.'

'I find that most things in life are negotiable,' Bailey commented. 'We'll make him a counter offer. He's not likely to go shopping around for other bids, is he?'

De Salis was still reluctant to let slip his vision of a spectacular defection, complete with banner headlines and a roundup of Russian agents, bringing personal encomiums from a grateful prime minister.

'You realise that Johnny may back off completely.' He appealled to C with his eyes, but the chief was playing silent umpire now and seemed to think Bailey was winning on points.

'It's a risk,' Bailey said. 'I admit that. But my hunch is that your chap likes the smell of cordite, and might like a chance to get back at his own bunch if he thinks they've let him down badly. That's what we can play with.'

'What are we going to pay him?' C intervened.

'A hundred to start him off, and fifty a month if he produces,' Bailey said briskly.

C noted the figures on a desk pad.

'Bit cheesy, isn't it?' de Salis sniffed.

'It's more than some of our chaps in the field are getting,' Bailey observed.

'There's also the matter of the girl.'

'I hadn't forgotten the girl. How much does she know about this?'

'All I know is, he wants us to help get her out of the country.'

'Can't he use his own network?'

'You don't seem to understand, Colin. His network has collapsed, and the Gestapo could pick both of them up any day of the week. That's one of the reasons he's come to us.'

Bailey smoothed the hair at the back of his neck. 'We mustn't do anything to show our hand. Do you know what passport Johnny is using?'

'It's Czech, I believe.'

'That makes things simpler. At a pinch, we'll find a Czech passport for the woman.'

Bailey's mind turned to a rustic inn near the Czech border, where he had lunched during a shooting holiday in Saxony.

'If necessary, we'll point Johnny in the right direction. Once he's out, I want to set up a meet. I'd like to take a look at this chap myself.'

4

Johnny decided to run on the day his photograph appeared on a wanted poster at the post office. It was an ancient picture; it showed a boy of seventeen in the uniform of a naval rating. He wondered where the police had dredged it up. The youthful face was hardly recognisable as that of a man now prematurely grey, weathered and scored by the life he had lived, and the caption identified him as 'Johann Heinrich Lentz,' a name that few people in Berlin had ever heard. All the same, the photo told him that their time in Germany was up.

He had met twice with de Salis since the Englishman returned from London, full of promises but little hard cash. De Salis told him he would receive the bulk of his money when he was safely out of Germany and could be thoroughly debriefed. Nonetheless, de Salis tried to squeeze him for more and more information, especially about Max. The Englishman showed him a list of Russian names and asked him to talk about each one. He recognised most of them – OGPU and Fourth Department men – but he made the conscious decision to hold back. The

British might be playing games with him, trying to suck him dry before they paid up.

At their last meeting, de Salis brought a passport for Sigrid. It was Czech – not British, as Johnny had specified – and this was a source of new suspicion. But at any rate the passport matched his own. De Salis advised him that if he wanted to slip out of Germany without attracting unnecessary attention, he should make his way to an inn south of Chemnitz, near the Czech border. The mention of Chemnitz filled Johnny with black foreboding. It was at Chemnitz, ten years earlier, that the Communist Party leaders royally screwed up the Hamburg revolt.

'Is that all?' Johnny asked. 'Just the name of a country inn?'

'Bailey says it will work,' de Salis said defensively.

'Well, I'm glad I haven't put you to excessive trouble,' Johnny parodied de Salis's own style.

'We're not babysitters,' the Englishman said huffily.

De Salis gave him a telegraphic address to memorise. It belonged to a Savile Row tailor.

'When you're out,' de Salis instructed, 'order a hacking jacket. Size forty-two if you're in contact with the opposition, forty-four if you're not.'

Back in the apartment, Johnny spent more than an hour getting his own passport ready for the trip. He had altered his appearance in minor ways, by dying his hair and putting on spectacles. He pasted a new photograph in the Czech passport to reflect these changes. To transfer the rubber stamp of the Czech police from one to the other, he used a hard-boiled egg. He peeled the egg while it was still hot from the pan and rolled it carefully over the original stamp until the imprint was transferred to the egg white. When he rolled the egg over the corner of the new picture, the stamp reappeared, only slightly paler. He then ate the egg for his breakfast. His job was clumsy compared with the work of the old forgery factory on the Lindenstrasse, but the Gestapo owned those premises now. It would do.

He showed both the passports to Sigrid.

'Brigitte Jelinek.' She tested the foreign syllables of the

last name. 'Yours is easier. Alfred Wittling. But it doesn't sound Czech.'

'It sounds Sudeten Czech.'

'Aren't all of them Hitlerites?'

'Not all. But I'll practice being one for a day or two, if you don't mind.'

He had explained the escape plan to Sigrid in some detail, letting her believe that he had got his directions from the Fourth Department. She approved the general idea and came up with a refinement that he liked. The forced inactivity of the past days had made her listless and depressed. The apartment had become a prison cell. Now, at the prospect of breaking out, she was as chirpy as a bird. She was actually singing when they boarded the train.

They had to change trains at Dresden. As the passengers came out of the cars, they were herded into line by black-uniformed guards. The nails of their boots clacked against the concrete. Johnny glanced along the platform. At the head of the line, a self-important SS officer was installed at a make-shift desk. A roll of fat hung over his collar like a dewlap.

Johnny squeezed Sigrid's arm lightly, nudging her forward. He fell back a few paces. He doubted that his passport would stand up to close inspection. If he was taken, at least they would not be taken together.

She glanced back, doubtful and afraid, and a small vertical crease appeared between her eyebrows. He looked away.

The SS guards worried at the flank of the column, like sheepdogs.

He saw Sigrid shuffle to the head of the line, heard her laugh at the officer's jokes. The SS man returned her passport without even opening it. Her looks were her safe-conduct.

The line shunted forward, then stopped.

The man in front of him was becoming agitated. He put his suitcase down, picked it up immediately, then dropped it again.

'What's going on?' he appealed to Johnny. His accent might have been Polish. 'Are they going to arrest us?'

The man was swarthy, with tufts of black hair on the

back of his hands. The SS officer wasn't going to give him the nod, not with that hooked nose.

'Will you carry this for me?' he mumbled, indicating the suitcase. It was the cheapest sort, cardboard, with a strap around the middle.

Johnny shook his head.

'I can pay you.'

'Keep moving!' an SS guard bellowed.

That instant, the Jew lost his sanity. He dropped his suitcase and dived over the edge of the platform. It looked like a bad fall, but he picked himself up and started scuttling across the tracks, towards the shelter of some freight cars on a siding.

The guard released the safety catch on his rifle and took aim. Two more SS men shouldered their way through the line and brought up their submachine guns.

'Not yet!' the SS officer bellowed. He strutted over to the edge of the platform, gauging the distance between the runaway Jew and the freight cars. When the Jew stumbled and fell across the tracks, the officer waited patiently as he struggled to get up.

Still on his hands and knees, the Jew looked back at the platform, puzzlement written all over his face. All was still, as if the whole scene had been captured under glass.

Then the guard nearest Johnny spoke. 'Look at his fat rump. I could hit him with my eyes shut.'

'But we're sportsmen, Frick,' the commandant said pleasantly.

He waited until his quarry was almost out of danger, until he had his hand on the railing at the back of the caboose, before he drew a bead along the barrel of his Luger and squeezed off a couple of rounds. His aim was excellent. The first bullet found its mark at the midpoint between the victim's shoulder blades. As it crumpled, the body seemed weightless and insubstantial, an emptied sack.

The SS officer stuck his gun back into his holster and returned to business.

'Next!'

Several suspects had already been herded to the far end of the platform.

Johnny lit a cigarette. It pleased him that it took only one match.

'Next!'

He walked up to the desk.

'Papers!'

'*Jawohl, Obersturmführer*,' he responded, promoting the SS officer by at least two ranks as he offered his fake passport.

'A shithead Czech,' the officer said with disgust, leafing through the passport. 'You don't look like a Czech.'

'I'm no shithead Czech,' Johnny replied in the same tone. 'I'm as good a German as any. Heil Hitler!'

Reflexively, the SS man returned the salute.

'Sudeten. Well now, that's different.' He returned Johnny's passport. 'You'll be joining the Reich soon enough, *Kamarad*. Come see us again before we come to see you!'

The final stage of the train journey was uneventful. At Chemnitz they hired bicycles and pedaled south with backpacks and picnic lunches, like any number of ramblers in those first days of spring. The crocuses were out, and you could smell the sap rising in the forest.

They were close to the border when they found the rutted dirt road Colin Bailey had remembered. The inn at the end of the road hadn't been discovered by tourists. They ate their lunch among local people, both Czechs and Germans. They didn't hurry the meal. Johnny ordered dessert and liqueurs, although Sigrid only toyed with her main course.

Johnny finally paid the bill, and they slipped out the back way, through the owner's private apartments. A schnauzer trotted out and snapped at their heels, but nobody came to stop them. When they walked out the back door, Sigrid froze. There, clearly visible above the pines, was the pointed roof of a watchtower.

'It's all right,' Johnny said, clasping her by the waist. 'We just crossed the border. Half the inn is in Czechoslovakia.'

He tried to give the words a ring of triumph, and she let him press her to his chest. But the warmth of the spring afternoon was not inside him. They were out of Germany, but they had not stopped running.

5

At the end of that week a messenger from Colin Bailey's tailors arrived at his flat with a box of detachable collars and a telegram, confirming his belief that the long-established firm of Plunkett & Rice was one of the most reliable institutions in England. The telegram contained an order for a hacking jacket and specified a forty-four chest measurement. It announced that forwarding instructions would be sent from Paris.

The second telegram relayed the information, in suitably disguised language, that Johnny had arrived safely in Paris and was installed in a small hotel in the fourteenth arrondissement. While Bailey consulted a boat train schedule, Diana started laying out clothes. He noticed she had picked one of their larger suitcases.

'I really think an overnight bag will be quite sufficient,' he called out to her.

'Not on your life,' she rejoined. 'You don't imagine I'm going to let you go to Paris by yourself, do you?'

With the children away at school and a fortnight to go before the Easter break, he could not think of a convincing excuse to leave her at home. It meant they would have to stay at the Lancaster. Her family had *always* stayed at the Lancaster. Caught in Paris at the start of the war, her mother had arranged with the management to have her Rolls-Royce driven to Calais, from whence it had been ferried across the Channel on a Royal Navy destroyer.

In the room up under the eaves of the Hotel Fouché that looked out over a choppy sea of blue rooftops, a bottle of Moët sat untouched in an ice bucket. Johnny had ordered it – and the white and yellow roses he had strewn everywhere, even across the bed – to celebrate Sigrid's birthday. He was suddenly in no mood for a celebration. He was trying to keep his voice low and calm, to betray none of the fear and anger that was in him.

She had told him she was going shopping, that she wanted to go alone so she could surprise him. She had come back empty-handed, but with news that had floored him.

'Slow down,' he said. 'Tell me the whole thing again from the beginning.'

Sigrid frowned with impatience. She was excited and happy and couldn't understand why he was being difficult.

'I went to Editions du Carrefour,' she repeated. That was one Paris address everyone in Berlin knew. The vast publishing house was the hub of Münzenberg's operation. It had scored a resounding success with the publication of the *Brown Book* on the Hitler terror. 'I asked for Willi Münzenberg.'

'Just like that?'

'I didn't see anything wrong, Johnny. We know he's in Paris. I want to get back to work.'

'Aren't you enjoying yourself?'

'Do you expect me to go on holiday while the Fascists are devouring Europe?' she rounded on him.

'All right. What name did you give them?'

'The old one. Firelei. Willi would remember that. But he wasn't there. At least, the receptionist wouldn't say. They made me wait more than an hour in an empty office.'

'Didn't you think of leaving?'

'They didn't want me to leave. You can understand that, can't you? They've every right to distrust strangers. I could have been an assassin.'

The solemnity with which she said this made him want to laugh, more at himself than at her. He was reminded of the lecture on revolutionary discipline he had given her when she had complained about Max.

'What happened then?'

'Max arrived with his bodyguards. He was charming, Johnny, absolutely charming. He said he's been looking

227

for us for two weeks. He sent men to the flat in Berlin to help get us away, but we had already gone.'

'Very thoughtful of him. Did he say when he arrived in Paris?'

'No.'

'But you told him when we arrived.'

'Why shouldn't I?'

Thank God I sent the cable to Smollett in London, Johnny thought. If Max found out I'd been in Paris for four days without making contact with my controllers, I'd be as good as dead. There'll be enough to explain as things are.

He resolved to put a bold face on things, opened the champagne, whirled her around the room and took her out for a late supper at a bistro near the Pont Neuf. He considered laying it all on the table that night but held back because of the doubts that kept flooding in. Had her visit to Carrefour been as naive as she said? Why hadn't she told him where she was going? How deeply was she under Max's spell?

Max had sent an invitation with Sigrid for both of them to dine with him the following night. The tone of the message was friendly. It was a summons, all the same.

I'll have to keep up appearances, Johnny thought. If it's a trap – he pressed his elbow against his side, feeling the bulk of the Mauser under his armpit – I'll take Max with me.

But first he had to meet an important Englishman from London. He hoped the man had better answers than de Salis.

In the morning he slipped out and sent a telegram to the tailoring firm of Plunkett & Rice, explaining that he had gone on a diet and therefore required to have his jacket taken in two inches.

Colin Bailey chose the Île St Louis, his favourite corner of Paris, for his first meeting with Johnny. Across the street from the bistro was a splendid apparition: a burnished horse's head, nostrils flaring, glowing in the dozy afternoon sun like an idol. Bailey noted that it was the sign of a butcher's shop dealing in horsemeat. This observation deepened his suspicion that the French were not altogether to be trusted. How could one vest complete confidence in a people whose better classes, it seemed, were given over to practices Diana regarded as lower than cannibalism? He resolved not to mention the incident to her. Diana much preferred horses to people.

Bailey was excited about the interview that lay ahead of him but edgy as well. Hennessy, a tall, gangling young man from the embassy who bore an unfortunate resemblance to a praying mantis, had reached him at the Lancaster just before he'd left, with the news of Johnny's eleventh-hour telegram to his tailors. To Bailey, the message that Johnny was back in contact with the Russians was reassuring. The man was unlikely to have sent the cable if he were playing a double game, and it seemed he was now in place to perform the role that Bailey had scripted for him. There remained the task of making sure of the man, of winning him completely to a job that would be not only dangerous but devastatingly lonely. If Bailey had read his man right, the danger might be more of a lure than a deterrent. But to cope with the loneliness of a double life, Johnny would need a sense of purpose as strong as the faith that had sustained him through his years in the revolutionary underground. Bailey knew he could not supply that; but he might help to mould it from the materials he found.

He knew his man as soon as he entered the restaurant – back to the wall, corner table, eyes on the door. The face was strong but troubled, Bailey thought, capable of – no, prone to – excesses of passion.

They drank the new Beaujolais, and since Johnny had no interest in the menu, Bailey ordered each of them a dozen *belons* and the steak *au poivre* to follow.

'I got your message,' Bailey said, when the waiter was out of earshot. 'Are you being followed?'

'I don't think so. But I spent all morning getting here, just in case.'

Bailey nodded his approval.

He looks bloody miserable, Bailey thought. Better start on the upbeat.

'I wanted to tell you that the prime minister is deeply grateful for the information you have given us. He asked me to send you his personal thanks.'

'The prime minister? Oh.' Johnny frowned and leaned forward. 'Have there been any arrests?'

'There won't be for a good while yet,' Bailey assured him. 'And when there are, we'll make damn sure there's nothing to tie them to you.'

At this, Johnny seemed to relax a little, and he consumed his oysters with relish.

I mustn't push him, Bailey reminded himself. Let him open up in his own sweet time.

'I'm going to see Max tonight,' Johnny suddenly announced. 'André, if you like.'

'I know who you mean. Tell me about him.'

'He is the most brilliant man I know. There was a time when I think I would have died for him. He killed my best friend.'

De Salis was right about this, at least, thought Bailey. Here was something to build on. Little by little, Johnny told him most of the story.

Then Johnny interrupted himself and said, oddly, 'In a way, I don't blame Max.'

'I'm not sure that I follow.'

'He pulls the trigger. He doesn't aim the gun. It's the party that does that.'

'You're saying that your quarrel is not with the individual, but with the cause.'

'Not with the cause,' Johnny came back fiercely. 'With those who have stolen it.'

Careful, Bailey cautioned himself. In part of himself, Johnny still believes.

'With the system, then,' he suggested.

Johnny didn't dissent from this.

'What are you planning to do about it?' Bailey challenged him.

'Heinz said he was going to Trotsky –' the German went off at a tangent '– before they killed him.'

'Did you consider that yourself?'

'No.'

'May I ask why not?'

'Because you can't fight Stalin with speeches.'

Closer, Bailey thought. We're halfway there.

But a few minutes later, Johnny cut across his questioning. 'Did you bring my money?'

'Well, yes. I have something for you.'

'Ten thousand pounds?' The corners of Johnny's mouth twitched.

'Not quite, I'm afraid. I can let you have a hundred for now. Actually, I wanted to suggest a more permanent arrangement.'

'Meaning?'

'Fifty a month.'

'This is not what I discussed with your man in Berlin.'

'But is that what you really want? So you can run a pub by the sea or grow cabbages? Forgive me if I'm presumptuous, but you don't strike me as the kind of man who'd be happy in early retirement.'

'What exactly are you suggesting?'

'I'm suggesting we join forces for the long haul.'

'You mean you want me to spy for you.'

'Put it that way if you like. The way I view it, you have a score to settle, and we are in a position to help you do it. Isn't that why you came to us in the first place?'

The waiter came with the steaks, and Bailey held his breath. Had he pushed it too far?

The waiter left and Johnny said, 'I'll let you know after tonight.'

In Paris, Max behaved like a millionaire on holiday. At least he did that night.

His driver called for them at the Hotel Fouché and whisked them off to the Café de la Paix. They ended up at a White Russian nightclub complete with gypsy singers and Cossack dancers, and Max insisted on ordering caviar with the vodka. He seemed entirely unperturbed about the risk of being identified as the wrong sort of Russian.

He expressed no suspicions about their escape from Germany. On the contrary, he toasted Johnny's imagination. But Johnny's stomach tightened as he watched all this show of hilarity, trying to keep his head clear while the bottle swung back and forth like a pendulum.

When the thunderbolt came, it was not what he most expected, but worse than anything he had feared.

'I talked to Marlowe today,' Max announced, looking at Sigrid. Johnny knew the name from the cable traffic he had seen in Berlin. It was a code name for the resident director of the OGPU in Paris, who operated from behind the cover of an architect's studio decorated in futuristic style on the Rue de Seine. It was curious, this Russian penchant for literary code names – novelists for military intelligence, playwrights for the chekists. 'It's all been cleared,' Max went on.

'Wait a minute!' Johnny exclaimed. Sigrid's face was shining. 'Did I miss something?'

'No need for secrets in the family,' Max beamed. 'Sigrid is going to work for us. Shall we drink her health?'

Oh, no, Johnny thought. You can't do this a second time. Not with Sigrid.

'This is something Sigi and I have to talk over in private,' he said.

He got to his feet a trifle unsteadily and took her arm. 'Come on. We're going now.'

He came perilously close to baring his soul to Sigrid that night. He told her that Max was a killer, that Stalin and his people had betrayed the cause they both believed in, that because of them, the mightiest Communist movement in the world outside Russia had stood frozen like a rabbit in the headlights of an oncoming car, in the face of the Nazi jackboots. She wouldn't hear him.

'You're jealous,' she informed him. 'You're jealous because I'll be working for Max instead of you. Didn't you teach me that these things are not for us to decide? That the party decides?'

I taught you too well, Johnny told himself. Now I shall have to wait until you hear the same screams that I hear and wake from this dream.

Helene had been right after all.

Over the next week he met Bailey several times. They spent the best part of a day in a flat in Neuilly loaned by a retired colleague of Bailey's who had decided to live abroad because, as he put it, the English were best admired from a distance. The apartment was adorned with mildly porno-graphic sketches of *grisettes* and spiky, inhospitable plants that belonged in a different climate.

Bailey didn't like the way Johnny was drinking. He was drinking like a Russian, drinking himself towards oblivion. Something had evidently happened involving Max and the girl, but Johnny refused to talk about it. On other subjects, however – from the order of battle in Moscow to Fourth Department operations in Oslo – he talked freely, with a wealth of detail. He pulled back abruptly only when Bailey asked about the woman who had lived with him at the Richmond address.

'Some things I'll never give you,' he said angrily.

'Yes. I respect that.'

Communications became the biggest worry. Johnny had been in touch with the Fourth Department man in Paris and had been told he would probably be recalled to Moscow. Though the Russians saw British spies under every bed, the Intelligence Service did not maintain a station in Moscow – a dereliction about which Bailey had often complained to C. British agents inside Russia were handled by officers stationed in neighbouring capitals: Reval, Helsinki, Prague. Bailey undertook to send a special courier to Moscow in the event Johnny was recalled. They discussed possible meeting places and settled on two: the bathroom of an Armenian restaurant and the Arbat metro station. Johnny would send a postcard to a cover address, setting the time and place for the initial contact by means of a simple code.

'If there's any sign of trouble,' Bailey promised, 'we'll get you out. You have my word on that.'

Pray God they don't keep him in Moscow for long, Bailey thought. We need to keep a good man alongside him. Otherwise isolation will start wearing him down, and the bottle will make him careless. Pity about this woman trouble. Although it's helping to bind him to us.

Gingerly, Bailey broached one last item of business.

'You mentioned that a few of your colleagues feel as you do about Stalin.'

'More than a few. We German Communists are all displaced persons.'

'Would you be willing to talk to any of them on our behalf?'

Johnny did not reject this out of hand. He thought for a bit before saying, 'Too risky. They wouldn't trust me. The way things are, everyone goes around looking over his shoulder. They would think I was a provocateur, a second Emil.'

'Perhaps there's someone we should talk to directly.'

'I'll think about it.'

6

The first requirement for a case handler, in Bailey's estimation, was the same as for a bird-watcher or a fly fisherman: the capacity to wait. He wanted to enlist Johnny's help in recruiting a second agent from inside the ranks of the Comintern, not only to increase his sources but to silence the whispering demon – the soul of Section V – that lived on his left shoulder and was still cackling in his ear that despite all the evidence, despite his gut instincts, there was an outside chance that his new agent was a plant, a phantasm created by Comrade Max. But Bailey did not push his suggestion, and his patience was rewarded.

He was taking a morning glass of champagne with Diana in the elegant courtyard of the Lancaster when a boy materialised with a note on a silver salver. From it Bailey learned that Johnny was waiting for him in a church on the Rue des Augustins.

Half an hour later, he was kneeling beside the German.

'I met someone from Germany,' Johnny whispered. 'His name is Karl Vogel. I told you about him. Do you remember?'

234

'Karl – you mean the boy who worked for Heinz Kordt?'

'He came for help,' Johnny went on. 'All Kordt's people are under suspicion, but he's a useful man. He's a good shot, he can handle himself. He told me he is on probation. He's in France illegally, living from hand to mouth, no better than an Algerian. But one of Marlowe's people came to him and said they're considering him for a job. I think it involves a Russian defector, the one who used to work in Stalin's office. He asked me what he should do.'

'What did you tell him?'

'I told him to act according to his conscience. I can't be involved. If you want to try something, that's your affair. I just thought you would like to know.'

'Where can I find this Karl?'

Johnny told him.

Bailey could think of more appetising sights before break-fast than a row of gutted steers slung from steel hooks. At five in the morning, Les Halles was crowded and bustling. Bailey lengthened his stride to avoid a thin rivulet of blood and followed an opulent pear-shaped figure, embellished with a boutonniere and a waxed moustache – evidently the buyer for one of the fashionable restaurants – between the stands of butchered meat. Bailey was dressed in his civilian uniform, complete with umbrella and homburg hat, as if he were on his way to his club.

He spotted Karl fairly quickly. He was wearing a blood-ied apron and was engaged in hoisting a carcass out of the back of a truck. This struck Bailey as suitable employment for a man who, by Johnny's account, had spent a good part of his life disposing of other types of bodies.

Bailey would not, under normal circumstances, have in-volved himself personally in an approach to a meat porter. However one looked at it, Karl Vogel was a very small fish. Yet he could provide useful bait. There was a chance of catch-ing the Russians red-handed in an assassination attempt. But Bailey's main interest was in quelling that little devil on his left shoulder. If there were any indication that Karl had been forewarned about his approach, he would have to accept that as proof that his instinct about Johnny was wrong. By informing Johnny of the exact time he would attempt the approach, he had invited the other side to arrange a trap – if Johnny were reporting to them. Bailey had taken certain precautions against that contingency.

'Slumming a bit, aren't we, darling?' Diana squeezed his arm and leaned over to inspect a heap of blood sausage.

It was perhaps unorthodox to take his wife along, but after all she had been in the game and was much handier with a revolver than he. Furthermore, the expedition was a diversion from the little shops set like jewel boxes along the Rue St-Honoré. Diana had already replaced her entire spring wardrobe and was working her way through the summer collections. In any event, Hennessy from the embassy was loping along on his stiltlike legs beyond the sides of beef. All height and no width, Hennessy in profile looked like a stick insect.

'Is that him?' Diana said, watching the flex of Karl's muscles as he swung the carcass onto his back.

'That's him.'

'He's not bad looking, in a caveman sort of way. But he could do with some care and feeding.'

Karl swung his burden up onto a hook and wiped his hands on his apron.

'Excuse me,' Bailey addressed him in faulty French. 'Do you have a few minutes?'

Karl growled something and headed back for the truck.

'There's money in it for you.'

Karl paused and looked at Bailey with cold suspicion.

'We could use a healthy young man.'

This was too much for Diana, who started giggling.

'That is to say,' Bailey went on, 'we have a proposal for you. Perhaps we could have breakfast and talk it over.'

Karl shrugged and gestured towards the truck.

'Do you think he understands French?' Diana whispered.

'Karl,' she addressed him in German, somewhat better than Bailey's French. 'I do think you ought to stay and talk with us.'

'Why do you call me Karl?' He glowered at her.

'I think it suits you,' she smiled beatifically. 'Do come and talk to us.'

There was something utterly disarming about Diana's smile. Karl hesitated. It was his foreman who settled things by bawling at him to get back to work. He tore off his apron and hurled it at the man in disgust. The apron snagged on the hat of the portly restaurant buyer, who sailed on, oblivious.

Karl's eyes darted back and forth between Bailey and Diana as they ate in an all-night café across the road. It was one of those magical places where people who have not yet gone to bed rub shoulders with those who have just finished half the day's work. What passed for breakfast was not, inevitably, what one would expect at the common table in the dining room at the Senior. Karl devoured an entrecôte steak, more raw than cooked, and washed down with copious draughts of red wine. To Bailey's alarm, Diana joined in the wine and ordered a crock of onion soup. Bowing to circumstance, Bailey called for coffee and a glass of calvados.

Karl's table manners were disappointing, but he was no fool. He guessed they were English and – once assured they were not seeking to hire a gigolo – he guessed the rest.

Bailey concluded there was nothing to be lost by bluntness. He made his proposal, and reinforced it with a fat envelope that he placed next to Karl's wineglass. The boy affected not to see it. A few minutes later, he announced he would need to think things over. He agreed to a second meeting at a couscous dive on the Left Bank, and at a more civilised hour. They let him leave the café first.

'What do you think?' he asked Diana.

'He's hungry,' she observed, contemplating the plate Karl had scraped clean.

'Yes,' Bailey agreed, noting that the envelope was gone. 'I wonder if he's hungry enough.'

He had his answer the next morning, when he received a distress signal from Johnny. They met in Notre-Dame cathedral, which was jammed with tourists.

'You seem to be developing a penchant for churches,'

Bailey remarked. 'Are you planning to convert to Catholicism?'

Johnny explained that Karl had called on him again, highly agitated, and divulged everything that had happened at Les Halles. Once again, Karl had wanted to know what to do.

'So what did you say?'

'I told him to go to Marlowe at once,' Johnny reported. 'He was nervous, so I made the arrangements myself.'

'You did the right thing,' Bailey assured him.

The next step was to see whether Karl would keep his appointment at the Algerian restaurant, and whether the Russians would try to play him as a double. Bailey, of course, would attend the rendezvous, to ensure that no suspicion fell on Johnny. Naturally he would take his babysitters. But not Diana. She would be left to make another blitzkrieg assault on the Rue St-Honoré.

Afterwards Bailey told himself he ought to be grateful that the Russians, in the main, were not overly subtle. He suspected that if Max Fabrikant had had charge of the operation things might have worked out rather differently. But Max had apparently left Paris.

Karl kept his appointment at the Casbah restaurant, and they consumed a lunch that later sat in Bailey's stomach like a slab of cement. Karl was nervous and showed it by talking and drinking far more than seemed natural. He even made an attempt to tell a joke. Bailey was convinced that this, in a German, was a sign that a man was acting out of character.

As before, Karl left first.

Bailey lingered for a bit, drinking coffee in the hope that it might dissolve the weight in his stomach.

When he strolled out into the spring sunshine, they came at him – two heavies in long coats, a third at the wheel of a car with the engine running. He didn't see the fourth until he backed into him and the man clamped an arm around his throat, blocking off the windpipe, while letting him feel the hardness of the gun jammed up against his ribs.

Hennessy and his men had the drop on the Russians, and they moved fast. But it might not have been fast enough to save Bailey had he not managed to swing his fist back between his attacker's legs, hard enough for the man's hammerlock to loosen. Bailey doubled over, wrenching at the arm with the gun, and his assailant toppled over in a clumsy arc and was left wriggling on the pavement like a beetle on its back. The pistol went off in the course of the struggle, and an ear-piercing whine went up from an old Moorish lady, invoking the Prophet.

Bailey surveyed the damage. No serious injuries. His men had their guns on the Russians; but the Russians had their guns out, too. There were police whistles from beyond the Boulevard St-Michel, and klaxons that were getting louder.

'It's a standoff,' he announced to Hennessy. 'Let's get out of this quietly while we can.'

In the car, nursing a bruised elbow, he said to Hennessy, 'It's quite fantastic. I believe they intended to abduct me. In the heart of Paris.'

'It's happened here before,' Hennessy said drily. 'Quite often, in fact. I'm afraid they're simply not house-trained.'

Bailey briefed his Paris man on how to deal with Johnny and on what to say if the striped-pants brigade chose to make waves. Though the approach to Karl had ended in a fiasco, Bailey had the satisfaction of knowing that Johnny had proved his sincerity. The devil at his left ear had stopped clucking. He decided it would be best to leave on the early train, to avoid any embarrassing questions. His mind turned to Diana's hatboxes. Making room for them on the train might be even more difficult than communicating with Johnny in Moscow.

5

The Long March

Insurrection is a calculus with very indefinite magnitudes, the value of which may change every day.
— *Karl Marx*

1

When Johnny was ordered to return to Moscow alone, he obeyed, though he felt his heart was breaking. He said goodbye to Sigrid at the hotel, so as not to prolong the leave-taking.

'I'll go to General Berzin,' he told her. 'I'll get you assigned to work with me. You're not going to refuse, are you?'

'Don't be silly.'

The tears came then, and he felt her heart flutter as he held her to his chest, so he knew she wasn't lost to him completely.

'I'll be back before you know it,' he said with more conviction than he felt.

In Moscow, General Berzin kept him waiting for a week. When he was finally received at the Fourth Department, he requested to be assigned to Paris. Berzin shook his head. 'It's already been decided,' he said. 'We need you in China.'

'Then I request to be accompanied by my companion, Sigrid Eckhardt.'

Berzin made a note of the name. 'I won't promise anything,' he said curtly. 'And frankly, you'll be better off on your own. This isn't a job for a woman.'

Bitterly disappointed, Johnny listened as the chief of the Fourth Department outlined the urgency of his mission.

The Japanese were in Manchuria, threatening Russia's back door. A Communist insurrection in China would force the Japanese to turn their attentions south. If the Communists won, they would treble the population under Soviet rule, adding four hundred million Chinese to two hundred million Russians. Then the revolution would be unstoppable.

The Chinese rebels had made themselves a fortress up in the mountains of Kiangsi, where they were running things like the first Bolsheviks. They had shot the landlords, closed the temples, abolished marriage and private property. But their enemies were gathering strength. With money from the financiers and gang lords of Shanghai, Chiang Kai-shek was mustering troops and planes for an extermination campaign against the Kiangsi Soviet. Hitler had sent General von Seeckt – the man Johnny had once been ordered to kill – as the head of a German military mission that was advising Chiang's forces. The Communists were desperately in need of weapons, training, organisation – and a viable military plan.

'Your first stop is Shanghai,' Berzin told Johnny. 'That's the gun sight through which we take aim at China.' The brains of the insurrection, the Comintern advisers assigned to the Far Eastern Bureau, were in Shanghai. 'It'll be like old times for you,' Berzin added cheerfully. 'You'll be fighting von Seeckt, and you'll find a lot of your old German comrades in China. The German civil war, ass-deep in the rice paddies. By the way, a particular friend of yours is in charge. Emil Brandt.'

Johnny stared at him.

'It should be quite a reunion,' Berzin suggested.

'It certainly will.'

The mention of Emil revived his spirits a little.

Maybe I'll find a way to pay the bastard back, he told himself. I'll have that satisfaction, at least.

'I want you to be completely candid in your reports,' Berzin said, as if he had read Johnny's thoughts. 'Let me know whether I can believe what Shanghai is telling us.'

'Oh, yes,' Johnny said, 'I'll be candid.'

Wherever they send me, he thought, it's the same play. Only the backdrops change.

He wrote to Sigrid and found a carrier pigeon to take the letter to Paris. His messenger was a voluble Argentinian revolutionist. Like most of the Argentinians who turned up in Moscow, he had an Italian name; everyone called him Verdi because, with his shaggy mane of grey hair and his staring eyes, he looked like a distracted composer. He was en route to Rio and São Paulo. Brazil, he told Johnny with amazing confidence, would be the next Communist power. But like other Latin Americans Johnny had met in Moscow, Verdi spent so much energy winding himself up verbally that it was doubtful whether there would be any left when the time came for action. Johnny ventured to say as much. Instead of taking offence, the Argentine said, 'You don't understand the Latin temperament. It's hard for you wurst eaters, because you come from such a cold climate. You get men to risk their lives by imposing an iron discipline. What do you call it? Cadaver horseshit?'

'*Kadavergerhorsam*,' Johnny corrected him. 'The obedience of corpses.'

'In South America, to get men to risk their lives, to make a revolution, we have to talk a lot. That's how we attain that fever pitch of excitement in which nobody cares what it costs. In that way talk makes action inescapable.'

He makes revolution sound like a crime of passion, Johnny thought. He decided not to prolong the argument, in case something that was said should lose him his carrier pigeon.

His words to Sigrid were tender and full of longing. He asked her not to give up her painting.

It's the artist in her that will bring her back, he told himself. Her conscious mind might be able to rationalise the things she would see in her work for Max into neat, bloodless categories; the artist in her couldn't.

For more than a week he sat on the Trans-Siberian Express. He rarely stirred from his berth except to go to the lavatory or to visit the dining car, where the tables were embellished with dishevelled bouquets of paper flowers and dusty black bottles of wine that never seemed to be opened. The piles of birch logs along the rail bed were black at the core, silvered along the trunks, as if coated with frost.

Vladivostok looked like a city at war. There were submarines in the harbour and flotillas of radio-controlled motorboats, stuffed with explosives, that could be used like monster torpedoes. In the rail yards he saw freight trains with tanks and howitzers and more submarines lashed to their flatcars. He was subjected to repeated identity checks and practiced, on Soviet soil, the role he would play when he stepped off the steamer to Shanghai.

His papers identified him as one Arne Paulsen, born in Minneapolis, Minnesota. The experts at the OMS had assured him that the passport was real enough, the property of an American citizen of Finnish extraction who had decided to migrate to Russia for the sake of socialism and world peace. From Johnny's viewpoint, it had one flaw. He discovered it only on the voyage south from Vladivostok, when he started trying to forge Paulsen's signature. Try as he might, the man's handwriting was almost impossible to reproduce. It seemed as tangled and twisted as a blackberry patch. He did not give up. He needed to be able to toss off a plausible version of Paulsen's signature, because the OMS had arranged to wire ten thousand dollars in the American's name to the Hong Kong and Shanghai Bank. He was still scratching away when he saw the skyscrapers of Shanghai rise out of a flat horizon of yellow mud and flooded paddy fields.

He had been instructed to check into the Palace Hotel. Its Victorian façade looked homely amongst the white palaces of the Bund, overlooking the warships and sampans on the muddy river. He discovered a second defect in his passport when he made his leisurely progress, some hours later, along the Bund to the confident domed tower of the Hong Kong Bank. Brass lions guarded its portals, their features rubbed smooth by the hands of numberless Chinamen anxious to absorb the predator spirit they embodied.

A British clerk, impervious to the heat in his starched collar, dark coat and striped trousers, received Johnny with all proper decorum and begged him to take tea while he verified that the sum in question had indeed been transferred for Mr Paulsen's benefit. He was gone for less than five minutes and showed no emotion when Johnny informed him that he wanted to have the entire amount in cash.

'Perhaps I might just have your signature, sir. And your passport. I won't keep you a moment, sir.'

This time, the delay was appreciably longer, and Johnny thought he saw someone – an authoritative-looking individual with muttonchop whiskers and half-moon spectacles – peer at him from a discreet remove beyond a glass partition. He became uneasy as the minutes ticked by. He was half resolved to get up and leave when the clerk came back, polite and impersonal as before.

'I see that your passport has expired, sir.''

'Why, yes. I've been travelling quite a bit. But I had it renewed.' Johnny was prepared for this. The passport had indeed expired, but the Comintern's experts had doctored it. It bore the stamp of the American consul in Tokyo, extending it for one year.

'Would you mind very much if I asked why it has been extended for only twelve months, sir?'

Johnny could only guess at the point of this question. 'Well, I'll be going back to the States before it runs out again,' he said lamely.

'I see.'

The clerk rang a bell on his desk. Johnny tensed, but it was only the signal for a cashier to come in with the money, sorted into packets of crisp new bills.

He signed a receipt for the total, minus the bank's commission, and the clerk returned his passport.

'A pleasure to do business with you, sir.'

'Likewise.'

'Would you like an escort to your hotel, sir? I must warn you, the streets can be quite dangerous for a newcomer.'

'I'm sure I'll survive.'

2

Shanghai was the perfect setting for intrigue. It was many cities, not one, and in all of them allegiances could be bought and sold as cheaply as a man's life or the body of a nine-year-old girl. There was the colonial dream of number three, the Bund, home of the Shanghai Club, where the taipans gulped their *stengahs* at the longest bar in the world. There were the cabarets and stylish villas of Frenchtown. There were the glittering lights and the streetcars of the Nanking Road, with its famed emporiums – the Sun Sun, the Wing On – where the mistresses of Chinese generals and Green Gang mobsters came to shop. There was the stifling, noisy round of the cotton mills, the shoe factories, the silk filatures, where children were worked for fifteen hours a day, or until they dropped. There were the Americanised millionaires who raced around in their big cars with armed bodyguards on the running boards. There were twenty-five thousand women who hawked their bodies. There were followers of every flag in the world – nine flew over the International Settlement, guarded by its fierce, bearded Sikhs – and plenty willing to sell themselves to any or all.

The Communists, though, were not so easily bought. That made them different from the other political factions and elicited grudging admiration from Hugh McIvor of the municipal police. Inspector McIvor, a young man prematurely aged by the Orient – and, no doubt, by the quantities of gin and quinine water he infused as a prophylactic against malaria and misanthropy – was something of a specialist on Communism.

McIvor had no fixed opinions about Chinese politics. One warlord looked much like another. Only their prices varied. His job was to keep Shanghai open to European commerce. The Communists, who appealed to the misery of the slums and to popular hatred of the 'foreign devils', were therefore his main opponents.

McIvor's Chinese detectives kept watch on a list of houses and flats whose tenants were thought to be associated with the Communist International. More than a few of these addresses belonged to Americans. There was that foul-mouthed woman writer on the Avenue Dubail in Frenchtown, stocky as a lumberjack, who looked as if she cut her hair with a lawn mower. She had spent time in Russia and seemed to be the first port of call for every transient radical. McIvor suspected her of running a message centre for the Russians, but her passport was genuine and he could not have her deported without further evidence. One of her visitors was a fellow from Seattle who called himself Walsh and had no visible means of employment. McIvor had heard rumours that Walsh was high up in the Communist Party USA. Perhaps they imagined in Moscow that Americans had some special affinity with the Chinese – or that possession of a US passport conveyed some kind of immunity.

McIvor was intrigued by what he had learned about another American recently arrived in the settlement. He called himself Arne Paulsen and had collected a large sum in cash from the Hong Kong Bank. There was an oddity in his passport, which one of McIvor's contacts at the bank had been shrewd enough to spot. The passport had expired, and Paulsen had it renewed at the American Consulate in Tokyo. It was not unusual for an American consulate to extend an out-of-date passport with a rubber stamp, to save its bearer the delay of waiting in a foreign city for delivery of a new travel document. But the standard extension was for two years, not one. McIvor had checked this with the American consulate in Shanghai. Furthermore – he had since received word – though the passport number matched the records, the American consul in Tokyo had never heard of a man called Arne Paulsen.

McIvor ordered two of his Chinese detectives to maintain close surveillance. The results, though disappointing, confirmed his suspicions.

The man calling himself Paulsen was tailed to the Avenue Dubail, where he paused outside the woman writer's apartment building but did not go in. The detectives lost him when he paid a visit to a small shipping agency off the Bund. They watched for him outside, but he did not re-emerge. McIvor assumed that he must have found his way out through the partners' entrance and warned his men to be more alert. Paulsen did not return to his hotel that night. One of McIvor's men spotted him in the street, quite by chance, two days later. He was followed to a Szechuan restaurant on the Nanking Road, where he took lunch but was not seen to speak to anyone except the waiter. In the afternoon, the suspect was observed loitering on the Bubbling Well Road near the Buddhist Temple.

When he entered the temple, the policemen followed, determined not to be cheated a second time. But to their consternation, they found their quarry was gone. A white man, a stranger to Shanghai, had become as invisible as a native pickpocket.

This satisfied McIvor that the man was a professional and knew his job. He decided to visit the hotel in person and elicited the fact that the American had paid for a week in advance. The assistant manager agreed to show McIvor the room. All he found was a forlorn suit on a hanger and a pile of laundry waiting for the maid. No personal papers, and the money from the bank had gone.

He assured the assistant manager that there was no cause for alarm, but he wished to be informed as soon as Mr Arne Paulsen returned. He had no confidence that this event would take place.

The Chinese girl who pressed up against Johnny in the temple said, 'Did you see the five T'ang horses?'

'No,' he responded without looking at her. 'There were two, not five.' Then, quickly, 'I'm being followed.'

'Come with me now, please.'

Within two minutes he was running behind her through a warren of narrow streets, crouched low to escape the awnings of the street peddlers. Two minutes more and he was lying in the back of a pushcart under coarse hessian sacking and, above it, a load of hot peppers, holding his nose to avoid sneezing. Within two hours he was in the hold of a junk, heading lazily south from the frantic docks of Hongchew towards the southern port of Swiatow.

From Swiatow, he travelled west by riverboat, pony and finally on foot, up stony mountain trails no wider than a man's body, into liberated China: the Soviet Republic of Kiangsi.

3

Johnny had been in south China for nearly five months when C asked Colin Bailey to lunch at White's. Bailey kept the appointment with some misgivings. In his experience, C invited his subordinates onto private territory when he wanted to mount a sudden flank attack. He wondered whether the chief wanted to pursue that awkward business in Brussels, where a member of the service had been caught with his fingers in the till, filching some of the visa money collected from Jews en route to Palestine.

They drank gin and french at the bar, where the appearance of the Prince of Wales caused not the slightest commotion. C made a point of introducing Bailey.

'Perfectly decent chap,' C remarked after the Prince had moved on. 'Rather underrated. It's a pity about that American woman.'

'A bit soft on the Germans,' Bailey ventured to suggest. C affected not to hear.

He delayed his attack until port and cigars had been served in the smoking room.

'You know Adam de Salis is in town,' C suddenly remarked. 'He asked to see Johnny's file. Since Johnny was, in a manner of speaking, his discovery, I couldn't actually refuse, could I?'

'Of course not,' Bailey said automatically, trying to conceal his annoyance that de Salis had been poaching on his territory.

'Adam thought that some of this China stuff smells a bit high.'

'Oh, really? What precisely does he object to?'

Johnny's reports from Manchuria had been spotty, and there had been a lapse in communications when he was up in the mountains in Kiangsi. But since he had come back to Shanghai and settled into a flat on the Avenue Molière, in Frenchtown, his reports had been regular and, to Bailey, a source of mounting fascination.

Johnny described a powerful revolutionary movement that was being led to certain destruction by its foreign controllers. The Communists had scored their biggest military successes by hit-and-run tactics, striking the enemy where he was weakest, melting away whenever they were outnumbered, giving up territory to save lives. Now, under the strategy laid down by Emil Brandt, they were painting themselves into a corner.

Emil – who had never set eyes on the province of Kiangsi – had convinced himself that the rebels' mountain fortress was impregnable. Under the gun and the lash, forced labour battalions were sweating to throw up earthen walls to make it stronger still. In his own reports to Moscow, Emil boasted that the Red Army mustered more than half a million men and could withstand any force the government hurled against it. According to Johnny, there were only half that number, and many of them were armed with sticks and knives. True, the forests of Kiangsi, laced with narrow paths where soldiers could advance only in single file, would be costly to storm in a frontal attack. But the defenders were vulnerable to a protracted siege. Their food supplies were low. All their salt had to be supplied from the outside. If they were squeezed for long enough, their own followers would rise up against them.

Von Seeckt understood this. Steadily, stealthily, he was moving on Kiangsi. His weapon was a garrotte. Johnny had seen the chain of concrete blockhouses and tidy forts, joined up by new military roads and bristling coils of barbed wire, that von Seeckt was building all around the Communist base area. Week by week, the lines were being tightened. Week by week, it was harder to smuggle food and weapons through. In Kiangsi they began to feel the bite of the wire against their throats.

The Comintern advisers who had been there had given Emil the same advice: break out of the trap; open escape routes; give up as much land as necessary, but save the Red Army. Some argued that in order to survive the Communists must be ready to seal an alliance with anyone who was ready to fight the Nanking government. Overnight, a powerful ally became available. Its appearance was almost miraculous, a gift of the gods. In the province of Fukien, next door to the soviet republic, the Nineteenth Route Army raised the standard of revolt. Its leaders were nationalists, not Communists, but they were opposed to the landowners, the warlords and the Japanese. Join forces with them, some of the Communists urged. Then we can break out of von Seeckt's ring of steel and open a road to the sea. The Russians will send guns to us from Vladivostok.

Emil was deaf to all these entreaties. The soviet republic is secure, he insisted. The rebels in Fukien are bourgeois opportunists. Those in our camp who promote their cause are Trotskyite adventurers. Until we have overthrown the chiefs of the Nineteenth Route Army and replaced them with Communists, we can have nothing to do with them. Emil had ordered an American journalist on his payroll – whose Shanghai-based publication, *China Forum*, was financed with secret Comintern funds – to write an article quoting fictitious interviews with rebel leaders in Fukien province to make these points. He had later denounced the same journalist as a Trotskyite, forcing him to flee from Shanghai.

So, while Emil hunted Trotskyite adventurers, the military rebels in Fukien were left to face the onslaught of Generalissimo Chiang's brand-new tanks and warplanes. Von Seeckt's influence had begun to tell. For once the government soldiers did not turn and flee at the sound of battle. The Fukien rebels were crushed, and the Communists were left in utter isolation to face the next extermination campaign. The generalissimo bragged that he had marshalled nine hundred thousand men to wipe them off the map of China.

In Johnny's account, Emil Brandt had set himself up as absolute dictator of the Communist party in China. He enforced his authority with bullying and threats of denunciation to Moscow. At the same time he lived in abject terror of incurring Stalin's disfavour. His mind moved in a parallel reality. By repeating and inflating his fabrications over and over, he had convinced himself that they were truer than the evidence of his own eyes.

Bailey knew the depth of Johnny's hatred and contempt for Emil Brandt and made allowances for this in assessing his material. Even so, he found the head of the Far Eastern Bureau an intriguing psychological study. A man addicted to his own illusions. What would become of him when his illusions – as Johnny predicted with such assurance – exploded in his face?

'De Salis's point,' the chief of the Secret Service was saying, 'is that Johnny's reports from Shanghai are too good to be true. He's telling us that without anyone's help the Communists are going to blow themselves up. Wouldn't you agree that's the gist of it?'

'More or less,' Bailey concurred. 'He says the Kiangsi soviet can't hold out for more than six months.'

'Which is, of course, what we would wish to hear.'

'I'm not sure I follow.'

'De Salis believes it possible that Johnny has been turned, and that these reports from China are part of a deception plan.'

'With what motive?'

'To keep us smug and inert while the Communists make another grab for Shanghai. It's the richest prize in the East. There's more silver in the Shanghai banks than anywhere else on earth.'

'I don't see it,' Bailey objected. 'An insurrection in Shanghai would be doomed unless they got help from outside. There's no help in sight.'

C reflected on this before asking, 'Do we have any independent confirmation of what Johnny is telling us?'

'Well, Killen thinks he's on the right track.'

Killen was their man in Shanghai. Only recently arrived

in China, he had a job as a griffin – a junior assistant – at the offices of the British Cigarette Company.

'Killen hasn't had much experience though, has he?' C observed. 'Against his opinion, we have to weigh the wireless intercepts.'

Recently deciphered traffic had included a message from Emil to Moscow, restating his confident prospectus for the Communists in south China. His figures, of course, had been wildly at variance with Johnny's.

'I suppose it boils down to whether we trust our man or not,' Bailey remarked. 'For my money, he's proved himself several times over.'

'Adam suggested we put it to the test.'

De Salis believes . . . Adam suggested . . . one of C's more irritating habits was to attribute his own doubts to a third party. It saved him from having to go into the firing line before he had made up his mind.

'May I ask in what way?'

'By using Johnny to stop some of the Red leaders in Shanghai. Emil Brandt, for one. The fellow who poses as a music teacher. And that other military expert, what's-his-name –'

'Otto Braun.'

'Just so. I understand we've already had an inquiry from the Shanghai police.'

A Scot called McIvor, a police inspector, had indeed paid a call on James Killen. It seemed his detectives had followed Johnny to Killen's home – evidence of a lapse of security on the part of both the Russians and Bailey's own service.

'I expect the locals are jittery,' C went on. 'The government didn't do much last time the city was under attack. If we break the back of this conspiracy now, we can do them and ourselves a favour.'

'I don't agree,' Bailey said mildly.

'Let me be sure I understand you. You're worried that Johnny will be blown. Is that it?'

'He might be blown. But there is something else to consider.'

'Well?'

'If Johnny's reports are reliable, the last man in Shanghai we would wish to see behind bars is Emil Brandt. He'll wreck the whole Communist enterprise in China without any assistance from us. The policy called for is masterly inertia.'

'Are you serious, Colin?'

'Yes. But I admit the situation does have its humorous side.'

When C failed to respond immediately, Bailey knew he had won his argument. His approach was not quite as passive as he had indicated to his chief. He had culled from Johnny's reports the names of the most effective Communist organisers. Feeding Emil's – and the Russians' – paranoia about Trotsky's influence, Bailey had arranged to have Trotskyite materials mailed to some of them anonymously. He had resolved to deliver the Chinamen on the list to the police when the appropriate occasion presented itself. They included the man code-named 'Slavein', who was the main link between the Far Eastern Bureau and the Chinese party. But for the moment, as he had advised Killen in Shanghai, they must be content to watch and wait.

4

For Johnny, living in the Shanghai underground under a new identity, waiting was impossible. He found relief in action, as always, in flouting the rules of all his employers by involving himself personally in risky operations. He staged holdups, smuggled guns off a freighter on the Whangpoo river under the noses of the police, planted explosives in a car belonging to the Blue Shirts, Chiang's dreaded secret police. The younger Chinese Communists he helped to train – the ones who had a vocation for death – admired him for it.

He, in turn, admired them. They gave freely of themselves, asking nothing in return, with a generosity of spirit that was totally alien to the carping, conspiring party bigwigs in Berlin and Moscow. These young Chinese reminded

Johnny of his own youth, and of Heinz – and then of the men who had murdered him. He had a mournful suspicion that his Chinese commandos would end the same way. He did not feel he was betraying them when he smuggled his reports to Killen, Bailey's man in Shanghai. It was the men in charge of the Chinese revolt who were the betrayers: carping graduates of the Lenin School, less Chinese than Russian; lost souls like Emil Brandt, who toadied to Moscow to cover up his terror and lack of conviction.

Johnny had toyed with the idea of shooting Emil one night, when rumours of a police raid had sent the members of the Far Eastern bureau scuttling out of a meeting and he found himself alone with Brandt on a blacked-out street, silent except for the distant thunder of an angry crowd and the howl of police klaxons. What saved Emil then, and helped to sustain Johnny now, was his realisation that Brandt was doing the job himself. All Emil's grovelling to Stalin would not save him, surely, when his mistakes in China resulted in another rout. Johnny was scrupulous in relating the full magnitude of those mistakes in his private correspondence with General Berzin.

When he needed women, they were never far. Within Emil's organisation, as in Moscow in the old days, it was as natural to go to bed with any consenting partner as to go to the bathroom. It was accepted, too, that for people who lived with the daily prospect of violent death, the urge was stronger than in others. It was not necessary to confine the appetite to party members. In the city of Shanghai, one house in twelve was a bordello. The women were of every age, shape, colour and nationality. Some of them, inevitably, were 'swallows' in the service of the party, or the police.

Now Johnny was on his back in a room above the Cockatoo Club, a cabaret on the Avenue Joffre, hands folded behind his head, eyes closed, a cigarette dangling from his lower lip. The girl who was working to arouse him with her lips and fingers was patient and skillful. May had the wide cheekbones and blue eyes of her Russian father, the simian grace of her Japanese mother. He had been with her before. He liked her because she was beautiful and clever and never shammed pleasure she did not experience. At least not with him. She had confessed to him that she was utterly indifferent to what took place on her bed.

He found her a useful source because of her other lovers. One of them was a banker who was sending millions abroad in Shanghai silver dollars that could be resold for ten or twenty per cent more than their face value in London or New York because the American treasury had decided it needed to hoard silver as well as gold. May had promised to find out what ship would carry the next consignment. One act of piracy could pay for a hundred machine guns, five thousand rifles. But the bags of silver coins would be heavy. And he would need a friendly captain.

'Have you been drinking?' May asked.

'Not enough. Let's have some cognac.'

'As you like.' The boy was waiting outside the door. She gave him his instructions and said, 'You're sad tonight. Are you thinking about your wife?'

'No.' The ash spilled from his cigarette. May brushed it off his bare chest and kissed his nipples, the way he might have kissed hers. He began to feel mildly aroused. But he said, 'Let's talk. Who else have you been seeing?'

'You'll be jealous.'

'On the contrary. You know it excites me.'

'Very well. But give me a cigarette.' He helped her light it, and she went on, 'I saw Tu Yu-seng. Do you believe me?'

'Of course. He's your protector, isn't he?'

Tu Yu-seng – Big-Eared Tu, they called him, because his ears stuck out like bat's wings – was the boss of the Green Gang. It was said that nobody could run a bar or a cabaret or a gambling den in Frenchtown without paying him. It was also said that he controlled the detective section of the police in the French Concession. The taipans sipping whisky at the Long Bar or tea at the Astor House might never admit his existence, but they, too, paid their dues. Nor did Tu's influence end there. The generalissimo, Chiang Kai-shek himself, had taken the vows of the Greens as a young man – terrifying vows that bound a man to give his life to the society, if demanded, and guaranteed that the society, in exchange, would always protect him. The Greens had carried out their part of the bargain in 1927, when their gunmen and axemen went through the streets killing Communists. The generalissimo would be paying his dues to the end of his days.

May held her cigarette between thumb and forefinger, like a Russian.

'Where did you see him? Here?'

'I went to his house.'

'What's it like?'

'Like an emperor's palace. There were mechanical birds, singing in a tree with gold and silver leaves.'

'I don't care about the birds. Why did he send for you?'

'You don't think I have talent?'

She lay back with her legs apart and blew smoke at him.

'Of course.'

'There was a party,' she explained. 'There were generals from Nanking, even the finance minister. A German, too.'

'A German? What German?'

'An officer from the front. I don't remember the name.'

'Von Seeckt?' He screwed an imaginary monocle into his face. 'A man in his fifties? Very arrogant, very Prussian?'

'All of that, but not in his fifties. His name was similar, though.'

Johnny thought hard. He had made a personal hobby out of studying the members of the German military mission that was planning the destruction of the Reds in Kiangsi. He had drawn up a plan to assassinate von Seeckt. It had been approved. But he had been forbidden to take part himself, and one of the Chinese involved had lost his nerve at the last moment and thrown his grenades too soon, missing the general's car and turning a dozen nameless civilians into chopped meat.

He had not reported the episode to James Killen, his well-intentioned but rather insular British contact. One day, given the chance, he might mention it to Colin Bailey. He thought Bailey would understand. Von Seeckt and Emil Brandt were two sides of a German evil. But one of them was going to self-destruct. It was best to focus his hatred, for now, on the one that might not.

He mentally rehearsed the names of other members of the German advisory team, which Hitler had recently doubled in size: Falkenhausen, Zorn . . .

'Steinitz,' he suggested. 'Colonel Martin Steinitz. Is that the one?'

'It might be –' May yawned. 'Why are you so interested? You ask too many questions. What are you? A policeman?'

'I don't pay you to ask questions. And I pay you well enough, don't I?'.

'Not as well as Tu.'

'Did you sleep with him?'

She crossed her legs and hugged herself as if she felt a chill. 'Not him. One of his lieutenants. He carries the marks of the smallpox – everywhere.'

'Who went with Steinitz?'

'Some girl – a Russian, I think. You know what they are. The latest fashions, furs, and not two bits of *cash* to scrape together. She looked like a model from Chanel. But hard, very hard. I think your Colonel Steinitz likes that. He really fell for her.'

'What is her name?'

'They called her Lena. I never saw her before.'

'But you can find out, can't you?' He took a handful of Mexican silver dollars – still the preferred currency in Shanghai – and shaped them into a neat stack on the bedside table.

The boy came with a bottle of Martell. Johnny paid him off, too.

'Is that all you want?' May asked, after draining her glass. She straddled him, letting her breasts swing over his face.

'No,' he said, closing his eyes again. He was no longer in Shanghai. He was with Sigrid, in a room in Paris where the afternoon light spilled through the shutters and dropped to the floor like ripe sheaves of wheat.

May loved to be taken out. That satisfied her that she moved in a different dimension from the taxi dancers downstairs at the Cockatoo Club or the varnished Chinese whores who paraded two abreast down the Nanking Road, with their amahs at their heels. Like all the denizens of Shanghai, she also loved to gamble. So Johnny took her to the Canidrome. The greyhound she picked in the third race was so heavily drugged that it collapsed on all fours in the home straight. May was outraged. He consoled her with champagne, but she was still fuming when he broached the reason for their meeting.

'What did you find out about Lena?'

'She's too skinny for you,' May snickered.

'Did you find out where she lives?' Johnny persisted.

'I can go one better. Colonel Steinitz found out, too.'

'You mean he visits her?'

'I gather he is infatuated.'

'Give me the woman's address.'

May told him, and he made a mental note. The apartment was on the wrong side of Soochow Creek. He knew the area slightly. Some affluent Chinese lived there, but no Europeans, except for a few White Russians.

'We could go to a dinner dance,' May suggested. 'We could go to the Cathay.'

The woman would have made the perfect wife for one of the English taipans, Johnny thought. Indifferent to sex but in love with appearances. The Cathay produced one of the starchier evening entertainments on offer in the settlement. Members of May's profession got in as long as they were suitably attired and not obviously oriental.

'Not tonight,' he said.

'Are you going to see Lena?'

'Perhaps. I don't know.'

'Why do you care so much about this German officer?' May looked angry. 'I bet I know. I bet you're a Communist.'

'What do you have against Communists?'

'They pretend that sex doesn't have a price.'

'If I were a Communist, would you betray me?'

'It would depend on what I was paid.'

Johnny watched the sweat gleam on the lean, dark back of his rickshaw driver. The man's leathery feet in their straw sandals drummed noiselessly on the pavement. The night smelled of camphor and oil. On sampans pushed nose to tail on the muddy bank of Soochow Creek, families were eating and swapping tales, their laundry hung out on oars that made some of the boats look like wounded flying fish.

They were still in the settlement, but they had left the wide boulevards of the European city. There was no sign of the shells and bombs that had gutted whole streets in Hongkew only two years before, when the Japanese had landed troops at Shanghai. The singsong houses and restaurants, the pawnbrokers and silver shops had sprung back, rank and prolific as tropical weeds. A brass band thumped out a tune from an upstairs window above a department store, primitive but effective advertising. The people in the street were a sea of blue.

He touched the shoulder of the rickshaw puller with the toe of his shoe.

'*Man, man!*'

He dismounted at the end of Lena's street. There was a herbalist's shop near the corner with ginseng and dried frogs on display in the window. There was also a black car blocking half the narrow street. Two Chinese toughs loitered on the driver's side, smoking cheap cigars. Opposite was a dress shop with a copy of a Molyneux evening gown in the window. On the second floor, Lena's apartment.

Johnny had come with no fixed plan except to watch and to open his lungs. The hot season was on its way; in the night the humid exhalations of the mud flats rose up through the cement and tar.

Lena and her colonel interested him. He had heard something from Otto Braun about this Steinitz. He was a passionate Hitlerite, according to Braun, but also a soldier who knew his business. He had helped to draw up the plans for Chiang's extermination campaign. If he was dallying in Shanghai for reasons other than personal pleasure, it was no doubt to arrange the delivery of a new shipload of arms or to squeeze more money out of the Chinese bankers who paid for the generalissimo's campaigns.

Steinitz was a promising target. If the girl could be bought — or persuaded — they could find out the colonel's secrets through her.

The idea was seductive. It might even be a way to strike at two enemies at once and drive the last nail into Emil's coffin. Moscow trusted conspiracy more than common sense. Anyone with his eyes open could see that the Communists in the south were lost unless they changed their strategy. Otto Braun could see it; he had actually asked the centre to recall Emil to Moscow on the grounds that his policy was suicidal. Braun had the Kiangsi leaders on his side, including the big, flat-faced peasant philosopher, Mao Tse-tung. But the Central Committee was in Shanghai, and it was run by recent graduates of the Lenin School whose dogmatism made Torquemada look like a freethinker. They would back Emil as long as Moscow did. In the fights that broke out between Emil and Braun, Johnny tried to avoid taking sides. When forced to state his position, he deferred to Emil. But his secret reports to Starik were a damning cumulative indictment. Firsthand evidence, through Steinitz, of the plan to crush the Kiangsi soviet — the plan Emil had done everything to advance — would surely settle Emil's hash when the accounts were drawn up in Moscow.

Failing that, Johnny thought he would quite enjoy putting a bullet into Colonel Steinitz.

He went into the corner pawnshop. There seemed to be a great many samurai swords. He went out the door on the other side, leading into a street the Chinese called Iron Road. He saw it was possible, by climbing over fire escapes and pocket gardens, to get to the back of Lena's building.

He retraced his steps and saw Steinitz march briskly towards his car. He had a handsome, haughty face, marred by the jagged white seam of an old scar that must have been stitched up in haste. He was carrying a leather satchel.

Johnny waited for several minutes after the car moved off. Then he went through the entrance next to the dress shop. On his left, there was an open door: Chinese in black pyjamas playing mah-jongg. They watched him pull back the metal grille and step into the lift, but nobody questioned a European.

He tapped on Lena's door.

'Who's there?' The girl called out in English.

'I have a message from Colonel Steinitz,' he responded in German.

For what seemed like a long time there was no response. He wondered if she was inspecting him through a concealed peephole. He pressed his ear up against the door. He could hear Mozart on a scratchy recording.

He knocked again and was rewarded with the scrape of metal as she released the bolts inside the door.

But she didn't open it. She merely called out, 'Come in.'

Even as he turned the handle, he knew it was a trap. The room was a black hole. In the first instants he could see nothing. He only sensed her movements as she slipped behind him, too late to fling himself out of range. The touch of the silk rope against his throat was exquisitely smooth and cool. But he clawed and grabbed at her hands, trying to prise them loose. There was amazing strength in the woman's arms. The garrotte is not a weapon for women – at least, not for many. The room was a pattern of purplish blotches in front of his eyes when he managed to grab a fistful of hair and wrench her head over to one side. Instantly, the vice around his windpipe was relaxed. He could hear the light rhythm of her panting as she darted across the room.

He made a leap at her, caught hold of a leg and went crashing on top of her. Glass and porcelain exploded across the floor. She wrestled and bit. She broke something over his head – a bottle or a vase – and went gouging for his eyes, two fingers extended like the talons of a bird of prey.

'You're a fighter. I have to give you that,' he said when he finally had her pinioned, her arms twisted up behind her back.

He heard a sharp intake of breath. Perhaps he was holding her too tight. But he had no intention of starting another round.

He found a light switch. She was wearing black silk pyjamas. Her skin glowed against them like ivory. Her eyes were pale and bright, ice-blue. One of them would be very black by morning.

'Good God.' He released her arms. He was too shocked for a moment to say anything more. Finally he said, 'Is this how you receive all your former lovers?'

'Only the ones who deserve it,' Helene replied, and laughed till her ribs hurt.

In the little ways, at least, Helene was the same. After sex, or after a fight, she demanded to eat. Johnny took her to a place where Europeans rarely went. The restaurant advertised its cuisine with a newly fried chicken, varnished to a bright vermilion and suspended above the door. Most of the Chinese customers ate standing up at a counter, but there were a few tables at the back.

'I didn't know you at the door. But I knew you weren't from Steinitz,' Helene explained, pausing in her demolition of a plate of fried dumplings.

'What did you think I was?'

'Police. Or Gestapo.'

'Gestapo? Here? But why?'

Her chopsticks moved from the dumplings to a bowl of saffron-coloured rice.

'Because Steinitz is one of us.' She took a mouthful and said, 'We have been very careful. He is closely watched. The Greens have people everywhere. But who can object to a kept woman? It's only human, isn't it? Besides, they think I'm a White Russian. Who else would live in this part of Hongkew? And they saw Steinitz meet me in the house of the grand vizier, no less. You know that's what he likes to be called, don't you? Big-Eared Tu.' She wiped her mouth. 'The man is disgusting. But he truly is the grand vizier of Shanghai.'

'How did you manage the introductions?'

'I met Steinitz before, of course. In Berlin. But none of his people know that. They saw him falling in love with me in Tu's house. What do you think of that?'

'Not bad. How did you get invited?'

'An acquaintance. One of those gentleman who likes Chekiang silk and dainty feet and doesn't care where he finds his money.'

Johnny realised that a powerful Chinese, a member of the Green Gang, perhaps even a relative of Big-Eared Tu, had been recruited by Helene's network.

'It's dangerous work,' Johnny observed. In Shanghai, by his observations, a bribe worked only until a bigger bribe was available.

'More dangerous since you decided to drop in on me,' she countered. 'You stumbled in like a pathetic amateur. You could have got all our heads cut off.'

'Believe me, I had no idea of the relationship. I thought it was a stupid affair of a bar girl, someone who could be bought. Nobody warned me about Steinitz. They didn't even tell me you were in Shanghai.'

'Emil Brandt isn't the only game in town,' Helene sniffed. 'And it's just as well.'

He got into the habit of visiting Helene when Steinitz was out of Shanghai, in Nanking or at the front. They drank together and talked about the old days, and about Sigrid.

'Poor Johnny,' Helene said to him. 'Don't say I didn't warn you. It was the same when Sigi and I were kids. Everybody wanted to give her the treats, she looked so sweet and innocent. Besides which, she was the littlest one. Whenever we had a fight, I'd get belted for it. I was the tomboy, the bad girl, the one who was always running away from home. But guess who won most of the fights? She did.'

For Johnny, talk about Sigrid, however banal, was better than nothing. He had received only a few short letters from her, not much better than postcards. One was postmarked Brussels, another Copenhagen. She made no reference to the long letters he had written her, painting word pictures of the city that he thought might please her. He wondered if she had even received them.

If there had ever been jealousy or hostility between him and Helene, it had been leached away by the passage of time. Sitting with her, completely at his ease, he thought at times they were almost like an old married couple. But there remained an unbridgeable gap defined by professional caution. They could talk about Heinz and laugh at the games the three of them had once played together, and Johnny could express his contempt for Emil for denouncing Heinz to the party. This much was common ground. But Johnny did not dare to go further. He could not attack Max, not to a woman who, by all appearances, remained one of Max's most devoted protégées. He must let nothing slip that would tell her what he had become, nothing to hint at the driving purpose that had supplanted his lost faith in the party: the determination to put a bomb under the little Stalins, and the big one in Moscow too, with the help of British Intelligence.

On her side, too, Helene was reticent. Johnny became certain that they shared a common contact in the Shanghai underground, the shadowy Latvian who posed as a music teacher and represented the OMS. This was the man to whom Johnny delivered his money from the Hong Kong Bank. But Helene never mentioned him. And though she talked about Steinitz's courage and conditions of life at the front, she did not share his reports. Once, though, she asked him to deliver a coded message to the radio man who operated from a room above a sewing shop on Sad Donkey Road. The text was incomprehensible to him, but he made a copy and passed it on to Colin Bailey's man.

Helene was available; she made that plain enough. She changed her clothes in front of him in a matter-of-fact way that said, take it or leave it. He left it. They carried too much baggage.

He slept with May when the mood took him but stopped frequenting the Cockatoo Club. He arranged to meet her at her own studio, a few blocks from the Quai. May liked the new arrangement, because it meant she could pocket the money she would normally have to pay out to the pimps. She forgot that in Frenchtown the pimps were scrupulous about collecting their dues.

On a night of fireworks and whirling dragons – a festival

for red-faced Kuan Ti, god of war and peace – Johnny went to the apartment near the quai. The left pocket of his jacket sagged with silver dollars, the bonus he intended to give May. With her information, he had arranged the hijacking of a cargo of silver bound for San Francisco and the American commodity markets.

The success of this operation was not the only reason for his high spirits. Emil and his dour Polish wife had finally been recalled to Moscow. This followed a blazing session at the Far Eastern bureau at which Emil was outvoted seven to two and Otto Braun came close to calling him a traitor. The Kiangsi soviet was finished. The Red Army had suffered a bloody defeat. The population under Communist control had shrunk to one third the original number. Cut off from the outside world, denied even salt, the peasants were turning against their commissars. All of Emil's creative bookkeeping could no longer disguise the real state of affairs. Without salt the Red Republic of Kiangsi would go under. The remnants of Mao's guerrilla army would have to flee for their lives or be ground under the treads of the generalissimo's tanks. Though the official version had it that Emil was returning to help organise the next world congress of the Communist International, Johnny was certain that in Moscow he would be presented with the bill for one of Moscow's most costly failures. Best of all, he had confirmation that his own departure from China was imminent. Emil had suggested that they leave on the same boat. The poor dreamer apparently saw Johnny as a witness for the defence.

He climbed to May's landing and rapped twice on the door. There was no answer. He tried his key but found that the door was already unlocked. When he threw it open, he was assailed by a stench so overpowering that he took a step backward involuntarily. The ceiling light was on. The bulb was weak, but it showed him more than he wanted to see. May was sprawled on the bed, the knuckles of her left hand grazing the floor. From her nostrils and mouth, thick rivulets of slime oozed down, fouling the bright satin of her dress. It might have been vomit, but the smell was a compound of shit and gasoline. He knew what it meant. In China a favourite method of interrogation was to force a mixture of petrol and excrement through a hose into the suspect's nostrils, until his belly swelled up. The next step was to jump on the victim's stomach so the filth erupted from his nose and face. He was unlikely to hold much back after that – if he could still talk.

May had nothing to add to whatever she had told her questioners. From her navel to her vagina, her stomach had been laid open. The butchery was precise: the gash was deep but almost perfectly straight. It must have been made in one or two strokes from an axe or a cleaver. The flies had begun their work. Her spilled intestines were black with them.

May was wearing red, the colour that brought good luck.

Johnny supported himself against the door frame, trying not to gag. He could not help himself. The waves of nausea reached his gorge, and he spat bile.

People were moving about on the floor above. He wiped his mouth clean and half ran, half fell down the steps into the cascading lights of the festival.

He tried to stop the singing terror behind his eyes, to force his thoughts into order. An ordinary pimp, angry that May was making money on the side, would have contented himself with giving her a beating and threatening to cut her face; no pimp lightly discarded a source of income. Interrogation with liquid shit was a favourite method of the generalissimo's secret police. Murder with an axe was a specialty of the Greens. They worked hand in glove anyway. Perhaps they had connected May to the theft of the silver consignment. What had she told them under torture? Were they out looking for him?

The singing in his head grew louder, drowning out the fireworks and the bands. May knew Helene's address, and that he had gone to see her.

The mounted Sikhs along the Bund cradled their short carbines, indifferent to all the Chinese exuberance. They showed mild interest in the white man who was hurrying along on foot, deaf to the entreaties of the rickshaw drivers.

Privileged servants of the Raj – whose attitudes were faithfully mirrored in the Shanghai Municipal Council – the Sikhs had an exquisite sense of protocol. Only orientals and Russians walked in Shanghai, and weren't the Russians half-Asiatic anyway?

6

Helene wasn't at home. He jimmied the lock and found that her flat had been ransacked. In the bedroom, even the pillow and the mattress had been ripped open, leaving duck feathers all over the floor.

He decided to go to the radio man in the huddled quarter of Chapai, outside the settlement. But the huge wrought-iron gates of the settlement were closed, and the police were checking identity papers. It was a bad omen. On the night of his festival, Kuan Li, the spirit of a mighty general of the Three Kingdoms, had decreed war.

Johnny took a rickshaw to the Metropole and telephoned James Killen.

'I was starting to worry about you,' the Englishman said. 'I'm afraid the balloon's gone up.'

'What balloon?' Johnny's English was serviceable but far from idiomatic.

'The natives are restless.' Killen sounded much too relaxed. Too many whiskys at the Shanghai Club? 'The Greens found out one of their people has been doing favours for your lot. Or he decided to sell you out. Things are a bit muddled, I'm afraid.'

'Who are you talking about?'

'The name is Tu Hsiao-lin, or some noise like that. They call him Little Tu, because he's related to the other one, or One-Leg Tu, because he's got a gimpy leg. The family sounds like a collection of missing parts, what? The fellow seems to know rather a lot. The police are trying to take things in hand, but the Greens have a way of settling their own affairs.'

So Johnny's instinct had been right. Helene's contact in

the Green Gang had sold her out. And God knew who else. He thought of May, and the singing in his ears deadened him to Killen's languid voice on the end of the line.

'Hello? Are you there?'

'You'd better make yourself scarce. You can come here if you like.'

'No. I'll call you later.'

He went to Frenchtown, to the Latvian with a little card on his door that announced that he was a graduate of the Paris Conservatoire and offered lessons in violin. There were sentries in the street – a boy with a shoebox, a rickshaw-puller who wasn't begging for customers. Johnny made a sign to them as he turned to enter the building, and they signalled 'all clear'.

The Latvian received him with an outsize revolver in open view on top of his piano. The man was skin and bone; his round Polish wife carried enough weight for both of them. She was busy packing.

'As you see, we're leaving tonight,' the Latvian announced. 'The Greens are running amok with the right addresses. They have killed a hundred Chinese, maybe more. That's not the worst of it. The municipal police have got Slavein.'

Johnny was stunned by this new information.

Jui Tsien-pa, code-named 'Slavein', was the top Chinese Communist organiser in Shanghai and the vital link between the Comintern team and the local networks. He was in a position to identify every member of Emil's group – except, perhaps, for the music teacher.

The music teacher continued: 'There is a ship in the harbour, out beyond Hongkew. The *Chungking*. The captain and the crew are party members. It is on charter to Sovexport. It will sail for Vladivostok at first light, or whenever we say. Emil and his wife will be on it. So will we.' He glanced at his wife. 'You knew Slavein as well as anyone. You'd better come too.'

'Did the police get anyone else? Any of our own people?'

The Latvian squinted at him through glasses as thick as Coke bottles.

'Nothing is certain. At least one person is missing.'

'Who?'

'The one you know best.'

'Helene?'

The Latvian nodded. 'She told me you had met. You know it was a breach of security.'

'It wasn't intentional.'

'She told me that, too. All the same, you should have reported it.'

'Do you know where she is?'

'The Greens have her. They are going to make a present of her to the generalissimo and the German mission.'

'Can't we stop it?'

The Latvian unhooked his glasses and rubbed the bridge of his nose.

'I don't think you know chess,' he said wearily. 'You must learn to give up a pawn to capture a knight. You give up a bishop to save your own queen. Helene is gone. It's not your fault, so accept it. And be on the *Chungking* before first light.'

Perhaps the madness that took possession of him had to do with the gunpowder quality of the night. The popping of rockets and the clamour of noisemakers were interspersed with the rattle of automatic fire, mostly from the far side of Soochow Creek; it all seemed part of the celebration. Or perhaps what spurred him was Killen's languor and the Latvian's checkerboard abstraction, and the frustration of leaving only another set of cicatrices on the suffering body of China. Or May, the taxi girl who had come so close to the oriental ideal of detachment in life, only to lose it in her unspeakable death. Or perhaps it was that Helene was not merely Sigrid's sister but a part of his life, something he could love or hate, resent or revere, but not cut out without major surgery. Whatever the reason – though he did not doubt that Helene would kill him with her own hands if she ever discovered what he was – he had no intention of leaving her in the hands of the men who had butchered May.

He went to Teng, a cell leader he had trained to blow up

ships, and found the quickest and most independent of his Chinese recruits. Teng had led one of the combat squads that had taken part in the seizure of the silver ship. Johnny also knew that he had risked his life in Frenchtown in an attempt to assassinate the finance minister, the brother-in-law of the generalissimo.

Teng undertook to find out where Helene was being held. It took him more than two hours to return with the answer. Johnny passed the time swatting mosquitoes in a fetid room in the Old City. The street lamp was directly opposite the window. Each time someone passed by, a shadow was thrown against the wall behind him – a shadow with pointed ears when an alleycat jumped up on the sill.

'She's in Frenchtown,' Teng reported. 'Not at Tu's house, but nearby. The place is a fortress. We would have to use bombs or grenades. Even if we got through, we would probably find her dead. It would be safer to try an ambush. They are taking her to Nanking in the morning.'

Johnny pictured the route their cars would take to the North Station. They would have to pass through the International Settlement. That gave him an idea. Perhaps he could make use of the languid Mr Killen after all.

McIvor, of the municipal police, dealt with the Greens at arm's length. He regarded them as hoodlums who would be put away in any civilised country but were much too powerful to be broken – or ignored – in Shanghai. They virtually ran the police in Frenchtown. Even in the settlement, his own domain, he knew that many of his Chinese agents had taken the vows of the society. He turned a blind eye to this, as long as the Greens did not attempt to prey on the European community. It was not his job to reform native customs. But a report that the Greens were abducting a respectable white woman to put her in a warlord's harem – that was enough to make his blood boil. The Frenchies might turn a blind eye to that sort of thing, but not the settlement, not so long as McIvor had any say in the matter.

The tip came from an unlikely source: James Killen. They had met a number of times on business matters, never socially. Despite his lowly official position at the British Cigarette Company, Killen gave himself the airs of a nabob, playing polo, running a racehorse, dining out with members of the Municipal Council. McIvor, of course, was aware of Killen's *sub rosa* functions but had found him generally unhelpful in responding to inquiries about Comintern activities in Shanghai. However, Killen had done him a singularly good turn within the last forty-eight hours by providing a lead to the top Communist organiser in the city. The fellow's arrest was a feather in McIvor's cap. So the Inspector was more receptive than he might otherwise have been to Killen's rather unorthodox plan of action.

Little Tu rode in person with his prize in the second of the three black limousines. He was sure that when he arrived with her in Nanking and presented Chiang and General von Seeckt with the head of a German spy, rich rewards would be heaped on him and the rest of his clan.

He lit up a fat, stubby Havana, the type they called a Rothschild. The woman wore a veil, as if she were in mourning. It partly camouflaged the marks his men had left on her face the previous night, when she had been repeatedly beaten and raped. There was a swelling the size of a pigeon's egg next to her right eye. A bodyguard sat on the other side of her with his Thompson on his lap.

There was a traffic jam at the bridge over the Soochow Creek, some altercation between a chauffeur in a sedan and some pushcart owners whose load had been spilled in the road. Tu leaned out his window, yelling for them to clear the way. This part of the riverbank, next to the bridge, smelled of raw sewage.

There were more Sikh policemen in evidence than usual. One of them came over to the other side of the car and peered through the window at the Thompson and the girl.

Tu told his driver to honk the horn. Soon all three cars were blaring in unison. The crush of pedestrians – workers in blue denims, women in black pants and blue tunics, half-naked beggars – pressed in on the cars. A British officer in tropical kit strolled up with a swagger stick in the crook of his arm. His ginger moustache extended the narrow line of his upper lip.

'Good morning,' McIvor addressed Little Tu, leaning into the car. 'It's Mr Tu, if I'm not mistaken.'

The bodyguard made no effort to conceal his Thompson.

Little Tu was not perturbed. Perhaps this Englishman, like the French, wanted his squeeze.

'What is the delay?' he asked McIvor.

'Too many people in a hurry, that's all. We'll have it cleared for you in a moment. Excuse me –' he looked at Helene's face '– is the lady feeling quite well?'

'Quite well,' Little Tu chorused.

'She looks to me as if she might be suffering from heatstroke.'

'We're on our way to the family doctor now.'

How long must this fool go on? Tu asked himself.

As it happened, McIvor did not have the opportunity to pursue his questioning, because another, larger European with a lock of fair hair falling over his forehead came shoving through the crowd and yelled, 'Stop them! They've got my wife!'

'Will you please step this way, Madam?' McIvor said to Helene as he opened the car door, though it was Tu who had to get out first.

'Would you please be so kind, Mr Tu?'

There was the rattle of safety catches being released. Tu looked at his bodyguards, and they at him. Were even the Greens bold enough to risk a shoot-out with the settlement police in broad daylight? Since nobody was quite sure, the Sikhs had their carbines ready. Looming over the cars, they looked as if they were out to shoot rabbits.

Reluctantly Tu moved his bulk. Helene sat still for a long moment, so that McIvor started to wonder if she had been drugged.

Johnny came forward and took her arm, half guiding, half lifting her out of the car. She seemed to need his support as they moved to the pavement. McIvor had the odd impression that part of the crowd opened to receive them and wrapped itself round them like a blanket. Or a shield.

Little Tu's eyes looked ready to burst from their sockets. He screamed and pulled out a heavy pistol, taking aim at the heads of the Europeans, which bobbed up above the crowd.

McIvor cracked him smartly on the funny bone with his baton. Tu yelped and dropped the gun. His bodyguard was less fortunate. Seeing his boss in trouble, he brought up his Thompson. The bearded Sikh by his window shot him just above the ear. The bullet tore through his cranium and settled in the rich leather of the back seat.

McIvor watched the woman in the veil and the unexplained man go down the embankment. Among the thousands of sampans in the mud, there was one that seemed to be waiting just for them.

When Colin Bailey received Killen's report on Johnny's last days in Shanghai, he fired back a very chilly reprimand. Killen might very well have blown Johnny's cover, and for what? To smuggle out a dedicated Communist agent whom Johnny had every reason to fear! Poor McIvor would have a thrombosis if he ever learned who he had helped to safety. And how would Johnny explain himself in Moscow?

The episode had quite conceivably ruined an otherwise highly successful monitoring job. Johnny's predictions had all been on target: the Communist rebellion in south China was growing fainter day by day. Bailey had seen no harm in delivering up the most effective Chinese Communist in the Shanghai underground, fingered by Johnny months before, at this stage of the game. He only wished he could have laid hands on Mao. By Johnny's account, he was one of the few men in China who actually knew how to win a revolutionary war.

Johnny's effort to play the Scarlet Pimpernel and his involvement with some barroom floozie who had been dissected by mobsters confirmed Bailey in his view that women would be the fellow's downfall. For his own sake and that of the Firm, he had to be kept on a tight rein. If Johnny survived whatever lay in store for him in Moscow, Bailey promised himself to see to this in person.

7

For much of the journey back to Moscow from Vladivostok, Helene was dazed and disoriented. She couldn't keep
food down or look in a mirror. When the questioning
began in Moscow, she could remember nothing of her last
forty-eight hours in Shanghai. They didn't believe her at
first. But finally they brought in a doctor who diagnosed
partial amnesia. Her sanity was not impaired. The doctor
prescribed a prolonged vacation at one of the spas in the
Crimean peninsula.

'You ought to go with her,' the doctor told Johnny.
'You look as if you've had a touch of yellow fever.'

But Johnny had something else to do. He found out that
Sigrid had returned to Moscow and had stayed for a time
at the Lux Hotel. But she had left two months before,
leaving no messages. At the Fourth Department and at
Comintern headquarters, people denied all knowledge of
what had happened to her. He went to Starik, who had
promised to look out for her.

'You've come to the wrong department,' General Berzin
told him.

He telephoned to the Lubyanka and asked for Max. He
had to explain himself to three men in succession before they
told him that Max was not in Moscow, but that someone
would be coming to see him. He had expected that.

It was after midnight when the chekist came to his hotel
room. He introduced himself only as Genrikh. He was slim
and well-tailored and trailed a faint odour of expensive
cologne.

'I have a letter for you,' Genrikh announced.

He watched while Johnny scanned it.

It was in Sigrid's hand, but the feel was all wrong. It
read as if she were taking dictation. She had been posted
to Copenhagen. She hoped he was well. It was a polite
note to a stranger.

There was a sentence he read and reread. She had had a
miscarriage. His child. And she had never told him.

He glowered at smooth, polished Genrikh. 'Why wasn't

I told? What happened to her letters? She must have written to me before.'

'Don't shoot the messenger boy.' Genrikh smiled beat-ifically.

Copenhagen. It might just as well have been the South Pole. 'Why is she in Denmark?'

'It's livelier than Moscow. It's not something to be sneezed at, a posting abroad.'

Johnny calculated that his hands could just about circle Genrikh's thin, perfectly barbered neck.

The chekist may have read that thought in his eyes, because he said, more seriously, 'She is working for Max. Copenhagen is his new base.'

He was made to write the chronicle of his time in China, then to write it again. Then they questioned him at Ozhod-Niriat and the Fourth Department. He wasn't called to the Luby-anka, but OGPU men sat in on some of these sessions. They hovered silently, like vultures. He told as much of the truth as he could, and in every version the villain was Emil Brandt. He wondered whether Emil was experiencing equally gentle treatment. Come October, Johnny's prophecies were proven right. The Chinese Communists – those that were left – abandoned their base in Kiangsi. Mao squeezed the shattered remnants of the Red Army through a gap that he found in von Seeckt's iron ring and led them off into the wilderness. Nobody knew where the trek would end. Like a psychotic mother, the Comintern smothered its babies and promptly got pregnant again. Johnny had attended enough crib deaths to recognise the pattern. If he had experienced doubts about his double role in the presence of the brave young guerrillas of Shanghai and the peasant fighters of Ki-angsi, the behaviour of the men from the Big House – as the Latin Americans in Moscow called the Comintern – satisfied him that he had chosen the right course.

Piatnitsky asked Johnny to come and see him. 'You've done all right,' Piatnitsky told him. 'You seem to have a way with people. Both Emil and Otto Braun speak highly about you, and they don't have much time for each other.

You can pick your own assignment.' Piatnitsky held up a finger. 'With certain limitations.'

'Yes.'

'You can go back to China. We have to get guns to Mao's forces overland. You'd be reporting to Berzin and the Fourth Department.'

'What's the alternative?' Johnny asked. He did not think he had anything new to learn about China.

'You can go to Brazil.'

His mind flashed back to what Verdi, the Argentinian, had said about how South Americans talked themselves into making revolutions.

'What is the nature of the operation?'

'Armed insurrection. You're going to kick out the government and put in our man. He's here in Moscow. You'll find him quite unusual.'

'What resources are available?'

'Do your own homework. There is a young officers' movement opposed to the government. There is only a small urban proletariat, but millions of hungry peasants who can be organised. The requirement is that the revolution should take place by January 1936.'

Piatnitsky said all this in a deadpan manner, and Johnny began to realise that the head of the Orgbureau was no enthusiast for the project. Johnny was bemused by the idea. The two most powerful Communist movements outside Russia had just been dealt crushing defeats. What had persuaded the Comintern that it could succeed in a country of sambas and sugar cane when it had failed in Germany and China?

Piatnitsky's tone encouraged Johnny to risk a provocative question.

'Isn't this a sideshow?'

'No!' the Comintern chief said sharply. He got up and started pacing, his hands clasped behind his back. 'I haven't explained very well. This project has the personal interest of someone very high up. The orders come from the top, the very top. Do you understand?'

'Yes.' So the plan for Brazil had Stalin's personal backing.

'We are prepared to spend whatever it costs – millions

of dollars, if necessary. Our best operatives are to be made available. So I wouldn't call it a sideshow.' Piatnitsky's tone had turned from indifference to almost open disgust. 'Well? Are you going or not?'

'I'm going. Who will be in charge? Guralsky?'

Guralsky was the veteran chief of the South American bureau of the Comintern. He had personally recruited many of the local Communist leaders.

'The South American bureau is getting a new boss. Emil Brandt. As a matter of fact, he asked to have you on his team.'

Piatnitsky saw Johnny's expression and added, 'I read your reports from China. They were accurate. Not a word –' he stopped Johnny from speaking. 'I would prefer that you didn't say it. Emil was chosen for this mission by someone very close to the top. Are you still with me? End of story. The man must be given credit for recognising his deficiencies. Why else would he ask for you?'

Emil's promotion was emblematic of what was happening in Moscow – how much so became obvious to Johnny in December, when the whole vast organisation of the Comintern was shaken by the news that Kirov, the second most powerful man in Russia, had been shot dead in his office in Leningrad. How the assassin had managed to smuggle himself and his revolver past all the security guards was a mystery. It was said that the killer had previously been seen in the company of OGPU men who reported directly to Dzerzhinsky Square. In any event, Kirov's slaying was blamed on Trotskyites in high places and the 'Zinoviev clique' in the Communist International. Old Bolsheviks were rounded up. Overnight, Piatnitsky and his files vanished from his office. It was rumoured that the head of the Orgbureau was being grilled in the cellars of the Lubyanka. Closed sessions of the Comintern were interrupted by pistol-toting chekists in black coats who hurled accusations at platform speakers in full view of the foreign delegates. 'Less literature!' they bellowed when their victims tried to explain themselves. A man's record was worthless unless it demonstrated undeviating loyalty to Stalin. It was plain that the only men Stalin trusted completely were those he had created out of the muck. The city stank of fear.

But Emil took all this in his stride. Emil, Johnny discovered, had a protector, and Dmitri Manuilsky was the right man to have on your side in Moscow at the close of 1934. Manuilsky was Stalin's creature in the Comintern. From Shanghai, Emil had fed him a string of poisonous backchat, reporting – or inventing – the anti-Stalin gossip of his rivals and even his superiors at the Big House. In Stalin's Moscow, Emil's willingness to betray his comrades counted for infinitely more than success or failure in China.

When they met, Emil was so effusively cordial that Johnny became convinced that the new chief of the South American bureau had ratted on him too. As more and more old faces disappeared from the Big House, it struck Johnny that maybe he and Emil had survived for the same reason: in a climate of generalised distrust, the plausible liar has a better chance of saving his skin than anyone who presumes to speak his mind.

Emil introduced Johnny to the others who would lead the rising in Brazil.

Chief among them was a tiny, taciturn man with delicate features. Indrawn and mystical, he carried a faint aroma of the cloisters. He had been living in a house in Moscow with his mother and sisters for several years. In Brazil they called him the Knight of Hope. It seemed that, a decade before Mao, he had led a Long March of his own through the interior of Brazil, from the parched backlands of the northeast to the great falls of Iguaçu. The revolutionary lieutenants who had marched in his column were scattered all over Brazil. Some had become colonels or governors. They were expected to rise and join the revolution when this little man gave the word. His name was Luis Carlos Prestes. It was hard for Johnny to imagine him on horseback, waving a sword.

Yet Prestes' quiet fanaticism was not unimpressive. The army would rise. He could vouch for it. He had letters from his comrades in all the major garrisons. He even had supporters in the police and on the general staff. Several state governments would turn against the president once they saw that the movement was serious. The peasants would take up arms and chase the landowners into the sea.

After meeting Prestes for the first time, Johnny asked Emil, 'Do you like the Brazilians?'

A vacant look, the same one Johnny had observed when he had come back from Kiangsi and reported facts that Emil found inconvenient, took possession of the other man's face.

Emil said, 'I haven't given the matter the slightest thought.'

Johnny spent time with the files. Just six months before, in June, the South American bureau, under its former management, had drawn up an exhaustive report on the prospects for Communist takeovers in the various countries of the hemisphere. The prospectus for Brazil was discouraging. 'In Brazil,' Johnny read, 'the Communist party is only weakly connected with the masses, and in this respect it is on a downward grade.' The authors of the secret report found 'great objective possibilities for the development of the revolutionary movement' in the radicalism of junior army officers, popular hatred of the foreign banks and the misery of the peasants, especially in the north. But nothing in their findings suggested that the revolution was at hand.

A summons came from Manuilsky. Perhaps Stalin's man had the answers.

Manuilsky fingered a moustache that seemed to be made of cotton wool. He might look like a favourite uncle, but he cultivated the manners of a boorish petty official. He kept Johnny standing while he went through a sheaf of papers.

'Another bloody German,' he finally greeted Johnny. 'Moscow is full of you people.'

And whose fault is that? Johnny thought.

'So what do you think of the Popular Front?' Manuilsky challenged him.

'I think it requires study.'

'That's a sensible answer. I see you're a strawberry from our patch after all.' Manuilsky gave him a shrewd look. 'Sit over there, on the sofa. Let's have some brandy.'

The stuff he poured was good French cognac, not the Armenian product.

'What do you think of our Knight of Hope?'

'He has a certain quality. It's hard for me to picture him in uniform.'

'You know what they say about the Portuguese. They don't kill the bull. It's the same with Brazilians. Prestes spent three years marching up and down the country, with hardly a shot fired in anger. But he's their hero. We work with what we've got. At least he's no Chiang Kai-shek. He's a good party member, and he'll do what he's told.'

'But in Brazil the party is insignificant.'

'It doesn't matter. Prestes will give us the army. We can buy up half the state governors with money or promises. What you have to do is kill the bull.'

Manuilsky embarked on a speech about what a Communist victory in Brazil would mean. It would be the decisive step towards creating a federation of soviet republics in all of South America. It would knock the stuffing out of the British and American banks. Faced with a knife at its soft underbelly, the United States would be powerless to act outside its own hemisphere. And with Brazil in its pocket, the Soviet Union would control the one raw material it lacked: rubber.

Manuilsky replenished their glasses and said, 'It will also show Hitler we mean business.'

He paused to assess Johnny's reaction.

Johnny raised his glass. 'I'll drink to that.'

They clinked glasses.

Manuilsky looked at him approvingly and said, 'I'm going to do you a favour you won't forget. I'm going to take you to see the boss.'

8

The next day Johnny received orders to meet Manuilsky at his office at midnight. Since Stalin didn't sleep at night, official Moscow was obliged to be insomniac too.

They took the road along the embankment to the Moskva gate. The river gleamed dully, like pewter, under the thin ice.

Militiamen stopped them under the arch. Their officer snapped smartly to attention at the sight of Manuilsky's papers. There were soldiers with heavy machine guns at the entrance to the vast palace courtyard.

The Kremlin guards in the lobby were a head taller than Johnny. They dwarfed the man who was hopping down the wide staircase. He was birdlike with his narrow, slightly hunched shoulders and hard, bright little eyes.

Manuilsky went up and pumped his hand. He mumbled a joke, and they both laughed. The chekist was looking at Johnny.

'Comrade Yezhov,' Manuilsky said, 'This is Johann Lentz, one of our Germans.'

'A pleasure,' Yezhov said. His stare was like a slap across the face. He nodded, and hurried out of the building.

'Yezhov is one of the most powerful men in Moscow,' Manuilsky whispered as they crossed an echoing reception room at the top of the stairs. 'He may get Yagoda's job. Of course,' he added, so softly that Johnny had to strain to make out the words, 'Yagoda is Jewish.'

Stalin's secretary slid out from behind the padded door. 'The *Vozhd* is waiting.'

The Vozhd. It was a curious form of address, just starting to creep into newspaper editorials and official speeches. It was stronger than the English word 'leader'. Its resonance was the same as that of 'Führer' in German.

The Vozhd did not look much like his statues. Stalin was short and squat. His skin was yellowish and deeply pitted. His eyes were puffy and narrowed into slits, so that the whites hardly showed. He wore brown boots and a cotton *rubashka*, and his pipe wheezed like an asthmatic as he sucked at it.

Manuilsky made the introductions. Stalin motioned for Johnny to sit in a low-slung chair and returned to his own desk, which was set high up on a specially built platform so that Johnny had to tilt his head back to see the leader's face.

He expected to be quizzed about the Brazil mission or

perhaps about China. Stalin's opening shot caught him completely off guard.

'You're a German. Do you believe that Hitler has the support of the German people?'

'Many of them,' Johnny conceded.

'Thousands of former Communists have joined him.'

'I'm afraid that's true.'

'And he rules with a rod of iron. All opposition has been ruthlessly crushed.'

'There is still opposition. But of course it is forced deeper and deeper underground. The Gestapo is a very effective organisation.'

Stalin grunted.

'If the Japanese strike us,' he went on, 'will Hitler make war on us, too?'

'I'm in no position to judge. But I think Germany is still weak. Hitler will wait till he has built up his war machine.'

'And you think a conflict with Hitler is inevitable?'

'It's in his book –' Johnny began.

'I've read his book, fuck your mother!' Stalin burst out. 'All the sermon mongers in that *lavotchka*, that clip-joint you work for, spout it at me. I think I know Hitler better than any of you. It's not our system that he hates. It's the Jews. When he wrote *Mein Kampf*, he believed that the Jews were running the Soviet Union. Am I right?'

Johnny said nothing.

'If we show him that we know how to deal with the Jewish problem, what do we have left to fight about?'

Johnny was shaken by this but remained perfectly still.

'We have more in common than either of us has with any of the bourgeois democracies. Germany and Russia are both victims of Versailles. We have been allies since the war, regardless of who sat in the Berlin Chancellery, united against the Western capitalists. We have no quarrel over territory. Hitler has designs on Poland. Well, there is enough of Poland for both of us. Hitler and I understand the nature of power. As for Britain and France, they are rotting, pustular invalids. They are too feeble to hold on to their empires. Their colonies are waiting to be shared out among those who are not scared to act. The United States is too busy making money to fight.'

The words rushed out in Stalin's thick Georgian accent, so that Johnny missed a few, but not the terrifying thrust of the argument.

'Hitler must see this!' The Vozhd shouted. 'He must be made to see it!'

Manuilsky nodded, his hands folded piously in his lap.

'We'll show him who's running Russia,' Stalin went on. 'And we'll make him respect us. There is a big German community in Brazil. If we succeed in Brazil, he'll take notice. What do you think?'

'There's no question about it,' Johnny agreed.

Everything he had learned since he had first turned the stiff, water-stained pages of Heinz Kordt's diary should have prepared him for this revelation. But when it came, the raw cynicism and power lust of Stalin's statements left him breathless. Stalin lampooned the most famous advocates of the Popular Front – he called the French writers 'shit-eaters' – and heaped contempt on the democratic leaders in the West. He saw enemies on all sides. He quizzed Johnny for material to add to the prosecutor's dossier on Piatnitsky and other 'deviationists' in the Comintern. Johnny obliged, so far as memory and imagination would serve him. He was sure that Stalin would not have bared his deepest instincts unless he had been informed by Manuilsky that Johnny was 100 per cent reliable. Johnny made every effort to live up to that reputation. One false note after Stalin's revelations, and he would join Piatnitsky in the bowels of the Lubyanka.

The conversation ended after three in the morning.

Johnny came away convinced that the Brazil operation was different in kind from the Comintern's previous revolutionary adventures. The South American bureau wasn't being sent to make a revolution. It was being sent to Rio to stage a coup d'état – to impress Hitler and to cut the ground from under the feet of those who argued that, in a world that contained Hitler and Mussolini, the Communists must make common cause with all the forces opposed to Fascism.

2

A Country of Gods and Men

(1934–1936)

Walk slowly in processions or the saint
will fall.

– Brazilian peasant proverb

6

Our Man in Rio

We of the Game are beyond protection. If we die, we
die.
  Our names are blotted from the book.
                            — *Rudyard Kipling, Kim*

1

There was a mournful sameness about railroad hotels,
Johnny thought. The same sense of transience, of imminent
loss. The beds always looked as if someone had just got
out of them. The whores in the street were brisk and
businesslike, seeking out clients who had time to kill,
but not enough to start living. In the Grand Hotel in
Copenhagen – railroad hotels always had names like that –
Johnny's room had a pitch pine dresser, a two-bar radiator
that crackled as if it were frying insects, a mud-coloured
portrait of an unknown burgher and twin beds. The bed
nearer the window had the lumpier mattress, but he picked
it for the view of the great gabled roof of the central station,
mottled and grey. On top was a spire out of Grimm's fairy
tales and a clock that had stopped at the precise hour they
had left Moscow.
  'Hurry up!' Helene rattled the door handle from outside.
'I'm starved!'
  'Coming!' Johnny called back. He closed his suitcase and
shoved it into the closet. There was no point in unpacking.

They had been given forty-eight hours in Copenhagen – just enough time to call at the Westbureau and collect travel papers and final instructions – before the onward journey to Genoa and a 'spaghetti boat' full of Italian emigrants bound for Rio.

When Manuilsky had told him that Helene would accompany him to Brazil, Johnny had protested that she wasn't well enough to do the job. Manuilsky had pointed out that she had made a remarkable recovery after her return from Shanghai, which was true. Johnny had explained that there were personal problems. When he had requested point-blank that Sigrid should be sent in her sister's place, Manuilsky had lost his temper.

'Do you think we're sending you to Brazil to screw in the sand dunes?' Manuilsky yelled at him.

'I think I've earned the right to choose my own assistant.'

'The choice has been made. What's the matter with you? You know we don't tolerate romantic attachments. Get a new woman. If you don't like it, give me your papers. There are plenty of others who would give their left ball to go.'

That had silenced Johnny.

I have to get to Copenhagen, he had told himself. At least that far. Colin Bailey would be waiting for him; Johnny had mailed the postcard, and a courier from Bailey had met him at the Arbat metro station. But there was something more urgent. Sigrid was in Copenhagen. He had to find her. He must try to get her away from Max – if she would still have him.

That first night in Copenhagen, he sat with Helene at a restaurant table in front of an open fire. The wood smoke carried the smell of sour apples. The food was wonderful – a soup made from morels, ham in puff pastry, little delicacies of the sea – but Johnny didn't notice.

Helene looked up and said, 'I'm sorry it's me. I didn't ask to go to Brazil. You know that, don't you?'

'I know.'

She pushed the crumbs on her plate into little stepped pyramids. 'You're still in love with Sigi, aren't you?' she challenged him.

'I haven't changed,' he conceded. 'I don't know about her. There was a letter – not a good letter.'

'You went looking for her today, didn't you?'

He hesitated. He had spent nearly three hours after they'd arrived trying to find Sigrid. He had asked about her at the Vesterport, a big, blocky construction in the centre of town. The Westbureau of the Comintern had its secret headquarters on the third floor, behind the brass plate of an obscure engineering firm. Johnny's contacts had professed never to have heard of Sigrid. He had gone to Smollett, the Fourth Department man, who had been transferred from London. Smollett knew nothing about Max's operations but had volunteered to ask about the girl. He had warned that it might take some time. In his frustration Johnny had even gone to Wollweber, the German boss of the Westbureau, a vulgar bully with eyes like slits in a bulging gourd. He had gone even though Smollett had warned him that there were nasty rumours about Wollweber – specifically, that the German had been trading information with Gestapo agents, ratting on comrades who had presumed to criticise his leadership. Johnny had found Wollweber cordial to begin with, and liberal with his akvavit. But when Johnny had asked about Sigi and Max, the Comintern chief had jabbed a finger at his chest and cautioned him not to go sticking his nose into business that didn't concern him.

Johnny met Helene's eyes.

Can I trust her?

There was a bond between them. In Shanghai it had saved her life. In London it had saved him from arrest. Helene felt something for him – not love, perhaps, but loyalty and affection. But surely that was a reason for her to stand between him and Sigi, not bring them together, especially if she could sense the force of the temptation that had been tugging at him since he arrived in Copenhagen: the temptation to abandon a life of loneliness and lies, to sweep Sigrid up and take her somewhere they could be simply man and woman, without counting the cost to others. And beyond all of that, she still belonged to Max.

'Did you find her?' Helene prodded.

He thought, what have I got to lose? If I leave Copenhagen without seeing Sigrid, God knows if I'll see her again.

'Nobody admits to knowing her,' he reported. 'Wollweber told me to piss off.'

'That sounds like him.' She took a slim panatella out of her bag and held it over the candle. 'Would you like me to find Sigi for you?' she asked coolly.

'Are you serious?'

'Perfectly serious. If you're sure it's what you want.'

'But why?'

'You've lived for thirty-five years,' she said through the white haze, 'and you've managed to learn absolutely nothing about women.'

'That's not fair.'

'It's accurate.'

'Not quite. I've learned that you'll never cease to surprise me.'

2

Tiny lights winked on and off in the trees like swarms of darting fireflies. Colin Bailey paused to inspect the strings of lights that were threaded through the drooping branches of a blue spruce.

'The Danes say every bulb in the Tivoli Gardens works,' he remarked to Johnny. 'Do you suppose it's true? I can't find a dead one on this tree. Good Lord, there must be millions of them –' his glance took in the copses of illuminated trees, a blazing Persian palace, a Chinese theatre where the light shimmered on a curtain shaped like a peacock's tail, the bright pavilions and peep-show arcades. 'They're a meticulous people, the Danes. Something German in that, I suppose. And yet not like the Germans at all. What about over there?'

Bailey pointed with his umbrella to a beer garden by the lake. The water looked very black, the swans inanimate – decoys sliding on glass.

'Whatever you say,' Johnny responded.

They sat at a table in the open air. On the other side of the beer garden a troop of husky young Germans were booming out drinking songs in their own language, making their trestle tables rock like rowing boats on the swell. They looked like a group advertisement for the Hitler Youth, but they were probably harmless, Johnny thought. Tourists looking for beer and girls. He was grateful for the uproar. It would make it very hard for anyone to tune in to his conversation with Bailey.

A bouncing waitress came with their beer. She wore a plunging bodice despite the nip of winter in the air, and Johnny smiled at her.

Habit or nervousness? Bailey asked himself. Johnny was the reverse of relaxed. Bailey sensed that his nerves were stretched taut.

'I'm sorry I couldn't give you more notice,' Johnny said when they were alone.

'I've been waiting for your message since we got confirmation you were safely out of Shanghai. That went all right, did it?'

'No complaints.'

That's two borders we've helped you across, Bailey thought. We'll have to watch it the third time.

'Your reports from China were flawless,' Bailey told him. 'If Uncle Joe had read them, he might have learned something.'

'They weren't exclusive. I sent almost identical reports to Moscow. They changed nothing, as you know. In Moscow, there are two categories of facts – convenient facts and inconvenient ones. My assessments came under the second heading.' He took a pull on his beer. 'By the way, I met Stalin last week. He's not very tall.'

Bailey sat riveted while Johnny recounted the story of his nocturnal call on the Vozhd.

I'll go to Winston with this, Bailey promised himself when Johnny described the depths of Stalin's longing to impress Hitler. The London clubs – including the cabinet room – were full of comfortable chaps who held that the

Nazis and the Russians could never make a deal, almost as many as believed that Hitler meant no real harm. That same week, he had listened to a Tory peer who had insisted that Hitler's territorial appetites could be satisfied with a nice little slice of Portuguese Africa.

Johnny started to explain his new mission.

'Brazil?' Bailey echoed him. 'What the devil do the Russians want with that?'

Bailey's knowledge of Brazil was – to put it charitably – sketchy. He knew that Brazil was a very large and very green chunk on the map of South America, that it spoke Portuguese instead of Spanish because of a fifteenth-century Pope, and that slavery had been legal until long after the American Civil War, when a homegrown Brazilian emperor had abolished it just before the slaveowners kicked him out. He dimly remembered one or more articles on Brazil that Kipling had published in the *Telegraph* before the Great Crash. They were about jolly native festivals and thundering hydro-electric turbines; Kipling was rather good on man-made thunder. Then there was that planter fellow Bailey had once met in Kuala Lumpur, a man grown fat and florid and whiskery in the tropics, who clapped his hands to summon the servants. This Malayan planter had spun a long-winded tale about how he had struck a tremendous blow for Britain – not to mention his own pocket – by smuggling rubber plants down the Amazon in the teeth of crocodiles, piranhas and manhunters with rifles and machetes who had orders to kill anyone who tried to break the rubber monopoly. The man had complained bitterly, a quarter of a century after the event, that he deserved a peerage, or a knighthood at least, and had implored Bailey to intercede with the King.

Oh, yes, there was that polo player. Carlos something. Pal of Diana's. Goes about reeking of pomade and making eyes at girls. No. On second thought, he was an Argentinian.

This, then, was the sum of Bailey's knowledge of Brazil. The store was not increased by service reports he might have forgotten or overlooked. In 1935 British Intelligence did not have one single case officer *en poste* anywhere in South America. Bailey thought it would be injudicious to divulge this inconvenient fact to Johnny.

The way Johnny explained things, Stalin had set his sights on Brazil for two reasons: to blow his critics in the Comintern out of the water·and to show Hitler that he was no slouch when it came to grabbing *Lebensraum*.

'How much of a chance do you suppose the Russians have got?'

'They've got a front man called Prestes. He doesn't look like anything much, but he talks a lot less than most South Americans, and to better effect. He's something of a national hero. As long as he doesn't go about draped in the red flag, he could pull in quite a following.'

Johnny explained the master plan for the revolt, as it had ripened in Moscow. Geography was important. The country was vast, the rivers ran the wrong way and the mountain ranges were in the wrong places; over huge areas, land communications were nonexistent or agonisingly slow. It would probably be impossible to seize the whole country with a single blow. At the same time, if the revolution succeeded in several regions – above all the north, where the peasants were starving and ready to risk everything – it would take months for the government to organise a counterattack. If a rising in the north were combined with lightning coups in the capital and major cities like São Paulo, the counterattack might never come at all. The Russians were confident that Prestes had enough friends who wore epaulettes – even generals at the Ministry of War – to make that happen. The Brazilians weren't fighters. To be sure, they were not averse to killing each other in knife fights in the slums, or in land wars between peasants and the hired guns of the backlands 'colonels', or in pursuit of bizarre millenarian visions. But when it came to deciding who was going to sit in the presidential palace, the rival factions would line up their forces in fierce military array and set to frantically counting noses. Then the weaker side would discreetly abandon the field.

'I begin to see,' Bailey remarked. 'They say the Portuguese don't kill the bull. Your people are ready to kill the bull, and that makes everything different. So you'll be the military adviser?'

'The military specialist' Johnny modified this. 'I have been appointed to the South American bureau. It means that with Emil and Prestes – and the Argentinian – I would take part in the strategic decisions.'

'Excellent!' Bailey steepled his fingers, trying to calculate the effects of a wrecking job on the Soviet gang in Rio. It would give a definite boost to British influence in South America. It would be a stinging humiliation for Manuilsky and all of Stalin's cronies in the Comintern. It would probably help the Reds like Willi Münzenberg and the French lot, who were campaigning for a Popular Front against the Nazis and had been getting kicked in the teeth up till now. Bailey's mind ranged over the reverse scenario. If Stalin succeeded in turning Brazil into the second Communist power, a whole continent would be in jeopardy. The Americans could probably be counted out as allies in a future war; they would be too busy having kittens over what was going on south of their border. There was also the chance that Stalin would do a cynical swap with Hitler. You take Brazil, with its million-odd Germans. We'll take the Baltic states and a nice chunk of Poland . . .

It dawned on Bailey that there might, just might, be something even bigger at stake.

'For God's sake,' he burst out. 'This is Uncle Joe's private hobbyhorse. If it all blows up in his face, on top of the way he's treating all the Old Bolsheviks in Moscow –'

He cut himself off just as he was about to add: we might be able to put the skids under the bugger.

He kept the completion of the thought to himself, not because of the jumbling of metaphors, though that was scarcely pardonable in a Wykehamist, but because these were very early days and it simply wouldn't do to get overexcited. He hadn't even worked out how he was going to service his agent on the other side of Rio.

He said merely, 'It's splendid. You'll hold all the strands

in your two fists. You can make or break this revolt whenever we choose.'

'I could,' Johnny remarked.

Bailey did not like this repeated use of the subjunctive. 'Something's worrying you, Johnny. Let's have it.'

'I'm not going to Rio.'

Bailey stared at him. 'Would you care to amplify that?'

'I've decided to get out.'

Bailey sat very still. 'Is this a – sudden decision?'

'You could say so. I decided today. Will you help me?'

Bailey hesitated.

Steady, he cautioned himself. The man is close to breaking. I mustn't put on the screws, mustn't scare him worse than he's scared already. Not unless I have to.

'I might help if I knew the circumstances,' Bailey suggested mildly. 'Are you under suspicion?'

'No more than all of us are.'

'It's the girl, then. The painter.'

Johnny did not dissent.

'Is she in Copenhagen?'

'She's in Oslo.'

'How did you find out?'

'Her sister told me. She works for the same people.' Johnny rubbed the corners of his eyes between thumb and forefinger. He added, 'Helene and I are supposed to be travelling to Rio together.'

'And this is the same Helene who went after de Salis in Berlin.'

'We don't talk about that.'

Bailey let the Berlin episode ride. He asked, 'Did Helene tell you why the other one went to Oslo?'

'She's doing a job with Max.'

'Did Helene tell you the nature of the job?'

'I don't think she knows.'

'But you're planning to run off to Oslo and look for the girl, just like that – without knowing where she lives or what she's doing.'

'Oslo isn't London or Paris,' Johnny countered with stubborn determination. 'I have some friends. I'll find her.

With or without your help.' He was tired of the grilling. 'All I need from you is the money that belongs to me. Thirteen hundred pounds.'

'A bit more than that, with the interest accrued.' Bailey endeavoured to sound like a helpful bank manager. Johnny's salary was deposited in an escrow account at Coutts' in the City.

Softly, softly, the Englishman told himself. In his hurry to get to his girl, Johnny may be starting to see *me* as the enemy.

'You can have your money whenever you like,' Bailey announced. 'But there's something I ought to ask you. If your girl is in Oslo with Max, there's obviously a sensitive job involved. Why would Helene court suspicion by running around asking all sorts of indiscreet questions on your behalf? Why would she tell you even if she knew before?'

'I've asked myself the same things,' Johnny said. 'Helene is an unusual woman.'

'She is also a Russian spy,' Bailey responded, letting the steel show. 'I don't want to appear insensitive, but it must surely have occurred to you that Helene is putting you through some kind of test. Do you think she'd pack you off to Norway without telling Max?'

'It's possible,' Johnny conceded, remembering the episode in Moscow, when Helene had told the secret police about his talk with Emil.

'It's more than possible, in view of what's going on in Oslo.'

Johnny was startled. 'Do you know something about it?'

'We've had Max under observation for some time. He's made several trips to Norway, sniffing after a well-known compatriot of his. A certain Lev Davidovich Bronstein. Am I making myself clear?'

The shock of recognition showed in Johnny's face.

Of course, he told himself. The Norwegians had given Trotsky asylum. Everyone knew that Stalin would stop at nothing to see Trotsky dead – and Max was an expert at what the chekists tactfully described as *mokrie dela*, 'wet operations'.

'What sort of impression do you think it will make if you walk in on Max and your girl unannounced in the middle of a plot to kill Trotsky?'

'I can't imagine that Sigrid is involved.'

'Why else would Max take her along?'

Johnny said nothing.

'If you go to Oslo,' Bailey pressed on, 'they'll nail you as a Trotskyite agent, or worse. You can see that, can't you? What good would you be to Sigrid then?'

'I'll take her away,' Johnny countered defiantly.

'Are you sure she'd go?' the Englishman said softly. 'Have you done anything to prepare her? If you'll forgive me for saying this, you have a way of picking women with minds of their own.'

'It's my neck,' Johnny said fiercely, clenching his fists. But a voice inside him said, Bailey is right.

Later they walked by the lakes, accompanied by the scudding of oars and stifled giggles from lovers who were out there in dinghies. It reminded Johnny of an afternoon on the Wannsee, when Sigrid had blotted out the sun.

He said, 'I've thought it over. I'll go to Rio.'

'I think you've made the right decision.'

Bailey heaved a sigh of relief. The stuff about Trotsky was a stab in the dark. His agents had lost sight of Max several weeks before. It was plausible enough, though, and had worked like a charm with Johnny, who was nobody's fool. Now it would be interesting to check with the Oslo station whether his hunch about Trotsky was correct.

Johnny stopped at the water's edge. The wind had picked up, driving ripples across the lake. 'I want you to understand this is the last job I'll do for you,' he announced. 'Afterwards, I want out. And I want Sigrid with me. You have to promise you'll make that possible.'

'Agreed.'

'How are we going to stay in contact?'

'That's an easy one,' Bailey said decisively. 'I'm coming out myself.' Now that he had convinced Johnny to carry on – not through deception, he told himself, so much as informed speculation – Bailey had no intention of leaving his man in the lurch. 'By the way,' he went on, 'what cover have the OMS chaps given you this time?'

'I'm supposed to be an Austrian cigar importer, on a busman's holiday with my sister.'

'What name?'

'Franz Gruber.'

A smile flickered across Bailey's face. He murmured, '"Silent Night".'

'I beg your pardon?'

'Franz Gruber is the composer of "Silent Night".'

'I doubt whether the man who fixed my passport has much time for Christmas carols.'

3

There was nothing to compare with Christmas in England, Bailey thought. There were snowmen in the park, while Snow White and the Seven Dwarves revolved in Selfridge's windows. He took the girls to see Father Christmas in the grotto behind the toy department, before he drove down to Odiham to see C. in his country retreat.

He found the chief stomping around in plus-fours and muddy boots in his tack room. The place smelled of leather and wet dogs. Three of the latter – a mastiff and two black Labradors – greeted Bailey with a show of teeth and voice projection that would have driven away all but the most determined visitor.

C. announced that he had been shooting with the King. He congratulated himself that he had shot a dozen more birds than HM but had managed to fudge the count so as not to commit the sin of lèse-majesté.

C. was startled when Bailey informed him that Johnny was en route to Rio. He wanted to know what Stalin hoped to accomplish.

Bailey explained. He had done some homework and dwelled on the fact that sizable British interests were at stake. British companies owned the railroads and had a stake in other utilities.

'Of course, we can't rely on the Americans to do anything. Roosevelt doesn't see that Communism is a danger. His ambassador in Moscow is hooked on Stalin. There's really nobody we can deal with on this in Washington. Hoover is quite impossible. They don't have anything that resembles a secret service. Their attitude is even worse than the Foreign Office's.'

This argument seemed to impress C. more than anything else.

He agreed to sign a chit.

On New Year's Eve, Bailey was on platform eleven under the sooty arches of Waterloo station, boarding the train for Southampton. For two hours, ensconced in a cosy, cream-painted Pullman, he watched the home counties flash by, chartreuse watercolours under the rain. The steward brought madeira and cherry cake.

At the docks the revels were in full swing. Young hearties whirled their noisemakers and kissed their girls while a band thumped out songs of farewell; 'Good Night, Sweetheart' was the favourite. Nobody had eyes for the trim military figure proceeding up the gangway onto the deck of the RMS *Arthurian*. The crowd was given over to the cheerful chaos of leavetaking, to last-minute packages and flowers and smuggled embraces, and champagne parties that spilled over from the staterooms onto the boat deck.

As Bailey followed a steward below, a girl hopped, giggling, out of a nearby cabin, champagne flute in hand. He had a brief impression of dramatic violet eye shadow and a flying feather boa before she skated along the floor and landed in his arms. He caught her by the elbows, at the cost of getting the contents of her glass all down his shirt front.

'Whoops!' the girl laughed up at him.

'Rather a waste of champagne,' Bailey observed.

'Perhaps you'll let us make amends.'

Bailey looked for the source of the new voice and found

a young man brandishing a bottle of Veuve Cliquot. The stranger was tallish, strong-boned, not stocky, with the supple, wide-legged gate of a man who is equally at ease on a horse or a rolling deck. His hair was chestnut brown, his moustache a touch lighter. His face was flushed with good health, but his skin was the kind that freckles rather than tans. He was well dressed in an offhanded way, in country tweeds and a soft collar, above which a smudge of lipstick burned against the side of his neck.

'Happy New Year!'

'I hope it will be,' Bailey said, accepting the proffered glass of champagne. 'In the meantime, I've always found this a rather good prophylactic –'

The girl burst into another fit of giggles.

'– against mal de mer.'

'Harry Maitland,' the young man introduced himself. His handshake was firm, not bone-crushing. He was confident of his place in the world.

'Colin Bailey. Maitland –' the older man brooded on the name. 'I knew a Maitland at Winchester. Rather a keen batsman.'

'That would have been my father, sir.'

'Really?'

'We're having a little farewell party,' Maitland said, gesturing towards his door. 'You'd be very welcome to join us.'

'I think not,' Bailey said, peering in at a crowd of bright young things. 'But thank you for this.' He returned the empty glass. 'How far are you going?'

'To Rio.'

'Then we'll have plenty of time to talk.'

In his own cabin, Bailey indulged himself for a few minutes in cosy memories of going up to Scholars' Hall at Winchester at six of a winter's evening to toast thick slices of bread on the end of a bamboo pole over the blast furnace of the hulking double stove the boys called the Simon and Jude.

In the distance he heard the cabin boy pattering down the corridors, banging a gong and piping, 'All ashore that's going ashore!'

He could summon up only a blurred image of Maitland senior, a bluff sportsman who hated bullies, one of life's spenders. His face darkened as he reflected that Maitland senior was one of England's missing generation, his name inscribed in stone along the cloisters that served as the school's war memorial, on the roll call of those who had fallen in Flanders fields.

Bailey stayed below until the ship's siren howled, the last visitors were shooed onshore and the *Arthurian*, with the pilot's tug at her bow, had completed her tricky passage round the bar and was steaming south across open water to Cherbourg on the green coast of Normandy. Then he made a leisurely ascent to the saloon, ordered whisky and soda and decided that he did not care for the public rooms. The designer had copied the grandiose style of the Cunard liners, but the chairs were jammed in together so that someone's ear was at your neck, while the inevitable skylight, under the sodden curtain of clouds, submerged the whole scene in the cold penumbra of a fish tank.

Seven times around the promenade deck, by Bailey's calculation, made a mile. He shifted a florin from one pocket of his flannels to the other at the completion of each circuit. After three miles he returned to the deck chair he had reserved on the port side to take his morning bouillon.

He was soon engrossed in a folder of cuttings from the *Telegraph*; his girl had dug out the old Kipling articles. Bailey was reading about the Brazilians' passion for gambling when Harry Maitland loomed up.

'May I join you?'

'Please.' The deck chair next to Bailey was unoccupied. 'You know Brazil, do you?'

'I've lived there for four years, on and off.'

'Do you know this game called –' he consulted the clipping '– The Beasts?'

'Oh yes,' Bailey laughed. 'The *jogo do bicho*. Everyone plays it. You bet on an animal – a lion, say, or an elephant. Each animal controls four numbers. If they come up in the daily lottery drawing, you've won. It started as the bright idea of a man who wanted to induce people to visit the zoo. It sprouted up all over the place. Everybody plays. It's illegal, of course, but in my office the locals buy and sell tickets in full view of their supervisors.'

'And what kind of office would that be?'

'I work for Rio Light. That's the power company.'

'You're an engineer, then?'

'My job is public relations, mostly. Not awfully import-ant, I'm afraid. But it gives me an excuse to live in Rio.'

Bailey started to draw him out. Maitland had the endear-ing self-effacement of the sort of Englishman who sails the Atlantic single-handed and talks about it as if he were describing Sunday lunch at a pub. All that Maitland *père* had bequeathed was a mountain of debt, so, when he came down from Bailliol, Harry had been urged to pay court to his senior aunt, a formidable dowager who controlled the family purse strings. Her most beloved possession had been a vicious Pekingese called Harold.

'Things were going pretty well,' Harry reported, 'until she asked me to tea to discuss her will. Naturally, this was an exciting occasion. I sat down on the blue sofa a bit too quickly. I heard something crunch, but I didn't dare look to see what it was until Aunt Hermanie had gone off in search of the dog. I stood up and found I had squashed poor Harold flat. She was calling and calling in the other rooms. Inspi-ration seized me. There was a rubber plant by the windows. I pulled it out of its pot and popped Harold underneath. I left as soon as was decent, without being detected. But I am afraid my aunt's suspicions fell on me in the end. I received a note from her lawyers, informing me that she had cut me out of her will. That was the end of my inheritance. And I must say, I feel I owe a debt to old Harold.'

'How so?'

'He drove me to Brazil, in a roundabout way. I was faced with the imminent prospect of joining the salaried class.'

Maitland made this sound like a sentence to prison.

'You could have taken a rich wife,' Bailey observed.

'I gave it some thought. Then I picked up *The Times*

and found an advertisement in the agony columns. They wanted an extra gun for an expedition to Brazil, to look for an explorer who had disappeared in the territory of the Xingu Indians.'

'Major Fawcett.'

'You read about it, then.'

'You never found Fawcett,' Bailey pointed out.

'No, but I found Brazil. It's – well, it's extraordinary. A country of gods and men.'

'And Rio?'

'Rio is simply the most beautiful place in God's creation. The Cariocas say that when God took seven days to create the world, he spent six of them on Rio de Janeiro.'

Bailey cocked an eyebrow at this gush of enthusiasm.

'Not very Wykehamist,' he said with mock rectitude, alluding to their old school's reputation for turning out dry logicians. 'I believe you're a romantic, Mr Maitland.'

Harry grinned and swept the hair off his forehead.

'I'm told revolutions are as common in South America as elections in England,' Bailey remarked.

'A revolution is their version of an election. That's why they're usually kind to the losers. The other party may get in next time.'

'What about the Communists?'

'There are Communists, of course. They don't play by those rules. But I don't think there's much room for communism in a country where, if you're hungry, you can pluck a banana off a tree.'

'I do hope you're right.'

Bailey had decided that he liked Harry Maitland. Some of the boy's opinions were naive and superficial; that was to be expected. But he had a quality that appealed to Bailey. More than mere youthfulness, it was his air of constant, delighted expectation. While so many of his class and generation in England – the young men Bailey met at Diana's dinner parties – were suppurating with world-weary cynicism or spouting half-digested nonsense from an unreadable dialectician, Harry gave the impression that he was one of those who would ride over the edge of the world for a dare, or just for the joy of the riding.

Maitland began telling him about a Communist effort to spark a labour dispute at the power company. The Communists had tried to make a big issue out of the fact that foreign employees were paid much better than the Brazilians. Bailey was impressed with Harry's account of how he had personally contributed to the failure of the strike by paying a left-wing journalist to write articles that had set the organisers at each other's throats.

But Bailey's attention strayed with the appearance of a new face at the far end of the deck. He caught only a brief glimpse because the man whipped round immediately, giving them a fine view of his back. But Bailey was sure he knew him. He was young, even younger than Maitland, but his ravaged face was that of a much older man, leached and striated by what life had dumped on him. Bailey was sure that he, too, had been recognised. Neither he nor Karl Vogel would be likely to forget their last encounter at an Algerian dive in Paris.

'Excuse me –' Bailey took Maitland's arm, interrupting his narrative. 'Have you seen that fellow before?'

Maitland shook his head. 'Perhaps he wandered up from below.' Harry inspected the object of Bailey's curiosity more closely. The stranger certainly didn't appear to belong on the first-class deck. 'He may have boarded at Cherbourg, of course.'

'We dock at Lisbon, don't we?'

'Why, yes. We're due in a couple of hours.' Maitland was struck by the change in the older man's manner. All his ease was gone; he had the aspect of a pointer that senses a bird is about to break cover. 'Are you going ashore?'

'I think I will,' Bailey said. He watched Karl's back until he had ducked out of sight behind the *Arthurian's* funnels. 'I can do without the salted codfish,' Bailey went on, regaining his aplomb. 'But Lisbon's a splendid city. Shall we take in the sights together?'

The *Arthurian* dropped anchor at Lisbon, dwarfing a school of sardine boats, and the passengers who were going onshore started to assemble along the railings. Bailey had changed into a lightweight suit and a panama hat. It wasn't quite as warm here as he had expected, and there was a brisk wind coming in from the Atlantic.

With mounting nervousness he watched Karl boarding one of the ship's boats among a crowd of second-class passengers. Bailey knew, from Johnny and other sources, that there would be a Comintern liaison office near the docks, as in all major European ports, probably disguised as a seamen's club. He did not know whether Karl was still a member of the *Apparat*. It was conceivable that the young German had finally burned his boats with the party and was running off in search of a new life in the New World. But Bailey didn't much believe in coincidence. It seemed more likely that Karl was on the *Arthurian* for reasons related to his own: that Karl, too, had an assignment in Rio. If Karl headed for the Comintern bureau on shore, that would settle the matter.

It might also blow Bailey and his mission out of the water. There were more sophisticated minds in Stalin's secret service than the ones Bailey had had to contend with outside the Casbah restaurant in Paris, and they were unlikely to set any more store by coincidence than he. If Karl reported that he had sighted the same British Intelligence officer who had approached him in Paris en route to Rio, an inquisitive chekist – perhaps Max Fabrikant – would start making connections. Almost inevitably, the inquiry would lead to Johnny. Bailey realised that more than his own mission was at risk. Johnny's life was at stake.

Maitland appeared at his elbow.

'Ready?' the younger man asked nonchalantly, nodding towards the boat that was filling up with first-class passengers.

'Oh, yes, of course.' But he detained Maitland for a moment before they climbed down into the boat. 'I may have a spot of bother,' he began.

Maitland heard him out and seemed to take it in his stride, even though the sum of his knowledge of Colin Bailey up to this point was that he had been at school with his father, held a presumably boring civilian job in the War Ministry and was an amateur naturalist who was spending his holiday in Brazil to look at birds and animals.

Karl had a long head start, and, when they reached the docks, Bailey feared they had lost him. The steep, narrow streets leading away from the harbour were crowded with people. A horse-drawn cart lumbered past, blocking the view and spattering a fresh load of dung over the toes of Bailey's brogues. He swore softly and jumped up on a packing crate to get a better look around.

There. He spotted the German's sandy, close-cropped hair and navy-blue coat. Karl was ambling along a street lined with shops and honky-tonks like a man without a care in the world.

'Give me a good start,' Bailey told Maitland. 'There's no need for you to get involved. I just want you to watch my back. All right?'

'All right.' Maitland grinned at the prospect of an adventure.

Bailey trailed Karl as the German followed a circuitous course through snaky side streets. At one point Karl turned left towards the harbour, then rounded a corner and walked back parallel to the way he had come. He was either lost, or enjoying a simple outing – or checking whether he was being followed.

Bailey hung back, hugging the doorways and trying to stay out of sight.

Then Karl broke into a half run and dashed around another corner. Bailey quickened his stride, anxious not to lose him.

He rounded the same corner. Karl was nowhere to be seen. But two blocks away, in the direction of the port was a down-at-the-heel seamen's club, a likely cover for the Comintern office. Could Karl have reached it already? Even taken at a sprint, the distance seemed too great.

Bailey hesitated. There were alleys off to both sides of the street. He peered down one of them. There was a smell of rotting fish. He heard a faint scuffle and the clang of metal and advanced a few steps. Probably nothing more than an alley cat scavenging the rubbish bins.

He turned on his heel and saw Karl, face tensed and pale, lunging at his belly with a knife.

Bailey flung himself to one side, twisted his ankle and came down in a sprawling heap.

Bailey rarely carried a gun and had not deemed it necessary to go armed on board a cruise ship. As he rolled to avoid Karl's plunging knife, he realised that the omission was likely to prove fatal.

He managed to seize hold of the German's wrist and wrestled with him for control of the knife. It was a losing battle. The point of the blade nicked his ear.

Then another figure erupted into the alley. Harry Maitland charged at the German like a bull, knocked him to one side and twisted the knife out of his hand.

But Karl wasn't easily dispatched. Bailey had felt his strength; his sinews were tempered steel. He lashed out at Maitland, dealt him a terrific blow on the chest and went gouging for the eyes, his fingers spread like claws.

Maitland was breathing hard, and Bailey saw him go down as he scrambled to his feet, ready to take on the German again.

But before Bailey could make his move, Maitland struck out with his feet, one after the other. He made an amazing sight, suspended above the ground on the palms of his hands, his legs driving high into the air. His right foot connected with the side of Karl's jaw, and the German dropped like an ox under the slaughterer's mallet.

'Are you all right?' Maitland inquired, dusting himself off.

'Thanks to you.'

Bailey limped over to where Karl was lying.

'My God,' Maitland said. 'I haven't killed him, have I?'

'I'm not sure,' Bailey said mildly, pressing his ear to the German's chest. He heard an irregular flutter.

He squatted on his haunches, took Karl's head between his hands and wrenched until he heard a distinct crack.

'I'm afraid there's no hope for him,' Bailey said blandly.
Maitland stared at him.

'I saw what you did,' Maitland said.

'You saw nothing.'

'We have to do something.'

'I agree. I think we have both earned a stiff drink.'

'Look, I don't want to be boring, but we have to go to the police.'

Bailey was still crouched over the dead man's body, rummaging through his pockets, inspecting the lining of his coat. He picked up Karl's knife, slit a seam, and extracted a small square of linen that had been stitched inside. He gave no sign of having heard Maitland's last statement.

'I said, we must go to the police,' Maitland repeated.

'Listen to me, Harry.' Bailey got to his feet and looked the younger man squarely in the eyes. 'I am engaged in a secret mission for the War Office. Do you understand what that means?'

'I – I think so.'

'That man –' Bailey jabbed his foot at the body '– was a Russian agent. These are his credentials.' He held up the linen square covered with minute characters. '*Aut disce, aut discede.* Have you forgotten the last bit?'

'*Manet sors tertium caedi,*' Maitland recited dutifully.

It was the Latin tag that was framed on the wall of the ancient hall at Winchester College that was known simply as 'school'. The translation was even more awkward than the original: 'Either learn or leave. There remains a third lot, to be beaten.'

'Exactly,' Bailey said.

Maitland still appeared unconvinced.

Bailey put his hand on his shoulder and said quietly, 'Harry, are you ready to serve your King?'

Maitland stiffened. 'Of course.'

'Good. Then help me get this fellow out of the light.'

Bailey had seen enough of killing on the battlefields of France to detest the idea of taking life. Karl's death weighed on his conscience. He told himself that what had been begun in self-defence had ended with the plain acknowledgment of necessity; it was Karl's life or Johnny's. He had no means of holding Karl as a prisoner. He could imagine the prune-faces that would have greeted him at the embassy in Lisbon had he turned up with a wounded Bolshevik and asked them to lock him up. He could not afford complications with the Portuguese authorities. And of course there was no question of releasing Karl, once he had shown his colours.

His reasoning was flawless. But it couldn't screen out the image of the downy hair on the German's face, the remembered pulse of his failing heart, the echo of the sickening crack as his neck was broken. It is hardest to kill when the enemy has a human face.

Back on board the *Arthurian*, he set to encrypting a telegram to London. He preferred the easy-to-remember Playfair system to book codes or any of the more elaborate ciphers. It was based on a single word. He selected one that he liked – 'phantasmagoria' – from the short list he had committed to memory. He took a sheet of paper and wrote it out as two sides of a square with the initial P in the top left-hand corner, omitting duplicate letters as he went along. This gave him the following construction:

P H A N T S M G O R I
H
A
N
T
S
M
G
O
R
I

He proceeded to fill in the letters of the alphabet, as follows:

```
P H A N T S M G O R I
H A B C D E F G H I J
A K L M N O P Q R S T
N U V W X Y Z A B C D
T E F G H I J K L M N
S O P Q R S T U V W X
M Y Z A B C D E F G H
G I J K L M N O P Q R
O S T U V W X Y Z A B
R C D E F G H I J K L
I M N O P Q R S T U V
```

Using this table, he could turn each letter of his cable into one of several grid references. The letter A, for example, appearing several times inside the box, could be cross-referenced as HH, or NG, or OR. He translated the words of his message directly into the code, without making an original. When he had finished, he tore the sheet of paper bearing the table into tiny pieces and tossed them out to sea on his way to the ship's radio room. As the cable would be presented to C., it began: 'I have to inform you that an unfortunate incident at the start of the voyage set the operation at risk. It has been happily resolved.'

When he had satisfied himself that the telegram had been safely transmitted to a cover address in London, he went looking for Harry Maitland and found him in the saloon.

'I gather that Veuve Cliquot is your blood group,' Bailey said, signalling the bartender. 'Now I want you to tell me where you learned kick boxing. I saw something similar in the Orient. But you're the first white man I ever saw fight like that.'

'In Brazil they call it *capoeira*. I'm not really very good. You should see the *moleques* – the street kids – foot fight in Bahia. It's a ballet.'

As he listened to Maitland talk, Bailey reflected that the two of them were now committed to each other. It struck him that Johnny would probably like Harry too.

5

'You smell the land before you see it,' Maitland remarked.

They had spent nearly two weeks crossing the Atlantic. Now the sea breeze had dropped away, and in place of the tang of salt water, Bailey breathed in the ripe, heavy scent of the tropics. It was intimate and overpowering, like a moist palm pressed over his face. It carried the sweet-sour odour of the jungle, the whole relentless cycle of germination and decay.

The blue haze ahead of them slowly resolved itself into the profile of islands and mountains. On the port side Bailey could make out red-roofed villas and royal palms along a white crescent of sand overhung by the riotous greens of virgin forest.

'Your hotel is over there.' Maitland pointed at a palatial building facing the sea. 'It's extraordinary to think that Copacabana was almost undiscovered ten years ago. It's hard to conceive of a city so rich in natural beauty that it could turn its back on a glorious beach like that.'

Frigate birds escorted them through the mouth of the vast Guanabara Bay, guarded by the twin forts of São João and Santa Cruz, where antique cannon poked their muzzles through the sturdy sea walls. Maitland drew Bailey's attention to the changing colours around them. As the water grew deeper, it turned coppery, like a river.

'That may explain why the discoverers called the place River of January,' Maitland observed, enjoying his new role as guide. 'They thought they had entered the mouth of a great river.'

Bailey was fascinated by the mountains that framed the city and its circling beaches. They rushed down at the water like horses reined in at the last moment, before toppling in. Each had a personality of its own. Maitland pointed out some of the landmarks: the smooth, steep peak of the Sugarloaf; Gavea, flattened and windswept like the mainsail of a caravel; the hunched back of Corcovado, where the giant statue of Christ the Redeemer, arms outstretched, kept vigil over the city; the ominous Fingers of God stabbing the sky away to the north, ragged cloud streamers trailing from their tips.

Nothing in that skyline stayed constant for long. Bailey watched the coastline open and close and open again like a fan, as the *Arthurian* steamed on past the tributary bays of Botafogo and Flamengo and the baroque green filigree of the old customs house towards the docks.

'From one corner to the next, from one day to the next,' Maitland said, 'Rio is never the same. She's a beautiful woman you can never own. Or predict.'

Bailey looked back the way they had come and saw the horizon changing contours again, until the promontory of Niteroi looked like the head of a crocodile lazily basking in the sun.

Harry's a romantic fool, he thought. But perhaps Maitland was right, all the same. This city was a woman, and its welcome was a dance of the veils, both tempting and deceiving.

Bailey's hotel was a marbled palace facing the bright sweep of Copacabana, beyond an avenue lined with palms and a mosaic forecourt that looked like a Miró canvas in black and white. A maharaja and his retinue were in the lobby. When Bailey threw back the French doors to his balcony, he had the Sugarloaf to his left, a white fortress to his right, the shining blue of the Atlantic in between. He luxuriated for a while in a bathtub as deep as a well. Then he put on his white dinner jacket and descended to the hotel terrace to wait for Maitland, who had insisted on showing him the town. The colours were all impossibly vivid. The water of the pool was turquoise. The mountains that reared up above the palms and rubber trees turned from chartreuse to curação as the light fell. A grand old man in a pinstriped waistcoat with a long white apron below that fell to his ankles brought mineral water in a silver bucket and a local cocktail, a *caipirinha*, which proved to be a glass of fierce cane alcohol caressed, not weakened, by the pulp of a lime. The liquor seared its way to Bailey's stomach, leaving a heady warmth and a sweet, slightly oily taste on the tongue.

'You can taste the Amazon,' Harry Maitland remarked, taking another seat at the table. 'Do you like it?'

'I'd rather taste Loch Lomond,' Bailey smiled. 'But I'm sure I will soon be acclimatised.'

There was no dusk. The sun died in a burst of flame, and the sky hung down in folds of purple velvet.

Bailey felt the throbbing before his ears became attuned to it, a steady, insistent pulse that stirred the heavy fronds of the shade trees and the slender, supple women on the terrace in their shimmering Paris gowns. It came from all directions.

'The rhythm of Africa,' Maitland said softly. 'The samba schools are practising for Carnival. Every neighbourhood, however poor – especially the poorest – has its own school of samba. We can go to one, if you like. Later the drummers will play for the *candomblé*.'

'The *candomblé*?'

'For the spirits of Africa. They came with the slaves and became the masters.'

'But this is a Catholic country.'

'Oh, yes. But go to any church, and behind the plaster saint you will find a Yoruba god with his axe or his sword.'

Bailey listened to the drums and to the voices that came skirling over them down the hillsides from the shantytowns. He had hardly noticed the heat before. Now he found he was mopping his face with his handkerchief.

'Well,' he said to Maitland, 'what local customs were you planning to initiate me into tonight?'

'We have a dinner invitation.'

'We?'

'Well, I do, if you wish to be precise. But you will be more than welcome. Of course, we need only go if you think it would amuse you.'

'May I ask who is the host?'

'Doctor Alcibiades.'

'I beg your pardon?'

'I suppose we would call him Doctor Guimaraes in England. But in Rio everybody is known by his first name, even the President.'

'I imagine that if we had first names like Alcibiades, nobody would bother with our surnames either. At least it suggests an acquaintance with the classics. As I recall, the original Alcibiades was an Athenian drunk who tried to conquer Sicily. What is your one?'

'He's the mayor of Rio. Which means a damn sight more than Lord Mayor of London. In terms of power, if not respect.'

'Do you know who else is invited?'

'His parties are unpredictable. There are people who dare not refuse an invitation, and people who dare not accept. You see, before Alcibiades entered politics, he was the city's leading authority on –' Harry cleared his throat '– social diseases.'

'I can see why he's an influential man.'

'He speaks excellent English. He went to medical school in Boston.'

'I see. Well, I suppose that's as close as one comes to the King's English in these longitudes.'

'Shall we go, then?'

'Why not? But do me one favour, will you, Harry? Just say I'm a friend of your father's. If anybody asks, you might say I'm on holiday, looking at tropical wildlife.'

'Then you'll have a lot to talk about to Alcibiades. He's one of Brazil's leading naturalists.'

He said this straight-faced, and Bailey was pleased to note, once again, that the younger man was quick. He had confided in Harry, to a degree, after the affair in Lisbon, without specifying either the exact nature of his employment or the reason he had come to Rio. He was confident that Maitland would do nothing to cause an embarrassment.

6

Doctor Alcibiades' house was a red-tiled villa in Flamengo, about equidistant from the British embassy and the presidential palace. They drove there in the open car Harry called the Beast. It was a Hispano-Suiza touring car. When

Harry had to brake for a streetcar, there was a low growl from under the hood, as if the Beast were trying to slip the leash.

The streetcar was jammed. The conductor clambered over the passengers contending for space on the running board like a referee trying to pull apart a rugby scrum.

'See the tram?' Maitland said to Bailey. 'The trams give you the key to what Rio society is like. Everybody uses them, even the millionaire who built your hotel. So naturally, they reflect every nuance of the class structure. On the first-class trams, a male passenger is admitted only if he is wearing a jacket and tie – preferably, of course, a linen suit worn only once before it is laundered and pressed – and perhaps a boater. A man of humble means will give up his seat on the tram to a man of a higher station, regardless of age. The English colony over in Niteroi has its own tram. Naturally, Brazilians – your old-style Englishman still calls them Portuguese – are not allowed on, any more than they are admitted to the British Club.'

The streetcar jangled past, and the Beast leaped over the intersection.

'By and large,' Bailey observed, 'the great talent of the English abroad is for *not* going native.'

They were received at Doctor Alcibiades' house by a black butler with enough fruit salad on his splendid white uniform to equip an admiral. The party spilled out of the house, across a wide terrace and gardens bordered with bougainvillaea. All the Brazilians seemed to be drinking scotch whisky. Their host was sleekly handsome. His shining black hair capped his skull like moleskin. He had the longest eyelashes Bailey had ever seen on a man.

Maitland squired Bailey around the terrace, making introductions – a newspaper publisher, a popular artist, a very anglicised Canadian with a monocle who had something to do with the power company. Bailey's eye fell on a woman who was by herself in a circle of men. She was dressed conservatively in comparison to the other beauties at the party, who were flaunting the most daring of the Paris fashions. Her jewels were discreet. Her dress was basic black, and the neckline was high, though it failed to conceal the boldness of her figure.

Bailey thought she looked the way Emma Bovary ought to have looked, just after the fall.

'She's quite a knockout, isn't she?' Maitland murmured, following Harry's glance. 'She's the publisher's mistress. I believe her name is Ariana. I expect her presence is causing quite a stir. All the wealthy Brazilians keep mistresses, but they're not supposed to show them at affairs like this.'

Bailey noted that a very fair-skinned woman in red – presumably the wife of one of Ariana's admirers – kept glaring menacingly in her direction. A small, lively figure detached itself from the circle around the woman in black.

'Good evening, Harry,' he greeted Maitland. 'Do you suppose Rio Light could arrange a blackout tonight? It might spare some of our friends the wrath of their wives.'

'I wonder if that's all that would happen. Colin, I am honoured to present Colonel Plinio Nogueira. Colonel Plinio is the man who makes it possible for us to sleep safe in our beds.'

'Or someone else's,' the colonel said pleasantly.

Colin Bailey inspected him more closely. Plinio was immaculately turned out in a dark, tailored suit whose quality was discreetly advertised by the fact that the last button on each cuff was left unfastened. The arch of the eyebrows and the silky moustache curling up slightly at either end suggested a capacity for humour. His high colour indicated not only a pleasing variety of ancestors but that – in one of the biblical tags he liked to recall from his Catholic education – the colonel had looked at the wine-cup when it was red.

'Colonel Plinio is the chief of the Department of Political and Social Order,' Harry explained.

The colonel clicked his heels and made a little bow.

'You are also English, Mr Bailey?'

'Very much so, I'm afraid.'

'I have always liked the English,' Colonel Plinio announced. 'Even if they do not invite us to their club. I was in London some years ago, and I visited a haberdashery on

Savile Row. I have a penchant for ties, you know. It is one of my *serious* vices.'

Bailey examined his neckwear, a burgundy silk foulard with a subdued equestrian pattern.

'I had selected half a dozen ties – my collection fills a whole wardrobe – and when the time came to pay the bill, I found, to my embarrassment, that I had no money on me. The sales attendant, one of that superior breed that can pass for housemasters at Eton, was perfectly charming. He asked if I had some means of identification. I had not so much as a visiting card. You see, I had changed my clothes and left my hotel in rather a hurry to keep a rendezvous – a somewhat delicate story I mustn't bore you with here. I told the attendant that I would return to collect the ties later. Still unperturbed, he said, "That's perfectly all right, sir. May I examine the label in your suit?" I was too astonished to refuse.

'Can you guess what happened? The attendant glanced at the label on my inside-breast pocket. Fortunately, it was the label of a well-known tailor, also on Savile Row. The attendant said, "That will do admirably, sir." They wrapped up my purchases and let me walk out with them, just like that.'

'A man with the right tailor could never belong to the criminal classes,' Bailey remarked.

'There it is!' Colonel Plinio exclaimed in triumph. 'The quintessence of English social philosophy. To the Raj!'

'I see that your Colonel Plinio is something of a humorist,' Bailey remarked to Maitland after the policeman moved on. 'And something of a ladies' man to boot,' he added, noting that Plinio had returned to the assault on the tantalising woman in black.

'I'm rather surprised to find him here,' Maitland observed. 'His chief and Doctor Alcibiades can't stand each other.'

'And what are Plinio's relations with his chief?'

'Ambiguous. Like Plinio's relations with most people.'

'I see that you've brought me into the middle of some intrigue.'

'I thought it might be the kind of entertainment that agreed with you.'

Bailey's eyes twinkled. He was sure now he was going to enjoy Brazil. 'What can you tell me about Plinio's chief?'

'Well, of course Plinio heads the political police. Filinto Müller, the chief of police for the federal district, is his boss.'

'Müller? Is he German?'

'Of German descent. There's quite a large German community here. I'm sure the German embassy must be cultivating Müller. So are the Greenshirts, our local storm troopers. They turned out an honour guard to help him celebrate his birthday. But Müller is an ambiguous character, too. He was one of the *tenentes*, the revolutionary lieutenants. He even marched with the Prestes Column, though when he bailed out they started calling him a coward and a traitor. Things are never black and white in Brazil.'

Bailey nodded, surveying the two or three brown faces among the guests.

'You seem to be remarkably well informed,' he told Maitland.

'Well, it's a small society here. Much like anywhere else, I expect. If you can sit a horse properly, you're already halfway there.'

Dinner included some of the heady delicacies of Bahia – *vatapá*, *acarajé* – washed down with Chilean wines. The wife of the Canadian monocle was seated on Bailey's left. She was called Stella, and she talked about life with a robust vulgarity that didn't go with her husband's aroma of mothballs.

'Oh, there's no colour problem in Brazil,' she announced, in response to a question. She leaned closer and whispered in Bailey's ear, 'Because the Portuguese will do it with anything on two legs.' Then, in a more normal voice, 'You don't see many blacks here, of course. You won't see them in the Jockey Club enclosure either. But the Brazilians don't exclude people because they're black. They exclude them because they're poor. If you've got money, you're as white as alabaster, whatever your grannie happened to be.'

A band played tangoes on the terrace after dinner. When the band paused after its first set, Bailey could hear the drums talking again from the hillsides. Doctor Alcibiades made the round of his guests, puffing on his cigar.

'I am told you are something of a naturalist, Mister Bailey,' the mayor addressed him.

'Just an amateur.'

'I'm sure you're too modest. Would it amuse you to see my collection?'

'I'd be delighted. Does it have any special focus?'

'Oh, yes.' Alcibiades smiled. 'I am especially interested in reptiles.' His liquid brown eyes shifted to Colonel Plinio. 'Perhaps this might amuse you, too, my dear Colonel?'

'I wouldn't miss it for anything.'

Doctor Alcibiades led them down a dimly lit corridor that made a right angle bend and along a covered walk smelling of palm oil, where servant boys were sleeping in hammocks. Bailey calculated that the villa must contain at least thirty rooms.

A guard dog rushed out of the shadows, teeth bared, pawing at the air when it reached the end of its tether. A man rose out of the darkness behind it with a rifle under his arm. He spoke to the dog, and it lay down.

'I see you are well protected, Doctor,' Bailey remarked to his host.

'More than is necessary, I think. We Brazilians are a pacifistic people. But my friends in the police insist.'

They came to a large greenhouse, and Alcibiades unlocked the door with a key that was fastened to his watch fob. Bailey noticed that some kind of talisman was also attached, a small gold fist with the tip of the thumb pushing up between the index and middle fingers.

The mayor turned on the lights, and Bailey saw that both sides of the greenhouse were occupied by large glass cases with wooden hutches and miniature rock gardens inside. In one of the nearer cases, a jet-black reptile advanced on the glass in a series of sudden, whiplike movements and raised up, flicking its tongue. The thing was as long as Bailey.

Doctor Alcibiades picked up an odd implement – a pole with a piece of thick, bent wire on the end, like one tine of a fork – unlatched the case, caught the black snake under its middle, and tossed it straight at Harry Maitland.

'Just hold that for a minute, will you?'

Bailey looked round for something heavy and picked up a rock. Colonel Plinio, who had been hovering at Maitland's right elbow, staged a lightning retreat. He was now by the door, clutching a Smith & Wesson. Harry had managed to catch the heavy, squirming reptile. Its tail thwacked against his thigh. Sweating lightly, he manoeuvred till he had a hand round its neck, just below the head. Its jaws opened and closed. It was as cold as a tombstone.

Doctor Alcibiades surveyed the disruption he had caused and burst out laughing.

'I see you really are a novice, Mister Bailey. Otherwise you would have been able to reassure our young friend Harry. That little beauty is a mussurama, a cousin of the North American king snake. He's harmless to men. He even enjoys human company. Here, put him on the table.'

Harry dropped the snake onto a surface the size of a billiard table, with a slightly curved, glassy rim.

'Snakes are highly specialised,' Alcibiades went on. 'Especially in their eating habits. There are some that live exclusively on birds, others on frogs or lizards or even spiders. A very few species are cannibals. This fellow is one of them. He dines exclusively on his fellow snakes. In your honour, gentlemen, I will provide a demonstration.'

He opened another of the glass cases and fished around with his hook among a pile of rocks and dead branches. A smaller snake lunged out of its hiding place towards the open door. Alcibiades caught it at the last instant, pinned its head and dropped it on to the table at the opposite end from the mussurama.

It reared up, threw back its pointed head, and opened its jaw to reveal huge fangs dripping with yellow venom.

'The ace of spades, to perfection,' Bailey said. 'She's a pit viper, isn't she?'

'Very good, Mr Bailey. We call her a *jararaca*. She is

related to the fer-de-lance. Men can sometimes survive her bite for many hours, even a whole day. But not pleasurably. Now watch, please.'

The bigger snake was not intimidated by the viper's display. It rippled gently across the table, till it was brushing the viper's side, as if seeking to make friends. For a moment the viper was perfectly still. Then it struck with such speed that it was merely a blur before Bailey's eyes, until he saw its fangs drive deep into the back of the larger snake.

The mussurama seemed utterly oblivious to what had just happened. In a slower but decisive movement, it rounded on its assailant, prisoning the viper's lower jaw inside its mouth. It swung the viper aloft, then brought its body slamming down against the hard surface. After several minutes, the viper seemed to have been thrashed into insensibility.

The bigger snake opened its jaws to their fullest extent. In a series of prodigious gulps, it began to swallow its victim whole.

When its meal was over, its body was unevenly distended, like a string of sausages.

Alcibiades contemplated his cannibal snake with proprietorial affection. 'Doesn't that remind you of our distinguished colonel of police?' the doctor addressed his English guests. 'Courtly, a friend to all mankind – and especially, to all womankind – and yet capable of consuming any of us. My dear Plinio. I do hope I haven't offended you.'

'On the contrary. I am flattered, of course.' Plinio rose to the occasion with a smile and a little bow. 'But, being a simple policeman, I lack the subtlety to grasp your analogy completely. If I am not mistaken, this little pet of yours – the mussurama – devours only snakes that are dangerous to other species, such as man.'

'That is so.'

'Then tell me, my good Alcibiades –' Plinio patted the cold skin of the mussurama, stretched taut over the undigested body of its victim '– would you compare yourself to this useful animal – or his supper?'

7

Johnny's Rio was very different from the city of lights that Harry Maitland was showing off to Colin Bailey.

At the hour when the RMS *Arthurian* was steaming into the Bay of Guanabara, Johnny was at a deserted beach, hidden in a fork of the mountains a few miles west along the coast. He was teaching four skinny Brazilian boys, and a skinnier Basque who was old enough to be their father, how to make bombs.

The scene looked more like a cooking lesson. Each man had an empty jam tin and a supply of phosphorus and other chemicals.

Johnny's simplest instructions took time to convey. His Portuguese was still rudimentary, although he had been going twice a week to the home of a language teacher on a shady street in Botafogo. The man was a positivist who made Johnny practice excerpts from the writings of the master, Auguste Comte. This was less than adequate for explaining street fighting tactics or the handling of explosives.

Vasco, the Spaniard, knew some English. So Johnny would call out orders to him, and he would translate for the others.

'The proportions must be exact,' Johnny lectured. 'Once you have prepared the bomb –'

'*Las proporciones deveran ser exactas.*' Vasco piped across him. In his excitement, he was using his native Spanish instead of Portuguese.

'– don't sit around twiddling your thumbs. Lose it fast. It's like a grenade without a pin, so don't go knocking it over by accident. The mixture will detonate on impact. Does everybody understand?'

After the pause for translation, the response was five sets of grinning teeth.

'All right. Go to it!'

Johnny walked up and down the white sand, watching them. They were one of the cells selected for special training by Nilo, the party organiser in Rio. Two of them had been in the army, though you wouldn't guess it from the way they handled explosives. At the end of Johnny's week-long course – which ranged from the Leninist theory of imperialism to secret communications and homemade bombs – each man was supposed to be ready to teach others.

It was going to take a damn sight longer than a week, Johnny thought. Still, he could not fault their enthusiasm, even if it was slightly unorthodox. In the midst of one of his mini-tutorials on scientific Marxism-Leninism, the Spaniard – a painter and a former anarchist – had got carried away and started spouting Bakunin. 'I suffer because I am a man and wish to be a god!' Vasco quoted with trembling passion. The Brazilians had applauded, not knowing exactly who Bakunin was. The Brazilians seemed to have been nurtured on *Les Misérables* rather than *Das Kapital*. Some of their notions came from even less scientific places. Zé Sampaio, the slim mulatto at the end of the beach, had brought Johnny photographs of his friends. Johnny was surprised to learn that all of them were dead. 'They are my spirit friends,' Zé amplified. 'They visit me every week.'

Johnny found that all of this made it easier for him to play the role of ideological mentor.

I teach them one mythology, he told himself, and they blend it into their own, the way the Roman army borrowed Mithra from the East.

There were moments when he actually enjoyed himself.

He noticed that Vasco was shovelling phosphorus into his jam tin.

'Go easy on that!' he called out to his interpreter.

Vasco nodded and grinned and threw in an extra scoop of saltpeter.

All of the bombs were ready. They were primitive devices, but they could be produced quickly, cheaply and in bulk, and Nilo claimed that in Rio alone there would be five thousand civilians willing to use them.

'One at a time!' Johnny shouted. 'Zé! You go first! The rest of you – on your bellies!'

Vasco had not finished translating when Zé hurled his bomb, which brought down a royal palm and left a smoking crater where it had stood.

When the Spaniard's turn came, he whooped, 'That's the Special Police barracks!' and flung his bomb at a conical rock fifty feet away. The bomb fell short and rolled on its side. The only sound was the crash of the breakers.

'*Coño*,' Vasco swore in Spanish. He started loping along the beach towards the unexploded bomb.

'Vasco!' Johnny yelled, propping himself up on his elbows. 'Don't touch it!'

It was too late. Vasco already had his fingers round the can. The moment he lifted it off the sand, the bomb went off.

Vasco howled. His face was blackened, and most of his moustache had been burned off. He was squeezing his hands. From between the fingers, blood spurted high into the air in narrow jets.

Johnny ran to him and prised his hands apart. The right one was normal. On the left hand, the thumb was intact. But above the knuckles, there was only a charred, bloody stump.

Johnny started tearing strips off his shirt, to make a tourniquet.

'Zé! Get your car!' he shouted to the young mulatto, who worked as a taxi driver and acted as chauffeur to the group.

Vasco was sobbing and mumbling incoherently. Something about a wedding ring. Johnny scoured around in the burned grass and found it, a simple gold band with two sets of initials inside. Gently, he pushed it onto the third finger of the Spaniard's right hand.

Johnny had memorised the address of a doctor, one of the ones who would not report a gunshot wound – or bomb damage – to the police. He ran a clinic on the Rua Chile that Johnny had used for secret meetings with Nilo. On their way there in Zé's taxi, Johnny said, in an effort to buck Vasco up, 'You're bloody lucky to be alive. And it wasn't your right hand. You'll still be able to paint.'

'I'm left-handed,' the Spaniard said, and spat out a broken tooth.

Johnny and Helene had disembarked in Rio three weeks before, the advance guard of the South American bureau.

Their landing was choppier than Bailey's. They had to fight their way through a crush of Sicilian and Neopolitan peasants who were being bullied by petty officials. The customs inspectors behaved as if they had all week to examine each bag, until Johnny slipped one of them a handsome tip. Instantly a dozen small boys sprang into action, and they saw their suitcases being hustled away in different directions. Johnny went racing after the one that contained the books he needed to encipher and decode messages – innocuous-seeming editions of Victor Hugo and a guide for commercial travellers.

Outside the customs hall Johnny paid off the unwanted porters and deposited their bags in a locker. They walked to the contact address they had been given, a hole in the wall off the Praça Maua. It was full of sailors. Whores of every shape, age and colour leaned over the gallery above, cooing to attract the men. There was a mulatta in a yellow dress, beautiful except for the gap in her front teeth, who was munching on roasted peanuts. She tossed some of the shells at Johnny and called down in a voice that ended in a screech, like a parrot's.

'I think she said I'm too old for you.' Helene winked at him.

They found a table by the wall, half inside, half out. They sipped sweet, strong *cafezinhos* and waited. The scene in the street was a riot of colour, almost a carnival. Strolling musicians stopped to serenade them. A shifty-eyed man sidled up and thrust out a forearm festooned with a half-dozen watches. When Johnny turned away, he uncurled his fist and showed Helene a palm full of dull reddish stones that might have been rubies. The women moved by on dancing hips.

A boy wandered along with a cart, selling hot roasted peanuts in little twists of paper. He had made a brazier out of a rusty can; the coals were glowing at the bottom. He tossed a few nuts onto each of the café tables, then retraced his steps, trying to make a sale.

Absentmindedly, Helene started cracking the shells and popping the nuts into her mouth.

'They're good,' she said to Johnny when the boy came back. 'Let's buy two bags.'

The smallest Brazilian banknote Johnny had on him was worth more than the boy's entire stock.

The boy plucked it from his hand and started trotting off round the corner.

'Hey!' Johnny called after him. 'Where's my change?'

The boy looked back over his shoulder, grinned, and crooked his finger.

'Come on,' Johnny said to Helene. He threw some money on the table and hurried after the boy.

There was a taxi double-parked in the next street, with its engine idling.

A man with slicked-down hair leaned out the back and said, in the voice of an announcer on the World Service of the BBC, 'I do hope you had a good trip.'

This was Johnny's first introduction to the man who was known in the underground as Nilo.

Nilo was the head of the Communist network in Rio and number two in the party's national organisation. Like Prestes, he owed his advancement to the Russians. Guralsky had picked him up in Buenos Aires, years before. Nilo had little else in common with Prestes – or any of his other comrades in the Brazilian Communist Party.

Behind Nilo's back, Johnny learned, they joked about him as *O Milionário*, The Millionaire, because he received a handsome annuity from his mother. While he was still in short pants, she had taken him to Europe to do the Grand Tour and left him at boarding school in England – and not just any boarding school. Nilo was the first Communist of Johnny's acquaintance who had gone to Eton. In his present milieu, that made him as exotic as a stuffed toucan in a cage might have seemed in a London drawing room.

Nilo became Johnny's constant companion in those first weeks. As he studied the Brazilian, Johnny wondered whether his conversion to the revolutionary cause was bound up with the playing fields of Eton, with some slight he had resented and remembered. Though he talked like an

English toff and affected English tailoring, Nilo had a settled hatred for the masters of the Raj. Beyond this, it was hard for Johnny to fathom his motivation. Nilo was widely read and would shoot off ideas – usually lifted from French and English literary reviews – like fireworks displays. But there seemed to be no fixed anchorage for his beliefs. Certainly he did not allow them to interfere with his pleasures, and he felt no obligation to share his annuity for the sake of the brotherhood of man. Perhaps he was in it simply for the game, playing at revolution the way he had played at other things – at being an army officer (he had been discharged after getting his commandant's daughter pregnant and declining to marry her) or an entrepreneur (he had tried to make a fortune selling orange juice to the Americans, but the bottom had fallen out of the market).

Johnny discovered another side of Nilo the night Colin Bailey was dining with Doctor Alcibiades.

On previous days, when Johnny was not busy with the training sessions on the beach, Nilo had helped him to scout out the enemy dispositions in the capital. They had inspected the guard posts around the Catete and Guanabara palaces, the layout of the Special Police barracks on the hill of San Antonio, the airfields and the military garrisons. Johnny had found a gap several hundred yards long in the security fence around the main air base. He had made sketch maps showing where the roads and the railway lines must be cut to prevent government reinforcements from reaching the capital. Using information from Nilo and other contacts in the party, he had started making lists of which military units in the capital district could be counted on to join the revolt, which would stay neutral, which would have to be beaten into submission.

That night, Nilo picked him up at the clinic on the Rua Chile, where the doctor was stitching up Vasco's wounds.

'You've been working too hard,' Nilo announced. 'I'm going to take you out on the town.'

'Then I'll fetch Helene. I told her I'd meet her for dinner.'

'Leave her at home tonight.' Nilo winked. 'I want to show you the city's other weak points.'

Johnny nearly cried off. But on the other hand, why not accept Nilo's invitation? The man was too self-indulgent to be threatening. It wouldn't hurt to get drunk with him, if that was what Nilo had in mind. In a few weeks more, when Emil and Prestes and other members of the bureau arrived, Johnny knew that his life would be far more taxing, much more closely confined.

Besides, he did not particularly relish the prospect of another long evening alone with Helene. A frost had crept into their relationship since Copenhagen. He felt, once again, that she was watching him. He had no proof that Bailey was right – that she had played the role of a provocateur for Max – but there were times when he thought she was acting as if she felt guilty. They had not talked about Sigrid since Denmark, and the fact that Helene did not ask about the decision he had made deepened his suspicions. On the steamy nights when he couldn't sleep, Johnny would walk the beach and stare across the ocean that divided him from Sigrid. Back in his room, he bared his soul to her in long, impassioned letters. He had written one about Trotsky and the crime Stalin had done him, and the greater crime that might already have been committed – though there was no news of that in the papers. He wrote a twelve-page confession, a desperate plea for understanding and forgiveness. He mailed none of these letters. Night after night, with the ink still wet on the last sheet, he would hold a candle to the pages and watch them turn yellow, then black.

Nilo's tour started off with dinner in the Rua Ouvidor, washed down with quantities of whisky and soda and a superior red wine – a Macul – from Chile. Nilo gossiped about other members of the party leadership. He joked about Miranda, the party's secretary-general, and his illiterate mistress, making them sound like a pair of country bumpkins.

Nilo's a snob, Johnny thought. And he wants Miranda's job. He's a fool to show me his hand after a couple of drinks.

Nilo and Miranda were polar opposites. Miranda was a bantam rooster, cocky, dedicated and energetic. Johnny liked him immediately. Unlike Nilo, Miranda actually belonged to the working class in whose name the revolution was being waged, the first man in his family to go to school. His strength came from his roots. When he talked about class oppression, you could tell that he knew what he was talking about from the callouses on his hands. His woman – the one Nilo poked fun at because she couldn't read – was a slender beauty from Bahia who had been raped at the age of ten by the owner of the great villa where her mother scrubbed floors.

Miranda is worth twenty of you, Johnny thought, watching his guide. If there were more like Miranda in other countries, I might still belong to the party.

After the meal Nilo lit up a cigar and proposed a stroll before the *digestivos*. They rambled down into Cinelandia. Along both sides of the boulevard men and women were strolling with their own sex, in twos and threes. Some of the girls were escorted by older women. They were all dressed to the nines. They exchanged languorous looks and blown kisses. From time to time one of the boys would let out a complicated wolf whistle that reminded Johnny of an animal in pain.

'Romantic love,' Nilo said mockingly. 'In Brazil, if you find that your bride is not a virgin, you can call the police and have the marriage annulled on the spot. So if you're courting a girl from a bourgeois family and she's willing, she'll probably tell you to use the back door. Some of our native duchesses develop rather a taste for that.'

He smirked at Johnny, who tried to conceal his mounting contempt.

'If she's not willing,' Nilo went on, 'when you're finished with mooning about down here, relief is just a few blocks away.'

He led Johnny into the winding streets of the Lapa district. They moved in a river of pastel lights. Girls called down to them from the balconies. Johnny saw the pink sign of a club, the Babylônia.

'I have a fondness for this area,' Nilo announced. 'One

of my father's friends brought me here, at his request. To make me a man, as he put it. That's still the way with the old families. I'll be eternally grateful. It made me one up on those buggers at Eton.'

'Would you describe that as a socialist attitude?' Johnny sniped at him. 'Oh, I don't know. It's certainly fraternal, wouldn't you say? I know that it goes on in Moscow. They sent me a couple of little numbers who did wonders for my socialist orientation.'

Yes, Johnny thought. They would have.

A girl came out of the Babylônia Club wearing a strapless red dress. Her skin was wild honey. The tight satin of her dress defined the rhythmic lilt of her hips. She was followed by an American with a panama hat tilted back on his head and a linen suit in need of pressing. A doorman in a turban rushed to help them into a taxi.

'She'll squeeze him for five dollars,' Nilo commented. The going rate in the shuttered houses along the streets of Lapa was ten or twenty *milreis*, the equivalent of fifty cents or a dollar.

'What about the police?' Johnny asked.

'The police are paid off. We're safer from the police here than in any other part of the city.'

They stopped for a drink at a street café and instantly drew a small crowd. Street hawkers offered beads and curios, even a live parrot. A musician serenaded them on a strange, echoing instrument that resembled a zither. Another twanged at a long, single-stringed *berimboim*. Urchins rushed up, palms outstretched, fingers slyly groping at Johnny's trouser pockets. The waiter shooed them away, flapping his napkin.

'*Para manjar*,' one of them pleaded.

Nilo threw him a coin. He sat there, the tip of his tongue flicking the side of his mouth, like a lizard's, as the girls sauntered by, and Johnny wondered why he had been brought on this outing. If Nilo were interested in hired sex, why take a witness? More probably, Nilo was trying to elicit his own weakness. Beneath the Old Etonian veneer, this unlikely Brazilian was evidently that crude, and that stupid.

330

'This is the middle circle,' Nilo announced. 'You must see the others too.'

The tour of the *zonas* took them past elegant townhouses in Santa Teresa, where the most recondite sexual passions were catered for discreetly behind the wrought iron filigree, to a corner of Leme where pederasts congregated, and finally to the roughest, most colourful of the red-light districts, the Mangue. It was near the docks and reminded Johnny of furtive boyhood visits to the Reeperbahn, except that here the girls in the bright-lit windows were darker and the busy streets opened off an avenue lined with royal palms. There was a canal beside the palms. Under soft moonlight, the scene looked as timeless and beautiful as a vision of ancient Egypt. The smell spoiled the illusion; the canal was an open sewer. The whores of the Mangue were of all ages and stages of decay. In front of a swaggering group of sailors – Johnny saw from their hatbands that they were off an Italian ship – a huge, toothless *mulata* hoisted her skirts up above her waist and danced a little jig.

Johnny felt faintly queasy. Nilo laughed and steered him in a different direction.

'I have another confession to make,' Nilo announced. 'I have a weakness for working-class girls. There is nothing more erotic to me than the sight of a well-endowed woman on her hands and knees, scrubbing the floor. Do you believe me? It's also a matter of breeding. We had a housemaid on the plantation, quite a pretty one. My father didn't need to send me to Lapa. So you see, my instincts are truly with the people.'

He laughed at his remark and clapped Johnny on the shoulder.

'I picked up a girl here once,' he went on. 'Coffee coloured, wonderful teeth, hips made for child bearing. I paid her well. You know, you can buy it here for the price of a bottle of soda. But you know what she most wanted? She wanted to sit in a bathtub, a real bathtub. She had never used one. Of course, that was all before I saw the light.'

Johnny decided then that if anything unpleasant should happen to this Brazilian because of him, he wouldn't lose much sleep over it. Nilo seemed as self-serving, as indifferent to the plight of individuals, as any coffee baron, any backlands *coronel*. Johnny's mission in Rio would be easier – he thought – if the men he met under assumed names were all cynical adventurers like Nilo or toadies and fabricators like Emil. That would have made Johnny's task of betrayal a positive pleasure. The hard thing was, there were real revolutionaries too, men and women in whom he recognised something of himself. There was Miranda, and Prestes, and Verdi, the romantic Argentine, and Livia, the stunning Communist poetess who had become Helene's special friend in Rio. There was Helene. Lost soldiers, all of them, as Heinz had said – whether they knew it or not.

8

Johnny and Helene were living in a white frame building a rifle shot away from Colin Bailey's hotel, facing the beach at Copacabana. The establishment styled itself the Valhalla Guest House. As this improbable name implied, the pension – run by a bosomy widow from the state of Paraná called Hildegard Kapp – catered almost exclusively to visitors with Teutonic bloodlines.

The Valhalla was one of Nilo's discoveries. He insisted that Johnny and Helene would attract less attention at a place where everyone spoke German. Frau Kapp, for her part, was delighted with her new guests, rapturous after Johnny expressed a fervent admiration for the Führer. She plied them with tortes and implored them not to spend too much time on the beach, because the sun's rays were ruinous for the kidneys. The better class of Brazilians, according to Frau Kapp, went bathing before breakfast and were never seen on the beach after eight in the morning.

While Johnny trained saboteurs and scouted government defenses, Helene was fully employed in preparing the ground for the senior members of the South American bureau who would soon be arriving in Rio. She scoured the classified pages, looking for apartments for rent, and found a luxurious flat for Emil in Ipanema, on the Rua Paulo Redfern. She took a lease on a more modest apartment, a few blocks away, that would be convenient for meetings. She bought a Baby Ford with operational funds – she would act as Emil's driver and bodyguard when he arrived – and drove it into the Rio traffic as if she were opening a billiard game.

The morning after Doctor Alcibiades' party, Colin Bailey strolled the Avenida Atlântica and took a seat at a sidewalk café facing the water, half a block away from the Valhalla Guest House. He downed two *cafezinhos*, while several boys hopped about, offering to shine his shoes or arrange an assignation with one of their sisters. Bailey contemplated hiring one of them to carry a note to Johnny. Then he saw a tall, striking blonde come out of the *pension* and climb into a little black Ford. He knew Helene immediately from the photographs. She was superbly turned out in a suit with high, padded shoulders and a tailored jacket that drew attention to her narrow waist. She wore a wide-brimmed hat and dark glasses. Bailey wondered who she was setting off to meet. The Ford lurched out into the traffic.

With Helene safely out of the way, Bailey decided to risk a frontal assault on Valhalla. A Negro boy answered the bell. He became nervous and flustered when Bailey asked for Senhor Gruber, and apparently spoke no English. He ended by slamming the screen door in the Englishman's face.

Bemused by this reception, Bailey walked round the block and found that the guest house had a service entrance at the back. He was testing the door when a lace curtain was pulled back and the snout of a long-barrelled pistol poked through the window.

'Johnny?' Bailey called out.

'Hold on.'

When Johnny unlatched the door, his gun tucked away beneath his jacket, he was apologetic.

'I wasn't expecting you so soon,' he told Bailey. 'I told the boy to tell anyone who asked for me that I was out.'

'Is there some problem?'

'I was worried about the police. These Brazilians aren't very security conscious.'

They took a walk on the beach, and Johnny told Bailey about his excursion with Nilo. He made the Brazilian sound like the type who had become a radical because he'd failed to get into the First Eleven at Eton. Bailey resolved that when he got back, he must get Diana to ask her brother, another old Etonian, whether he remembered anything of this Brazilian. Apart from his nervousness about the police, Johnny seemed in good form. But the meeting did not end well for Bailey. He took off his shoes to walk on the sand, and, distracted by a ravishing Carioca in a scandalously skimpy swimsuit, he managed to step on a jellyfish. He hardly noticed it at the time, but he ended up spending much of the night soaking his foot in cold water, until the drums from the *favelas* started pounding inside his head.

Bailey's subsequent meetings with Johnny took place on safer ground. The Englishman came to favour the warren of gaming rooms at the back of his hotel, which habitués called the Necrôpolis. There was a grand casino on the second level of the hotel, with an endless supply of free champagne for the fashionable clientele who turned out to play roulette and blackjack. But Bailey ruled this out as a suitable place for a meet after his first brush with the *physionomiste* who had a perch in the lobby. *Physionomistes* had a photographic memory for faces. Casinos employed them to screen out professional cardsharps and other undesirables. Bailey also had found uses for them. This one, unfortunately, was worthy of his keep. He told Bailey that he remembered him from Divonne, though Bailey had visited the casino there only once in his life, and that had been a decade before, at the least.

In the Necrôpolis, evening dress was not a requisite, and the management did not bother with complimentary champagne or canapés. The *physionomiste* was replaced by a couple of obvious heavies in lounge suits. The rooms were packed with compulsive losers, mostly Brazilians.

The Necrôpolis struck Bailey as an ideal place for a brief meeting or a brush contact, and he taught Johnny the old roulette ruse. To decide the date and place of the next meeting, he would place his chips on red or black – meaning the Necrôpolis itself, or a beachfront café – and then on two separate numbers, for the day and hour.

Bailey learned from Johnny's reports that the principal conspirators would not arrive until after Carnival, travelling by steamer via Montevideo. A radio man was en route from California. There were plans to arm peasant leagues in the north. Nilo and Miranda were confident of their support in the armed forces and expected it to grow dramatically once a front movement, in which the Communist involvement would be disguised, was launched.

Two problems still confronted Bailey: how to communicate with his agent once he had returned to Europe and what, if anything, to tell the Brazilian authorities.

At the end of his first week in Rio, Bailey went around to the embassy to send his mail and pay his respects to His Majesty's Ambassador Plenipotentiary, Sir Evelyn Paine. The British Mission was pleasantly situated on a leafy boulevard in Flamengo, fronting the sea. The window behind Sir Evelyn's desk was a picture postcard, with the Sugarloaf in the right-hand corner. Summerhayes, the Head of Chancery, had counselled Bailey to seek a morning interview. Sir Evelyn was apparently in the habit of taking a siesta in the afternoons, leaving the business of the embassy in charge of his wife, who treated the striped-pants contingent as an extension of her domestic staff.

Bailey found Sir Evelyn preoccupied with arranging his seasonal escape to Petrôpolis, where the president had his summer palace, before the start of Carnival.

'Damned lot of noise and African mumbo jumbo,' was Sir Evelyn's description of the latter. 'A poor excuse for an orgy.'

'Kipling enjoyed Carnival here.'

'I can't think why,' Sir Evelyn said stuffily. 'You'd be well advised to get away before it begins.'

Sir Evelyn made it plain that, from his point of view, Bailey's departure could not come too soon. He presumed to inform the head of Section V that he belonged to the 'old school'. In other words, Sir Evelyn thought that diplomatists should not be required to dirty their hands by consorting with spies. Bailey refrained from pointing out that his own 'school' was rather more ancient than the ambassador's; it could trace its genealogy at least to Moses' spies in the land of Canaan.

'I've been instructed to assist you,' Sir Evelyn said, rattling through the small phalanx of medicine bottles arrayed on his desk. 'But I do hope you're not going to cause any fuss.'

Bailey accepted Summerhayes' invitation to lunch at the British Club, near the racetrack. The club was full of the types he had used to avoid at Simla. Summerhayes told him in a conspiratorial whisper that the members were engaged in a last-ditch effort to keep up standards; they were trying to keep Americans out.

Summerhayes resembled a melancholy greyhound, but he had a dry sense of humour that appealed to Bailey and seemed well informed on the Brazilian scene.

'I'd like to pick your brains for a bit,' Bailey announced after the second gin.

'How can I help?'

'Tell me about President Vargas.'

'Getulio? That's what they all call him in the street, you know. Let's see. He's five feet four, goes about in white suits and smokes black cigars and has sons named Luther and Calvin – which is quite a feat in a Catholic country, you know. He's also a fanatic about golf, although he plays so badly I'm afraid even Sir Evelyn has trouble losing to him graciously. He's a very mild-mannered dictator, as dictators go. He got in because of a revolution, one of those typical Brazilian affairs in which almost nobody gets shot.

'Some of the coffee planters backed him because the old government wouldn't do anything for them when coffee prices fell through the floor after the crash on Wall Street. A lot of the *tenentes* – the young nationalists in the military – sided with him too. And of course the cowboys. He's from the south, from gaucho country. He's a reformer, in his way. He's brought in a new constitution and is moving in a more liberal direction. He's doing a lot for the middle class and for the cities. The people who hate him are the old establishment, especially in São Paulo, and various regional warlords who are used to running their own show and don't like the fact that he's increased the power of the federal government. And some members of this club,' he added, cocking an eyebrow. 'They think he's an upstart, especially since word got around that he received Sir Evelyn at his summer palace wearing his pyjamas.'

'Is it true?'

'It was a Sunday morning, one gathers. Brazilian men think it's perfectly proper to be seen in pyjamas on Sundays, provided they are freshly pressed.'

'What is the president's attitude towards Britain?'

'Relations are correct. Getulio plays golf with H.E., as I mentioned. We have some useful connections in the government. But of course the Americans and the Germans are gaining a great deal of influence. They both have vigorous partisans in the government.'

'What do you see as the biggest threat to our interests?'

'Well, there is tremendous pressure to cancel the foreign debt. I don't know whether you heard about Souza Dantas. The head of the Bank of Brazil, you know. He went to the United States on a mission and horrified the bankers by announcing that Brazil couldn't afford to pay its debts. Vargas showed some common sense; he promptly reassured everyone that Brazil would go on meeting its obligations. When Souza Dantas got off his boat at Rio, he was met by an honour guard of local Fascists – they call themselves *Integralistas* – in their jackboots and green shirts. I happened to be meeting the same boat, so I saw the whole thing. It was quite uncanny. The Greenshirts let out Red Indian war whoops –'

'Did you say Red Indian?'

'Yes. Brazilian Fascists are frightfully keen on being indigenous.'

'What an extraordinary country!'

'The Greenshirts borrowed their war cry from the Tupi Indians. It goes something like this. *Anaué!*'

A florid gentleman at the next table turned and gave Summerhayes a withering glare.

Summerhayes blushed and lowered his voice. 'The long and short of it,' he pursued, 'is that both the Fascists and the Communists stand to gain from the financial crisis, and the place is full of woolly-headed subalterns who will join any revolt as long as it's sufficiently picturesque.'

'We may be able to offer some assistance,' Bailey said quietly.

When they went in to lunch, Summerhayes was visibly excited.

'I take it you told H.E. about this,' the Head of Chancery said over the roast veal.

'Not in any detail. I think it's best not to involve the embassy any more than is strictly necessary, don't you?'

Bailey explained what he had in mind. He would need a friend at the embassy to pass on cables that could not be entrusted to the commercial services, and to help in an emergency.

Summerhayes would be useful, but as a catcher, not a bowler. Bailey had no intention of entrusting Johnny to anyone from the embassy. Sir Evelyn's languour might be contagious and was almost certainly terminal. Besides, Bailey had already found the man for the job.

Harry Maitland lived on the fringe of the Tijuca rain forest, in a Gothic Victorian house with a high, pointed gables and a wide verandah where hammocks were slung under mosquito nets. The forest smelled of rain. All along the winding road, the bright coral reds of impatiens – the Brazilians called them Shameless Maries – blazed among the green.

As Bailey mounted the steps, he was greeted by a low barking sound from close at hand, followed by a series of piercing whistles. He looked around for the dog and found a bird in a cage.

'It's a *curupião*,' Harry told him. 'A natural impressionist. Actually, it was a present from our friend the mayor. I imagine he keeps birds to feed to his snakes. Come in and have a drink.'

The drinks were served by a girl with smiling eyes who moved at a gently rolling gait, more a dance than a walk, that made her whole body quiver. Her skin was cinnamon; her billowing white skirts were trimmed with gold. Her assurance and the way Harry looked at her told Bailey she was more than a housekeeper.

'Her name is Luisa,' Maitland said. 'She is from Bahia.'

The smells of *dendê* and coconut oil wafted through from the kitchen as Luisa prepared some of the favourite dishes of her native city – little crabcakes, sizzling in the dish, *ximxim de galinha* and a sugary dessert, made with beaten eggs, that looked like a mass of fine yellow hair.

It was a farewell dinner, and Bailey was glad that Harry had decided to share another part of his life with him.

Bailey had made his proposition the day after his lunch with the man from the embassy.

'There's no money in it to speak of, I'm afraid,' Bailey had warned. 'Although of course we'll see that you're not left out of pocket. No glory either. And you'll be pretty much out on a limb. If you get into trouble, the embassy will deny all knowledge. You'll be working for a service that doesn't officially exist.'

'No thanks if I succeed and no help if I fail?' Maitland grinned, paraphrasing Buchan.

'That's about it. But you'll be helping both your own country and your adopted one – and a chap I think you are going to like enormously.'

Bailey didn't need to dress up the offer to feel confident that it was one that Harry couldn't refuse. How could a man who would sail up the Amazon in search of a lost explorer turn down another adventure? Besides, Harry was perfect for the job. He had proved that both in Lisbon and at dinner with the mayor. He had both spunk and connections, as well as the ability to think on his feet. He was going to need all of them.

Bailey was not disappointed.

Harry's questions were all practical, to do with how to

arrange safe meetings and how to send secure messages. Bailey was able to give him all of a day's instruction in basic tradecraft. They went to inspect some possible dead drops. Bailey was pleased that Harry had some ideas of his own, including a church collection box, though he had to rule out a few of them as impractical.

Bailey stressed again, as they smoked cigars after dinner, that Johnny must be protected at any price. If it became necessary to alert the Brazilian authorities, it must be done in such a way as to hide the source. Perhaps, if the occasion arose, Maitland would be able to build on his relationship with Colonel Plinio.

'I'll be sorry to miss Carnival,' Bailey said. He did not mention the cable that had persuaded him to return on the next boat. Things were coming to a head in Copenhagen where – acting on Johnny's information – he had set in motion an operation involving a certain Captain Werner of Russian military intelligence.

It seemed hotter and stuffier outside, as if the rain forest were swallowing the air, and Bailey began to perspire under his light jacket.

He shook hands with Luisa. Her touch was warm but dry.

He said, 'It was a magical dinner. And you're very beautiful.'

'I'm afraid Luisa doesn't speak English,' Maitland said.

But Bailey felt that she answered him with her eyes.

As they strolled towards Harry's car, a circle of dancing lights by the roadside drew Bailey's attention.

They were candles, surrounding a curious arrangement of objects – a bottle, a cloth, cigars laid over each other to form a cross, a clay figurine or doll.

Bailey bent down to take a closer look. He reached for the doll.

He felt the restraining pressure of Luisa's hand, light yet firm, against his arm.

She murmured something in Portuguese.

He felt the warmth of her skin. She carried the faint, bewitching aroma of burnt cloves he had smelled before, borne in by the breeze across the Bay of All Saints, when his cruise ship had laid anchor at Bahia, en route to Rio.

'What is she saying?' he appealed to Harry.

'You musn't touch that. It's a *despacho*, an offering to one of the spirits. Those who ask favours must bring gifts.'

In the car, Bailey said, 'Luisa believes that stuff, doesn't she?'

'She's a daughter of Yemanjá.' Harry did not volunteer any further explanation.

Bailey remembered the gold talisman he had seen on Doctor Alcibiades' watch chain and asked about it.

'It's just a *figa*,' Harry explained. 'A good luck charm. Many Brazilians wear them.'

'So this – voodoo – is widespread?' Bailey had begun to notice other *despachos*, scores of little candles flickering in crevices along the road.

'Call it voodoo if you like. It works for some. There are spiritists in the government. Even among Prestes' followers.'

'Do you believe in it?' Bailey suddenly asked him.

'I believe in the power of all faiths,' Harry said. 'I've seen things – no, let that pass. I believe what Unamuno wrote. To believe is to create. We create gods out of our need, and they are none the less real.' Harry smiled at his own solemnity. 'I told you this was a country of gods and men.'

Back at the hotel, folding shirts for the journey ahead, Bailey thought about Harry and Luisa, and then about Kipling. On the face of it, Sir Evelyn was right. It seemed out of character for Kipling to have fallen in love with the land of Carnival. It was hard to imagine a greater contrast than that between the life and attitudes of an Englishman under the Raj and those of the Brazilians. But then again, not *entirely* out of character. The part of Kipling that was Kim would revel in Brazil and its freedom from the taboos of his tribe.

7

The Art of Insurrection

For a cornered mind, salvation lies in action.
Jan Valtin, ★ Out of the Night
★ Pseudonym of Richard Krebs, former Comintern
operative.

1

As the Baby Ford crested the rise above the docks, Johnny
had a view of two elderly Brazilian warships. They looked
as immobile as the stone fort at the mouth of the harbour.
On the other side, above the baroque cathedral, shanties
clung like mussels to the side of a granite mountain. Scores
of them had been washed away during the rains, but they
had sprouted up again as fast as the xuxu weeds and the
Shameless Maries. Soon they left the city behind and were
travelling across swampy flats towards another mountain
range, smoky in the distance. From the passenger seat,
Johnny looked out at the brown faces of women and
children at wayside stalls selling manioc root and *caldo de
cana*, sugarcane juice. Then they were climbing. Two small
boys waved at the car and held up an enormous bunch of
ladyfinger bananas. As Johnny looked back, one of them
tore off a piece of the fruit and squeezed from the bottom,
gulping down the mashed banana that came out like tooth-
paste. The road tilted up a steeper incline, and at last they
left the soggy heat of the Rio summer below.

Strange flowers blazed like jewels among the rocks; the *gravatá* plants were torches, tongues of yellow fire above the vivid orange stalks. Johnny wondered what Sigrid would make of this carnival of colour. He could see her now, her eyes bright, her lips pursed, capturing with her brush the things he couldn't name. With the image came the hollow pain of absence, so that the rockslide on the road to Petrópolis was almost a welcome diversion.

As a driver, Helene lacked experience, not confidence. Johnny gripped the doorframe to steady himself as she hurled the Baby Ford round a succession of hairpin bends, claiming the whole road as her property.

'Easy!' Johnny cautioned her after she flung the car back into her own lane to avoid a collision with an oncoming bus. The bus driver leaned out his window, shaking his fist.

Helene was flushed and happy, her hair mussed by the wind. His nervousness only seemed to heighten her pleasure. She slammed her foot down on the gas pedal again.

They screeched around a blind corner. On Johnny's right was a jagged wall of rock. To the left, beyond the narrow shoulder, the land fell away abruptly. Thousands of feet below, he could see the silver tracery of a stream at the foot of the gorge. He thought, We're travelling on the rim of a glass.

He heard the sound – like a distant drumroll – before either of them saw the first boulder that came tumbling across the road.

Helene hit the brakes, too hard. The Ford went into a skid. She clutched at the wheel, wrenching it the wrong way. They missed the fallen rock and went lurching straight for the cliff. Johnny grabbed the wheel, fighting for control of the car. By the time he had brought it shuddering to a halt, the left front wheel was suspended over the gorge.

'Get in the back,' he ordered Helene.

'You're heavier,' she snapped back, determined not to show fear at the vertiginous drop below her. 'You get in the back.'

It was not the place to argue. Gingerly, he hoisted himself over the back of his seat and manoeuvred into the space behind. With the weight in the car more dispersed, Helene tried to start the engine.

On the first two attempts, it spluttered and died. She had the choke full out, and was pumping the accelerator.

'You're flooding the carburettor,' he warned her.

Quietly but firmly, he told her what to do.

She let him drive the rest of the way to the summer capital. The smell from the high grass on the outskirts of Petrôpolis was pleasurable and oddly familiar to him. It brought back something of his boyhood. It was like the smell inside the tea chests he had used for games of hide-and-seek.

He said, 'If we take that road again, you'd better bring your parachute. And one for me, too.'

Helene laughed. She was proud of the fact that she was one of the handful of foreign women who had completed parachute training with the Soviet Air Force.

They parked just off the main square, by the canal that divided the avenue in front of the summer palace of the last emperor of Brazil. Johnny could glimpse its pink façade through the exuberant foliage of a tropical garden.

They walked to the café. There was an L-shaped counter in the front section where stand-up customers chose pastries and hot dishes from a large selection under glass. Sit-down customers were served in the back, where every wall presented a reassuring view of the range of alcohol on offer; backed by mirrors, the bottles on display were multiplied into infinity.

At that hour of the morning the back room was deserted, except for the flies and a young man drinking coffee. Johnny recognised him; he had attended one of the bomb-making courses at the beach. In the underground, they called him Escoteiro, or Boy Scout. He was very dark, with lustrous, curly hair, most of which was hidden by the broad-brimmed straw hat he had jammed down over his forehead.

Boy Scout smiled at Johnny and made a thumbs-up sign.

'They're all in there,' he said, pointing to a door with a handwritten sign that read *Privado*.

Boy Scout did not get up. As they passed him, Johnny saw the snout of the sawn-off shotgun under the table.

Six men and a woman were already assembled in the private room. Emil jumped up to greet the last arrivals. His face was bright with sweat, although he had torn off his jacket and tie. Under the great bulge of his forehead, his eyes shone with excitement.

'It's on the boil!' Emil exclaimed happily. 'There's no stopping it, absolutely no stopping it!'

'Hear, hear,' said Nilo, in his plummiest BBC voice.

His rival, Miranda, pumped Johnny's hand and kissed Helene on both cheeks.

The proximate cause of Emil's elation was sitting on a humpbacked sofa under a swooning portrait of the Virgin Mary, the kind that was sold outside churches. This conjunction made Prestes look distinctly like a seminarist, Johnny thought, even though the Communist chief was dressed like any modestly successful shopkeeper, in a white suit with black shoes. Dangling from the sofa, his feet barely touched the ground.

'Welcome home,' Johnny said to the man Stalin had picked to lend a face to the revolt. 'When did you arrive?'

'Not long ago,' Prestes said evasively. 'We had some passport difficulties. Nothing serious.'

Johnny was intrigued by the woman sitting next to Prestes. She looked a real Amazon, tall and big-boned. Her head was curiously elongated, ending in a massive, square-cut jaw. She seemed the least likely person in the room to be doing crochet. At the sight of Helene, she dropped her crochet hook and swept her into a powerful embrace.

'This is Olga,' Prestes introduced her to Johnny. Her grip was as strong as his own. 'My bride of the Comintern. That's what we used to call the ladies in Moscow, isn't it?'

I don't remember that you ever had much time for the ladies, Johnny addressed him mentally. Except for your mother, whom you worshipped.

'Helene, you're enchanting, as always,' Prestes turned to her. 'I can see that you and my Olga are old friends.'

'We jumped out of a few planes together in Russia,' Helene remarked.

'Parachute training,' Olga amplified this. 'We're like sisters.'

That might be very true, Johnny thought. What was this strapping girl to Prestes? A surrogate mother? A baby-sitter from Max's organisation? Johnny was certain that there were deadlier weapons in Olga's satchel-sized handbag than a crochet hook.

'Olga goes with me everywhere,' Prestes said, patting her back. 'Our friends in the Big House think I need looking after.'

They made an odd couple, standing side by side. Olga was a foot taller than Prestes and at least sixty pounds heavier. Johnny could not help speculating about what might happen if she rolled on top of him in bed. Olga was attractive in her way, and he sensed a raw sexuality close to the surface. She returned his visual inspection boldly, with a smile on her lips, and he had the distinct sensation that she was mentally undressing him from top to bottom.

Prestes made the last introductions.

'You know Verdi, of course.'

Johnny was genuinely glad to see the voluble Argentinian, who made a great fuss over kissing Helene's hand, while his shaggy grey hair tumbled down over his eyes.

The last man in the room was introduced as Tatu, which meant 'Armadillo'. It seemed to fit. Tatu was one of the regional organisers from the north. His face was cracked and blackened like worn-out saddle leather. Every excess ounce had been stripped from his frame under the northern sun.

Johnny took a chair by the wall and glanced around the circle of faces, some eager or elated, others watchful and appraising.

The high command of the Brazilian revolution was assembled, for the first time, on Brazilian soil.

Emil banged his fist on the coffee table. 'We begin!'

The revolution Stalin had planned for Brazil was supposed to move along two parallel tracks.

Track one was a front operation, of the kind Willi Münzenberg was constantly promoting in Europe. The guiding principle was simple: thousands, perhaps millions, of people who would never knowingly support the Communists could easily be recruited to a front organisation secretly controlled by the party that campaigned in the name of such admirable causes as world peace, social justice and anti-Fascism. Lenin had called the people who were duped in this way 'useful idiots'; Johnny had heard them described by his superiors in Moscow as 'shit-eaters'.

The creation of the National Liberation Alliance – the ANL for short – was announced before an excited crowd at the João Caetano Theatre on March 30, 1935. The guiding slogan was 'Bread, Land and Liberty!' The speakers called for the seizure and breakup of the big estates, for the repudiation of foreign debts and the expropriation of the foreign-owned monopolies. The ANL's executive included three retired naval officers; this was calculated to enlist navy support for a revolt. Only one of these ex-mariners, Roberto Sisson, had any clear conception of the strategy behind the new movement. The audience was swelled by trade unionists from the Federation of Seamen and the National Federation of Railwaymen, both of which – Johnny learned – were largely controlled by the party. The taxi drivers', bank clerks' and textile workers' unions were also represented in force.

One of the youngest speakers was a fiery orator called Carlos Lacerda. Just before he took the rostrum, he was approached by Major Costa Leite, a veteran of the Prestes Column and a member of Prestes' intimate circle.

'We think it would be a good idea,' said Costa Leite, 'if you nominate Luis Carlos Prestes as honorary president of the ANL.'

The tone was that of a military command.

When Lacerda mentioned Prestes' name on the platform, he was received with a resounding ovation. Huge banners bearing Prestes' name that had been smuggled into the hall by party members were instantly unfurled.

Soon hundreds of voices were raised in the new marching song of the ANL, sung to the tune of the national anthem:

Crimson are our Brazilian souls,
Erect, brave and handsome youth
Of clear minds and strong physique
We fight for bread, land and liberty.

It was no competition for the *Internationale*, Johnny thought, when he heard this ballad for the first time. Still, the ANL rapidly gained strength, attracting swarms of new adherents every time its activists clashed with the police or the Fascist Greenshirts. In Rio, ANL organisers backed demonstrations by workers and bank clerks demanding an eight-hour day and a minimum wage. In Minas, they helped tenant farmers fight eviction by the rapacious landlords. Through two dozen newspapers and bulletins, they appealled to liberals to join them as the first line of defence against fascism. The name of Prestes was a magnet, just as the Brazilian leader had promised. To most of those who rallied to his name, Prestes was seen not as a Moscow-line Communist, but as the Cavalier of Hope, the idealistic hero of a revolt that still evoked *saudade* – romantic yearning – because its objectives had never been clearly defined.

The ANL did not flaunt the red star or the hammer and sickle. The fact that it was under the fist of the Communist party – and therefore the South American bureau – was carefully concealed. What was the point of having a front if everybody knew what was in the back room?

Track two was the secret effort to trigger an armed insurrection. The Comintern vested its hopes in Prestes' old comrades, some of whom were now colonels and state governors and police captains, and in the underground work of spreading sedition and training military cells in which Johnny was playing a leading role. At Johnny's suggestion, party and ANL sympathisers in the various garrisons organised new social clubs where soldiers who came along to play Ping-Pong or enjoy a few beers could be drawn into social discussion. In his lectures to his five-man cells, Johnny stressed the need to focus on issues of immediate concern to the sergeants and corporals – living conditions, terms of service, the behaviour of unpopular officers, the use of troops to suppress strikes by workers who came from the same social background.

Only a handful of men in the Brazilian Communist Party were told the true nature of the plot. Only Nilo and Miranda knew about the deadline set in Moscow: the revolution was supposed to be unleashed no later than January 1936.

It soon became clear to Johnny that the Brazilian party was riddled with jealousy and suspicion. Veteran party members resented the fact that Prestes – once denounced by the Communists as a 'petit bourgeois adventurer' – had been parachuted in by Moscow as their new leader. At the same time Emil and his team were wary of anarchist and Trotskyite heresies among the party faithful, and perhaps with some reason, since in its original incarnation the Brazilian Communist party had been in large part a creation of anarchists.

It was plain to Johnny, at that first gathering of the general staff in Petrópolis, that jealousy and suspicion reigned even within the South American bureau. It was a matter of temperament as well as tactics. Nilo and Miranda vied with each other in offering more and more optimistic accounts of the progress that had been made.

'Five thousand officers have joined the ANL!'

'The governors of Ceará and Amazonas have sworn to join us!'

'Great news from Recife – they're ready to set up a soviet republic in the interior!'

Tatu, the northerner, would sit silent through most of this, scratching his nose. Verdi, the Argentinian, was openly sceptical, harping on inconvenient facts: the party was small, the class struggle in Brazil was at a primitive stage, President Vargas was popular even on the left. At

349

one of the meetings, when tempers flared, Verdi accused Nilo of being a 'victim of passion'.

Emil was desperate for success but wary of being deceived again, as he had deceived himself in China. Sometimes, when the others had vented their opinions, he would turn to Johnny for advice, as if Johnny were some kind of referee. Johnny distrusted this excess of deference. Whenever he was obliged to give his views, he sided with Nilo, who was positively baying for blood, or with Prestes, who talked as if he wanted to launch the revolution the next day.

Let's hurry it along, Johnny told himself. The sooner it blows up, the sooner I'll be out of here.

This proved to be almost a terminal miscalculation.

2

It was a soft day in early June, and the sky hung down between the mountaintops like a sodden towel. Harry Maitland was waiting for Johnny at the very centre of the Jardim Botánico, at the end of an avenue of royal palms. A rococo fountain bubbled gaily where the paths crossed, but it was overshadowed by an enormous silk-cotton tree beyond. The massive trunk reared up for a hundred feet before dividing into branches, crooked like the brackets of ritual candelabra. There was a sense of brooding power about that solitary giant, made ominous by the dark of the sky and the pendulous deformity of one of the limbs. What hung from the tree might have been a wasp's nest, but it was hard for Johnny to conceive of a wasp's nest twice the length of a man. Everything in nature seemed exaggerated in Brazil, and anything would grow. Perhaps that was why the botanical gardens were so often deserted. They were silent now, except for the low thrum of the insects in the tract that had been turned into a corner of the Amazon Jungle.

The two men broke their walk at a curious stone table, set on a hummock in front of a gazebo. In one direction the eye fell to a yellow lagoon, almost completely covered by giant Victoria Regina lilies; in the other, it rose above waves of green foliage to the slopes of Corcovado. The Redeemer was lost in the mists.

'I've got some messages for you from Colin,' Maitland reported. 'He wonders if you can verify an address in Paris.'

'What is it?'

'74 rue du Rocher.'

'That's easy. It's an OMS apartment, rented in the name of a Portuguese who is a secret party member. Alfonso Figueiredo. I was given his name once in case I needed help with travel documents and visas.'

'Thank you. I think that will be very helpful.' Since their first meeting, Harry Maitland had been impressed by Johnny's exact memory for dates, cover names and addresses, even after downing a litre of brandy in a late-night drinking session. But there was something that fascinated Harry far more than the mnemonic skill or the boozing capacity; it was the sense that he was in the presence of a man who had taken the world on his shoulders. More often than not, there had been tension between them. When Johnny's judgement was questioned – sometimes simply in order to elucidate a point – he would flare up, ready to lacerate Harry as a rank amateur, fumbling under the weight of the preconceptions of an amateur of his social class. Maitland had to practise being patient. It was an unfamiliar exercise, but he was helped along by the sense that he was learning all the time, not merely as Colin Bailey's proxy in Rio, but as a man.

Johnny said, 'What else?'

'The other bit's personal, I think. Colin asked me to let you know that Max and Sigrid are in Paris.'

'I see. Thank you.'

So they didn't get Trotsky. Not this time. At least Sigi was safe, and in a place that she loved. But still Max's captive. Perhaps his willing captive . . . *No.* Johnny tried to shut off the jeering rush of thoughts and images. He could not allow himself to dwell on any of that.

He reported to Harry, 'They're sending me to the north.'

'Where?'

'Bahia. Recife. Then the backlands.'

'To train the party underground?'

'To assess our military capacities,' Johnny specified. 'But there's something more. Emil has made me his ambassador to Lampião.' He saw the surprise in the young Englishman's face and added with a grin, 'I'm afraid I talked myself into it.'

Lampião was the most notorious bandit in Brazil. At the mention of his name, a picture flitted through Harry's mind, something he had seen in a Rio newspaper: a blurred daguerrotype of a man in funny pebble glasses, dressed all in leather, with crossed bandoliers over his chest and a rifle in his fist. The wide brim of his hat, studded with silver coins or amulets, was turned up at the front, lending him an oddly Napoleonic aspect. The toe of his boot rested on the corpse of a fallen enemy. Lampião had been credited with killing hundreds of men. He had earned his strange-sounding nickname by squeezing off rounds from his Winchester so fast (it was said) that the rifle barrel glowed like a street lamp.

'I don't understand this at all,' Harry said. 'Lampião is no Robin Hood, and he's certainly no revolutionary. His men tried to attack the Prestes Column when it marched through the north eight years ago.'

'That's what Tatu said to Emil,' Johnny responded. 'But Emil is convinced that the bandits – the *cangaceiros* – are our natural allies. In his head he's still in China. The bandits made up about half of Mao's forces. You see, revolutionaries are always trying to fight the last revolution. Just as generals are forever trying to fight the last war.'

'But why did Emil pick you to send to Lampião?'

'He asked what I thought of the plan, and I said it was inspired. You know that's the game I've been playing, Harry. Egging them on. You didn't find fault with it before now, did you?'

'No,' Maitland agreed. He had discussed all of this in general terms with Colin Bailey. The spymaster's instinct was the same as Johnny's: that the agent's role should not be merely to pass on information but to act as agent provocateur, goading or luring the conspirators into over-reaching themselves.

'But I don't like the smell of this,' Harry went on. 'By all accounts, Lampião isn't the most hospitable host to uninvited guests. Has it occurred to you that Emil may be trying to get you killed?'

'It's occurred to me,' Johnny agreed. 'But I'll manage. Tatu is coming too. He doesn't like the idea any better than I do, so I think I can trust. him. And he knows the lie of the land.'

'But how does Emil propose to win over Lampião?'

'With money. He's got lots of it.'

'Where is it coming from?'

'I brought ten thousand US. Emil arrived with fifty thousand more. I've heard that a man from the OMS flew in to São Paulo this week with still more. And there are local contributors.'

'Who?'

'Businessmen paying protection money, out-of-work politicos hoping to get their jobs back – I can't tell you for sure. But I ran into something interesting the day after I last saw you. I was running a little seminar on anti-military techniques, specifically aimed at sergeants. You know the kind of pitch. Why are your officers treated better than you? Why can't you pay for a decent house for your family, or your mistress at least? The usual stuff. I had a minor brainwave. The people I'm working with aren't long on theory. Most of them are functional illiterates. Pictures work better than any number of speeches. It struck me that it might be very effective to hand out photographs showing the rich at play – mansions with sixteen gardeners and three swimming pools, that sort of thing – so the sergeants can take a good look at how the top dogs live. I got a camera for one of our boys and told him to go around the city taking pictures. He came back with a good selection. Well, Nilo happened to drop in when we were discussing which photographs to use. He loved the whole idea. Of course, he comes from a wealthy family himself. He was keen to see which of his family friends were going to have their villas expropriated. He looked through the pictures and started laughing as if his sides would split. Then all the wind went out of his sails.'

'What happened?'

'He didn't like one of the photographs. In fact, he pulled it out of the batch and put it in his wallet. He said it wasn't appropriate. He wouldn't give any further explanation.'

'Can you describe the house in the picture?'

'I can do better than that. I got the negative from Escoteiro. I didn't have time to have it developed.'

He took an envelope from his pocket and handed it to Harry, who extracted the negative and held it up to the light.

Even with the image reversed, Maitland recognised the high walls, the wrought-iron gates, the ornamental pond among the shade trees.

He was looking at the house of Doctor Alcibiades, snake collector, mayor of Rio – and the man in charge of the police.

Why would Nilo seek to protect Alcibiades? It was not inconceivable that the doctor had a hold over Nilo; given the millionaire Communist's sexual proclivities, he may well have had occasion to consult a venerealogist. The alternative explanation was that the doctor was in on the plot. Perhaps he was even one of the anonymous local paymasters. That possibility was unsettling. If the man who controlled the capital was part of the conspiracy, then its chances of success were far greater than the British – or Johnny – had anticipated.

3

Johnny dined with Helene at Gladstone's, a lively bistro just off the Avenida Atlántica. The little marble tables were jammed tight together, but they had no trouble finding a quiet nook at this hour of the evening; Gladstone's crowded up after midnight and stayed open until its last patrons left for work – or their beds.

'What did you do today?' Johnny asked casually.

'I was typing reports for Emil all morning,' she said, lighting a slim black cigarillo. 'Then I met Proust.'

'Who the hell is Proust?'

'Your radio man, of course! You mean you don't know about him?'

'Are you talking about Harvey?' Johnny had been informed on his return to Rio that a wireless specialist, a Californian called Harvey Prince, would accompany him on the first leg of his trip to the north. As far as Johnny could make out, the job of the radio man was to set up a communications link between Emil's general staff and the local command in Recife.

'I've decided to call him Proust,' Helene said mischievously. 'I think he's one of the boys. You'd better watch your back, dearest. He's awfully pretty.'

She glanced at the menu.

'Then I had to fix Emil's toilet,' she went on. 'Honestly, the man is as helpless as a child. The bowl overflowed, and when I went back, the filth was seeping out over the living room floor. So I struck my blow for the cause with a plumber's devil. Then I made some deliveries. Then I went home and lay in the bath until the hot water stopped running. Quite a heroic day, wouldn't you say?'

She yawned ostentatiously.

'Oh, but I mustn't forget,' she added. 'We have a new lodger at the Valhalla. And I have a new admirer. He's asked me to go to the new Ginger Rogers movie with him. You don't object, do you, brother dear?'

'Who is he?' Johnny asked suspiciously.

'His name is Hossbach. Our landlady and everyone else calls him Engineer Hossbach. I don't know whether he has a first name.'

'German?'

'As Bavarian as a beerhall.'

'What's he doing in Rio?'

'That's the best part, Johnny. Can you imagine a pig

looking devious? That is the picture of Hossbach, when I asked. He muttered something about a contract with one of the government departments. But you must ask him yourself. He says he's very anxious to meet you.'

Johnny resolved to take a look at the new lodger before he left for the north. But on their return to the boarding house he was told that Engineer Hossbach had not yet come back from dinner. Johnny fell asleep with a Portuguese dictionary in one hand and a copy of *Os Sertões*, Euclides da Cunha's haunting account of millenarian revolt in the backlands of the north, open across his chest. His dreams were filled with ragged bands of flagellants fired with a vision of an imminent Kingdom of God. He was wakened by Helene banging on the thin wall between their rooms. He responded by pounding with the heel of his shoe.

'You're lying on your back!' she called out to him. 'Roll over before your snoring wakes up the whole of Copacabana!'

'Is that any way to talk to your brother?'

It was strange how such banal, domestic intimacies could still forge a bond between them, as the thinnest fibres, wound tightly together, make the strongest rope. For a moment, lying wide awake on his lumpy mattress, he considered going to her, sharing her bed for a few hours.

Instead, he pulled out an old pipe and filled it with his favourite navy cut tobacco. Then he put on his bush jacket, khaki pants and a pair of light boots and hiked along the beach, wondering which was more real – the images from da Cunha that had taken life in his dreams or the abstract dreams of Emil, for whom Brazil, like China, was a country of the mind. There were candles by the water and what looked like an entire steak dinner. Even the dogs, it seemed, would not touch an offering to the old gods. How did that fit into Emil's schema?

The sky had lightened by the time he recrossed the avenue and approached the Valhalla Guest House, so he had a clear sight of the grey hulk that rose up from the verandah like a whale surfacing for air.

'Good morning! It's Herr Gruber, isn't it?' The words came out in two bursts. The grey hulk could now be identified as a large German in a striped bathing costume. He had his arms folded behind his neck. He threw himself back on the deck, then raised up, as he continued his sit-ups.

'You must be Engineer Hossbach. My sister mentioned you.'

Hossbach abandoned his sit-ups and pumped Johnny's hand. Running on the spot, he said, 'Delighted, delighted. Come on, I'll race you to the water.'

'Perhaps later –'

'Nonsense. One must keep up a regime.' He slapped Johnny on the shoulder and went bounding down the steps. On the pavement he wheeled around and marked time, shunting his knees up and down with such fanatical dedication that Johnny couldn't help himself; he grinned and went loping after Hossbach.

'Have to keep *fit*!' Hossbach roared as they jogged between the palms. 'The Latin races are *soft*! The mongrel races – just look around!'

Johnny let Hossbach beat him to the water's edge. Or perhaps he merely flattered himself that he had conceded the race because, despite his bulk, the German was surprisingly fleet.

'Did I tell you there is a forfeit?' Hossbach asked, standing in the surf with his hands on his hips, swaying his head from side to side.

'What forfeit?'

'I would like your permission to take your sister out.'

'I understand she's already accepted. Besides, I can't remember when she asked me for permission to do anything.'

'But that's not right,' Hossbach said, with apparent earnestness. 'A fine Aryan girl like that. It is the duty of the head of her family to protect her.'

'I think you'd better explain that to her yourself.'

Helene was going to have a merry time with her suitor, he thought.

'Then perhaps I may ask for another forfeit.'

'I suppose you can ask.'

'I would like to invite you to have dinner with me. I have found an excellent place. Fine Bavarian cooking. Only Germans go there.'

'You forget I'm not German.'

Hossbach laughed and patted his arm. 'German, Austrian, what's the difference? Wasn't the Führer born in Austria? We are all the same *Volk*.' He winked at Johnny. 'Besides, your lovely sister told me about your sympathies,' he added conspiratorially. 'We may be able to do one another some good.'

'Naturally, I'll be pleased to assist you in any way possible. Helene didn't tell me what line of business you're in.'

'I'm trying to land a certain contract for German business.'

'Then you're dealing with the Brazilian government?'

'With some officials, yes. But business here isn't easy. These people have no sense of punctuality. I could do with the benefit of your experience. What do you say to that dinner?'

'It would give me great pleasure. But I'm afraid I have to go away on business.'

'I believe your sister said you deal in cigars.'

Johnny inclined his head.

'What an agreeable profession. You'll be going to Bahia, I suppose? Isn't that where they make the best Brazilian cigars?'

Johnny nodded again. 'Do you know Bahia?'

'Niggertown,' Hossbach spat, with sudden violence. 'My boat docked there overnight. The Negroes are entirely given over to sex and superstition. If you want to know why this country is weak, look there.'

'You seem to have learned a lot about Brazil in a short time,' Johnny remarked in a neutral tone.

'I was in Bahia, and I was in Blumenau,' Hossbach said. 'Two different poles, one indicating the problem, the other the solution. Do you know Blumenau? You don't? But you must go. I can even arrange it for you. It's in Santa Catarina, in the south. A German community, true to its race, with German newspapers and German schools. There are a million *Volksdeutsche* in Brazil. Think what they would accomplish if they were shaped into a single fist!'

'I see that we have a lot to talk about,' Johnny said. 'But for now, I'm afraid I have a boat to catch.'

'Don't worry about your sister. I'll look after her while you're away.'

'I'm quite sure you will.'

He left Hossbach on the beach, engaged in a new bout of calisthenics. His large, heaving figure seemed to hold magnetic fascination for a small tribe of brown-skinned boys, who had squatted nearby to watch. Hossbach talked and looked like a coarse buffoon, with his pink, bulging face and his yellow hair, cropped so close that the skin showed through. But Johnny had glimpsed raw cunning behind those piggy eyes, and he was persuaded that the engineer was no more engaged in legitimate import-export business than he. Hossbach's visit to Blumenau suggested that he might be an envoy from the foreign section of the Nazi party, which was reaching out aggressively to mobilise German communities all over the world in the Führer's cause. Equally, Hossbach could be a Gestapo agent, sent to hunt down the anti-Nazis who were seeking exile in South America in ever-increasing numbers, and to make friends in the local police.

Either way, Hossbach's arrival at the guest house was an unwelcome complication. They would need to take soundings, to find out what Hossbach was really up to. Johnny was confident that whatever a woman could wheedle out of a man, Helene would get.

4

The great city of Recife sprawled across two muddy rivers behind a reef, like a giant crab. Up in the hills, in the leafy quarters of Dos Irmãos and Madalena, were the mansions built on sugar, patrolled day and night by police and private guards. Down in the muck were the *mocambos*, squalid encampments of wooden shacks that were slowly sinking into the swamp. Infants and yellow dogs fought over scraps among rotting heaps of garbage. Adults and older children went digging for crabs in the mud.

'It is the perfect cycle,' Tatu explained. 'There is a type of crab peculiar to this coast. It feeds on decomposing flesh – human flesh. These unfortunates live on the crabs. When they die, the crabs live on them.'

Johnny looked back. The American, the radio man, was only halfway up the slope, even though Johnny was lugging the heaviest part of his equipment. Harvey Prince had acquired a following. Bare brown children with saucer eyes, their stomachs distended by malnutrition, hobbled along beside him on stilt legs. Harvey kept coughing into a handkerchief. The American had dressed like a big game hunter, down to the leopard-skin band around his hat. Now the trousers of his very new, very expensive safari suit were caked with mud and more dubious substances, and he looked ready to throw up his breakfast.

Though Johnny had taken an instant dislike to the young Californian, he could feel passing sympathy with his reactions. In the *favelas* of Rio and the *barracos* of Bahia, where the steamer had docked, there was beauty even in the most abject poverty. Johnny remembered the broken streets around the Terreiro de Jesus, in the old upper city of Bahia, where black chickens ran across the cobblestones and wildflowers grew out of the crumbling walls. What man in his right mind would swap that for gas cooking and running water in a sooty industrial suburb in Liverpool or Chicago or Berlin? But in the *mocambos* of Recife, poverty was terror. It reduced a man, body and soul, to an alimentary canal that was never filled.

Johnny puffed steadily on his pipe. The smoke helped to obscure the stench of ordure and advanced decay. At the top of the rise was a circle of one-room huts, only a small step up from the shanties below, and a larger building with a pitched roof and, rising from it, a wooden cross. This house of God had little in common with the hundred baroque churches and cathedrals that raised their glories above the city. With their Italian saints and their altars of gold and silver, they did not speak to the *mocambos*; they were rich men's apologies to God for lives spent without concern for his laws, eleventh-hour payment for indulgences by people who despised the judgment of others but were terrified, on their deathbeds, of a final reckoning. This church was different.

The man who came to greet them wore rope sandals under his cassock. He walked stoop-shouldered as if to conceal his height.

He gave Tatu the briefest embrace and asked, 'Did you bring the morphine?'

Tatu handed him a parcel, and the priest vanished into the nearest hut through a crowd that was waiting in line, three abreast.

'He's everything to these people,' Tatu explained. 'Doctor, teacher, miracle worker. They call him Father Badó.'

'Badó? But that's an insult, isn't it? Doesn't it mean simpleton, or half-wit?'

Tatu smiled. 'His name is Baudouin. But the children couldn't say it. Now he makes everyone call him Father Badó. He says it fits.'

They sat in the priest's own quarters to wait for him. He cooked, slept and studied between the same four walls, his bed a rough hammock, his table an upturned packing case.

'They say he was to become professor of theology at Louvain,' Tatu remarked. 'But he came to Recife. Father Badó says that a man with a heart who sees the *mocambos* has no choice except to become a revolutionary.'

'So he belongs to the party?' Harvey asked eagerly.

'No,' Tatu shook his head impatiently. 'Though the archbishop talks about him as if he does. He's a friend, a man of trust. His communism is from the heart.'

Tatu explained that since Father Badó had become active in the interests of the poor, he had been threatened with one ecclesiastical sanction after another and finally forbidden to celebrate Mass. The Archbishop had asked the superior of his order to send him back to Belgium. Deaf to all the complaints of the hierarchy, Father Badó went on with his self-appointed mission, losing patience only when grateful families brought him ex-votos – little tin replicas of limbs or organs he had supposedly cured – as if he were a saint in one of those gilded churches in town.

The priest rushed in and plunged his hands into a bowl of water. He rinsed them vigorously, then rubbed at his face with a wet towel.

'I'm a terrible host,' he apologised, shaking hands with the newcomers. 'No soda, no tea, not even coffee – imagine, to be in Brazil without coffee! But –' he wagged a finger triumphantly '– I do have *cachaça*, and when a poor man has *cachaça*, he can live without a great many lesser things.'

They all accepted, except for Harvey, who mumbled something about an upset stomach.

The Belgian priest threw a shot glass of the fiery spirit down his throat, snapped his jaws shut, then opened them again in a gasp of pleasure or pain, perhaps both.

'I have a friend – a Jesuit – who warned me that if I drink too much *cachaça*, I will start to hallucinate. I told him I hallucinate already!'

Johnny was refilling his pipe. The priest followed his motions with visible interest.

'Do you mind?' Johnny asked politely.

'Let me smell before I tell you.'

Johnny lit the pipe and Father Badó sniffed ostentatiously.

'That's good!' he enthused. 'Latakia?'

'It's a London blend. It has some Turkish in it.'

'I knew it. Once I understood something about smoking. But here, I am content with my little *mulatas*. Ah, thank you –'

Apparently on cue, Tatu presented him with a box of black cheroots.

'I will share these with Floriano,' he announced. 'He is the local witch doctor. We never argue about matters of theology.'

'Only about cigars?' Johnny suggested.

'You have it!' Father Badó laughed. 'Only about matters of substance.'

Behind all his surface jollity, the priest looked utterly exhausted, ready to drop.

'My friend Tatu doesn't come bearing gifts for no reason,' Father Badó prompted.

'Father, we are going to the interior. We need to make contact with certain men.'

'Which men?'

'With Lampião and other captains.'

The priest's face darkened. 'You're making a mistake,' he said curtly. 'It is not the way, even if you could persuade them to join you.'

'You have always told us that to see what men are reduced to here is to become a revolutionary,' Tatu appealed to him. 'Can we make a revolution without guns and men who are trained to use them?'

'You were away for the rally,' Father Badó answered him obliquely. The priest was active in the National Liberation Alliance, the party's front movement. The movement had organised a big demonstration in front of the governor's palace, to call for the breakup of the big estates and the expropriation of the foreign monopolies. Thousands had turned out.

'The authorities were terrified,' Father Badó told them. 'They met us with machine guns and cavalry. As the crowd advanced towards the palace, the order came for the cavalry to charge. There they were – three hundred men on horseback, sabres flashing. They broke into a trot. The hooves shuddered against the cobblestones. We could see the horses snorting and steaming, the moist upper lips of the troopers. Everyone was scared, but the soldiers were more scared than the demonstrators. There was a girl from Rio with us, a dramatic speaker. To listen to her was like listening to opera. She squeezed through the ranks and ran out in front of the horses. I thought she would be trampled to death. She had her arms outstretched. Her voice rose, wild and terrible, above the shouts and the thunder of hooves. "Soldiers, shoot your lieutenant!" And again, "Soldiers, you belong to the people! Shoot your lieutenant!"

'We could see the officer, leading from behind, as you would expect. Some of the soldiers in the front rank faltered and reined back their mounts. They weren't going to ride over a girl. The officer pulled out his revolver and yelled out threats, ordering them on. Then one of the troopers wheeled his horse around and rode back. Others followed. The line broke and the crowd surged forward. We could see the officer, bellowing and shooting his pistol into the air. Finally, his fear got the better of him. He galloped off, calling over his shoulder to his men to follow. The soldiers were not ready to fire on the people. For three days, the movement owned the streets. It was like a fiesta.'

As the priest talked, Johnny watched a cockroach the size of his big toe scuttle out of a crack in the wall and drop to the floor.

'You see what can be done without violence,' Father Badó said.

'It's from Gorky,' Johnny remarked.

'I beg your pardon?'

'The girl from Rio must have read Gorky's *Mother*. The trick may not work the next time. Sometimes violence is necessary.'

'Are you a Russian?'

'No. But I've travelled in Russia.'

'Is it true that they have closed the churches?'

'Many of them.'

Father Badó sighed deeply. 'That will happen here, too,' he said, 'unless the church takes the side of the people.'

'So you'll help us?' Tatu intervened.

'I will give you a letter to a father at Juazeiro.' The priest's tone was one of resignation. 'He is like a chaplain to these people. But you must be careful. His vision is not the same as ours.'

'May we ask one more favour?'

'What is it?'

'May we use your chapel? To store a few things?'

The canvas sack with Harvey's radio equipment had been left near the open door.

Father Badó frowned. 'You know I am forbidden to give Holy Communion. But my church is still consecrated ground.'

'That's why the police will never search it.'

The priest studied the two foreigners. 'Is either of you Catholic?'

'My father was Episcopalian,' Harvey said brightly.

Father Badó snorted and looked at Johnny.

'I'm a seeker,' Johnny said.

'That's not such a bad answer,' the priest responded. 'When I came to Brazil, I lost my faith. I'm still searching for it. But as long as you are searching, your soul is alive. You may use my church,' he said, getting up. 'But you must promise to do nothing to endanger my mission. There are many families that depend on me.'

'You have our word,' Johnny said, warming to this *cachaça* priest in rope sandals.

5

The wood-burning locomotive huffed around a great bend in the line where soldiers stood guard over the tracks. The railroad workers had been fighting a running battle with the British-owned company for months. The soldiers were there to stop the strikers' families from blocking the tracks. They were not happy poking their bayonets at women who rocked their babies in their arms and waved little green-and-yellow Brazilian flags. In the daytime, party organisers slipped in and out of the Great Western railyards, singling out foremen and scabs for attack, sowing the seeds of more disruption. At night some of the same organisers gathered in the bars and honky-tonks where the troops from the nearby barracks at Socorro passed their free time. The soldiers were happy to accept a few free drinks, and many of them listened to the talk that accompanied the beers. Most of them had been sent down from Natal, because the state government did not trust its own enlisted men. They wanted to be back with their own families, not bullying those of other men.

Father Badó was not the only priest who had joined the movement. Captains and lieutenants, as well as sergeants and other ranks, had formed cells inside the barracks and met in secret with the party's regional directorate. In the huge railyards of the Great Western Company, the largest concentration of industrial workers in the north would be in the vanguard of the rising. And on the way to the train, Tatu showed Johnny the blackened skeletons of mansions that had been razed five years before, in the revolution that had brought President Vargas to power but had done nothing to change the condition of the poor; they were proof that the passivity of the *mocambos* had its limits.

Tatu, so reticent and retiring in Petrópolis, took on new life now he was back among his own people. But he was obviously nervous about the trip to the interior. He kept finding excuses to put it off, until Johnny and the Californian – who had acquired a Colt .45 and an appetite for adventure – announced that they were ready to leave by themselves.

Beyond the narrow belt of green coastal plain, the land for miles on either side of the tracks had been stripped bare. Every tree had been cut down to feed the furnaces of the locomotives. Beyond this man-made desolation they entered a desolation that escaped man's control, a tormented landscape of thorn trees and dried-up gullies that was worse than open desert, because it narrowed the horizons.

They completed the journey to the down-at-heel river port of Juazeiro on a truck without springs. Father Badó's friend glared at them through the one clear lens of his spectacles; the other had been blacked out. He wore a heavy silver crucifix, but the stains on his cassock could probably have revealed his eating habits for the past three months. His long beard was matted and rank. His manner did not improve after he had scanned the letter from the Belgian priest. But he allowed that he might know where to find Lampião. Of course, his church was poor; the roof was falling in. With the famous Father Cicero gone, fewer people made the pilgrimage to Juazeiro.

'The tears of the Blessed Virgin no longer flow.'

This mystified Johnny. He looked at his companions and volunteered to make a modest contribution to the Lord's work in Juazeiro. All three of the travellers were weighted down with padded money belts stuffed with gold and silver coins with which they hoped to buy the bandits' support. The holy man of Juazeiro undertook to provide them with a guide to an isolated ranch two days' ride into the backlands, where Lampião had last been heard from.

More of their money went on the horses, lean, miserable beasts that hardly looked strong enough to support Johnny's weight. Alceu, the guide appointed by the priest, supervised the purchase, and it was obvious he was getting a commission from the sellers. Alceu was wall-eyed with a stubbly chin, pointed like a fox.

The priest came to see them off.

'You're Communists, aren't you?' he said.

'What if we are?'

The priest merely shook his head. Johnny pressed his heels against his horse's narrow flanks. As they moved off, kicking up a little cloud of dust, he heard the priest humming.

'*E tempo de muricy*,' Tatu sang along to the tune. '*Cada um cuida de si.*'

'What are you singing?' the Californian asked.

'It's an old ballad of these parts,' Tatu said.

'How do the words go?'

'It's time to die,' Johnny translated. 'Every man for himself.'

Harvey swallowed and adjusted his bandanna. 'That's quite a send-off.'

The guide stood in his stirrups and pointed. 'There!'

It was odd to see the man straight-backed. For hours he had seemed more asleep than awake, lolling forward against the neck of his scrawny mare.

Johnny peered into the distance. He could see nothing

except the eternal *catinga*, the forest of thorn trees that clawed and cut deep, like a frightened, squirming cat. He was glad Tatu had made him buy leather chaps and a leather jacket, though it was hard to breathe inside them in the brilliant, diamond-sharp light of day. Now the forest of thorns was ghostly in the dusk. Land and sky seemed to meld under a fine shower of ash. The earth, baked hard by the sun, could hold warmth no better than moisture. He felt the chill coming down, seeping into his bones.

Without warning, the guide yanked at the bit, forcing his mount to turn in a narrow circle. He jabbed with his spurs and the little mare carried him past the other riders in a surprising burst of speed.

'Alceu, wait! Where are you going?' Tatu shouted at him.

'I did my part!' the guide yelled back. 'No further!'

Tatu looked ready to ride after him.

'Let him go,' Johnny ordered. 'We must be almost there.'

He could make out something now – a wisp of smoke, perhaps from a cooking fire.

'But how will we find our way back?' Tatu protested.

'We have a compass.'

Whatever lay ahead, Johnny was anxious to get to it. He was beginning to savour the anticipated pleasure of very ordinary things, like drinking from a rainwater barrel instead of a sour, brackish hole in the clay, of getting out of the saddle and out of the boots that pinched his ankles, of sitting within four walls with company – however unpalatable – that he could see.

Crossing that wilderness on unmarked trails, they had never been truly alone. People loomed up out of nowhere and vanished again like wraiths: cowboys slouched in their saddles like Alceu, at the tail of a sorry herd of half-starved cattle; families of *retirantes*, broken by the drought, fleeing on foot towards a death by salt water; ragged bands trooping the other way, deeper into the backlands, with a mystic fire in their eyes, on their way to the miracle priest who had made real blood flow from the host in the mouth of a poor woman taking Holy Communion. Once their path had crossed that of a gang of bearded, sun–blackened *ja-gunços*, quick with a gun or a knife, who escorted them in utter silence for a mile or so. Johnny kept his hand on the butt of the Winchester slung behind his saddle till they melted away into the scrub.

'They'd as soon kill you as look you in the eye,' the guide had laughed. 'They'll wait till you're asleep, or your back is turned.'

Now Johnny could see a house in a clearing, a modest place built of rough–hewn logs, with a barn behind and a fenced–in enclosure where a few horses were loose.

A sound unlike anything he had heard before carried across the thorn trees. It reminded Johnny of the pieces of an old tin roof, sawing against each other in a driving gale. He realised he was listening to a harmonica.

Tatu turned very pale.

'*Mulher Rendeira*,' he said. 'It's the song of Lampião.'

'It's what we came for, then,' Johnny responded, kicking his horse on.

'I don't like it,' Tatu protested, keeping pace a head behind. 'Where is everybody? They must see us coming.'

The mouth organ stopped playing in the middle of a bar.

'There's someone now,' Harvey called out. 'He's waving to us!'

Johnny could make out a silhouette at the very edge of the clearing, among the thorn trees, indistinct in the gloom, except that the man seemed impossibly tall. His arms were spread, but not in greeting. Perhaps it was only a scarecrow.

No. Johnny was close enough now to see the man's eyes, which were dark and alive. The man's shirttails hung loose and flapped against a branch like washing on a line. His outstretched arms were rigid, nailed to the thorn tree in a grim parody of the crucifixion. His boots and his trousers were gone. All that lived in that body were the ants, which had occupied the sockets of the eyes and the bloody refuse that hung between the legs.

'Jesus,' the American gasped. His immediate reflex was to reach for his Colt.

'Put that away!' Johnny growled at him.

Tatu's instinct was swifter, and possibly surer. He threw himself over the neck of his horse and galloped off in the direction the guide had taken.

A bullet whistled after him.

At the same instant, someone in the shadows threw a rope around Harvey's neck and dragged him off his horse. The big revolver went off, kicked and fell from his hand.

Johnny found himself looking down into twin shotgun barrels.

'Get down,' the man behind the shotgun ordered. 'It's the same to me whether you die now or later.'

Johnny obeyed. More bandits loomed up out of the scrub. There must have been twenty of them, several of them sporting bits and pieces of army or police uniforms.

They searched Johnny, removing his belt, his pistol and his watch.

There were whoops of elation when they found the money belt.

They made him take off all his clothes down to his undershorts, trussed his hands behind his back and hauled him inside the house.

They flung him on the floor in the kitchen, where a wood stove was burning. The one who appeared to be their chief hacked at a slab of charred beef with his knife while he asked questions. His face was knotted and seamed like old wood, and he wore a silver earring and silver bracelets on his wrist.

'We heard about you before you even got to Juazeiro,' the bandit announced. 'They call me Captain Elétrico. Even the bushes talk to me.'

'You're making a mistake, Captain. We have come in friendship. There are letters to prove it.'

'What letters?'

One of Elétrico's men extracted the packet from Johnny's saddlebag. The bandit chief stared at them, obviously baffled.

'Shall I read them to you?'

'You? You can't even speak Portuguese like a man. *You* read –' he threw the bundle at a man wearing eyeglasses.

The first letter was addressed to Captain Virgulino Ferreira, better known as Lampião.

'You are lucky you met me instead of Lampião,' Captain Elétrico declared. 'He is not such a patient man.'

The letter had been drafted by Emil with advice from the chief of the party's regional directorate for the north, a man code-named Cato who was known to Johnny only through his reports. This Cato shared none of Tatu's caution, perhaps because he did not share the same risks. He burned with the same fever as Emil and the leadership in Rio. He had even advised that conditions were ripe for creating soviets among the peasants of the north – the China trap all over again.

The bandit in spectacles stumbled through the letter to Lampião, missing syllables and punctuation marks, and succeeded it making it sound like exactly what it was: an awkward translation from a foreign language and, behind it, a foreign thought process. The letter began with flattery, hailing Lampião's heroic exploits and anointing the most notorious of the *cangaceiros* 'the legendary champion of the oppressed'. A lengthy passage followed which described the development of class struggle in Brazil and the need for an anti-imperialist revolution.

The Electric Captain grunted and yawned and scratched his private parts through most of this. He blinked at a reference to 'the latifundist class'. He muttered something to the reader, who paused.

'Hey,' he addressed Johnny. 'You saw that piece of dogmeat outside?'

'I saw it,' Johnny said, thinking of the corpse impaled on the thorn tree.

'He used to farm this place. Does that mean he's a latifundist?'

'How many acres did he own?'

'Who can say? There aren't any fences in the *caatinga*. He had three women to himself, though. And he was ass-buddy with the colonel.'

'Then he was a latifundist.'

'Good. Go on reading,' he ordered his man.

The next section was about the need to carve up the big estates and give the land to the tiller.

'Chickenshit,' Captain Elétrico interrupted. 'What do you think this land is worth? It's cattle and water holes that matter, and horses and women. You think Lampião cares who owns this godforsaken wilderness? You think I give a shit? You think any lousy cowboy will fight over that?'

'There's more,' Johnny said.

The reader squinted and stumbled on. The last part of the letter was all that mattered. Emil made the proposal he believed the bandit chief couldn't refuse. The revolutionaries would help him to take vengeance on his enemies. They would provide him with money, thousands of American dollars, to buy guns. In return, the *cangaceiros* would place themselves at the disposal of the revolutionary high command as a mobile guerrilla force.

'You see,' Johnny commented. 'The gold you took from us was just a down payment.'

Captain Elétrico was plainly intrigued by this promised fortune, but puzzled.

'You are here, showing me these things,' he said. 'What have you got to do with any of us? Where do you come from? You talk as if your mouth is full of rocks.'

'From Germany. From the other side of the ocean.'

'From Germany.' The Electric Captain rocked with laughter. 'Most of us here haven't been further away than Piancó. Recife, Olinda, those are already foreign countries. And that fancy boy you brought with you. Where is he from?'

'He's from California. From the United States.'

'Ah, these gringos like to use the back door. Isn't that right?' He nudged one of his companions, who was whittling away at a stick with a wickedly curved knife, and all the bandits started to snigger. Captain Elétrico's assessment of Harvey was evidently the same as Helene's.

'High command – revolution – all these fat words,' the bandit chief went on. 'They mean nothing without a man. Who is your man?'

'Prestes,' Johnny replied quietly.

'What?' The Electric Captain looked thunderous.

'Carlos Prestes.'

'Is he here?' The bandit erupted from his seat and squeezed Johnny's throat with his thumbs. 'Tell me where.'

'Not here,' Johnny gasped. 'Not – in – Brazil.'

The bandit released him abruptly, dropping him so the back of his head thudded against the bare floor.

'You know Piancó?'

Johnny shook his head.

'Four days' ride north of here. That's where I'm from. My brother was there when Prestes' men came to Piancó, eight years ago. They're good Catholics in Piancó, they don't want anything to do with the Reds. There was a priest called Padre Aristides. He decided to make a stand against the Prestes Column. He barricaded himself inside a church with some of the townsfolk. My brother was one. Prestes' men had them outnumbered. They were gauchos, throat slitters from the south. When they captured the church, they cut the throat of every man inside and dumped the bodies in a mass grave, without honour. My brother is in that grave.'

The Electric Captain was flushed, and breathing hard.

'So you see,' he went on, 'I won't be joining *Capitão* Prestes. You're a very brave man to come here and use his name. Or a very stupid one. Chain him to the stove,' he ordered his men. One of them produced a leg iron that looked like a relic of the slave trade. The metal was rusted but solid.

The heat of the fire scorched Johnny's bare skin.

'What are you going to do with us?'

'I could sell you to the state police. But this is something personal. Because of Piancó. You're a man, and I'll treat you like one. In the morning, you'll see why they call me Captain Elétrico.'

The night was lacerated by the American's screams from another part of the house. It was only too easy to picture what they were doing to him. Johnny struggled with his ropes and singed his wrists trying to burn through them by pushing up against the hot iron of the stove. He had almost succeeded when one of the bandits came in and slouched down in a chair. The manacle bit into the flesh of his leg; he couldn't shift it.

Between the screams and his efforts to wriggle out of his bonds, Johnny brooded on the web of folly and likely betrayal that had dragged him into this hell. If the massacre at Piancó had really happened, how could Emil and the others have deluded themselves that a revolt bearing the name of Prestes would be welcomed with open arms in this wilderness of thorns? The one-eyed priest at Juazeiro must have known what their reception would be. Perhaps Emil knew, too. It occurred to Johnny that the priest was not the only one who might have been happy to see them riding off to their deaths.

Not here, a voice tolled inside Johnny's skull. I'm not ready.

The sense of waste rose up in his gorge.

It was absurd. He had survived the Gestapo and the OGPU only to find his life in the hands of a scruffy Brazilian bandit with a ridiculous name.

He started laughing. It became uncontrollable, rocking his whole body, until a bandit came and kicked him in the ribs to shut him up.

He woke at first light. The stove was dead, and his hands were numb. There was movement outside, the sound of horses whinnying and stamping their hooves in the dust. The bandits were preparing to move out. There was a strong smell of petrol or kerosene.

Captain Elétrico swaggered in, wearing Harvey's safari jacket under his leather vest. He was sporting his full regalia, complete with crossed bandoliers and a brace of pistols in his belt. He had a rifle slung from his shoulder and, on his head, his high leather hat, hung with amulets and silver stars. 'I'm a tidy man,' he announced to Johnny. 'I always clean up after myself.'

He proceeded to sprinkle kerosene from a rusty can along the outer wall.

'Nobody can say I'm not a fair man, too.'

He bent down and inspected the solid links of the chain that bound Johnny's foot to one of the thick iron legs of the stove, which was bolted to the floor. Satisfied that the chain would not give, he sawed through the ropes around Johnny's wrists. Johnny felt prickling pains as the blood began to flow back into his hands.

'An old place like this shouldn't take too long to burn,' the bandit said. 'But I'm giving you a chance.' He set his knife down on the floor. Johnny calculated that it was just within his reach, but the captain had his boot on the blade.

'Maybe you'll roast. Or maybe you'll cut yourself loose. It's possible. Of course, you won't walk so good.' Elétrico's lips curled back to display a row of ruined yellow teeth.

Johnny stared at the knife and the leg iron, and the bandit's meaning dawned on him in a sudden, sickening perception. He would never be able to saw through the chain before the fire consumed the house. But he might just have time to hack off his own foot, there above the ankle.

The bandit played with a box of matches. He struck one, but merely to light his cigar. He struck another, and blew it out.

He started backing away towards the door.

'Goodbye, gringo,' he said, striking a third match.

Johnny grabbed for the knife, got up onto his knees and hurled it at the man with the hat full of stars.

I won't die alone, he promised himself.

He aimed for the face, but his fingers were stiff. The knife flew low, missing its target.

Any soldier knows that the third light is unlucky. The dagger tore into the bandit's abdomen, just below the belt.

He howled and clutched at the wound.

The lighted match, loosed from his hand, fell to the floor, and the room exploded into blue and yellow flame. Blinded by fire and smoke, the bandit reeled backwards. Something clattered to the floor. Johnny leaped at Elétrico, but the gap between them was too great. The leg iron stopped him in midflight, and his face hit the ground too fast for him to cushion the fall. Choking on the acrid smoke, blood streaming from his nose, he writhed and clawed helplessly, like a tethered animal. Then his hand closed on something that hadn't been there before – the barrel of the bandit's rifle. He yanked at it, hoisted it up under his arm, pushed the muzzle against the chain and fired. Slivers of metal like tiny razor blades sliced at his face and chest. But he was free.

Elétrico had managed to hobble to the door.

Johnny hurled himself at the bandit and brought him down in a rugby tackle. They landed in a flailing heap on the verandah. Johnny rolled to keep the captain's body between himself and the *cangaceiros* who were gathered in the clearing, levelling their rifles and shotguns over the necks of their horses. The Californian was with them. They had dressed him in a cotton shift like a girl and roped him to the saddle tree of a heavy, black-bearded ruffian who was sporting Harvey's hand-tooled San Antonio boots.

Elétrico was grappling for one of his pistols, but Johnny was stronger. He wrenched the gun out of the captain's hand and jammed it up behind his ear.

'Tell them to back off,' Johnny ordered.

The bandit hesitated. His breath came in short, fetid bursts.

'Tell them to back off,' Johnny repeated, 'or I'll blow the back of your head off.'

Elétrico gave the command. The horses backed off a few paces.

'Now tell them to sling their rifles and dismount. Very slowly.'

Grudgingly the *cangaceiros* obeyed. Johnny was nervous of pushing them too far. It was hard to tell how far Captain Elétrico's authority carried.

Johnny could feel the heat of the fire at his back. The timbers of the porch creaked and swayed.

Painfully, he got onto his feet and used Elétrico as a human shield as he inched his way down the steps away from the burning house.

'Now tell them to cut the gringo loose.'

Harvey's captor laughed as he slit the young Californian's bonds and gave him a pat on the rump.

Harvey shrieked like a madman and snatched the fat man's rifle from its harness. He fired wildly. The bullets vanished among the thorn trees. Some of the horses panicked and ran off. The *cangaceiros* went diving for cover, drawing their pistols.

'Harvey, *no!*' Johnny bellowed.

'They're going to pay,' the Californian sobbed. His whole body was shaking. 'Those cocksuckers.'

He fired at Blackbeard, who was rolling over on the ground. The bullet went wide again.

'Stop it *now!*' Johnny yelled again. 'You'll only get yourself killed!'

He said to Elétrico, 'Tell them there'll be no more shooting. Tell them to lay down their guns.'

The spell would not last much longer, Johnny thought. He could see some of the bandits widening the circle, edging away to the right and left, so that he would not be able to watch all of them at once.

He fired a single warning shot that made one of them dance.

'Stay in your places!' he roared. 'Harvey! Get two – no, three – of the horses. And for God's sake, take some of their clothes.'

Five miles from the railroad terminus, Johnny told Prince he could have the honour of disposing of the hostage. The Californian shot Captain Elétrico once in the chest and once, for good measure, in the balls. Then he threw up. There was blood amid the bile.

Johnny made no comment then or during the three hours they had to wait for the train back to Recife.

6

Colin Bailey had precious little time in those days to worry about Brazil. He made a second trip to Copenhagen to follow up on Johnny's leads. Working with an old friend in the Danish security police, he was able to roll up a whole Soviet illegals network. To deflect suspicion from Johnny, they tried to make it look like a lucky strike. The police, supposedly on the trail of a gang of counterfeiters, conducted a house-to-house search in the street where the illegal was living.

Bailey went on to Berlin. De Salis had removed the clerk in the passport office whom Johnny had identified as a Russian agent, but there was deep concern about leaks to the Germans.

'The Gestapo has no need to crack our ciphers,' de Salis had cabled, 'so long as it can listen to His Majesty's Ambassador on the telephone.'

For once, Bailey found himself in complete agreement with Adam de Salis. For nights at a time, the residency was left in the sole charge of a German porter who could be presumed to be working for the Gestapo. The ambassador, a fervent believer in the idea of a natural alliance between Britain and Germany, shared all the secrets of the embassy with his telephone.

Two years of firsthand experience of the Hitler regime had worked changes in de Salis. He had developed a network of anti-Nazi sources in business and the German military. From them, and from some of the would-be refugees who streamed daily into the passport office, de Salis chronicled the German race to re-arm. He had become convinced that Hitler was hell-bent on a war of aggression and could no longer be contained by his generals. He was disgusted by the foreign secretary's efforts to curry favour with Hitler on the dictator's terms. The British government and the British press seemed determined to give Herr Hitler the benefit of the doubt. De Salis's newspaper had suppressed an article he had written on the growth of the Luftwaffe, on the grounds that it would offend the German government and cause children in London to have nightmares of being bombed in their beds.

'The government must be made to see the writing on the wall,' de Salis insisted.

This was a new Adam, a bit alarmist, perhaps, but a welcome change from the vain intriguer Bailey had sparred with in the past. Bailey was pleased to acknowledge a new ally. In the summer of 1935 there were few enough men of influence in London who had taken Hitler's measure. Churchill was one and Vansittart another. But theirs were isolated voices in the House of Commons and the Foreign Office. Even that silly peacock Ribbentrop had not quite managed to rupture the British establishment's love affair with the Nazi dictator by greeting the King, at a diplomatic reception, with a stiff-armed salute and a cry of 'Heil Hitler!'

One of Bailey's own colleagues dismissed a report on Hitler's designs on Austria and Czechoslovakia as a plant, the probable work of 'Jews and Bolshevists'. Like all establishments, Whitehall was hostile to intelligence that contradicted its fixed opinions.

Johnny's account of his night call on Stalin had caused a passing stir but was too exotic to take root. Nobody in Whitehall believed in the possibility of a deal between the German and Soviet dictators. The general view was that Hitler's ambitions lay to the east, not to the west, and that it was clearly in Britain's interest to keep him pointed that way. Bailey, too, was convinced that the moment when an understanding might have been possible between Moscow and Berlin had passed. Reviled by the Nazis, Soviet Russia was becoming a popular cause amongst the people who were most alarmed about the rising tide of fascism. After long hesitation, Stalin had decided to break out of isolation. He had signed pacts with the French and the Czechs. According to an interesting tidbit from Johnny, apparently gleaned from Emil Brandt, the much-delayed Seventh Congress of the Comintern would definitely take place in July; the Popular Front against fascism would be the order of the day.

When Bailey got back from Berlin, he found several cables and letters from Rio waiting for him. Harry Maitland had been scrupulous about filing his weekly reports. It was plain that he was enjoying his work and had established a good rapport with Johnny. If his style was at times exuberant, his judgment was shrewd enough. The longest of the telegrams described a disastrous expedition Johnny had made to the northeast. It seemed he had been lucky to save his skin. An American who had accompanied him had suffered a complete nervous breakdown. The whole thing had the flavor of a bad horse opera. Harry suggested that Emil must have read too many of those Wild West adventure stories that had been all the rage in Germany a few years ago.

Failure to sign up the bandits for the revolt had not slowed the momentum of the Comintern operation. Emil and his associates had drawn up a list of cabinet ministers who would be appointed to a 'national revolutionary government'. The men selected were not openly Communist. They could be relied on to take party orders because they were secret members or because, through greed or ambition, they had placed themselves in the party's debt.

In another message Maitland described a curious complication in Johnny's life. There was a new lodger at his guest house, a German called Hossbach, who was paying court both to Johnny and his 'sister'. At their last encounter, Hossbach had boasted of his prowess as an aviator. He claimed to have served under Göring and to be on intimate terms with the former air ace who was now the second most powerful man in the Reich. He had told Johnny that he was holding himself in readiness for 'the call'. He was taking a keen interest in German refugees who were coming to South America and had sought to enlist Johnny's help in spying on a Jewish research scientist who had once worked for I.G. Farben. Johnny had played along, affecting sympathy for the Nazi cause.

One detail fascinated Bailey. Engineer Hossbach boasted that Göring had told him that Germany would soon have the most powerful air force on earth, able to bomb Paris or London into the stone age. According to Hossbach, Germany now had more than two thousand combat planes and eight thousand trained pilots.

Bailey snatched up the report and rushed down the corridor to C.'s office.

'I'm afraid it will have to wait till this afternoon, Major,' the chief's secretary said, glancing up at the clock on the wall. 'He's running late for a meeting at the War Office.'

'It's about that.'

C. was about to slip out the back way through his private apartment. He was dressed up in his admiral's uniform with all the decorations. He had a habit of reverting to naval garb when he was going to do battle.

'Johnny's come up trumps again,' Bailey announced.

'Colin, I've no doubt your man can walk on the waters, but Brazil is a very long taxi ride from the Air Parity Committee, and they're waiting for me now.'

'I think you'll want to see this first,' Bailey insisted.

C. squinted at the cable, then reread the section that mentioned the number of German pilots.

'Good lord,' he said softly. Then, in his familiar bark, 'You didn't plant this, did you, Colin?'

'I've only just opened my mail.'

'Have you seen Winterbotham's report?'

'I'm not privy to the details, of course.'

But he knew the gist of it. He could hardly fail to. Since Hitler had boasted to the foreign secretary, at their last meeting in Berlin, that the Luftwaffe had reached 'parity' with the Royal Air Force, the top priority for every department of British Intelligence had been to find out exactly what this meant and whether the Führer was bluffing. Group Captain Winterbotham was the head of the firm's air intelligence section. He had been fighting a running battle with Whitehall – and, in particular, with the Air Ministry – over the official estimates of German air power. The conventional wisdom was that Hitler was talking through his hat and that the Luftwaffe was years behind the Royal Air Force. The marshals and mandarins at the Air Ministry insisted that Germany had no more than four thousand trained pilots at its disposal. Cobbling together information from various sources, including members of de Salis' network, Winterbotham had calculated that the true figure might be twice as high. C. had defended his estimate at the often testy sessions of the Air Parity Committee, set up to adjudicate on this single issue. But the voice of C.'s service remained in a minority. For the most part the august members of the committee believed what they wanted to believe: that Germany was weak, that German industry was as inefficient as British industry, that it would take Hitler many years to rebuild. Now, it seemed, an agent in Brazil, half a world away, had supplied what it required to win the argument – proof from the horse's mouth.

C. had reason to be excited. The stakes were high. The country's whole defence programme now hung on the agreed estimates of German strength. But a Secret Service victory in a battle with the other arms of the bureaucracy would bring more immediate gains.

'This could be worth another hundred thousand to us in the Secret Vote,' C. remarked, with satisfaction.

'I trust we can afford to give Johnny a bonus.'

'Oh, I should think so. Now I have to run. I can't wait to see the expression on a certain air-vice-marshal's face.'

7

Harry Maitland parked the Beast under the palms and strolled under the long colonnaded portico of the member's entrance to the Jockey Club, a white marbled palace worthy of a viceroy of India.

A reporter from the English-language paper was lounging near the betting counters, studying the racing form and the well-heeled patrons of the club. Spotting Maitland, he drifted across the tesselated floor. He was sporting a straw boater, a beard in the style of George V which was obviously dyed, and an Old Harrovian tie to which Harry was perfectly sure he was not entitled.

'They think they're at bloody Royal Ascot, don't they?' He greeted Harry with a blast of whisky and stale tobacco, wagging his finger at a group of men in silk hats and women decked out in furs, despite the heat.

'How are you, Monty? Filling up the gossip column?'

Desmond Wild gave him a sly look. Maitland suspected that Wild supplemented his journalistic earnings by charging prominent members of the Anglo-Brazilian community a fee *not* to publish what he found out about their extramarital affairs. Monty was certainly not averse to writing a puff piece or to passing on a tip when the price was right. Maitland himself had made use of him on occasion, though he preferred, by and large, to deal with Brazilian reporters; they had better access to local politicians, drank less and came cheaper, by and large, than Desmond Wild.

'I just saw His Imperial Majesty's Ambassador Extraordinary,' Wild reported. 'He was fairly *seething*. They've given his usual table to a bloody Yank.'

'Who is it?'

'That oil man from Houston. Don't say you don't read my paper, dear boy. He gave a bash that was the talk of the town. He took over the Golden Room at the Copacabana Palace. The place was *drowning* in champagne.'

'I suppose you helped bail them out.'

'I did my bit,' Desmond Wild allowed. 'Speaking of which, what would you say to a stirrup cup?'

They went up the wide marble stairs to the terrace, which commanded a sweeping view of the track and the mountains beyond. Corcovado reared up to the left. It was the start of the season, and the terrace was crowded. Every table was marked out as private turf by a bottle of Chivas or Johnny Walker Black with a tape measure along the side. Wild's eyes glinted at the lineup.

A white-jacketed headwaiter bobbed up, apologising that the restaurant was completely full. His soft, pale features and half-closed eyes made him look like a calculating grouper. Casually Harry displayed a wad of thousand-cruzeiro banknotes, and a free table miraculously appeared.

'There's the Yank,' Wild announced, once he had armed himself with a stiff single malt. 'Mister Courtland Bull. I gather he lives up to his monicker. And just look who he's asked to lunch. Our pinko mayor. Now *that's* an interesting conjunction.'

Maitland turned without haste. The Texas oil man was in his early sixties and ruggedly handsome, his deep tan set off by a mane of white hair. He was laughing around a big cigar, flanked by two young, exceedingly well-developed women who laughed with him. Doctor Alcibiades' attention flitted back and forth from his host to the neighbouring tables, where a number of wealthy Brazilian men affected not to see him. It was not clear whether their objections were personal or political. Some members of the Jockey Club regarded the mayor as a dangerous demagogue who stirred up trouble by flirting with the unions and making speeches on the plight of the poor. Some might have more private reasons for avoiding Doctor Alcibiades, at least while in the company of their wives; Maitland guessed that more than a few had had occasion to visit his VD clinic in previous years.

Their eyes met briefly. Doctor Alcibiades nodded and smiled.

Wild had a point, Johnny thought. It *was* an odd conjunction: the 'progressive' mayor and the Texas oil baron. Especially since Doctor Alcibiades had landed himself in hot water with the established oil companies by imposing a freeze on gasoline prices in Rio.

'I'll take the Sugarloaf on the left,' Wild said, admiring the blonde who was seated between the American and the mayor, making an inviting show of cleavage. 'What do you say? Oh, I forgot. You like them darker, don't you?'

To avoid rising to the bait, Harry called a boy to place a bet for him on the second race, on horse number six.

'*Vencedor*,' he specified. 'To win.'

Wild was impressed by the sum Maitland was betting.

'Pretty sure of yourself, aren't you?' He consulted his form sheet and shook his head. 'She doesn't stand a chance. Melpomene. Bloody silly name for a filly, anyway.'

He took another look at the form sheet. The horse was owned by a São Paulo syndicate. A thought struggled to the surface of his consciousness like a fish rising up out of a murky aquarium.

'You own a piece of a horse syndicate, don't you?' he

said to Maitland, almost accusingly. 'Do you own a piece of this nag?'

'I might,' Harry conceded.

'Fuck. I put a bundle on number three. Carlota.'

When the boy came back with the betting slips, Wild asked him to put some money on Melpomene for him. He then made a great show of having mislaid his wallet.

'You wouldn't mind, would you, old man –'

Harry cut short the entreaties by loaning him the equivalent of about ten dollars.

'I'll pay you back if I win,' Wild said generously. 'I can't wait to see the look on Sir Evelyn's face if I do. I told him Carlota was a sure thing.'

'Let's hope he doesn't listen to you.'

The British Ambassador was sitting at a table a few steps above them on the other side of the terrace, his view of the track obscured by the constant coming and going of waiters and patrons on the level below. Sir Evelyn was looking distinctly peeved. Lady Maude was drinking a good deal of champagne and lecturing in a high, nasal voice. Summerhayes was at their table, trying to make himself invisible. Harry assumed the mousy woman in a chintzy frock who made up the party must be Summerhayes' wife.

The horses were at the starting gate. The jockeys' garb was confusingly similar. Most of them wore tunics in varying shades of red, and St Andrew's cross, in gold or bright orange, was in great demand as an embellishment.

Lady Maude watched the race through opera glasses, barracking for Carlota, the favourite, as stridently as any of the punters who lined the railing below the members' stand. Harry noticed that Courtland Bull paid no attention to the race. He had swapped seats with one of the women and was talking animatedly to Doctor Alcibiades, punctuating his points with his cigar.

Melpomene led from the beginning and won the race by nearly five lengths.

'Bloody hell!' Wild yelled in high excitement. 'It's a good thing I ran into you. How big a piece of that filly do you own?'

'Oh, about two per cent, I should think.'

'Well, if she repeats that showing at the Derby' – like other Anglos, Wild persisted in calling the Grande Prémio do Brasil, the biggest event in the local racing calendar, the Derby – 'Courtland Bull will be taking you to lunch. Excuse me.' He got up so hastily he dropped cigarette ash down the front of his jacket. 'I must go and pick up my winnings.'

Across the terrace Sir Evelyn tore up his betting slips and strewed them over the tablecloth in disgust. The blonde at the American's table clapped her hands and kissed everybody within reach. Harry was intrigued by the relationship between Doctor Alcibiades and his host. Was Bull Petroleum trying to undercut the other oil companies and grab the Brazilian market for itself? Or was Courtland Bull planning to move some of his oil rigs south? There had been speculation – little better than rumour – about some big offshore oil deposits along the coast of Bahia. But those were not in the gift of the mayor of Rio de Janeiro. However, Doctor Alcibiades had the ear of the president, and of other people besides.

It struck Harry that Desmond Wild had been gone for rather a long time. Still, Wild could never be accused of hurrying to settle his debts. No doubt he had repaired to the other bar or the betting counters below.

'Maitland?' The voice was querulous.

Harry looked up to find the British Ambassador hovering over his table, puffed up so that it seemed he was about to pop his collar stud.

'Good afternoon, Sir Evelyn. May I offer you a drink?'

'I've got a bone to pick with you, young man. What the devil do you think you're up to, using my embassy as a postbox? Summerhayes tells me you've been coming in every week, sending off cables none of us can read.'

The ambassador was talking loudly enough to be overheard at any of the neighbouring tables.

'Sir Evelyn, I hardly think this is the appropriate place –'

'I won't tolerate my embassy being used for any of this shady business!'

'Sir Evelyn –'

'I want to see you in my office first thing on Monday morning, and I shall want some satisfactory answers. Otherwise, I shan't hesitate to speak to your employers. I'm sure Rio Light will take a responsible view.'

'Shall we say nine?' Harry responded, as calmly as possible.

Sir Evelyn looked at him as if he had gone quite mad.

'I shall receive you at ten,' he said frostily.

The interview did not go well. In the course of the weekend Harry had prevailed on an acquaintance at Cable & Wireless to open up the shop and send a coded telegram to London, asking Colin Bailey for instructions on how to proceed. When Maitland arrived at the embassy on Monday morning, he was made to cool his heels for nearly half an hour before he was admitted to the ambassador's presence. Sir Evelyn had the transcript of Colin Bailey's reply on his desk.

'Perhaps you would start by translating this,' he said, handing the message to Harry.

'It will take me a little time, sir.'

'I am prepared to wait.'

'I'm afraid I also need special equipment. If you'll give me an hour –'

'Oh, very well,' the ambassador acquiesced grudgingly.

Harry drove home to decipher the cable. Its twelve-letter key was based on a parallel-text edition of Xenophon's *Anabasis*, which Maitland and Bailey had both studied in the original at school. The choice of the book on which the simple code was based had less to do with fond memories of Winchester than with Bailey's sense of whimsy. The *Anabasis* was the story of a long march. Prestes, the Communist figurehead, had conducted a long march of his own; Emil, the controller, had been responsible for another.

Harry drove back to the embassy with his notes.

To his discomfiture, Lady Maude was present at the second interview. She offered him tea and settled herself, stiff-backed, in the leather chair in front of the bookcase.

Harry remembered one of Bailey's remarks about the ambassador, an allusion to a Russian novel about a man who was incapable either of getting out of bed or doing anything worthwhile when in it.

'Use your own judgment,' Bailey had cabled, 'but protect our source at any cost.'

Maitland quoted this to Sir Evelyn, along with a few other selected passages.

'Well, I'm waiting,' the ambassador rejoined.

Harry gave a brief summary of the facts he had assembled from Johnny's reports. The Communists' hopes centred on the movement in the north, where there was talk of rallying an insurrectionary force of a hundred thousand men, and on Prestes' old comrades in the military, some of whom now held strategic positions in the armed forces and the government. The Communists were strong in a number of trade unions, especially the railroad workers and the taxi drivers, but their popular base in the cities was still weak. They had been training paramilitary cells to carry out acts of sabotage against key buildings and communications. Their front organisation, the National Liberation Alliance, was gathering support by advertising a few simple slogans attacking the Anglo-American banks, the big landowners and the Fascist Greenshirts. The aim was a violent revolution under the banners of nationalism and social justice that would be handed over to the Communist party once Vargas was overthrown. The operation was well funded and was under the supervision of a team of veteran revolutionists from Moscow. It was gaining momentum now that Prestes had returned to Brazil and was in personal touch with his admirers.

'You must tell Getulio at once,' Lady Maude interrupted, addressing her husband.

Sir Evelyn nodded. 'I was hoping to play nine holes with him on Saturday,' he reported.

'No, dear. You must go to him today.'

Maitland cleared his throat. 'If I may say so, I think it would be premature to go to the Brazilian authorities.'

'Nonsense,' Sir Evelyn admonished him. 'We are dealing

with a grave conspiracy. The government must be alerted, so it can take appropriate measures. I know the president well. He remembers his friends. This will do no harm to British interests. On the contrary, we can expect a more sympathetic hearing at Guanabara Palace.'

'There are some operational matters to be considered.'

'Operational matters?' Sir Evelyn's expression implied that Harry had just broken wind in his presence.

'The conspiracy is still in its formative phase, and we do not yet have sufficient information to identify all the ringleaders. If we are patient, we have the chance to bag all of them.'

Harry thought that his appeal to masterly inertia might reach Sir Evelyn. But his formidable wife intervened once more.

'If we merely wait,' she pointed out, 'the balloon may go up while we're all in our beds. Before we know it, we'll have a Bolshevik mob storming the embassy.'

'That is most unlikely,' Maitland countered, with as much patience as he could muster. 'You see, we have an excellent source. A source that must be protected.'

'Who is this source?' Sir Evelyn challenged him.

'I'm afraid I'm not at liberty to say, sir. But he is a remarkable man who has already rendered immense service to Britain.'

'That's all very well, but Maude has an excellent point. We can't just sit on this type of information. I've made up my mind. I shall seek an audience with the president.'

'Might I make one suggestion?'

'Well?'

'If you do talk to Vargas, you might tell him our information comes from sources in Europe – a wireless intercept, something of that kind.'

'What are you suggesting? That the president can't keep a secret?'

'He is bound to discuss the matter with his cabinet and his police chiefs. We can't tell which of them may have been compromised. In any event, you know the Brazilians. They're a talkative lot.'

Sir Evelyn did not dissent from this.

He was in a markedly better humour when he rose from his desk to indicate that the interview was over.

'I know your family,' he said to Harry. 'I can't imagine how you got in so deep with Bailey and his gang of eavesdroppers.'

'I'm afraid I was always the black sheep.'

President Vargas agreed to see His Majesty's Ambassador on the morning of June 20. Sir Evelyn put on his morning coat and his full decorations and drove to the Palace of Guanabara in the embassy Rolls. The Union Jack stood up stiff and correct on its little mast above the fender. The ambassador was welcomed by an honour guard in white uniforms and helmets with horsehair plumes. The uniforms were in need of pressing, Sir Evelyn noted with a jaundiced eye, and the headgear could have done with more than a touch of brass polish. The honour guard presented arms in a fashion that would have made a British drill sergeant swoon.

Sir Evelyn was received by the president in the grand salon. For part of the time, the president's daughter, a lively, pretty young thing whom he called Alzarinha, was present. She seemed to have almost as much influence in the palace as Lady Maude exercised at the British Embassy, though Sir Evelyn would not have welcomed the analogy.

Vargas smiled and listened and smoked his long cheroots. He was small and dumpy and would have gone totally unremarked in any crowd but for the fact that his portrait hung on the wall of every school and post office and government office in the country, always smiling. The Brazilians said he had the ability to be silent in twelve different languages. He was an anomaly in a continent of shouting, swaggering caudillos. He had come to power through a revolution made by politicians and military men against the old oligarchy of the São Paulo coffee barons. He had held on to power not by force of arms but by a balancing act. His supporters ranged from Greenshirt sympathisers and regional bosses to near Socialists like

Doctor Alcibiades and *tenentes* who had marched with the Prestes Column. Getulio Vargas himself seemed to defy definition. Perhaps that was why he had survived numerous plots and an armed revolt by the Paulistas. Certainly he was avoiding showing himself in this interview. His inscrutability was such, Sir Evelyn thought, that he might be practising to be a Chinaman.

The president's manner changed abruptly when the ambassador mentioned that Prestes was in Brazil.

'How is it possible?' Vargas said, puffing faster on his cheroot. 'We have proof that Prestes is in Moscow. Here –' he scrabbled around among the papers on his desk and produced a newspaper. The characters were Cyrillic, Sir Evelyn noticed; it was a Russian paper. It was folded to an inside page.

Vargas showed Sir Evelyn the blurred photograph. Prestes was clearly recognisable among other foreign Communists, and there was no doubt about the locale. They were posing in front of Lenin's tomb.

'This newspaper appeared less than a week ago,' Vargas commented. 'One of our diplomats arranged to send this copy on the *Graf Zepelin*. How is it possible that Prestes could arrive here before the airship?'

'I don't know,' Sir Evelyn replied. 'Perhaps the photograph is a hoax. We have positive information from sources in Europe that Prestes has been here for more than a month.'

From that moment Vargas was all attention. To Sir Evelyn's satisfaction, he put off an appointment with the German Ambassador to prolong the conversation.

'We will take the most energetic action,' Vargas announced.

'If I may say so, *Senhor Presidente*, the appropriate course would seem to be energetic *watching*.'

Sir Evelyn was rather proud of this formulation.

At the end of the audience the president invited the ambassador and his wife to join the First Family in their box for a performance at the Teatro Municipal. Lady Maude would be pleased.

Two days later, President Vargas held a cabinet meeting at which he discussed the plan for a Communist revolution in Brazil. Secret Comintern documents supplied by the British Embassy were passed around the table. The conservative defence minister expressed the view that it was necessary to 'break the backs' of the plotters without delay. The National Liberation Alliance should be banned immediately. Others preferred a waiting game.

Four days after that, on the morning of June 26, O Globo ran a scream headline on its front page: THE COMMUNIST PLAN FOR BRAZIL. What followed was a bloodcurdling report drawing extensively on an unidentified Communist document. It contained directives for a 'preparatory phase' in which nationalism would be made the 'spinal cord of the movement'; any hint of 'internationalism' would be 'eliminated'. At the given time, a swift and furious coup d'état would be launched simultaneously in the north, in the vital Rio-São Paulo-Belo Horizonte triangle, the country's economic hub, and in the south. Trained cells would seize the electricity centres, the telegraph stations and the radio transmitters. Anti-Communist officers would be shot without mercy, 'preferably at their own doors or inside their houses', and special forces would range the streets in trucks, using machine guns to cow any attempted resistance.

Harry Maitland read the newspaper over breakfast and flung it down in fury. Someone inside the government had cooked up his own version of the Zinoviev Letter. The 'Communist document' cited in the newspaper was a forgery, but a forgery based on the facts. Whole paragraphs had been lifted from the Comintern documents Harry had been ordered to supply to the embassy. O Globo's account conformed very closely to Johnny's description of the plan Emil Brandt was trying to execute. Emil and the others in the South American bureau were bound to suspect a leak.

He arrived at the office in a black mood, which was not relieved by the spectacle of Desmond Wild lolling behind his desk. Wild, with his unerring nose for a liquor source, had found the bottle of scotch Harry kept in a desk drawer and had helped himself to a double. He had also helped himself to one of Harry's favourite cigars, the private stock he had had shipped direct from Havana.

'Make yourself at home, why don't you?'

'Now, don't be a prune, old boy. I come bearing gifts.'

'I'm surprised they let you up here. Have you paid your light bill recently?'

Wild treated this as beneath his dignity. Harry noticed he had acquired a monocle, which hung uselessly from a silk cord around his neck.

'I thought you might like a scoop,' Wild pursued. 'One of my native bearers moonlights as a typesetter for the Commie paper.'

'*A Manhã?*'

'And the same to you.'

'So?'

'Well, he tells me they're all rather het up about this stuff in *O Globo*. The Reds are going to put out a counterblast, a special edition. They've got a front-page story that claims that old Getulio was fed a lot of info on the Reds by none other than our intrepid ambassador. Perfidious Albion meddling again, trying to squash the glorious workers' movement. That kind of thing.'

'It's a red herring,' Harry said flatly. 'The usual propaganda lies. Would it inconvenience you terribly if I used my desk?'

'I think there's more to it.' Wild moved languidly in the direction of the sofa, whisky in hand. 'My chappie says the other lot have really got the wind up. You wouldn't know anything about it, I suppose?'

'Why should I?'

'Well, you really ought to, my dear. Aren't the Bolshies supposed to be planning to black out Rio Light so they can cut our throats in the dark?'

'You should ask Sir Evelyn.'

'I tried. He won't take my calls. I expect he's still hopping mad about that horse in the second. I tried Summerhayes, too, actually collared him on his way to the embassy. He scuttled off like a frightened rabbit.'

A messenger tapped on the door and entered immediately

with a note for Maitland. He recognised Johnny's hand-writing on the envelope. He glanced at the contents quickly and tucked the note away in his pocket.

The fact that Johnny had taken the risk of sending a message to him here – even though the language was suitably camouflaged – confirmed Maitland's worst fears. His man was in danger.

'You'll have to excuse me,' he said to the journalist.

He met Johnny at noon in the little museum of mechanical toys on top of the Sugarloaf, fifty yards from where the cable cars stopped.

'You might have warned me,' Johnny said.

'I didn't know it would be blown up all over the press,' Harry responded lamely.

'I only heard about it last night,' Johnny pursued. 'Emil received a full report from someone who has access at the highest level of the government. He has seen copies of all the papers your ambassador gave to Vargas. You should never have trusted these people.'

'And?'

'Emil told me he thinks the Secret Service got its information in Europe, by deciphering radio signals or intercepting the mail to one of the letter drops in Paris. He may have been testing me.'

'Have you been watched?'

'With Helene in town, I'm always under surveillance,' Johnny said grimly. 'But it will get worse. I'm sure they'll send an investigator from Moscow.'

'What can I do to help?'

'Stage a diversion.'

Maitland thought for a moment. Johnny had supplied the addresses of several safe houses in Paris that were used for Comintern traffic from South America.

'I could ask Bailey to fix something in Paris,' he suggested. If the Russians knew that one of their letter drops had been blown, that might deflect suspicion from Johnny.

'Better to do it here,' Johnny said.

Maitland understood. If the Comintern was looking for a traitor, it was his task to deliver one.

8

'We go forward!' Emil boomed over the hubbub around the Spaniard's dining room table. 'Then all these nervous Nellies will have to choose. They either shit or get off the pot.'

The sensational press coverage of the Communist plot had not resulted in any damage to the underground. The police had attacked left-wing speakers in the Praça Maua with their truncheons and beaten up a few union leaders, but that was nothing out of the ordinary. However, inside the National Liberation Alliance and even the Communist party itself, the publicity had sparked off a heated debate. Some people said the leadership was forcing the pace, moving before it had created a solid base of support. The old charge levelled at Prestes by the Communists before Moscow had taken the Cavalier of Hope under its wing was being revived: that Prestes and those around him were romantic militarists, closer in spirit to Blanqui and Bonaparte than to Marx and Lenin. There were doubters even within the ranks of the South American bureau itself. In his cups, Verdi, the Argentinian, was heard to describe Emil as a 'comical Chinese warlord, surrounded by sleep-walkers'. Emil demanded – and received – a formal apology for the remark.

Emil decided to shunt the sceptics out of the way by packing them off to the north to make speeches. Seven chiefs of the National Liberation Alliance were shoved on board a steamer headed up the coast. The fact that they were accompanied by twice as many police agents was of no consequence to the chief of the South American bureau.

Emil was a man in a fever dream. With the critics neutralised, he was free to rush ahead with the next stage of the operation. Johnny encouraged him. Johnny even helped to draft the new manifesto that Emil insisted must be issued in the name of the ANL.

The ANL had a big rally planned for July 5, the anniversary of previous armed risings. There was quite a turnout. The crowd did not look very revolutionary; the men all wore hats and their best Sunday suits, as if they were going to church.

A nervous young man in a bow tie was on the platform, looking over his notes. Carlos was a fine orator, but prone to stage fright. Before leaving his home, he had played 'The March of the Toreadors' over and over on his Victrola, to prime himself for his performance. On his way into the theatre, a squad of Integralistas in their green shirts and their stupid Sigma armbands had jeered at him and threatened to rough him up. He knew their leader; they had been at law school together. It anguished him to think that more of the intellectuals of his own generation were gravitating to the Fascists than to the left. Even at the Academy of Letters, the country's literary establishment applauded politely when the leading anti-Semitic ideologue of the Greenshirt movement delivered long harangues, decked out in a pith helmet and his full regalia. Of course, it was the lure of action, strongest of all for men who lived sedentary lives filled with abstractions.

The band struck up a tune; the meeting was under way. Carlos was scheduled to speak second. He hardly listened to the opening address, delivered by a former navy officer who was hopelessly adrift in his own syntax. Another military figure appeared from the wings and glided swiftly behind the speaker's podium. Carlos knew the man. He was a former army captain who had marched with Prestes and held a vague position on the organising committee of the ANL.

'You're to read this,' the captain whispered in his ear, thrusting a script into his hands.

'I don't understand. I've already prepared my speech.'

Carlos glanced at the first lines. They read like a cannon roll, like a barrage from the old guns at the Copacabana Fort. Never having met Johnny, Carlos could hardly know that some of the most inflammatory sentences had come from his pen. The whole thing amounted to an open declaration of war on the government.

'I can't read this,' the young Brazilian protested.

'Look at the signature.'

Carlos turned to the last page. The manifesto was signed by Prestes. It ended with a battle cry: 'All power to the ANL!' It was an open appeal for the overthrow of the government.

'This is madness.' Carlos began to shake violently. 'You'll get us all arrested.'

'The orders come from the top. Do as you're told, or I'll read it myself and denounce you as a coward.'

The opening speaker had reached his final peroration. The applause was punctuated by catcalls from the Greenshirt supporters and undercover cops in the crowd.

Carlos was being introduced.

'It's suicide,' he said unhappily.

'Stop pissing in your pants and get up there.'

A few days later, Harry Maitland joined the crowd that had gathered outside the ANL headquarters. Most of the windows on the upper floors had been smashed. Policemen were engaged in throwing file cabinets, furniture and type-writers down onto the pavement below. Thousands of copies of *A Manhã* and other left-wing publications were blowing along the street.

The government had answered Prestes' declaration of war – edited and inspired by Emil and Johnny – by banning the ANL and ordering a roundup of leftist union organisers. The Communists had thrown away their legal facade.

Their critics on the left – especially the anarchists and Trotskyites – denounced the party's tactics and claimed that its followers had been deceived by police spies and agents provocateurs. Harry wondered if they realised how much substance there was to their charges. In the decisive meeting of the Communist leaders before the big rally, Johnny had helped to fuel Emil's passion. Verdi predicted that the government might shut down the ANL if its spokesmen made an open appeal for revolt. Johnny countered that the government probably wouldn't dare go so far but that, if it did, it would be doing the revolution a favour. The country would become polarised; the president's reformist pose would be exploded; liberals would move to the left. Above all, many more people would recognise that an armed uprising was the only way forward and be drawn into the party underground. This was the argument that won out.

As Harry watched the police completing their demolition job at the ANL building, Colonel Plinio strolled out the front door, his panama hat tilted rakishly across his forehead.

He greeted Harry in high good spirits.

'They shot themselves in the foot this time, didn't they? Let's have a drink to celebrate.'

They went to the Confiteiria Colombo, where a string quartet was playing among the potted palms in the depths of a bustling hall lined with mirrors and mahogany. Above Plinio's head, painted schooners under full sail ploughed a sea of glass.

His day's hunting over, the colonel was in a philosophical mood.

'We are a gentle people,' he remarked, surveying the powdered ladies in white gloves who were sampling the Colombo's famous pastries and 'Petrôpolis bread', toast prepared with butter and Parmesan cheese. 'We are also too much addicted to the French and their endless talk about *liberté*. Voltaire, Victor Hugo, Romain Rolland. They – and the anarchists, of course – are far more seductive to us than Marx. But what is freedom? In the real world, freedom can be comprehended only by the boundaries that contain it.' He sipped his drink. 'Like pure alcohol,' he went on, 'liberty can be enjoyed only in dilution, and there are few men with the stomach – or the table manners – to withstand the higher proofs.'

8

Prince of Shadows

Faust:
When you will introduce us at this revel,
Will you appear as sorcerer – or devil?

Mephistopheles:
I generally travel without showing my station,
But on a gala day one shows one's decoration.
– Goethe

1

'There are times I don't know you at all,' Verdi remarked to Johnny. 'You're an intelligent man. You know that Emil is wrong. Yet you go along with him. You even encourage him.'

'Mine wasn't the only voice,' Johnny said quietly. 'The Brazilians took the same line.'

'They're victims of passion.' The Argentinian swept his hair off his forehead. 'Nilo, Prestes – they can't always help themselves. But you – you're a professional. You've been with Emil, you've seen him make the same mistakes in China. Then he nearly got you killed in the north. That's why I can't fathom you.'

'Put a sock in it,' Helene cut in rudely. 'The decision was made. There's an end of it. If you want to do postmortems, go and work for a coroner.'

'Sometimes I think I do –' the Argentinian began daringly, but Helene silenced him with a look.

He knows what I know, Johnny thought, feeling a closer sympathy for Verdi, who looked and smelled as if he had started drinking even earlier than usual that day.

He's heard the screams too.

Helene was steering the Ford with one hand, nursing one of her baby cheroots in the other. She spotted a gap in the traffic and whipped over to the left.

'This is close enough,' she announced, pulling up in front of a bank. The Pan Air office was just round the corner.

'Will you wait for me?' Verdi said. 'I won't be two minutes.'

Helene shrugged and glanced at Johnny.

'Two minutes,' Johnny said.

They watched the Argentinian circumnavigate the little crowd that had gathered round a *bicheiro*, to bet on the elephant or the rooster.

'I'm surprised he didn't ask one of us to come in and hold his hand,' Helene said with quiet contempt. She glanced at her reflection in the plate glass windows of the bank. 'We look like bank robbers in a getaway car.'

Verdi came back, visibly agitated.

'They say I must get an exit visa from the police,' he reported. 'The Pan Air agent says he will go with me to the station. Do you think it's safe?'

He appealed to Helene with moist spaniel eyes. He met that ice-blue stare. 'It's your decision,' she said curtly. 'You can swim to Buenos Aires, if you'd rather.'

Verdi looked miserable.

'I'm sure it will be all right,' Johnny tried to encourage him. 'There's nothing wrong with your passport, is there?'

'We can't sit here all day,' Helene announced, revving the engine.

'All right. I'm going.'

Helene rammed the Ford into gear and left Verdi standing on the sidewalk.

'You were a bit brutal with him, weren't you?' Johnny said.

'He's just another Hamlet. We can't afford them. He ought to be sitting at home writing clever little philosophical essays that nobody reads. Emil is right to send him away.'

Verdi had been instructed to go to Buenos Aires to meet the leaders of the other South American Communist parties and report on their attitudes. Emil had not forgiven the Argentinian for comparing him to a Chinese warlord.

'It is also possible that Verdi is right,' Johnny remarked.

'That wasn't what you said at the meeting.'

'A man is allowed to change his mind.'

'Not about some things, Johnny.' The unexpected choice of phrase, and the savage wrench at the wheel that sent the car hurtling towards a group of passengers alighting from a streetcar made Johnny wonder if he had pushed his luck too far.

A week before Sir Evelyn had called on the president, Johnny and Helene had moved from the boarding house to a small apartment in Botafogo. The front windows overlooked the cemetery of John the Baptist. This was a graveyard for the rich. The marble busts were stern images of bourgeois rectitude, complete with pince-nez, wing collars and imperials. Sculpted maidens wept over them soundlessly, their Grecian robes in calculated disarray. In the foreground, just inside the cemetery wall, a wounded lion with an arrow sticking out of its back howled its last from the top of a marble plinth.

It was almost nightfall when Verdi appeared on Johnny's doorstep together with a small suitcase and a wife to match, a nervous, dark-eyed girl called Rosario.

'You must help us,' said Verdi breathlessly. 'We have nowhere to go –'

'Come in, come in.' Johnny took his arm and half pulled him into the sitting room, which opened directly off the landing.

Rosario perched on a corner of the sofa, her hands folded in her lap.

'Who is it?' Helene called from the bathroom.

'It's okay!' Johnny shouted back.

Before he had finished pouring Verdi's brandy, she came padding out, still dripping from the bath and swathed in a huge apricot towel. Helene could subsist on a handful of rice, but not without perfumed soap and soft towels.

'Shit.' She glowered at Verdi. 'What do you think you're doing here?'

'I'm sorry,' the Argentinian apologised, not daring to meet her eyes. 'I had to get Rosario away. I think the police are onto me.'

Johnny handed him his drink. 'Tell us everything that happened. Take it slowly.'

'I went to the police station,' Verdi began. They had insisted on taking his fingerprints and told him they would have to retain his passport for a few hours, to complete the necessary formalities. He had been instructed to come back at the end of the day.

'I sensed something was wrong,' Verdi continued, 'so I paid the Pan Air man a few dollars to go back for my passport. The police wouldn't give it to him. They claimed it was a forgery. They said they had checked my fingerprints and believed I was a dangerous man, a man on the run. They told him to tell me I was required to call for my travel documents in person. The man in the airline office is *muy simpático*, no friend of the police. But you know what he said to me? He said, "Are you really a dynamiter?" What would you have done in my place? Naturally, I got away as fast as I could.'

'So you led the cops here,' Helene commented, peering around the edge of the curtains.

'I wasn't followed!' Verdi jumped up, his voice rising to a falsetto. 'I swear it!'

Johnny went to the window. 'There's no one,' he pronounced.

Verdi crumpled into the sofa.

'What are we going to do with them?' Helene demanded. In her anger she had let the towel ride up to the tops of her thighs. Verdi was watching as if this, too, were part of his ordeal. His wife blushed and stared at the floor.

'Why don't you get dressed and get us all something to

eat?' Johnny suggested calmly. 'I'll go and alert the others.'

'Johnny —' she followed him into the bedroom. She watched him from behind as he checked the magazine of his pistol and slipped it back into the shoulder holster under his jacket.

'Johnny —' her lower lip trembled.

He saw this in the mirror·as he combed his hair. The instant of weakness — was it fear or suppressed fury? — softened her, as did the nakedness of her shoulders, rosy and moist from the bath.

'Yes?'

As he turned to her, her lips made a little bow, and he thought she was going to kiss him.

Instead she said, 'Those two are dead weight. It's stupid to risk ourselves for them.'

'Maybe. But take care of them, all the same.'

'I worry about you, Johnny.' She traced the line of his jaw with her finger. She smelled of sandalwood.

'You needn't.'

'But I do. You're too patient with the bleeding hearts. You never used to be this way.'

'Are you trying to tell me something?'

'Just take care they don't start bleeding over our floor.'

The threat was not specific, but it was there in her tone and in the cool indifference with which she swung out to the bathroom and pulled off the towel. Naked, with the door open, she proceeded to shave her armpits, as if he had ceased to exist. Her long, firm body was as white as one of those statues in the cemetery.

Verdi did not leave for Buenos Aires, but he got his passport back. Prestes, whom Johnny found dining with Emil at the German's luxurious apartment in Ipanema, undertook to fix everything. Even Emil seemed nervous about the method he proposed.

'Don't worry about it,' the Brazilian reassured him. 'I know my people.'

Prestes wrote a letter to the police, asking them to return the travel papers of a special friend, and signed it with his own name. The letter was hand carried to the central station by a reserve army officer wearing his captain's uniform.

The next morning, Johnny waited for the messenger on a bench in the Praça Maua, next to a stand where they sold watermelons and sweet *caqui* fruit, which looked like fat, overripe tomatoes. He did not expect his man to arrive.

When the captain appeared, beaming from ear to ear, Johnny got up and strolled about, affecting not to see him. He also unbuttoned his jacket, so he could get at his gun quickly.

The captain took the cue. He breezed past Johnny and paused to inspect a mound of papayas. As Johnny came abreast of him, he slipped Verdi's passport into his hand.

He could not refrain from whispering, 'Piece of cake.'

Johnny fully expected detectives to seize him at any moment. He spent more than three hours before he satisfied himself that he was not under surveillance, even taking a ride out into the harbour with a boatload of sightseers.

When Prestes was told what had happened, he was jubilant.

'You see,' he enthused, 'the revolution has allies everywhere! We even have friends in the police!'

When Harry Maitland heard the story, two days later, he found himself trapped in a state between sleeping and waking for much of the night, as his mind groped for a satisfactory explanation. The easiest to accept was that Colonel Plinio's men were more subtle than Johnny had counted on and had succeeded in staying out of sight when they tailed Prestes' messenger. For why would the police release the passport of a known subversive – let alone a courier from the most wanted man in the country – if not in the hope of following them to bigger game? No doubt there were a few Communist sympathisers in the police, but it would be madness for them to risk exposing themselves in such an obvious way. Anyway, the orders must have come from high up, perhaps from Colonel Plinio himself.

Harry pictured the faint smile on Colonel Plinio's face as he had watched the duel between the viper and the boa in the mayor's snake house. What game was he playing now?

Was he confident to the point of carelessness because he had a spy of his own inside the conspiracy? Did he want the conspiracy to run its course so as to crush it more completely – or because he wanted it to succeed?

'Piece of cake,' Prestes' courier had murmured to Johnny.

Colin Bailey had said something similar to Harry when he had asked him to work for the Secret Service.

The memory of the Christmas pudding he had been made to eat at home, as a boy, rose up out of Harry's subconscious – a pudding so heavy they used to joke that if they dropped it, it would make a crater in the floor. He had been induced to eat it only by the promise of silver threepenny bits hidden among the raisins. He remembered the sense of being cheated when he worked his way through a whole piece and found no threepenny bits.

2

Johnny met Maitland at the Necrôpolis. It was a simple brush contact by the roulette table. Johnny put his chips on red, and then, as everyone watched the ball, he slipped his report into the pocket of Harry's dinner jacket. The ball landed on a red number. He did not forget to pick up his winnings.

He was standing in line in front of the cashier's grille when a thick, rather guttural voice called out, 'Gruber! Johnny Gruber!'

Johnny stiffened as if someone had poked a gun between his shoulder blades.

Very slowly, he turned and saw a large Germanic figure barrelling at him through the crush of players.

'You fuckhead!' Engineer Hossbach greeted him. 'Did you think you'd given me the slip? Where've you been hiding? Where's that cold-assed sister of yours?'

Hossbach had a hand on his shoulder and wouldn't hear of parting company until they had inspected some of his favourite night spots and killed a bottle or two. Johnny was so relieved Hossbach had failed to notice Maitland that he went along with the German's proposals.

It proved to be quite a productive evening. Hossbach was in a talkative mood, boasting that he had been promised a big job in Berlin and dropping the names of connections at the German Embassy as well as the anatomical details of various women he claimed had enjoyed his favours.

'It was a stroke of luck, running into you like that,' Hossbach said. He leaned his face nearer to Johnny's. 'I might have a job for you. The money's good. Enough to pay for every floozie in this dump.' He waved his arms expansively over the crowded floor of the Babylônia Club.

'Tell me more.'

'One of our best men is coming from Germany. He'll be needing some local help. Nothing to do with the embassy, mind. I've been told to find a few men who can keep their mouths shut.'

That would rule *you* out, Johnny thought.

He said, 'What's it about?'

'It's a spot of debt collecting, that's the size of it.'

'What sort of debt?'

'The kind you have to pay.' Hossbach smirked. 'A blood debt. We got a tip that a big Red is coming to Rio. He killed some of our boys in Germany. The idea is to settle the account.'

Johnny thought, he could be talking about *me*.

'How will you find this Red?'

'Our man is bringing a photograph. And we know the kike started in Antwerp, so he's probably got diamonds to hock. That's how those bastards pay their way,' he added with assumed authority. 'So we've got lots to play with.'

Johnny realised he had impersonated a Nazi lover too well in his previous conversations with Hossbach. There was no chance of backing out easily now the German had put this many cards on the table.

'Why don't you go to the police?' he suggested.

'The Brazilians are soft.' Hossbach curled his lip. 'We know how to take care of these things. Well, are you in?'

'You know you can count on me,' Johnny agreed. 'But I don't know much about guns.'

'No need to start pissing on the floor!' Hossbach guffawed. 'We'll handle the serious business. You're a sales-man, aren't you? We'll find out where the Yid is hiding out, and you can make him an offer he won't be able to resist.'

A whore Hossbach couldn't resist, in a dress slit to the waist, saved Johnny from spending the rest of the evening at the Babylônia Club. He even managed to slip away without giving an address.

'I've got a girl waiting for me, too,' he announced, as the whore jiggled her bust under Hossbach's nose. 'I'll call you tomorrow.'

On the streetcar back to Botafogo, he went over the conver-sation in his mind. There was no longer any doubt who Hossbach worked for – or that the Gestapo had a source close to the Comintern operation in Europe. *The kike . . .* was the Gestapo on the trail of Emil, or somebody else?

I'll talk about it with Helene, he decided. It struck him that he had just been handed a chance to do something highly pleasurable – to give the Gestapo a kick in the balls – and improve his standing with the South American bureau at the same time.

He was in excellent spirits as he turned into the street near the cemetery. There was a light on in their apartment. Helene must have finished earlier than expected or brought some of the typing home. She did that sometimes, and he was then able to steal a look at the secret directives Emil was sending out.

Johnny turned his key in the door. There was an odour of tobacco from light Virginia cigarettes, like the Argentinian smoked. But Verdi and his wife had left several days before, and Helene still favoured her black cigarillos.

Johnny reached for his gun as he swung the door open. He saw the battered soles of the man's shoes, stretched out across the ottoman. A record was playing on the Victrola, one he did not recognise. It sounded like a funeral dirge. He ducked down and burst into the room behind the gun.

'I see you've started the revolution already,' said the man who was lolling in the armchair, smoking American cigarettes. There was a big revolver in front of him, on the coffee table. He made no move for it. Instead he turned up the volume on the victrola. The voices were reaching a crescendo.

Dies irae, dies illa
Solvet saeclum in favilla
Teste David cum Sybilla.

'Beautiful, isn't it?' said the man in the chair. He began to translate: 'On that day of wrath, the world dissolves into ashes . . .'

Johnny put his gun away. He shut the door and stood beside it as if waiting for permission to sit down.

'What is the music?' he asked.

'Verdi's *Requiem*. Do you suppose our Argentinian deserves one?'

Johnny slumped onto the sofa without responding.

'Not much of a welcome, Johnny,' said Max Fabrikant. 'Are you so sorry to see me?'

'Surprised, that's all. Nobody told me you were coming, Max.'

'Leon. You have to call me Leon. I'm supposed to be a Belgian.'

'What are you doing here?'

'What do you suppose? Land reclamation.' Max added with seeming anger, 'You're living in a swamp! All of you! I wouldn't expect too much from some of the others, least of all from your Brazilian half-breeds, who can't tell black from white. But *you*, Johnny! You disappoint me.'

'What have I done?'

'Come closer to me.' Max patted the edge of the sofa closest to his chair. 'I want to look into your eyes so I can tell when you're lying. Then you can explain to me why.'

Johnny experienced the same sense of panic he had felt at school, when the headmaster had summoned all the boys to assembly and announced that he knew that one of them had been smoking in the toilets. The headmaster had called for the guilty boy to step forward. Johnny had had to wrestle with himself not to confess. In the end it was an innocent boy, a boy who had started shaking and burst into tears, who had been held responsible and suspended from school. That was the way it went. Johnny was no more – and no less – frightened now than then. But he looked steadily into the inquisitor's eyes.

'There's a spy inside your circle,' Max announced. 'Is it you?'

Johnny tried to see only his own reflection in Max's eyes. 'No.'

'You've been in contact with a Gestapo agent, a man called Hossbach.'

'Yes.' He felt slightly dizzy. It could hardly be coincidence that Max was asking about the man he had just left.

'Why didn't you report your meetings with this man?'

'Helene knew everything,' he defended himself. 'What more do you want?'

'You should have written your own reports. How can you tell what Helene puts in hers?'

The angle of this attack was so bizarre that Johnny found it impossible to take it seriously. The pressure in his chest lifted; he wanted to laugh in Max's face.

He couldn't restrain himself. He was spluttering as he said, 'Max, dear Max. Have you come here to accuse me of working for the Gestapo?'

'This isn't a joking matter.'

'Very well, let's talk about the Gestapo. I saw Hossbach tonight. It was a chance meeting – there's room for chance in life sometimes, isn't there? He thinks I'm a good little Nazi, so he asked for my help. They're hunting one of ours.'

'Who?'

'I haven't quite worked it out. Perhaps you'll be able to. Hossbach described the target as a big Red and a kike.'

Max did not flinch at the coarse epithets. 'Emil?' he suggested. 'Olga?'

'I couldn't know at the time,' Johnny said, 'but it seems to me now that Hossbach was talking about *you*.'

'What are you saying?'

For the first time Johnny had the satisfaction of seeing Max on the defensive.

'Well, I don't know if you're Jewish,' Johnny went on, milking the situation for all the pleasure he could derive. 'But you're certainly a Belgian now, aren't you?'

'Stop farting around and get to the point!'

'*Kamarad* Hossbach says the target started his travels in Antwerp. Also that he's carrying diamonds.'

Max did not respond immediately, which was why Johnny was certain he had found his mark.

It was Johnny's moment to attack, and he seized it. 'I ask myself,' he said, 'whether Hossbach is working for you – or you are working for him.'

'You bastard!' Max was on his feet, with his fist clenched.

'You try it,' Johnny said, not stirring from his place. 'I've got a few years on you and a good few pounds as well, and I haven't had a decent fight since Emil tried to get me killed in the north.'

Max's fury slowly subsided.

'We need to work this out,' he declared, after Johnny had poured them both a stiff brandy.

It was a very long night, as long as any Johnny had spent with Heinz in the days when his world was merrily on fire.

Max ordered him to maintain contact with Hossbach and offered to increase his expenses so he could keep a safe house, an address to supply the Gestapo man when he – inevitably – would ask. Johnny agreed. At the start of the conversation, he had been convinced that Max had somehow contrived the whole episode with Hossbach in order to frame him. Max's emotional response to his accusation had persuaded him he was wrong. There *were* coincidences in life, he told himself. The roulette ball sometimes landed on the same number twice.

When Max returned to the main purpose of his mission, he talked to Johnny as a trusted comrade, not a man under suspicion.

'There is a British spy in the organisation,' Max announced. 'Who would you nominate?'

I mustn't jump into this, Johnny cautioned himself. It would be smarter to condemn by faint praise.

'What about Nilo?' Max prodded him. 'He went to school at Eton, didn't he?'

'I don't think he was very popular at school. He doesn't love the British.'

'He doesn't love his mother,' Max observed. 'But I am informed that he still takes an allowance from her. They call him the Millionaire, don't they? He could be bought.'

'Only with girls.'

If he wants to waste his time watching Nilo, Johnny thought, that's perfect. But let it be his own choice.

There was only one bad moment, when Max remarked, 'In my experience the man who calls loudest for blood is usually the provocateur. Wouldn't you agree?'

'Sometimes.'

'So why have you been hurrying everything along? You sided with Emil over that idiotic manifesto that got the ANL banned, didn't you?'

He's already talked to Helene, Johnny realised. That was probably why she seemed to be staying out all night.

'I have my orders,' Johnny said. 'They come from Manuilsky —' he paused '— and from Stalin. If you intend to question my judgment, you should take it up with them.'

Max stared at him for a long time before he permitted himself to smile.

'You've learned a few tricks, Johnny Lentz.'

'I've had the very best instructors.'

'I have one piece of advice for you. Don't forget who your friends are.'

'I'll never do that,' Johnny promised, thinking of the friend Max had murdered. 'Speaking of friends,' he went on, 'I want you to tell me about Sigrid.'

'I admire your restraint in waiting all this time to ask.'

'Is she safe?'

'Perfectly safe, except from mosquitoes.'

Johnny blinked at him. It was too much to hope for.

'I brought her to Rio,' Max confirmed. 'I know she wants to see you. Johnny, I don't know quite what you think of me, but I'll promise you this, I won't stand in your way.' He took a swallow of brandy and added, 'Unless there are compelling professional reasons.'

The qualification did not diminish what Johnny felt: a soaring sense of elation, of flying without wings. Here, in this magical country that shattered every prejudice and preconception of the Old World, she would at last be his. Whatever Max had done to her, whatever he had tried to make of her, would not matter a damn in Brazil.

3

A violet–blue sail flapped across the windshield, so close, so vivid that Sigrid raised her palm to protect her face.

'It's a butterfly,' she said in wonder, as it dipped, caught an updraft and glided off into the highest canopy of the rain forest. 'I've never seen one so big.'

'That's how it is here,' Johnny said, slowing the car to negotiate a hairpin bend. 'The country knows no limits.'

Guavas grew wild along the road. The forest blazed with flamboyants and mimosas, the yellows and purples of the *ipe* blossoms, the hot, rowdy pinks of the impatiens that sprang up everywhere. Johnny stopped the car at a bend that hung over the green gorge like a balcony. When he turned off the engine, the silence seemed complete, until Sigrid began to listen properly. Then she heard bird song, the whir of insects, the bubble of water in secret springs, the scuffle of unseen monkeys or squirrels among the foliage.

'I saved this place for you,' he said. He took her hand and led her along a low stone parapet to a clearing that opened out like a piazza. In the middle was a stone table with narrow stone benches on either side.

He drew her with him to the very edge of the cliff.

'Look.'

She followed his pointing hand. The sensation was giddying. The ground fell away at her feet. She felt she was leaning over the neck of a horse as it hurled itself down the mountainside, charging at the sea miles below. She shut her eyes and clutched at Johnny's arm, and felt his hand close over hers.

When she looked again, the sensation was different. A curious sense of calm and completion began to steal over her. What opened out below her appeared as a vast natural amphitheatre. There, at the very centre, was the circling bay of Botafogo, turned to mother-of-pearl by the distance and the harbour mists. The peaks around it were islands in the haze. There were no sharp edges. Everything was rounded and opaque. The forest enclosed the whole panorama like a pair of broad, cupped hands.

'It's perfect,' Sigrid whispered. 'It's the landscape of dreams.'

He led her back to the stone table. 'It's called the Emperor's Table.'

'Why?'

'The last emperor of Brazil – Dom Pedro – picked the most breathtaking view in Rio and set his picnic table to command it. Now it belongs to us.'

Her face was shaded by a wide-brimmed straw hat. Her dress was foamy white and reached to midcalf. She was even more beautiful than his dreams, her body fuller, her movements more confident. But when he looked directly into her eyes, a shutter seemed to fall.

'You're different,' he said to her.

'Did you think it would be the same?'

'I don't know. But I waited for you, all the same.'

'You shouldn't have waited.'

'What are you saying?' Johnny wanted to shake her. But there was a stronger longing. He took her by the waist and tried to kiss her. She kept her mouth closed and slipped away from him.

'Is it Max?' He couldn't contain himself. He rushed on, 'Are you in love with Max?'

'Does it matter?'

'Of course it matters.'

'You haven't learned very much, Johnny.'

She said it with such weariness, such resignation, that he fell silent.

'Max didn't take me to Copenhagen to sleep with me,' she went on. 'You know him. You know that's true. He came to me once, just once. He didn't force me.'

'Then why?'

'He had been ordered to kill a man.'

'He's used to that.'

'Yes. But he talked about how much harder it is to kill when you have time to take a good look at your victim, to notice the little, ordinary things that make him human – the way he lies in his sleep, the hairs on the back of his hands, the sound of his breathing. It wasn't an easy assignment. I think Max was scared. He certainly had reason to be. There was a very good chance he would not return alive.'

'And you made love to him because of that?'

'Because it was my duty.' She folded her arms across her chest. 'You should know. That's what you taught me, isn't it? That we're all soldiers under orders?'

He turned his head, to look out over the glorious view of Rio with sightless eyes.

'Were there others?' he pursued.

'What makes you think you have the right to ask me these things?' she erupted. 'Did you take monastic orders? Are you telling me you never went with another woman?'

'No more than was necessary.'

'Hah! And you think you're entitled to ask me what *I* did in bed!'

'Sigrid, I waited for you. In every way that counts, I waited for you.'

'What about Helene? Did you sleep with her too?'

'No.'

She stared at him, ungiving.

'Have you seen Helene?' he asked quickly.

'Yes, of course.'

'What did she say?' He was suddenly terrified that Helene had invented something to try to turn Sigrid against him.

'Nothing that matters. But I think she's still in love with you.'

'You're wrong. We're not together by choice. The

414

situation doesn't amuse her any more than it does me.'

'Yet you made a choice in Shanghai.'

'She told you about that?'

'She told me you saved her life.'

'I would have done it for any comrade. It doesn't change anything. If you want to know, I think Helene hates me.'

'Love and hate are closely related.'

'Like sisters?'

'Like sisters,' she agreed, and pursed her lips.

He tried to touch her again, but she twisted away. Why did she keep this distance between them? Surely she wasn't jealous of Helene?

He felt slighted, and because of that, he chose words that would wound her.

'They told me you were going to have a baby.'

'What business is it of theirs?' she rounded on him. 'Whoever "they" are.'

'It was ours, wasn't it?'

'How could anyone tell?' she struck back at him.

'*Was it ours?*' he shouted. He shook her so violently that her hat tumbled off and rolled away into the forest.

'You're hurting me.'

He relaxed his grip. The tears welled up in her eyes. She tried to turn her face away, so he would not see, but he forced her to look at him.

'Sigrid –'

'Of course it was ours.'

The wind blew threads of red-gold hair across her face. He smoothed them gently back into place.

'Why?'

'I heard nothing from you.'

'But I wrote to you every week!' Even as he said that, he knew what had happened. The secret police had intercepted the letters. How had Max put it? There was no such thing as a personal conversation.

'How could I keep a child in Russia?' she went on. 'By working in a factory? I don't even speak Russian.'

'Our people would have looked after you. General Berzin promised me.'

'Oh, yes?' she said bitterly. 'How? By taking the baby and putting it in a communal crèche?'

'Who told you that? Max?'

'He ought to know.'

'That bastard.'

'Don't blame Max. He's the only one who helped me. He even found the doctor, a man from the Kremlin clinic, not one of your backyard butchers. The doctor says I might still be able to have children. It's the Russian way, isn't it? The average woman in Russia has six point five abortions in her lifetime.' She tried to make herself sound like a statistical yearbook, but her voice was breaking.

'Fuck the average woman in Russia!'

'I imagine you did.'

With the tears running down her cheeks, she started laughing. He felt giddy. Suddenly he was laughing and crying, too. He caught her in his arms and pressed her tight against his body, and this time she did not pull away. Their lips met. He tasted salt and wild honey. He struggled with the hooks of her dress.

'Wait.' She pushed her palm against his chest. 'We have to find my hat.'

They held hands and walked into the rain forest. The air was heavy with the scent of bougainvillaea. They came to a little clearing where orchids grew wild among the under-growth. He picked one for her. She smelled it and tucked it behind her ear, smiling and frowning at the same time.

'I can never remember which ear is the right one.'

'They're both perfect.'

She made him wait while she took off the lacy white dress and hung it from a bough. She flirted with each button as she stripped him of his clothes. The light, filtered through the branches, dappled her skin. He spread his shirt over a bed of dry leaves. Then he swept her up into his arms and laid her tenderly on it, as if he were taking her for the first time. A shaft of light plunged down from above his head.

She looked up at him and said, 'You're wearing the sun in your hair.'

Above him she saw a pair of *pássaros de sangue*, the blood-red birds of the jungle, flash past.

He touched her breasts, her thighs, and each time she started giggling. He ran his fingers along the inside of her leg, and she was convulsed. He grazed her neck, and she reared away, panting with laughter. Her skin was a mass of nerve endings.

He lay still, propped up on his elbows, smiling but puzzled.

'I'm sorry,' she said, trying to stifle a new fit of giggles. 'I'm ticklish everywhere.'

She took him by the upper arms and drew him down on to her.

'Come to me.'

She shivered as he entered her. His face under the sunburst was that of a dark lord.

They lay silent for a long time afterwards, holding each other and listening to birdcalls like bells and wind chimes.

He said, 'I was wrong. It is the same. Each of us may be different, but *we* are the same.' He sat up and looked at her. 'I won't let anything take you away from me again.'

'You can't say that.'

His words had broken the magic circle. She started picking up her clothes.

'You're the only thing real I've had to hold on to,' he persisted. 'I won't give you up now that I've found you again.'

'Isn't there a character in Dostoyevsky whose only hold on reality is a toothache?' she countered, trying to make light of it.

'I'm serious.'

'Not now, Johnny. Let's not be serious now.'

On the drive back to the city he asked about Copenhagen.

'What was it like there, working with Max?'

'It wasn't an easy time. You know Max was ordered to kill Trotsky?'

'I didn't know,' Johnny lied. 'But I guessed as much

when I heard you were both in Norway. Evidently he didn't succeed.'

'Trotsky is well protected. He has a whole private army. Max asked me to help find a way past the guards.'

'And you agreed?'

'Naturally,' she said briskly. 'Trotsky is a traitor, a British agent.'

Johnny glanced at her sidelong. She spoke with no sense of irony. She believed it.

'What was the plan?'

'Max showed me a place where some of Trotsky's people met. He told me to cultivate one of them – Trotsky's private secretary – and show him my pictures. I was to offer to paint Trotsky's portrait.'

'Did you?'

She shook her head. 'The secretary didn't trust me. I think he preferred boys. In the end Max shot him.'

'And if they'd let you into the house? What would have happened then?'

'Max had a poison. I was supposed to smuggle it in with my paints. Max said the death would look completely natural, like a heart attack.'

'You were prepared to go that far?' Johnny was horrified.

'I don't know for sure,' she said thoughtfully. 'In the abstract, perhaps. But I didn't see Trotsky's face. I could only know if I saw his face, as close to me as yours.'

They rode together in silence for a few minutes. He realised that, despite their enchanted hour in the forest, he would have to be more careful of her than of any of the others.

4

The boulevard press, as Emil liked to call it, ran horror stories every week about the Red plot to destroy Brazil. There were broad hints planted by the government that old-time politicians – even some who were tied to the coffee barons of São Paulo – were secretly involved.

In the wealthy beach suburbs of the southern zone, Emil and his general staff fired communiqués back and forth, far less troubled by the police than by the uncomforting presence of Max Fabrikant. Emil's reports to Moscow, transmitted by radio via the Soviet Mission in Montevideo, were uniformly optimistic. They inspired Wang Ming, the Chinaman who spoke on behalf of South America at the Congress of the Comintern in Moscow, to declare that an anti-imperialist revolution was at hand in Brazil.

These rival accounts, however exaggerated, were not without foundation. The country's political history had been a chronicle of coups and countercoups, mutinies and regional revolts. There was a floating population of veteran intriguers who were willing to gamble on any new rising against the central government: out-of-work governors who wanted their places back, local dynasts who wanted to stop Rio meddling in their private fiefdoms, restless *tenentes* (some generals or *interventores*, virtual dictators of remote states) who were bored with inaction. For some of them, especially those who had marched with Prestes a decade before and still revered his name, the ultimate aims of the conspiracy were of secondary interest; at any rate, as long as the conspirators didn't go around banging their drum too loudly. It was the promise of change – sheer movement, not direction – that made them eager to join up.

For the vast majority of the Brazilian people, who could neither read the newspapers nor place Russia, or perhaps even Rio, on a map, expectations of an impending revolution took exotic forms. Myth travelled further and faster than the speeches of politicians. In the marshy slums of Recife, Father Badó heard a curious rumour that Princess Isabel, who had freed the slaves, had been resurrected to rescue their descendants from the yoke of the landowners and the shopkeepers. In a garrison in the *pampas* country of the Rio Grande do Sul, which had produced both Vargas and Prestes, a young lieutenant told his comrades that the government had insulted the honour of the army and urged them to throw in their lot with a new movement of the patriotic officers that was preparing to claim satisfaction.

In Salvador da Bahia, a baker who attended a clandestine gathering of the ANL volunteered to inject a powerful laxative into the bread he supplied to the local barracks, maintaining that this would immobilise the government's soldiers on the day of the revolt. He announced that he was ready to do this to avenge police harassment of spiritists and practitioners of *candomblé*.

Emil sat in his apartment on Rua Paulo Redfern with his fan and his spiked pineapple juice, writing directives in English or German for others to translate. Harry Maitland saw him by chance one morning, taking a stroll along the beach at Ipanema with his taciturn, kinky-haired wife, Lenka. Emil was wearing a felt hat and a baggy suit without a tie. Lenka wore a dress of shapeless brown stuff that trailed to her ankles and a scarf over her lustreless hair. They might have been on the beach at Odessa. They were as utterly remote from the country they had been sent to revolutionise, Harry thought, as visitors from another galaxy.

Yet, as he sifted through the information he gleaned from Johnny and matched it against other, less confidential sources, he worried that Emil might have stumbled on a winning formula. It is generally easier to recruit people *against* an existing state of affairs than *for* some proposed remedy. When the National Liberation Alliance had been banned, attention had been focused on government repression, not the Communist element in its program, and liberals who had previously spurned it took up the cudgels on its behalf. The conspirators did not advertise their objectives. They were willing to latch on to any group that had a grudge against the government, promising money and advancement.

The fact that there was a double agent inside the Comintern team was no guarantee that the revolution would fail. The tsarist secret police had had highly placed agents inside all the opposition groups, including the Bolsheviks; they had also been powerless to stop either of the revolutions of 1917. Colin Bailey had seen fit to remind Harry of this comforting analogy in a recent letter. There were questions Johnny could not answer. Which of the generals at the Defense Ministry had promised to support a coup? Nilo had made a tantalising reference to one who could be counted on. What was the new source of funds for the South American bureau that its agents were spending so lavishly? Was Doctor Alcibiades committed to the plot?

If the decision to launch a coup were taken tonight, would Johnny know about it?

This last question worried Johnny as well as his control. Since Max had arrived in Rio, security around Emil and his colleagues had been tightened considerably. Max had gone to ground somewhere; Johnny had been unable to discover his address. Sigrid had a place of her own, a room in a boarding house in Copacabana, where Johnny sometimes stayed overnight. But he knew that she also stayed with Max and at other safe houses dotted around the city. Helene no longer brought documents home. She was more careful than before about what she said to Johnny about her own activities. The Brazilian leaders, including Prestes, had been ordered to change their lodgings. Johnny had been asked to booby-trap a safe for one of them – he had little doubt it was for Prestes himself – but did not know where the safe was being conveyed. For fear of police infiltration, regional leaders, especially Cato's group in the north, had been given much greater autonomy.

Worst of all, it had to be assumed that Johnny was under suspicion. Maitland's meetings with him had become more furtive and less frequent. Since the incident with Hossbach, the two men no longer used the Necrópolis. They used cemeteries a good deal, the graveyard of the rich at Botafogo as well as more anonymous plots up on the hillsides. Brazilians gave graveyards a wide berth at night, when demons and spirits were abroad.

Often Johnny seemed nervous and hypersensitive behind a jocular veneer. He had been in contact with Hossbach again and had been ordered to await instructions for a meeting with the Gestapo man who was arriving from Berlin. If anything came of it, it might serve to divert Max's attention for a bit longer.

But Harry thought he had hit on a more useful way to relieve some of the pressure on Johnny.

Harvey Prince, the radio man for the South American bureau, interested Maitland. Johnny had lost contact with the young Californian since their traumatic visit to the northeast. He had heard talk that Harvey was going to be sent home; then that he had insisted on finishing the job he had been sent to do. Johnny thought that Prince must be living in the Southern Zone, because of the speed with which messages were sent and delivered from Emil's apartment. But Johnny did not know the address. The only lead was that Helene had made a disparaging remark about Prince's car. Harvey Prince was posing as an idle American playboy and drove a yellow custom-made convertible. There could not be many cars like it in Rio.

Maitland was on his way to the beach on a quiet Saturday morning when he spotted the car quite by chance in front of a pharmacy on the corner of Copacabana Avenue and the Rua Chile. He parked the Beast in the next block, got out and made a show of inspecting a jeweller's display window. He did not have long to wait. The fair-haired young man who came out of the drugstore wearing sunglasses and a white leisure suit matched Johnny's description.

A car buff could hardly fail to notice the Beast; Harry left it in the parking space and hailed a taxi. The driver had turned his dashboard into an altar with religious medallions and plaster images of the saints.

'Follow that yellow car,' Maitland instructed him. 'But don't get too close.' He remembered Johnny's caution about the number of taxi drivers who had been to the bomb school and added, with a grin, 'It's for a bet.'

The cabbie smiled back.

Wherever Harvey Prince was going, it wasn't home. They went through the tunnel, out of the Southern Zone and along the breezy embankment. Soon they were heading downtown. The yellow convertible parked near the main post office. Harry told his driver to stop, gave his driver a large bank note and showed him a second.

'Wait for me,' he said.

The cabbie nodded happily.

Most of the counters inside the main hall of the post office were already closed. Maitland got into line behind the American; a plump brown woman with four squalling children had taken the place in between.

He could not hear what Prince said to the man behind the counter through the squeals of the children.

But thanks to the tendency of all Brazilian officialdom to reverse English first names and surnames, Prince was having some difficulty making himself understood.

'There's nothing for you, Senhor Gordon,' the clerk reported.

'My name isn't Gordon,' the Californian said, with some irritation. 'It's Wood. Gordon Wood.'

The clerk rummaged among his pigeonholes again and produced two airmail letters.

'*Obrigado*,' Prince said curtly, thrusting them into his pocket.

'*De nada*, Senhor Gordon.'

Maitland had intended to purchase some stamps in case the American was watching his back, but the woman ahead of him embarked on a marathon complaint that had something to do with a change of address. So he slipped out of the post office in time to see the yellow convertible sailing away up the Avenida Rio Branco.

'We follow?' his cab driver grinned, turning on a little wire fan for his customer's benefit.

'We follow.'

The yellow convertible led them straight back to Copacabana, to a small apartment building on a shady street only a few blocks from the corner pharmacy where Harry had first caught sight of Harvey Prince. The American was neglecting even the most elementary precautions; perhaps he was in a hurry to read his mail. Harry saw the yellow car swing into a narrow lane beside the apartment house that presumably led to a parking area behind.

'Keep on,' he instructed the taxi driver.

'Did we win the bet?' the driver asked when he dropped

Maitland off a few blocks further on, in front of a *botânico* that sold herbal remedies and religious articles.

'I certainly hope so.'

He passed a few minutes in the *botânico*, inspecting potions guaranteed to bring back an errant lover or eliminate a rival and ugly black statuettes of Exú, the devil, with a lolling red tongue and pointy teeth. Then he strolled down to the beach and spent an hour enjoying the spectacle of the most sensuous women in the world parading in various states of near nudity while he contemplated his next moves.

He felt sure that the letters from the United States were personal. Colin Bailey had managed to run a background check on the radio man. Harvey Prince was an orphan. His father, a first-generation immigrant from Galicia, had been active in the Wobblies but had ended his life by blowing his brains out after long years of unemployment and the strain of living with an alcoholic wife who had died, not long after, of cirrhosis. As a teenager, Harvey had been adopted by a wealthy San Francisco art collector who flirted with the local Communist Party; there were strong indications that their relationship had been something other than filial.

He's perfect, Harry thought. A family history of psychological instability, homosexual tendencies that were probably frustrated by the rules he was required to observe in Rio, the recent trauma in the *sertão* – enough to tip any man's balance.

Harry waited until Monday before he revisited Prince's apartment house. As he turned the corner, he saw Helene come out of the building in a hurry. He drove on. He called at his bank before he went to the central post office.

'Anything for Senhor Wood?' he asked a different clerk.

'No, Senhor. Nothing.'

'I'd like to rent a mailbox.'

He received the expected response: nothing was available. The tactful display of a few banknotes rectified this. He was offered a box almost big enough to hold a body.

'Haven't you got something smaller?'

He signed the form 'Gordon Wood' and added the address of the Copacabana apartment house. The rental charge

424

was a fraction of the tip that he left. He received two keys.

He returned in the afternoon to check the box and deposited a plain envelope addressed to 'G. Wood'.

The next steps would require help.

Maitland was still thinking about them when he got home. The *curupião* barked at him from its cage on the verandah. He responded with a wolf whistle, which it mimicked to perfection. There was a smell of palm oil from the kitchen, but it had to contend with a stronger, fouler odour that made him cough as he entered the living room.

'Luisa!' he called out. 'Is something burning?'

Luisa rushed out of the kitchen in her apron, blushing and apologetic.

'I'll take it away,' she said. 'No problem.'

She reached for a little incense burner she had slung from the inside door.

'Luisa? What is that stuff?'

'Nothing. It makes the house clean.'

'Clean? I thought we were on fire. Let me see that thing.' He inspected the contents of the incense burner, a heap of blackened crystals. He sniffed again. 'Garlic?'

She nodded.

'Coffee?'

She nodded again.

'What else?'

'A little brown sugar.'

'No, there's something more pungent.'

'You don't want to know.' She smiled, showing all her teeth. Somehow, when she smiled like that, it was quite impossible to be angry with her.

She swirled out to the kitchen.

'Luisa. It's one of your spells, isn't it?'

'It guards the house.'

'Against the evil eye, or something like that?'

'Something like that.'

'Listen, I've told you before. I don't mind what you do outside this house, but I won't have that mumbo jumbo in here.'

'But it's for you, Senhor Harry,' she said seriously.

425

He did not pursue it. He assumed she had been to see her voodoo priestess again – the Mother of the Saint, Luisa called her. You couldn't fight the old religion in Brazil. The Holy Inquisition had tried and lost, and it was unlikely that any of its latter-day competitors would do better. It was a living faith; the images and the rituals, older than those of the Christians, revived by the struggle to preserve them during the brutal exodus from Africa and the harsh centuries of slavery, had not grown tired and worn with hollow repetition. To believers, the *orixás*, the spirit kings who were mediators between men and an unseen, inaccessible god, were present at every turning in life, to protect or to punish. They were also jealous lords who demanded constant propitiation. Hence the chicken or the goat Harry would sometimes find tethered discreetly behind the barn at the back of his house and the rows of candles glimmering under the trees.

They sat together at dinner. The scene would have shocked the crinolined ladies of the English colony but would probably have startled few Brazilians. Here and in the bedroom they were simply man and woman. Harry wished at times that there could be, in the outside world, some greater equality between them, but Luisa herself would have been the last to demand, or accept, it. In their moments of passion she called him '*meu principe*'. He would have been hard put to explain the depth of his feeling for her. It went beyond lust, beyond loyalty and affection, but he would never have dared to call it love. Yet he found it quite impossible to imagine being without her.

Looking at her, he thought of a possible solution to one of his problems. 'That friend of yours – Teresa –' he began. 'Didn't you tell me her boyfriend was in trouble with the police?'

'They caught him breaking into an apartment. He told them he was making a delivery and found the door open. He's very clever with locks.'

'Did they put him in jail?'

'No. They just gave him a beating, so they could rob the apartment themselves.'

'Where is he now?'

'He's got a job as a doorman at one of those places in Lapa.' She made a face. 'You know the ones.'

'I'd like to meet him.'

'Why?'

'I'd just like to meet him. Will you arrange it for me with Teresa?'

The next step required help from a very different quarter. Summerhayes, from the embassy, was flattered to be asked to lunch at A Rotisserie, on the Rua Ouvidor. The restaurant was widely regarded as the city's finest, with prices to match.

Summerhayes wiped his mouth daintily with his napkin after polishing off a desert of crepes doused in Grand Marnier and said, 'Your expense allowance from the light company must be a damn sight more generous than HMG's. Or do we have Colin Bailey to thank?'

Maitland eluded the question.

'Actually,' he said, 'I've got a slight favour to ask.'

He explained what he had in mind, and for a moment Summerhayes looked ready to disgorge his excellent lunch.

'Sir Evelyn would have apoplexy!' he protested. 'I can hear him now.'

'The British Mission does not engage in shady business,' Harry volunteered, in a reasonable impression of the ambassador's voice.

Summerhayes stared at Harry in amazement.

'But we owe it to our chap, don't you think?' Harry went on. 'After all, we did rather land him in the soup.' He added, more confidentially, 'I wouldn't be at all surprised if you get a mention in the Birthday Honours List when we pull this off.'

'Really?' Summerhayes started to perk up again.

'Sir Evelyn won't know,' Harry promised. 'I give you my word. We'll even keep Lady Maude in the dark.'

Summerhayes began to giggle.

After two glasses of port he said, 'There's one thing that still bothers me, Harry. Can we be sure I can meet this chappie without any of his friends spotting me?'

'I'll take care of that,' Maitland said as he lit his cigar.

6

In a modest house on the Rua Sá Ferreira, Helene concentrated on the chessboard. Max seemed distracted. He smoked and stared idly out the window while he waited for her to make her move. She realised that in moving his bishop he had carelessly exposed his queen. She leaped to attack.

'Sorry, Max.' She removed his black queen from the board, leaving him with only two major pieces, a rook and the bishop. His mind obviously was elsewhere. He did not even bother to inspect the damage.

'Do you want to concede?' she prodded him.

'Not quite yet.'

Barely glancing at the board, he drove the bishop forward, capturing a pawn and placing her in check.

Max got up and stretched his legs, leaving her to work the rest out for herself. She started to move her king to capture the bishop, then realised it was covered by the rook. Her king was hemmed in by her own pieces. It had nowhere to run. In her eagerness to seize the enemy queen, she had neglected the danger.

'The whole secret of chess,' Max remarked, 'is in the art of sacrifice.'

'You knew I couldn't resist the queen.'

'Not the first time.'

He watched her study his end game before she replaced the chessmen in their original places. She was quick. She wouldn't fall for the same trick twice.

'I want to ask you something,' she announced.

'I'm listening.'

'Why did you bring Sigrid to Rio?'

'She's useful. Do you object?'

'It complicates things.'

'I assume you are referring to Johnny. Are you jealous?'

'Don't be absurd! We haven't got time for these romantic

follies, that's all. People make mistakes. It increases the risk to everyone.'

'When the wick is lit, the brain goes out,' Max recited.

'So why did you give her back to him?'

Of course she is jealous, Max thought. You can throw something away and still want it back when you see someone else using it. This was a weakness he might be able to use.

'I showed you the answer,' he said to Helene.

She stared at Max, then at the chessboard. Watching her, he saw that she understood. Max was playing against Johnny, and Sigrid was the queen he had carelessly left exposed.

'What makes you sure that Johnny is a traitor?' Helene challenged him.

'If I were sure, I wouldn't need to test him.'

'If you're worried about the Hossbach business —'

'I'm not worried about Herr Hossbach,' Max said dismissively. 'Not even his masters. But there's a mystery about Johnny. I don't like mysteries unless I create them.'

Max had to admit to himself that he had been weak in relation to Johnny. He had begun to suspect him when Heinz Kordt had made his surprising escape from Hamburg, leaving the corpses of two professional killers behind. Yet Max had always been willing to thrust his suspicions aside. He knew he had given Johnny several reasons to hate him. Yet he felt a curious fondness for the younger man. This emotion was so out of character that it was hard for him to account for it. His vocation required him to doubt every man's motives and convictions; yet he had taken Johnny's on trust. Perhaps he had been vulnerable precisely because, in his world of shadows, he needed to believe in *someone*.

But it was less easy for him now to suppress his doubts about Johnny. British Intelligence had shown its hand in both Copenhagen and Rio. Johnny had been in both places; he was the obvious link. He had warned Max about a Gestapo plot against his life. But that could not clear Johnny of suspicion of a link with the British; there were more than two sides playing this game.

Even now, Max wanted to be proved wrong. He was watching all the leaders of the South American bureau, setting traps. Helene and the Romanian who rented the safe house on Rua Sá Ferreira – a man whose face was unknown to the other Comintern agents – were his eyes and ears. If Johnny was a spy for the British, Max felt sure that one of the two sisters would finally deliver him up: Helene because of jealousy, or Sigrid because lovers grow careless of their own safety.

The Romanian was bored and felt frayed around the edges. He had spent a whole week tailing various members of Emil's team around the city and had precious little to report to Max. The least interesting of all was the American, Harvey Prince. He stayed shut up in his apartment most of the time. He usually ate lunch alone at a little seafood place round the corner. He seemed to have no contacts outside the bureau. The fuzz on his upper lip indicated he had started to grow a moustache.

Now the Romanian was halfway through a wasted Saturday morning, dozing over a *cafezinho* at a sidewalk cafe diagonally across the street from the American's flat. Ragged brown-skinned boys buzzed around the tables like flies, holding out their palms for money or scraps. A pavement artist set up his easel and offered to produce an instant portrait. The Romanian waved him away. A few tables away, a lanky man in a navy blue blazer lingered over his breakfast rolls, distancing himself from the commotion in the street behind a copy of the London *Times*. He had been there when the Romanian had arrived. The Romanian did not pay him much attention.

When Harvey Prince came out of his building, evidently on his way to lunch, the Englishman folded his paper neatly, settled his bill, and set off across the street. On the far side he quickened his stride to overtake Harvey Prince. His walk was erratic; he appeared to bump into the American. He said something – perhaps an apology – and moved on briskly. Prince had stopped short. He was turning something over in his hands. It was a letter or a small packet. He peered around nervously, stuck it in his pocket and then hurried round the corner into his usual restaurant.

It was nearly three the next morning when Harvey Prince was roused by a violent drumming on his door. He rolled out of bed naked and put on a light cotton robe. He had a raging thirst and the beginnings of a sore throat.

He squinted through the peephole and saw the girl courier, the hard-assed bitch they called Erna, with a man he didn't know. The man looked tough. Prince didn't like his eyes. They seemed to reach out, even through the peephole, to catch him by the throat.

'Jeez, Erna,' he complained as he released the bolt. 'Don't you people ever sleep?'

He was swinging the door open when it was hurled back so suddenly that it hit him in the face.

A second blow, from the man's gloved fist, brought down on his chest like a hammer, knocked him to the floor.

'Holy shit –'

A swift kick aimed at the kidneys silenced his protest. His dressing gown flapped open. His body was very pale.

Max Fabrikant inspected it with that same brutal stare.

'Look,' he said to Helene. 'It's pointed, like a dog's.'

Harvey brought up his knees and wrapped his arms around them. He seemed to be trying to roll himself into a ball. He was shaking and making little whimpering sounds.

Max sat down on the edge of the bed and started fiddling with a short length of pipe. It dawned on Harvey Prince that it was a silencer.

'I don't believe in lengthy introductions,' Max announced. 'I'm sure you're not a fool. You will spare yourself – and me – a great deal of unnecessary exertion if you cooperate.'

'I don't understand –'

'We'll start with the letter you received this morning. The letter from Mr Summerhayes.'

'I don't know anyone called Summerhayes!'

Max sighed. 'You were seen together, outside your apartment.'

'But I never saw that man before in my life!'

'You're lying. Is he your boyfriend?'

'What do you think I am?' Prince screamed.

'We both know what you are. I am here to find out what you have done. Where is the letter?' Max had finished screwing the silencer on to the barrel of his pistol.

'I don't know what you're talking about.'

Helene looked at Max. 'Let me try,' she said.

He nodded.

She took the burning cigarette from his lips and went over to Harvey Prince. The American was sweating heavily. He did not want to know what she intended to do with the cigarette.

'In the desk,' he said hastily. 'The top drawer.'

Helene found an airmail envelope addressed to Gordon Wood. 'From the United States,' she reported to Max.

'Let me see that.'

Max scanned the letter – four pages scrawled in a large hand, with exaggerated loops. He scowled over the explicit passages.

'What is this?' he demanded. 'Pornography – or a code?'

Harvey's cheeks were scarlet. 'It's from an old friend in San Francisco.'

'And delivered by Summerhayes of the British Embassy? What is this? The Homintern?'

'I don't know how he came by the letter. It must be a mistake. Or a provocation. My friend writes to me care of the post office.'

'All right. You've already confessed to a serious violation of party discipline. Now show me the letter Mr Summerhayes gave you.'

'That's it! I already told you –' his voice rose to a shrill as Helene pressed the burning stump of the cigarette under his scrotum, pinning him with her knee and her free arm so he couldn't wriggle away.

'We're wasting time,' Max interjected. 'Search the apartment.'

Helene looked disappointed. 'What about him?'

'I would advise you to stay exactly where you are,' Max said to Prince. 'The female of the species –'

They found a collection of nude photographs, copies of several secret messages that should have been destroyed, a bundle of love letters from San Francisco, a key and a thousand dollars in US currency.

'Why did you keep these?' Max demanded, shoving the documents under his nose. 'To send to your little pen pal in California?'

'I don't know. It must have been an oversight.'

'How about the money?'

'I don't know where it came from. I haven't been paid since last month.'

Max snorted.

'And this?' he held up the key. 'I suppose this is the key to your gas tank.'

'I never saw it before.'

Helene had lit a fresh cheroot. She nudged Harvey lovingly with it, on the calves and the soles of his feet. He screamed in pain, and somebody in a neighbouring flat started to bang on the wall.

'What is it?' Max pushed him. 'A safe deposit box?' He glanced at the letter again. 'Or a mailbox?'

'I don't have a mailbox.' Prince was sobbing. 'Oh, Jeez. My mother raised me for this?'

At a more respectable hour of the morning, Max left Helene with the American and went to the post office.

'Excuse me,' he said to a clerk. 'I found this in my box.' He showed the clerk one of the letters to Gordon Wood, carefully resealed. 'It's happened before. But I suppose it's understandable. Mister Wood's box is next to mine, isn't it? Three-four-seven?'

The clerk checked his records and shook his head disparagingly.

'No, Senhor. It's five-two-one. I regret the inconvenience.'

'That's perfectly all right. Glad to be of assistance.'

Half an hour later, Max retrieved both the boomerang letter and a plain envelope, containing an enigmatic post-card and two hundred pounds sterling.

Got him, Max thought. But he wasn't happy. It was all too easy, too amateurish. And why, after all, would Harvey Prince rat on his comrades for money? His adopted father in California was loaded with it. Perhaps he had simply snapped after his ordeal in the north and wanted to take it out on everyone he held responsible. Or else he had been set up.

The Romanian intercepted him on his way back to Harvey Prince's apartment.

'We've got to get away,' he said urgently. 'The police are all over the place.'

'What happened?' Max thought of the irate neighbour, beating on the wall.

The Romanian ran a finger across his throat. 'He jumped. Broke his neck.'

Harvey Prince's flat was on the third floor. In Max's experience, unless you were six floors up, instant death could not be guaranteed. He supposed they were lucky the American had not lived to explain his reasons to the police.

'What about the woman?'

'She got safe away.'

'And the radio?'

'That, too.'

Max felt sure that Helene had thought to take the com-promising documents with her. They had done a thorough job in ransacking Harvey Prince's apartment. The police would find nothing to tie him to the conspiracy.

The American had killed himself because he had been found out. That seemed to put Johnny and the others in the clear.

Yet Max's mood as he retraced his steps to the safe house on the Rua Sá Ferreira was sombre. It had ended so quickly and so neatly. He distrusted neat conclusions. Life, as he had observed it, was extremely untidy.

9

Eyes of the King

To measure up to all that is demanded of him, a man must overestimate his capacities.

– Goethe

1

The place was an hour's drive from Maitland's house, in a rough neighbourhood on the way to Caxias. Off the main road, the streets soon deteriorated into dried-up creekbeds, meandering strips of baked mud rutted and cratered by the last rains. The car jounced from one pothole to the next. It was like driving on the face of the moon.

The road forked ahead. There was a street lamp at the corner, and a band of young men were clustered under the light, playing pool at an improvised table. They hooted and whistled at the handsome, unfamiliar car.

This was the end of the town. Beyond the pool players, there were no more streetlights. The darkness was complete, save for the occasional glow of a kerosene lamp or candle behind the window of one of the low houses – some little better than mud huts – that fanned out at widening intervals into the tropical forest. Rio Light was not doing much business in these parts.

'Keep left,' Luisa instructed him.

She waved at the boys around the pool table as the Beast crawled by, and the whistles multiplied. She had her party dress on her lap, wrapped up in a piece of crepe paper, but she had put on her special beads, blue and white for Yemanjá, the goddess of the waters.

'Are you sure this is the way?' Harry demanded after a jolt that travelled all the way up his spine.

'We're nearly there,' Luisa smiled.

Harry was not reassured. She had said this three times since a police patrol had stopped them at the top of the hill. The sergeant had made out he just wanted to give them a friendly warning.

'This is not a healthy neighbourhood for a gentleman of your class, Senhor,' he had informed Harry. 'Not so late in the evening.'

He had stared boldly at Luisa, at the beads and amulets at her neck, the fine lace garments that poked out of their wrapping, and demanded in overly familiar terms to know who she was and where she was going.

Luisa had pursed her lips, ready to give the policeman a piece of her mind, but Maitland had interceded.

'We are visiting relatives,' he had said smoothly. 'And we are running late. Now may we proceed?'

The sergeant had not dared to stop a wealthy foreigner in a Hispano-Suiza. He shrugged and said, 'I wouldn't go in there myself, Senhor,' and jabbed a finger under his eye to emphasise his point.

'I wonder what that was all about,' Harry said as they drove on.

'The police do it all the time,' Luisa replied casually. 'It is because Ivan's *terreiro* is so famous.'

'Do they arrest people for going to the ceremonies?'

'No. Except for the dark side.'

'You mean black magic?'

'The *Quimbanda*. Yes. If a man dies because of a spell, then the police come. But they also come to frighten us away.'

'Why?'

'Because they're frightened of what they can't see. Because some of their big bosses want a Brazil of white men, nothing of Africa, nothing primitive, everything from

436

countries of snow and ice. Some of them even want to ban Carnival!'

'I can promise you that's something that will never happen.'

Harry was mulling over this exchange when a dog lurched out into the glare of his headlights. He jammed his foot down on the brake pedal and came to a stop only a few paces short of the animal, which proceeded to squat down in the middle of the road. It was a bitch and astonishingly ugly. Its splotched yellow-white hide might have been cobbled together from several unmatched pelts. Its swollen teats hung out from its belly like a cow's. Harry honked his horn experimentally. The dog blinked at them and yawned without stirring. It was either dazed by the lights or utterly unaccustomed to cars. He honked again, repeatedly, until the dog raised itself up and hobbled directly across their path. Luisa gasped and clutched at the talisman at her throat when she saw it had only three legs. It disappeared into the deeper shadows at the side of the road.

'It's a bad omen,' she whispered as Harry moved the gearshift.

'It wasn't a pretty thing, I'll grant you that.'

'It's a message. I don't know if it's for you or for me, or for both of us. We must tell Ivan. He will know what to do.'

'Now hold on. I agreed to sit in on your cousin's confirmation. That's all. I have no intention of getting mixed up with any witch doctor.'

'He's not –'

'I know, I know. He's the Father of the Saint, and all that. Even if he does call himself Ivan.'

'He's a *babalão*,' she said seriously. 'A man of great power and respect.'

'Then you tell him your problems. I'm just the chauffeur.'

'There's no need to be afraid.'

'My dear, I am not in the least afraid.' His tone was patronising, but he was gripping the steering wheel too tightly. There was a terrible smell in the air, compounded of dried excrement and putrefying flesh.

'It's there,' she said, pointing to a low wall with a substantial cement-block building set back among the trees.

'Charming. It smells like a slaughteryard.'

He glanced at his watch. It was a few minutes past midnight. Harry's enthusiasm for this nocturnal expedition had begun to wilt even before they had left the house. It was impossible to live fully in Brazil, even for twenty-four hours, without becoming aware of a world of magic and mystery. You might try to avoid looking at it squarely; it was there nonetheless, looking at you. A girl he had met at an embassy party, the fashionable widow of a coffee planter, had bribed his previous housekeeper to slip a love potion under his mattress, some concoction sewn up inside the body of a toad. The potion was supposed to make Harry fall in love with his pursuer, but he had detected it from the stench before it had worked its spell. At least that was what Luisa had said when he had told her the story.

In bustling, money-mad São Paulo, Harry had visited a hall as big as St Paul's where educated, affluent men and women came by the hundreds to hear mediums convey messages from the spirits of the dead. Those who were sick lined up to have their tumours or inflamed appendixes extracted by an illiterate who operated with a rusty kitchen knife without benefit of anesthetics or disinfectants, guided by the spirit of a dead surgeon.

In Copacabana, on New Year's Eve, he had found the beach transformed into a forest of candles. Elegant couples in evening clothes and barefoot kids from the favelas jostled for space. They brought their dreams and their gifts to the water's edge in the hope that Yemanjá would hear them and carry their offerings away in her long tresses, which streamed across the beach like waves. This told the lucky ones their secret desires would be granted.

To hurried visitors from colder climes, this was all hoo-doo and hocus-pocus, the sort of thing civilised people had outgrown in the Middle Ages. Major Mackenzie, the choleric Canadian who presided over the fortunes of Rio

Light, was fond of observing that 'idolatry and moonshine' were proof of the debility of the country's racial stock, and a reason why Brazil, for all its vast natural riches, would never catch up with his native land in its economic development until 'practical men' – white men, of course, and Canadians or Scots for preference – took charge.

As he had told Colin Bailey, Harry did not pass judgment on these things. He recognised the power of the African religion in the lives of its initiates, who did not refer to it as voodoo (a bastard word derived from the language of the Fon people of Dahomey, whose slaves had mostly gone to Haiti) but as *candomblé* or *macumba* or *umbanda*, names drawn from the tribal-memory of the Yoruba. The gods of *candomblé*, like those of other men, were jealous lords, as unpredictable as the forces of nature to which they were so intimately related. They demanded blood sacrifice. They took possession of their worshippers and rode them like horses. Knowing this much, Harry had never presumed, before that night, to intrude on a gathering of their devotees.

Luisa had talked him into it by describing the night's entertainment as a quite ordinary event in the social cycle, a bit like a child's first communion or a bar mitzvah, an occasion for family festivities. A girl called Elza, Luisa's distant cousin – how distant it was impossible to say, given the uncertainty about their fathers – had spent a month in seclusion, preparing for this final rite of initiation into the cult. Over the past weeks Luisa, playing surrogate mother, had sent live animals and special delicacies, as prescribed by Ivan the witch doctor, to the *terreiro*. Harry had lost patience with her when he learned that she had dipped into her slender savings to pay for a cow and two goats. He suspected that, whatever else was going on, Ivan Pessoa and his friends were not going hungry. He became curious to get a good look at this witch doctor with the Russian forename who had such a reputation – so Luisa claimed – for making and breaking spells.

But he decided to go only at the last moment, when he came home from the office and realised that he was sup-

439

posed to be dining with the Mackenzies. Stella Mackenzie was a good sort, until the last couple of gins; her breezy, cheerful vulgarity reminded Harry of a barmaid at a pub he liked on the Fulham Road. But Major Mackenzie, with his monocle and his one-eyed opinions, was insufferable. Listening to him was almost enough to make Harry sympathise with the Reds, who wanted to put a bomb under Rio Light. Worse yet, Summerhayes would be in attendance, and Harry had been studiously trying to avoid him since that miserable business involving Harvey Prince. Summerhayes had come beating on Harry's door, quite hysterical, when news of the American's death had appeared in the press. Summerhayes had managed to convince himself that a witness would come forward to identify him to the police and that there would be a dreadful scandal. The prospect of Lady Maude's rage seemed to terrify the poor man even more than the chance – which Maitland considered too slight to be worthy of discussion – that the government would declare him persona non grata. He had refused to take comfort from anything Harry could say, reproaching him with the eyes of a faithful hound that has been beaten for no reason he can comprehend. All in all, Harry was happy to seize on an alternative to Stella Mackenzie's soirée.

He now realised that the slaughterhouse stink was rising from a little cabin that stood on the left side of the path. The cabin was no taller than Harry, but the door was a huge slab of wood hewn from a single trunk and secured with some serious-looking bolts and padlocks.

Harry made a show of holding his nose.

'You can smell Exú,' Luisa said, squeezing his arm.

'I smelled him a fair way off.'

'He must be fed before the rituals,' she added with an air of authority. 'And the birds and the animals must all be black. Otherwise he will come and play tricks.'

Exú was the devil. At least that was how he was often represented, at the head of a great host of lesser demons. But in this temple, Satan was better-treated than in Christian churches. He wasn't cast out. He was asked very politely to stay in his own house just outside the *terreiro*, guarding the paths.

They passed knots of people smoking and talking in low voices and reached an open space, walled in on three sides. The floor was beaten earth strewn with fresh leaves. There were benches along two of the walls, men sitting on one side, women and girls on the other. The atmosphere was reassuringly, disappointingly normal, even in the uncertain light of the hurricane lamps slung from the ceiling. It might have been a church social, except for the offerings of cane brandy and manioc flour laid out beside the candles in a magic square – and the snakes.

Harry did not notice them until he had almost walked into one. A shadow passed across his eyes. He stopped short and found himself staring into the open jaws of a viper. He stood frozen until a girl started laughing. She was a pretty, catlike little thing in swirling yellow skirts, with a turban wrapped tight around her ears. She saw his eyes move in her direction and stuffed her hand across her mouth, still bubbling over with mirth. The snake had not moved.

Harry let out his breath and ducked his head under the jaws of the dead viper. He saw now that there were snakes suspended from the roof at each corner of the *terreiro*.

Luisa embraced the little brown girl in the yellow skirts and led her over by the hand.

'This is Elza.'

Elza looked up at Harry, wide-eyed, and burst out laughing again.

'I must go and dress,' Luisa announced. 'There is Ivan.'

Harry followed her glance. Ivan certainly did not look like a witch doctor. He was short and light-skinned, with curly grey hair and a neat grey beard, wearing a loose cotton shirt that hung down over a copious paunch, smoking and gossiping with his parishioners. Luisa said a few words to him. He turned. His bright, intent eyes seemed to be searching for something behind Harry. He nodded and patted Luisa's cheek.

Harry found a place on the bench reserved for the men

441

and steeled himself for what Luisa had warned would be a long night.

Ivan vanished into one of the rooms that opened off the main hall and reappeared with an iron rattle. He jangled it lazily, and three black men took their places behind the tall, pot-bellied drums. The drums talked for what seemed like an eternity. Over them, the voices of Ivan and the senior drummer rolled monotonously, invoking the *orixás* in their own language. Harry's eyelids began to grow heavy. He glanced furtively at his watch. But little by little, the beat became more insistent, the chorus more peremptory. One by one the initiates rose from their places and joined a conga line. Luisa was among them, dancing between an elephantine black grannie in spectacles and a trim, tidy little Portuguese matron. They shuffled and whirled with surprising grace. The rhythm was subtly infectious. Before he was aware of it, Harry's feet were marking time.

Suddenly a terrible howl went up, and Grannie Elephant fell as if she had been literally bowled off her feet. Her weight carried her through the thicket of arms that was raised to catch her, and her shoulder landed in Harry's lap. The drums talked louder, faster, Ivan's voice rose higher in praise, and the other devotees whisked Grannie Elephant away, removing her spectacles and her shoes so she would not damage herself as she wheeled about, eyes tightly closed, in a strange rolling motion, emitting groans and wails, bent over at the waist as if someone were riding on her back. Harry had not had time to recover from this spectacle when there was a piercing shriek, and Elza went careening across the dance floor. They caught her before she went down, and soon she was stalking about, bent over at the waist, eyes shut, like a hunter in the long grass.

Self-hypnosis, Harry thought. Or very effective playacting. It was horribly contagious. Ivan looked well under. The white man seated next to Harry, who had seemed fairly remote from the proceedings, screamed and lurched out into the circle of the possessed. At the same instant there came a bellow of pain and rage that made Maitland think of a wild animal falling into a pit full of sharpened stakes. To his dismay he realised that this noise was coming from Luisa, who was bucking and prancing, a mount for her savage god.

One by one, the possessed were led out into the *roncó* – the sanctuary – through one of the doors behind the drummers. Some of them returned in procession, under a shower of wildflowers and fresh-cut herbs, decked out in the regalia of their patron saints. Luisa wore blue and white, for Yemanjá, with a silver helmet, a mirror, a sword and a veil of shimmering strands that gusted in front of her face. Her eyes were still closed.

The dancing and singing went on until dawn and climaxed in a deafening ovation that must have carried all the way to Rio. Lesser spirits – the spirits of children and ancestors – now made their entry. Elza came hopping up to Harry with a brace of pacifiers in her mouth, giggling and drooling like a mischievous infant.

'Do you like our *candomblé*?'

'It's charming,' Harry said. '*Me encanta.*'

'*Es encantado!*' Elza shrieked and clapped her hands. 'He's spellbound!' She skipped away and tried to piggyback on Luisa's shoulders.

To Harry's relief, Luisa looked more or less normal.

'What did it feel like?' he whispered to her.

'I don't remember.'

'Well, do you actually see them – these *orixás*?'

'Not see them, not the way you mean. But after – it's difficult to say. It's like feeling a thickness in the air, like seeing colours that don't exist.'

He might have pursued this, but Elza darted up and handed him a bottle of beer and a plate of *farofa*, rice and some unidentifiable grey meat.

'Breakfast?'

'Breakfast.'

'She's really very pretty,' he remarked to Luisa, watching the lilt of the girl's body as she went to serve the others.

'You should see her without her turban. They shaved her head.'

He dug his fork into the rice, downed his beer and murmured to Luisa, 'Can we go now?'

'First you talk to Ivan,' she said firmly. 'For the *registro*.'

Ivan received him in a cell-like room, a third of whose space was occupied by a massive wooden sideboard laden with statues of the *orixás*, cauldrons, piled necklaces and curious talismans of wood and iron. The place smelled of blood and incense. Harry did not look too closely at the bones and feathers sticking out of a pot in the corner.

Ivan squatted on one side of a straw mat, his bare feet wide apart, and motioned for Harry – who had been told to leave his shoes at the door – to sit on a low chair opposite, his feet resting between the priest's. There were formalities to be observed; ritual greetings in the language of the Yoruba, an offering to Exú to open the paths. Ivan wrote out Harry's full name on a piece of paper and recited it several times in the course of a long incantation. Then he gave Harry an object to hold in either hand, a seashell and a piece of carved bone. He made Harry rub them quickly together behind his back and then hold out his hands, concealing the contents. Ivan picked one, examined the contents without comment, and cast the cowrie shells. For thousands of years, these had been the most popular oracle of the Yoruba. Each pattern had scores of possible meanings, to be drawn from oral memory – from thousands of verses handed down from one priest to the next – and by testing and retesting, casting the shells over and over again.

'It is not good,' Ivan said at last. 'There is death and sickness. We must discover the source of the evil.'

He cast the shells again.

'One source of the evil is a spirit,' he pronounced. 'A spirit that was separated from its body too violently, so that it lingers, not knowing where to go.'

He looked up sharply. 'Have you killed a man?'

'No.'

Ivan frowned, and Harry found himself thinking about Harvey Prince, and then about the young tough Bailey had killed in an alley near the Lisbon docks.

'There is danger from others who are living,' Ivan went

on. 'A fire is growing strong, very close to you. You have not yet begun to feel its flames.'

He threw the cowries again and started to tell Harry about his family and his earlier life. His statements were remarkably accurate, down to the stillbirth of Maitland's younger brother.

Harry felt increasingly nervous and uncomfortable. Perhaps Ivan does have psychic powers, he thought. Or perhaps I'm reading too much into his guesses.

'You were born with a *caixa de mistérios*,' Ivan announced. 'A box of mysteries. You must take care to keep secret what is meant to be secret. The walls have ears.'

Ivan's fingers moved back and forth, casting and recasting the shells. He paused to dab his finger in a saucer of some oily vermilion mixture and pressed it against the roof of his mouth. He asked Harry to do the same.

'To make the telling easier,' he explained.

The taste was not as offensive as Harry had expected.

'*Xango te defiende*,' Ivan said, with greater force. 'Xango defends you. But there is another who is angry. You must appease them both.'

Ivan explained what this would entail, and Harry tried hard not to make a face.

Ivan looked hard at him. 'This is not a game,' he said flatly. 'You have invoked a power. It will show itself to you.'

Afterwards it was Luisa's turn. Harry drank some more beer and watched Ivan's congregation at play, dancing to music on the radio as if the party were just beginning. He wondered how these people found time to sleep, let alone work. The neighbours were obviously either stone deaf or part of the gathering. He tried to dismiss what Ivan had said. The man was a fortune-teller, admittedly more convincing than the gypsies who read palms or tea leaves at Brighton Beach, but no different in kind.

But when Luisa came back, she looked worried, almost desolate.

She did not speak for a long time after they got into the

car. They were climbing towards the house at the edge of the rain forest when she said, 'You must do what Ivan said.'

'I don't have your way with chickens,' he countered, laughing it off. 'Besides, I used to give donations to the RSPCA.'

'What is RSPCA?'

'Oh, never mind.' In his worn-out condition, he did not feel up to explaining the RSPCA and the English reverence for all forms of animal life.

'Another can do it for you,' Luisa pursued, 'but it won't be the same. There will be consequences.'

'Look, we've both had a long night. Let's have a decent breakfast and get some shut-eye, shall we? Thank God it's the weekend.'

When she said, 'Cook your own bloody bacon and eggs,' he realised she had picked up more English than he had given her credit for.

2

Emil Brandt padded out of the kitchen in his underwear, carrying a tumbler and a bottle of scotch.

Lenka did not look up from her sewing.

'You said you weren't going to touch hard liquor till the end of the week,' she reminded him.

'So I couldn't wait.'

She rammed her foot down on the pedal of the ancient Singer sewing machine, and the needle whirred.

'Do you have to do that?' Emil appealed to her, collapsing into the armchair next to the fan. 'We're not in Minsk.'

'It helps not to look at you,' Lenka said savagely.

'So you don't care to look at your husband any more? You're not such a bathing beauty yourself.'

'You're falling apart. Who's going to tell you except me?'

He sighed while she followed the needle, hemming a tablecloth they would probably never use.

'You're a hard woman, Lenka.'

'So how else would I still be with you?'

He drank and leaned closer to the fan to dry the sweat from his face. The heat was killing him, and the summer still lay ahead. He felt sorry for Lenka but sorrier still for himself. He hardly slept any more. He felt as if insects were crawling under his skin.

It had been worse since the American had died. Max Fabrikant had come storming in, demanding to see copies of every communication that might have passed through the hands of the radio man, ordering the rest of them about like children or mental defectives. Emil had been obliged to report the episode to Moscow, of course. In an attempt to cover himself, he had reported that he had been wary of Harvey Prince for some time and had severely restricted his access. Emil doubted whether this would counteract the poison Max was spreading. Max must have found out by now that Emil had personally recruited Harvey Prince during his stopover in New York. Prince came recommended by one of Emil's most trusted agents, a man he relied on in the old days when they joked that he was the czar of the American Communist movement. Emil had no reason to distrust either Harvey Prince or his sponsor. The boy had his failings, for sure, and he was close to a crack-up after that business in the north, but Emil privately refused to think of him as a traitor. In fact, he suspected something very different: that Max Fabrikant had cooked up the whole affair in order to destroy him.

Emil knew he had powerful enemies in Moscow, people who would never forget that he had once presumed to criticise Stalin's policies and called for a united front with the Social Democrats to stop the Nazis. He had been taught the error of his ways in Moscow, in vertical tombs in the cellars of the Lubyanka where ice formed on the walls and the nights were scarred by the screams of fellow inmates. At the end of his re-education, he publicly abased himself. He wrote syrupy tributes to Great Stalin, the genius of the age. He crawled before Manuilsky. His persecutors wanted Heinz Kordt, so he gave Kordt to them, along with many others. Betrayal became a habit, even an obsession. Eagerly, he sought out old comrades who dared to challenge Stalin's judgment and denounced them as spies and Trotskyites. In China as in Moscow, he hastened to show he had learned his lessons: that there was no truth except Stalin's; that a Communist would be judged, first and last, by his tireless devotion to the Leader.

I did all this, Emil thought, and they still won't trust me. Is it because I'm German? Or because I'm a Jew? Or because I was already a party organiser when Trotsky and Zinoviev stood at Lenin's right hand?

He had read the resolutions of the Seventh Congress of the Comintern, whose deliberations had extended through most of the month of August. The delegates got to their feet and cheered when Dimitrov announced the start of the Anti-Fascist Decade. With Hitler openly rearming, with Mussolini's legions rolling into Abyssinia and Japanese officers taking snapshots along the Great Wall of China, Moscow had finally approved the policy Stalin had rejected so savagely until now: a broad front against the Fascists. The change came too late to help Germany or those, like Heinz Kordt and a younger Emil, who had been condemned as 'premature anti-Fascists'. And Emil, suffering the tropical heat in a city thousands of miles from Moscow, wondered whether the change was real. It did not affect his own mission. His orders were the same. Moscow's tone was, if anything, more imperative, more strident.

When Harvey Prince killed himself, Emil confided some of his doubts about the planned revolution – for the first and only time – in a memorandum to Manuilsky. Of course, he attributed the problems he saw to the sloppiness of the Brazilians and the irresolution of his colleagues in the South American bureau.

The reply from the Big House was stinging. The letter was hand carried to Rio from the Soviet Mission in Montevideo by the new wireless operator assigned to replace Harvey Prince. It was signed by Manuilsky himself.

'Loyalty will be judged by results,' Manuilsky's letter

concluded. 'If you fail, no excuse will be sufficient. There are serious charges pending against you.'

This passage reminded Emil of a famous dictum of Frederick the Great, one he had once been made to copy out over and over in Gothic script when he had angered a schoolmaster in Cologne: 'The world judges our actions not by our reasons but by the success that crowns them.'

Manuilsky's letter brought the nightmares closer. Emil woke up between three and four every morning out of howling nightmares in which he was being dragged through the basements of the Lubyanka or across the frozen tundra. His terror was increased by every new report about the purges in Moscow, which had already swallowed up tens of thousands of old party loyalists. It seemed that nobody was safe – at least, nobody who had been imprudent enough to join the party before Stalin had become general secretary. Now Stalin's hatchet man had put him on notice of the penalty for failure in Brazil.

Whatever the cost, he had to go forward. The risk of detection by the Brazilian police paled into insignificance in comparison with Stalin's displeasure.

But who could he trust?

Not the Argentinian, who didn't have the stomach for action.

Not Johnny, who had every reason to hate him.

Not Helene, the bitch informer whose stare could freeze a man's balls off. Helene's transfer was the one good thing to result from Prince's suicide. Max had decided to ship her out, on the grounds that one of the Californian's neighbours might be able to identify her to the police as a regular visitor to the apartment.

But Max still had his woman spy. Sigrid had taken over Helene's work. The younger sister might be the deadlier of the two, Emil told himself. Because she seemed softer, more vulnerable, it was easier to let your guard drop.

Least of all could he trust Max Fabrikant. Max isn't here to help make a revolution, Emil thought. He's here to finish me.

Moscow had sent new men to Rio to reinforce Emil's

team: a Lithuanian who specialised in the labour unions, a wireless operator from Tokyo, a Fourth Department man who had gotten himself into some scrape in Denmark and was lucky, by all accounts, to have landed another foreign assignment. None of them had been approved by Emil. More than ever, he felt under hostile eyes.

He banged out to the bedroom and started getting dressed.

'Are you going somewhere?' Lenka called to him.

'I have to meet Nilo.'

'That one! That playboy! He's *meshuggeh*. You shouldn't listen to him.'

'Who would you have me listen to?' he roared at her, struggling with his tie. 'To the Argentinian? All he wants is to go home and eat *empanadas*.'

'Maybe he's got the right idea.'

'Nilo's a good boy. He's got guts.'

'They're the ones who get you killed.'

Emil was not inclined to argue. He had a blinding pain behind his left eye, the result of an abscess above a tooth he should have had pulled out long ago. But who had time for any of that? He had a revolution to make.

There was quite a crowd in the waiting room at the clinic on the Rua Chile. But when Emil mentioned his cover name to the receptionist, he was ushered through to the surgery straight away. He raised his hand in salute to the young white-jacketed doctor who was probing around his patient's groin and walked briskly on into the back room. Nilo was stretched out on the sofa, leafing through a copy of the *Psychopathia Sexualis*.

'What did you find out?' Emil demanded.

He had sent Nilo to Recife as his personal emissary, to report on the progress of the revolt. He wanted to believe the stream of gung-ho reports from Cato, the regional chief of the underground, but he needed a second opinion.

'They're straining at the leash. We can't hold them much longer. Cato says that unless we move by the end of the year, the whole thing will blow up in our faces.'

'It's Cato's job to keep things under control,' Emil commented.

'You have to understand the pressure that is building. The sergeants can't wait much longer. At the end of the year, hundreds of them are going to join the unemployed.'

Emil nodded. This was one of the grievances he had set out to exploit. Nervous of left-wing influence in the barracks, the government had decided to retire hundreds of sergeants whose five-year contracts of service expired in December, instead of signing them up for another term. Only a handful of these NCOs were Communist sympathisers, but since word of the impending layoffs had got around, plenty were willing to take part in any action that would guarantee them a decent wage.

'We can seize the north tomorrow,' Nilo announced. 'It's not just the sergeants. Even the army commander in Recife is ready to join us. But we can't afford to delay. We have to catch the tide.'

Emil grunted. 'And what about Rio?'

'You see where we're sitting.'

Emil glanced around at the twin bookcases, one of them filled with jars of pickled specimens, the framed diplomas, the flattering portrait of the mayor above the desk. The clinic had belonged to Doctor Alcibiades before he took charge of the city government. All of its staff were secret party members.

Emil had never met Alcibiades, and did not much like the way he looked in his picture. That face belonged in a silent movie, the kind Valentino played in. How could you count on a man whose eyelashes were that long?

But Alcibiades had proved himself in more important ways than by allowing his old clinic to be used for secret meetings. The mayor had channelled nearly two hundred thousand dollars to the Communist underground. The money was laundered through a charitable foundation dedicated to bettering living conditions in the favelas. Emil was not unaware that most of this cash was supplied by Alcibiades' business friends and that the biggest single donor was Courtland Bull, the American oil millionaire.

Bull's yacht had become a familiar sight these past months, basking at the mouth of the Bay of Botafogo like a gleaming white whale.

Emil relished the humour in the situation. Courtland Bull was paying for a revolution that would blow him out of the water. The American obviously thought he was buying himself a president and all the concessions a president could dispense. He was driven by greed, just as Alcibiades was driven by ambition and pride. Emil had had some experience in harnessing those emotions. He intended to do so now.

'What I say now is between the two of us,' Emil said to Nilo. 'Is that understood?'

'Perfectly.'

'I want you to go to Alcibiades as soon as you can manage it without being observed. You will tell him that the date for the rising has been set.'

Emil mentioned a Saturday in December, and the Brazilian's face lit up.

The man has the confidence of a sleepwalker, Emil thought.

Emil proceeded to list the things he would need from the mayor. On the night of the revolt, the Municipal Guard, which was under the doctor's personal control, was to seize the police headquarters and arrest a number of high officials, including the minister of war and the minister of justice, on the grounds that they were involved in a Fascist plot against the life of the president. Simultaneously, the army and air force officers who were secretly pledged to Prestes would neutralise all armed resistance in the capital, while civilian assault teams took control of the railroads, the telegraph and the docks.

Emil had calculated the odds many times, in discussions with Prestes and the handful of other Brazilians he trusted. He had concluded that the rising had a reasonable chance of success in Rio and in the north, even without mass support. But São Paulo would be contested territory, and the south would probably fight. In a country so immense, so fragmented, the capture of Rio would be merely the prelude to civil war – unless the Communists could disarm their opponents psychologically by presenting themselves as the defenders of the republic against some more sinister force.

He thought he had found a way to do it.

Its shock effect would be tremendous. It would create a national explosion of sympathy for the revolt. But what it required was so alien to the Brazilians' way of doing things, to their celebrated tolerance and *simpatia*, that he did not dare to discuss it even with Prestes. After all, no head of state had ever been assassinated in Brazil.

'There's one thing more,' he told Nilo. 'We'll need a floor plan of the Guanabara Palace. I want to know where every guard is posted.'

Nilo considered this for a moment and said brightly, 'There's a back gate. I've seen it myself.'

Emil stared at him.

'You can get in through the Fluminense Club. It backs on to the palace gardens.'

'What's the Fluminense Club?'

'Honestly, Emil. You've been here half a year and you haven't heard of the national sport?'

'Oh. Yes, of course.' Emil looked mildly embarrassed. Fluminense was one of the most popular soccer clubs in the country. 'What is the security like?' he pursued.

'At the Fluminense Club? I suppose they have a night watchman. What more would they need?'

'And on the other side of the wall?'

Nilo shrugged. 'Maybe a marine or two, having a quiet smoke. Do you want me to find out? It's not difficult. I know one of the coaches at the club.'

'Find out everything you can. But don't tell anyone else about this.'

'May I say something?'

'Of course.'

'If you're planning to grab the president, I'd like to be there in person.'

Emil shook his head.

'Why not?'

'Because you don't have a green shirt in your wardrobe.'

Emil began to explain what he intended. He found he had not misjudged his man. A smile spread slowly over Nilo's face.

3

Max has put everything into little boxes, Johnny thought, and nailed them up tight.

He suspected that it was because of Max that he had been excluded from several important meetings. He felt he had been relegated to the outer circle, reduced to the role of a mere technician showing Brazilians how to make bombs. Helene's abrupt departure should have allowed him to breathe easier. But the effect was just the opposite. Sigrid had taken her place, and it took far more concentration to keep his guard up with the woman he loved.

He realised the extent of the danger when he came to her room in the night and found her waiting for him in a flimsy negligee, her skin rosy and sweet-scented from the bath.

'Take me now,' she breathed. 'I can't wait any longer.'

He took her in his arms and carried her to the bed. He was about to enter her when she pressed her palm up against his chest and said, 'Why do you walk in the cemetery at night?'

His mind reeled. He went to cemeteries to meet Harry Maitland. He always took every possible precaution to ensure that he was not being followed. But with Max, every possible precaution might not be enough.

His desire ebbed away. He fell onto the bed by her side, pulling up the sheet because of the sudden chill that had entered the room.

He said, 'That's a strange question. Have you been following me? Or did Max tell you to ask me?'

'I need to know the answer.'

'All right,' he said fiercely. 'Here's your fucking answer. I walk by myself at night because I can't sleep. Because I can't forget all the friends I've lost.'

'Friends like Harvey Prince?'

'Not him.'

'Because he was a British spy?'

'I don't know anything about that!'

'If he wasn't a spy, then why is he dead?'

Because he was born to be a victim, Johnny thought. Like you – unless I can get you out of this.

'If Max wants to interrogate me,' Johnny said, 'tell him to do it himself.'

'I didn't mean to upset you –' suddenly, she was all woman again, snuggling up against him, letting him feel the soft pressure of her body. 'I saw you coming out of the cemetery in Botafogo when I was driving back from a meeting.'

'And you didn't offer me a lift?'

'I didn't want to embarrass you.'

'What do you mean, embarrass me?'

'How could I know what you were doing?'

Liar, Johnny thought. You were never there. But one of Max's watchdogs must have been. If Max knew anything definite, he wouldn't have sent you on this fishing trip. But I'll have to be much more careful.

'Johnny,' she implored him, caressing his lower back, 'don't hold it against me. It was just something I had to get out of the way. Would you rather I kept these things bottled up?'

'Is there something else you want to ask me?' He looked at her intently. He thought he saw a shadow pass before she buried her face against his chest. Was it shame or fear?

'Just make love to me,' she murmured. 'I need you so much.'

You're not lost to me yet, he told himself.

All real desire had left him, but he worked to make her body sing, until he saw her eyes widen and felt the trembling explosion within her.

When she lay still beside him, he saw Max's face, like a physical presence in the room.

You bastard, he thought. You try to turn all of us into mechanics.

When Max questioned him again, it was not about the cemetery.

The three of them were together in the new apartment Johnny was renting, a stone's throw away from the marina and the Gloria church. Max had brought another recording, an opera in French that Johnny had never heard before. It was Meyerbeer's *Le Prophète*. There was a booklet with the libretto, in the original and in an ungainly English translation. Leafing through it, Johnny found the story of a young man chosen by the Anabaptists – a millenarian religious sect – as their prophet and proclaimed King of Leyden in a violent sixteenth-century crusade. His mother had been forced to deny him; the girl who loved him had killed herself when she saw what he had become. Resolved to destroy the sect, he perished by setting a fire which consumed the palace in which he and the Anabaptists were banqueting.

'Very diverting,' Johnny remarked, tossing the booklet back at Max, who was humming and waving his arms about like a conductor. 'You have a curious taste in light entertainment.'

'I chose it for you, dear boy. Of course, Meyerbeer takes scandalous liberties with the historical record. But it occurred to me you might find his version rather familiar.'

'If you're trying to provoke me –'

'I wouldn't dream of it! I should come to you for lessons in provocation!'

Max smiled and held out his glass to Sigrid, who hurried out to the kitchen for another bottle.

Johnny thought, he's playing with me.

'Have you seen your pet Nazi lately?' Max asked.

'I saw Hossbach two days ago. We had a few drinks.'

'What happened to the Gestapo man you said they were sending to catch – how did you describe it? – a certain kike from Antwerp?'

'He's here,' Johnny reported. 'But I haven't met him. Hossbach said the plan has been changed.'

Even boozy Hossbach has become careful of me, Johnny reflected.

'But he showed you the photograph, at least?'

'Oh, yes. He showed me the photograph. It was you, all right. Hossbach told me to keep my eyes open.'

'I would very much like to meet this friend of Hossbach's who carries my picture around in his wallet,' Max said thoughtfully. 'Do you suppose you could arrange a meeting?'

'I could try.'

He watched Max take his drink from Sigrid. In Johnny's eyes, Max's words and movements were offensively possessive. Max said, 'There's a good girl,' as if he were petting a domestic animal. What infuriated Johnny most was that Sigrid seemed unconscious of any slight.

At that instant a grisly scene flashed through Johnny's mind: the scene of a shoot-out between Max and the Gestapo, leaving all of them dead.

Why not? he thought. Nobody would be able to blame him – and Sigrid's tether would be broken.

But Max would never let himself be caught so easily.

'I could try,' he repeated, more assertively. 'Of course, we would have to find the right bait.'

'We'll think of something.'

The recorded voices of the Anabaptists rose to a crescendo and Max abandoned the conversation to join in the chorus:

Suivez-nous, amis! Dieu le veut,
Dieu le veut! C'est le grand jour!

Two nights later, Johnny kept a rendezvous with Hossbach at the Babylônia Club. The doorman greeted him with a grinning salaam, and a couple of the bar girls blew kisses. He was becoming a regular.

'Hello there, Johnny. Better get that down you quick, before the ice melts.'

Johnny took the cocktail that was waiting for him.

'Look at the bouncers on that one.' Hossbach smacked

his chops, eyeing the new girl, who was attempting to sing 'Night and Day'. He snapped his fingers for the waiter. 'Give the lady a glass of champagne,' he instructed. 'Tell her to come over here when she's finished the set.'

'Very good, sir.'

'Well, then.' He turned back to Johnny. 'What's up? You said on the phone you had something interesting for me.'

'Are you still interested in that kike from Antwerp?'

'*Natürlich*. Did you hear something about him?'

'Better. I saw him today.'

'How is that possible?' Hossbach narrowed his eyes until the whites were invisible between the folds of flesh. The effect reminded Johnny of Wollweber, the Comintern boss in Copenhagen.

'I was in a jewellery store around the corner from the Copacabana Palace, looking for something to impress a little lady I discovered. Your man walked in and asked for the manager. I saw him go into the back room. I'd bet he was trying to peddle some of those rocks you mentioned.'

'You're sure it's the same man?'

'Pretty sure. I never forget a face. He was a few years older than the man in your photo, but I'd swear it's the same one. He had Jew written all over him, and he was dead scared.'

'What did you do?'

'I waited till he got outside. He looked ready to run when I approached him, but I spoke to him in English, as if he was an American tourist. I told him the people in the store were thieves and that I'd get him a good price if he had any more stones to sell.'

'Did he buy it?' Hossbach's face was damp with excitement.

'He said he'd call me.'

'Wait here.' Hossbach hauled his weight off the chair and went to use the telephone in the hall.

If they're hungry enough, Max had said, they'll bite.

Hossbach was gone at least fifteen minutes. When he came back, he had a lot of notes scrawled on the back of an envelope. He used them to fire off a series of questions his boss had obviously just dictated, taking more notes as Johnny gave his replies. What were his father's and mother's Christian names? Where had he gone to school in Vienna? Military service?

'It sounds like your boss is a careful man,' Johnny remarked, hoping that the cover story of Franz Gruber – the Austrian whose identity he had assumed – was strong enough to withstand a Gestapo investigation in Vienna, at least until this operation was over and he could vanish from Engineer Hossbach's life.

'Listen, it's nothing personal,' Hossbach said clumsily. 'In my business, we can't be too bloody careful. Here's what we want you to do. If Dorfman gets in touch –' Dorfman was one of Max's many aliases '– tell him to meet you at the Alpino, and make sure you give us at least three hours' notice.'

Johnny shook his head. The Alpino had a largely German clientele.

'I told you, the Jew is scared,' he pointed out. 'He'll want to pick his own time and place.'

Hossbach considered this and said, 'Okay. But make sure to give us enough warning, so we can set it up right.'

'I don't think he'll call,' Johnny played the sceptic. 'If he's as important in the Communist party as you say, why would he take the risk?'

This little twist helped a lot, because Hossbach became the one defending the whole implausible proposition.

'I know these sons of bitches,' the Nazi said. 'They like to feather their nests. My guess is he's doing a little business on the side with Uncle Joe's money.'

'Speaking of which –'

'You don't need to worry.' Hossbach pulled out his wallet and flicked several large banknotes across the table. 'I know how to look after my pals. There'll be plenty more if this comes off.'

Johnny dabbed holy water on his forehead and made the sign of the cross. He bent his knee before the high altar before slipping behind the pews and along the left side of the church towards the confessionals. Light filtered through stained glass made a batik pattern of blues and greens on the stone floor.

He entered the second confessional and leaned his head close to the grille.

'Bless me, Father,' he intoned. He added quickly, 'I was followed, but I gave them the slip in Cinelandia.'

'Max's people or Hossbach's?' Harry Maitland whispered from the priest's side of the confessional.

'Max's, I think.' He recounted what Sigrid had said about the cemetery. 'Max probably wants to see which way I'll run.'

Johnny described Max's plan to deal with Hossbach's employers.

'You can't go through with it,' Harry told him. 'It's a lunatic scheme. If the thing misfires, you'll get yourself killed.'

'That may be one of the attractions for Max.'

'I don't understand why Max would be willing to risk the whole Rio operation merely to bag a few Nazi thugs.'

'He's not risking the operation,' Johnny pointed out, 'he's risking *me*. Besides, the Gestapo has got his scent and he doesn't like that.'

'Don't go,' Harry urged him.

'I have to go. It's a direct order. I think it's also a test. If I do the job right, it may be a bit easier for me to find out what the hell is going on.'

'Then at least let me give you some backup.'

'What backup? The police? They'd probably arrest me instead of Hossbach's friends. Besides, it wouldn't be very easy to explain.'

'I was thinking of myself.'

'Thanks for the thought, Harry. But you'd better stay out of this. I don't know where Max will be, but he'll be watching. You can bet on that.'

From behind the screen Maitland heard Johnny rising to leave.

'Three Hail Marys,' Harry called after him. 'And all the luck on God's earth.'

In the street market under the old aqueduct, the cacophony was immense. It sounded as if all the Furies had been loosed at once. It took a minute or two for Johnny to distinguish the separate elements in the storm of sounds: the shouts of the porters as they shouldered their way through the crowded passages, their wares stacked high on top of their heads or swaying from poles across their shoulders; the shriek of caged parrots and macaws; the rattle and creak of pushcarts; the dull thud of the butchers' meat axes; the clack of cheap wooden clogs; the insistent babble of hawkers arguing over a price; the braying of tethered goats; the squall of a lost child.

Max's instructions had been precise. Johnny was to telephone Hossbach thirty minutes before the meet, thus denying the Nazis time to set up an elaborate ambush. The rendezvous would be on the harbour side of the market, near the wharves where they hauled up freshly caught fish. The long, low building that housed the fish market itself had half a dozen exits.

'Don't carry a gun,' Max had warned Johnny. 'They may become suspicious and search you. A gun would be hard to explain.'

'Don't you want to take them while you have the chance?' Johnny had asked.

'Not immediately.'

It seemed that Max's plan was to identify the enemy and have him tailed to his lair. To a counterintelligence mind, Johnny knew, it made sense to leave an identified enemy in place. An identified agent could be monitored. He might be used as a channel for false information. If his weaknesses were learned, he might even be turned against his own masters. If they killed the Gestapo man from Berlin, he would be replaced by an unknown successor, and their advantage would be lost.

But the plan left Johnny highly exposed. It would be up to him to satisfy the Germans, when Max failed to arrive, that he had not been laying a trap. Hossbach swore copiously over the telephone when Johnny told him the arrangements for the meeting. When Johnny set down the receiver, he hesitated for a few minutes before he took the Mauser out of his belt.

I'll be naked without it, he thought, turning the big gun over in his hands. Damn Max's orders. I'm not going into this unarmed.

He tucked the Mauser back into place.

The stink of raw fish was hard to take on an empty stomach. Slim, dark-skinned men were pulling wriggling eels out of a boat and tossing them into buckets. Outside the blotchy facade of the market building, women squatted behind panniers of bright parrot fish, squid and cuttlefish.

Johnny looked at his watch. He had been waiting nearly twenty minutes. I'll give it five minutes more, he told himself.

A hawker came up with two buckets of fish slung from a pole. He swung one of the buckets under Johnny's nose. The fish had been dead for a very long time.

'Four for one milreis,' he intoned.

Johnny shook his head.

'Five?' the hawker proposed hopefully.

'I'm not interested.'

'The fish are fresher inside,' the hawker said confidentially. 'The fat man told me to tell you.'

Johnny toyed with his pipe for a bit – the beauty of a pipe was that it always gave you an excuse for delay – before he strolled into the fish market. The stench inside was overpowering. He blew out clouds of smoke to drive it away. A girl in a maid's cap and apron watched as one of the vendors gutted a large, fatty fish.

Hossbach loomed up out of the shadows. There was a second man with him, nicely turned out in a crisp linen suit and a panama hat.

He looks like a meat porter all the same, Johnny thought.

'This is Dr Zeller,' Hossbach said.

As the stranger came closer, Johnny tried not to stare. There was something horribly familiar about that coarse, bulging face.

I know you, he thought.

'What happened to your pal?' Zeller challenged him.

'Maybe he spotted you,' Johnny suggested. 'Maybe he just got scared.'

'That's two maybes too many.' Zeller's tone was less than friendly. 'I hope you're not pissing around with me, Gruber.'

The way he blustered and pushed himself up too close made Johnny sure. Take away forty pounds and about half as many years and he was looking at Willi Rausch, the schoolyard bully who had killed his father. Willi Rausch, the model Aryan, who had grown up to find there was a seller's market for his talents.

Suddenly Johnny's desire for revenge was all-consuming. His hand crawled towards his back, flirting with the butt of the Mauser.

I could take him now, Johnny told himself. Hossbach too. But there must be others. A coward like Rausch wouldn't risk himself without plenty of backup.

Rausch was squinting at him.

'Haven't we met somewhere?'

'I don't think so.'

'I never forget a man,' said Rausch. 'Weren't you in Hamburg?'

'I've never been in Hamburg.'

There's no more time, Johnny realised. I have to do it now.

A flash of movement beyond the archway that led to the loading area caught his eye. There was a chance – just a chance – of narrowing the odds.

'There he goes!' Johnny yelled.

'What? Are you sure?'

'It's Dorfman!' he called over his shoulder. He was off and running between the trestle tables, and the Germans went crashing along after him – two, no, there were four of them now. He had flushed the others from cover.

'Go round the other way and cut him off!' Johnny shouted to Hossbach. 'He'll try to get away round the side!'

He heard Rausch and Hossbach barking at each other.

463

He hopscotched over some baskets of crabs and barely escaped a collision with a majestic black woman in the white headdress and voluminous skirts of Bahia. He lurched into one of the tables, producing shrill cries of fear and alarm. His hand closed over something before he careered on. As he neared the archway, he risked a look back. Rausch was stumbling along after him, breathing hard, and a second German had nearly caught up. The others must have gone out the front. The odds were improving.

'He's in there,' Johnny announced to Rausch, pointing to a mound of crates that rose to the height of a man's head.

Rausch peered about, clutching a Luger. The porters milling about outside goggled at him.

'*Raus!*' he snarled at them, brandishing the gun. 'Get out!'

The alleyway emptied at once.

'I don't see anything,' Rausch said warily. 'Kurt –' he motioned to his bodyguard. 'You go take a look.'

He watched Kurt go zigzagging towards the crates.

'There's something about you I don't like,' he said, turning to Johnny. 'If you're pissing with me –'

He broke off because for a fleeting moment he saw the glint of light on metal. His scream died in his throat as Johnny drove the point of a fish knife into his neck behind the windpipe. The last sounds he uttered were like those of a cat trying to spit out a hairball.

It was doubtful whether he heard Johnny breathe, 'That's for my father.'

Johnny dropped to the ground.

Where was Kurt? The bodyguard had vanished behind the crates. There was a truck parked a few yards away, to the left. On his belly, with his Mauser out, Johnny wormed his way towards it.

A shadow fell across his path. He tried to bring the gun up but failed, because at the same moment he felt a shooting pain in his right arm, and his hand went numb.

'*Klugsheisser*,' Kurt swore. He must have seen what had happened and crept around behind the back of the truck. He had stamped his foot down hard across Johnny's wrist.

Johnny lashed out with his good hand, trying to pull the German down, but Kurt jumped away, kicking the Mauser out of reach.

Kurt was evidently undecided whether to shoot Johnny on the spot or wait for Hossbach, who couldn't be far away.

Johnny rose onto his haunches.

'Down!' Kurt jabbed the gun at him. 'Get down!'

If this is the end, Johnny thought, I'm not going to meet it on my belly.

In his painful squatting position, he steeled himself for a desperate leap. Kurt was only a few feet away, holding the gun out in front of him like a duelist.

If I can just move fast enough . . .

At the instant he propelled himself forward off his aching calves, the shot rang out. It did not stop Johnny's forward momentum. His head butted into the German's chest, toppling him backwards. He clawed for the throat. The two men rolled together, and Johnny was half blinded by the blood that gushed over his forehead.

With a kind of wonderment, he realised that the blood was not his. Kurt's face was very white, paler than fish-belly white, around the red crater where one of his eyes had been.

Johnny released the body and retrieved his Mauser. When he peered over the side of the truck, a bullet zinged past his ear, punching a hole in the stucco wall of the fish market behind. The sniper must be in the window of one of the buildings across the alley. He must have a rifle, to be firing at that range. When he stuck his head out again, he was driven back by a second shot.

'Get your ass out of there, you bloody fool!' Hossbach called from somewhere away to his left. 'Can't you see it's an ambush?'

Johnny squeezed off a couple of rounds in the general direction of the sniper. Before he made his run for safety through the archway into the market, he risked one more look. He was rewarded with a glimpse of two men at a window. One was squat and swarthy. The other was aquiline, almost elegant as he puffed his cigarette. Max Fabrikant.

As Johnny hurled himself through the doorway, a bullet kicked up the dust where his feet had just been.

'Were you trying to kill me?' Johnny challenged Max afterwards.

'The better question is, were you asking to be killed?' Max responded calmly. 'Nobody told you to play fishwife with the man from Berlin.'

'He recognised me,' Johnny pointed out. 'It was him or me. In any event, I had a score to settle.'

'We all have scores to settle. Some of them have to wait.'

'Why didn't you kill Hossbach, too?'

'I didn't come to Brazil to hunt Nazis. Nor did you. Actually, I went one better than killing Hossbach. I gave you an alibi.'

This was true, up to a point. In the melée and the confusion of flight, it had apparently not occurred to Hossbach to inquire more carefully into the circumstances of Rausch's death. He had appeared to accept Johnny's explanation – that one of the ambushers had been lying in wait with a knife – and, above all, the testimony of his own eyes. He had seen Johnny trading shots with a Red sniper. In a hurried nocturnal meeting, Hossbach had advised Johnny to get out of Rio as soon as possible, and given him an address to contact in Buenos Aires. Naturally, Johnny had agreed to these proposals.

'Come to think of it,' said Max, 'it might not be such a bad idea if you were to leave. Helene's in BA. She'll look after you. I can arrange it.'

'For Sigrid too?'

'I need her here.'

'Why? To hunt Trotsky supporters?'

Max's eyes flashed. For an instant Johnny was reminded of the inexplicable fear he had experienced when this man's gaze was first turned on him in Berlin.

I have many reasons to fear you, Johnny addressed him mentally. But I'll never succumb to you.

Max said, with strange, stiff courtliness, 'You presume on our friendship.'

There was something in the tone that made Johnny feel an unwanted, unexpected stab of sympathy, because it suggested to him that in Max's life, perhaps he really was the closest thing to a friend.

Johnny said, 'I'm needed here too.'

4

Heedless of reverses, Emil's team forged ahead with the making of a revolution. Prestes spent several weeks writing to old comrades, appealing to shared nostalgia for the days when, as rebel *tenentes*, they had tramped from one end of the country to the other. Some replied apologetically that he had been away from Brazil for too long, that he didn't realise how much things had changed. 'I long to join your movement,' one major wrote, 'but because you have accepted the embrace of the Communists, this would be like loving a girl with syphilis.' Others were silent. But there were a few who were ready to rise and who guaranteed the support of whole garrisons. Prestes' confidence in their eventual success remained unshaken.

Bangu, the party boss in Bahia, reported that the people were ready to revolt en masse. Cato sent urgent messages from Recife warning that the pot was bubbling over; revolutionary enthusiasm – whipped up by the bitter strike at the Great Western railroad and the shabby conditions in local barracks – could not be held in check for long. The ANL, officially banned, continued to organise under the slogan of 'Bread, Land and Liberty', targeting the land barons and the Greenshirts and the Anglo-American companies like Rio Light and Standard Oil. Cash flowed in via Youamtorg, the Soviet trading company in Montevideo, as well as from the local sources Harry Maitland was trying to investigate. Plans for a general strike were well advanced. The railwaymen were committed; so were the seamen and the workers at the huge Malvillis and Bonfim textile factories in Rio. The graduates of Johnny's training courses were active all over Brazil; pro-government commanders would be surprised in their barracks by a combined assault by armed civilians from outside and rebel soldiers from within. At the appropriate time, the capital would be blacked out by bomb attacks on the towers and accumulators of Rio Light, spreading panic and confusion in the ranks of the government. Lists of reactionaries who were to be shot were circulating, especially in the north. Under Emil's supervision the conspirators had even drawn up a list of cabinet ministers who would figure in a provisional revolutionary government, to be headed by Prestes. Dr Alcibiades was to be appointed Minister of Public Health.

Inevitably there were doubters. Toward the end of October 1935, a veteran Brazilian Communist, João Batista Barreto Leite, penned a letter to Prestes counselling caution; he was promptly expelled from the party. Roberto Sisson, the key organiser in the ANL, who had hand-carried secret instructions on preparing an armed rising to regional chiefs in the north, wrote in a similar vein. He knew too much to be kicked out. He was advised that the revolution had been postponed indefinitely and was shut out of all further planning.

There was a doubter even on the Comintern's general staff in Rio. Verdi, the Argentinian, asked Johnny to have a drink with him after a meeting largely concerned with plans to disrupt the Central do Brasil, the railroad that linked the capital with São Paulo.

'I don't understand Emil's confidence,' Verdi complained. 'Bangu writes from Bahia that the masses are ready to revolt, and Emil swallows it. I went to Bahia. You know who's really in charge there? A mulatto baker who believes in spirits and hates intellectuals. They had a woman on the committee, a popular novelist and beautiful as well. The idiot baker drove her out. He called her into his office and lolled there in his sweaty undershirt, picking his big toe. He told her she had to make sixty-seven changes in her new book because it wasn't sufficiently socialist. I doubt if he could read it. How are we expected to make a revolution with these cretins?'

Verdi took a great gulp of red wine and added, 'Either Emil is completely intoxicated or there is a missing element. What do you think?'

'I think he's a man who can't afford to go home empty-handed.'

But Johnny was thinking that Verdi was right. Unless Emil had taken leave of his senses, he must have a card up his sleeve – one that neither the Argentinian nor Johnny had been permitted to see.

Verdi mentioned that he had written an editorial for a special edition of the Communist paper, to be issued on the day of the rising. This suggested that Emil had set a deadline. The revolution was going to happen. Johnny's immediate task was to find out when.

He lay between sleep and waking, very much alone. After the episode at the fish market Sigrid had spent three full days with him. She was loving and unthreatening, and they even had time to go sailing out in the bay, on a little skiff he rented at the marina.

She lay on the deck, sunning herself, letting the sea breeze stream through her hair.

She said, 'I wish we could always be like this,' and for a few hours he was completely happy.

But now he was locked in the familiar cycle of absence and distrust. Sigrid disappeared for days at a time, and sometimes he could only guess at what she was doing. She told him once that she had gone to São Paulo with Max. In his mind Johnny connected this with rumours that a leading Trotskyite had arrived in Brazil. Enemies in the family, he reflected, were often the deadliest kind.

As he lay there watching the strip of light under the shutters grow brighter, he thought about others who had been close to him: his father, who had predicted, in his soft, sad way, what would happen to the Communist movement; Heinz, who had seen it come to pass, and whose death still cried out for justice; Helene, who had heard the screams but kept the faith. He tried to picture her in Buenos Aires, tried to fathom what sustained her. Perhaps she was duelling with the Nazis; according to Verdi, Argentina was a hotbed of Gestapo and Abwehr agents. That was what all of them needed – a good clean fight, a just war against unambiguous enemies. Not this dirty war, waged in a permanent penumbra.

He heard the scratch of a key in the lock and sat up in bed.

'Sigi?'

'Good morning.' She slipped into the bedroom and kissed him lightly on the side of his face, still crumpled from the pillow. 'You look like a child when you're just waking up.'

'I'm still asleep,' he smiled at her. 'You'll have to help me wake up.'

He opened his arms to her, and she kissed his lips. She smelled like a sunlit garden.

'Later, sweetheart,' she said gently. 'I've come to collect you. There's a job Max needs you to do.'

'What sort of a job?' he asked warily. He had only recently been reminded that an assignment for Max was most likely to get you killed.

'It's a security job,' Sigrid said. 'He wants you to booby-trap a safe.'

'I'll need to get my stuff.' His tools and explosives were stored in Grajaú, at the home of Vasco, the Spanish painter who had blown some of his fingers off playing with bombs on the beach.

They drove to Grajaú, and Johnny emerged from Vasco's house with a bulky black leather bag, like a doctor's.

Their final destination was a modest house in Meier, a working-class district in the northern zone, a long ride from the affluent beach suburbs Emil and the foreign comintern agents preferred. Brown-skinned children ran shouting across the road, chasing a ball, peering in the windows of the car.

A big German shepherd barked at the two Europeans from behind a screen door. As Johnny climbed the steps, it reared up on its hind legs, pawing at the wire, so that its teeth were almost level with his face.

'Down, Príncipe!' a woman called from inside.

The dog went on barking and leaping until she came and hauled it down by the collar. The barks subsided into a low rumble rising up from the belly.

'He's shy with people he doesn't know,' the woman apologised, releasing the catch on the door to let them in.

She smiled at Johnny, and he recognised her at once. She was Prestes' woman, the one he had met at Petrópolis. She was wearing a sort of smock over baggy cotton trousers.

'Carlos isn't here,' Olga said. 'But Max told us you would be coming. The safe is in the next room.'

The dog followed at Johnny's heels, sniffing and snarling, his hackles raised.

Johnny turned and held out his hand. The dog shied away, baring his teeth.

'He'll make friends in his own time,' Olga said reassuringly.

It was not at all certain the dog agreed. When Johnny took another step towards the bedroom door, Príncipe made a run at him.

'Príncipe!'

Johnny stood perfectly still. The dog drew back and started barking again.

'Look, it would make things a lot easier if you two took him out for a walk,' Johnny suggested. 'Would you like to go for a walk?' he asked the dog, who kept on snarling but cocked his head in anticipation.

Olga did not look entirely happy about Johnny's suggestion.

'I promise I won't raid the liquor cabinet.' He smiled at her.

'All right.' She smiled back. 'I'll just open the safe for you.'

He watched from the door as she dialled the combination, conscious of Sigi and the dog watching him.

'I always thought I had a way with animals,' he remarked to Sigrid.

471

Olga had the safe open. She took a pistol from the top shelf and tucked it inside a capacious handbag.

'How long will you be?' she asked him.

'Less than an hour, I expect.'

'We'll be back sooner than that,' Sigrid announced, taking Olga's arm.

'Good boy,' Johnny said to the dog, and he meant it.

When the women left with Príncipe on a chain, he picked up his bag of tricks and went into the bedroom. The safe was American-made, the same type as Emil's. It would be child's play to wire it up. He started moving papers about to make room for the dynamite.

On top of the stack was a six-page document, a directive from the leadership of the Communist Party of Brazil, addressed to branch organisers around the country. Johnny scanned it quickly. The contents were mostly generalities. The directive announced that the time was propitious for action, that local party officials – hiding their Communist affiliations – should intensify agitation on every level to install a People's Revolutionary Government with Prestes at its head.

He glanced at the paper underneath. It was the draft of a letter, to be signed by Prestes. What it contained was so explosive that Johnny pushed it back into the stack after skimming the first paragraph. He went through the apartment from room to room to check that nobody was in hiding. He peered out the windows to see if anyone was keeping an eye on the place from outside and saw only the children playing ball. Still not satisfied, he went out onto the porch. There was no sign of Olga and Sigrid or of anyone more suspicious than a delivery boy taking groceries into a house nearby. He went back inside and bolted the door.

Now he studied the draft letter more carefully, trying to memorise every detail. It was addressed to the commanding general in Recife. It advised him to be ready to seize full control on December 14, the date set for a general uprising throughout the country. It stated that the courier who brought the letter would provide a verbal report on the preparations that had been made in other army garrisons.

With rising excitement Johnny ferreted through the other documents. There was a notebook with a list of officers and sergeants – some identified by pseudonyms, others by their real names – who had promised to join the revolt. There was enough information to identify some of the couriers. There were sketch maps of Rio and other cities, showing where bombs would be planted and barricades set up, but these were less interesting; he had drawn some of them himself.

Johnny began scribbling notes on a scrap of paper. He allowed himself only ten minutes, realising that the women might return at any moment. When the time had elapsed, he took off one of his shoes and concealed the information he had stolen inside his sock.

He had not quite finished wiring the safe when he heard the dog bark outside. He hurried to the door, not fast enough to get it open before Olga had tried her key.

'You bolted the door,' she challenged him.

'I thought the maid might come,' he responded, as casually as he could manage.

'Have you finished?'

'I'll just need a few minutes more.'

The dog shouldered his way past the women, bounded over to Johnny and started licking his hand.

'I don't know what you've done to him,' Johnny said, looking at Sigrid. 'But it seems to have worked wonders.'

'I told him to give you the benefit of the doubt.'

5

Colin Bailey was in his favourite corner of the smoking room, dallying over a glass of port and a copy of the *Economist*, when the club porter came in.

'Telephone call for you, Major Bailey.'

The booth was in the lobby, in front of the porter's cubbyhole.

'Yes?'

'It's Norton here, Major. Cecil Norton, at Plunkett's.'

'Yes, of course, Mr Norton. How are you keeping?'

'Very well, thank you kindly, sir. Very well indeed. It's about those shirts you ordered.'

'They're ready, are they?'

'Shall I send them round, sir?'

'That won't be necessary. I'll stop in myself.'

It was a pleasant stroll up Regent Street, through the white light of November. Plunkett's front window on Savile Row was understated: a couple of bolts of excellent worsted, a striped jacket with the sleeves off, ready for sewing. Bailey went up the stairs and through the cutting room into the tiny back office, where a bright, birdlike little man with a tape measure draped over his shoulders winked at him and produced a Cable & Wireless envelope.

'I was out to lunch when it arrived, Major,' Norton explained. 'I called you as soon as I came in.'

'I'll never have reason to complain about service at Plunkett's, Mr Norton.'

'Always a pleasure, sir.'

Communicating with Maitland via the embassy in Rio had become more trouble than it was worth, in Bailey's estimation. Summerhayes, who had seemed a decent enough fellow, though a bit dry, was having kittens over the death of that young American – not without reason, Bailey had to concede. In his opinion, Harry's effort to set up Harvey Prince had been an ill-conceived, amateurish operation with negligible results. He doubted whether it would deceive a professional like Max Fabrikant. Still, his rebuke to Maitland had been coached in the mildest possible language. He couldn't fault the boy for trying. He had told him to use his wits – and he was, after all, an amateur. But Bailey had cautioned Harry to take no further initiatives without proper consultation and to avoid the embassy altogether. Plunkett's was more understanding, by and large, than the Foreign Office.

Bailey went back to Broadway and set about deciphering Harry's telegram, which ran to nearly three pages and must have dug quite a hole in his expense allowance. The cable conveyed both urgency and puzzlement.

Maitland had learned from Johnny that the Comintern had set a date for an armed uprising in Brazil: December 14. It seemed that Johnny had been able to lay hands on extraordinarily detailed information regarding the plans of the conspirators, including the names of senior military officials who had promised to join the revolt. He had come by all these facts in a rather unlikely way. He was a man who was under suspicion, or so he had told Maitland. He had been shut out of policy meetings and believed himself to be shadowed for much of the time. He thought that even his mistress was spying on him. Yet, by his own account, he had been left alone in the flat of the top Communist organiser, at leisure to ransack his private papers. The only explanation he could render was some ridiculous tale of a dog that barked or didn't bark, or both.

What was Bailey to make of all this? He could not rule out the possibility that Max Fabrikant was now in control and was playing Johnny back against the British. Harry was convinced that his agent was telling the truth, so far as he understood it, but Harry might not be in a position to judge. It was equally possible that the episode at Prestes' flat had been a hoax arranged by Max to expose Johnny while feeding false information to Johnny's handlers. The date for the rising could be pure invention, the list of supposed conspirators a concoction designed to send Bailey and the Brazilian authorities – if they were informed – chasing after the wrong hare.

Bailey judged that at least some of the information was authentic and highly compromising. Several of the army officers who were named, and at least one of the couriers, had figured in previous reports from Johnny. But that would fit the profile of a professional deception operation, which required a kernel of truth – a *kanva*, as Max Fabrikant would say – to make the lie believable.

What if Johnny's entire report, including the date of the planned insurrection, was accurate? That opened another question in Bailey's mind. Had his agent simply been fantastically lucky? Or was he *meant* to see the papers in Prestes' safe?

Bailey was a great believer in luck. Unless you were born lucky, in his view, you had no business dabbling in intelligence.

But luck often walked in company with other people's interests. Was it conceivable that there was somebody else close to the Communist leadership who wanted the conspiracy to fail?

Bailey could not answer his own questions, yet he felt certain the answer lay with one man: Max Fabrikant. He had tried to fathom that restless intelligence, to project himself inside Max's mind. But the gulf of character and circumstance that divided them was immense. Max's behaviour since he had arrived in Brazil had been curiously contradictory. He was clearly attached to Sigrid, yet he had sent her back to Johnny's bed. He distrusted Johnny, but he had not taken the simple step of getting him recalled to Moscow.

Max might despise Emil, the man in charge of the plot, but it was difficult to imagine the chekist propelled by anything as trivial as personal spite. Max was a ruthless, highly efficient instrument of his masters; his whole life represented the triumph of the Russian state party over personal loyalties, of *raison d'état* over philosophy and morals. He was also a chess player. If he had staged the scene in Prestes' apartment, it was as a gambit in a larger play authorised by Moscow.

Bailey sighed. He had concluded early in his career in counterintelligence that one of the worst mistakes was to over-estimate the subtlety of your opponents.

Max might be baiting a trap. On the other hand, his people might simply have made a cock-up.

Sitting in London, Colin Bailey could not determine the truth. In the meantime, the Communists were gearing up for a coup d'état, and Harry needed guidance.

We have to run with it, Bailey decided.

He picked up his pen and started drafting a reply to Maitland. He suggested that at this stage Harry should take his friend Colonel Plinio into his confidence without, of course, disclosing the source of his information.

At the mayor's dinner party in Rio, Colonel Plinio had lyricised his visits to London, and Bailey had not failed to do his homework. He had found that his own bootmakers on St James's Street, made shoes for the colonel from his personal last. Bailey concluded that a Brazilian with a private last at the finest bootmaker's in London must be both a confirmed Anglophile and capable of discretion.

These were desirable qualities for what Bailey had in mind. It was plain now that there were many influential men in Rio, even in the police, who could not be trusted. There were those like the mayor who were flirting in secret with the Communists. There were also the Fascist sympathisers, well represented in the police, who might seize on new evidence of a Moscow plot to eliminate anyone they did not like the look of, or even to justify a coup of their own. De Salis had reported from Berlin that a team of Gestapo officers had left for Rio at the invitation of Colonel Plinio's chief, to provide certain technical instruction for the Brazilians. Bailey had no intention of making Hitler's friends a gift of Johnny's information.

No, Plinio was their man. He was an opportunist, no doubt, but for that very reason he could be easily influenced. It would not escape the colonel's attention that the British could help him to earn a substantial reward from his government, perhaps in the form of his boss's job.

More than a month before, Bailey had started to clear the ground by arranging for the bootmakers in St James's to furnish Colonel Plinio with an exceptionally fine pair of paddock boots, charged to Bailey's own account. Plinio had not disdained this offering.

In Bailey's mind there was only one satisfactory way for Harry and the colonel to proceed.

'Think of yourself as a midwife,' he wrote to Maitland. 'Your task is to force an early delivery.'

He rather liked his analogy. But to ensure that Harry did not miss the point, he went to some pains to explain it in detail.

He had almost finished encrypting the text when one of the lights at the base of his black telephone flashed on.

'Yes?'

'It's Rowecliff here, Major. There's a young man been waiting for you over half an hour.

'Tell him I'm on my way.'

In his excitement over the news from Rio, he had completely forgotten his appointment.

He gave the cable to one of the girls to send off and took a taxi to a house off the King's Road that had had a For Sale sign up for as long as anyone could remember. The real estate agent whose name appeared on the sign was less than helpful when prospective buyers called to ask about it.

Bailey entered the house, using his own key, and found Nicholas twiddling his thumbs in the drawing room at the back, overlooking a small walled garden. Nicholas was one of the new crop of Oxbridge men, slightly baffled by his present environment. He was very good-looking, with curly brown hair worn a little too long at the back. Bailey had interviewed him personally. He thought that the boy would do nicely for an opportunity that had just presented itself on the other side of the world from Brazil. According to de Salis, the wife of the new German Ambassador to Istanbul was a holy terror, given to jumping into bed with any man bold enough to make an advance.

Bailey eyed his new recruit speculatively.

'Do you know Turkey at all?'

'No, sir. I'm afraid not.'

'Well, never mind. How would you like to do some fucking on the Secret Vote?'

10

The Bomb Factory

A decision that is quick but wrong is worth more than one that is correct but too late.

— Luis Carlos Prestes

1

The revolution began three weeks ahead of schedule, and the Comintern team in Rio first heard about it over the radio.

It began far away to the north in Natal, the old port city on the bulge of Brazil, on a coast lined with strange, steep sand dunes pleated like skirts that gave way, farther north, to immense salt flats so white that they hurt the eyes.

There had been trouble brewing in the local garrison. On Friday an unpopular lieutenant called Santana had been shot in the back by one of his own men. He had them loaded up like mules in full battle kit, despite the heat. When the shot rang out, his fellow officers came running from the mess. Nobody would admit to pulling the trigger, but the officers placed half a dozen known dissidents under armed guard. They were going to face a court-martial on Monday morning.

The court-martial never took place.

Saturday, November 23, was graduation night in Natal. The new governor and the notables of the town were assembled in the Civic Theatre to applaud each other's speeches and hand out prizes to the honours students of the

Escola Santo Antonio. The band introduced each speaker with a patriotic tune. It was missing the trombone that evening. Sergeant Quintinho, a self-taught musician who donated some of his free time to the band, had other business to attend to back at the barracks. Everybody liked Quintinho, even if he came from Pernambuco – you might as well say Timbuktu – and held rather advanced opinions for a man who had never set foot in a schoolhouse.

The governor was lost in an interminable sentence. His plight seemed desperate; he had repeated his phrase about 'the flower of northern youth' twice over, and there was still no sign of a verb.

The punctuation, when it came, was explosive. Three rifle shots cracked out, then a staccato burst of machine-gun fire. It sounded as if the firing was coming from just outside the doors. Some members of the audience tried to crawl under the seats in front of them. A big man in the second row, a cotton planter, shoved his way to the aisle and stood there brandishing a pistol.

'Show me a Communist!' he bellowed. 'I'm ready for those sons of bitches!'

He squeezed off a couple of rounds that blacked out one of the chandeliers and brought down a shower of plaster dust and tinkling glass.

The governor abandoned his hunt for a verb and ordered the band to strike up 'Réunir'.

The music could hardly be heard above the din. Women screamed as another burst of automatic fire stitched a zigzag line across the double oak doors. The cotton planter, panicking, hurled himself into the frightened mob that was trying to squeeze through the side door, using his pistol as a club.

'They're setting fire to the theatre!' someone screamed.

The governor took his wife by the arm and hurried her out through the stage entrance. The police chief and a dozen army and government officials fled after them.

'Go to your posts!' the governor yelled at his followers outside. 'I entrust the city to you! Fight to the last man!'

Without further ado the governor rushed to the house of

an old business partner whose beautifully engraved cards declared him to be the Honorary Consul of the Republic of Chile.

'I claim political asylum!' the governor shrieked at his astonished friend. 'Quick, man! Put out the flag!'

The shots were interspersed with the sound of breaking glass as looters raided the stores.

The honorary consul produced a small, somewhat faded Chilean flag.

'Haven't you got a bigger one?' the governor said doubtfully.

'I'm sorry. But you could go to the French shipping company,' the consul added brightly. 'They've got a tricolour as big as a house.'

'Raul –' The governor's wife squeezed his wrist.

He peeked out the window and saw a squad of soldiers with their caps reversed, rebels from the Twenty-first Battalion, those trouble-makers Vargas had transferred up here from Recife. They had expropriated a supply of hooch and were swilling it from the bottle. There were rowdies in civilian clothes trooping along with them and a few men in the uniforms of the Civil Guard, that gang of political brigands he had just ordered disbanded. Nobody seemed to be resisting them. As he watched, some of them broke down the door of a fine townhouse down the street. He recognised the man who came to argue with them; he was a young engineer, the heir to a wealthy family that supported the governor's party. One of the men in civilian clothes was poking him with his rifle. The engineer's wife tried to push between them. The others dragged her away by the hair and threw her down in the gutter. They shot the engineer right in front of her.

The governor's wife fell into a dead faint.

'Don't think you're not welcome,' the honorary consul said to the governor. 'But there are two Mexican corvettes in the harbour. You'd be much safer on board.'

'If I go, you go too,' the governor snapped.

The neck of the decanter shivered against the glass as the consul poured them all drinks.

'I never knew there were so many Communists in Natal,' he said unhappily.

While the governor hid behind the flag of Chile, resistance to the rebels centred on the police barracks, whose rear windows looked out over coconut palms and muddy shacks along the Pontengui River.

The white stucco facade had developed eczema; it was scarred and pitted by hundreds of bullets from the rebels who had occupied the houses across the street. They were using the sign for target practice. It used to read 'Regimento Policial Militar', but only the initial 'R' had survived.

It was hard for the men inside the police barracks to tell what exactly the rebels wanted. Some voices in the mob were cheering the name of the federal defence minister, a notorious reactionary. Others shouted the names of Prestes and the National Liberation Alliance. Somebody was proposing an assault on the Young Ladies' Academy, an expensive boarding school for the the landowners' daughters. This idea was received with enthusiastic roars. It was getting impossible to tell soldiers from civilians; the mutineers from the barracks were arming people at random and swapping clothes with the crowd. Quite a few jailbirds had got hold of rifles. The warden of the state prison was a well-known bleeding heart, little better than a Red (if you asked the police chief's opinion). He had taken to letting some of his prisoners go home every night. It would be no surprise if he were in on the plot.

The chief of police found that fewer than forty of his men had stayed to defend their barracks. They were supplemented by a handful of army officers, including the newly appointed commander of the Twenty-first, a colonel from the south. The colonel was strutting up and down, inspecting everyone as if he were on a parade ground.

'We'll show this rabble what we're made of!' he announced to the chief of police. 'Where's your bugler?'

'Noberto!' the police chief barked at a young man who was trying to make himself scarce. 'What do you want with him?'

'Get up on the roof!' the colonel ordered the unhappy bugler. 'Sound the call to arms!'

Noberto appealled to his chief with spaniel eyes. The police chief shrugged.

'You are a symbol of the heroic resistance,' the colonel informed him.

The bugler climbed out the back window and started scaling the wall. They knew when he had reached the top, because the snipers in the houses across the street started blasting away with everything they had — rifles, pistols and machine guns. The men inside the barracks raised a ragged cheer when the strains of 'Unido' rang out, only slightly off key. Then the bugle fell silent in the middle of a bar.

Several men rushed to the back windows.

'Did those bastards get him?' the colonel shouted.

'No, sir,' someone called back. 'He's climbing down the wall.'

The colonel rushed over to see. The ground fell away sharply between the street and the river, and the back side of the barracks was a full story higher than the front. Noberto had tossed away his bugle and was crouched on a window ledge, trying to pluck up the courage to jump.

'Get back to your post, you coward!' the colonel bellowed at him, brandishing his service revolver.

This settled things for Noberto. He jumped at the same moment the colonel fired. The bullet went wide, anyway. Some of the other policemen cheered when they saw the bugler fall on his hands and knees in the soft mud, pick himself up and go zigzagging off into the shacks along the river.

'Your men haven't got a pair of balls between them,' the colonel informed the police chief.

'Then why don't you go and join *your* men across the street?'

The colonel turned an ugly shade of red and went to inspect the gunners. The defenders' heavy artillery consisted of two Hotchkiss machine guns and an old Maxim gun. From the sound of things and the quantity of shattered glass on the floor, the attackers had superior firepower. But there was no sign of casualties on either side.

One of the policeman had methodically blasted out every pane of glass in the building directly opposite. Satisfied with his accomplishment, he swung the Hotchkiss round to inflict the same demolition on the house next door.

After a whole night of fireworks in which they fired off almost their entire stock of ammunition – a hundred thousand rounds – the defenders agreed to stage an orderly retreat at breakfast time on Sunday. They all took off their uniforms, descended on ropes from the rear windows of the barracks and splashed across the river to take shelter among the stilt shacks on the far side.

The city of Natal was now entirely in the hands of the rebels. In the course of the battle for the police barracks – the only military engagement of any note – the rebels had expended three hundred thousand bullets and wounded a grand total of twelve men. Ten of the twelve had been winged as they fled across the river.

A revolutionary junta set up shop in the Vila Cincinato, a government palace on the outskirts of town. Its apparent chief, a slender mulatto who was a cobbler by trade, presided over meetings with a cavalry sabre in his hand. His finance minister, the town postmaster, scented them with his fancy cigars. Sergeant Quintinho, the illiterate trombone player, was appointed minister of defence. A plump, bearded lawyer whom everyone called 'Papai Noel', or Father Christmas, was named minister of public works. He was the chief of the Communist underground in Natal, the recipient of secret messages from Recife addressed appropriately, if insecurely, to 'Santa'.

This Santa was delighted but somewhat bewildered to find himself a member of the first soviet ever formed in Brazil. He had received just three hours forewarning of the rising, when Sergeant Quintinho had hauled him out of his favourite bar in the middle of a lazy Saturday afternoon. 'Orders from the top,' Quintinho had said. Santa was slightly miffed that the orders had gone straight to the barracks, passing him by. This suggested that the leadership in Rio trusted the sergeants who had joined secret cells inside the army more than properly constituted party officials like himself. But Santa wasn't a man to hold grudges. What did it matter, when the wind was obviously blowing their way? The government of Natal had deflated like a tired meringue. The message would carry clear across Brazil. Santa read the announcement on the radio. It ran on the hour, every hour, in between recordings of the *Internationale* and popular songs of the north.

It was carnival time in the town. Santa came across some kids who were trying to set fire to a streetcar.

'No, no,' he intervened. 'Don't destroy your own property. The *bondes* are free! They belong to the people!'

The kids got the idea, soon enough. They piled into the tram and shunted off, looking for girls.

The revolution needed a treasury, so Quintinho and the other members of the junta drove down to the local depository of the Bank of Brazil. The manager refused to open the vault. He made out he had swallowed the key. Quintinho sat on his stomach but succeeded only in bringing up the man's breakfast. Someone ran down to the docks and came back with a blowtorch, which the finance minister naturally claimed as an appurtenance of his office. Half an hour later, their pockets stuffed with cash, the members of the junta were ferrying moneybags and gold bars out to their truck. As they made their triumphal progress back to the Vila Cincinato, Quintinho threw fistfuls of banknotes to the crowd.

'Revolution is fun!' he proclaimed.

2

In the early hours of Sunday morning, a man on a motorcycle sped through the sprawling industrial zone that lay between Recife and the big new army barracks at Socorro, out near the railyards. The road was almost deserted. Rounding a bend, the courier saw the rear end of a truck, pulled up a quarter of a mile ahead. He had almost caught up to it when the driver pulled out into the middle of the road without bothering to signal. The driver was a real road hog; when the motorcyclist tried to pass, he swung his wheel viciously, blocking off the left lane. The courier sounded his horn and tried to get round the other side. He was almost abreast of the driver's cabin when the truck lurched over to the right, forcing him off the road. His front wheel hit a ditch, and he flew out of his saddle, landing a dozen feet away in a heap of broken bones.

The truck screeched to a halt. A trim man in a pearl grey suit jumped out of the passenger side and made straight for the leather pouch that hung from the saddle of the motorbike. He found what he wanted immediately: a letter in a plain manila envelope. He scanned the contents under his flashlight, refolded the letter and tucked it away inside his breast pocket. He produced a second letter from his other inside pocket and placed it in the messenger's pouch. Several men who had been concealed in the back of the truck stood around, waiting for him to complete this operation. One of them, a huge mulatto dressed like a stevedore, was holding a Thompson submachine gun. In his hands it looked like a toy.

'Give me that,' the man in grey ordered. He took the Thompson and gestured towards the motorbike. 'See if it still works.'

The black man tried to kick life into the motorcycle. The engine spluttered and died.

'Enough,' the man in charge said impatiently. 'Take my car. They won't know the difference. Ask for Lieutenant Lamartino. You've got that?'

'Yes, sir. Lieutenant Lamartino. What if someone else is on duty?'

'Say you've got a message from your sister.'

The mulatto smiled broadly.

'There won't be any problems,' the man in grey assured him. 'Most of their officers are in town getting drunk.'

There was a big guitar festival in Recife that night, and the officers of the garrison had hired a special bus. They were not likely to hurry back before they had made a thorough inspection of the cantinas and the bawdy houses. Besides, the regional army commander had been summoned to Rio to attend some meeting at the War Ministry.

'Put the motorcycle in the back of the truck,' the man in grey ordered his other men.

'What about him?' one of them asked, pointing to the motionless courier.

'Get rid of it.'

'Yes, Colonel Falcão.'

At eight that Sunday morning, the duty officer at the Socorro barracks, Captain Mindelo, looked out his window at battalion headquarters and saw a crowd of soldiers with their caps back to front. He recognised some of the usual loudmouths, sergeants and corporals who had been bitching since word got around that they were going to be dumped when their five-year terms expired next month. He had been keeping an eye on them since that incident on the railroad. A week or two before, a platoon had been sent from the barracks to clear the track around the Crab's Bend. The Communists had called another strike and produced a horde of women and children to sit along the railbed and stop the trains from getting through. The platoon commander, Lieutenant Santa Rosa, wasn't going to stand for any nonsense. He ordered the civilians to clear the tracks. This inspired a volley of catcalls and obscene gestures. So he told his men to fire into the air. Shots rang out, and one of them dropped Santa Rosa. He got a bullet between his shoulder blades and died on his way to hospital. The Reds put it around that he was killed by one of his own men. Captain Mindelo didn't know whether to believe this or not – the c.o. had told him in confidence that the fatal bullet was from a pistol, not a rifle – but it did not help anybody's nerves. He had received an anonymous letter warning him that any officer who stood against the people would share the fate of Santa Rosa. Some of his own company sergeants played deaf when he issued commands, so that he had to repeat them in a louder voice, trying not to show rage – or fear. Now the time had come to draw the line.

'What the hell is going on?' he yelled out the window.

'Everardo!' The shout came from one of his friends, Lieutenant Lamartino. They had served together in São Paulo. '*Você e dos nossos*! You're one of us! Join the people! We're counting on you!'

'Have you taken leave of your senses?' the captain shouted back. He was making some quick calculations. He had ten or twelve men in the HQ, including a couple of officers he could rely on. So long as they could hold out, he controlled the arsenal. He ordered his people to load their weapons and cover all sides of the building.

Then he strolled out onto the steps with a swagger stick in the crook of his elbow.

'You're hung over,' he said to his friend the lieutenant. 'Or still drunk. Go and sleep it off.'

A private soldier drove his rifle butt into Mindelo's stomach, and the captain rolled in the dust.

The soldier took aim.

'No!' Lamartino intervened. '*Isso não se faz assim*! It's not done that way!'

Captain Mindelo got to his feet, brushing the dirt from his tunic.

'Kill him like Santa Rosa!' the rebel private urged. 'Then the rest will surrender.'

'You belong with us,' Lamartino appealed to the captain. 'The government has fallen. Haven't you heard? Why fight for a lost cause?'

'Go fuck yourself.'

Captain Mindelo backed into the headquarters building and was actually inside the door before the shooting started.

He tried the telephone. To his amazement it worked. There was a list of emergency numbers, and he worked through them in sequence. There was no answer from army HQ or the governor's office. Of course, the general was in Rio, and the governor was travelling in Europe. But you would expect someone to pick up their phones. Perhaps Lamartino was not lying. Perhaps the revolution had already triumphed. Nervous and frustrated, Captain Mindelo tried the third number on the list. It belonged to the secretary for public safety.

To Mindelo's relief, his call was answered on the very first ring. The secretary himself was on the other end of the line.

'Falcão.'

'Colonel – Your Excellency – this is Captain Mindelo. I am the duty officer at Socorro.'

'Well?'

'I'm sorry to disturb you, but there is a revolt in progress.'

'How long can you hold out?'

'How long –'

'Give me your exact dispositions,' Falcão snapped.

'It's hard to be exact. We are surrounded. Except for the arsenal and the headquarters itself, the barracks is in their hands.'

'You will soon receive reinforcements. You will hold out for two hours. You hear me?'

'Yes, Colonel Falcão. Two hours. And then?'

'Then give them whatever they want.'

Colonel Falcão, the secretary for public safety of the state of Pernambuco, was no stranger to revolt. As a young army cadet, he had taken part in the rising in Rio in 1922. Two years later, he had been in São Paulo, in the thick of another insurrection. He had joined the revolution that brought Vargas to power and played guerrilla saboteur, cutting telephone lines to stop the loyalists from calling in reinforcements. Twice a loser, once a winner. Thanks to a helpful tip from his friend Plinio Nogueira in Rio, confirmed by news of the mutiny in Natal, Falcão was confident that this time he would even the score – and win bigger than before.

As soon as he received the first telephone call from Captain Mindelo, he rushed around to the home of the acting governor, who came to the door in person in his freshly starched pyjamas as if this were the most ordinary Sunday of the year.

Falcão informed the acting governor that a revolution was being attempted and demanded to know what measures he meant to take.

The poor man hesitated and blinked through his thick lenses and burbled something about how there must be no shooting.

'You're under arrest,' Colonel Falcão told him.

Within the hour he had locked up two other members of the state cabinet – the secretaries of justice and finance, old adversaries of the colonel – on the grounds that they were secret Communist sympathisers.

He talked to Mindelo every half hour. Amazingly, the rebels had still not cut the telephone lines. Shortly before 11:00 A.M., the colonel learned from Mindelo that the mutineers, several hundred of them, were on their way to the city, accompanied by some of the strikers from the railroad.

Commending himself on his sense of irony, he decided to meet them in the Largo da Paz – Peace Plaza – a large and leafy public square that lay athwart the main road from the barracks to the city centre. Falcão had mustered a hybrid force consisting of a couple of companies of loyalist troops from the old Soledad barracks downtown, uniformed policemen and plainclothes detectives, officers of the merchant marine, firemen and street-car drivers, and a few sporting gentlemen from the Planters' Club. Falcão's men were outnumbered by the rebels and their armed hangers-on. But the colonel knew, as the rebels did not, that thousands of government troops with howitzers and heavy machine guns were already approaching the outskirts of Recife. They came from garrisons in the interior and from as far away as Paraiba and Maceo and João Pessoa. The colonel had wired for help as soon as he received confirmation of the rising in Natal.

In the Largo da Paz a police captain shouted at the rebels through a loudhailer, offering terms of surrender. The police had set up barricades, blocking off the exits that led to the city centre. The mutineers responded with bullets. Rebel troops ran into the church on a corner of the square and climbed up inside the bell tower to take potshots at Falcão's men behind their barricades. Others set to digging trenches across the middle of Peace Plaza.

'Shoot to kill,' Falcão ordered his men.

He withdrew to a modest hotel nearby to draft a radio message. This was part of his bargain with Colonel Plinio Nogueira, who had supplied such gratifyingly accurate information on the Communist underground in Recife – right down to the location of the secret radio transmitter hidden in the church of the activist priest the locals had dubbed Father Badó.

'The vast majority of the suffering masses of Recife have risen as one man,' he scribbled. 'Don't fail us now!' He crossed out the second sentence as too plaintive, and substituted, 'The hour of victory is at hand!'

He added a few lines and signed the message with the code name of the chief of the regional directorate of the Communist party: 'Cato'. Cato had left his lodgings in the middle of the night, but Falcão's detectives had kept him under constant surveillance. The colonel was confident the Communist leader would be silenced before he could send a contradictory signal.

Father Badó could hardly object. At that moment, he was enjoying the hospitality of a cell in the House of Detention that the other prisoners described, with reason, as the Matchbox.

3

In Rio it was a perfect Sunday morning. There were sailboats out in the bay. They looked like flying fish beside the gleaming white bulk of the yacht *Slidell*, where the Yankee millionaire Courtland Bull gave parties that had filled the gossip columns for more than a week. By the pool at the Copacabana Palace Hotel, a circle of habitués honed their appetites on seasoned Scotch whisky. The president was at the golf club, in excellent spirits despite the fact that he had managed to land his ball in a sand trap for the third time in as many holes. Roberto Sisson, navy captain (retired) and honorary president of the illegal National Liberation Alliance, was in a less ebullient mood at the House of Detention. Together with a hundred and fifty other suspected 'subversives', he had been arrested in a dawn raid by the police. The raid had not stirred a ripple on the placid surface of Carioca life. Many families were still abed, sleeping off Saturday's *feijoada*. The men of the house went to the door in their freshly pressed pyjamas to take in the newspapers. The headlines were devoted to new attacks on the mayor by the local version of the League for Decency, which was demanding a halt to casino gambling, and to Mussolini's exploits in darkest Abyssinia. News of the remarkable happenings in the north would not reach the populace at large until late in the day.

Johnny was down at the marina waiting for Sigrid. He had hired a skiff and was checking the rigging. He had a day planned for them that would match the weather, a day of lolling about among the islands, a picnic lunch with some cold white wine, another chance to revisit that afternoon on the Wannsee that first brought them together as man and woman.

There she was now, pushing back her windblown hair with the palm of her hand, casually turned out in a cream cotton jersey and a navy skirt, padding along in rubber-soled shoes. She stood on the edge of the jetty looking down at him, her expression unreadable behind her dark glasses.

'Did you forget our lunch?' he shouted up at her. 'I brought the wine!'

'We're not going!' she called back.

He grabbed hold of the capstan and swung himself up onto the pier.

'What's the matter?'

'Haven't you heard?' That little vertical line like an exclamation point, appeared between her eyebrows. 'It's begun.'

'Where?'

'In the north. In Recife. There was a radio message.'

'And?'

'You really don't know?'

Harry might have warned me, he thought. No, he corrected himself, Harry was right. It was better that his surprise was real. Harry had hinted that he was going to take steps to 'move things along'. Johnny could make a fairly good guess at what those steps had been. A word with a government minister, or more likely a friend in the police. An agent provocateur in the north sending false signals in the name of Prestes or Emil . . . the revolution had started according to Colin Bailey's timetable, not Moscow's.

'The police are out in force all over the city,' Sigrid reported. 'They say the president is going to declare a state of siege. Many people have been arrested.'

'Emil? Prestes?'

'No. The leadership is intact. There's going to be an emergency council. They told me to get you.'

The high command of the revolution assembled that night in a doctor's house on Rua Correia de Oliveira. Emil and Nilo were late and Prestes passed the time while the others were waiting for them hunched over a rosewood secretary, scribbling notes to old friends. Johnny glimpsed the contents of one of these messages, addressed to André Trifino Correia, the adjutant of a battalion in Minas Gerais: 'We are about to have the revolution. Here we cannot wait longer than two or three days. I am counting on you.'

Miranda paced up and down, slapping a balled fist into the palm of his other hand, while Verdi lolled on the sofa, working his way through a bottle of *vinho tinto*. They looked as if they had been up all night.

There was a whistle from the lookout in the street, and a few seconds later Sigrid came through the door. She had tied a scarf around her head and wore a man's loose jacket and culottes.

'Where's Emil?' she asked Johnny.

'Still not here.'

Verdi rolled off the sofa. 'Is there word from Moscow?' he asked her eagerly.

'The message is for Emil,' she said crisply.

So she had come from the radio man. Johnny could picture the scene: a wireless buried under the floorboards somewhere in a house on a hill, carried upstairs at night when they wanted to transmit. It wouldn't be powerful enough to reach Moscow Centre. They would try to get messages through via Youamtorg in Montevideo. They must have been signalling frantically since the first news had come through from the north.

'You can give it to me.' Verdi smiled at Sigrid, holding out his hand.

She looked at Johnny, over the Argentinian's shoulder.

Johnny said, 'What difference can it make?'

'As you like.' She took out a folded sheet of paper. Verdi pounced on it.

Johnny followed her out into the hall. 'What about Max?' he whispered. 'Is he going to cancel the operation?'

She looked at him so sharply he wished he had not asked the question. 'What makes you think Max would tell me?' she countered. 'Besides, it's not his decision.'

'Of course,' he agreed. 'Are you coming back tonight?'

'I can't say.'

He suddenly feared for her, racing back and forth in the new car – the Opel – between the doctor's house and the radio man and Max's bolthole, with the police out in droves.

He said, 'For God's sake, be careful.'

There was the hint of a smile when she replied, 'You're a fine one to talk.'

Their lips brushed. Then she was gone into the night.

'You see?' Verdi's voice rose shrilly from the living room. 'They've got their heads screwed on right in Moscow! They don't want this thing to go off at half cock!'

He read the contents of the message out loud. It struck Johnny as the reverse of a clear directive. The centre requested more detailed information on the progress of the revolt in the north and recommended that Emil or his nominee should return to Moscow as quickly as possible to review the situation. Yet the message allowed Emil plenty of rope to hang himself if he chose. 'We have full confidence in the judgment of the South American bureau,' it concluded.

There were a couple of low whistles from the lookout, and then Emil came barrelling in with Nilo at his heels. It struck Johnny that they were both in suspiciously good spirits.

'Sorry we're late,' Emil said briskly. 'Let's get to it!'

The revolt was spreading like wildfire in the north, he reported. He had been in radio contact with Cato, in Recife, and Bangu, in Bahia. It would take the government days to mobilise sufficient troops to retake the coastal cities. If the conspirators struck in Rio now, those reinforcements would never be sent.

'In Rio we are unstoppable,' Prestes volunteered.

Only Verdi expressed open dissent. He started quoting the signal from Moscow, and Emil snatched it away from him.

'This changes nothing,' Emil announced, when he had scanned the contents. 'There's no time for consultations. Moscow will back whatever decisions we take.'

Verdi complained that the premature risings in the north could be the product of police provocation.

'Suppose you are right,' Emil responded. His tone was patronising, almost insulting, 'that would merely prove that the police don't know their business. If the actions in the north were triggered by police spies, they'll find they have started something they can't stop.'

'But the raids in Rio this morning —'

'What damage did they do? Answer me that. The police rounded up the usual suspects. They didn't bag a single man we depend on. You see? They're still fumbling in the dark.'

'Or leading us on,' Verdi suggested gloomily.

'I saw Jorge this morning,' Nilo intervened on Emil's behalf. This Jorge was a popular writer of leftist leanings, a supporter of the ANL. 'He told me the police raided his apartment. They confiscated every book that was bound in red.'

495

Everyone laughed except Verdi.

Emil made inventory of the units they could count on. There were reliable cells inside the Third Regiment, a short drive away from the presidential palace and the barracks of the Special Police. Communists in the Second Regiment, which supplied guards for the War Ministry, were ready to seize the commanding generals and the army headquarters. Revolutionary cadets and instructors at the Aviation School would neutralise the air force base next door.

Emil asked Johnny to report on his commando teams. In neutral tones, Johnny described how the men he had trained would cut road and rail links to São Paulo and the huge military complex at Vila Militar, and black out Rio Light.

Then Prestes held up the sheaf of letters he had just written to his admirers in garrisons in the interior, directing them to act without hesitation as soon as they received word from him.

'You always leave out the navy,' Verdi interjected.

They all recognised that the navy could be a decisive factor in a battle for Rio, with its long-range guns, its planes and its crack corps of marines, who supplied body-guards for the president. Despite all the propagandising by Sisson and the other ex-navy men on the council of the ANL – and Johnny's own efforts – the Communists had made few friends in the fleet and almost none within the officer corps. Unlike their counterparts in the army, Brazilian navy officers belonged to an exclusive caste, monied, white and patrician, hostile to ideas of social reform.

'If the navy moves against us, we're sunk,' Verdi pressed his point.

Prestes dealt with this. He puffed out his chest and declared, 'I can personally guarantee that the navy will join the revolution.'

Johnny noticed that even Emil appeared thunderstruck by this intervention.

'I have received certain pledges,' Prestes went on. 'The navy is on our side.'

There was no way for Johnny to tell whether these pledges were real – or whether Prestes was hallucinating.

Johnny said, 'That decides it, doesn't it?'

He was rewarded with a look of sheer misery from Verdi, who returned to his bottle, and a broad beam from Emil, who roared, 'We move within forty-eight hours! *Wenn schon, den schön!*'

Verdi stifled a belch with his hand. 'I beg your pardon?'

'If it's got to be done,' Emil translated freely, 'do it right!'

What troubled Johnny most was Emil's extraordinary self-confidence. The only reason for it he could fathom – unless Emil himself was a provocateur, which Johnny considered improbable – was that there was a strand to the conspiracy that had been kept hidden even from the other members of the South American bureau.

What could it be?

He stumbled across a possible clue when he went back to Vasco's house, which was being used as an armoury for his sabotage squads, to check on the distribution of arms and explosives.

'We're five Thompsons and six revolvers short,' the Spaniard reported.

'I don't understand.'

'A kid came around with an order signed by Nilo. I couldn't very well send him away empty-handed, could I?'

'What kid?'

'They call him Escoteiro.'

Johnny remembered the young tough who had played bodyguard at the meeting in Petrópolis, the one they called Boy Scout. He had been running errands for Nilo for several months.

'A charming young gentleman,' Vasco commented with distaste. 'He bragged about how he's been given a really big job. You know what he told me? He said he's been preparing for this for months. He said he had a dog, an animal he grew up with. He butchered it, hacked it to bits and disembowelled it. He said he wanted to drive out pity, to harden himself so he can kill without flinching.'

'Absolutely charming,' Johnny observed. 'What would he consider a really big job?'

'He shot off his mouth about sticking a needle up Getulio's backside. But he clammed up when I asked for more. It's hard to believe a kid like that has it in him to do more than make a nuisance of himself on the bleachers. He was dressed like he was going to the game.'

'What game?'

'Well, he was sporting a Fluminense tee shirt. I told him he was a bit late for this season.'

Johnny could not make much sense out of this, except that Nilo was arming gunmen for purposes that remained obscure to him. But the remark about Getulio – President Vargas – stuck in Johnny's mind. Vargas was still regarded by many Brazilians as a genuine reformer, a man committed to social justice and improving working conditions. His administration included progressives; Doctor Alcibiades was one of his appointees. Though the Vargas reforms had been denounced in the Communist press as a sham, Emil's team privately acknowledged that the President's liberal reputation was a major obstacle to the revolution that was being planned.

Was it possible that Nilo and whoever was behind him – Emil or Max, or the two of them in concert – had decided to remove that obstacle by killing the president?

No, Johnny told himself, such a plot would be madness. The assassination of the president would rally the whole country against his murderers.

He tried to put himself inside Emil's mind, the mind of a desperate man who had been warned by Stalin and his creatures that no excuse would be accepted for failure in Rio, a man who had learned to trample on every moral scruple, every shred of loyalty, in order to pleasure the murderous paranoia that reigned in Moscow.

If I were Emil, Johnny reflected, I wouldn't hesitate about killing a president, if that were the key. But it would have to be done right.

Then he realised how the job might be accomplished.

On the afternoon of Tuesday, November 26, after frenzied preparations, the members of the South American bureau agreed that the revolt would start in Rio at two o'clock the following morning. Prestes signed orders that were to be carried to trusted agents inside the garrison and others that were to be taken to São Paulo and the south by couriers who would leave from the Pedro II station.

The previous day, Johnny had warned Harry Maitland that 'the balloon was about to go up'. They had taken their normal precautions, meeting in the Gloria church. Now there was no time for elaborate subterfuge. Early on Tuesday evening, for the first and only time, Johnny risked a visit to Harry's home in Tijuca. He crept round the side, peering in through the windows like a burglar. He saw a handsome mulatto woman singing to herself as she stirred a pot in the kitchen, and then at an upstairs window he saw Harry himself, fiddling with his bow tie. He tossed a small stone at the insect screen. The second one caught Harry's attention.

'What the devil –'

Harry peered down and saw the strongly built figure in the shadows.

'Hold on. I'm coming down.'

In urgent, staccato sentences, Johnny explained the last-minute arrangements for the rising. Maitland was relieved to learn the exact locations of the bombs that were to be planted at Rio Light, including one in Major Mackenzie's office. He was pensive when Johnny confided his suspicions of a second plot, concealed from the full membership of the South American bureau. He would suggest to Colonel Plinio that the president's guard should be reinforced, even though there was nothing solid to go on.

Johnny mentioned that Prestes had been trying to set up a personal meeting with Doctor Alcibiades. The conspirators were counting on the mayor to play a decisive role in the plot.

It occurred to Harry that the very best way to monitor the night's entertainments might be to carry on exactly as he had planned. He had been invited to a reception at Doctor Alcibiades'.

But first he had some telephone calls to make.

4

As evening deepened, the Cariocas gave themselves over to familiar pleasures. In Lapa they sang serenades of transient love. In the smart casinos the chandeliers blazed on whirring roulette wheels and outrageous décolletés. Along the beaches couples snuggled among the dunes and packs of feral boys – the 'captains of the sand' – roamed in search of sport. The city seemed too normal, Harry thought. He wondered whether it had been the same in Paris the night before they stormed the Bastille. As usual, there were a dozen fashionable parties to choose from. But, also as usual, *the* party to be seen at was at Doctor Alcibiades'. Rarely if ever had a bachelor been known to be such a consummate host. But then, with half the women of Rio at his feet, the handsome mayor had no lack of counsellors.

Harry drove up to the gates of the villa but was stopped by an apologetic policeman who asked if the Senhor would mind parking farther up the street. He found a space a couple of blocks away, and when he strolled back the same policeman checked his name against a list, making the standard confusion of first name and surname so that Harry had to assist him.

'Your security is very thorough tonight,' Maitland remarked, noting that a squad of Special Police, in their bright-red kepis, were patrolling inside the high wrought-iron fence. It occurred to him to wonder whether all the extra guards were there to screen the guests coming in or to stop some of them, and possibly their host, from coming out.

'There you are, dear boy,' Desmond Wild assailed him, whisky in hand, as he entered the main salon. The journalist looked subtly different, and Harry realised that this was due less to his startling red cummerbund than to the thing that was perched on top of his pate like a beaver on a rock. Harry could not help staring at it.

Wild was quite unabashed. He patted his hairpiece lovingly. 'I got it through the mail,' he reported. 'Stella Mackenzie says it takes off about ten years. What do you think?'

'I'd say it takes off more than that.'

Harry tore his eyes away and examined the crowd. There was the predictable array of beautiful women, some of them competing for the attention of Courtland Bull, who was holding court on the far side of the room near the French doors. Harry spotted a couple of cabinet ministers and several high-ranking officers in dress uniform. He recognised Admiral Wilson Cavalcanti, the navy's chief of operations. There had been a fuss about him only a few days before, when the newspapers published a photograph showing him giving the stiff-arm salute at a Greenshirt rally, and there were calls for his resignation.

The admiral was the centre of another little group.

'I see that Cavalcanti is still in circulation,' Harry remarked.

'He's in his element. The place is positively crawling with Fascists. See that horse-faced Kraut with him? That's Wolfgang Trott from the German Embassy. He's one of yours.'

'I beg your pardon?'

'Cloak-and-dagger type.'

'I'll overlook that.' Harry scooped a drink from a passing waiter's tray. He wondered how a Fascist admiral fitted into Doctor Alcibiades' lifestyle. Perhaps the mayor was simply playing the old political game, being all things to all men. Or perhaps, if he were secretly involved in the Communist plot, he calculated that a party attended by men like Cavalcanti would supply him with a perfect cover – and an unassailable alibi in the event that the plotters failed.

'I must go and pay my respects to our host,' Harry announced. 'Have you seen him?'

They both peered around.

'The doctor seems antsy tonight,' Desmond Wild observed. 'He's been rushing off to the telephone. Do you suppose something's up?'

Stella Mackenzie rescued Harry from the rest of the conversation, squeezing him to her ample bosom as if she intended to smother him.

'Darling Harry,' she gushed. 'The major's hot for your blood tonight. But I'm going to protect you.'

'Come and tell me all about it, Lovie.' He winked at Desmond Wild and steered her safely out of earshot. One more gin, he thought, and they would have to carry Stella out.

'The local constabulary are all over head office,' she explained jerkily. 'They put one of the major's engineers in the jug. Something about a bomb, was it? They said you knew all about it. The major's on the warpath because he wasn't informed.'

'I'll sort it out in the morning. There's really nothing to worry about.'

'But it's not the bomb that got him so upset. It's the buses.'

Harry glanced around nervously, but nobody seemed to be paying any heed to what Stella was saying. Colonel Plinio had called him in some agitation just before he had left for the party, to report that saboteurs had done a pretty good job of knocking out the motor pool at Vila Militar, smashing up transmissions and gear shifts and setting a fire in the main garage. This would delay the arrival of loyalist troops for hours if things got out of hand downtown. Harry had promptly volunteered to put Rio Light's fleet of buses at the disposal of the government. He had tried to telephone Major Mackenzie to prevent a blow-up but had learned from Stella's maid that his boss had already left home. It was bad luck to run in to the Mackenzies at Alcibiades' party, and he had no intention of risking a scene with the major, whom he could see advancing resolutely through the throng.

'That drink looks pretty sick,' he said to Stella, seizing her glass, now empty except for the last sad ice cubes. 'Let me get you the other half.'

Stella rewarded him for this gesture with a wet kiss.

He got to the other side of the room and pointed a waiter in Stella's direction. Then he slipped out onto the patio, where he caught sight of a man who struck him as almost as unlikely a guest as Admiral Cavalcanti, a muscular fellow with heavy-lidded eyes who had turned up in a lounge suit instead of black tie. He looked more German than Brazilian. He would have looked all wrong in any kind of civilian rig, except maybe a pair of boxing shorts. Harry had seen him once or twice at official functions, always in uniform. He knew him by reputation as the most feared interrogator in Rio. He was Captain Honorio Schmidt, the head of the Special Police, that athletic corps of bruisers the local wits had dubbed the Tomatoheads.

'Good evening, Harry.'

Maitland turned to the source of this port-flavoured voice and found Colonel Plinio smoothing his moustache. Unlike Schmidt, the colonel was in uniform, with his cap under his arm.

'I see your men are out in force tonight,' Harry remarked to him. 'You've even got Honorio Schmidt guarding the back door.'

'So we do.' Plinio acknowledged the captain with the most distant of nods, and it was plain to Maitland that these two were very far from being friends.

This encouraged Harry to whisper, 'I thought Schmidt spent most of his time torturing people.'

'Tsk, tsk.' Plinio clucked the mildest of reproaches. 'You have lived in South America long enough to understand that here a man is put in jail so that he can confess.'

'Unfortunately, that philosophy is not unique to South America.'

'You are absolutely right. My good friend Honorio, as you may have observed, is a student of the German philosophy. Did you happen to notice Herr Trott?'

'I did.'

'He has been sent here to assist us at the recommendation of Captain Schmidt.'

'Trott is Gestapo, then?'

Colonel Plinio sighed and consulted his watch. 'Nearly eleven,' he said. 'We still have over three hours to wait.'

'I wonder how many of Alcibiades' guests will still be here.'

'You may well ask.'

'I've been trying to work out why they were all invited in the first place. Admiral Cavalcanti, for example. It's hard to imagine that he has anything much in common with the mayor. And shouldn't he be at navy headquarters, if there's a general alert?'

The Colonel played with his whiskers. 'You're missing something that's perfectly obvious, my dear Harry.'

'Which is?'

'The common denominator. They weren't invited to the other party. Either by Prestes or the president. We are attending a *salon des refusés*.'

Much as he enjoyed Plinio's bon mot, Maitland's curiosity wasn't slaked by it. He felt certain that their absent host was embroiled in the Comintern plot – though he had only the most circumstantial of evidence to go on – and that the guest list was somehow connected.

'Did you find the bomb?' Harry asked under his breath.

'All three of them. I don't think Alcibiades' chandeliers will go out before the party is over.'

'Where did they plant them?'

'Exactly where you said. One in Major Mackenzie's office. Two at the generator.'

'I'm trying to avoid the major. He's upset about the buses.'

'I'm sure the government will be happy to pay for the gasoline.'

'And there's no sign of trouble yet?'

'Not a squeak. We picked up two couriers at the railroad station.' He caught Harry's look and added quickly, 'We're not altogether novices, Harry. We let them board their trains. If anyone was covering them, he will report to Prestes that they are safely on their way to Minas and São Paulo. The guard at the War Ministry and the Vila Militar has been changed. The duty officers were part of the conspiracy, as you thought. It was all done with perfect discretion. The war minister has put out a general alert, to take effect after midnight. We've sent out word that it's a routine fire drill. You don't look happy, Harry. Have I left anything out?'

'I don't know.' Maitland had a crawling sensation at the back of his neck. Johnny's instinct could be right. The vital element might still be missing.

'Where is the president?' he said suddenly.

'I believe he went to the theatre. It's Toscanini tonight. Did you know Toscanini once conducted at the Teatro Municipal? The president has a special fondness for his work. The performance must be ending about now. You know, the president is concerned to give the impression that everything is exactly as normal. He has been quite impeccable in that.'

'I'm delighted to hear it. And after the theatre?'

'He'll go home to bed. He's not a man for late-night parties.'

'Who's guarding the palace?'

'The marines, of course. I think he likes their white uniforms. But they're good men. The best the military have.'

'And they belong to the navy, as in England.'

'Naturally.'

'And that means that Admiral Cavalcanti gives them their orders.'

'Well, the marines have their own commander.'

'But the chief of naval operations is his superior, isn't he?'

'Look here, Harry. I'm not an authority on matters of navy protocol. Why don't you go and ask the admiral himself?'

Maitland frowned.

'Is there something you're driving at?' Colonel Plinio asked him.

'I just can't seem to put my finger on it. You remember I told you about one of Prestes' men, the one the others call Boy Scout?'

'I do.'

'Were you able to find out anything more about him?'

'Your description would have fitted a hundred young men who have burned out half their brain cells on alcohol or ideology. Thank you.' He took a glass of champagne from a waiter. 'Does he matter so much?'

'I keep thinking about his threat.'

'Not very specific, was it?'

'Listen, it had to do with the president. That may be what we've missed.'

'You mean an assassination attempt?'

'Yes.'

Plinio allowed himself a gentle smile.

'I don't see that the idea is particularly funny.'

'Forgive me,' the Colonel said. 'You live among us, but you don't think like us. I know my Brazilians. Carlos Prestes may be a Communist, he may be ready to lie down and lick the dirt off Stalin's toecaps, but he would never authorise the murder of Getulio Vargas. He's a Brazilian, and a Brazilian of a certain class. Within that class we're not given to killing each other. This may, I admit, be a serious political defect. But it's not un-English, is it? Assassination is for Spaniards and Russians. And possibly Germans,' he added, glancing at Honorio Schmidt, who had been joined by Trott, the Gestapo representative. 'People who burn with the absolute. Besides, the Communists know that if they killed the president, the whole country would unite to mourn him and bury them.'

'The leaders of the revolt aren't Brazilians,' Harry said quietly. 'They're countrymen of Herr Trott.'

Plinio tweaked his moustache. 'Hmmm. Well, we'll find out soon enough, I suppose. I may drop by the palace and check that Xuxu's tucked up properly for the night. I expect that, like the rest of us, he won't want to miss a thing.'

Harry found it odd that the chief of the secret police referred to his president by the same pejorative nickname – Xuxu – as the Communists Johnny was dealing with.

Colonel Plinio put his cap on his head, clicked his heels and gave a comical salute.

'By the way,' he said, as an apparent afterthought, 'are you coming to see the fireworks?'

'I wouldn't miss them for the world.'

5

The beach was a narrow strip of sand in the cleft between the Sugarloaf and a rocky promontory that struck out into the ocean like a giant paw. The sand, now white under a crescent moon, was pink in the afternoons in the light reflected from the sheer, polished slopes above the royal palms, so they called the place Praia Vermelha, the Red Beach. To Prestes' supporters in the Third Regiment, whose barracks faced the sea, the name seemed auspicious.

Chief among them was a high-strung, voluble captain from the south. He had a knack for holding an audience, even though he delivered his lectures in a monotonous, rather tinny voice and his stature was less than heroic. With his small, squat body, his tiny head and jutting beak of a nose, he strongly resembled the macuco bird, and the nickname Macuco had stuck to him. His influence over the soldiers was the more surprising because he did not belong to the regiment. On the contrary. He had been sent to Praia Vermelha under guard, sentenced to twenty days' detention for spreading sedition among the garrisons of the south. The Fascists had tried to shoot him in Porto Alegre after the court-martial, so his family had prevailed on the General Staff to let him serve out his sentence in the capital.

The regiment treated him with the respect owed to an officer and a gentleman. He dined in the mess. He was allowed to take up residence in a family apartment in Copacabana and to come and go from the barracks as he pleased. He soon made contact with the handful of Communists and the larger amorphous group of Prestes admirers in the barracks. He arranged to circulate Communist broadsheets especially aimed at the sergeants and corporals whose terms of service were about to expire and at the ill-equipped conscripts who were crowded into ramshackle wood-and-stucco pavilions put up for the famous Exposition of 1908 and never expected to last. He singled out the men with the stomach for a fight and schooled them, in one-on-one meetings, in the techniques of insurrection.

Fewer than a dozen men out of the seventeen hundred in the regiment had any exact notion of what was being planned. Fewer than four dozen, despite Macuco's efforts, could be counted on to give instant support to an armed rising. But the little captain from the south was not intimidated by the odds against the conspirators. He was a student of Lenin and Mussolini. His bible was a well-thumbed volume of Curzio Malaparte's essay on the coup d'état, which he had read aloud to some of his recruits. He was convinced that revolutions, of whatever hue, had nothing to do with the masses; the ones that succeeded were the work of a small and dedicated elite advancing to power over a bovine majority that lacked the imagination and the will either to join or to resist. In this vision of things Macuco found a soul mate in Nilo.

While Harry Maitland took the air on the mayor's patio, Macuco was on his way back to the regiment on a bicycle after attending a secret meeting near his flat in Copacabana. In his pocket he carried the letter Nilo had pressed into his hands. He was so elated by its contents that he whistled as he pedalled along. The letter, signed with the magical name of Prestes, appointed Macuco to the command of the Third Regiment of the People's Revolutionary Army. His new commission would take effect at 2:00 A.M., when he was charged with seizing the barracks. At 3:00 A.M., he was to lead an assault on police headquarters and the presidential palace.

The Urca casino, across the avenue from the barracks, was ablaze with lights. The place was a Venus fly-trap for off-duty officers who preferred philandering to politics. Macuco's grin broadened as he saw it looming up. If he had his way, some of his brother officers would see more of the casino than they had contemplated tonight.

As he jumped off his bicycle, he noticed that there were

a lot more sentries about than usual. A whole platoon with machine guns was deployed along the street side of the barracks.

Macuco started walking his bike through the line, and a fresh-faced conscript trotted up with his rifle at the ready.

'Halt!'

'*Boa noite, calouro*,' Macuco said casually. 'Hello there, greenhorn. Don't you know me?'

'Password!'

'Password? We don't bother with passwords! What do you think this is, a boys' club?'

He heard the rattle of the rifle bolt and began to feel distinctly unhappy. The kid was nervous and green enough to let that thing in his hands go off. It might just be a training exercise, he thought. But if there were an alert and they searched him and found the letter –

His only recourse was to brazen it out.

'Where's your officer?' he demanded. 'I'm carrying special orders.'

He took out the compromising envelope and waved it in the boy's face. The soldier looked confused but did not give way.

Macuco saw the duty officer striding briskly across the patio. He was delighted to recognise Lieutenant Otelo, his closest friend in the regiment. Apart from Macuco, there were only two commissioned officers in the regiment who belonged to the party; this lieutenant was one of them.

'*Tudo bem*,' the lieutenant said to his jittery sentry. 'The captain is expected.'

'What's going on?' Macuco whispered to him as they walked towards the barracks.

'They've ordered a general alert.'

'And put you in charge of the guard? That's a bit of luck.'

'Not just luck. The colonel picked Avelino for duty officer. But he started bitching that he had a date, so I offered to swap places with him.'

'They locked up the arms, I suppose?'

'That's the bad news. Julião's in charge of the arsenal. He'll fight us.'

'Only if he gets the chance.' Macuco grinned. 'I'll take care of him myself.'

'So we're going to do it?' The subaltern's face was shiny with excitement.

Macuco showed him the letter. 'Go to David and Alvaro,' he ordered in an undertone. 'Tell them to spread the word. I'll go to the others.'

When Macuco came out of the barracks, it was almost 1:00 A.M., a clear, bright night. Everything was black and white – the sentries, the revellers coming and going from their cars to the casino across the way – as distinct as in a movie. But Macuco did not spot the colonel until he loomed up from somewhere among the palms, in uniform, with his service revolver at his belt.

'It's a bit late for you, isn't it, Captain?' Colonel Ferreira challenged him. 'Don't you have better things to do this time of night?'

'I don't sleep so well, sir.'

'What are you doing here?'

'The same as you.'

'I beg your pardon?'

'Well, there are plenty of rumours floating around. I thought I'd see if any of them are true.'

'You'd do better to get a good night's sleep.' Colonel Ferreira's tone was not unkindly; it was almost avuncular.

Macuco mimicked it to perfection. 'At your time of life, you're the one who ought to worry about getting your rest.'

'Damned impertinence!' the colonel erupted. 'Go to your lodgings before I forget you're a guest and have you locked up.'

'I'm afraid you're in no position to give that order.'

'Lieutenant!' Ferreira called.

Otelo hurried over to them.

'This officer is to be placed in solitary confinement.'

The lieutenant swallowed and looked at Macuco.

'I am assuming command,' Macuco said coolly. 'Colonel Ferreira will be *our* guest tonight.'

The revolution in Rio was starting nearly an hour ahead of schedule because of a social indiscretion. So much the better, Macuco told himself. Even if there had been a leak, they would have plenty of time to secure Red Beach before the other side was ready for them.

6

Harry Maitland lingered at the mayor's party long after Colonel Plinio left. At Doctor Alcibiades' villa, nobody took account of the clock. It was nothing unusual for his entertainments to last until dawn. One of the guests was playing 'Lili Marlene' on the baby grand. Harry was surprised to see that the pianist was Courtland Bull. He played more delicately than Stella Mackenzie sang. She swayed over towards Harry, moaning the chorus in a tone that reminded Harry of a dog trying to move on an injured leg. He caught her arm before she had sloshed more than an inch of gin and tonic over his white dinner jacket.

'Kiss me, Harry,' Stella said, puckering her lips and throwing herself backwards in a parody of Hollywood passion so that he had to fling his arms around her to save her from falling.

He got her upright, gave her a chaste peck on the corner of the mouth and beat a hasty retreat.

Harry noticed that Admiral Cavalcanti had disappeared. So had several of the army officers and the German attaché, Wolfgang Trott. Then Captain Schmidt came marching briskly through the salon, sidestepping the dancers. Instead of going out into the front hall, Schmidt veered right and disappeared down a corridor that led to the library and the private wing. Harry presumed the policeman had gone in search of a lavatory or a telephone. But Schmidt had not returned when, several minutes later, a man who looked more like a bodyguard than a servant came out of the same hallway, crossed the salon, and whispered something to Courtland Bull that caused the American to cease his piano playing. Bull kissed the hands of his claque of lady admirers and followed the messenger back the way he had come. Harry got a better look at the servant this time and thought he had seen him in the background the night Alcibiades had shown off his snake house. The servant was a real charmer: flat-faced, swarthy skin, woolly eyebrows that met in the middle and resembled a hairy caterpillar crawling across his low forehead.

It looked as if Alcibiades had summoned the oil millionaire to a meeting somewhere in the private wing. The mayor had made only a couple of fleeting appearances in the course of the entire evening, interrupting the merry-making at one point to deliver a brief word in praise of the immense philanthropic efforts of the Bull Foundation and of Mr Courtland Bull personally. These had allegedly brought new hope to the poor of Rio de Janeiro.

Harry was still puzzled by the connection between Doctor Alcibiades and the oil baron. He had little doubt that Courtland Bull had returned to Rio in high hopes of making a financial killing. He had done his homework with some help from Desmond Wild and an American press cuttings service and knew that Bull was not renowned in his home state of Texas for either philanthropy or progressive leanings. At an oilmen's gathering in Houston, he had publicly berated President Roosevelt for his 'good neighbour' policy in South America, which ruled out the use of military force. In Bull's opinion, the Roosevelt approach was a license for 'communism and the theft of US property' all over the continent. Yet the Bull Foundation was making generous donations to Doctor Alcibiades' community clinics. The obvious explanation was that Courtland Bull saw the mayor as a coming man in Brazil and wanted to get him in his debt – so deeply in his debt that, if he got greater power, he would have no option but to hand over whatever concessions the Texan demanded. Desmond Wild had heard stories that Bull was mixed up with a consortium that was trying to sell the Brazilian navy some fancy new destroyers and minesweepers. That might explain what Admiral Cavalcanti was doing at the party. South of the Rio Grande – and north of it, too – money tended to talk louder than ideology.

Yet Harry could not satisfy himself with this simple line of reasoning. He felt instinctively that something much deeper and more dangerous was involved. Whatever was taking place in Alcibiades' private rooms must be bound up with the conspiracy that was unfolding in the rest of the city. Was Courtland Bull aware of the Communist plot? Had the mayor invited his strange collection of Nazis and right-wing admirals and generals in order to immobilise them – or to use them in some way?

It was past 1:00 A.M., Harry saw, and he sensed that it was now urgent to have the answers to these questions. He set off down the corridor in the footsteps of Courtland Bull. The hallway ended abruptly in another that led off both to right and left. There was an old German woodcut on the wall. It showed St Denis, the patron saint of the French and of syphilitics, receiving the supplication of pockmarked reprobates. A memento of Alcibiades' former life.

Maitland hesitated. The library was off to the left, he remembered. The door was slightly ajar, and there was a light on within. He edged towards it.

'The Senhor wishes something?'

He wheeled round at the sound of the gruff voice and found Caterpillar behind him.

'I thought I might use the telephone,' Harry said.

'The senhor will find a telephone in the main lobby.'

'Perhaps I might see Doctor Alcibiades,' Harry changed tack.

'The Doctor is not available.'

There was no chance of talking his way round this brute, Harry concluded. He would have to backtrack and start again.

He was moving back along the corridor with Caterpillar shadowing his every step when he heard an inhuman wail.

It seemed to be coming from the other direction, from

the end of the hall that led out into the back garden and the reptile house.

The wail turned into a low groan, punctuated by a few human syllables.

Maitland slipped by the guard and hurried towards the source of these sounds. Caterpillar was behind him but made no further move to block him until he got out the side door on to the verandah.

The groans were more distinct now. Maitland fancied that he heard a few words in English, even his own name being called.

'The Senhor must go back inside the house,' Caterpillar announced, interposing his bulk on the path that led to the snake house.

'Somebody's been hurt,' Maitland protested. 'We must go and see.'

Caterpillar drew a knife. The moonlight danced along the blade. He signalled for Harry to go back inside.

Instead, Harry struck out with his right foot. He had calculated the distance nicely. The toe of his patent leather shoe clipped the servant's humerus. He squealed, and the knife tumbled from his hand; his lower arm flopped down uselessly, as if the limb had snapped at the elbow. But he looked as if he might still have some fight in him, so Harry delivered another kick to his groin that laid him out on his back.

'You there! What are you doing?' a new voice challenged him. Harry saw a young officer in a red cap advancing between the trees and kicked the knife away into a pool of shadow under the shrubbery.

'This man is a thief,' Maitland announced to the policeman. 'He's been stealing from the guests. Find Senhora Mackenzie and ask her to make the identification.'

His tone was sufficiently haughty and his tailoring so faultless that the young police officer swallowed any objections. He left the semiconscious Caterpillar in charge of one of his men and set off in search of Stella. Harry calculated that her condition might divert the policeman for a good few minutes more.

The groans had stopped. Harry rushed to the reptile house and found it padlocked. He pressed his ear to the door. He could hear a faint, rasping sound from within. It might have been somebody's hoarse breathing. He crept around the corner of the pavilion and peered in through a small window, streaked with dirt. Not enough light filtered through for him to make out anything very clearly. He could identify some of the glass cages, a cactus plant or two, a hairy thing on the floor just below him that must be one of the rodents or small animals the Doctor fed to his pets. A careless keeper must have let it out by mistake.

Then Harry realised that what he was staring at was not an animal. It was Desmond Wild's astonishing mail-order toupee.

He tapped on the window pane. 'Desmond?'

He was rewarded with another groan, fainter than before.

He went back to the door and examined the padlock more closely. It was stout but badly rusted. With his penknife he soon managed to prise it open.

He found Desmond Wild lying on his belly, sweating hard, with a nasty blue pallor about his face.

'Harry – thank God –'

'What happened?' Harry managed to roll him over and got his back propped up against a planter.

'Bloody snakes –'

Maitland could see the bite marks now, at least two sets of them, on the left hand, and another at the side of the neck. He slashed at the neck wounds with his pocket knife and tried to suck out the poison, spitting blood over the concrete floor.

'Too late –' Wild moaned. 'Got to stop them –'

Was he talking about the pit vipers? Between his ministrations, Harry glanced carefully around the darkened pavilion. He saw no sign of a snake on the loose.

He repeated his exercise on Wild's hand, wondering how long it took a double dose of the jararaca's venom to finish a man. There was only one hope: that Doctor Alcibiades had an antidote ready to hand. He must find the mayor at once. Desmond Wild was already delirious.

'Fluminense,' he was raving, as if he were barracking at a football game. 'Fluminense.'

'Hang on, old man. I'll be back in a couple of minutes.'

Maitland hastened back inside the villa. As he headed towards the library, he thought he could guess at least part of what must have happened. Wild had stuck his nose into something, and Alcibiades – or one of his guests – had gone to desperate lengths to silence him. He knew that by going directly to the mayor, he risked exposing himself to similar treatment. But Wild's life was at stake.

'Ah, there you are, Maitland! Where in damnation do you think you're off to? I've got a bone to pick with you!'

It was Major Mackenzie, lurching along the hallway. He seemed in only a marginally steadier condition than Stella. For once Harry was delighted to see him. It would be no bad thing to have a witness. There was surely a limit to the number of guests who could vanish at the mayor's party.

'How are you, Major? Why don't we both go and pay our respects to our host?'

'That's all very well, but about my buses –'

'I think he's in the library.'

Harry took the major's arm and escorted him, protesting, up the corridor to the library door, which was now closed.

Without hesitating Maitland turned the knob. As he swung the door open, he sensed that the whole scene inside had been frozen. An extraordinary group was assembled within those panelled walls, and every member of it was staring at the intruders. There was Doctor Alcibiades, of course, his back to the bay window; Admiral Cavalcanti and two men from the General Staff; Captain Schmidt and the German attaché; and Courtland Bull, who was stretched out on a studded leather chesterfield, holding up a cigar between finger and thumb as if he had been using it to emphasise a point.

Doctor Alcibiades was addressing the group in an over-dramatic voice, and Harry had no doubt that he had embarked on this soliloquy for the benefit of the new arrivals.

'The name of the disease derives from a Latin poem of the sixteenth century,' the mayor was saying. 'A poet–

physician called Fracastorius invented a shepherd called Syphilis who was cursed with the pox because – so we are told – he raised forbidden altars on the hill. An engaging conceit. Wouldn't you agree, Major Mackenzie?'

'Well, I, er –' The Major took refuge in a mild coughing fit.

'Are you enjoying the party, Harry?'

'Very much so, Doctor. I'm sorry to intrude, but one of your guests needs urgent medical attention. He seems to have been bitten by a snake.'

The men in the library mastered themselves pretty well, assuming they had something to hide. Their faces expressed the appropriate blend of curiosity and concern. But Harry noticed that the mayor exchanged a quick glance with Admiral Cavalcanti before saying, 'I'll come at once.'

As they left the library, Harry saw Cavalcanti pick up the telephone.

Major Mackenzie was flustered. 'What's this about snakes?' he demanded. 'And what is my wife doing with that policeman?'

There, indeed, was Stella, hanging on the shoulder of a Special Police lieutenant.

'It's some frightful mix-up,' she yawned. 'I think it's to do with the buses.'

They all trooped along behind Harry and the mayor, who stopped to unlock a small room that smelled like a laboratory and removed a vial from a glass case.

If this was an antidote, it came too late to help Desmond Wild. Doctor Alcibiades felt the journalist's pulse, rolled back his eyelids and pronounced him dead.

He then made a great show of searching for a viper, presumably escaped from one of the containers.

'I can't think what your friend was doing messing about in here,' he remarked to Harry. 'These reporters like to pry into everything.'

Maitland picked up Wild's hairpiece and arranged it on top of his skull. It looked slightly more realistic now that the poor fellow was dead.

'I'm afraid we shall all have to wait for the coroner,' the

mayor informed them. This was obviously absurd, with the police already on the scene of what appeared – at least to the Mackenzies – to be a tragic accident. Doctor Alcibiades was trying to detain them for his own purposes. The major started to protest.

'I'll just go and call Desmond's wife,' Harry announced in the midst of Mackenzie's outburst.

'I didn't know Wild was married,' Alcibiades said warily.

'Oh, he never showed her in public much.' Harry raised an imaginary glass to his lips. As he hurried back to the villa, he saw an officer in white dress uniform – Cavalcanti – striding off towards the stables and the private parking area. Harry avoided the library and returned to the main salon, which was fast emptying. He used the phone in the front lobby to call Colonel Plinio, who answered at the second ring.

'I'm glad I caught you.'

'Harry? I can't talk to you now.'

'What's happened?'

'The shooting has started. It seems the Reds at Praia Vermelha can't tell the time.'

'Well, it's started here, too. One man is dead. The admiral left in a hell of a hurry.'

'I don't understand.'

'There's no time for that now.' He could see Doctor Alcibiades watching him. Fortunately, the mayor had been detained by some of his other guests. 'What does Fluminense mean to you?'

'It's a football club.'

'Yes, but is there some other significance?'

'Well, some Cariocas think it's a religion, like Manchester United fans. It's an odd time to be talking about it, Harry.'

Fluminense. It had been Desmond Wild's last word. And according to Johnny, it was the logo on the jersey that Boy Scout had been wearing when he came to collect his submachine gun. Was there a link?

'Where is the Fluminense Club?'

'Harry –'

'This could be important.'

'All right. Surely you've seen it. The club is just behind the Guanabara Palace.'

'That must be it!' Maitland exclaimed.

'I simply don't have time for this.'

'Meet me there as fast as you can. If you can't make it, send me some of your best men and tell them to look out for me.'

He hung up and was out the door before the mayor caught up with him. He tried to slow his step as he weaved through the crowd of leave-takers among the fountains. He heard a voice calling his name but ignored it. There was safety in the crowd. Surely Alcibiades would not risk ordering the guards to stop him in front of so many people who knew him.

He got out into the street and ran east, towards his car. Nobody tried to stop him. He jumped behind the wheel, and the Beast roared away in the direction of the presidential palace. He took the avenue along the embankment and saw a company bus hurtle past, heading for Praia Vermelha.

They were going to kill the president. He was sure of it now. It had also dawned on him that Prestes' crowd were not the only people who were plotting a coup. There were at least two conspiracies, not one; Doctor Alcibiades was the hinge between them.

There were troops out in force in front of the little barracks across the street from the German Embassy. As Harry cruised up the Rua Farani towards the palace, he saw an official car coming through the gates. The marine guards saluted; one of them stepped out into the road and waved for Harry to stop and let the limousine pass. He recognised the War Minister in the back. The government was starting to take things in hand.

He slipped the Beast into gear. Glancing into the rearview mirror, he saw an American car behind him. The driver turned in at the gate. One of the marines came up to question him. The guard looked in the back of the car and saluted smartly. Harry could see the white dress uniform, the soft, blurred features that lay too much to one side, as if a sculptor moulding the head from clay had tired of his work and pushed it away with the flat of his hand. It was Admiral Cavalcanti, and the marines were letting him through.

There's nothing I can do about it, Harry told himself. If he tried to explain his suspicions, even Colonel Plinio would think him insane.

He drove to the end of the street, rounded the corner and pulled up near the members' entrance to the Fluminense Club. The sidewalk was deserted. The door to the club was locked, the windows shuttered and barred. His pen knife would not work this time. There was no sign of life inside the main building. He walked up the street, inspecting the high fence. It might be possible to shimmy over and get into the grounds.

I'm probably making a complete fool of myself, he thought.

He made a tentative jump at the fence, got a hand on the ledge, but was nicked by something sharp – probably broken glass – and let himself fall back.

At the same instant a truck came screeching around the corner. The driver swung up onto the pavement, so that Harry had to flatten himself against the wall to avoid getting hit. Half a dozen men in civilian clothes tumbled out of the back. Harry looked at the odds and decided to leave his gun in his pocket. It was better to try to bluff his way out. But if this was Boy Scout's mob, that would not be easy.

A black sedan double-parked next to the Beast.

To his relief, Harry saw Colonel Plinio get out.

'I'll handle this one,' he shouted to the men who were menacing Maitland with their pistols.

'Breaking and entering, Harry?'

'I wasn't sure you'd come.'

'O ye of little faith. Allow me to introduce Doctor Mota, the manager of the club.'

Harry shook hands with a tall, saturnine man with slicked-down hair. The club manager did not look amused at being rousted out at two in the morning.

'I told Doctor Mota that you had information about a break-in,' Plinio said.

As the manager fumbled with a bunch of keys, the colonel asked in a whisper, 'What's all this about a dead man?'

Harry explained what had happened to Desmond Wild. 'And Cavalcanti went straight from the mayor's house to the palace,' he added. 'I saw him go inside.'

'What of it? A patriotic officer, guarding his president from a Red revolt? The admiral's trying to make his come-back, that's all. I hope you're not wasting our time.'

Doctor Mota had managed to open the door. He led them into the trophy room, where he satisfied himself that nothing was missing.

'I can't think what else anyone would want to steal.'

'If we wanted to get into the palace from here, how would we do it?' Harry asked.

'There's a door on the basement level,' the manager reported. 'But it's locked and bolted from the other side. The president's secretary has the key.'

'Will you show us where it is?'

Their heels clattered on the stone steps. There was a strong odour of chlorine and wet towels, but no indication that anyone had been down there since nightfall. The manager kept switching on lights.

The door to the palace gardens certainly looked like a formidable obstacle. It was lined with sheet steel. Harry noticed a faint smell of oil, as if the hinges had been lubricated not long before.

He tried the handle. The heavy door swung open silently, and they looked out across sculpted gardens towards the pillared façade of Guanabara Palace.

'It's unthinkable!' Doctor Mota exclaimed. 'And where are the guards?'

'I think I see one of them,' Harry remarked. He pointed to a pair of boots jutting out from under a clump of bushes.

The colonel's men pulled the body out into the moon-light. The marine had been stripped to his underwear.

'He's been garroted,' Maitland announced, inspecting

the thin red line around the neck. 'Piano wire, I should think.'

Colonel Plinio turned to one of his men. 'Euclides, go back into the club and telephone the president's secretary. Tell him we're coming in.'

'What if they're already holding the palace?' Maitland interrupted. 'Remember, at least one of the attackers is wearing marine uniform.'

Plinio thought about this for an instant and said, 'You're right. We'll have to chance it.' He detailed Euclides to call for reinforcements and to check the state of affairs at the guardhouse at the street entrance to the palace.

'You'd better clear out,' he said to Maitland. 'This business isn't for foreigners.'

'Not on your life. Who brought you here in the first place?'

Colonel Plinio's retort was swallowed up by a sudden burst of fire from the palace.

'Stay behind me,' he instructed Harry. Then they were all running along flagstoned paths, splitting into two groups at the foot of the terrace, where two broad flights of steps led up to the top.

A bullet whined past Harry's ear, and he looked up and saw a pretty, dark-haired girl taking aim at him from an upstairs window.

'*Comunistas miseráveis!*' she screamed above the shooting. "Communist bastards!'

Harry recognised the president's younger daughter. 'Don't shoot!' he called up.

The First Family appeared to have barricaded itself on the second floor. A gun battle was raging around the main staircase. It was hard to tell friend from foe in the thick pall of smoke; some of the drapes had caught fire. Men in marine uniforms and a few in civilian clothes were trying to storm the stairs. They were being held off by a smaller group on the landing, in the same medley of attire. Neither the attackers nor the defenders seemed sure whose side Plinio's men were on, and the policemen were equally confused.

There was a pause in the shooting while everyone tried to assess the new odds.

'Look at that one!' Maitland pointed to one of the marines crouched in the stairwell. 'He's wearing street shoes!'

'Give yourselves up!' Plinio ordered the attackers, using his best baritone. 'Your cause is lost!'

This was received with a volley of fire that failed to drop a single policeman. The colonel's men took cover behind the furniture and blazed away as if they were in competition to see who could exhaust his ammunition first.

'Where's the rest of the guard?' Plinio muttered.

'You might also ask, where is Cavalcanti?' Harry responded.

Caught in a crossfire, the attackers soon lost their fight. Several made a run for the doors, were wounded or intercepted and gave themselves up. There was a young one, a better shot than the rest, who seemed bent on holding out. He had crawled away to reasonable cover behind the bannisters and winged two of Plinio's men. But soon he was the only one left fighting. There was a door behind him, now riddled with bullet holes. He had not yet tried to use it for escape.

'I'll bet that's Escoteiro,' Harry whispered to Plinio. 'Let's try to take him alive. If you cover me, I'll try to get around behind him.'

Crouched low, Harry made a zigzag dash for the corridor behind the staircase. He found a terrified maidservant who showed him how to get into the drawing room on the far side of the staircase.

He saw that the drawing room door opened inwards. He turned the handle and was gingerly pulling it towards him when several bullets splintered the wood. One of them cut a neat slit in the sleeve of his dinner jacket. He threw himself to the floor.

At the same instant the door flew towards him, just missing his head, and a solid weight dropped on his shoulders. The reek of blood and urine filled his nostrils. He rolled onto his back and found himself clutching Boy Scout's head to his chest. The boy terrorist stared at him out of one glassy eye. The other had been blown away. Harry's hands were sticky with blood and grey matter and ooze that he did not care to analyse. He started to wriggle free of the body, trying not to throw up.

Then, through the smoke, he saw something that made him forget the state of his stomach. The lobby was full of white uniforms, and at their head Admiral Cavalcanti was levelling his revolver at Harry. He held the gun like a duelist, his right arm outstretched, his left folded away in the crook of his back.

Harry rolled again, but his foot snagged in the belt of Boy Scout's stolen uniform. Cavalcanti's finger tightened on the trigger.

His attention riveted on Maitland, the admiral did not see Colonel Plinio until he struck. Very precisely, Plinio cracked the butt of his own gun against the admiral's wrist.

The bullet went wide, and Cavalcanti dropped his revolver, cursing violently.

'I'm sorry, Admiral,' Plinio said blandly. 'But you nearly made an irreparable mistake. This is one of our friends.'

Maitland got to his feet and met Cavalcanti's eyes. They were pink with hate. He wondered if the admiral had really made a mistake.

'Did you kill this one?' Harry challenged him, tapping Boy Scout's body lightly with the toe of his shoe.

'What of it?'

'Was it necessary?'

'He was Communist scum. Who cares how they lose their skins?'

Colonel Plinio took out his cigar case and offered it to Harry and Cavalcanti. The admiral shook his head impatiently.

'You might dismiss your men now,' Plinio remarked to him. 'The police have everything under control. By the way, where were your marines when the president was under attack?'

'The Reds staged a diversion at the front of the palace.'

'That's very interesting. We obviously missed quite a lot.'

Colonel Plinio noticed the president's secretary trotting down the stairs and excused himself.

He returned almost immediately with a beatific smile on his face.

'I regret to inform you, Admiral, that it is my duty to place you under arrest.'

'I am answerable only to the military authorities!'

'And to the President of the Republic.'

'What is the charge?'

'Treason and attempted assassination.'

'This is a farce! You have no evidence!'

'On the contrary. The president has just received a personal telephone call from Doctor Alcibiades, our honourable mayor. I believe you know him. Doctor Alcibiades made the denunciation.'

Cavalcanti gaped, then exhibited a mastery of nautical abuse that awed everyone within earshot.

'Are you ready, Admiral?' Plinio pursued. 'Or would you prefer to be left alone with your revolver? I believe that way is preferred by officers of the old school in some countries. No?'

Cavalcanti glowered at him, and Plinio motioned for the detectives to disarm him.

'You see,' the colonel murmured to Harry as they made their exit together. 'We're Brazilians. Even the worst of us. We don't kill the bull.'

7

On a damp day in London in early December, Colin Bailey put aside Maitland's report and pictured the man who had written it. He imagined Harry, on his verandah in Tijuca, listening to the birdcalls in the forest and puffing at his cigar while the lovely Luisa brought *caipirinhas*. Or perhaps he had gone south to his ranch, to fish for *dourado* with a bright spoon on the end of his line – silver, of course, was best – or to chase roebuck through the pampas grass in a mock-up of a West Country hunt. He had certainly earned a holiday, and Bailey would have liked nothing better than to chuck the London drizzle and join him.

Only two military units in Rio joined the Communist rising in the early hours of November 27. One was the Third Regiment, which never managed to leave Praia Vermelha. The commandant managed to get away from the rebels and held them pinned down for a time with the aid of a loyal machine gun company, while the government sent reinforcements round in the buses of the power company. The War Minister took personal charge, talking to the commandant from a public telephone at a gas station on the corner of the Avenida Pasteur. The rebel chief, a bantam captain they called Macuco, refused an offer of conditional surrender. At first light, the government sent warships and fighter planes to shell and strafe the barracks into submission. The flimsy wood and stucco pavilions caught fire like dry tinder. At about one in the afternoon, the surviving rebels gave up the ghost. They were marched through Botafogo in front of jeering crowds. Macuco and the other ringleaders were locked up in an old prison ship, the *Pedro I* that was resurrected for the occasion.

The other unit that rebelled was the School of Military Aviation out at Campo dos Afonsos, fifteen miles west of the city, next to the headquarters complex in the Vila Militar. This was a cadets' affair led by a Communist instructor. The Air Force regulars at the base next door were alerted in good time. But the school was hard to isolate, because the security gate was unfinished and there was not even a simple fence around most of the perimeter. Captain Socrates drove in at the wheel of a roadster packed with his friends. Though apparently drunk, he arranged the seizure of arms and training planes, shot a loyalist lieutenant and marched off at the head of his cadets to capture the air base next door. His party was met by government troops, shot up pretty badly and the whole business was over by sunup.

The revolt never got started in the Second Regiment or at Army HQ, because the leads from Johnny enabled the authorities to arrest all the key conspirators before the deadline arrived at their destination. Prestes' couriers to garrisons outside Rio never left.

The population at large was never involved. Confronted with the prospect of imminent rout, Communist labour organisers disregarded their orders to lead a general strike. The special edition of the Red paper, *A Manhã*, calling for a mass rebellion was seized by the police before it could be distributed. There were a few acts of sabotage – the vital switch point at Barra do Pirai on the Rio–São Paulo line was blown up – but they had no effect on the outcome of events.

The defeat of the coup attempt in Rio coincided with the collapse of the risings in the north that had triggered it. The ragtag army that invaded Recife's Largo da Paz was shot to pieces by regular army units with field guns. The most notable achievement of the revolt in Recife was that the celebrated German airship, the *Graf Zeppelin*, en route to the city on a journey that had started in Bathurst, had to alter its flight plan.

Hearing rumours of disaster, the festive junta that had held power in Natal since Saturday night boarded a merchant ship in the harbour and tried to make off with the money it had looted from the local bank. They were pursued and overtaken by two navy cruisers. 'Santa', the Communist chief, was found to have his share of the loot sewn up inside his trouser cuffs. Rebels fleeing inland were hunted down by gunmen hired for the job by the local land barons.

What was the meaning of the whole affair? Bailey had one version in front of him – a torn-out page from the New York *Times* forwarded by a friend in Manhattan. The *Times*' man on the spot, a certain J. W. White (filing from Buenos Aires to avoid Brazilian censorship), gave the Communists a clean bill of health. In his judgment, the revolt was 'not communistic, as reported by the federal authorities. It was socialistic and strongly nationalistic'. The demands of the rebels were said to be 'mild'.

Bailey had read far too much of this sort of thing over the years to let it anger him. He had read it in cables from ambassadors as well as newspaper articles. Sometimes he detected the hand of a Goebbels or a Willi Münzenberg. More often it was a matter of people believing what they wanted to believe and screening out conflicting evidence. This was known to happen in intelligence, as in other trades; hence the difficulty he experienced in persuading some of his colleagues that Hitler was as much of a menace as Stalin, or vice versa. There were relatively few people, in Bailey's experience, who found much satisfaction in unearthing facts that flouted their preconceptions. Yet a willingness to confront facts of that kind – even a delight in so doing – was, in his estimation, one of the hallmarks of an intelligence professional.

So he sat mulling over the questions that Harry's report, though masterly in its way, had left hanging.

One thing was clear: Johnny had played his role superbly. Thanks to his information, a police agent had triggered the mutiny in Natal weeks before the revolt was supposed to begin. A clever bit of provocation by the police chief in Recife had ensured that the second barrel went off, forcing the hand of the Comintern chiefs in Rio. Thanks to Johnny again, the planned coup in Rio was dead in the water hours before it began.

Yet the affair could have ended in tragedy if the assassination plot had succeeded.

There were several things that intrigued Bailey.

Was there a Gestapo agent – perhaps Nilo – inside the South American bureau?

What role, if any, had Max Fabrikant played in the events of November 27?

Had the Fascists mounted a provocation of their own, hoping to use the murder of the president by Reds as a pretext to seize power for themselves?

Whose side was Doctor Alcibiades on?

Bailey had not exhausted the list when C. called him on the direct line.

'Would you care to stop in for a spot of tea?'

Bailey stowed his papers away, shut up the filing cabinet and reversed the little cardboard sign that read 'Open' on one side and 'Locked' on the other.

'Norton at the Foreign Office sent round another billet-doux from their chap in Rio,' C. said casually, when they were settled on either side of the teapot.

'Sir Evelyn Paine?'

'Quite so.'

'Is he bleating again?'

'On the contrary. He seems to be pleased as punch. The president called him in to express his undying gratitude to His Majesty's Government for saving the country, or words to that effect. Sir Evelyn would be glad to be told, at some point, exactly what he did.'

'I'll look into it.'

'I gather your young friend Maitland has done rather well. Bring him over so I can get a look at him next time he's in London.'

'With pleasure.'

'But you might tell him to try not to behave quite so much like something out of John Buchan's thrillers.'

Diplomatically, Bailey allowed this to pass without comment.

'Your chap Johnny doesn't cease to astonish me,' C. went on. 'I thought we might do something for him, to show appreciation and all that.'

'What did you have in mind? A bonus?'

'Good heavens, no. I thought I'd ask the prime minister to get him a gong in the Birthday Honours. Naturally, we couldn't allow any mention of it in the papers. But the gesture would count for rather a lot, don't you think?'

'Johnny had an Iron Cross once,' Bailey observed. 'I believe he chucked it overboard.'

C. looked at him as if he had just broken wind.

'I am referring to the Order of the British Empire,' C. said grimly. 'It would mean something to Johnny if the King presented it in person.'

'Good God! The man's a bloody foreigner!'

'Quite so.' Bailey's expression was respectful but unyielding.

3

The Path of the Dead

(1936)

We Communists are all dead men on leave.
— *Eugène Leviné,*
leader of the 1919 Munich revolt, shortly before
he faced the firing squad

11

The Chinese Method

I was not averse to the idea of shooting a property
owner simply because he was a property owner, so it
was reasonable that the propertied class should punish
me for my intentions.

– Graciliano Ramos,
Memórias do Cárcere

1

The days slipped by, and Rio returned to its normal pur-
suits. Driving along the Avenida Atlântica, it was hard to
believe that the country had just escaped a revolution. Even
the principal conspirators were not acting like hunted men.
Harry Maitland made a tour of the beach suburbs and
caught a glimpse of Emil and his wife taking their consti-
tutional along the beach. Emil had his jacket over his arm
and had rolled up his sleeves. He wore suspenders and a
grey felt hat tilted back from his forehead. He was an
alien presence, a world removed from the copper-skinned
beauties lazing on the beach. But he did not look like a man
about to jump into a ditch. He might have been taking his
summer holiday at Sochi, on the Black Sea.

Harry was puzzled that Emil and his team had not simply
cut and run after the failure of the revolt. What were they
waiting for?

Johnny brought some of the answers in the early days of

December. They met at one of their old haunts, a crowded gaming room in the Necrôpolis, at the back of the Copacabana Palace Hotel.

He's nervous, Maitland thought, watching Johnny from across the roulette table. He wasn't surprised when Johnny bet on red, signalling that he wanted a personal meeting somewhere else. Maitland placed some chips on number four, one of several locations both men had memorised. Johnny bet on twenty-four, which gave them the hour.

Their rendezvous took place at midnight in a seamen's tavern near the docks.

'Are you all right?'

Johnny was swaying a bit.

'A drink too many,' he said. 'I'll live.'

'Is Max on to you?'

'He has suspicions.'

'Nothing more?'

'That's enough, isn't it?' Johnny came back savagely. 'He'll move when he's ready. Not before.'

'What's going on? Why haven't they tried to get out?'

'They think they're still in business.'

'What?'

'You heard me. They're planning to try again.'

'Who?'

'Emil. Prestes. Nilo.'

'They're crazy.'

'Perhaps. But Emil has persuaded Moscow to back them.'

'I can't believe it.'

'Believe what you like. I brought you a copy of his report.' He handed over a squat manila envelope.

'How did you get it?'

Johnny gave him a lopsided grin. He said, 'I've been in this business for longer than you. No offence, Harry.'

'Of course not.'

Play it long, Colin Bailey urged in his cables. If you jerk on the line, the big fish will break it.

But Harry didn't like it. Johnny refused the stack of

white five-pound notes he offered, the bonus Colin Bailey had finally extracted from C. and the misers in the accounts department. Perhaps Johnny's disinterest was a professional reflex. What was he going to do with the cash in Rio? But Johnny also seemed reticent and evasive. He refused point-blank to talk about Sigrid now, which Maitland thought was a bad sign. Maybe shared adversity was pulling him closer to old comrades.

The Comintern network began to fall apart a few days before Christmas, on the night Vasco's house went up in smoke. Johnny had described the Spanish painter's home in Grajaú, where explosives were hidden in the cellar and under the stairs and the walls were covered with surrealist canvases of melting clocks and women whose bottoms turned into cellos. By Johnny's account, Vasco had to be awarded full marks for guts, if not for brains. Since he'd lost three fingers from his painting hand in that accident on the beach, he had been training himself to hold a brush in the other hand. He even practised gripping a brush between his toes. According to Johnny, his footwork was pretty good.

In the wake of the mass insurrection that never took place, Vasco had been left sitting on top of three hundred homemade bombs and a truckload of dynamite. Harry first learned what had happened from his morning copy of O Globo.

It wasn't clear how it started. A cigarette, carelessly dropped on the floor, sparks from the charcoal stove in the kitchen, a lamp overturned in a domestic squabble, a child playing with matches . . . Johnny's hunch was that canisters holding the two components for a binary explosive, the chemicals he had described to illiterate recruits as 'rat poison' and 'salt and pepper', had been allowed to get damp in the closet under the stairs. The soggy cardboard was eaten away, the chemicals mixed – and the roof of Vasco's house blew off.

The Spaniard rolled out of the place with his clothes on fire and a terrified child in his arms. Distraught neighbours, their own houses ablaze, called the fire brigade and the police, who went in for Vasco's two-year-old daughter. She was charred like a nicely barbecued chop but still living. The neighbours were ready to tear the little Basque limb from limb, though he swore blind that he thought the boxes he was storing contained only fruit and eggs. The police probably saved his life. They hauled him off for a spiritual session on the *morro* of San Antonio, the headquarters of the Special Police.

Vasco knew quite a few of the Comintern bosses, at least by sight, because of all the boozing and talking that had gone on in his upstairs living room. And of course he knew Johnny, though only by the cover name 'Pedro' that he used among the party's military cells.

When Harry learned of Vasco's arrest, he concluded that the time had come to roll up the Comintern team in Rio, and advised Bailey accordingly.

With Vasco and hundreds of local Communists in jug, it was surely only a matter of time before Emil's group accepted defeat and scattered to the four winds. Harry wanted to catch them before they got away. They had a good deal to answer for.

There was still a risk that Johnny could be blown. But in Maitland's view the risk of using the most sensitive information from his agent – the covers and hideouts employed by Emil and his team – was much less than before. If the Russians wanted to find an informer, there would be a long list of suspects to choose from, starting with the little Spaniard. Max Fabrikant would not be easy to shake off. But with any luck Max would soon be enjoying the hospitality of one of Colonel Plinio's lockups.

Bailey agreed with this assessment. His cheerful response came back by cable: 'Shop the buggers!'

2

Betrayal is easier for little men, Harry thought. Easiest for those, like Iago, who were so stunted in spirit that they could consume their lives in the service of the 'green-eyed monster', jealousy, or in pursuit of trivial advancement. Johnny was built to larger proportions.

In the months he had known the German, even though most of their meetings were hurried and furtive, Harry had found much to admire and even more to identify with: the restless appetite for adventure, the readiness to gamble against the odds. He had never known Johnny to be meanspirited, even in discussing the men he had most reason to hate.

So Maitland was not altogether surprised when Johnny balked at the final stage of betrayal. The Englishman had anticipated a long conversation and a deal of soul-searching, so he had prepared his ground carefully. He had rented a flat in Flamengo with a view of the bay and filled one of the kitchen cupboards with single-malt scotch.

'The place is yours whenever you need it,' he told Johnny.

Maitland cooked dinner himself. It was spaghetti bolognaise, one of the few dishes he was confident about preparing. He was not offended when Johnny showed more interest in the whisky than the food.

'Colin and I both feel that it's time to roll things up,' Harry said tentatively. Johnny listened while he rehearsed his reasons.

Then he astonished the Englishman by quoting one of Iago's lines from *Othello*: 'I follow him to serve my turn upon him.'

He laughed at Harry's expression. 'You see, my visits to the Richmond Theatre weren't entirely wasted.'

Johnny's smile faded. He had heard grim stories about what the police were doing to the Communists who had been rounded up. The Brazilians might eschew capital punishment, but they were quite inventive when it came to torture. It was one thing to betray the plan for the revolution; it was quite another to deliver up comrades to the certainty of physical abuse. In many ways it would be easier for him to shoot Emil or Max himself – he had thought of doing so, more than once – than to turn them over to the police.

He said to Harry, 'Who do you want?

537

'All of them. The whole South American bureau.'

'Prestes, too?'

'Prestes most of all.'

No, Johnny thought. I won't give them Prestes. The man is washed up, whether he knows it or not – a sleepwalker stumbling about in a violent dream. Let him run back to Moscow, if Stalin still wants him.

Johnny said, 'I don't know where he lives.'

Maitland was fairly sure he was lying but resolved not to push the issue. In part of his being, Harry realised, Johnny still belonged to the revolutionary cause. There were people and things he would never betray.

Emil was not one of them. In Johnny's eyes, Emil had blood on his hands – the blood of Heinz Kordt and of thousands of young Chinese herded to the slaughter. If Johnny had had second thoughts, they would have been academic; he had already given Maitland the address of Emil's luxury apartment in Ipanema.

Nilo also deserved whatever was coming to him, Johnny thought. Miranda was one of those – Johnny now knew – who had helped talk Manuilsky and the Comintern into believing that Brazil was ripe for revolt. Johnny would lose no sleep over him. Verdi, the *simpático*, eloquent Argentinian, had proved more clear-sighted than the others, which possibly made him more dangerous.

Johnny was drinking too much whisky and knew it. But he didn't slow his intake. He didn't like playing God with people who had shared the same trenches.

One more name was unavoidable.

Harry mentioned it first. 'What about Max?'

'I don't know where to find him,' Johnny responded. This time his answer was truthful. He had not seen Max since before the brief, premature spasms of the risings in the north. From what Sigrid had let drop he was convinced that Max was still in Rio, but had no idea where he had gone to ground.

'We have to deal with Max,' Harry observed.

'You mean, before he deals with *us*,' Johnny completed the thought for him.

'Exactly.'

'Did you have anything particular in mind?'

'Sigrid.' Harry watched him as closely as a surgeon making an incision. He knew he was cutting into the most sensitive part of Johnny's life, the part he had always refused to expose.

Johnny shied away angrily. 'I won't have her involved,' he said flatly.

'She's our only way to Max.' Since Johnny did not contradict him, he risked the next sentence. 'And this is the only way you can get her away from Max.'

'What do you want to do?' Johnny's words came slowly and painfully.

'Put a tail on her.'

'No!' Johnny shouted. 'You can't expose her to the police! If it has to be done, I'll do it myself.'

'Please think it over, Johnny. She's bound to spot you. She's a professional. She's been trained by the best. A man your size and colour can't just blend into the Carioca street scene. Brazilians might have a chance.'

'No,' Johnny repeated, shaking his head.

'It doesn't have to be the police,' Harry said patiently. 'I'll organise everything myself. I can hire a few smart kids. I'll make out I'm a jealous husband. They don't have to know anything more than that.'

Johnny thought this over for a bit, pacing round the room. He reminded Maitland of a large animal circling its cage.

Suddenly, Johnny rounded on him.

'You could do it anyway,' he said. 'You could set watchers on me and follow Sigrid when she leaves me.'

'I could,' Harry agreed, 'but I won't. Not unless you give your consent. You matter a damn sight more to me than Max Fabrikant.'

This must have been a turning point, because the next time Johnny spoke, he said 'I'll help you. But you must promise me you'll get her away safely.'

'You have my word.'

This will be the end of it, Johnny pledged himself, and

Sigrid. We'll leave together, and that will be the end of betrayals.

But the figure of a player on a Richmond stage loomed up out of memory, mocking him. He heard the actor's lines as clearly as if he were squeezed into those cramped front stalls instead of standing at the window before the shadowed, sensuous curve of the Sugarloaf:

> So I will turn her virtue into pitch
> And out of her own goodness make the net
> That shall enmesh them all.

3

The police took Emil and his wife in the flat in Ipanema. Emil watched with a bemused smile as they tinkered with the safe. When they attacked the steel door with a blowtorch, he squeezed Lenka's hand. He had watched Johnny booby-trap the safe with enough explosives to blow all of them into the sea. There were worse ways to die, he thought.

His smile faded when they opened a hole in the steel shell and there was still no explosion. There were more than a thousand documents inside, plus his address book and receipts for payments to agents in Brazil.

'Johnny,' he murmured under his breath.

'What's that?' one of the policemen rounded on him.

'Nothing.'

I'll give them nothing, Emil promised himself. Not even that. If I start talking, it will never end.

He tried to take Lenka's hand again, but they tore her away.

In the police barracks, when the questioning began, he puffed out his chest and said, 'I could tell you these things, but I won't. You can do what you like. I have been tortured by the police before. Even in China.'

The one behind the table with a face like a skull gave a thin smile of recognition.

'We are an underdeveloped country,' he said. 'But not in this.'

They took Miranda and his girl. They caught Verdi. They got the Romanian. The surviving conspirators roamed the city like vagabonds, from one transient address to the next.

The police released Miranda's mistress, Elza, after only a few days in captivity. She was a pretty, illiterate country girl, little more than a child. Nilo, who had managed to elude the police dragnet, was convinced that she had been blackmailed into working as a police spy. She seemed to be allowed extraordinary access to her man inside the House of Detention; this weighed against her more heavily than anything else. Nilo claimed she was passing on whatever she gleaned about the Communist underground to the Department of Political and Social Order.

The girl was lured to a safe house rented by Nilo and interrogated for several hours. Max was the chief inquisitor, but he remained offstage. Sigrid drove back and forth between his hideout and Nilo's flat with lists of questions and rough transcripts of what the girl had said.

In the early hours of the morning Max pronounced the death sentence.

There were five men present in Nilo's apartment when it was carried out. Nilo wanted to garrote her; he maintained that this was the quietest way and would sow terror among other potential police spies. They found a length of clothesline in the laundry and looped it around Elza's neck. But they were rank amateurs at the business of killing. The first man who tried to choke off the girl's life lost his nerve. Nilo poured strong liquor for all of them and told another to try again, while Elza lay gasping, blue-faced, on the floor. The second executioner was so terrified he lost control of his bowels. It was quite a long evening before they were ready to bury the body, rolled up in a rug, in a garbage dump up in the hills.

Johnny was not invited to this entertainment.

He heard about it from Sigrid. She was oddly detached.

as if she were describing a scene from a film, as if the murdered girl existed only on celluloid.

'Was it really necessary?' he asked.

'She knew the punishment.' She frightened him when she added, 'I would have done the same.'

You can't mean that, he pleaded with her silently. This is the madness that Max has induced. At the same moment he was trying to push away the sense of guilt that twisted his stomach. He had given the police Miranda – and the Communists had claimed Miranda's girl, who meant the world no harm.

Later Sigrid responded naturally, even ardently, to his caresses. But he found that his sexual desire was less potent than the image of the terrified girl with the rope sawing at her neck.

When Sigrid left him in the early morning, Harry Maitland's men were watching.

Left alone in the apartment, Johnny felt chilled to the marrow, despite the muggy heat. He threw his head back against the pillows, because everything in the room was churning. He was trying to stay afloat in an empty, hostile sea.

It wasn't easy to follow a car in Rio without being spotted. Private automobiles were still a rarity; even the wealthiest Cariocas patronised the streetcars (first-class, to be sure) or took a taxi. Harry Maitland had allowed for this. He had engaged four trackers: one on a bicycle, posted at the corner nearest Johnny's flat, two in taxis, one in a Ford. It would have been easier and certainly less costly to turn the whole affair over to Colonel Plinio. But Harry did not want to break faith with Johnny. He had to be the one person in Rio Johnny could trust unconditionally.

In any event, Harry's painstaking preparations paid off: by the end of the morning his trackers had identified three separate addresses that were new to Maitland. By the end of the day he was reasonably certain that one of them, on the Rua Guerreiro, was Max's bolthole.

At this point keeping faith with Johnny involved one

further complication. Johnny had insisted that, when the police closed in on Max, Sigrid must be with *him*, safely removed from the scene.

Harry intended to keep that promise, too.

Almost a week later, Johnny lay on the sofa of the apartment in Flamengo that Harry had rented for him, listening to the rain. It fell in sheets, blocking off his view of the bay. It had even silenced the drums rehearsing for Carnival. A sour taste of tar bubbled up from his pipe, and he tossed it aside.

She must come soon, he told himself. It's been nearly three hours.

He had managed to persuade Sigrid to come for a drive up into the hills, out of the sweltering city.

The sudden, torrential rain had turned their side road into a mudslide, and they had had to reverse back down. He had clutched at one excuse after another to prolong their outing. He had found a little restaurant whose outside walls were adorned with murals depicting its specialties – turkey, suckling pig, rabbit – and ordered two bottles of wine to give himself an excuse to dawdle at the table. She'd become impatient, driving too fast for the wet road, so that they'd skidded on the way back to the city and dented the right fender on a slow-moving oxcart, whose owner had to be pacified with enough *milreis* to pay for a new bullock.

When they parted, he prayed that the thing was over: that the police had come and gone from the house on the Rua Guerreiro, that Max had been exorcised from their lives for good. That she was coming back to him. He had told her to meet him at the new address in Flamengo. Harry was the only other person in Rio who knew it. Max's people couldn't touch them here.

He heard the scratch at the door, like a cat asking to come in, and rushed to open it.

She was holding a little umbrella but was soaked to the skin. Her eyes were wild, her breathing shallow and too fast. She looked on the edge of tears.

'What's happened?' His alarm was unfeigned.

'The police – oh, God. I think they took Max.'

'You saw them?'

'They were in the street, outside the house.'

'You came straight here?'

'Of course not. I went to Danton.' This was a code name for the new radio man, whom Johnny had never met.

'And?'

'The same story.'

He fussed over her, fetching towels from the bathroom, pouring stiff drinks, trying not to show the tremendous sense of relief that suddenly possessed him.

It's over, he thought. Within twenty-four hours, two days at most, they would both be on a boat bound for Buenos Aires. They might run into Helene; Johnny had learned that, after Max had sent her south, she had stayed on in Buenos Aires to run the Comintern liaison office there. But there was no reason for Helene to suspect anything. She would know by now that the whole operation in Rio had ended as a rout. He and Sigrid would be accepted as two of the survivors.

After Argentina, Europe. He would take Sigrid to England. He would have to tell more lies to begin with, but later she would understand. She had to.

He felt her forehead. She was running a fever. But already she was on her feet, picking up her bag and umbrella.

'I can't stay,' she said. 'I have to go back, to make sure —'

'You're not leaving,' he said firmly. 'I'll go. I want you to lie down.'

'Johnny?'

'Yes?'

'What will they do to Max?'

'He'll get by. He's a professional. Eventually Moscow will arrange a trade.' He said whatever came into his head. But he realised as he spoke that it was all too glib. His rosy sense of relief had ebbed away, giving place to more complicated less complacent emotions. In part of himself he was sorry for Max, sorry for what the interrogators would do to him, sorry that Max had survived more formidable opponents to end up in a Brazilian cell. But fear was the larger emotion: fear that Sigrid would never be free of Max's mystique, fear that he would always have to lie to her.

He watched her staring around at the unfamiliar surroundings, the low-slung leather chairs, the coloured prints of sailing ships on the walls.

'How long have you had this place?' she asked.

'Not long.' He didn't like the tilt of her question. 'Listen,' he said, 'I want you to take a nice hot bath and go to bed. I'll go and check on Max.' He remembered, just in time, to ask, 'What's the address?'

No amount of bad weather could stop Carnival. The Avenida Rio Branco was afire with plumes and satins and sequins. Even inside the penitentiaries, they took up the chorus of *Cidade Maravilhosa* and *Pierrot Apaixonado*.

Max Fabrikant was hundreds of miles removed from this scene, comfortably ensconced in a suite at the Crillón in Buenos Aires, a fitting address for a Belgian businessman of evident means. He had explained to a sympathetic clerk that his luggage was being sent on after him. He could pick up the basic necessities at the elegant emporiums along the Calle Florida, behind the hotel.

He had eluded the police trap that Harry Maitland and Colonel Plinio had laid for him in Rio by purest chance – luck, if you were a gambler at heart. Max had taken his morning stroll later than usual and had paused to read the newspapers over a *cafezinho* at a restaurant around the corner from his apartment on the Rua Guerreiro. Even a novice would have found it difficult not to notice the four men who got out of the unmarked car that pulled up directly opposite his building.

Max indulged in a second coffee, sipped it slowly and read the editorials before he resumed his stroll. He observed that plainclothes detectives were covering both the front and back of his building.

He walked on in the most leisurely way in the world but his mind clamped down like a steel trap.

Johnny, he told himself. It had to be Johnny.

He had changed his lodgings after Emil was arrested.

Only Sigrid knew where to find him. He was certain that she hadn't consciously betrayed him. That same morning, shortly before he had left his apartment, she had telephoned to report that Johnny had a new address – something Max was quite sure no one in the party had authorised. At the time he had accepted the information merely as proof that Johnny's survival instinct had not atrophied. Now it enlarged all the other question marks over Johnny's activities in Rio. What had Johnny been doing in the cemetery in Botafogo after dark? Why hadn't Emil's safe blown up?

I abandoned my duty, Max reproached himself. I sheltered Johnny because I became an emotional fool, because I imagined I saw something in him I once had, because he is worth – even now – a thousand snivelling Emils. He betrayed the revolution, and I smelled it. But I still refused to interrogate him – I even avoided seeing him – because he was the one person in my life I needed to believe was above suspicion.

I'm going to make all of that right, Max promised himself.

Max left Rio the same day on a steamer registered in Panama and bound for Buenos Aires. The police were all over the docks, but he met the captain of the boat in a waterfront tavern and bribed him to have his passenger smuggled on board inside a packing crate. Deliberately, Max did not entrust his fortunes to any of the Communist cells that survived around the docks. In the age of Stalin and Hitler, he had learned, faith was uncertain; the venal side of man was one thing you could count on.

Now Max's room at the Crillón was quiet except for the scratch of his pen against the writing paper. He waited for the ink to dry, then folded the letter and tucked it inside a plain envelope.

He straightened his tie, put on his hat and took the elevator down to the marbled lobby.

The uniformed doorman ushered him out.

'Would you like a taxi, sir?'

'No. I think I'll walk.'

'Perfect day for it, sir.'

The girls along the Calle Florida wore light summer dresses and exuberant hats. He picked out one of the boys who were ogling them and beckoned with his finger.

'*Señor?*'

'Would you like to earn some money?'

'*Si, señor.*'

'I want you to deliver this for me, as quick as you can.' He held out the envelope and an Argentinian banknote with an impressive number of zeroes.

The boy goggled at it.

'All right?'

'*Macanudo, señor!*' the boy exclaimed happily. He raced off after only the briefest glance at the inscription on the envelope. It was addressed to the military attaché at the German Embassy.

'I'm getting you out tonight,' Maitland told Johnny on the last day of Carnival. Colonel Plinio had told him of Max's escape. Colin Bailey agreed that it had become too dangerous for Johnny to stay on in Rio.

'Sigrid comes, too,' Johnny said.

'Naturally.' Maitland cleared his throat. 'Does she know – anything?'

'I haven't told her.'

'Will you – I mean –'

'Maybe. When she's ready.'

Harry wondered then, as he had wondered often during the time they had spent together in Brazil, at the hidden reserves that kept this man going, that enabled him to withstand the appalling loneliness of his double life.

He gave Johnny the address.

'You must be there no later than six in the morning. I'll see you on board myself. How will you introduce me?'

'I'll think of something. She knows I have my own contacts. She won't ask too many questions. After all, she's a professional.'

Johnny told Sigrid to meet him at the Babylônia Club. It was a place where a single woman wouldn't raise eyebrows.

He had gone there with Hossbach. The fact that the place had a sizable German clientele was an asset rather than a liability, in Johnny's estimation. It wasn't the sort of place where the police would expect to find Communists on the run.

He had told Sigrid nothing about the boat, nothing about the escape plan. He preferred to face whatever questions she might raise at the last minute. Besides, he knew she had been to see Olga. He couldn't risk letting anything slip.

In the early evening – the eve of Ash Wednesday – Johnny fought his way through laughing crowds to the safe house in Flamengo. He wanted to pick up a few of his belongings and destroy any papers he would no longer need.

He made a bonfire in a metal wastepaper basket. It gave out more smoke than he had expected. As he struggled with the broken sash of the window above the sofa, he saw them in the street below, their red caps bobbing as they piled out of their truck. Special Police.

They might have been coming for one of his neighbours, but instinct told him they had come for him.

I must have been followed, he thought. Only two people knew that address: Sigrid and Harry Maitland. Whatever Sigrid might suspect, she would never tip off the police.

But she might have told Olga, Johnny realised. Or Max. Could she have told Max? Johnny thought back to the morning they had stopped at a rustic café on the winding road to Petrópolis, the morning Max was supposed to be arrested. Sigrid went to the rest room and was gone for what seemed like a very long time . . .

This is madness, he told himself. The police weren't coming for him. They were going to somebody else's apartment.

But he could hear the clatter of their boots on the concrete steps. He peered down the fire escape. They were coming up that way, too. They must have his building surrounded.

A terrible, debilitating lassitude crept over him.

Let them come. Let it end.

He trained his thoughts on the girl he loved, waiting for

him alone and scared among the dubious clientele of the Babylônia, and his energy began to seep back.

There was still a way out. He had tested it before. He had never liked to live in a place that had only one back door. He flung himself out the back window, onto the little platform at the top of the fire escape, and was greeted with a volley of rifle shots that ricocheted off the wall.

He clutched at the pipe running up to the roof and started to haul himself up, hand over hand.

Then he was running stooped across the rooftops, trying to keep his balance as he weaved to avoid the shots from below. There was a sudden, searing pain across his leg. He gasped and felt himself slithering down the steep angle of the roof. He flailed out with his arms, seeking support. His legs shot out into space. He was gone. No, not quite. He grabbed hold of the gutter. It creaked but held. A bullet drove brick dust into his eyes. Mustering all his strength, he heaved himself back onto the roof, threw himself at a chimney and clung to it. Then he was off again, willing himself not to feel the pain, not to remember that one of his legs was dragging, a dead weight that could no longer support him. The red caps were jumping up and down in the street, trying to follow his passage.

Afterwards it was hard to imagine how he had made it to the end of the row of houses, down another fire escape and through the swirl of samba dancers into the side door of the church before they caught up with him.

Inside the church there was the smell of incense, the sweet melodious chime of organ music. Lighted candles spluttered in a brass stand at the back. Johnny took a spill from the box, lit it and placed it beside the others.

He saw a rubicund priest, preceded by shiny altar-boys swinging censers, moving towards the altar to conduct evening Mass. The pews were mostly deserted; the last night of Carnival was no time for Portuguese priests. Johnny slipped past the side altar, with its great gilded image of the Virgin, and found the door to the vestry. The largest cassock in the closet failed to cover his calves, but it would have to do.

The rest of the night had a dream quality tinged with the musky scent of the *lança perfumes* the young swells in their flash convertibles were spraying into the sashaying crowd.

Johnny emerged from the church as a mock priest in his stolen cassock and lurched towards Lapa. As he approached the door of the Babylônia Club, the pink lights of the sign overhead stained his face like grenadine in a milky cocktail.

The dream turned to a nightmare when he entered the club and saw Sigrid sitting with Hossbach and a second German.

His first instinct was that whoever had sent the police for him must have sent the Gestapo for her. But he could not walk away and leave her. He resolved to brazen it out. He calculated that the Germans wouldn't risk a gunfight in public. He would find a way to get Sigrid to safety. When he joined the table, Hossbach's drunken maunderings and the other German's distant curiosity began to persuade him they both had a real chance. Hossbach seemed to suspect nothing. The encounter was purely accidental.

Johnny's first instinct was sounder; there is a limit to coincidence. He learned that as dawn broke on Ash Wednesday, lying flat on his back inside a ring of Special Police, with the muzzle of his own pistol jammed against his teeth, so that the end of Carnival tasted of blood and gunmetal.

4

Sigrid made sure the police had gone before she slipped out of the Babylônia Club. The rain was coming down in buckets, washing out the last night of Carnival. She huddled in the doorway while the doorman ran to the end of the street to fetch her a taxi.

She watched the red fez bobbing back towards her under the huge candy-striped umbrella, minus the taxi.

'I'm sorry, Senhora,' Zé apologised. 'With the rain, and all the people going home . . . perhaps one of the gentlemen could take you.' He glanced back at the door to the club.

'It's all right. I can walk.' She clutched her light stole to her throat.

'But your beautiful hair!' Zé was mortified. 'Wait!' He rushed back inside and returned with a handsome umbrella with a mahogany handle banded with silver. 'Take this.'

She saw the monogram. 'But it belongs to someone.'

'The cheapskate hasn't given me a tip in weeks. You take it.'

'You're marvellous,' she said, and gave him a peck on the cheek.

Zé Pimenta beamed and saluted with his pasteboard scimitar.

She lingered as if waiting for the downpour to ease.

'The police gave everybody a scare,' she remarked.

Zé spat. 'The boss must have forgotten to give someone his squeeze.'

'Did they arrest anyone?'

'Not here.'

'I saw a priest as well. I thought somebody must have died.'

Zé laughed until he was doubled up. 'If somebody died in the sack,' he confided when he was sufficiently recovered, 'they'd drag him up the street.' He pointed to the entrance of a rival establishment. 'Bad for business.' He started chuckling again. 'And that wasn't a priest. That was Senhor Gruber. He's a real joker.'

'Did he leave alone?'

'He had his pals with him. A couple of Germans in their bibs and tuckers. It looked like they were out to make a real night of it.'

Zé watched appreciatively as the girl trotted off. That one was a looker, all right. A lot more class than you usually saw at the Babylônia. It was a crime to let a girl like that walk herself home.

The rain stopped as suddenly as it had started, as she crossed into Cinelandia, pursued by wolf whistles from the elegant young rowdies in a passing convertible. One of them tried to spray her with cologne. She smelled musk and tired lilacs.

A drunk came out of a doorway with his pants around

his knees and staggered after her, mouthing obscenities. She tried to walk faster, but her high heels snagged in the cracks of the broken mosaic sidewalk. She took her shoes off and padded on in her stockinged feet.

Her chest was tight, her breathing shallow, when after a few false turns she found the address Johnny had given her. She hesitated at the foot of the steps. The place looked like a sailors' dosshouse. There was a blue light in the front window, behind a torn shade. The hallway reeked of urine and stale beer. There was something sprawled across it, a mound of flesh that shook and shivered with its snores.

She looked back along the street and saw two men in tight-waisted suits and fedoras, like the detectives from the club.

She gripped the furled umbrella and stepped gingerly over the sleeping hulk. It gave a terrific snort and rolled over on to its back, so that she had to skip sideways to avoid a flopping arm. At the same instant a hand reached out of the shadows and clamped her shoulder.

'You'd better come in here.'

The voice was quietly authoritative. She moved with it, into the room with the blue lamp. The other furnishings consisted of a bed with an iron frame, a scuffed dresser with a bottle of whisky on top and an armchair with the stuffing hanging out. There was a pile of soiled sheets in the corner, partially concealed by a tan leather suitcase.

'Not quite the Ritz, I'm afraid.'

The man was about Johnny's height but younger, with a warm, open face. You didn't learn his kind of English in a language course. She knew there was something very wrong about that.

She felt ready to drop, but she stayed on her feet, close to the door, when he offered her the chair. A moth was trying to batter itself to death against the lamp.

'Would a drink help?'

'I don't think so.'

'I could try to rustle up some breakfast,' he said doubt-fully.

She was trying to read him from his eyes, his hands, the

552

way he crossed his legs when he sat down on the end of the bed. There was nothing threatening about him. The hands were sensitive, the hands of a painter or a surgeon.

'Who are you?'

'A friend of Johnny's.'

'The nameless kind?'

'You can call me Harry, if you like. I do think you ought to sit down and rest.' He was eyeing her muddy stockings.

She lowered herself into the armchair. It was the first concession.

'Where is he?'

'I don't know. We met at the Babylônia Club. There was a police raid. He said it would be safer if he left first.'

'Go on.'

'He'd been shot.'

'Shot?'

'Not seriously. But he lost a lot of blood. And he was dressed like a priest.'

Maitland frowned. Johnny must have fled into the church where they sometimes met – it was only a few blocks from the safe house. Had he tried to leave a message?

She repeated what the doorman had said about the Germans. She remembered that one of them was from the embassy. Maitland made her describe them, just to be sure. There was no doubt about it. Johnny had left the club in the care of the Gestapo. It was not encourageing news. However dim-witted, Hossbach had had plenty of time to mull over what had gone wrong at the fish market and to formulate some questions Johnny might have trouble fielding.

Sigrid asked, 'Is he safe?'

'I'm sure everything will be fine,' Harry sought to re-assure her. 'He's a hard man to stop.' He looked at his watch. 'Besides, we've got plenty of time. Why don't you curl up for a bit? I'm sure Johnny will turn up.'

She shook her head, but he could see she was fighting to keep her eyelids open. She accepted a swallow of whisky, and ten minutes later, she was fast asleep in the armchair. It wasn't an easy dream. Her teeth chattered a bit, and her head rocked against her shoulder. Gently Maitland took the cover from the bed and draped it over her.

When he raised the blind almost two hours later to let the morning light into the room, she woke immediately, sitting up wide-eyed like a cat.

'Johnny –'

Maitland had had time to go over all the possibilities. That Johnny was being held at the German Embassy or a Gestapo hideout. That he had been turned over to the police. That Max's people were onto him. That he was safe but forced to lie low for the time being.

Since he knew nothing for certain, except that the boat for Buenos Aires would be leaving within the hour, he decided it was best to lie a little.

'He's been held up,' Harry said. 'He wants you to go on ahead. He'll be joining you soon.'

'You saw him?' she asked eagerly.

'There was a message.'

'Why didn't you wake me?'

'I thought you needed your strength. Look, we'll have to get our skates on.'

'Skates?' This colloquialism eluded her.

'I promised Johnny I'd put you on that boat.'

'But my clothes –' She looked ruefully at her rumpled party dress, her ruined shoes and stockings.

'The morning after Carnival, people make allowances. You'll find everything you need for the voyage in here.' He hoisted the suitcase. 'I hope they fit.' He handed her an envelope. 'Money, tickets, passport. There won't be any problems,' he rushed on, leaving no space for objections. 'You know who to contact in Buenos Aires?'

She obediently recited the Comintern cover address Max had told her to memorise, a language school on the Calle Florida.

'There is something you must do first,' Harry instructed her. 'As soon as you arrive – before you talk to *anyone* – you are to call on this man.' He showed her a card and let her study it until they were both satisfied she had committed the contents to memory. The name was one of those funny

English ones that belonged in a cottage with a rose garden and a privet hedge: Bradbeer.

'I won't leave without Johnny,' she said defiantly.

'You must,' Harry said patiently. 'It's what he wants.'

'Then let him tell me himself!'

He saw the fear and suspicion in her face and assumed it was all bound up with Johnny. 'I'll get him out,' Harry promised. 'He means a lot to me, too.'

She finally acquiesced, but her expression did not change.

She's got every right to be bloody scared, Harry thought. Johnny disappears with a pair of Gestapo hoods, and now she's being batted around between unexplained Englishmen.

He got her on board the boat and tipped the steward to take her flowers and champagne. He lounged around the harbour till he saw the steamship leave. He hoped that Bradbeer would have sense enough to know how to play her. It was a damn tricky thing to spell out in a telegram.

He had something more pressing to worry about now. What had become of Johnny?

5

If Johnny stood on tiptoe, he could touch the ledge of the tiny barred window high up on the wall. If he pulled himself up, like a gymnast on the parallel bars, he could see the spire of a church planted on top of a rocky hill. He had attempted this exercise only once, because the guard who kept watch behind the Judas hole in the steel door had rushed in and beaten him about the kidneys and on the inside of the knees with a rubber truncheon. The guard had gone on thwacking at the soles of his feet when Johnny had fallen to the ground; he had had to bite his lip till it bled so as not to cry out.

He had been made to stand in the middle of that vertical tomb with its shiny walls, rocking lightly from side to side, wishing that he were a horse that could sleep on its feet without falling. It was the second day; he could tell that from the light outside. He was not completely alone, because he could hear the clatter of the wooden clogs – the *tamancos* – of other prisoners in the exercise yard, and at night his neighbours would tap on the wall in a simple, interminable alphabet code. Three taps for the letter C, then sixteen for O, and he had to memorise each number, swaying on his aching legs, in order to work out that someone who believed in him just because he was here was spelling out COURAGE.

The furnishings of the cell consisted of a canvas hammock with the ropes removed in case the prisoner thought of hanging himself and a stinking open latrine in the concrete floor, which he had been permitted to use only once, before the first interrogation. He had flung the useless hammock over the hole; it did not relieve the stench.

He rocked on his heels like a pendulum, back and forth, back and forth, each time closer to the wall, till his shoulder was scraping it, till he let his weight relax against it, till he was sliding down onto the floor. The clammy concrete under his backside felt better than a feather bed. He did not hear the clack of boots along the corridor, the jangle of keys against the lock; he was lost to all that.

'On your feet!' the warder screamed.

They were beating him again on his feet, his buttocks. They slapped him across the face repeatedly because he still wouldn't wake up, and he tasted salt. They got him by his armpits and hauled him up, but when they let go, he fell down again. They kicked him in the balls, not hard enough to make him black out completely, just hard enough to make him yell and get his eyelids open.

'That's enough!' another voice called out. 'The captain's ready for him!'

Somebody thrust some clothes into his arms – not his own but a pair of filthy pyjamas several sizes too small and *tamancos* that chafed his toes. They pushed him out of the door, along the hallway, down the flight of metal steps that rang under their heels. Through the gaps Johnny could see the creature they kept in a cage under the stairs. There was a bald patch on the top of his head, pink and round like a monk's tonsure, from which the matted strands of hair stuck out like straw; he had his hands over his ears, trying to shut out the clash of metal. When Johnny and his escorts reached the foot of the steps, the creature crouched against the bars of his cage, a big man whose force was spent. He stuck his palm out between the bars, begging for food or cigarettes, and the guards jeered at him.

'Emil?' Johnny croaked, not quite believing.

'Know this one, do you?' One of the guards moved to the cage, thrust his fist under Emil's chin, and forced the head up so that Johnny could see his eyes. They rolled in their sockets, milky and unfocussed as marbles.

'Come on then,' the guard taunted the man in the cage. 'Say something to your friend.'

'Oh, God –' Johnny stared at the hand, still held out in supplication, at the rigid, hooked fingers, at the blackened, suppurating scabs where two of the nails had been pulled out. 'I never meant this,' he mumbled in a low voice, in German. Emil Brandt gave no sign of recognition. One of the jailers spat into his cupped palm. As they shunted Johnny away, he craned his head back and saw Emil dab a finger into the spittle and sample it with his tongue. His face was full of wonder.

The interrogation room was like any other. Indifferent to day and night, windowless, the harsh blue–white glare of a high-wattage bulb stabbing at the prisoner's eyes.

They made him stand in front of the table, and the same thin-faced policeman who had taken down his answers the first day droned through the same set of questions.

'Name?'

'Franz Gruber.'

'Birthplace?'

'Vienna, Austria.'

'Family?'

'An estranged wife. Erna Gruber.'

'Occupation?'

'Importer.'

'Religion?'

This is where they bogged down before.

'I have no religion,' Johnny said, as he had said the first time.

'That is not an answer. I am not permitted to leave any of the spaces blank.'

'Put down seeker, then,' Johnny said, remembering what he had told the *cachaça* priest in Recife and wondering whether Father Badó had ended up any better than Emil.

'*Pesquisador?*' the thin man looked up from his paper. His face in the shadow was that of a hungry carp butting the glass of an aquarium. '*Que espécie de culto é?*'

'Just put it down.'

'I'll put down Pentecostal,' the carp said brightly. 'They've heard of that.'

The next instant he was on his feet.

'Leave us,' Honorio Schmidt said curtly, flicking a riding crop across the palm of his idle hand.

Thoughtfully the chief of the Special Police tilted the lamp away so it was no longer shining directly in Johnny's face. He picked up a straight-backed chair and set it in front of the table.

'Sit,' he instructed Johnny, taking his own place on the other side of the table. 'I believe you smoke.' He offered his leather cigar case. 'Whisky?'

Johnny refused none of these offers. He suspected none of them would be repeated.

Captain Honorio pushed a tumbler of scotch across the table. Johnny took one gulp, then another. It was stupid to drink on an empty stomach, but he didn't care. He wanted to blot out the image of Emil reduced to a dribbling idiot in a cage. His fatigue was not enough to overcome it. His hatred for Emil and what he represented was not personal enough to justify it. So he sucked at his glass and puffed at his cheroot as if he expected them to be snatched away at any moment.

'You spoke to your friend, Herr Brandt,' the policeman said softly. 'What did you say to him?'

'I don't know what you're talking about.'

'When he came to us, he was very arrogant. Like you. I put a few questions to him, and do you know what he said?

He said, "I know but I shall not tell." He said he had experienced every kind of torture in many countries. Even the Chinese method. He defied me to do better. You see the result. He underrated us. I hope you do not make the same mistake. Have some more whisky.'

Johnny drank it, though his head was starting to swirl.

'I want you to know that I respect you. Not your exalted political convictions but you, the man. Others have identified you. Your little Spanish friend, the one you taught to make bombs, talks about you like a lost lover. We have documents – heaps of them – that mention a certain Pedro. We know that is one of the names you use. We even know the name you were born with, Herr Lentz.'

Johnny kept his lips glued to the glass. It was a long time since he had heard anyone address him by his family name. It hardly belonged to him now.

'I am going to ask very little of you,' Captain Honorio pursued. 'A capable stenographer is waiting to take down your confession. In case you are tired, I have prepared an abbreviated version for you –' He held up the document. 'All it requires is your signature. Here.' He handed over several closely typed pages.

'This is absurd,' Johnny said after several minutes. 'I've never heard of most of these people.' His prepared confession named various prominent Brazilians as members of the conspiracy. Some of the names were strange to him; others were simply bizarre. Among the alleged plotters was Colonel Plinio Nogueira, the head of the political police. Honorio Schmidt was playing some game of his own. The really puzzling thing was that the document referred to various crimes Johnny had supposedly committed in Germany.

'It's a joke,' Johnny went on. 'Even if I sign, who would believe any of it?'

'We don't need to fuss with all of that. Here, use my pen. Then you can get some sleep between real sheets.'

Johnny struggled to reason through the fog of exhaustion and cheap whisky. What harm would it do to sign? Sigrid was safe – well she must be, mustn't she? Or else Schmidt would have mentioned her. Harry Maitland would see her through. Harry was the man he needed now. Harry would sort it all out with the government and put this cocky mock-German back in his box.

Why wasn't Harry here?

Was it possible he didn't know what had happened?

'You're making a mistake,' Johnny said to his interrogator. 'It's clearly a case of mistaken identity. I'm a simple businessman. There is –'

He did not finish the sentence because Captain Honorio erupted from behind the table and kicked his chair from under him. His cheek came to rest in a puddle of whisky.

'Someone – will vouch –' Johnny groaned.

'Yes.'

'There's someone – who will vouch –'

'For you?' Captain Honorio was engaged in polishing the toes of his boots on his prisoner's buttocks. This appeared to give him considerable satisfaction. 'Who is this simpleton? Well? I'm waiting!'

There was no response from the captive, who was lying on his belly, making a noise between a moan and a snore from which it was no longer possible to segregate syllables.

The policeman cracked his riding crop across the prisoner's face. It drew blood but no clearer message.

'It would have been easier to sign,' Honorio said to an audience of one. He strode back to the table and pressed the buzzer.

His assistant came in and ventured a floppy salute.

'Has His Excellency arrived?'

'Yes, Captain.'

'Then please show him in.'

Wolfgang Trott, who had taken to styling himself Graf von Trott in the company of Brazilians of German stock, came into the chamber at a brisk march and greeted Honorio with a floppy version of the Hitler salute.

He inspected the large body laid out on the floor and remarked, 'He looks ready for shipment. Are you finished with him?'

'Not quite. He hasn't signed yet.'

'Perhaps I might be of some slight assistance.'

Captain Honorio inclined his head.

'We don't have a great deal of time,' Trott went on. 'My superiors are very anxious to spend some time with your friend. There is a German ship leaving for Hamburg on Thursday.'

'There are some formalities that must be concluded –'

'I do trust there will be no unnecessary delays.'

6

Maitland allowed himself several hours before he called Colonel Plinio.

He started with the safe house in Flamengo. It had been swept clean. You would never have guessed that the flat had been ransacked from top to bottom, unless you were looking for the telltale signs: the slight indentation in the rug where a heavy wardrobe had been moved, the floorboard that had been nailed down too firmly, so you could see the fresh impress of the hammer.

He went to the church. He dropped a few cruzeiros in the slot, took a spill from the box and lit it with a match. As he placed the burning candle in the tray beside the others, he probed the narrow crack at the back of the marble ledge. He found a sticky wad of chewing gum. Nothing for him.

He tried their other mailboxes, including the niche behind the wounded lion in the Cemetery of John the Baptist. Nothing.

He called home. Luisa sounded flustered but relieved to hear him. Some strangers had been to the house. Something to do with fixing the electric meter. That didn't sound right. He wasn't aware of any fault in the meter.

'What did they look like?'

'Like cops. They didn't take anything. I never let them out of my sight.'

He drove out to Copacabana, to Hossbach's boarding house, not sure what he hoped to accomplish. He was rewarded with a glimpse of the German sitting on the verandah with his landlady, eating sandwiches and drinking beer. This reminded Harry that it was lunchtime and that he was supposed to be helping to entertain some visiting Canadians in the private dining room at Rio Light.

When he whipped into a no-parking space on the Avenida Marechal Floriano, in front of the company building, it was past 2:00 P.M.

A spinsterish secretary followed him into his office.

'You look like something the cat threw up,' she said with evident satisfaction.

'Any messages, dear?'

'The major called down three times. He didn't sound very happy.' Harry could hear the voice. When Major Mackenzie gave vent to emotion, his teeth rattled. It made him sound as if he were crunching ice cubes. The pink message slips and the envelopes on the desk were all routine.

The long face of Olga, Prestes' companion, peered mournfully out of a newspaper photograph. 'Have You Seen This Woman?' He wondered who had given them the picture.

He got rid of the secretary and tried Colonel Plinio's direct number. The colonel was not in his office. Like half of Rio's population, he was probably at home, giving up work for the beginning of Lent.

He hesitated before dialling Plinio's home number.

If the police were holding Johnny, then the colonel must know about it – and should have called Harry. With the wave of arrests, Johnny was more and more vulnerable. Any one of his comrades might betray him under interrogation. One recourse might have been to confide completely in Colonel Plinio, who had been sniffing after Harry's source. But Colin Bailey had ruled this out on the grounds of the lack of security inside the Brazilian police, and Harry, remembering the ambiguous role that Captain Honorio had played on the night of the coup, thoroughly agreed with him.

He had instructed Johnny that, if he were ever captured by the police, he should ask for Colonel Plinio Nogueira by name and tell him that Maitland would vouch for him as a legitimate businessman.

The fact that Plinio had not been in touch suggested either that Johnny had not been arrested or that the policeman was trying to dredge as much as he could out of him through his own delicate devices.

I'm declaring an interest and probably not gaining a bloody thing, Harry told himself.

But what choice did he have? If the Gestapo – or Max's boys – had Johnny hidden somewhere in the city, he was going to need help to find him. And if he wasted too much time, he risked finding his man too late to save him.

Plinio answered his home telephone in person. He sounded pleasurably dozy.

'My dear Harry. Why aren't you sleeping it off, like everyone else?'

'I'm afraid my employer doesn't recognise hangovers.'

'Oh, yes. Your galloping major. What can I do for you?'

'I was wondering if you made any interesting arrests last night.'

'None that I heard about. The usual crop of drunks. Have you got any particular reason for asking?'

'A chum of mine seems to have turned up missing. I thought he might have had a few too many.'

'Not quite my parish. But of course I'd be happy to make inquiries. What is the name of your friend?'

'Gruber. Franz Gruber.'

'He's German, then?'

'Austrian, actually. He's rather good on cigars.'

'It will be a pleasure to make his acquaintance. Can you give me a description, just in case?'

Harry did his best to oblige, not leaving out the priest's disguise, which seemed to appeal to the colonel's sense of humour. He wondered, as he talked, whether Plinio was toying with him. He had just hung up when Major Mackenzie barrelled into his office.

'Jolly nice of you to grace us with your presence, Maitland!'

'I'm sorry about the lunch –'

'I think we ought to have a chat about your future with this company.' The major jammed his monocle into his face.

Harry got up from his desk. 'Certainly, sir. Perhaps at a more convenient time –'

'It's convenient now, thank you very much! Two buses damaged beyond repair by your Brazilians,' he snarled, 'and no sign of compensation!'

Harry didn't dare look at him for fear of bursting out laughing. He looked out the window instead – and saw several men in uniform engaged in trying to hook up the Beast to a tow truck.

'Bloody cheek!'

'Are you talking to me, Maitland?'

'No, sir. Some idiots are trying to tow my car away.'

'I gave strict instructions that the street in front of the building is to be kept clear,' the Major said primly. 'Since the bomb scare, you know.'

Which would have been a damn sight more than a scare if I hadn't scotched it, Harry thought.

'But that's my car!'

'We all live by the same rules here,' Mackenzie said, with pure malice. 'But if you're worried about your paintwork, I dare say someone will drive it to the lot for you.'

'I'll do it myself.' Harry was rapidly losing his sense of humour.

'No, you won't. We have a few larger things to settle. Agatha!'

The spinster secretary tripped in.

'Mr Maitland is going to give you his car keys. There we are. Be a good girl and take them down to Jaime, won't you? Tell him Mr Maitland will pay the fine when he comes down.'

The secretary smirked.

'What fine?' Harry was ready to explode.

'Company policy. If you spent any time at all in the office, you might have heard about it.'

Maitland sighed and slumped back into his chair.

God, I'm tired, and I've got a slab of pig iron jouncing

up and down above my eyes, and I've lost Johnny, and I have to listen to this idiot preach about company manners.

I wonder if Jaime can even drive.

He craned his head round so he could see down into the street, two floors below. The company detective, all smiles, was climbing into the Beast. He made a little bow to the passers-by.

'Maitland. I say, Maitland! Are you listening to me?'

'Oh, yes, sir. Every word.'

'You could show a bit more –'

The next word was no doubt 'respect', since the major's style was nothing if not predictable, but it was choked off by a roll of thunder that blew out the window behind Harry's head and set the desk shaking.

The shock of the explosion threw the major off his chair. He picked himself up, minus the monocle, and rushed to the window.

The Beast was a pile of junk metal. The headless trunk in the front seat was recognisable as human only because of the arm that dangled over the side of the car. The other arm was gone. The bystanders were scattered across the pavement like fallen leaves. A security guard was doubled up against a lamppost, heaving his guts out.

'They p-put a bomb in your car,' the major stammered.

Maitland was picking splinters of glass out of his hair. He could feel a trickle of blood down the back of his neck.

They could have done it with a timer, he thought. They must have planted it somewhere else. It was too public here, and besides, he'd only been in the building half an hour. Unless they had simply lobbed the thing from a passing car. He would have to talk to the people outside. Either way, he was being followed by someone who meant to stop him.

He experienced the odd sense of calm that comes at the heart of a crisis.

'I don't think you'll have any trouble stopping people from parking outside,' he remarked to Major Mackenzie, who stared at him as if he had gone utterly insane.

7

They had Johnny swinging on an iron bar. It ran inside his knees, biting into the flesh. They had his wrists and his ankles tied together behind his back, so that if he relaxed his grip, he spun round like a top until his head ached.

He tried to think of anything except the questions they repeated over and over.

Where was the girl known as Sigrid or Firelei?

Where were Prestes and his woman?

What were his relations with Harry Maitland?

He tried to imagine himself on the Wannsee with Sigrid in the time before his world blew up in his face.

He was dimly aware that they had brought him a visitor.

'Very colourful,' the man remarked to the police captain.

'How are you, Johnny?' he addressed the prisoner in perfect German, with a trace of a Silesian accent. 'How do you like the parrot's perch?'

Johnny's leg muscles relaxed for an instant, and he saw Wolfgang Trott leering at him upside down.

'We have devised certain refinements that maybe of use to you,' Trott remarked to Honorio Schmidt.

He took something from his pocket; Johnny couldn't make out what it was.

'Would you have such a thing as a hammer?'

Schmidt went to the door and called out an order. An athletic young man stripped to the waist came in with the hammer. Honorio and his guest both looked fondly at his pectorals.

'Cut him down and I'll show you,' Trott said.

Honorio nodded. Tarzan untied Johnny's bonds and let him fall onto the concrete.

'Now you see –' Trott held up a small convex disk of black plastic. 'You fit the cap over the pupil, like so.' He jammed his thumb and forefinger into the socket of Johnny's right eye, forcing the lids apart. He inserted the cap, and the light died.

'You must do this very tenderly. Like an act of love,'

Trott continued his lecture. 'Otherwise you will blind the suspect and very quickly drive him out of his wits.'

He tapped very gently, and it seemed to Johnny that a red-hot poker was being driven through the eyeball into his brain.

'Now we'll test the results,' Trott said. 'Which question is at the top of your list?'

Honorio was on the point of replying when there was a rap on the door, and a sergeant in a red cap came in and saluted.

'I ordered no interruptions!' Honorio screamed.

'I'm sorry, sir, but —'

'Get out!'

A dapper figure in a wide-brimmed panama hat tripped around the sergeant, preceded by a white cloud of cigar smoke.

'I wouldn't dream of interrupting your sport, my dear Honorio, but could you possibly spare me a minute?'

'This is not your department.' Schmidt glowered at Colonel Plinio.

'That's precisely what I wish to discuss. Preferably among Brazilians.' He cocked an eyebrow at Wolfgang Trott. 'We *are* still on Brazilian territory, aren't we?'

Trott, red-faced, seemed to be looking for a place to hide the hammer.

'Graf von Trott is here in an advisory capacity,' Schmidt said woodenly.

'Quite so, quite so. But you will forgive us, I trust, Herr Trott?'

Trott clicked his heels. 'Let me know when it is convenient,' he mumbled to Honorio Schmidt.

'You mean, to take delivery of your property?'

Trott's embarrassment increased. He rushed out of the interrogation room.

Blood was running out of Johnny's eye.

'Get that seen to straight away, will you?' Plinio ordered Schmidt's half-naked assistant, who led the prisoner out once his boss gave the nod.

'So you found out about the deportation order,' Honorio

said when the two of them were alone. Plinio was perched delicately on the edge of a straight-backed chair, his hands folded over the ivory knob of his cane, his trousers hitched up a fraction to preserve their immaculate crease.

'You were in rather a hurry, weren't you?'

'I have the chief's approval, and the justice minister's signature. It's out of your province.'

'But my dear fellow, it was never in my province. That's where you made a big mistake. You've overstepped your authority. Political information is my bailiwick. Your people are merely mechanics, employed to assist in extracting it. This prisoner – this Gruber – belongs to me.'

'It's my operation from start to finish. If you don't like it, you can go and talk to the chief.'

It was no secret in Rio that the chief of police was much closer, personally and politically, to Captain Honorio Schmidt than to the colonel. The chief was a frequent dinner guest at the German Embassy.

'I must congratulate you,' Plinio said urbanely.

'I beg your pardon?'

'I was thinking that your spiritual sessions with Gruber must have been stunningly successful, if you're ready to turn him over to our German friends so quickly. May I see the interrogation reports?'

They went to Honorio's office. Half an hour later, several long, closely typed pages were produced.

'During the subversive events that lately deflagrated in this capital,' the document opened in the recorder's rotund style, 'the subject claimed to be a merchant of tobaccos, living in sybaritic luxury in the Southern Zone.'

'There's nothing here,' Plinio pronounced after a quick glance. 'He's told you nothing.'

'Our investigation is still at a preliminary stage –'

'And you're putting him on a boat to Hamburg on Thursday!'

'You're well informed.'

Colonel Plinio saw no reason to disclose that his source was the muscular young man whom he had sent out of the interrogation room. One of Plinio's detectives had caught him engaging in acts of public lewdness with other men among the dunes at the Leme end of Copacabana beach. The colonel had spared the young Special Police athlete any embarrassment in return for occasional scraps of information.

'What I'd like to know,' Plinio pursued, 'is what Herr Trott promised you. A death's head tiepin? An audience with Himmler? Or is it a matter of something you both wish to hide?'

'You're being childishly offensive.' Honorio's jug ears, never his best feature, had turned bright pink. 'You can read the deportation order for yourself.' He pushed it across the desk. 'It is a perfectly straightforward matter. Lentz, alias Gruber, alias Pedro and other names, entered Brazil illegally, using forged papers, and is being deported to his native country, where he is wanted for murder.'

'I see.' Plinio found the deportation order more informative than the interrogation report. It seemed the Gestapo had quite a dossier on the man Harry Maitland had described as his friend. He was wanted on several counts of murder. 'I'll tell you what we'll do,' the colonel went on. 'We will settle this like civilised men. You let me have the prisoner for a few days, and I'll see if he wants to sing to me. Then you and Trott can play with him as long as you wish. Agreed?'

'I told you, I have special authority –'

'I have a few friends of my own, Honorio. Shall we call one of them?'

He scrawled a telephone number over Schmidt's pristine blotter. The captain studied it. It was one of the direct lines to the palace.

Honorio accepted that for the moment he was outgunned.

They strolled out into the courtyard. As his escorts took delivery of the prisoner, Colonel Plinio spotted Honorio's athletic assistant, still shirtless, hurrying towards the garage.

'Do you really think you should let your playmates run around during working hours without their clothes?' Plinio asked pleasantly.

That evening, Colonel Plinio received Maitland at home. The house was out beyond the golf club, modest but newly painted and full of happy children, who were shooed out of the sitting room but peeked in through the crack in the door at the tall, sandy-haired stranger.

The colonel proposed champagne or cognac.

'I drink nothing else at home,' he declared. 'Life has taught me to know my blood group.'

The brandy, a very superior Hine, arrived chilled to the point where it had lost all bouquet. Harry was surprised by the colonel's lapse. His taste in all other respects was impeccable.

'You'll find it rides easier in this heat,' Plinio remarked, reading his guest's expression. 'It would be a crime to dilute it, don't you agree?'

Harry suppressed his misgivings. The cognac slipped down smoothly, all right, but he thought the flavour was barely distinguishable from that of Coca-Cola. It might, of course, have been his palate that was at fault; he was hardly in the mood for a wine tasting.

'I found your friend Gruber,' Plinio suddenly announced. 'He actually asked for you by name.'

'Where is he?'

'At this precise moment, he's on his back in the infirmary. I'm afraid Honorio didn't lose any time before putting him on the grill.'

'Is he badly hurt?'

'He'll live. At least, as long as he's in Brazil.'

'What do you mean?'

'The Gestapo wants him sent to Germany. The justice minister has actually signed the deportation order. I saw it myself.'

Harry froze. Deportation to Germany was a death sentence.

'We've got to stop it,' he said. 'We'll go to the president

if we have to. Dammit, Johnny just saved your government. You ought to be giving him a medal.'

'That wouldn't make him very popular with his Communist friends,' Plinio observed, pleased that Maitland had admitted what he had guessed from the first phone call – that this Gruber was the agent Harry had refused to identify.

'Plinio, I want him out of jail tonight. It's not much to ask.'

'It may be more than you think. I doubt if he's fit to travel. But in any event, my hands are tied. My chief gave me a direct order this afternoon. I am to deliver your friend into the custody of Herr Trott on Friday.'

'Then call the palace. Go to the president. Explain the situation to him.'

'The president is in Porto Alegre. And if I bypass my chief, he'll have me thrown out of my office.'

Harry bit his lip. It was obvious why the Gestapo wanted Johnny back in Germany: they wanted to pay him back in their own sweet time for what he had done to Willi Rausch and milk him for whatever he had to yield on comrades who were still at large. Why Plinio's superiors were so accommodating was rather more of a mystery. The most likely explanation was that money had changed hands. But it was also possible that someone high up was scared that Johnny knew something that could destroy him, something about the plot to kill the president.

I could try to mobilise Sir Evelyn and the embassy, Harry thought. Cable Colin and ask him to get the Foreign Office to make a fuss. It would all involve time and bluster and the inevitable leaks – which would pretty much guarantee that Johnny's cover would be blown for good.

No, there was only one satisfactory solution.

He explained it to Plinio, who professed to be scandalised. After another brandy and two glasses of champagne, however, the colonel allowed that he might be swayed by the prospect of a handsome contribution to his personal insurance plan.

'With all this buzz and ferment,' he conceded, 'a man in my position can never tell where he's going to be next week. I sometimes think there would be worse places to come to roost than a cottage in one of the sunnier home counties. But of course, England is so expensive –'

They shook hands on it.

'I don't suppose you found out who wrecked my car,' Harry said before they parted company.

'I am afraid that for once, the city is mute. It is a most unusual thing.' But he confided that he had assigned detectives to keep a discreet watch on both Herr Trott and Engineer Hossbach.

8

At night, in the infirmary, he woke screaming from a nightmare in which they were trying to gouge out his eyes and screamed again when he realised that his sight was gone. The orderly came running to quiet him.

'There,' he murmured, loosening the bandage, so that Johnny could see a stripe of light under his left eye. 'There.' The right eye was heavily padded.

He lay back in the dank sheets and listened. He heard a train whistle and the thrum of pistons from somewhere nearby and, from nearer still, what sounded like amateurs' night on the radio. Except that they would never sing 'The Hymn of the Poor Brazilian' on the government radio. That was marginally less popular with the regime than the *Internationale*.

The singing stopped, and a rotund, humorous voice rang out across the exercise yard the prisoners had dubbed Red Square.

'Tonight, dear friends and comrades, Radio Libertadora will instruct you in the high metaphysical Theory of the Two Suppositions, according to which everything must turn out for the best. If you will only learn this theory, you will understand that there is no reason at all to be apprehensive. None whatsoever. We will either, *primo*, be released, or *segundo*, remain in jail. If the first, well and good. If the second, we will be tried and either *primo*, be acquitted or *segundo*, be condemned. If the second –'

Johnny's attention wandered. He wondered why the guards did not interrupt the prisoners' entertainment. Security at this prison was obviously rather more relaxed than in the barracks of the Special Police. They called the place the Pavilhão dos Primários, which made it sound like a primary school.

The absurd-sounding name deepened the black irony of his situation. The same men who were driving Emil insane were planning to hand him over to the Gestapo, trussed and basted like a chicken. Yet *they* would have been the ones in the cells – as prisoners, not jailers – if he had not ensured the failure of the revolution. He knew he could not afford to dwell on this. He thought of Harry with his freckled, open face, so boyish and so brave.

Whatever lies they had told him in the interrogation room, Sigrid must be safe. Harry had promised that. Harry would keep his word.

He told himself, Harry will get me out of this.

'– if we are executed,' the rotund voice was rounding up, 'we will either *primo*, go to Heaven, or *segundo*, to the other place. If the first, well and good. If the second, we will meet all our friends. It could happen to anyone.'

There was laughter and heckling from the windows across the yard. It darkened Johnny's mood; this solidarity did not include him.

In the morning he persuaded the orderly to change the bandage so he could see out of one eye, at least. The coffee they brought him for breakfast was sickly sweet, probably heavily laced with bromides. He tossed it back all the same. But he couldn't swallow the bread. He tried to divert himself by moulding a set of tiny chessmen out of the crumbs. A wave of fatigue rose up and engulfed him before he had finished. When he rose out of it, he found a swarm of cockroaches devouring the last of his pieces.

From the window of the infirmary he could see the coppery glint of water under palms and recognised the Mangue canal, which he had first explored with Nilo on his tour of the city's low life. Nilo, the millionaire terrorist, had survived the wreckage better than he.

He dozed off again and was roused by the clatter of wooden clogs, to find one of the *faxinas* – common criminals whom the guards allowed to perform services for tips – hovering at the foot of his bed.

'These are for you.' He thrust a brown paper bag into Johnny's arms.

Johnny looked inside and found two packs of cigarettes, a clean shirt, a loose pair of cotton trousers and a pair of canvas shoes.

'I don't have any money –'

'It's taken care of,' the trustie winked at him. The lumps on his bald cranium would have made a phrenologist's day. 'Harry says you're to meet him outside at ten tonight.'

'I don't understand –'

The *faxina* winked again and gestured towards the double doors that led to the prison pharmacy. 'Through there.'

Johnny still did not understand, and hardly dared to hope. He slapped a hand to his wrist, to check the watch that was no longer there.

'Wait,' he said helplessly. 'How will I know when it's ten?'

'It's when the radio starts, isn't it?' The trustie shrugged and shuffled off in advance of an orderly.

He was alone in the infirmary when a shrill whistle from across the exercise yard, followed by rhythmic clapping, announced that Radio Libertadora was on the air.

He eased himself out of bed, put on his new shoes and hobbled over to the double doors. The pharmacy was deserted, too. The outside door was secured, but the key had been left in the lock.

It was raining outside. The guard who should have been stationed in front of the building was probably inside, keeping dry.

'Johnny!'

The call came from a taxi with its light off and the engine running.

Harry Maitland opened the back door and helped him inside.

'Here. Put this on.'

Harry handed him a coat and hat. Johnny felt the weight of a gun or a bottle in the pocket. There were a hundred questions he needed to ask.

'Sigrid –'

'She's safe. I promise.' Then Harry put a finger to his lips and they rode in silence to the Pedro II station.

The night train for São Paulo was actually on time; the vintage engine had a splendid copper-bound smokestack, enormous driving wheels and an old-fashioned cowcatcher in front.

An official whose uniform would not have shamed a field marshal inspected their tickets at the gate. He cast his eye over Johnny's attire.

'I profoundly regret that the Senhor is not permitted to board the train.'

Johnny tensed and thrust a hand into his pocket.

'Is there some problem?' Maitland asked calmly.

'It is a company regulation. Gentlemen passengers must be correctly dressed.' He looked pointedly at Johnny's bare neck.

'*Muito boa*,' Harry rose to the occasion.

He fished in his holdall and produced a Winchester tie. It looked rather loud to Johnny with its bold stripes of red, brown and blue. But Harry winked at him, and he knotted it hastily around his neck.

The station official smiled his approval and ushered them through. 'I knew there must be a reason I've held on to that thing,' Harry said when they were comfortably ensconced in a Pullman.

'I don't imagine I look much like someone who went to an English public school,' Johnny remarked, pulling the tie away from his throat.

'Perhaps not,' Harry smiled. 'But I have the feeling we're classmates just the same.'

12

Manhunt

Like a woman, a horse does not like the weak; still
less does it respect them.

– Alvisi,
Aphorisms

1

From among the flowering trees above the house, a sound
rang out like the clang of a blacksmith's hammer striking
the anvil. The hammer fell again, and Puck, the roly-poly
tomcat who had adopted Harry and Luisa, jumped off the
pillow and bellied underneath the bed for cover, the way
he did during thunderstorms.

Luisa laughed at his timidity but got out of bed to check,
for the third or fourth time, that all the doors were locked.
The call of the *ferreiro*, the blacksmith bird, was an evil
omen; it presaged violence, the clash of metal. And Ivan
had warned that the greatest danger to both of them would
come in this season, in the darkening of the moon.

She hated to be alone in the big, echoing house. Her
whole family could have fitted into the kitchen wing, at
the back, where she slept in a little room whose window
overlooked her herbal garden. Harry had called from the
office to say he was going to be away for a few days to
look at horses at his ranch in the south. She had never set
eyes on this estate, but he had once showed her photographs

of a cluster of neat, whitewashed bungalows and himself in a funny round cap and white breeches, drinking a stirrup cup in a circle of horsemen dressed in the same outlandish style. In one of the pictures was a gate and a painted sign that displayed a bushy-tailed animal she had never seen. It was a red fox, he explained. One of his partners had been a Master of the Hunt in Somerset, which was somewhere in his own country, on the other side of the ocean, where it was the custom for gentlemen to pursue these small, clever animals on horseback.

Luisa asked, 'Do you eat them?'

'Of course not,' Harry said, in high indignation.

'Then it's a *despacho*. A sacrifice.'

Harry chuckled and gave up trying to explain, leaving her puzzled and somewhat frightened, because these Englishmen were obviously homesick for their own country, which meant that one day, inevitably, Harry would leave her for the strange place beyond the waters where men wore red coats and called them pink.

Dudley, Harry's German shepherd, was lying in the coolest spot he could find, at the end of the hall. He gave a tremendous yawn as she padded out of the bedroom but dragged himself to his feet and came puffing along behind her. Dudley belonged in a different climate. The heat sapped all of his strength, and every time he went outside, she had to spend twenty minutes picking the ticks out of his coat. Still, his presence was comforting, especially tonight.

She checked the bolts on the front door and peeped out the bay window. The neighbours' lights were out, and the sky hung down like a black shroud. She could not see as far as the low stone wall at the end of the lawn. Behind her, Dudley staggered around in narrowing circles, ready to flop down.

She told herself not to be such a child, scared to be alone in the dark. She switched off the light and called the dog from the hallway.

'Come, Dudley. You can sleep with me.'

But Dudley did not obey. He stiffened. A low rumble came from his throat. Then he started barking, a deep-chested, serious bark guaranteed to deter all but the most determined visitors. He woke up the *curupião* in its cage on the verandah, and it tried to mimic him.

'Dudley?'

Hackles raised, the dog was nudging and pawing the front door. Luisa turned on the porch light and went back to the window. Beyond the pale circle of light, the darkness was impenetrable.

The dog would not be quieted.

It's an animal, she told herself, resolved to be sensible. A squirrel or a stray cat. Or even an armadillo. She had nearly tripped on one of them once, tending her garden.

Dudley's growls alternated with whimpers of frustration. He butted at the door so hard that the glass in the panels shook.

'All right.' She unlatched the door. 'Go seek.'

He barged past her and charged off into the night, his hackles so high he seemed to have sprouted a hump. The air was full of invisible midges. She brushed her arm across her face and retreated inside the screen door.

The dog was barking and snarling. He was going to wake people up.

'Dudley!'

The barking ended with a yelp, followed by a ragged, high-pitched whimper. Then nothing. The stillness that descended was unnerving. She listened carefully and could hear only the whine of mosquitoes, the feathery thud of the moths assaulting the lamp on the porch, the murmur of the wind among the leaves.

'Dudley?'

Nothing. Her hand was trembling as she locked the door.

I have to look for him, all the same.

He might have got stuck in the storm drain, chasing a smaller animal. Or in a trap. The people in the house on the north side had threatened to put out traps after something had killed two of their chickens. What would Harry say if the dog had been hurt badly and she let him lie out there until morning?

She found a flashlight in the kitchen and put on the white silk robe Harry had given her for her birthday.

The heat rose up out of the wet grass. She followed the wavering thread of light into the copse on the northern side of the property, where Dudley's barks had been coming from.

She moved among the trees. Suddenly, she stopped short, biting her lip so as not to cry out.

There was a man standing on the far side of the trees, a burly man with a weapon, a rifle or a shotgun, cradled in his arms.

He must have seen the flashlight. Should I run?

'What the hell is going on?' the man shouted out rudely. 'Don't you *Ingleses* ever go to bed?'

It was only Porcão, the neighbour.

'Have you seen our dog?'

'If I see that mutt near my chickens, I'll send him home full of holes.'

Luisa was too relieved to care what Porcão said. More confidently, she went back into the copse, jabbing at the undergrowth with her flashlight. Something glinted white in the arc of the flashlight. She hunted for the spot, found it. And dropped the flashlight.

For an instant she had seen Dudley's face, the jaws partly opened over his shiny alligator teeth, the swollen tongue lolling out at the side. She had also seen the black hollow at his throat, the jagged vent that ran down to the belly, the entrails that spilled out like writhing eels.

She opened her mouth to scream, but the sound was suffocated by a strong hand that was clamped over her lips, while a muscular arm tightened around her waist, hoisting her sideways and upwards till her feet were off the ground. Helpless, gagging, she saw the awkward shape of Porcão shambling back towards his house.

A long, bony face pushed up close to hers. It looked like a death's head.

'Where's the *Inglês*!' the skull whispered in Portuguese. 'In the house?'

She shook her head.

'Bring her inside,' Skull ordered his companions. She could see two more rising up out of the bushes. Plus the man who had her pinioned.

When they got her inside, she saw that one, at least, was a foreigner. His face was pink and sweaty. He had close-cropped blond hair and no earlobes to speak of. The man who had grabbed her was a huge mulatto, darker than she.

The bony one, who seemed to be in charge, flashed some kind of pass in front of her face.

'Special Police,' he breathed. 'If you don't want trouble, you'll tell me what I want to know.'

'She's just the maid,' someone else said. 'What can she tell us?'

'I wouldn't mind a maid like that,' the mulatto chipped in, with a coarse laugh.

'Where is Senhor Maitland?' Skull demanded.

'He's gone away for a few days.'

'Where?'

'I don't know.'

'Have you seen this man?'

They showed her a photograph with a police identification number across the bottom.

She shook her head.

'Why did you kill the dog?' she said to them, between tears and rage. For an answer, their leader hooked a finger over the neck of her silk robe and tore it from her shoulders. Her dark nipples were clearly visible under the nightie. The mulatto stuck his lips out obscenely and blew her a wet kiss.

'You want her, Jaime? Have her! It may loosen her tongue.'

He ripped the nightie away from her body. She tried to cover herself with her hands, and Skull laughed at her.

The mulatto hesitated. He was staring at the *guias*, the ritual beads – blue and white for Yemanjá – around her throat.

'What's the matter? You don't like her any more?'

Luisa cowered before them, her eyes shut tight, invoking Yemanjá and the other *orixás*. Lady of the waters, take this from me. Carry me away in the foaming tresses of your hair.

This is not my body, she told herself. Nothing they do can touch me. I will feel nothing.

But she felt a violent hand tear at the *guias*, breaking the strings so that the sacred beads went rolling away in all directions.

Other hands were laid on her, probing and defiling.

'Go on, Hossbach!' Skull cried out merrily. 'I can see you want to!'

But they stabbed at her secret places with something sharper than human flesh, with metal or glass, until she could no longer see the colours that could not be named or withstand the calvary of a body that was undeniably hers and was reduced to blurting out everything she knew or could imagine about Harry. They were particularly interested in the hollow inside the chimneypiece where they found his private papers and the mention of a *fazenda* in the south, on the borders of São Paulo and Paraná, with the carved face of a red fox on a sign.

2

'*Formé!*' the wrangler shouted. He flicked his whip for the benefit of the persistent black flies rather than the horses.

The horses knew just what was expected of them.

They formed up in a rough circle inside the corral, their tails brushing the rails, their heads pointing to the centre.

'Now,' the wrangler called to Harry, 'do you want to see if he still knows you?'

Maitland dropped from his perch on the rail, whipped his straw sombrero from his head and advanced, with the hat outstretched, towards a handsome grey gelding. He was big for a Brazilian horse, fifteen hands at least, with a broad chest and good quarters and a silver-black mane, left shaggy to keep off the flies. He cocked his ears forward and pawed at the red dirt with his neat black hooves as Harry approached.

'Hello, Winston,' Harry called to him, holding his hat upside down by the brim. The horse danced forward and nuzzled inside the hat.

'You cheated!' the wrangler reproached him with a grin.

Winston, disappointed at finding nothing inside the hat,

was trying to graze inside Harry's shirt. Maitland brought a lump of *rapadura* – raw brown sugar – out of his trouser pocket and let the horse eat it out of his hand.

Johnny came over. He had gained strength these past days at the ranch, but he still wore a patch over one eye. It gave him a piratical look.

'What is he?' Johnny asked. 'A thoroughbred?'

Inocencio laughed. The wrangler was a frontiersman, a mixture of Brazilian, Spaniard and Guarani Indian, lithe and quick, with a scrubby beard and skin like saddle leather.

'He's a mongrel, like me,' Inocencio said. 'Creole, mostly. Some racing blood on the father's side. He's fast, and he's a stayer. But he hasn't been ridden for a couple of months,' he added for Harry's benefit. 'You'd better watch him.'

'Have you still got my saddle?'

'We might be able to find it. What about your friend?'

Maitland turned to Johnny. 'Do you feel up to a ride?'

'I'm not in your league.'

'You could try Hilde,' the wrangler suggested, leading out a stocky little bay mare.

'But she's too small for me.'

'She's stronger than you might think,' Maitland interjected. 'She's a *coralera*. They breed them in Mato Grosso. Best horse you could want for cross-country hacking in these parts. And a lovely temperament to go with it.'

The little mare was snuffling and licking Johnny's hand. He said, 'I'll give it a try.'

Inocencio produced a Texas saddle with the tree cut down and strapped it on over a soft, loose-woven blanket.

'Don't jerk,' the wrangler cautioned. 'She's got a mouth like velvet. You only have to *think* what you want her to do.'

Maitland was already out of the corral, pressing his knees against Winston's flanks. The horse suddenly leaped into the air and jackknifed till its back legs and forelegs almost met. It was the best Harry could do to stay on, clinging to the mane.

Winston bucked sideways, and Harry hugged his neck, muttering old endearments and trying to get his left foot back into the stirrup.

Johnny trotted past on the coralera mare, looking as if he had been born in the saddle.

'Need any help?' he called back to Maitland, who smiled through his gritted teeth.

He clapped at Winston's sides with his ankles, and they galloped out across a sea of grass, where a herd of hump-backed zebu cattle, oddly Asiatic, were grazing placidly. They did not stop till they reached the bank of a shallow stream. Harry drove his mount on through the muddy water and over a lazy sandbank to the steep, slippery clay on the far side, hanging on to its tail with his left hand and looking out for caimans. When they raced back to the *fazenda*, they were driven by a single will.

Johnny trotted up on the little mare from the opposite direction and swung smoothly down from the saddle.

They took whisky and sodas on the verandah, and Harry said, 'I must say, you do seem to have made a remarkable recovery. What would you say to a spot of shooting tomorrow? Inocencio says he saw a ten-point stag in the swamps.'

'I can't waste any more time,' Johnny responded quietly. 'I have to get to Buenos Aires. Have you heard anything about Sigrid? Is she all right?'

He had asked the same question twenty times since they had boarded the train in Rio.

'She's fine,' Harry assured him. 'Probably a bit disoriented, but you'll sort that out. Bradbeer's a good man. He'll keep her out of trouble until you arrive.'

Harry expressed more confidence than he felt. He didn't like the tone of the cable he had finally received from Bradbeer that same morning. Bailey's man said there had been complications in Buenos Aires, without specifying what had gone wrong. Bradbeer strongly recommended that Johnny should take the roundabout route to the Argentine capital, via Paraguay. The British agent was going to arrange for a contact to meet them on the other side of the Paraná River, which Harry remembered as a nest of gamblers and contrabanders. With that evil-looking patch over his eye, Johnny would fit in beautifully.

Harry had yet to break the news of this unexpected detour.

'When do we leave?' Johnny asked.

'We've got a couple of choices. There's a British ship leaving from Santos the day after tomorrow.'

'Would that be quickest?'

'If we get through. I've been informed that our friends from Rio have got the ports pretty well covered. It would be safest to skip across the border into Paraguay. No one is looking for us there. We wouldn't lose very much time, because we can fly direct from Asunción to Buenos Aires. There's a mail plane twice a week.'

'So your vote is for Paraguay.'

'I think it makes sense, don't you?'

Johnny was frustrated by the prospect of a further delay before he caught up with Sigrid. But he tried to make light of the situation.

'I think you're being less than candid, Harry. I think you want to go overland to Paraguay so you can bag a few more deer.'

'It never hurts to keep one's hand in,' Harry grinned.

3

Luisa scrubbed herself until her palms and the inside of her thighs were chafed, and still did not feel clean. She dug a shallow grave under the bougainvillea and buried what was left of Dudley. Then she took another bath and put on her prettiest dress and her butterfly hat. She took the housekeeping money and walked down the hill to the bus stop. Some hired hands bouncing along in the back of a horse-drawn cart whistled after her.

'I'm in love with you!' one of them called. 'I'll make an honest woman of you!'

'So what do you call your wife?' another baited him.

She did not hear them. She was going to Caxias, to Ivan's *terreiro*. She was going for revenge.

She would give Ivan all the money she had and tell him

the strange, foreign name she had heard in the night. She would plead with him to speak the terrible name of Exú Caveira, Exú Skull, the dark power that closed off a man's paths and snuffed out his life like a candle.

4

It was two days' ride to the Paraná River, Inocencio said, unless the rains came again. In their saddlebags they stowed enough beef jerky, beans and rapadura to last a week. But in that country, no man who could shoot need ever go hungry. The woods and the marshes were teeming with wild pigs and tapirs, deer and muscovy ducks. As they followed a red dirt trail through the rain forest, Inocencio would lean from the saddle to scoop an orange or papaya from a branch.

Leaving Fox Hill, they had travelled for a time through massive stands of conifers – Paraná pines, Harry explained – with a distant view of a vast coffee plantation on the hills to the south. Now, they were surrounded by true jungle, laced with lianas woven together in the high canopy, far above their heads, so that they rode through a patchwork of light and shade.

Each of the three men had a rifle slung behind his saddle – the short-barrelled .44 Winchester that Harry favoured because it was light and the flat-nosed lead bullets were easy to find anywhere between here and Asunción.

Twenty miles west of Fox Hill Farm, they dismounted and left the horses in a clearing to graze at will. Harry's little mare, no mean forager, made straight for a *maté* plant; to a horse in these parts, the fruit of the *yerba maté* (as the Spaniards across the border called the plant) was as irresistible as catnip to your average feline.

Maitland and Johnny followed Inocencio for half a mile or so into a shallow, stinking marsh teeming with water fowl.

'The deer love it in here during the day,' he whispered, showing Johnny where to crouch. 'They get away from the ticks.'

Johnny was squatting in the stagnant water when Inocencio put a finger to his lips. A regal stag, six points at least – no, eight – was advancing among the trees. He stopped short and started butting his head against the branches. What was he up to?

Johnny watched the animal over the sight of his Winchester. The stag, not sensing danger, had paused to make his toilette; he was rubbing the fur off his antlers against the rough bark.

'He's yours.' Harry reached over and squeezed Johnny's shoulder.

Johnny watched the stag. There was a kind of majesty about him. The way he shook his head, the way he stood up with his chest thrown out, reminded Johnny of someone. Was it Heinz Kordt?

There was a scuffling among the leaves – perhaps a sloth changing position – and the stag reared up his head. The next instant, he was bounding away, across Johnny's line of fire.

Johnny swung the rifle, keeping the sight trained a few yards ahead of the deer. That was the trouble with a .44 Winchester. It threw its bullets rather slowly. You had to aim well in advance of your target.

Johnny went through the motions. At the last possible moment he tightened his finger and squeezed the trigger halfway back, then released it. He lowered the rifle and watched the stag complete his escape.

'You had him,' Maitland said, disappointed.

'But I didn't want him.'

Maitland shot him a quick glance and turned to Inocencio. 'I don't think venison agrees with our guest. Can we rustle up something else for supper?'

They bagged a *cateto*, a wild pig, back in the woods, and roasted it on a spit that night over a blazing campfire. The sweet-sour reek of the forest seemed more intense after sundown, but the stink from the roasting pig overwhelmed it.

Johnny wrinkled his nose.

Inocencio guffawed and said, 'He's got musk glands there –' he pointed to the short ribs '– like a skunk. Good eating, though. You'll see.'

He was right. It was better than any pork Johnny had ever tasted, though they all had to pay for it afterwards by picking the ticks off their bodies that had migrated from the drying hide of their dinner.

They couldn't sleep on the ground because the tiny blood-sucking ticks were everywhere. Inocencio slung his hammock at a discreet distance, on the other side of the fire, so the two foreigners could talk in English and drink *pinga* deep into the night.

Maitland lay back in his hammock with his hands behind his neck and a cigar in his teeth and looked up at the distant lights of the Southern Cross.

'Bradbeer's been told to organise a boat to England for you,' he remarked to Johnny through a veil of white smoke.

Johnny grunted and reached for the flask of cane brandy.

'I'm sure Colin will understand if you decide to pull out at this stage,' Maitland said gently, removing the cigar.

'It's not my decision to make,' Johnny responded curtly.

'I'm sure Colin won't put any obstacles in your way. After all you've been through.'

'I wasn't thinking of Colin.'

Of course not, Harry thought. He was thinking of the girl. Maitland prayed that Bradbeer had handled her with some degree of subtlety. She must be very confused and very frightened – and must by now have guessed part, if not all, of Johnny's secret role. It worried Maitland that Bradbeer had made no direct mention of the girl in the telegram that had been carried on horseback from the post office at Londrina.

'Did your man in Buenos Aires say anything about Max?' Johnny asked.

'No. I assume there hasn't been a sighting. Max would have gone back to Europe straightaway, wouldn't he?'

'Not necessarily. Not before taking care of unfinished business.'

'You think it was Max who got you arrested, don't you?'

'He was returning a favour.'

'How can you be sure?'

'It had to be Max. He must have obtained the address from Sigrid.'

'You might have been followed.'

Johnny shook his head. 'We were always very careful.'

'But Honorio Schmidt's information came from the Gestapo. Isn't it possible they started checking up on you after that business with Willi Rausch?'

'It's possible,' Johnny conceded. 'But they had information about me – party work names, personal things – that the Gestapo could only have known from an insider.'

'Are you suggesting that Max sent your dossier to the Gestapo?'

'Something like that. I'm sure he's done it to others.' He told Harry what he had learned in Copenhagen about the systematic betrayal of Stalin's critics inside the German Communist underground to Hitler's secret police.

Max Fabrikant was an enigma to Maitland. He was a man with blood on his hands, including the blood of some of the most vigorous anti-Nazis in Germany. Max had played his own game of provocation and betrayal in Brazil for ends that were still obscure.

'Have you ever considered that Max might be a double agent working for the Gestapo?' Harry asked suddenly.

'I've considered it,' Johnny replied. He thought of how Max had nearly got him killed in the shoot-out with the Gestapo at the fish market in Rio and then, at the last minute, had saved his life. 'I don't believe Max is working for the Germans,' he went on. 'The funny thing is, he couldn't have done much more damage if he were.'

In the dream, Johnny was walking with Sigrid in a warm northern countryside, perhaps in Portugal. The place was beautiful, but there was a stifling sense of unseen oppression. The land was occupied by some hostile presence. They were surrounded by children, not their own, yet children for whom he was responsible. They passed through formal gardens into a vast, many-storied mansion with endless galleries and corridors. Johnny knew this great house, its staff and its secrets, quite well; once he had been trusted here. But

the house was troubled. There was some terrible, unidentified danger growing close at hand. He realised they were
being hunted. He and Sigrid were suddenly running through
the house, looking for a way out. They stumbled through a
labyrinth of hallways and stairs before they found an ancient
elevator and rode down inside its rickety cage to a flagstoned
lobby, where each of the massive doors had half a dozen
panels, each with its own locks. All the locks had to be opened
simultaneously by the deft manipulation of a bewildering
series of catches and keys. Johnny found he could manage
this surprisingly easily. Outside, in a walled garden of fleshy
plants and running fountains, he sensed that he was nearing
the source of the danger. Beyond the wall rose the foreboding
bulk of another great house, or a castle. Sigrid and the children backed away, making for the far wall. But Johnny made
them hold hands and led them towards the danger. He joked
at the top of his voice and burst into snatches of song, as if,
by presenting himself as anything other than a fugitive, he
would not be taken for one. He saw armoured cars and
truckloads of enemy soldiers moving away from them in a
cloud of dust. There was a wonderful sense of imminent
liberation.

Then a shadow fell across his eyes. Something was
choking him, blocking his mouth and his nose.

He opened his eyes. The clearing was dappled with
morning light. Something warm and furry was dragging
itself across his face. He could not see it clearly, because it
was on the cheek under his bad eye. The movement tickled,
yet suddenly he wanted to scream.

'Don't move,' Maitland said softly. He was standing
next to Johnny's hammock, holding his rifle by the barrel.

The thing edged down the angle of Johnny's jaw. He felt
its hairy legs scrabbling for a purchase on the slope of his
neck. Beads of sweat broke out across his forehead. He dug
his nails into the palms of his hands until he broke the skin.

The thing dropped off his neck on to the hammock.

'Now!' Maitland ordered.

He did not need a second invitation. He flung himself
off, leaving Maitland to swing the butt of his rifle down

savagely, once, twice, till the cords of the hammock broke and the tarantula was a sticky black lump among the leaves.

Johnny took a series of deep breaths.

'If Schmidt had used one of those,' he said later, 'I would have told him anything he wanted to hear.'

From the rise they could see the peaceful, muddy expanse of the Paraná River, still many miles to the west. Inocencio produced an old brass telescope. Through it Johnny saw a flock of ibises, a couple of Indian canoes and a powerful motor launch that Inocencio pronounced to be a rum-runner's boat.

'There's a little river port downstream,' Maitland announced. 'We'll ride down in the morning and hire a boat to take us across.'

Inocencio did not like the mention of this particular town. The people were all thieves and bloodsuckers, he muttered, worse than the ticks.

'What he means to say,' Harry interpreted with a grin, 'is that one of his girlfriends' husbands ran him out of town.'

They camped near a stream. Maitland magicked a bottle of champagne out of the depths of his saddlebag and placed it in the running water to chill.

'It's your last night in Brazil,' he explained to Johnny. 'I thought it called for a celebration.'

They had an hour of daylight left, and Maitland proposed bagging a few ducks for the dinner table.

A strange, striped bird with a high black comb, two-pronged like devil's horns, fluttered away through the trees as they moved along the watercourse. Higher over the treetops, vultures sailed on their great wings.

Johnny scored the first hit. The bird dropped like a stone, somewhere on the far side of the stream. They sloshed across to the other bank and were still searching the undergrowth when Inocencio stopped and motioned for the others to remain still.

He stretched out full length and pressed his ear to the ground.

'What is it?' Maitland asked.

'Listen.'

They felt it before they heard it: a faint, rhythmic vibration under the leaves.

'Horses?'

Inocencio nodded. 'Six. Maybe more. One far ahead.'

'Two parties, then?'

'Or one, with a tracker.'

'Are they tracking us?' Johnny asked, his face lined with tension.

'They could be bandits, after the horses,' Maitland said. 'We'd better get them. Inocencio doesn't like to walk,' he added, trying to make light of it. Inocencio was already on his feet, running almost noiselessly through the woods. 'Johnny, I think you should wait here.'

'No. I'm coming, too.'

They could hear the riders clearly now, approaching at a fast clip.

They led the horses deeper into the woods. Winston was shying a bit. Maitland fed him a lump of rapadura to quiet him down and tied his reins to a tree, just in case.

They watched the trail from the cover of thick scrub.

The first rider to appear wore a red bandanna and the flapping grey pants of a gaucho, and a hat with bobbing corks hanging below the brim to keep the flies off his face.

'I know that bastard,' Inocencio whispered. 'They call him Throat Slitter.'

'What is he?'

'He's a bloodhound. He works on a German *fazenda* near Maringá. He killed three men in a fight.'

Throat Slitter got off his horse, a big bay, and inspected the remains of the camp. He sniffed the air and peered into the forest. Johnny could see his eyes, hard and glinty, like obsidian. The man seemed to be staring straight at him.

They heard the drumbeat of many hooves, saw a haze of red dust.

Throat Slitter put two fingers in his mouth and let out a piercing whistle.

The riders following him reined in just short of the clearing. There were eight or nine of them, lean, weathered and sunbrowned, except for the one who appeared to be in charge. He was wearing a sun helmet and an army officer's tropical kit with the badges of rank removed. He was too big for his horse, though the horse was a sturdy Arab grey. His face was bright scarlet from the heat and the exertion.

'Hossbach,' Johnny murmured.

Hossbach and his men dismounted, leaving their horses to forage. Most of them carried rifles. While Hossbach conferred with his guide, the others started fanning out into the brush.

Maitland would have liked to put a bullet between his eyes then and there – not just because of what had happened in Rio, but because he recognised several of the horses. They had been stolen from Fox Hill. One of them was a promising two-year-old he had hoped to enter in the Grande Prémio some day. Her rider was using a wicked snaffle bit of twisted wire. Her mouth would be ruined. Harry doubted she would ever see a racetrack after the way she had been used on that punishing trail.

He guessed that Hossbach must have flown down from Rio in a light plane. The German Embassy had a two-engine job he could have borrowed. Some of the big *fazendas* had landing strips. The German had boasted to Johnny about the number of Nazi sympathisers in the state of Paraná. He must have touched down at one of their ranches, hired his gang of toughs and set off overland by car or truck for Fox Hill, where he had picked up their scent – and Harry's horses.

Harry knew they had to make an instant decision. They could make a fight of it, but they were badly outnumbered. They could try to get away through the forest, but then they would have to abandon their mounts and try to hack their way to the river on foot. There was only one way they had a fighting chance.

'Inocencio.'

Inocencio was silently fuming. He clearly had his own

notions about the correct treatment for horse thieves.

'Senhor Gruber and I will draw them after us. See if you can get round behind them and drive off the horses. Then we'll make a bolt for it.'

Inocencio slipped away through the dense vegetation. The vines parted and closed behind him again like a curtain.

Hossbach hated the jungle. It stank, and it was full of biting, sucking things you couldn't see. It pressed in around you, closing in like the walls of a medieval torture chamber, till you were gasping for air. Twenty yards from the trail, he was lost. He stumbled along, breathing hard, terrified that he would lose sight of Throat Slitter's bobbing red bandanna and never find his way out.

He had volunteered for this job because he had a score to settle. Johnny Gruber duped him and murdered one of their best agents. Also, Trott had promised to recommend him for an important job in Europe if he succeeded. It had seemed straightforward enough: a surprise raid on a horse farm in a part of the country where half the ranchers spoke German. He hadn't reckoned with *this*.

Someone was calling him by name.

There it was again. 'Psst! Hossbach!'

The voice was coming from nearby. Hadn't the others heard it? Damn. Throat Slitter had vanished among the trees.

'Johnny?'

'Here! Over here!'

He fired in the direction of the sound twice, three times. There was no echo. The silence of that green hell seemed to mock him.

'Hossbach!'

He fired again and yelled for Throat Slitter and the others, who were pushing their way through the jungle to get to him, drawn by the shots.

He swung round to shout his orders, and that sudden motion may have saved him, because a rifle bullet hissed past his ear and got one of his men, who collapsed like a punctured balloon, in the chest.

Scared and sweating hard, Hossbach waved the others forward and staggered along after them sideways, covering the rear.

There was a tremendous volley from the other direction, over to the east, followed by the whinnying and stamping of hooves.

Throat Slitter came running back, shouldering his way through the rest of the men.

'Back!' he yelled out. 'Back! It's a trick.'

'Wait!' Hossbach cried out.

One of the men who hesitated was felled by a bullet between the shoulder blades. He dropped like a tree under the woodcutter's axe.

Hossbach was blundering after the others, tripping over roots and fallen branches.

He regained the trail in time to see his horse fly past, with the others stampeding behind. A mestizo on a black horse galloped along at their heels, firing his rifle into the air.

Hossbach took aim and squeezed off a couple of rounds, but the rider flung himself down against his horse's neck, so the bullets went wide. He aimed for the horse, but the trigger snapped on an empty chamber.

Hossbach swore. His men opened fire as two horsemen came darting out of the woods, but neither of them fell. He watched Johnny and the Englishman racing into the sunset.

'They're probably headed for Esperança,' Throat Slitter suggested.

'How far?'

'Fifteen, twenty miles.'

'Is there anywhere we can find horses in this godforsaken jungle?'

The guide rubbed his stubbly chin. 'Not unless we catch them ourselves.'

They started walking west, jangling spurs. They had a stroke of luck. They came across a saddleless straggler – a pretty palomino mare – chewing her way through a *maté* bush. Throat Slitter got a rope round her neck and unwound his Indian belly-belt, a dozen feet of tough, knitted wool that he wore around his waist. He tied one end of the belt around the horse's neck, just behind the ears, and made a turn around the nose. Gripping the other end, he had an improvised rein.

'I'll take her,' Hossbach announced.

Throat Slitter gave him a surly look but handed over the rein.

At his first attempt to hoist his bulk up onto the mare's bare back, Hossback slipped and fell heavily in the dirt. The men laughed.

Throat Slitter vaulted on to the mare's back and reached out a hand. 'Here. You can ride pillion if you want.'

There was pink murder in Hossbach's eyes, but he accepted.

5

Maitland was in excellent spirits, although the fisherman had charged him a small fortune to rent out his boat. It was a broken-down tub reeking of bilge water and gutted fish, but the diesel engine seemed serviceable enough. It was the best thing on offer in Esperança, a huddle of adobe huts with a couple of cantinas on a main street that was a blur of red dust and black flies. If Hossbach managed to follow them that far, he would be hard put to follow them any further in an Indian canoe or a leaky dinghy. On the strength of that, Harry had decided to sail all the way downstream to a point just above the Iguaçu Falls, within easy striking distance of their rendezvous at the Paraguayan town of Acarai. He had trailed a couple of lines over the side of the boat. There were dourados in these waters, and nothing in the world tasted better. There were piranhas, too, as he warned Johnny when he stripped off, intending to take a dip.

They had left Inocencio in Esperança with the horses. Harry had told him to go back to Fox Hill by a different route and alert a friendly officer in the state police that they had been attacked by horse thieves. Here on the frontier, you weren't forgiven for stealing a man's horse.

They caught a couple of dourados and cooked them on the primus stove at the end of the day. In the falling light, dark, vertical clouds bristled above the rain forest like spears. Harry could tell that the falls were near, from the swarms of butterflies with vivid black and red wings that danced across their bow. One of them perched above the wheel. When its wings were folded, the pattern resembled the number eight or the symbol of infinity. The falls had a magnetic attraction for these creatures. Harry fancied he could hear the distant thunder of the waters and calculated that they were half an hour, at most, from their landfall.

Johnny was throwing fish bones over the side.

He looked back and said, 'We have company.'

Maitland followed the pointing hand and saw the sleek motor launch he had watched through a telescope the day before. The one Inocencio had said belonged to contrabanders. The launch was coming on fast; nothing he had seen on the Paraná River would match it. He wondered whether the skipper was making for the same anchorage.

He slapped the side of his cheek. He had forgotten how ferocious the mosquitoes were on the Paraguayan side.

The launch was almost within hailing distance. There were a lot of people on board. Maybe they were pleasure trippers, not smugglers, as Inocencio, with his sour view of human nature, had maintained.

Maitland raised his arm above his head and waved.

The response was less than friendly.

The first shot, from a high-velocity rifle, cracked the glass in the sole surviving window of the wheelhouse, just beside Maitland's ear. The other bullets flew high and fell short.

Johnny was already hunkered down, sighting along his Winchester, waiting for the launch to get within range. Now they could see Hossbach in his desert tan and Throat Slitter's red bandanna. Hossbach's gang must have hijacked the launch at Esperança, or bought the captain.

Maitland tried to coax more speed out of the engine, till he heard an ominous clanking and the deck started to shudder underfoot. They could never outrun Hossbach's boat.

He took off his belt and used it to lash the wheel into place. Then he crawled along the deck, close to Johnny, and traded shots with the pursuers. It was hopeless. The launch was almost alongside, and the German had got hold of a Hotchkiss gun. It spat lead across their deck, driving wood splinters into Harry's legs and hands.

The launch came at them full throttle.

'They're going to ram!'

Johnny, the sailor, took charge. He yelled to Maitland to cover him and leaped for the wheel. He wrenched the boat around till they were hugging the Paraguayan shore. He saw a jumble of tin-roofed shacks and a sagging jetty – the place where he had intended to land – drift past. Muscovy ducks flapped, squawking, out of the mangroves.

The boat was gathering speed, but for the wrong reason. The current was tugging them along, down to the falls. The crash of the waters blotted out the thrum of the engines. In a few minutes, Johnny realised, he would have to run the boat aground or risk being dragged over the precipice.

Maybe he could lure Hossbach on to a sandbar. The big launch must have a deeper draught than the fishing boat. He veered round to the landward side of an island, into a shallower channel. The launch did not follow. He lost sight of it behind a wilderness of palms and lush tropical plants. The light was fading fast. Everything was indistinct except for the shimmering haze up ahead, the spray from the seething waters of Iguaçu.

The island dropped behind, and the launch hurtled at them, shuddering against their hull. Johnny heard a crash behind him. One of Hossbach's men had flung himself onto the deck. He grabbed the boathook and lashed out with it. He caught the boarder along the side of the jaw and knocked him over the side. He wrestled with the wheel, driving the boat in towards the shore. Their bow scraped against a basalt rock, but the pull of the river was now irresistible. The boat was being swept along like a cork towards the falls.

Johnny heard a cry of alarm from the bigger boat.

He called to Maitland, 'Jump!' Land was only a few yards away.

But Maitland was struggling with another boarder, lashing out with feet and fists. Hossbach took a blow to his chest but recovered and was after him with a knife, a kind of knife Johnny had only seen once before, in a Fourth Department weapons course. He did not throw the thing, he fired it. As Maitland's leg shot out again, aiming for the groin, Hossbach released a catch. The razor-sharp blade hissed from its socket and embedded itself deep in Harry's thigh.

Maitland gasped and fell backwards, so his head was dangling in the river.

Hossbach was scrabbling around among ropes and fishing lines for the Winchester. He glanced up, and his mouth dropped open as he saw Johnny thrusting down at him with the boathook. His last thoughts were lost as the hook tore his throat out.

On the other boat they were trying desperately to reverse engines. It was a lost cause. The falls were calling them.

'Harry!'

Maitland was trying to draw the knife blade out of his leg. It sliced into his hand, even through the folded handkerchief.

'Leave that! We have to jump now!'

'I don't think I can.'

There was a stubby promontory ahead, with branches that overhung the river. Johnny snatched up a coil of rope, tied one end around Harry's waist and twisted the other round his forearm.

He climbed up onto the roof of the wheelhouse. There would only be one chance. None, unless the branch held.

'Get to the side!' he shouted down to Maitland.

He saw the black silhouette looming up and flexed his leg muscles, willing himself not to feel the ache in his feet, still swollen from the beatings. He bent at the knees, like a diver. When he made his leap, he sensed it would fall short. They had taken too much of his strength. His fingertips grazed the branch he was aiming for, and he was falling, into that murderous current. He went under. He came up again, gasping for air. But the river was sucking him down. Then something slammed into his chest. He clutched at it and felt wood – a submerged root, or a tree trunk. It held his weight. He made the rope fast around it and tugged for Harry to follow.

He saw the Englishman fall, rather than jump, off the boat. He pulled him in, hand over hand.

They clawed their way up onto the rocks and watched the two boats, like lovers clasped in a suicide leap, sail over the falls.

6

Johnny pushed open the frosted glass doors of the Casino Acarai. Inside, they were playing a scratchy record of El Ultimo Beso on the phonograph. A pair of short, dumpy Indian girls in bright prints waited for custom at the bar. The raw light favoured neither them nor the peeling walls. Most of the patrons were clustered around the roulette table, slapping down wads of Brazilian, Argentinian and Paraguayan currency which the head croupier accepted imperturbably and distributed between the cash slot and his own pockets. He was a villanous-looking character with a pencil moustache, slicked-down hair and a static, risorius grin.

'How will I know the contact?' Johnny had asked Maitland.

'Bet on twenty-two,' was the answer. 'Only on twenty-two. Bet big, and at least three times.'

It was a variation of the old wheeze they had used at the Necrôpolis in Rio.

At that moment Harry was in bed under a mosquito net they had had to acquire for themselves in a dosshouse that styled itself the Hotel Acarai. Johnny had pulled the knife blade out of Harry's leg with his teeth and bound up the wound as best he could with a handkerchief and a strip off his own shirt. The gash would need stitches, but Maitland refused to trust the local medical profession or to run the risk of attracting curiosity. In the meantime he was numbing the wound – and himself – with liberal shots of a local *aguardiente* labelled Gotas d'Oro, or Drops of Gold.

Johnny studied the group around the roulette wheel, to see if he could spot Bradbeer's contact. They were an unpromising bunch: a portly dowager loaded down with flashy jewels and accompanied by an obvious gigolo; a near hysteric who turned away with his hand over his eyes each time they spun the wheel; a clutch of Argentinian sightseers. The head croupier had no fewer than three assistants. Each time he spun the wheel, they all pressed in around it, so that it was all but impossible for the players to see where it jumped.

Johnny squeezed through the crush and handed the croupier a fistful of Brazilian money. He received a small stack of mauve plastic chips. He placed about a third of them on twenty-two.

'*Bolas!*' the stage villain called, flourishing his croup close to the knuckles of a player who was trying to rearrange the chips he had already deployed.

Johnny didn't see where the ball landed and didn't much care.

His chips were whisked away.

He bet again. The winning number this time was thirteen. Nobody had it. The dowager started to blubber – whether because of her losses or because of the way her escort was feeling her up in public, it was impossible to say.

Nobody gave Johnny any sign of recognition.

He placed his remaining chips on the same number. This time, he paid attention as the ball bounced around the rim of the wheel. From his height he could see over the shoulders of the assistant croupier, who was stationed so as to block the patrons' view. The ball came to rest on twenty-two. It would be worth quite a bit to him, with the stake he had put down. He glanced at his pile of chips and counted eight of them.

'*Veinte-ocho,*' the stage villain called out.

Johnny waited for them to shell out. Instead, he saw one of the assistants haul away his chips, with all the others.

'*Espere –*' he burst out.

'*Veinte-ocho,*' the head croupier repeated, with that permanent leer. 'Twenty-eight.'

Johnny peered at the wheel. Sure enough, the ball was resting at twenty-eight. They had moved it.

The other players started spreading their chips. They didn't know the game was rigged. Or else they knew and didn't care.

Johnny was disgusted, because there was absolutely nothing he could do. He wasn't here to make a killing at the tables. Even if he were prepared to make a scene, it could only succeed in getting him arrested; the house had four witnesses to support its story.

He went to find the men's room. There were slices of lime in the urinal. He watched the steam rise from them and wondered about the contact. Perhaps Bradbeer's agent hadn't come that night or hadn't yet arrived. After all, no time had been set for the meeting.

He had not quite finished when the door opened. A man walked straight to the urinal and started unbuttoning his flies.

'Mr Maitland, I presume?' he said in excruciating English.

Johnny glanced sideways and met the plaster grin of the croupier who had stolen his money.

The croupier was well connected and evidently well on his way to becoming a very rich man. He supplied Johnny with a new set of papers, a ride to the capital and a seat on a plane bound for Buenos Aires. The plane turned out to be a four-engine French flying boat en route to Paris from Santiago via various South American capitals. The same company, unknowingly, had flown Prestes to Brazil to start his revolution.

Bradbeer met Johnny at the airport. He would have passed for a merchant banker, slightly at sea in his present surroundings.

As they drove into the city, he asked after Maitland, expressed the appropriate concern over his injury and then turned to practical matters. He had laid on a room for Johnny at the Crillón – damn the expense and all that, Johnny had bloody well earned it. Besides, it was a very decent pub and an easy walk from Bradbeer's flat. He had reserved a cabin on a British steamship, the *Mandalay*, leaving for Southampton and points south within the week. Now, would Johnny like to check into the hotel and rest up for a bit, or would he care to stop in at Bradbeer's place for a drink?

'Where is she?' Johnny demanded coldly.

Bradbeer cleared his throat. 'She never made contact,' he said.

'*What?*'

Bradbeer started to fidget. 'She did arrive safely. I looked into that. But you know what the instructions were. She was supposed to initiate contact.'

'You mean she simply disappeared?'

'I imagine she took up with her old gang. I mean –'

'You lost her. Damn you. You lost her.'

'Now, hang on a bit. I didn't have a hunting license, you know. I couldn't very well go rattling the cages of the local constabulary either, now could I?'

Johnny sat grimly with his arms folded. He was attacking Bradbeer because Bradbeer was there. It wasn't this Englishman's fault.

'It's still the same place, isn't it? In the Zona Rosa?'

'You can't just barge in there,' Bradbeer protested.

'No, of course not,' Johnny agreed, once he had confirmed the address. 'We'll talk about it after I get some rest.'

Bradbeer looked distinctly relieved when he dropped him at the Crillón.

The porter affected not to notice that Johnny's sole luggage consisted of an overnight bag he had picked up in Asunción.

He made a brief inspection of his lodgings and found that, on this occasion, the Firm had spared none of the little touches. He had a whole suite to himself, with a patio and a miniature fountain in which a cherub with a serious

602

bladder problem widdled around the clock. There was a bottle of scotch with an ice bucket and two glasses.

The second glass, useless because there was no one to share, enraged him. He picked it up and dashed it against the pink marble of the mantelpiece.

7

'I've been waiting for you, Johnny. I've been waiting for a very long time.' The flashing lights of the honky-tonk across the street drew blue and orange bars across her face.

'You look different in glasses.'

She touched the rims defensively with her free hand.

'We're both older,' she said, keeping the pistol levelled at his chest. 'You're going grey. Keep your hands where I can see them. Higher. That's better.'

She felt around inside his jacket for the Mauser. She checked the magazine and exchanged his gun for her own, which she tucked under her belt.

'You walked in like a choirboy,' Helene said, with a note of professional reproach.

'Where is she?'

Helene laughed. That hoarse, deep-throated smoker's laugh, like a frog's mating call.

'I don't think you ever understood women, my love. She's tougher than you. Maybe you picked the wrong one.'

'What are you saying?'

'She told me all of it. Your Englishman in Rio. Your Mr Bradbeer. How do the Americans say it? She fingered you.'

'May I sit down?'

Helene waved him towards the bed. She sat on the edge of the desk, looking down on him. They were in the Comintern liaison office in the Zona Rosa. Helene had been stationed here since Max had ordered her out of Rio. She had spent the last weeks rescuing boat people from Brazil – the revolution had collapsed completely with the arrest or flight of all its leaders – and waiting for Johnny.

Helene shook a cigarillo out of its pack and lit it with one hand.

She said, 'You don't look good, Johnny.'

'I've felt better. Do you have to point that thing at me?'

'It helps to remind me we're on different sides,' she replied.

'We don't have to be. I've never done anything to harm you. Or Sigrid.'

'Here,' Helene interjected curtly. 'She left you a letter. Read it if you want.'

He took the envelope. The letter inside covered less than a page. It was typed, so he could decipher nothing of the mind of the writer from the script. It appealled to nostalgia, to his most precious memories. Sigrid wrote about the black panther in the cage in the Berlin zoo, about the sonnet by Rilke that he had recited to her.

'Come to me quickly,' Sigrid wrote. 'Without you, I am behind bars.'

The words wounded him. He had to assume that she had left this message on Max's instructions, to lure him into a trap. But why had she invoked something so personal, something that belonged only to the two of them? Was she signalling that she still wanted to be with him, that she was literally a prisoner behind bars?

His hand was shaking when he gave the letter back to Helene.

'What have they done with her?' he demanded.

'Max took her to Paris,' Helene reported, watching him intently. 'There's more. They sent this after she left.'

He glanced at the second message. It was briefer even than the first: the six-line transcription of a radio signal from Moscow Centre. It congratulated him on his performance in Brazil and ordered him to proceed to Paris to receive new instructions.

It was all so transparent he wanted to laugh out loud. Did they believe he was so witless he would buy this at face value?

'I imagine you know what it means,' Helene commented.

'I know.'

It meant more interrogations, a forced march to Moscow, torture at the hands of secret policemen more expert than any Brazilian, the chance of a show trial, the certainty of execution. Unless –

He stared at Helene. There were no accusations in the letter or the telegram. Max wanted to lull him into a sense of false security, using his feelings for Sigrid to bait the trap. Max must have ordered Helene to play along. But she had disobeyed orders.

'You're not playing your part very well, are you?' Johnny challenged her. 'You were supposed to receive me with open arms and shunt me off to Paris as if everything was absolutely fine. You're letting Max down, my love.'

'Leave Max out of this!' she snapped at him. 'I want to know why you did it.'

'It's a long story,' he began, conscious that there was no longer any point in trying to dissemble. His best chance was to appeal to the bond that still existed between himself and this woman. 'It started with Heinz,' he went on. 'When Heinz told me that Stalin and Hitler were natural allies, I didn't believe him. When he showed me how the party was opening the door to the Nazis in Germany, I still didn't want to believe. Heinz had to die before I was ready to understand. You know how he died? Max split his skull open with a sledgehammer because Heinz was one of the few men left in Germany – or the whole world Communist movement – who wasn't afraid to tell the truth.'

'That's a lie!' There were bright patches of colour in Helene's cheeks, and her chest was heaving.

She knows, Johnny thought. She's heard the screams too. She wouldn't be so agitated if she weren't trying to deny them.

'Heinz wasn't a special case,' he proceeded, keeping his voice low and calm. 'In fact, his fate was entirely predictable. Why do you think they are butchering the Old Bolsheviks in Moscow? Why do you suppose Wollweber in Copenhagen gives the Gestapo lists of comrades in Germany who, once in their lives, made the mistake of criticising the party bosses, or the big boss in the Kremlin? Do you believe the revolution has to be built on the corpses of those who sweat in its service, like the Great Wall of China? Do you imagine that what you are doing for the Russian secret police has *anything* in common with socialism?'

'Shut up!' she yelled at him.

'Because you don't believe me, or because you do?'

It was the first time he had ever seen her look terrified. Even in Shanghai, he had never seen her like this.

'You know I'm right,' he said softly. 'You don't belong with these people any more than I do.'

She jumped up and brandished the gun at him.

'Shut your face!'

'Or what?'

The hand with the gun was trembling. She pressed the other hand over it to hold it still.

'You betrayed all of us. I don't want to hear any more about the reasons. You have lives to answer for.'

'And some that I saved.'

She was crying. She swept the back of her hand across her eyes angrily, to brush this sign of frailty away.

'There is only one honourable solution.' As she stood up, it struck him that – consciously or not – she must be seeking to impersonate her putative Prussian sire.

She held the gun out to him, butt forward.

'What precisely would you like me to do?' he said. 'Do you want me to blow my brains out?'

She said nothing.

'Revolutionaries don't have a code of honour,' he taunted her. 'Max taught me that we were supposed to practise Bolshevist elasticity.'

'Do it for her sake,' Helene implored him. 'They'll drag her through all of it otherwise. Her life will be wrecked.'

'You had all of this worked out, didn't you? That's why you waited. I'm not a Prussian cavalry officer, darling. I'm not going to do it.'

Her lips were trembling. Her eyes goggled as if she were on the brink of a seizure.

'I won't do it,' he repeated. 'But if you shoot me with

606

my own gun, I suppose it might look like suicide.' He got off the bed and advanced slowly towards her.

'Come on,' he coaxed her. 'We haven't been together in a long time. Let's stop this charade and talk things over calmly.'

'Don't come any closer. I'm serious.'

'Go ahead then. You'll probably do me a favour.'

He moved closer, till he could feel the pressure of the gun barrel against his chest. She still didn't shoot.

'Let's lose that, shall we?'

Gently, not rushing her, he took her wrist. At that moment he felt a tremendous warmth towards this woman he had once held and loved. She was a victim, too. He sensed that she was approaching the same crossroads he had reached when he had learned how Heinz had died.

'There's no fight between us,' he said gently, moving his fingers to pry the gun loose.

She began shaking uncontrollably.

'*No!*' The word was a bellow of pain, neither male nor female, barely human.

He forced her arm back, so that when she fired, the bullet drove into the plaster above their heads. She was fighting back, clawing at his face.

He did not want to hurt her. He kept murmuring her name like a lover.

She heaved towards him with her lower body and kneed him in the groin.

He buckled in a spasm of unbearable pain but remembered the gun. She was lowering the barrel, aiming for his face. He wrenched savagely at her wrist at the instant she pulled the trigger.

At last she dropped the gun, and fell into his arms.

'Oh, my love. I never meant this.'

The pistol had gone off at the base of her chin, ripping away flesh and bone and vocal cords. She died without a scream.

He rocked with the body like a dancer, careless of the blood that was oozing over his shoulder and the tears that made salty furrows down his cheeks.

He repeated aloud, 'We're both victims.'

13

The Gift

. . . neither do the spirits damned Lose all their virtue.
— *Milton,*
Paradise Lost

I

The black-headed gulls had returned in twos and threes to
St James's Park. These were the ones that were barren,
Bailey thought, or had lost their eggs or their young.
Beyond a white, fragrant cloud of meadowsweet, tufted
ducks swam in the pond among their broods. The incon-
stancy of ducklings had always intrigued him. Cut off from
the brood, they would waddle off to join anything with
wings. They seemed to have no sense of a separate identity.

Johnny, perhaps, had too much.

Bailey had met the boat at Southampton. Johnny was
tanned and gaunt, his leanness exaggerated by the suit that
Bradbeer had loaned him, which was too wide and too
short. His dark blond hair had turned gunmetal grey. He
was wearing dark glasses, and one of their first calls in
London was to an optician who told him he would never
see more than shadows out of his left eye. Johnny accepted
this with apparent indifference. They went to the Army
and Navy Store, where Bailey picked out a few suits that
fitted Johnny well enough.

'You can't go to Paris,' Bailey told him over sandwiches
at the flat in South Audley street. 'Besides, you've got a

date with the King. He's going to pin a medal on you.'

'You can keep your bloody medal.'

Johnny was evasive about what had happened in Buenos Aires, which was a bad sign. After many questions, he said that Helene had killed herself. He could not explain why she had done this with his gun, and Bailey let the subject drop. He could sense that Johnny was tortured by what had happened.

Johnny had plenty of questions of his own about Rio.

'There's some good news,' Bailey reported. 'Captain Schmidt has been relieved of his duties.'

'What about Prestes and the others?'

'The police got Prestes. Something to do with his dog. You did say he had a dog, didn't you?'

'Yes. Príncipe.'

'He loved the dog too much. Not a bad quality, I suppose. But not very professional.'

There were conflicting accounts of the arrest, Bailey explained. The one he favoured was that, even in hiding, the rebel leader wanted his dog to eat only the best. The police knew that his lair was somewhere in the working-class district of Meier and started keeping a watch on butcher shops in the neighbourhood. They spotted a young black maid who was regularly buying choice cuts of meat and asking for bones. They tailed her to a house on the Rua Honorio and stormed the house in the early hours of the morning. Prestes himself came to the door in his pyjamas. A strapping German girl thrust herself between him and the police, shouting 'Don't shoot! We're not dynamiters!'

'That doesn't sound much like Olga.'

'That's the information we have.'

'What about Nilo?'

Bailey shook his head. 'No trace.'

'That son of a bitch has a lot to answer for,' Johnny growled. He was thinking of the pretty little Bahian girl strangled with a clothesline in Nilo's apartment, and the double game Nilo had played with Doctor Alcibiades and the Fascists.

'They did lock up the snake charmer,' Bailey volunteered.

Johnny merely grunted. Doctor Alcibiades, the most duplicitous of all the Brazilians, was no longer of much consequence to him.

'What will they do with her? With Olga?'

Bailey took a sip of beer. 'I'm afraid there's talk of deporting her.'

Johnny clenched his fists. 'You've got to stop it!'

Bailey thought, he's identifying Prestes' woman with Helene – and with what the Gestapo intended to do to him.

'I don't see that there's much we can do. Except possibly to indicate polite concern. It's not exactly HMG's style to stick up for Stalin's agents. And you told us yourself that Olga is a dedicated Communist.'

'Can't Harry –'

'Harry's on his way back to England,' Bailey said firmly.

But Johnny wouldn't let it rest. 'A German Jew, a Communist – Can't you imagine the party the Gestapo will have with her?'

'I can imagine.'

A hundred and sixty pounds of tortured flesh was something other than human. It was on the way to becoming something else: a hero, or an informer, or a madman, like Emil Brandt. Johnny had travelled part of that road. He knew. But his grief and anger over Olga's fate was more personal, more specific.

In part of himself he still belongs to them, Bailey thought. He is at war with the ideology and the regime, but he won't abandon comrades who shared the same trenches when he still believed. And he identifies Prestes' woman with his own. If he could conquer this instinct, he would make a more professional agent. And less of a man.

'I'm going to Paris,' Johnny repeated.

'Yes. Of course you are.'

The vaulting roof of the Gare du Nord could not contain the din. Porters rammed trolleys piled high with expensive luggage through the crowd. The first-class travellers who eddied along in their wake babbled about the excitements of the autumn collections, the fabulous embroideries of Jeanne Lanvin, the daring cut of Madeleine Vionnet's crepe evening gowns, the fastidious touch of Mainbocher, the prodigy from Chicago. There were flocks of German and Polish refugees with their possessions on their backs and under their arms. There were men who were racing against the clock and men who were too obviously idling, watching others or watching to see if someone had his eye on *them*. Some of them were vaguely familiar to Johnny, couriers he had seen in one or other of the Comintern offices in the old days. But there was not a face he could put a name to.

Out in the street somebody pushed a leaflet into his hand. It sang the virtues of the Popular Front, the alliance of Socialists and Communists that was on the verge of taking power. Working men in dungarees trooped past on their way to a union meeting or a demonstration. They chanted the *Internationale* quite openly, interspersed with bursts of the *Marseillaise*, and some of the bystanders took up the chorus.

He walked to the Comintern hotel on the rue d'Alsace. Nothing much had changed. Nobody had touched up the paint or fixed the cracks in the masonry. Only the posters on the outside wall had been updated. In one of them – a caricature of a bourgeois politician sitting in Hitler's pocket – he thought he saw Sigrid's touch. The theme was crude, but the wildness of the design gave it unusual power.

It gave him an idea.

The man at the reception desk was the one he remembered. He never seemed to look you in the face, and his fingernails were still sorely in need of attention.

'*Bonjour. Est-ce que Monsieur Münzenberg reste toujours ici?*' he asked in his faulty French.

'Monsieur?'

He repeated the question. During his last stay in Paris, Willi Münzenberg, the Westbureau's propaganda boss, had been living quite openly in this establishment. Everyone addressed him by his own name.

But the clerk affected never to have heard of anyone called Münzenberg.

'I need to reach him urgently. It's a party matter.'

The clerk turned his back on Johnny to rummage among the pigeonholes behind the desk. Without turning around, he said, 'Your name?'

'Mattern. Fritz Mattern.'

It was the name he had used inside the German party. It was the name Willi Münzenberg would remember, if he remembered at all.

'Wait.'

The clerk shuffled into the back room. Through an opaque glass door, Johnny could see his silhouette. He was talking – to somebody, or into a telephone. Remembering how Sigrid had once gone looking for Münzenberg at the publishing house and had found Max instead, Johnny almost succumbed to a sudden impulse to rush out the door.

The clerk came back with a travel brochure and slapped it down on the top of the reception desk.

'This will show you the Métro stations, Monsieur,' he said in a loud, disgusted voice, the voice of a man worn out by inane inquiries from tourists.

'Thank you,' Johnny responded in English, equally loud.

He strolled out of the hotel, turned south past the old prison of St Lazare and then swung east along the rue du Paradis. When he was fairly sure that nobody had followed him from the rue d'Alsace, he turned over the brochure. On the inside back cover he found a scribbled address.

He took the Métro. The line went direct to Odéon, but he made a diversion, changing trains at Chatelet and Jussieu, before he walked up into the perfect spring sunlight of the Boulevard St-Germain. A girl in a floppy beret was playing Mozart on a violin. A quartet of mimes, their faces chalk white, turned handstands and held out their bowler hats for coins. Tourists and boulevard philosophers thronged the tables along the sidewalk. It was all stunningly normal, which made him feel conspicuous.

He hurried to the rue Jacob, the address the clerk had given him. It struck him, as he turned the corner, that the house was barely a stone's throw away from the GPU office on the rue de Seine.

Trap or no trap, he told himself, I'm not going to stop now.

There was an intercom hitched up to the bell beside the door.

'Mattern.' He gave the same name he had used on the rue d'Alsace. 'Mattern!'

The buzzer sounded and he pushed his way in, to find himself standing in a mousetrap, a boxlike foyer with a sealed door on the other side, from behind which they were presumably taking a good look at him through the peephole.

The door opened and a feral girl with frizzy red hair and a prognathous jaw gave him the once-over.

'Credentials!'

'I don't have them with me.'

Her lips curled back in a most inhospitable way. But Willi Münzenberg appeared from some other room, looking like an abstracted professor with his lank hair and rumpled corduroys.

'It's all right, Cilly,' he reassured his assistant. 'I know him.'

'I ought to say, I used to,' Münzenberg added for Johnny's benefit, as he squired him past rows of clacking typewriters into a private office. 'You're different. I would never have recognised you.'

'We've all changed.'

'That's true enough. Especially in Paris. You've come to the right place, Fritz Mattern. Before we know it, the Communists will be sitting in the Hôtel de Ville and the Elysée! For the first time in our lives, we're respectable!'

'Then why all the security?'

'That's because of the Fascists, more than the police.

With any luck, we'll soon be running the police.'
He lowered his voice and went on, 'I only wish we'd
had the sense to do this in Germany when there was still
time.'

Johnny said nothing. He stared at the posters and wood-
cuts on Münzenberg's walls, glorifying the alliance of
Socialists and Communists that Stalin had banned in Germany. How long would it last in France?

'I heard you were in South America,' the Comintern
propaganda chief said.

'Brazil.'

'Ah. That was a nasty business. We have counter-
measures organised. Solidarity committees in support of
the victims of reaction. We even have some titled English
ladies who have agreed to sail to Rio to intercede with the
government.'

'You must try to do something for Olga.'

'I want to make her the focus of the campaign. There are
some bureaucratic problems, of course.'

'There are?'

'Well, there are people close to the top who would rather
not advertise our role in Brazil.'

He means Manuilsky, Johnny thought. Manuilsky and
the big boss, Stalin. They got us into Brazil, then they lost
their nerve. Now they don't want to hear about anyone
associated with the operation. Let the Gestapo have them.
Does a man like Münzenberg, who has more brains, and
more guts, than the whole Executive Committee of the
Comintern put together, still believe in this gang? How
can he? Johnny would have liked to ask, but he had come
for something else.

'What can I do for you?' Münzenberg asked.

'I've just come back,' Johnny rehearsed his hastily concocted tale. 'My companion – Sigrid – has moved from her
old address. She told me she would be doing some work
for you. I thought you might be able to put me in touch
with her.'

Münzenberg's face clouded. 'I think you've come to the
wrong department, friend.'

'But I know she's doing work for you. I've seen her posters in the street.'

'She's done a few things,' Münzenberg conceded. 'But it's just a sideline, a hobby. Pity. She has unusual gifts.'

'Do you know where she lives?'

Münzenberg rubbed his nose. He could smell that something was wrong. Johnny counted on the fact that he had no high regard for the chekists.

'You might ask Ana,' he suggested. 'She's in the artists' group. The two of them used to be friends.'

The new address was an atelier in Montparnasse, down the street from the Closerie des Lilas, where the Symbolists had discussed a revolution of the imagination and where Lenin and Trotsky had plotted a more tangible one in the world before the war.

Johnny took a table in the window and ordered Pernod and black coffee. Waiting for the gate to open between trains at the Sèvres-Babylone Métro station, he had sensed someone watching him intently. When he whipped around, he caught a fleeting glimpse of a quite ordinary man in a dark grey suit and matching hat, who disappeared in the rush of passengers as the automatic gate swung open. He did not see the man again.

Bailey had offered to cover him. He had refused. Once Max's people picked up his scent, they would spot the tail immediately.

There was a cyclist across the street, taking too long to adjust his clips. He waved to a second cyclist, a girl with straw-coloured hair tied up in a scarf. They pedalled away together. Perhaps it was nothing.

His eyes were hot and sore, despite the dark glasses. He couldn't hold the coffee cup steady. His skin was moist, his body racked intermittently by malarial spasms. He forgot the French cigarette that was glued to his lower lip, and the ash crumbled over his shirt front.

In my mid-thirties, he thought, I'm already an old man.

Seeing him like this, would she feel pity, or simply contempt? He didn't want either. He wanted some kind of a life. Since their reunion in Brazil on the heights of the

Tijuca rain forest, he had known that she had to be part of that life. He had enough money in a London bank account to support them both in reasonable comfort for the rest of their days. They had fought their battles. They both bore the scars. They had earned the right to some measure of happiness.

But would she come? On the boat train from England he had tried to script in his head what he would say to her if he could find her before Max found him. There were tricks he could play, lies he could tell. He had even thought of arranging a setup to convince her that Max was in the pay of the Gestapo. These ruses might get her out of Max's reach, but they would turn on him later, like hissing snakes, and poison whatever trust had survived between them.

His only chance was tell her the truth and hope that the love they had both been schooled to suppress would prove stronger than doubt.

A girl was coming out of the atelier. Svelte, bobbed hair, dark rain cape. She had a bicycle chained to a railing. She bent to open the padlock.

Johnny tossed some money onto the table and hurried out of the bistro.

'Excuse me. You must be Ana.'

'Have we met?'

She looked wary, and he took off the dark glasses. 'I'm Johnny. Sigrid's friend.'

'Oh. She mentioned you.' Her expression changed to mild curiosity. She looked Johnny up and down as if assessing his potential as a lover.

He smiled. 'I've got a surprise for her. Do you know where she is?'

'I don't know where she lives.' Wary again.

'It's a surprise that absolutely won't wait.' Johnny winked.

'Well, in that case – we often go sketching together on Tuesdays, and have lunch afterwards. At the zoo.'

'The zoo at Vincennes.'

'Yes. I told her I couldn't go today, because I've got a date.'

616

'That's a shame. I hope I get to know you better. Maybe next week?'

'Why not?'

It took half an hour to find her in the sprawling park. She had set up a folding easel under the trees, in a grassy expanse where African antelopes roamed freely. She had attracted a gaggle of schoolchildren, who were craning over her shoulder to see the picture coming alive.

He came up from behind and started reciting the last stanza of Rilke's poem about the panther –

Nur manchmal schiebt der Vorhang der Pupille
sich lautlos auf . . .

and the charcoal broke against the heavy paper.

Some of the children giggled. A solemn little boy in glasses retrieved the stub of charcoal and offered it to the artist.

'*You!*' The points of colour in her cheeks exaggerated her pallor.

A teacher came bustling over, full of apologies, and shepherded the children away.

'I promised I'd come for you.'

Her lips opened and closed, but no words came out.

'Also, I got your letter.'

'How – how could you? Are you mad?' She looked around nervously at a couple eating ice cream on a bench, at a busload of American tourists festooned with cameras, trooping along behind their guide.

She said, 'This city is death for you.'

'I've come for *you*.'

She shied from him like a frightened horse.

'I've come to take you away. Since that night at the Babylônia Club, I've lived only for this.'

'Don't talk that way! You don't have the right!'

'Come.' Gently but firmly, he took her arm. 'Let's talk.'

Reluctantly she packed up her easel, and they sat under a sun umbrella among the school parties and the holidaymakers. He ordered a citron pressé. She left hers untouched.

'What happened to your eye?'

He explained – the prison, the Gestapo, the jailbreak, the chase downriver. He omitted Harry Maitland.

'You were luckier than the ones you betrayed,' she flew at him. 'How many lives have you destroyed?'

'I didn't set out to destroy anyone's life. I did what I had to do.' Jerkily, trying to hold her with his eyes, he began to tell the whole story, starting with the death of Heinz Kordt. He talked of how his glowing belief in the world revolution had been trampled down by Stalin's secret police, of how the Soviets and the Nazis were joined in an unholy alliance to create a world fit only for slaves.

'You can sit here in France and say things like that!' she burst in. 'Here, when the Popular Front is about to change everything!'

'The Popular Front is only a phase, a zigzag along the way. You'll see. The only man Stalin trusts is Hitler. They're made for each other.'

Furious, she slammed her fist down on the table, spilling her drink.

'Shit! You're talking shit!' The coarse word seemed truly foul from those lips. 'You think any of this fiction justifies what you've done? You sold us to the British for a hundred pounds a month!'

'They don't pay quite that well. And I didn't do it for money.'

'Then why?'

'Because a man must have a place on which to stand.'

She stared off into the distance.

'And because I heard the screams.'

She was breathing in long, deep drafts, perhaps to master her emotions. When she turned, her face was different. Her features were set. She seemed to have come to a moment of resolution.

'Give me a cigarette.'

It always made him uneasy to watch her smoke. The cigarette was awkward, even obscene, in her fingers. She took shallow puffs that did not reach her lungs.

'Where would we go?' she asked suddenly, and hope fluttered inside him like a wounded bird.

'We'll go anywhere you want,' he said eagerly. 'We'll change our names, make a new life. We'll have money, no need to go short –' He broke off. No, better not to dwell on money. 'We'll turn our backs on all of them. You'll be able to paint. I'll go fishing, set up a little business. We'll live like normal people.'

'How soon?'

'We can go today. Tonight. Whenever you like.'

She threw the cigarette onto the paving stones, stood up and ground it underfoot.

'I have some things to collect. I'll meet you at the Gare du Nord – there's a coffee shop –'

'I know the one.'

'Seven o'clock.' She said all this without meeting his eyes. She let him clasp her to him, briefly. Their mouths brushed. But there was no life in her. It was like holding a mannequin.

'Sigrid. Are you sure?'

'Oh, yes.'

'What made you decide?'

'I heard the screams, too.'

3

A major train station is not the ideal place for a clandestine meeting. The police tend to be more vigilant than in other parts of the city, and it is harder to spot a tail among droves of transients. But this was not what troubled Johnny as he retraced his steps to the Gare du Nord in the lengthening shadows.

She didn't ask about Helene. Is it possible she doesn't know?

Mingling with the last flock of commuters, he made a leisurely circumnavigation of the great station. At 7:00 P.M. sharp, he was seated on a stool within sight of the café, reading *L'Aurore*, while a boy in a sailor cap polished his shoes.

Around the edge of the newspaper, he saw her arrive. She was carrying a small suitcase.

She sits down. The waiter comes, with his napkin over his arm. She orders coffee. No, the waiter brings cognac. She looks at the clock behind the counter. Then she looks at her watch. She is nervous, flustered. That's as it should be. There is nobody following her. Nobody I can see.

He gave the bootblack a couple of coins.

'How would you like to earn five francs more?'

The boy looked uncertain. '*Monsieur est pédé, non?*'

'*Non.*' Johnny moulded his most reassuring grin. 'Monsieur is *not* a pederast. I want you to take a note to the lady in the café. The one sitting by herself.'

'That's all?'

He scratched a couple of lines on a scrap he tore from an envelope.

'Meet me at platform seven. Five minutes. No cage can hold us. J.'

He handed the boy the message and a five-franc bill. 'Don't talk to her. Just give her the note and leave.'

He slipped away through the crowd and took shelter behind a telephone kiosk.

He saw her take the note and try to call the boy back.

She's read it. She frowns and summons the waiter. She is leaving. She has not communicated to anyone. Everything is going to be fine.

He trailed her to platform seven, not daring to be sure. She was at the gate, looking lost. She was wearing a blue suit of a brisk, almost military cut and a little matching hat with a visor. She looked like anything but a Comintern agent on the run. She might have walked straight off the Schiaparelli stand at the fashion show. She was superb. She was the only woman in Paris.

He started swimming towards her, through the tide of people.

She glanced up and saw his head, floating above the others.

He was almost close enough to touch her when she put a cigarette in her mouth and snapped a thin gold lighter he had never seen her use before.

In the next instant, two bulky men bracketed him.

'Police,' one of them grunted.

He looked at the bulging face, the dumpling nose. They didn't make faces like that in Paris.

He wrestled with them, trying to break away.

He felt a sharp jab just above the kidneys. His knees sagged. They were hoisting him up, half-dragging, half-carrying him away.

'Excuse, please. Our friend is sick,' a voice wafted out of an echoing pit.

In his last flicker of consciousness, he saw a woman in blue, walking briskly away. She did not look back.

'I'm disappointed in you, Johnny. I once thought of you as my most brilliant protégé. You end up as a lovesick calf. I warned you against that woman the first time I met her. You should have listened to me then.'

Max was sitting at the end of a long refectory table. A brass chandelier hung down from a domed ceiling. The walls were white and uncomforting, bare except for a few sombre oils of men in dark robes. The place had the air of a former monastery.

They had propped Johnny up at Max's right hand, in a tall, ladder-backed chair. He was still groggy from the needle they had stuck him with at the station. His abductors were transformed, for the night, into waiters. The service was sloppy, the food of no interest to Johnny. But he noticed from the labels on the wines – a pouilly fuissé, followed by a médoc and a venerable armagnac – that no expense had been spared. 'It's our Last Supper,' Max had announced. The note of blasphemy was enhanced by the spymaster's appearance. He was wearing a white silk turtleneck inside his black sweater.

Max smoked between courses, during courses, incessantly.

'What have you done with her?' Johnny croaked.

'Me? I've done nothing. She's gone back to Moscow, with my blessing. End of story. Now we have to decide what to do with *you*.'

'How long did you know?'

Max blew out smoke and watched the circles rise above the chandelier.

'I suspected for a long time. I didn't have proof until Sigrid gave it to me.'

'You suspected in Brazil. Yet you let me remain in place. Why?'

Max signalled for the two burly waiters to go.

'We are all capable of mistakes,' Max said serenely.

'Nothing is that simple with you. You wanted Emil destroyed. Didn't you?'

'You needn't exorcise yourself about him.' Max steepled his hands.

'You sit there like a defrocked priest!' Johnny exploded at him. 'I hated Emil. Then I saw what those bastards did to him –'

'A fit of conscience? From you? That's rather quaint. I'm afraid it won't affect your sentence.'

Johnny subsided. Max was right. His outburst was grotesque.

'I was once in Siberia,' Max resumed. 'Did you know that? No, I was never a prisoner, if that's what you're thinking. But I was out of favour. It was a few years after our first meeting. I had not quite adjusted to the new order of things. I still imagined that Trotsky was some kind of genius. I hadn't learned whose back to scrub. So in order to educate me they sent me to run a logging camp in the northeast, where the temperature drops to eighty below. I made one friend, just one, in almost twelve months. He was a Chukchi. Have you ever met a Chukchi?'

'No.'

'Well, never take one on in a fight, at least not on his own terrain. They're an arctic people, primitive, superstitious. They live like wolves in places you would think could never support human lives. One day my Chukchi friend – he was a chief or shaman among the rest, face like a Buddha

– invited me to come and watch the wolves. He said there was a lot to be learned from wolves, said they are more like us than any other species. Only a wolf can look a man straight in the eye and sometimes stare him down. I was shit scared, I don't mind admitting it, but I went with him all the same, in a fur-lined parka and snowshoes, loaded up with guns and ammunition and vodka.

'He took me up into some ranges where you could see for miles and miles. All I could make out to begin with was a white wilderness. I couldn't tell north from south. Then he pointed out the ravens – the ravens follow the wolves in hopes of feeding off their kills – and then we saw the pack itself. Magnificent, their legs rolling smoothly as wheels.

'There were two wolves loping along behind the rest. They were what the old man had brought me to watch. They were lone wolves, both trying to join the pack. One was an outcast, driven out of the pack for some reason, probably illness. Wolves sense any contagious infection. When they were resting, the outcast would nip at his backside, as if he had worms. The other wolf had come out of the white void. If he got too close to the others, they would bare their teeth and run at him, driving him away. They weren't inclined to share their food or their territory.

'The whole drama was played out. While the pack was resting, the pariah put his tail between his legs and made another bid for acceptance. He approached the others with his ears flattened back, and we saw him try to lick the muzzle of the alpha wolf. They nipped and snarled at him till he ran away yelping. He saw the lone wolf, the outsider, and all at once his posture changed. His legs stiffened, his jaws opened, and the next second he was hurling himself on the outsider's neck. They tussled for quite a long time. The pack kept out of it. The pariah took some vicious bites, but finally he had the outsider at his mercy. He killed the way wolves generally kill. By ripping the guts out and letting the victim bleed to death.

'As we watched, he limped back to the pack. He must have thought he had vindicated himself in the eyes of his old comrades by killing the intruder. He didn't strut. He cowered and fawned, as before. When the alpha wolf snapped at him, he even rolled over on his back, and put his legs in the air. And you know what his old comrades did? They tore him to pieces.'

Max paused and filled two wineglasses to the brim with armagnac.

'Drink,' he urged Johnny. 'To our cousins the wolves!'

Johnny took a swallow.

'Do you know why I told you that story?'

Johnny waited.

'Because it's about Emil. He killed the outsider, he rolled on his back, and they would still have torn him to bits in Moscow if the Brazilians hadn't got him first.'

'It sounds to me as if the story is about *you*,' Johnny said quietly. 'You did the killing. Heinz Kordt. Miranda's girl –'

'At whose orders?' Max screamed at him, all his urbanity fled. 'At whose instigation?'

'The Gestapo would have given the same orders. There are times when a man has to say no to his orders, or become your wolf.'

Max hurled his glass at Johnny's head. Johnny bent to one side, and it smashed against the wall.

'I dedicated my life to the cause.' He was on his feet, breathing hard. 'When you were crapping in your nappies, I was fighting for the revolution –'

'Do you still believe in it?'

'That's a stupid question.'

'Do you still believe?'

'It doesn't matter what I believe. There are only two sides, and I am on the side of the party.'

'That's a stupid answer.'

'You're not entitled to any answers! I could shoot you now.'

'Go ahead. I wouldn't lose any sleep over it, anyway.' Johnny's indifference wasn't feigned. He felt leached of emotion, even fear.

Max sat down and reached for another glass. He gulped the fine Armagnac like water.

'Why did you kill Helene?'

'I didn't kill her. It was an accident.'

It struck him now that this was what Sigrid was talking about, when she said she had heard the screams.

He stared at Max, who was leaning into the table, his chin resting on his arms.

'Do you believe me? Not that it matters.'

'I would like to believe you,' Max said. 'For your own sake. That one loved you better, in her way, than the other. The worst mistake you made in your life was to choose the wrong sister.'

They talked far into the night, and little of the conversation had the quality of an interrogation. Max was violent, nostalgic, philosophic by turns, and his mood shifts became more vertiginous when the Armagnac was gone and he started working his way through a fresh bottle of vodka. By the end of it Johnny found it hard to keep his eyes awake, even though he knew what followed a Last Supper.

He was finally allowed to fling down on the bed in a room with heavy wooden shutters that were bolted from the outside. When he awoke, the room was still dark, and he was amazed to see from his watch that it was past 10:00 A.M. It seemed odd that neither of Max's house goons had come to rouse him.

He banged on the door. No answer. He rattled the handle and found the door was unlocked. That was even stranger. Surely he had heard the key turn in the lock the night before.

He dressed and set off down the corridor. The house seemed deserted. When he descended the grand staircase and went to the front door, no one came to challenge him. He looked out over a wide terrace to a formal garden that was being rapidly recovered by nature. The lawn was bright with dandelions.

He considered making a break for it, then and there.

No, he told himself. They want an excuse to shoot me in the back, to avoid embarrassments in Moscow.

He went back inside and began exploring the house more

methodically. Not a retired convent, after all, to judge by the lady in a wimple whose bosom was bursting out of her bodice in a cracked canvas in the hall. He followed the smell of coffee and warm pastry into the kitchen, and found Max Fabrikant breakfasting alone. He was still drinking – lukewarm vodka, out of a tumbler. He looked and smelled as though he had been up all night.

'Eat. Drink.' Max gestured to a chair.

'Where are Rosencrantz and Guildenstern?'

'I gave them the day off. So we could continue our chat.' Max could probably drink half the population of Greater Russia under the table, but his speech was furry, and his eyes looked out of focus. 'I thought you might want to hear another story.' The last word ended in a belch, which he made no effort to suppress.

'Of course.' Johnny poured coffee from the pot. Like the vodka, the coffee proved to be lukewarm. Judging that vodka tasted better than coffee at room temperature, he joined Max in a glass.

'One of the greatest witchfinders of medieval Europe,' Max began, 'was Nicolai Remigii, the hanging judge of the Duke of Lorraine. When old Nick sat on the bench, he had eight hundred women burned at the stake for witchcraft. He had an infallible technique for telling the guilty from the innocent. He would have his suspect bound hand and foot and thrown into a pond. If the woman sank, she was judged innocent. If she floated, she was consigned to the fire. Elegant logic, wouldn't you agree? Not unknown in our century, for that matter.'

He drank some more.

'In his dotage, Master Nicolai reached the conclusion that he himself was able to cast magic spells. He was of course a stickler for due process, not to mention a punctilious kraut, my dear Johnny. So he registered himself with the court as a master of witchcraft. And what do you think happened? Did they burn him at the stake? Of course they did. Don't you find that uncommonly illuminating?'

In his excitement, he had seized Johnny's wrist.

He's running a fever worse than mine, Johnny realised.

'Are you going to tell me who this story is about?'

'Ah!' Max sprang up and started hopping around in a lunatic jig. 'It's about all of us!'

Johnny waited for him to subside. When Max flopped down, the light went out of him. He rested his head on the table.

After a while, Johnny began to worry that he had blacked out and got up to investigate. But Max snapped back. He sat bolt upright and carried on as if there had been no interruption.

'I don't have friends, Johnny. You know that. Trust is a weakness in my profession. You were perhaps the closest I had to a friend. You and one other. I don't think you ever met him. I called him Mishka. He got on the wrong side of Yezhov. Now he has confessed that he was involved in the assassination of Kirov. He wasn't even in Russia at the time. And he is a Leningrad man. Kirov was his hero. They will shoot him. Naturally.'

The story was almost humdrum compared with what both men had lived, what each could be held accountable for. What intrigued Johnny was that the fate of this un-known Mishka – presumably a fellow chekist – had touched Max in a way that the fates of Heinz and Werner had not. Could it be because he believed that Mishka's fate presaged his own?

'Max. Something has happened, hasn't it?'

Fabrikant shrugged and reached for the vodka.

'They're coming at noon,' he said drowsily.

'Who?'

'I've been summoned back to Moscow. It's not a friendly invitation.' He swilled the booze around inside his cheeks like a mouthwash. 'They planned to spring it on me as a surprise. Fortunately, I still have a few people who owe me favours. I got a call during the night.'

'What will you do?'

Max lifted the crumpled napkin on the table in front of him, exposing a Makarov service pistol.

'Not that.'

Max wiped his mouth with the napkin and laughed. 'No, I don't think so. I haven't made up my mind.'

'What about me?'

'Take a lesson from old Nick of Lorraine. Be the one that sinks without trace. The door is open, Johnny.'

Johnny started walking towards the door, not quite believing. In the doorway he turned back towards Max.

'Did Sigrid really leave for Moscow?'

Max's laugh was a dry rattle. 'Forget her. Marry an English girl with – how do they say? – peaches and cream in her cheeks. Give her a nice warm fuck for me.'

4

'They shot Max,' Colin Bailey told him. 'Put him down like a horse with a broken leg.'

Several months had passed. Time enough for the European dictatorships to find themselves a handy little proving ground in Spain and for Johnny to have his audience with the dying King; he went on to a celebration dinner at the Savoy at which Harry Maitland turned up in tails and insisted on snaring the prettiest girl on the dance floor to partner Johnny.

Bailey had taken Johnny down to the cottage in Devon for a few days, sensing that the German was nearing a new emotional crisis. The Firm had given him a few jobs to do. He had conducted a short training course for recent recruits on sabotage techniques and Comintern methods, which had most of the new boys excited. He had been encouraged to jot down his memoirs, for the files at least; but this literary project seemed to be withering on the vine. The symptoms of Johnny's malaise were easy to read. He missed the action, and he needed a woman. More than a woman, a friend.

Diana, God love her, had put Johnny on a horse and carted him off to a show, where he caused quite a stir among some of the county girls – at least after Diana hinted that he was a titled archduke travelling incognito. This produced a batch of promising dinner invitations and a rumoured affair which was the talk of the county for a week or so, but it wasn't even half a step towards solving what a man who had lost his woman and his cause was going to do with the rest of his life.

Bailey was mulling this over one morning when he picked up his blackthorn stick and said to Johnny, 'Let's get some air.'

They drove down to Dartmoor in Diana's cheeky red roadster. Driving it always made Bailey feel as if he were just coming down from college. Johnny must have caught the spirit. He was smiling and joking by the time they arrived at Two Bridges, which was just an inn and a thatched cottage making eyes at each other from opposite sides of the road.

Johnny's mood darkened when he heard the news about Max. Bailey had saved it up for a few days, since he had taken the train down from London, not sure how Johnny would react. The man had the right to rejoice. Max Fabrikant had been mixed up with most of the tragedies in his life, including the loss of Sigrid. Yet he reacted to the news as if something in himself had died.

Bailey led them off at a brisk pace, marking the rhythm with his stick, along the river bank to a blackened cottage. Now their way ran beside an ancient wall of granite lumps patched with lichen, held together over the centuries by the gaps the wind whistled through. This was lean, rough country. A few bighorn sheep, their faces black, grazed among deformed clumps of gorse. Crows and ravens turning slow circles overhead greeted the travellers with a parched cackle that reminded Johnny of Max's parting phrase.

They picked their way over swampy downs to a stile and then a wooden ladder over a farther fence where tufts of sheep's wool hung down from the rusty prongs of the barbed wire. It was only midafternoon, and yet night was closing in. A great, blanketing mist dropped suddenly over the valley, swallowing Beartown Tor, away to the left. From the crest of a hill, peering over the moors, Johnny followed Bailey's pointing arm and made out what seemed to be a giant oak forest in the far distance.

But there was something awry. The trees tilted crazily down the tilt of the valley, cowering under some irresistible force. Closer up, Johnny realised that the oaks were dwarves, the biggest only three times his height. The wood had survived for centuries, scorned – or, more properly, feared – by the tin miners who had plundered the surrounding moorlands for fuel. The trunks of the tiny oaks were bent over, parallel with the ground. The roots snaked around granite boulders, probing far to find the sparse soil and safe moorings for their eccentric loads. Inside the forest, a cobwebby green haze covered everything.

'They call this Wistman's Wood,' Bailey explained.

Johnny had to bend almost double to follow him under the dwarf oaks. They found a comfortable perch on a rock and shared a tobacco pouch.

'Is it true that Harry Maitland is joining the Firm?' Johnny asked after a time.

'Yes. As a matter of fact, it is. We're lucky to get him.'

Bailey did not see fit to add that it had taken a certain amount of arm-twisting. He had not been above suggesting to Major Mackenzie via circuitous channels that, while HMG was duly grateful for the role played by Rio Light and Harry in particular in the recent distressing events in Brazil, it would be no bad thing if young Maitland were sent back to England. He had acquired some powerful enemies, and the change would do him good. Bailey gathered that Maitland had had woman trouble of his own. Luisa had packed up and left, gone back to the steep cobbled streets of Salvador da Bahia, leaving a puzzling message about how they belonged to the gods of their own peoples. With any luck an eligible young bachelor like Maitland, caught up in the social whirl of the West End, would get over it soon enough. Hadn't Bailey once done the same?

It would be harder for Johnny.

The German turned to look at him through the haze of pipe smoke.

'Was it worth it?' Johnny asked.

'Don't doubt that for a minute,' Bailey responded fiercely. 'If war comes, as it is bound to come —'

'Your politicians in London seem to doubt that.'

'Then damn the politicians! You and I know better. *When* war comes, we will need Brazil. Not just for the rubber and the coffee, but because it's the stepping-stone to North Africa, and that is the key to southern Europe. I don't know what the Americans will do when we have to get rough with Hitler, but just imagine what a difference Brazil would make to them if it were owned by Stalin's boys. Or Hitler's.'

He thought about Courtland Bull, the elusive Texan millionaire, financier of Brazilian plots. Bailey's man in Washington had reported that Bull was now lobbying to get himself appointed Ambassador to the Court of St James's. Bailey intended to put paid to that notion.

'Brazil was a sideshow, all the same,' Johnny said.

'The sideshows are often the best things at a carnival. I rate this one of the very best.'

A silence fell between them, punctuated only by the continuous low drone from minuscule winged insects, scaled down like the oaks, barely distinguishable from grains of dust in the filtered light but insistent, aiming for the eyes.

'I need a job,' Johnny announced.

'I've been giving that some thought. You know, I had it in mind to send Harry to the Hague. You two got along together pretty well, didn't you? You might even be able to teach him to order from a German menu.'

Johnny showed no particular interest till Bailey added, 'Wolfgang Trott has been appointed first secretary at the German Embassy in the Hague.'

'When do I leave?'

'Steady on. I'll have to cut through a mile of red tape.'

He sensed Johnny beginning to relax, with the promise of action again in his sights. They smoked and enjoyed the comfortable silence of people who share a language beyond words.

Johnny broke it by asking casually, 'Why is this place called Wistman's Wood?'

'Oh, it's a hoary old West Country yarn. The Wisht-Man was Old Nick, or something very close. He had a pack of bloodthirsty dogs called the Wisht-Hounds, and the locals thought they spied them ranging these moors by night. A dreadful load of piffle, truly. The trail they took – we followed it part of the way – was called the Path of the Dead. You see, they used to carry the coffins along that route for burial in holy ground at Lydford. I suppose it made quite a sight in the dead of winter, those lonely columns of serfs staggering along with the boxes on their shoulders.'

'The Path of the Dead,' Johnny repeated.

It wasn't a scene from West Country folklore that he saw. It was a series of faces rising up out of the mist of his own past. Heinz Kordt. Emil Brandt. Helene. Max Fabrikant. Sigrid. And then came faces scarcely formed, things from the future, the first rough pummelling of the sculptor's clay.

He raised himself to his full height, pushing back the foliage.

He said, 'We're on the right track.'

Historical Note

This is a work of fiction, but it is based on fact. There was a double agent code-named Johnny who worked for the British in the thirties. One of his many aliases was Franz Gruber. His real name was Johann Heinrich de Graaf, and he was born in the little town of Nordenham, across the River Weser from the port of Bremerhaven, in 1894. His work as an agent inside the Comintern and Soviet military intelligence resulted in some of the greatest – and hitherto unrecorded – successes of British secret intelligence in the era between the two world wars.

Through Johnny, the British were able to penetrate Soviet espionage rings in London, Copenhagen, Paris and Shanghai. He provided critical intelligence on Stalin's bid to make an alliance with Hitler and the Nazi military buildup, although it was ignored by the appeasers who subsequently came to power in Britain. Johnny helped to sabotage Stalin's ambitious plot to turn Brazil into the first Communist state in the Western Hemisphere.

Like many of the most valuable agents, Johnny was a 'walk-in'. He volunteered his services to the British intelligence chief in Berlin in 1933 out of bitter disillusionment with Soviet policy. He had had firsthand experience of how Stalin had helped to destroy the anti-Nazi forces in Germany and was secretly collaborating with Hitler many years before the signing of the infamous Nazi–Soviet Non-Aggression Pact that ushered in World War II. He had come to regard communism and fascism as twin evils and spent the rest of his life fighting both, often at great personal risk.

He loved two sisters, both Soviet intelligence operatives,

although in real life, only one of them actually went to Brazil.

Johnny had a happier fate than many of his comrades. In 1940, when Hitler and Stalin were openly allied, the Soviet secret police herded 530 German Communists, including some of his former friends, over the bridge at Brest Litovsk in Poland and into the hands of the Gestapo. Readers who are curious to know more about the love affair between Stalin and Hitler and what it meant to Johnny's generation will find fascinating material in the memoirs of a number of Soviet intelligence operatives and Communist organisers who ended up sharing his disenchantment. These memoirs include Walter Krivitsky's *In Stalin's Secret Service*, Alexander Orlov's *The Secret History of Stalin's Crimes*, Ruth Fischer's *Stalin and German Communism*, Eudocio Ravines' *The Yenan Way* and Jan Valtin's *Out of the Night*, all of which provided valuable background for my novel.

On the recorded events of 1935–36 in Brazil, an indispensable source is the magisterial series by Professor John W. F. Dulles, the doyen of Western scholars in this area. His books include *Vargas of Brazil, Anarchists and Communists in Brazil* and *Brazilian Communism, 1935–1945*, all published by the University of Texas. Among the Brazilian works I found helpful were Hélio Silva's *1935: A Revolta Vermelha*, Graciliano Ramos' *Memorías do Cárcere*, a marvellous guide to the personalities involved in the Communist revolt, and the recent sympathetic biography of Prestes' companion, *Olga*, by Fernando Morais. Ivan Pedro de Martins, who was in 1935 the youngest member of the Central Committee of the Brazilian Communist Party, was generous enough to share with me some of the vivid recollections that will be published in his forthcoming autobiography.

For the record, Rudyard Kipling did visit Brazil (in the late 1920s) and immediately fell in love with the country, like many visitors before him and since. His charming travelogues were published by Doubleday in New York in 1940 in a slim volume entitled *Brazilian Sketches* that is not included in the major editions of his collected works.

Unhappily, Johnny did not write his memoirs. But I

have been privileged to talk with people who remember him and with others who played a role in the events described in the novel. In the course of several trips to Brazil I have interviewed some of the survivors of the 1935 revolt and examined the police archives from that time, which contain hundreds of Communist documents from the safes – booby-trapped by Johnny – that failed to blow up when they were forced open.

But *Carnival of Spies* is, of course, a novel, not a historical dissertation. For dramatic purposes I have taken a few liberties; for example, the Fascist coup attempt in Brazil actually postdated the Communist rising by about three years. Many of the characters are fictional. They rub shoulders with various historical figures. Among the latter are:

Stalin
Dimitrov, Comintern leader
Manuilsky, Stalin's hatchetman in the Comintern
Piatnitsky, head of the Orgbureau of the Comintern
Berzin, chief of Soviet Military Intelligence.
Yezhov, OGPU chief and organiser of the Great Purge
Harry Pollitt, British Communist leader
Getulio Vargas, president of Brazil
Luis Carlos Prestes, Brazilian Communist leader
Olga Benario, his companion
Lampião, Brazilian bandit chief
Ernst Wollweber, German Communist leader active in Copenhagen
Otto Braun, Comintern adviser in China
Von Seeckt, head of Hitler's military mission to Chiang Kai-shek
Tu Yu-seng, criminal overlord of Shanghai
Willi Münzenberg, the brilliant Comintern propagandist who pioneered the art of using 'peace' slogans and 'solidarity' campaigns to recruit liberals for Communist causes. Münzenberg eventually broke with Stalin over his policy of collaboration with Hitler. He was found dead with a wire garrote around his neck in the woods

of Cagnet in southwestern France in 1940 – a victim of Stalin's secret police or the Gestapo, or both.

Three Soviet agencies involved in covert operations abroad are described in the novel. A word on each:

The Comintern

The Communist International, or Comintern, was founded in Moscow in March 1919. According to its programme, 'It is the aim of the Communist International to fight by all available means, including armed struggle, for the overthrow of the international bourgeoisie and the creation of an international Soviet republic as a transitional stage to the complete abolition of the State . . . The Communist International must, in fact and in deed, be a single Communist Party of the entire world. The parties working in the various countries are but its separate sections.'

Comintern advisers had extraordinary powers over local Communist parties, and in the course of the twenties they organised a wave of armed insurrections around the world, including the Hamburg revolt recounted in this book. All these military adventures failed; some brought the deaths of many thousands of party members. The Comintern ran training courses for foreign revolutionaries, notably at the Lenin School, just outside Moscow, which had 500 students in 1935, and in the M-schools, like the one at Bakovka mentioned in this novel, where Red Army instructors taught bomb making and assassination techniques.

In Stalin's time the Comintern – purged of its early, internationalist leaders – became simply an arm of the Soviet state, ruthlessly subjected to every cynical shift in Moscow's policy by the secret police and Stalin's trusted hatchetman, Dmitri Zacharovich Manuilsky, the son of a Greek Orthodox priest who turned up at the United Nations after the war in the guise of a delegate from the Ukraine.

The 'heart of the Comintern', according to Walter Krivitsky, was the OMS – the *Otdel Meshdunarodoi Svyasi*, or International Relations Department. This was the most secret section of the Orgbureau, headed by Osip Piatnitsky, the remarkable 'Old Bolshevik' described in the book who perished in the Stalin purges. The OMS arranged covert funding, transport and fake documentation and was charged with the security of Comintern operatives abroad.

The Comintern's regional directorates included the powerful Westbureau, which functioned from behind the cover of a publishing house on the Wilhelmstrasse in Berlin – as described in this book – until Hitler took power, when its staffers scattered and regrouped in Paris and Copenhagen.

The South American bureau, based in Buenos Aires until 1928 and afterwards in Montevideo, was the command centre for the Rio plot. For many years its dominating figure was August Guralski, a supple, sophisticated Lithuanian Jew who played a key part in recruiting Luis Carlos Prestes to the Communist cause. In Rio in 1935 the South American bureau was headed by a triumvirate that used the amusing acronymn GIN. The 'G' was for 'Garoto' (or 'Kid'), one of the code names for Prestes, who returned to Brazil on a fake Portuguese passport. The 'I' was for 'Indio', a party name for Rodolfo Ghioldi, a leading Argentine Communist. The 'N' was for 'Negro', a nom de guerre for Arthur Ewert (who often called himself Harry Berger), who had headed Comintern operations in Shanghai in 1932–34 and, like the fictional Emil, was not the least tragic figure in the Brazilian episode.

The attempted coup in Brazil was the Comintern's last ambitious experiment in overthrowing a target government by force of arms. For a few years afterwards, Stalin's reluctant decision to endorse Popular Front tactics – made public in the summer of 1935 by the Seventh Congress of the Communist International in Moscow – brought political and propaganda success, especially in France. But at the same time, the Comintern's most courageous and committed agents were falling victim to the purges in Moscow, and the signing of the Nazi-Soviet Pact threw the worldwide

Communist movement into utter disarray. After Hitler invaded the Soviet Union, forcing Stalin to align himself with the West, the Comintern became an embarrassment; it had been involved in too many plots against the Western allies. It was officially disbanded in 1943.

However, the Comintern is very much alive to this day in the guise of the International Department (ID) of the Central Committee of the Communist Party of the Soviet Union, which seeks to manipulate foreign political parties – not only Communist parties – for Soviet ends and has its own operatives posted at important embassies.

Soviet State Security

The Soviet secret police was formally organised in December 1917 as the All-Russian Extraordinary Commission for Combating Counter-Revolution and Sabotage, or Cheka for short. The word 'chekist' (or 'honourable chekist', in Soviet publications) is still used to describe members of the KGB. The first Soviet intelligence chief, Feliks Dzerzhinsky, described the role of his agency in the following terms in 1918: 'We stand for organised terror . . . The Cheka is obliged to defend the revolution and conquer the enemy even if its sword does by chance sometimes fall upon the heads of the innocent.'

Since the abolition of the Cheka in 1922, the Soviet secret police has been known by a bewildering chain of initials: GPU, OGPU, NKVD, MVD and KGB. To avoid confusion, Max Fabrikant's organisation is referred to throughout this novel as the OGPU. The initials stand for 'Obiedinyonnoye Gosudarstvennoye Politicheskoye Upravleniye', or Unified State Political Administration. This was the title used by Soviet state security between November 1923 and 1934.

Nikolai Ivanovich Yezhov, who is seen visiting Stalin and interrogating Johnny in the book, is, of course, a historical figure. He became chief of Soviet state security in September 1936 and presided over the bloody purges that claimed the lives of veteran Comintern organisers, Red Army generals and countless thousands of party faithful.

Max Fabrikant is a fictional character, but some of his European exploits are loosely modelled on the career of a Soviet master spy of Latvian origin who used the alias Michel Avatin and personally executed a number of alleged 'traitors'. For the record, a senior member of Avatin's service was dispatched to Rio in the fall of 1935 to ferret out spies within the Comintern team, and recommended the murder of the mistress of 'Miranda', the secretary-general of the Brazilian Communist Party.

Soviet Military Intelligence

Again, for the sake of simplicity, Soviet military intelligence (today known as the GRU) is described as the Fourth Department (of the General Staff). It was this organisation, rather than the forerunner of the KGB, that was responsible for most of the Soviet espionage coups between the two world wars. It produced spies of the calibre of Richard Sorge. It forewarned Stalin of Hitler's impending attack. However, Stalin preferred not to believe its reports; as Johnny reflects in the novel, Hitler was perhaps the only man the Soviet dictator was willing to trust.

General Jan Berzin, the Latvian head of the Fourth Department in this book, is another historical figure. He died in the purges, along with nearly all of his headquarters staff. According to the account of one Soviet intelligence defector, Berzin's death was a slow one; in the cells of the Lubyanka, his testicles were nailed to a block of wood.

ALSO AVAILABLE FROM
HODDER AND STOUGHTON PAPERBACKS

BRYAN FORBES

☐	26018 1	Familiar Strangers	£3.50
☐	35485 2	The Rewrite Man	£3.50

ROBERT DALEY

☐	35208 6	The Dangerous Edge	£2.95
☐	39019 0	Hands of a Stranger	£2.95
☐	33031 7	Year of the Dragon	£2.95

TERENCE STRONG

☐	41089 2	Dragonplague	£2.95

A. J. QUINNELL

☐	37179 X	Blood Ties	£2.95
☐	40719 0	Siege of Silence	£2.95

All these books are available at your local bookshop or newsagent, or can be ordered direct from the publisher. Just tick the titles you want and fill in the form below.

Prices and availability subject to change without notice.

Hodder and Stoughton Paperbacks, P.O. Box 11, Falmouth, Cornwall.

Please send cheque or postal order, and allow the following for postage and packing:

U.K. – 55p for one book, plus 22p for the second book, and 14p for each additional book ordered up to a £1.75 maximum.

B.F.P.O. and EIRE – 55p for the first book, plus 22p for the second book, and 14p per copy for the next 7 books, 8p per book thereafter.

OTHER OVERSEAS CUSTOMERS – £1.00 for the first book, plus 25p per copy for each additional book.

Name ....

Address ....

....